OXFORD WORLD'S CLASSICS

THE VIRGIN OF THE SEVEN DAGGERS AND OTHER STORIES

VERNON LEE, the adopted name of Violet Paget, was born in France in 1856. In her formative years, her family moved regularly around the Continent, before finally settling in Florence, Italy. Though she always considered herself an Englishwoman, this upbringing fostered in Lee a strongly pan-European outlook (after World War I, George Bernard Shaw called Lee 'the old guard of Victorian cosmopolitan intellectualism'). Intellectually omnivorous and driven, Lee began writing at a young age, producing over the course of a long career a steady stream of essays and books of history, biography, politics, travel, philosophy, aesthetics, music history, and literary theory. She wrote fiction as well, and while her early novel *Miss Brown* was poorly received, her Gothic stories and novellas were praised by contemporaries including Henry James and have been highly regarded by readers ever since. Her first supernatural tale, 'Winthrop's Adventure', was published in *Fraser's Magazine* in 1881, with other stories appearing in such publications as *The Yellow Book* and *The Fortnightly Review* before being reprinted, sometimes very belatedly, in story collections; the most famous of these, *Hauntings*, was published in 1890; the last, *For Maurice: Five Unlikely Stories*, not until 1927. Lee died in 1935, in Italy.

AARON WORTH is Associate Professor of Rhetoric at Boston University. He has edited Arthur Machen's *The Great God Pan and Other Horror Stories* and Sheridan Le Fanu's *Green Tea and Other Weird Stories* for Oxford World's Classics. His new anthology *The Night Wire and Other Tales of Weird Media* is published by the British Library.

OXFORD WORLD'S CLASSICS

For over 100 years Oxford World's Classics have brought readers closer to the world's great literature. Now with over 700 titles—from the 4,000-year-old myths of Mesopotamia to the twentieth century's greatest novels—the series makes available lesser-known as well as celebrated writing.

The pocket-sized hardbacks of the early years contained introductions by Virginia Woolf, T. S. Eliot, Graham Greene, and other literary figures which enriched the experience of reading. Today the series is recognized for its fine scholarship and reliability in texts that span world literature, drama and poetry, religion, philosophy, and politics. Each edition includes perceptive commentary and essential background information to meet the changing needs of readers.

OXFORD WORLD'S CLASSICS

VERNON LEE

The Virgin of the Seven Daggers and Other Stories

Edited with an Introduction and Notes by
AARON WORTH

OXFORD
UNIVERSITY PRESS

OXFORD
UNIVERSITY PRESS

Great Clarendon Street, Oxford, OX2 6DP,
United Kingdom

Oxford University Press is a department of the University of Oxford.
It furthers the University's objective of excellence in research, scholarship,
and education by publishing worldwide. Oxford is a registered trade mark of
Oxford University Press in the UK and in certain other countries

First published as an Oxford World's Classics paperback 2022

Impression: 1

Published in the United States of America by Oxford University Press
198 Madison Avenue, New York, NY 10016, United States of America

British Library Cataloguing in Publication Data
Data available

Library of Congress Control Number: 2022935478

ISBN 978–0–19–883754–1

Printed and bound in the UK by
Clays Ltd, Elcograf S.p.A.

ACKNOWLEDGEMENTS

BEYOND my gratitude to Luciana O'Flaherty and Kizzy Taylor-Richelieu at OUP for their usual support, skill, and professionalism, I must add a special thank you for their patience during the pandemic which dragged out the completion of this project for so long. Thanks as well to everyone else at OUP and Straive who worked on the book, including Nico Parfitt, Charles Lauder, Cheryl Brant, and Peter Gibbs. While I am attributing malignant agency to Covid, I will blame it also for any omissions in the following list of scholars, writers, and anthologists who helped me in some way (and in some cases with a significantly different conception of the book in mind) during the research process: Martha Vicinus, Franco Fabbri, Linda Hughes, Dennis Denisoff, Christa Zorn, Ana Parejo Vadillo, Mary Clai Jones, Darryl Jones, Jim Rockhill, Doug Anderson, Ioanna Iordanou, Don Cruickshank, Carolyn Burdett, Anita Savo, Jim Iffland, Benjamin Morgan, Mike Ashley, Jess Nevins, Otto Penzler, the staff of Godington House (the original of 'Okehurst') in Ashford, Kent, Jonah Siegel, Roger Luckhurst, Rosemary Pardoe, Marion Thain, Catherine Maxwell, Diana Maltz, Jonathan Foltz, Joe Bristow, Jill Ehnenn, Kristen Mahoney, Lindsay Wilhelm, Elizabeth Greeniaus, Patricia Pulham, and, last but very far from least, Sophie Geoffroy and Mandy Gagel, whose ongoing work of annotating and publishing Lee's letters is an incredible gift to all Lee scholars.

CONTENTS

INTRODUCTION

Readers who are unfamiliar with the stories may wish to treat the Introduction as an Afterword.

IN 1925, Vernon Lee, then nearing seventy, was invited by the London publishers Kegan Paul to contribute a volume to their phenomenally successful 'To-Day and To-Morrow' series, a line of pamphlet-like volumes by leading writers and thinkers of the day, delineating possible futures. This quintessentially Modernist project had grown from geneticist J. B. S. Haldane's provocative, proto-transhumanist manifesto *Daedalus; or Science and the Future*, whose enormous and immediate impact within educated circles (as well as that of Bertrand Russell's sceptical riposte, *Icarus; or the Future of Science*) encouraged Kegan Paul to keep the ball rolling; and so was born 'that brilliant series of little books', as T. S. Eliot called it, if a little sardonically.[1] In all, over a hundred 'brilliant' (and sometimes not so brilliant) 'little books' would appear: slender volumes bearing such titles as *Tantalus; or, The Future of Man* (by philosopher F. C. S. Schiller), *Aeolus; or, The Future of the Flying Machine* (by WWI flying ace Oliver Stewart), and *Halcyon; or, The Future of Monogamy* (by feminist writer and nurse Vera Brittain), and influencing figures including Aldous Huxley, James Joyce, C. S. Lewis, and Arthur Clarke. (Sadly, Evelyn Waugh's proffered manuscript, *Noah; or the Future of Intoxication*, was rejected.)

In keeping with the mythological conceit utilized by most of her predecessors, Lee titled her contribution *Proteus; or, The Future of Intelligence*, taking care, at the essay's outset, to ward off any confusion on the reader's part as to *what*, exactly, the elusive, shapeshifting deity of the Greeks represented to her. *Not* intelligence—at least, not directly—but the quasi-Kantian Real which this faculty seeks, for the

[1] Believing as he did that '[t]o be interested in "the future" is a symptom of demoralization and debility', Eliot's suggestion that 'the series will constitute a precious document upon the present time' is at least half barbed quip. T. S. Eliot, 'Charleston, Hey! Hey!', *The Nation and Athenaeum*, 40 (29 Jan. 1927). Reprinted in *The Complete Prose of T. S. Eliot: The Critical Edition*, vol. 3: *Literature, Politics, Belief, 1927–1929*, ed. by Frances Dickey, Jennifer Formichelli, and Ronald Schuchard (Baltimore, 2015), 595.

most part without success, to apprehend: 'Proteus, in my mythology, is the mysterious whole which we know must exist, but know not how to descry: Reality'.[2] In wrestling constantly with the Protean Real, 'Intelligence', which Lee primarily defines negatively (it is emphatically not 'Intellect', 'Reason', or 'Logic'[3]), must remain flexible, nimble, responsive to change. In fact, 'Intelligence' for Lee is not a fixed, or indeed 'natural', capacity at all, but a cognitive tool that evolves in reaction to contingent circumstances. Lee envisions a host of coming 'moral revaluations' and social transformations stemming from this evolution, while nimbly stepping back, time and again, from the brink of definite prediction.

What would Lee's departed Victorian contemporaries—friends and correspondents like Walter Pater, Henry James, Robert Browning, and John Addington Symonds—have made of *Proteus*? No doubt they would be initially nonplussed by the idea of 'Vernon Lee', a writer they associated, above all, with history and the past, turning futurologist. True, a careful reading of the text would dispel much of this sense of incongruity. Almost her last book, *Proteus* looks backwards as much as forwards; moreover, Lee is training the powerful lens of her historical consciousness upon intelligence itself—in fact, she comes close to identifying 'Intelligence' *with* historical consciousness, or what she calls 'thinking in terms of change': a habit, she asserts, which 'dates only from the days of Montesquieu, Voltaire, Gibbon and Condorcet'.[4]

But whatever else they might have thought of the book, it is almost certain that they would have been forcibly struck by the resemblance between its author and her chosen mythological figure. An intellectual fox if ever there was one, rather than a hedgehog (in the Greek lyric poet Archilochus' conceit), Lee cut an extraordinarily Protean figure in the world of (primarily though not exclusively) English letters for over half a century, publishing stories, novels, a play, and a steady stream of books and essays in a myriad of modes and on a myriad of subjects. She wrote history, biography, polemic, travel essays, philosophical dialogues, and monographs on aesthetics, politics, music history and theory, and literary theory, to give a partial accounting.

[2] Vernon Lee, *Proteus; or the Future of Intelligence* (London, 1925), 6.

[3] In this it resembles Coleridge's 'Imagination', while perhaps also looking ahead to such accounts of the mind's capacity for conceptual *poesis* as Arthur Koestler's 'bisociation' and Mark Turner's 'blending'.

[4] *Proteus*, 16.

Many of the 'manifold embodiments' (Lee's phrase describing the multifarious aspects of Proteus) of this prodigious oeuvre have been all but forgotten since her death in 1935, though a process of active scholarly rediscovery has been underway for some decades now, and not solely in literary studies. Yet her supernatural stories—or better, given their ambiguity, 'fantastic tales' as she herself called them—have never been entirely eclipsed, earning especially high praise from aficionados, and practitioners, of the Gothic tale. In assembling his influential 1931 anthology *The Supernatural Omnibus*, Montague Summers selected 'Oke of Okehurst' and 'Amour Dure' to represent the author he considered almost peerless, in her mastery of the form: pointing to M. R. James's skilful construction of atmosphere and attention to historical detail, Summers wrote, 'I know only one living writer who can be compared with him on this point. I refer to Vernon Lee (Violet Paget), from whose *Hauntings* I am privileged to give two stories . . . *Hauntings* is a masterpiece of literature, and even [Sheridan] Le Fanu and M. R. James cannot be ranked above the genius of this lady.'[5] Another James, warily ambivalent as he was about Lee and her fiction, expressed unqualified enthusiasm about the quartet of long uncanny stories which he received from her in 1890:

> Your gruesome, graceful, *genialisch* [ingenious] 'Hauntings' came to me a good bit since; but, pleasure-stirring as was the gift, I have . . . been unable to control what George Eliot would have called my 'emotive' utterance until I should have had the right hour to reassimilate the very special savour of the work . . . I have enjoyed again, greatly, the bold, aggressive speculative fancy of them.[6]

Well—perhaps the enthusiasm was not *entirely* unqualified; even as Henry James praises Lee's 'ingenious tales, full of imagination', he cannot resist sneering at the mould in which she has cast them: 'The supernatural story, the subject wrought in fantasy, is not the *class* of fiction I myself most cherish . . . But that only makes my enjoyment of your artistry more of a subjection.'

Very soon after being 'stirred' and, apparently, shaken by *Hauntings*, and for all his pooh-poohing of the form, James would resume writing

[5] Introduction, *The Supernatural Omnibus*, vol. 1: *Hauntings and Horror* (Harmondsworth, 1976), 36–7.

[6] Quoted in Carl J. Weber, 'Henry James and His Tiger-Cat', *PMLA* 68.4 (Sep. 1953), 672–9.

supernatural fiction himself, after a very long interval. More, while his early ghost stories, such as 'The Romance of Certain Old Clothes' (1868) and 'De Grey: A Romance' (1868), had been both conventional and comparatively paltry specimens of the genre, the products of James's second phase of supernatural writing, beginning with 'Sir Edmund Orme' (1891) and culminating in 'The Turn of the Screw' (1898), are not only finer but marked by a greater psychological orientation, a heightened degree of ambiguity. It is in just these qualities—in inclining towards what James termed the 'quasi-supernatural'—that they resemble such equivocal 'hauntings' as Lee's 'A Phantom Lover' ('Oke of Okehurst' in the collection she sent him). Yet while James's influence on Lee is acknowledged, the possibility of reciprocal influence is rarely considered.[7] This is symptomatic of many assessments—even highly positive ones—of Lee the 'weird' writer: she is lauded for her imagination and craftsmanship but seldom viewed as an innovator in the field, though her particular approach to engrafting the nineteenth-century European historiographical imagination onto a Gothic framework, for instance, strikes one as distinctively her own.

Beyond insight into the development of the form, and simple (or not-so-simple) enjoyment, Lee's 'gruesome, graceful, *genialisch*' fiction also offers us a lens for scrutinizing multiple aspects of European cultural history at the end of the nineteenth century. While her writing life was long, most of Lee's tales of horror and the fantastic were written in the 1880s and 1890s (though some would have to wait years or even decades for book publication), with settings—England, France, Spain, and above all Italy—reflecting the ever-shifting backdrop of her own peripatetic life. The ten-year span 1886–96 alone saw the publication of 'A Phantom Lover', 'Amour Dure', 'A Wicked Voice', 'Dionea', 'A Wedding Chest', 'The Legend of Madame Krasinska', 'The Virgin of the Seven Daggers', 'Prince Alberic and the Snake Lady', and 'The Doll'—tales which engage, in various

[7] E. F. Bleiler writes, for example, 'Written in line with the narrative theories of her friend Henry James, [*A Phantom Lover*] is a perplexing story; all that the reader comes to know is filtered through the personality of one man. . . . Thus (as with James's *The Turn of the Screw*), there has been speculation about what really happens in the story'; reading this, one might be surprised to learn that Lee's tale predates James's by a full twelve years. 'Vernon Lee', in Jack Sullivan, ed., *The Penguin Encyclopedia of Horror and the Supernatural* (New York, 1986), 256.

ways, such contemporaneous movements and themes as Aestheticism, Decadence, nationalism, sexual dissidence, and shifting gender roles, as well as any number of other literary, cultural, political, philosophical, and scientific currents circulating throughout Britain and the Continent during these years. Engaging with the past is itself a kind of wrestling match with Proteus, and Lee's own time was, and remains to us, in many ways an especially complex and elusive one. Her unsettling tales of obsession, possession, and transgression—'intelligent' in any and every sense—can also serve as a kind of borrowed 'intelligence' for twenty-first-century readers, in the sense in which Lee uses the word in *Proteus*: tools with which to better 'descry' the dynamic and multifaceted cultural milieu in which she worked.

A Childhood in Cosmopolis

In the wake of the Great War, George Bernard Shaw hailed Lee as 'the old guard of Victorian cosmopolitan intellectualism', marvelling that a twentieth-century Briton could be found who had remained immune to the 'war fever' which had swept across the nation in recent years ('Had she been Irish like me', he added wryly, 'there would have been nothing in her dispassionateness'). To Shaw, Lee's pacifist polemic *Satan, the Waster* 'prove[d] what everyone has lately been driven to doubt, that it is possible to be born in England and yet have intellect'.[8] In point of fact, as Shaw seems not to have known, the woman who would become Vernon Lee was born in France (though appropriately in sight, as it were, of England, in Boulogne-sur-Mer in the Pas-de-Calais), and spent her childhood shuttling between and among Germany, Switzerland, Italy, and elsewhere. These facts of her early life were crucial in fostering in Lee—born Violet Paget, in 1856—that quality of pan-European cosmopolitanism which Shaw so admired; as Lee recalled of her family life, 'We shifted our quarters invariably every six months, and, by dint of shifting, crossed Europe's length and breadth in several directions. But this was *moving*, not *travelling*, and we contemned all travellers.'[9] This early contempt for

[8] George Bernard Shaw, 'All about Satan the Waster', *Hearst's*, 38(6) (Dec. 1920), 25, 67.

[9] Vernon Lee, *The Sentimental Traveller*, 6. For more on Lee's cosmopolitanism, see Hilary Fraser, 'Writing Cosmopolis: The Cosmopolitan Aesthetics of Emilia Dilke and Vernon Lee', *19: Interdisciplinary Studies in the Long Nineteenth Century* (2019), 28.

mere tourists did not prevent Lee from later writing a great many books for their consumption, and in her nonpareil travel essays and other autobiographical writings we catch vivid glimpses of her continental upbringing: she writes of enchanted Christmases in Germany; of a succession of governesses Swiss and German, who exposed the precocious Violet, unsystematically but with contagious enthusiasm, to Schiller, Mozart, Goethe, and the Brothers Grimm; and of wandering the streets of Rome with her playfellow, the future painter John Singer Sargent, the pair of them 'bombarding' pigs with 'acorns and pebbles' one minute, 'hunt[ing] for bits of antique marbles [and] digging them out of the pavement with our umbrella ferrules' the next.[10]

Lee was the child of a second marriage, her mother, Matilda Paget (formerly Lee-Hamilton), having wedded the tutor she had engaged for her son Eugene's education. In the familial quartet thus forged, Henry Paget gives the impression of having been something of a supporting actor, with Matilda most definitely occupying centre stage. Contemporaries have left us a portrait of a diminutive, defiant throwback to an earlier age: a cosmopolitan woman in her own right, with the sensibility of an eighteenth-century *saloniste*. The great love of Vernon Lee's life, Mary Robinson,[11] would later write of Matilda's 'tremulous sensibility, her dominating will, her generous benevolence', adding, 'she was like . . . some friend of Buffon's, or patroness of Rousseau's . . . one could never think of her as wholly French or wholly English—"she came from Cosmopolis" ' (a reference, perhaps, to Paul Bourget's 1892 novel of that name).[12] Lee attributed, apparently quite seriously, this 'dominating will' to her mother's descent from

[10] Vernon Lee, 'J. S. S.: In Memoriam', in Evan Charteris, *John Sargent* (London, 1927), 233–55.

[11] Lee first met Mary, the daughter of a London banker, in 1880, and the two were devoted and passionately affectionate companions until Mary's devastating (to Lee) engagement to the Orientalist James Darmesteter in 1887. Soon after this, Lee began a long-term partnership with Clementina 'Kit' Anstruther-Thomson. The expressions used by modern biographers and critics to describe these relationships—'passionate friendship', 'romantic partnership'—are not euphemisms so much as labels acknowledging the difficulty of knowing whether these loving, emotionally intense relationships were also sexual; accordingly, scholars differ on whether Lee was a 'repressed lesbian' (as Vineta Colby calls her), an unrepressed one, or something more resistant to categorization.

[12] Madame Duclaux (Mary Robinson), 'In Casa Paget. A Retrospect. In Memoriam Eugène [*sic*] Lee-Hamilton', *Country Life*, 23 Dec. 1907, 935.

a colonial family which had made its fortunes in the West Indies before settling in Wales: 'It is the old slave driving spirit in the planter blood.'[13] It is not difficult to trace the origin of Lee's lifelong, Carlylean drive to work, to *produce*, at least in part, in her early internalization of this colonially inflected dynamic: as she would later write in her commonplace book, 'Myself is my strongest (& often worst) slave driver'.[14]

Equally important to her development was Lee's relationship with her half-brother Eugene, as well as the often-toxic dynamic generated by and within the Matilda–Eugene–Violet triad. (Again, Henry is the odd figure out—perhaps it is significant that, almost immediately after inventing the pseudonym 'H[enry]. P[aget]. Vernon Lee', Violet lopped off the preliminary initials.) Matilda Paget doted on her son; her letters to him at Oxford, with their affectedly Quakerish idiom, sound as if they were written by a hyper-solicitous maternal Polonius: 'Hast thou quinine pills with thee? If not, pray immediately desire a druggist to make thee up a scruple in 20 pills . . . Pray be on thy guard against the transitions of temperature!'[15] One does not need to be a Freudian to view Eugene as a quite literal casualty of this dotage: while in his late twenties, with a promising future in the Diplomatic Service ahead of him (albeit one about which he was highly ambivalent), he was transformed, with disconcerting suddenness, into a complete invalid, by means of a mind-forged paralysis about which we shall have more to say. When Eugene returned home in 1873, the hitherto nomadic Paget family ceased its wanderings and settled in Florence, anchored there, so to speak, by his immobile body, which appears in his own sonnets as a grotesque, even uncanny thing: he writes of the agony of 'keep[ing] through life the posture of the grave', bound to a

Hybrid of rack and of Procrustes' bed,
Thou thing of wood, and leather, and of steel,
Round which, by day and night, at head and heel,
Crouch shadowy Tormentors, dumb and dread.[16]

[13] *Selected Letters of Vernon Lee, 1856–1935*, vol. II, *1885–1889*, ed. Sophie Geoffroy (London and New York: 2021), 132.

[14] Quoted in ibid., lxiii.

[15] Quoted in Peter Gunn, *Vernon Lee*, 19.

[16] Eugene Hamilton-Lee, 'To the Muse' and 'To my Wheeled Bed', in 'A Wheeled Bed', *Sonnets of the Wingless Hours* (London, 1894), 3, 19.

Shadowy tormentors there may well have been, but in reality it was Violet who was most often stationed at his bedside 'by day and night', in perpetual service as a combination of nurse and amanuensis. In such circumstances, with Eugene's needs prioritized over hers for many years to come, it is astonishing that she found—or rather made—time to write, so much and so successfully.

Shortly before Eugene's return home, the fourteen-year-old Violet already had published her first work: a serialized story, written in French, following a Roman coin in its adventures through history. She was at work on her first Gothic tale, 'Winthrop's Adventure', as well: 'My story (the one I am now writing) is greatly mixed up with Italian music, so I have to read up on the subject.'[17] The origins of these tales, and of the intellectual obsessions of her adolescence more generally, lie in great measure in the summers the Pagets spent with the Sargent family. In long, as it were annotated, walks about Rome, Mrs Sargent gave Violet exhilarating object lessons in the power of the *genius loci*, the spirit of place, while she and John embarked on their own adventures of historical discovery. An 1872 visit to Bologna was particularly transformative: Lee would later recall how, as 'a half-baked polyglot scribbler of sixteen', she had spent 'ten days of historico-romantic rapture' in the old city, the two families together 'rambling . . . by moonlight, through the mediæval arcades and under the leaning towers and crenellations of that enormously picturesque and still unspoilt city'.[18] By day, Lee dragged John—who was, in her imagination, already '*the* great painter' of the future as well as '*the* comrade secretly expected to see in my vain self his equal and, so to speak, *twin*, in the sister-art of letters'—to the Accademia Filarmonica di Bologna, where they perused incomprehensible musical scores in superannuated keys and gazed up at the likenesses of Mozart, Handel, Haydn, and Gluck which hung in the neglected portrait gallery of the Accademia. One portrait in particular held them spellbound—that of Carlo Broschi, known as Farinelli, the superstar castrato singer of the eighteenth century, and as the two 'lingered and fantasticated in front of that smoky canvas . . . in the Bologna music-school', such

[17] *Selected Letters of Vernon Lee, 1856–1935*, vol. I, *1865–1884*, ed. Amanda Gagel (London and New York: 2016), 20.

[18] 'J. S. S.: In Memoriam', 248.

epithets as 'mysterious, uncanny, a wizard, serpent, sphinx; strange, weird, *curious*' fell from their lips.[19]

Like a protagonist in one of 'Vernon Lee's' history-haunted Gothic tales (she adopted the name in 1875), Violet had become all but possessed by the culture of a vanished place and time: the Italy of the eighteenth century. The fact that this period had been largely neglected by historians contributed, surely, in no small part to the subject's attraction to her; the teenaged cultural historian—for such she was—was staking out her own territory. 'I didn't care a pin about the Renaissance, or Antiquity, or the Middle Ages', she would later write, adding,

> I began to study that period—to read the books, even the newspapers, of the last century, which seemed to me full of actuality . . . I really did find my way into that period, and really did live in it . . . I had little or no connection with anything else. The eighteenth century existed for me as a reality, surrounded by faint and fluctuating shadows, which shadows were simply the present.[20]

The fruits of this intensive immersion in the all-but-forgotten cultural productions of eighteenth-century Italy were published in *Fraser's Magazine* (where Lee's first article in English, on 'Tuscan Peasant Plays', had already appeared), as lengthy essays on such comparatively recondite subjects as the Arcadian Academy (*Accademia dell'Arcadia*, a Roman literary society founded in 1690), music historian Charles Burney's 1770 journey through France and Italy, and the life and work of the once-preeminent librettist of *opera seria*, and bosom friend of Farinelli, Pietro Metastasio.

'Culture—Supernatural'

In this piecemeal fashion did Lee's first book, *Studies of the Eighteenth Century in Italy*, take shape (she would round out the volume with studies of the Italian commedia dell'arte and the Venetian playwrights Carlo Goldoni and Carlo Gozzi). Widely reviewed and, for the most part, well received upon its publication in 1880, the book would serve, in large measure, as her ticket of entrée into the literary and

[19] Vernon Lee, *For Maurice: Five Unlikely Stories* (London, 1927), xxx–xxxi.

[20] Vernon Lee, *Juvenilia: Being a Second Set of Essays on Sundry Aesthetical Questions* (Boston, 1887), 137.

intellectual circles of England the following summer. It also served as a breeding-ground for the first of Lee's 'culture-ghosts'—a coinage she came to regard, or to affect to regard, with a sense of embarrassment:

let me confess . . . that this correct ghost such as he was introduced to the reading public was distinguished by the adjectively employed noun *culture*; he was a 'Culture-Ghost' . . . the word *culture* signifying in the earliest 'eighties anything vaguely connected with Italy, art, and let us put it, the works of the late J. A. Symonds.[21]

The quotation is from the introduction to Lee's final collection of stories, *For Maurice: Five Unlikely Stories* (1927), in which 'A Culture-Ghost; or, Winthrop's Adventure' finally appeared in book form, unaltered beyond her lopping off the clunky first half of the original title. This is most definitely a 'culture-story' according to the above-quoted definition of 'culture', as are 'A Wicked Voice', 'Amour Dure', and 'A Wedding Chest', a tale of quattrocento Umbria which resembles a pastiche of Renaissance historian Francesco Matarazzo's *Chronicles of the City of Perugia*. There is some evidence that in writing these stories Lee considered herself to be pioneering a new Gothic form, or at least flavour:[22] replying to and, as it were, doubling down on, William Blackwood's rejection of her story 'Medea da Carpi' (later 'Amour Dure') for *Blackwood's Magazine*,[23] she tried, with equal lack of success, to sell the publisher on the idea of bundling it together with the earlier 'A Culture-Ghost':

I don't suppose it is much use asking, but before applying elsewhere, I should be glad to know whether you would care to publish this & another similar story of what I may term 'Culture–Supernatural' which appeared, & was much talked of, in the Jan 81 number of Longmans? They are highly finished little things, & I shd like to see them in a tiny volume.[24]

It may be worth probing this prospective category of 'Culture–Supernatural' a bit further, particularly as the concept of 'culture' was just then undergoing significant semantic change. This can be seen, for instance, in the emergence of 'cultural history', a field of study with

[21] *For Maurice*, xxxvi.

[22] Her 1880 essay 'Faustus and Helena', which theorizes the supernatural in relation to the aesthetic, shows that she was training her formidable analytical intelligence upon the subject as well.

[23] As 'Amour Dure', the story would be published instead in *Murray's Magazine* (1887), before being included in *Hauntings* (1890).

[24] *Selected Letters* II, 72–3.

which Lee's stories have a symbiotic relationship. It is a cliché to say of Lee's stories merely that they are 'haunted by the past' (the same could be said of most Gothic and horror fiction); what Lee brings to the fantastic tale, to a degree which few have done before or since, is an exquisitely developed historical consciousness, one in tune with the multidimensional conception of history associated particularly with the Swiss historian Jakob Burkhardt, author of *The Civilisation of the Renaissance in Italy* (1860). Such stories as 'Amour Dure' fuse the Gothic tale with this nineteenth-century historiographic imagination, imbuing the story with a formidable 'thickness' of historical particularity. Another likely influence on Lee was the novelist Elizabeth Gaskell, whose Gothic tales she seems to have envisioned as models for her own, writing her mentor Henrietta Jenkin (another important female influence in Lee's life) in 1874, 'I do not think that a regular magazine, Fraser for instance, would accept ~~stories~~ tales of the length & sort of Mrs Gaskell's ghost stories'[25] (apparently she was already scouting potential markets for her first 'culture-ghost'). It is not difficult to imagine Lee drawing inspiration from the carefully realized seventeenth- and eighteenth-century settings of such stories and novellas as 'Lois the Witch', 'The Grey Woman', and 'The Poor Clare' (the latter tale also features a portrait which anticipates Lee's 'Virgin of the Seven Daggers').[26]

Noteworthy, too, is the attention Lee pays to the modes and mechanisms of cultural transmission, her interest (perhaps inspired by that proto-media theorist of the Victorian age, Walter Pater) in the media of the past—inevitable harbingers of Lee's 'spurious ghosts', as she called them. There is, of course, nothing novel in the idea that the revenants of the past return to plague us through haunted or cursed objects, and the device of the haunted portrait in particular, whose iconic resemblance to its departed subject gives it a special place among such artefacts, is a Gothic trope of long standing. But consider, in 'Amour Dure', the multi-media assault which Medea da Carpi launches against the hapless cultural historian Spiridion Trepka, rather like a Renaissance version of Sadako from the Japanese horror film *Ringu*: she first appears to him in the 'dry pages' of

[25] *Selected Letters* I, 170.

[26] 'Our Lady of the Holy Heart, the Papists call it. It is a picture of the Virgin, her heart pierced with arrows, each arrow representing one of her great woes.' Elizabeth Gaskell, 'The Poor Clare', in *Gothic Tales*, ed. Laura Kranzler (London, 2000), 55.

history books; he then finds a miniature of her, a marble bust, a historical painting in which she appears, her handwritten letters, and a portrait in oils; he then begins to receive *new* letters written by her, with her punning device stamped in wax (he even writes, or perhaps channels, a haunting, and similarly punning, poem-song, 'Medea, mia dea'). Many media; invariably, however, Medea is the message.

Perhaps the story in which Lee most deeply probes the idea of culture as a dynamic, evolving concept is 'A Wicked Voice', her thoroughgoing revision of 'Winthrop's Adventure'. While both tales concern the haunting of a nineteenth-century man by a castrato singer from the past, the scene has shifted from Bologna to Venice, and the singer is now villain—a 'vocal villain', in Lee's phrase—rather than victim. Significant, too, is the emphatic recentring of the locus of the uncanny music in the 'voice' itself, as a detachable organ or object, rather than the singer. One suspects that the shifting media ecology of the intervening decade helped to shape, perhaps to inspire, this rewriting. Lee would later write that Farinelli 'would not have been merely a ghost but an awful, audible, deathless reality like Caruso quavering from a house-boat at Hampton Court, if gramophones had been invented a couple of centuries earlier . . . ignorant that gramophones were about to be invented, what would we [she and Sargent] not have given if some supernatural mechanism had allowed us to catch the faintest vibrations of that voice!'[27] Given that the technology first appeared between the composition of Lee's two stories,[28] it is tempting to see the later tale's account of a portable, disembodied *voix acousmatique*, contrasting with Winthrop's simultaneous, integrated experience of embodied singer and song, as a response to the new paradigm for the storage and mechanical reproduction of sound.[29]

Neither of the baleful arias in these stories (as 'mal-arias', they punningly mirror the malarial 'bad air' and 'fever' which also threaten the health of Magnus and Winthrop, respectively) kill their hearers, but both men are blighted by their experience, with Magnus suffering

[27] *For Maurice*, xxviii–xxix.

[28] Thomas Edison's phonograph in 1877, and Emile Berliner's gramophone (which by the twentieth century was a generic term for the machine in Britain) in 1887 ('Winthrop's Adventure' was composed in the early 1870s, with 'Voix Maudite', the original French version of 'A Wicked Voice', being completed in 1887).

[29] *Voix acousmatique* is Michel Chion's phrase. (Lee was also thinking about her friend and singer Mary Wakefield in similar terms at this time, fantasizing that her ravishing voice might be detached from her irritating self.)

from a particularly horrible (to a composer) form of haunting or possession. It is not a spirit which possesses him, however—a consciousness or personality—but an idiom, a way of thinking and writing, of expressing himself. And here we can see Lee figuring the strangeness of enculturation itself—the process by which we 'become ourselves' through, paradoxically, the internalization of texts and other cognitive technologies, alien artefacts from the past. Stricken with a bad case of the eighteenth century, Magnus laments, 'I am wasted by a strange and deadly disease. I can never lay hold of my inspiration. My head is filled with music which is certainly by me, since I have never heard it before, but which still is not my own' (p. 162). As an artist, he is no longer 'himself', no longer 'original'. But what does this really mean? Before his penetration by Zaffirino's infectiously 'languishing phrases', Magnus had been a perfect Wagnerite; now he is a perfect . . . Porporite, perhaps.[30] The transformation is only so disconcerting, so catastrophically threatening to his sense of self, because he had naturalized the Wagnerian idiom; culture, the story reminds us, both precedes and constructs the individual. As if to reinforce this point, the reader is presented with a series of seeming dichotomies between nature and culture which, upon closer inspection, resolve themselves into a spectrum comprising different kinds or levels of culture: Magnus leaves the city, site of high (as well as vulgarly popular) culture, for the country. But the country is itself defined, quite insistently, in terms of other forms of 'culture': agriculture, horticulture, sericulture. As Raymond Williams shows, over the course of the nineteenth century the residual meaning of 'culture' as the 'tending of . . . crops and animals' continued to give way to its modern sense, or rather multiple senses, including first of all the idea of human intellectual and artistic development.[31] In 'A Wicked Voice' (and to an extent 'Winthrop's Adventure'), Lee pointedly juxtaposes both of these meanings, as if to say: There is no escaping the grip of culture.

Mythologies

A second book by Lee, far less heralded then and today nearly forgotten, appeared at the same time as *Studies in the Eighteenth Century*,

[30] After Nicola Porpora (1686–1768), composer and singing teacher to Farinelli.

[31] Raymond Williams, *Keywords: A Vocabulary of Culture and Society* (Oxford and New York, 1983), 87.

a 'dainty little volume' (in the words of a reviewer) highlighting Lee's keen and abiding interests in folklore, philology, comparative mythology, and popular narrative traditions. Considered together, these two early books go a long way towards emblematizing her fantastic stories, which, not unlike the work of such Modernists as Joyce and Eliot, blend history with myth, two equally rich sources of inspiration to her.

Tuscan Fairy Tales (Taken down from the Mouths of the People) shows Lee taking on, or perhaps more accurately flirting with, the roles of folklorist and collector of *Märschen*. These roles had been pioneered by Jacob and Wilhelm Grimm, whose celebrated retellings of German and European folktales had occupied a special place in Lee's imagination since the days of her German childhood. After the Grimms came a veritable deluge, as nineteenth-century scholars sought to collect, preserve, and disseminate in written form a formerly ignored, and often despised, wealth of folk material—tales, poems, jokes, songs, proverbs—throughout Europe and elsewhere. Given that such orally transmitted genres had come to be seen as organically expressing the 'soul' of a people, it is no accident that the folklore hunters were particularly active in the two European 'nations' which were, precisely, not yet nations, that is to say, modern nation-states—namely, Germany and Italy. Lee's entry into the field should accordingly be viewed within the broader contexts of nationalism's rise in nineteenth-century Europe in general and, more specifically, the legacies of the recently consummated Italian Risorgimento (a presence in such tales as 'Dionea', 'Amour Dure', and especially 'The Legend of Madame Krasinska', where the bloody Battle of Solferino serves as the tragic catalyst for Sora Lena's anguished madness). In 1860, the year the revolutionary general Giuseppe Garibaldi landed his 'Expedition of the Thousand' in Sicily, the critic Alessandro d'Ancona had exhorted his countrymen to imitate the Grimms in documenting the popular narrative traditions of an aspirant nation, and the following decades—the 1870s in particular—saw the publication of a steady stream of Italian folklore collections,[32] harvested from the various corners of a nation only fully unified politically in 1871.

[32] Jack Zipes, Introduction to Thomas Frederick Crane, *Italian Popular Tales*, ed. Jack Zipes (Oxford, 2003), xvi.

Three of these collections—Laura Gonzenbach's *Sicilianische Märchen* ('Sicilian Folk Tales', 1870), Domenico Giuseppe Bernoni's *Fiabe e Novelle Popolari Veneziane* ('Popular Venetian Fables and Stories', 1873), and Rachel Harriette Busk's *Roman Legends: A Collection of the Fables and Folk-Lore of Rome* (1877)—are credited by Lee as inspirations for her own project:

It is no easy matter to obtain a glimpse of the popular mythology of Tuscany; nay, so disheartening are the suspicious reserve and assumed incredulity of the peasantry, that I long doubted whether any folklore really did exist among these people. But the rich collections of the folklore of Rome, of Venetia, and of Sicily . . . persuaded me that Tuscany could not be as barren of fairy tales as its sceptical and obstinate people would fain have one believe. Nor have I proved at all mistaken. Tuscany, at least the more remote parts, like the Val d'Elsa, the Garfagnana, and the neighbourhood of Carrara, whence all my stories have been obtained, possesses a very remarkable popular mythology.[33]

Here Lee presents herself as a mere, if scrupulous, recorder of (as yet unrecorded) orally transmitted material, amassing a trove of '*novelle*, *novelline*, [and] *fiabe*' and 'select[ing] ten of the most striking of those I have heard, without altering any point of the narration'. To be sure, the extent to which Lee truly extracted the handful of tales which make up her collection 'literally from the mouths of the people', as she insists, is difficult to know for certain. But there are reasons to be sceptical. No doubt she did spend time among the Tuscan *popoli*, gathering material; a letter of 1879 refers to the store of 'very curious facts about the life & ideas of these peasants, which I picked up last year while hearing fairy tales from them'.[34] But the omission, in the above-quoted preface, of any mention of the numerous existing Italian-language collections of Tuscan folklore with which Lee must certainly have been familiar,[35] with the implication that she was striking out into virgin territory, strikes one as disingenuous. One notes as well that the American folklorist Thomas Frederick Crane, while praising the manner of their telling, pointed out in a review that the ten stories in *Tuscan Fairy Tales* 'are only versions of tales already

[33] *Tuscan Fairy Tales*, 5–6. [34] *Selected Letters* II, 251–2.

[35] Recent collections of, or including, Tuscan folk material include *Le Novelline di Santo Stefano* (1869) by Lee's friend and editor Angelo De Gubernatis, Vittorio Imbriani's *La Novellaja Fiorentina* (1871), Domenico Comparetti's *Novelline Popolari Italiane* (1875), and Giuseppe Pitré's *Novelline Popolari Toscane* (1878).

printed in other collections'.[36] What seems most likely is that Lee saw an opportunity to corner the English-language market on the subject, particularly after the Englishwoman Harriet Busk's collection of Roman legends had demonstrated how little exposure the English-speaking world had had to the popular narratives of Italy, and assembled a slender collection drawing, in some proportion impossible now to determine, upon oral and written sources alike.

If the book's contributions to the study of folklore are slight, however, it yet remains a highly significant text when viewed in light of Lee's own development as a writer of the fantastic. Certainly there are themes and images in the particular stories Lee chooses to retell here which resonate with her own fiction, as in the Sleeping Beauty variant 'The Glass Coffin',[37] 'The Three Golden Apples', and 'The Woman of Paste', in which 'a sort of doll, but life-size' is supernaturally animated; one of the tales, 'The King of Portugal's Cowherd', even makes a brief appearance in 'Prince Alberic and the Snake Lady', a nod, perhaps, to family and friends familiar with her authorship of the earlier collection. More generally, from her earliest years Lee devoured folk and fairy tales, fables, legends, and myths from a myriad of sources and cultures, drawing upon them for inspiration in a number of ways. Her fiction bristles with references to classical mythology, biblical (and, in 'The Virgin of the Seven Daggers', Quranic) stories, the lives and acts of the Catholic saints, and the narrative cycle known as 'the Matter of France' (legends involving Charlemagne and his knights, which would be used by narrative poets of the Middle Ages and Renaissance), among other sources. Some childhood favourites, such as the *One Thousand and One Nights*, remained perennial resources for Lee the storyteller: she writes of 'help[ing] out the notion' of 'The Virgin of the Seven Daggers' 'by re-reading a book much thumbed in childhood, [Edward] Lane's *Arabian Nights*'.[38] Lee was influenced, too, as Pater and others had been, by the German poet Heinrich Heine's conceit of the survival of the classical deities in a post-classical world as monsters or demons (see headnote to 'Dionea').

[36] *The Nation*, 31 (22 July 1880), 63.

[37] The Brothers Grimm tell a version of this tale; Lee might also have read G. Pitré's specifically Tuscan version, 'La Scatola di Cristallo' ('The Crystal Casket'), published a few years earlier.

[38] *For Maurice*, xxi.

One collection which appears to have been a particularly rich source of ideas is *Curious Myths of the Middle Ages*, by the clergyman, novelist, and antiquarian Sabine Baring-Gould (1834–1924), whose other works include *The Book of Were-Wolves* and a sixteen-volume *Lives of the Saints*. Lee read the book in 1886, writing to her mother in July, 'I am sending off a copy of the book on Mediaeval Myth; I hope E. [Eugene] may find something in it. I will look out about the Were-Wolf book by the same author.'[39] Certainly Lee herself appears to have 'found something in it', to judge by the traces to be found in her own stories. Almost immediately after reading Baring-Gould's compilation, Lee began work on 'A Wicked Voice', with its young Norwegian composer trying to finish a Wagnerian music-drama based on the story of Ogier the Dane, one of Charlemagne's knights. Baring-Gould's treatment of the Ogier legend is slight, and Lee would have known of the figure from the *Chanson de Roland* and perhaps other sources as well. But it is suggestive that Baring-Gould links Ogier with 'Siegfrid [*sic*] or Sigurd', the mythical hero used by Wagner in the Ring operas *Siegfried* and *Götterdämmerung*, suggesting a possible spark for Lee's idea of a counterfactual Wagnerian opera. Longer treatments can be found in Baring-Gould of the legends of 'St Patrick's Purgatory', another key influence on 'The Virgin of the Seven Daggers', and of 'The Mountain of Venus', the story, used also by Wagner, of the knight Tannhäuser who tarries with 'the pagan Goddess of Love' in her subterranean palace, which Baring-Gould bundles together with other post-classical legends of the 'heathen' Venus/Aphrodite. Two Lee stories—'The Gods and Ritter Tanhûser' and 'St Eudaemon and his Orange-Tree'—spring directly from these tales,[40] while *Curious Myths* contains several possible sources for 'Prince Alberic and the Snake Lady' as well (see headnote to 'Prince Alberic'). As one soon learns when seeking to trace lines of influence in her work, however, it is dangerous to try to pin down the formidably widely read Lee to a single source; the wise reader will eventually make peace with the impossibility of running to

[39] *Selected Letters* II, 197.

[40] 'St Eudaemon and his Orange-Tree', which appeared in the 1904 collection *Pope Jacynth and Other Fantastic Tales*, has been called a 'cheerful variation of Prosper Mérimée's "Venus de l'Ille" ' (Colby, 241), but in fact both are retellings of a medieval story related by Baring-Gould.

ground each and every ingredient in her richly layered, overdetermined fantasies.

Brain Phantoms and Maniac Frowns

Lee lived during a transformative period in science and medicine, nowhere more so than within the many disciplines devoted to probing the mysteries of the human mind, seemingly every one of which left its mark upon Lee's writing. Philosophies and sciences of mind and brain should, indeed, be counted among her most important, yet least explored, influences. The nineteenth century alone saw the parallel emergence of modern psychology and neurology, with the birth of the latter being embodied in the Napoleonic figure of Jean-Martin Charcot (1825–93), dictatorial chief of the famous Salpêtrière hospital in Paris. Throughout Europe and beyond, there proliferated new disciplines, discourses, treatments, and methods of documentation and representation concerned with mental disorders, including those manifesting as ailments of the body; so, too, did new kinds of institutions: the modern hospital, asylum, and clinic. In her non-fiction writing, Lee engaged directly with virtually all of the cutting-edge psychological theories of the day; her work on aesthetic theory, for instance, drew upon—and in turn was often reviewed by—such prominent figures as evolutionary psychologist Karl Groos, philosopher of mind Theodor Lipps, experimental psychologist Oswald Külpe, and Théodule Ribot, author of *La Psychologie des Sentiments* (1896), whom Lee would later call 'my master' in the field.[41] While writing critically of William James's *The Will to Believe*,[42] Lee greatly valued his 1890 masterpiece *Principles of Psychology*. The end of the nineteenth century, of course, witnessed the birth of psychoanalysis, about which Lee expressed extreme ambivalence: calling the 'obscurantist' Freud her 'bête noire',[43] she was nonetheless forced to acknowledge in the aftermath of World War I that, despite the myopic focus of 'the Freudians' on sex as the master key to human experience,

[41] *Satan, the Waster*, xxv.

[42] In both 'The Need to Believe: An Agnostic's Notes on Professor William James', *Fortnightly Review* 66 (Nov. 1899), 827–42; reprinted in *Gospels of Anarchy and Other Contemporary Studies* (1908), and, at greater length and more polemically, *Vital Lies: Studies of Some Varieties of Recent Obscurantism* (1912).

[43] Peter Gunn, *Vernon Lee: Violet Paget, 1856–1935* (Oxford, 1964), 230.

'their insistence on hidden springs of our thought and action' represented a 'great gift to psychology'.[44] Later, in a lengthy introduction to the English edition of her friend Richard Semon's *Mnemic Psychology*,[45] Lee, roaming freely among the works of Ribot, German physiologist Ewald Hering, Samuel Butler, and Bertrand Russell, hinted that the work might contain the key to all future psychologies.

To be sure, and taking solely into account Lee's sheer intellectual rapaciousness—her first biographer, by way of noting 'the erudition of this provocatively articulate blue-stocking', unspools a dauntingly lengthy yet necessarily incomplete list of the subjects represented in her library at Il Palmerino, from Marxism to meteorology[46]—it would be surprising if she did *not* evince any interest in contemporary developments in the study of mind and brain. But it is difficult to escape the conclusion that Lee's interest in this particular subject was highly personal as well as intellectual, and often tinged with a decided sense of urgency. As her letters reveal, much of her reading in psychology was connected to, if not driven by, family efforts to treat her brother's, and sometimes her own, psychosomatic illnesses. Rather like someone surfing the Internet in search of alternative remedies for a chronic condition, Lee, in long-distance collaboration with Eugene and Matilda, was always on the lookout for possible new treatments: in September 1889, we find Eugene writing dubiously to Lee about the 'suspension treatment'—in other words, being hung up like a side of beef for hours at a time—recommended in his case to Mary Robinson (now Darmesteter),[47] and more enthusiastically of 'the wonderful effects recently obtained in Paris in diseases of the brain & spine by

[44] *Satan, the Waster*, 143.

[45] Semon, a nearly forgotten figure today, was an evolutionary biologist whose theories of memory were developed in the books *Die Mneme* (1904) and *Die Mnemischen Empfindungen* (1909); the latter was translated by Lee's friend Bella Duffy as *Mnemic Psychology* (Lee insisted upon using 'Psychology' in the English title, rather than the more accurate 'Sensations').

[46] Gunn, *Vernon Lee*, 8.

[47] The 'celebrated French doctor' making the recommendation may have been Charcot's former intern and eventual successor Fulgence Raymond, or possibly Charcot himself, though one would expect Mary to have named him. While Charcot had tried suspension on sufferers from Parkinson's disease earlier that same year, the procedure was more often associated with the treatment of syphilis-induced *tabes dorsalis*; perhaps this is why Eugene insisted, 'I am sure Mary described my case all wrong', immediately sending a follow-up 'memorandum begging her to show it to the Doctor in question... [s]uspension is quite out of the question in my case'. *Selected Letters* II, 556.

making the patient look at rotating mirrors; it produces apparently immediately a deep trance'. In response, Lee promises to track down 'the Rotary Mirror man'—this was Jules-Bernard Luys, author of the magisterial 'brain atlas'[48] *Recherches sur le système nerveux cérébro-spinal*—while suggesting that a course of hypnotic treatment, as recently advocated by psychologists Alfred Binet and Charles Feré, might represent a more promising possibility.[49] The great Charcot himself weighed in on Eugene's mysterious malady: 'I think the affliction comes under the category of cerebro-spinal neurasthenia, with peculiarities, however, which make it very different from the common type.'[50] But it was not until the eminent German neurologist Wilhelm Heinrich Erb took up the case in 1893, declaring Eugene's complaint to be entirely 'produced by a very high degree of auto-suggestion'[51] (as Lee had come herself to suspect), that his condition began to improve (though Lee's 'bête noire' in Vienna might have had something to say about the fact that Eugene's final recovery in 1896 coincided with the steeply declining health of Matilda, who died shortly thereafter).

Lee herself, meanwhile, suffered from depression and 'on & off seediness with neuralgia', and was subject to mental and emotional breakdowns, notably in the wake of Mary's 1887 engagement. She saw herself as foredoomed by both nature and nurture (both, significantly, deriving from Matilda) to mental instability, writing in 1894: 'I recognise now that my family is, on one side, acutely neuropathic and hysterical; and that my earlier years were admirably calculated . . . to develop these characteristics.'[52] Furthermore, while Lee's status vis-à-vis modern categories of lesbian identity may be complicated, she can hardly have been unaware that she would have been viewed as sexually non-normative, if not aberrant. Certainly many of her contemporaries so viewed her: some 'caricatured [her] for her passionate celibacy',[53] while her correspondent John Addington Symonds proposed her to Havelock Ellis as 'a possible case-history, for the section on Lesbianism', in what would become the pioneering medical

[48] John S. McKenzie, 'Jules-Bernard Luys and his Brain Atlas', *University of Melbourne Collections*, no. 6, 2010, 20–5.

[49] *Selected Letters* II, 558.

[50] Quoted in Gunn, *Vernon Lee*, 22.

[51] Quoted in ibid.

[52] Quoted in Colby, *Vernon Lee*, 2.

[53] Martha Vicinus, 'Lesbian Ghosts', in Noreen Giffney, Michelle M. Sauer, and Diane Watt, eds, *The Lesbian Premodern* (New York, 2011), 194.

textbook *Sexual Inversion* (1896).[54] We also know now that for years Lee did volunteer work, with her friend Amy Turton, at Florence's famous insane asylum, *l'Ospedale di Bonifazio*. In short, she had both an intellectual and, as caregiver and sufferer, a deeply personal investment in the mind and its disorders. It is little wonder that she explored these topics in her fiction as well.

Mental disorders feature most centrally in two stories with intriguing parallels, 'Oke of Okehurst' and 'The Legend of Madame Krasinska'. The former was first published by William Blackwood as a 'shilling dreadful'[55] bearing the more evocative title 'A Phantom Lover', and has been one of her best-known tales ever since. At one level 'Oke', which traces the slow unfolding of a *folie à deux*—or *à trois*—that ends in catastrophe, reads like a case study in abnormal psychology, much like Robert Louis Stevenson's (far better-known) *Strange Case of Dr Jekyll and Mr Hyde*. There are indeed quite a few parallels to be drawn between the two Gothic novellas, published within months of each other in 1886 (in the case of 'Oke' this was at Blackwood's urging, perhaps suggesting that he saw in the story a potential response to Longmans' coup in publishing *Jekyll and Hyde*). More than one reviewer compared Lee's tale—favourably—to Stevenson's. The *St James's Gazette* declared, ' "A Phantom Lover" is probably the best shilling story since "Dr Jekyll." It is short, it is startling', while *The Academy* enthused that the novella, 'alone among the recent numerous contributions to the literature of eeriness can be placed by the side of *The Strange Case of Dr Jekyll and Mr Hyde*', observing that 'its style [was] sometimes as matter-of-fact as a report by a mad doctor'.[56] Probably it was one of these that Lee sent to her mother in August 1886 with the comment, 'The enclosed review will please you: "Dr Jekyll" is a story by R. L. Stevenson; personally I consider mine very much better, but that is perhaps because I have no sympathy for the prosaic, unpicturesque kind of supernatural.'

[54] Phyllis Grosskurth, *John Addington Symonds: A Biography* (London, 1964), 223.

[55] A short, sensational novel aimed at a mass audience; 'A Phantom Lover' was Lee's only tale to be published in this form. A hugely prolific writer, she was never a 'popular', or financially successful, one.

[56] The *Academy*'s reviewer, William Wallace, went on to add, 'Vernon Lee's success is, in a sense, a more purely literary one than Mr Stevenson's. It is accomplished by means of the morbid, and not by the miraculous; and, unfortunately, the morbid plays only too important a part in real life.' *The Athenaeum* (28 Aug. 1886), 134.

(Writing to Stevenson himself earlier that month to let him know that she had asked Blackwood to send him a copy of 'A Phantom Lover', Lee refrained from dwelling on the superior merits of her tale, calling it 'a very humble offering from a very sincere admirer'.[57])

It is significant that the *Academy* reviewer, while both praising Lee's story and linking it with Stevenson's, likens it to a clinical report on a case of insanity. *Jekyll and Hyde* has been extensively analysed in relation to Victorian medical discourses: as a fictional exploration of contemporaneous theories of psychological duality, hysteria and other disorders, as a 'literary stud[y] of the unconscious', and, perhaps most of all, as a response to the influential ideas of Italian criminologist Cesare Lombroso, whose *l'Uomo Deliquente* (1876) pointed to visible, physiological signs, stamped upon the face, of innate psychological abnormality.[58] Every one of these approaches can be applied with equal salience and force to 'Oke'. Direct influence is a possibility—*Jekyll and Hyde* appeared early in January, while Lee was still at work on her story—but there is no need to presume it. She knew the work of Lombroso, writing of him, along with his fellow theorist of degeneracy Max Nordau, in her essay 'Deterioration of Soul'.[59] She might have been familiar as well with such Italian followers as Augusto Tebaldi, the head of a Pavian asylum, who had also visited Charcot's famed Salpêtrière. Two books by Tebaldi had appeared in the early 1880s; in the first, the reader was presented with a veritable photographic atlas of 'cretins', 'imbeciles', 'idiots', and 'maniacs', and other madmen and -women, and invited to read the truth of their inner maladies in the facial signifiers captured by the camera's eye. The 'maniaco', for instance, could be identified by the presence of 'le rughe longitudinali della fronte' ('longitudinal

[57] *Selected Letters* II, 223, 214.

[58] The quotation is from Edward S. Reed's *From Soul to Mind: The Emergence of Psychology from Erasmus Darwin to William James* (New Haven, 1997), 164; Reed treats the novella alongside nineteenth-century works of psychological theory as an original contribution to the emergent idea of an irrational unconscious. On the connection between *Jekyll and Hyde* and Lombroso, one might begin with Stephen J. Arata, 'The Sedulous Ape: Atavism, Professionalism, and Stevenson's *Jekyll and Hyde*', *Criticism*, 37(2) (Spring 1995), 233–59; Anne Stiles traces the possible influence of theories of the 'double brain' in the essay 'Robert Louis Stevenson's "Jekyll and Hyde" and the Double Brain', *Studies in English Literature, 1500–1900*, 46(4) (Autumn 2006), 879–900.

[59] First published in the *Fortnightly Review*, 59 (June 1896), 928–43, and included in her later book *Gospels of Anarchy and Other Contemporary Studies*.

lines of the forehead').[60] It is just this physiognomic peculiarity which appears on William Oke's ordinarily unremarkable countenance in times of stress or agitation; at their first meeting, the narrator remarks 'the only interesting thing about him—a very odd nervous frown between his eyebrows, a perfect double gash—a thing which usually means something abnormal: a mad-doctor of my acquaintance calls it the maniac-frown' (p. 40). If, as Lombroso and his disciples insisted, physiognomy is destiny, then the tragedy of the novella's conclusion is already written, as it were, in its first pages—a fact the narrator's painterly eye, functioning like a mad-doctor's camera, appears to intuit long before Oke's mountingly erratic behaviour might warrant concern. Again Lee's 'shocker' contains echoes of Stevenson's; her narrator sees Oke's hidden Hyde, but must depict his Jekyll: 'It was with this expression of face that I should have liked to paint him; but I felt that he would not have liked it, that it was more fair to him to represent him in his mere wholesome pink and white and blond conventionality' (p. 49). (Perhaps here, in the portrait *manqué* which would have revealed Oke's darker self, we also see an anticipation of Oscar Wilde's *The Picture of Dorian Gray*, written in 1889.)

Significant, too, is the ontological ambiguity of Christopher Lovelock, the long-dead Cavalier poet with whom Alice Oke is infatuated, provoking her husband's murderous jealousy; as with Peter Quint and Miss Jessel in James's 'The Turn of the Screw', it is possible to interpret Lovelock as either a 'real' apparition or the figment of a diseased imagination (another reason to take seriously the question of 'the Master's' indebtedness to Lee). It is especially interesting that Lovelock is described as a 'phantom' lover, rather than, say, a 'ghostly' or 'spectral' one,[61] given the emergent uses of 'phantom'—a word that straddles the supernatural and the psychological—as both noun and adjective in neurological contexts in the later nineteenth century (most famously, the American neurologist Silas Weir Mitchell had coined the term 'phantom limb' in 1871, in reference to the phenomenon experienced by many amputees). The psychological orientation

[60] Augusto Tebaldi, *Fisonomia ed Espressione Studiate nelle loro Deviazioni* (Padova, 1881), 125.

[61] It was Blackwood, presumably for marketing reasons, who insisted on changing the title (from 'Oke of Okehurst') in the original book publication, though Lee may have had a hand in choosing the new title, and she used 'The Phantom Lover' as the story's subtitle when including it in *Hauntings* a few years later.

of the tale generally, and Lee's conception of a 'phantom lover' particularly, may well have been influenced by her reading, including the work of her friend Paul Bourget and of Hippolyte Taine, whose account of the brain and its ontologically elusive 'fantômes' (see headnote to 'Oke') might have helped to shape Lee's conception of the Okes (Alice implies that she, too, experiences Lovelock—in how many sensory registers is left to the imagination—but this may simply be part of her sadistic play-acting). For his part, the narrator has evidently, like Lee, been reading up on the subject: shortly before the catastrophe of the tale, in an attempt to get his tormented host to 'see a good doctor' about his 'delusions' and 'morbid fancies', he 'pour[s] out volumes of psychological explanation', to which the distracted Oke can only reply, rather vaguely, 'I am sure what you say is true. I daresay it is all that I'm seedy. I feel sometimes as if I were mad, and just fit to be locked up' (p. 81).

Perhaps he should have been; certainly the narrator's 'mad-house doctor' friend would have considered Oke, with that danger sign etched upon his brow, a candidate for confinement. But if the spectre of the institutional remains at the margins of 'Oke of Okehurst', it lies closer to the heart of another story of insanity and possession, 'The Legend of Madame Krasinska', first published in early 1890 in the *Fortnightly Review*. One might indeed call this a tale of two institutions, the first being the benign 'asylum' operated by the order of the Little Sisters of the Poor in Florence, where the young, beautiful American widow Madame Krasinska, as Mother Antoinette Marie, finds her true vocation and where, the reader may infer, the tragic figure of Sora Lena, the 'hulking old' madwoman wandering the city's streets, might have found some measure of true 'caritas' or charity (another of the story's core themes), had it been in existence earlier.[62] While not herself heartless, at least according to the standards of her class, Madame Krasinska commits a heartless act, masquerading as the Sora Lena at a 'fancy ball'. Only her friend Cecchino (yet another of Lee's painter-characters) sees the cruelty in her choice of 'costume' (complete with a cunningly wrought mask she has fashioned of cardboard, using one of his sketches as a guide). But then, he is not of her station: the high-society revellers,

[62] The order came to Florence in 1882, establishing the refuge referred to in 'Madame Krasinska' in 1888—an event possibly inspiring in part the story, whose main action would seem to take place no later than the early 1880s.

valuing, like the late-Victorian Aesthete of caricature, artistic 'effect' above all other considerations, including (or especially) moral ones, are as delighted as he is horrified by her performance, which both dehumanizes and gothicizes the madwoman ('the thing'):

> [T]here walked into the middle of the white and gold drawing-room, a lumbering, hideous figure, with reddish, vacant face, sunk in an immense, tarnished satin bonnet; and draggled, faded, lilac silk skirts spread over a vast dislocated crinoline. The feet dabbed along in the broken prunella boots; the mangy rabbit-skin muff bobbed loosely with the shambling gait . . . the thing looked slowly round, a gaping, mooning, blear-eyed stare . . . There was a perfect storm of applause. (p. 170)

The cruelty may be collective, but the karmic punishment is individual, as Madame Krasinska begins to be infected, or possessed, by the madness of the woman whose semblance she has put on. At the very moment of this triumph of simulation, the original has hanged herself from a rafter in Florence's old Jewish ghetto ('Suicide of a female lunatic', reads the next day's headline); thereafter, Madame Krasinska becomes a progressively worsening case study in psychological 'alienation' in the most literal sense, with the Sora Lena's thoughts and memories intruding upon her own, mingling with them in what Lee presents as a proto-Modernist stream of blended consciousness, until finally she cries out, 'Ah, I am she—I am she—I am mad!'

Madame Krasinska's carnivalesque act of mimicry is thus performative in more than one sense, functioning as a supernatural invocation or invitation, an instance of what anthropologist James George Frazer had termed in *The Golden Bough*, published the previous year, 'sympathetic' or 'contagious magic'. Even without the benefit of magical influence, however, Lee worried that madness could be contagious, transmissible—perhaps especially between and among women. As we have seen, she was acutely aware that mental illness might be encoded in her own hereditary make-up, speculating about the family backgrounds of other women as well, including Lady Archibald Campbell. The case of her friend, the Anglo-Jewish poet Amy Levy, may be particularly relevant here: Levy had committed suicide in September 1889,[63] prompting Lee to write to her mother: 'But she had every right: she learned in the last 6 weeks that she was

[63] Albeit by carbon monoxide poisoning (the method used by Father Domenico in 'Dionea') rather than hanging.

on the verge of a terrible & loathsome form of madness apparently running in the family.'[64] It is unlikely to be coincidence that Lee dramatizes the suicide of the Sora Lena—and the near-suicide of the anguished, mentally deteriorating Madame Krasinska—in a house in the defunct Jewish quarter which Levy had recently immortalized in her essay 'The Ghetto at Florence'.[65]

It is telling, too, that the Sora Lena's—and later, channelling her, Madame Krasinska's—greatest fear is of institutionalization in the very hospital where Lee did charitable work:

> Oh, no, no, not that—anything rather than be shut up in a hospital. The poor old woman did no one any harm—why shut her up? . . . Don't speak of San Bonifazio! I have seen it. It is where they keep the mad folk and the wretched, dirty, wicked, wicked old women . . . The thought of that strange, lofty whitewashed place, which she had never seen, but which she knew so well, with an altar in the middle, and rows and rows of beds . . . and horrid slobbering and gibbering old women. Oh . . . she could hear them! (p. 181)

We can see a portion of this 'strange, lofty whitewashed place' in a celebrated canvas by Lee's friend, the painter Telemaco Signorini (1835–1901), the almost naturalistic *La Sala delle Agitate al San Bonifazio in Firenze* (The Ward of the Madwomen at San Bonifazio in Florence), also known as *Le Pazze* (The Crazy Ones) (1865). It is tempting to see in one of the shrouded, almost shapeless figures depicted there—perhaps the stoutish one standing to the right of the painting, head bent to one side, hands held, or bound, behind her back—the original of Sora Lena. Signorini's painting, no less than Lee's tale, constitutes a hauntingly vivid portrait of the anguish, as well as the repressive measures, endured by 'female lunatics' in the nineteenth century. One must keep in mind, however, that San Bonifazio, under the direction of psychiatric reformer Vincenzo Chiarugi and his successors, was considered a model of progressive, humane treatment: visitors to the asylum remarked upon the fact that the primary method of restraint was the comparatively less restrictive 'muff' (*manicotto*);[66] the Bolognese journal *Bollettino delle Scienze*

[64] This was possibly congenital syphilis; *Selected Letters* II, 565.

[65] Published in 1886 in the *Jewish Chronicle*.

[66] The Belgian psychiatric pioneer Joseph Guislain noted their use at San Bonifazio and elsewhere in Italy during a visit to Florence: 'Les moyens de répression se bornent presque exclusivement à l'emploi de manchons de cuir, que nous avons trouvés dans d'autres établissements de l'Italie.' *Lettres Médicales sur l'Italie* (Ghent, 1840), 157.

Mediche similarly noted the 'padded leather muff' which left the lunatics (*alienati*) at liberty to roam freely.[67] Is it too fanciful to imagine a connection between the prominence in Lee's story of the muff, as an article of women's clothing, and San Bonifazio's iconic instrument of constraint?[68] At the very least, we may safely conclude that Lee remained ambivalent about the 'best practices' then in vogue for treating the mentally ill, perhaps mentally ill women in particular.

Mind Reading

Anxieties regarding the relationship between mind and body, as well as those arising from the unknown, perhaps unknowable, contents of other minds, may also help to account for the prominence of dolls, puppets, and 'effigies' (a favourite word) in Lee's fiction—and, for that matter, life.[69] Literary critic Susan Jennifer Navarette, who reads Lee's fantastic stories as the product of a 'fin de siècle culture of Decadence', writes, 'The doll [in the story of that name] takes pride of place among the effigies, stone idols, marionettes, and puppets littering the lumber room and enchanted garret of Lee's imagination.'[70] These ambiguously alive figures recur throughout Lee's writing, from the egregiously Carlylean *The Prince of the Hundred Soups: A Puppet-Show in Narrative*,[71] to the 'allegoric puppet-show' she wrote in 1920,

[67] Quoted in Matteo Banzola, 'I Matti degli Altri. Viaggi Scientifici di Alienisti Stranieri in Italia (1820–1864)', *Storia e Futuro* (Feb. 2021), n.p.

[68] Muffs are associated with both women and serve repeatedly as a link between them: the 'delicate gray muff' into which Madame Krasinska thrusts the sketch of the Sora Lena; the Sora Lena's own 'great muff', the 'mangy rabbit-skin muff' Madame Krasinska wears in impersonating her.

[69] Lee collected puppets and organized puppet performances throughout her life; one visitor to Il Palmerino noted Lee's ancient Greek terracotta figurines 'fraternising' with her collection of 'coloured marionettes from Goldoni's comedy' (*Selected Letters* II, 284, lxiii).

[70] Susan Jennifer Navarette, *The Shape of Fear: Horror and the Fin de Siècle Culture of Decadence* (Lexington, KY, 1997), 157.

[71] Lee wraps her story in metafictional layers, with its supposed author, one 'Theodor August Amadeus Wesendonk', being rather transparently derived from Carlyle's fictitious Diogenes Teufelsdröckh in the 1836 novel *Sartor Resartus*. Where Teufelsdröckh's master metaphor had been clothing, Wesendonk's is the puppet: steeped in the writings of Hoffmann and other German Romantics, he becomes besotted with 'The comedy of masks, complicated with its child, the puppet-show', and *The Prince of the Hundred Soups*, one of a 'heap' of fragmentary manuscripts supposed to have come into 'Lee's' possession, represents a fictional exploration of his own recondite philosophy.

in response to a war which she viewed as a 'ghastly Grand Guignol', featuring an 'archangelic marionette . . . my Puppet Satan'.[72] A satanic puppet also features in one of Lee's last stories, 'Sister Benvenuta and the Christ Child', which centres upon a marionette performance at a convent, reaching its climax in a supernatural showdown between an infernal puppet which has been left behind ('Beelzebubb Satanasso, Prince of all Devils') and a mothballed effigy of the infant Jesus. And as we have seen, one of the folktales which Lee chose to adapt for what we may regard as her first collection of stories concerns a woman, 'handsome and rich, but quite alone in the world', who makes herself a surrogate daughter ('a sort of doll, but life-size') out of dough. This 'beautiful woman of paste' is animated by a passing trio of fairies; 'a creature of flesh and blood now', she yet remains a disconcertingly uncanny figure, with detachable body parts: one of the original, sepia-tinted illustrations shows her sitting, headless, surrounded by metonyms of domesticity—spinning-wheel, rafter-hung onions and herbs, a seemingly unperturbed cat—a kind of decapitated angel in the house.[73]

Lee's 1896 story 'The Doll', originally published in *The Cornhill Magazine* as 'The Image', can be seen as a revisiting of this early *fiaba*, much as 'Prince Alberic'—published the same year—revisits an archetype from folk material encountered by Lee long before.[74] In this ambiguously fantastic tale, a noble widower, 'half crazy' with grief, has a life-sized simulacrum of his wife fashioned of cardboard, satin and silk finery, and a wig made from her own hair. The narrator, an Englishwoman travelling in Umbria on one of her '*bric-à-brac* journeys', comes across the effigy decades later, while treasure-hunting in the Count's *palazzo*, where it has been taken from its closet into the laundry-room 'for a little dusting'. The long-neglected, nearly forgotten figure is in a sorry state: hands cobwebbed, frock and bodice 'grey with engrained dirt', 'a big hole in the back of her head'

[72] *Satan, the Waster*, vii, l.

[73] *Tuscan Fairy Tales*, 31–2. Looking disconcertingly like Lewis Carroll's Alice in John Tenniel's iconic rendition, the 'Woman of Paste' is shown absently dressing the hair of her own head, which rests in her lap.

[74] Introducing the story some thirty years later in *For Maurice*, Lee attributes its substance entirely to the imagination of her friend Pier Desiderio Pasolini—presumably the original of 'Signor Oreste' in the tale—but the more one probes the multifarious influences upon her fiction, the more one is inclined to take such assertions with a sizeable grain of salt.

(p. 254). An immediate 'fascinat[ion]' with 'the Doll', which for the narrator embodies, rather than merely represents, the long-dead Countess ('I made no distinction between the portrait and the original'), quickly becomes something very like obsession, as the Englishwoman perceives, or imagines, in the effigy the presence of a kind of consciousness. Consciousness, in such a condition, implies suffering, and in the end, the narrator buys the Doll in order to give it—her—the gift of oblivion, through immolation in a backyard pyre of heaped myrtle, bay, and chrysanthemum.

Interpretations of dolls, manikins, and similar figures in literature and film most typically revolve around the famous conception of the uncanny (*Unheimlich*) formulated by Freud in response to German psychiatrist Ernst Anton Jentsch's discussion of the anxieties produced by 'doubts whether an apparently animate being is really alive; or conversely, whether a lifeless object might not be in fact animate'.[75] In Lee's case, one suspects that other factors might also be at play: Eugene's own effigy-like condition, for example. But a concern with problems of intersubjectivity may be even more salient here, as evidenced particularly in 'The Doll'. Written immediately after the death of Matilda Paget, the story is at one level a fantasy of mindreading, in which the unnamed narrator, intersubjectively challenged in her relations with other human beings, intuits, with preternatural ease, the mind of the Doll-Countess (this effortless access symbolized, perhaps, by the hole in her head). How often, one wonders, must a young Violet Paget have sat scrutinizing her diminutive, labile, domineering mother's face, wishing that she could peer directly into her mind, and silently asking, 'What are you *thinking*? What do you *want*?'

In the non-fantastic interpretation of the story, of course, the Doll's head is empty, and the supposed contents of its mind are projected there by the narrator herself. But, as cognitive science tells us, that is all the contents of other minds *ever* are: a simulation, a mental model in our own heads. Lee appears to have had a particular difficulty, throughout her life, in constructing such models. To be sure, diagnosing the dead is a perilous business; moreover, the modern reader will find that many of the criticisms of Lee's 'abrasiveness' and

[75] For a productive reading of Lee's fiction in relation to Freud and the Uncanny, see Chapter 3, 'Painted Dolls and Virgin Mothers', of Patricia Pulham's *Art and the Transitional Object in Vernon Lee's Supernatural Tales* (Abingdon, 2008).

'want of tact' voiced so often by her contemporaries smack of sexism ('draw it mild with her on the question of friendship', Henry James warned his brother, 'She's a tiger-cat!').[76] But she was herself acutely conscious of, and perplexed by, a certain deficiency in the matter of 'reading' people. She seems to have been genuinely surprised, for instance, at James's deeply pained reaction to her all-too-transparent portrait of him as 'Jervase Marion' in her 1892 story 'Lady Tal', the incident prompting the above-quoted warning to William (he had not relished the experience of recognizing himself in 'the stout gentleman in the linen coat', 'a dainty but frugal bachelor', 'short [and] bald'). After the disastrous reception of her novel *Miss Brown*, which was both condemned for its 'putrescent' treatment of sex and resented, as 'Lady Tal' would be by James a few years later, as a roman à clef (Oscar Wilde, for instance, appears as 'an elephantine person [with a] flabby, fat-cheeked face'), Lee wondered in her journal whether she might not suffer from a form of cognitive or intersubjective 'colour-blindness', incapable as she had proved of anticipating the thoughts and feelings of reviewers and friends alike, and even of knowing her own mind during the novel's composition.[77] It is a striking choice of metaphor. Colour blindness, which had itself only begun to be studied scientifically around 1800, soon came to be employed analogically, to describe abnormalities or deficiencies of other kinds: John Addington Symonds and Havelock Ellis, for instance, used it to conceptualize homosexuality.[78] Lee's own usage interestingly anticipates accounts of 'mindblindness' in modern cognitive science, a field of study Lee would undoubtedly have found fascinating.[79]

If a certain mindblindness arguably cost Lee some friendships in the nineteenth century, however, most notably James's, it was unbending principle, deriving from her cosmopolitan sensibilities, which brought widespread opprobrium down upon her in the twentieth. As her beloved Europe drifted towards total, and in her view fratricidal,

[76] Quoted in Colby, *Vernon Lee*, 196.
[77] Quoted in Colby, *Vernon Lee*, 106, 110.
[78] Havelock Ellis and John Addington Symonds, *Sexual Inversion* (London, 1897), 134.
[79] 'Normal humans everywhere not only "paint" their world with color, they also "paint" beliefs, intentions, feelings, hopes, desires, and pretenses onto agents in their social world.' John Tooby and Leda Cosmides, Foreword to Simon Baron-Cohen, *Mindblindness: An Essay on Autism and Theory of Mind* (Cambridge, MA, and London, 1995), xvii.

war, she found it impossible to hold her tongue, much less to rally behind the Allied cause. George Bernard Shaw honoured Lee for her stance, but to many it looked like simple disloyalty. Opposition to the war ended the warm friendship which had sprung up between Lee and H. G. Wells (who called her his 'Sister in Utopia'); another former friend denounced her as a 'parasite', 'traitor', and 'spy', marvelling that Lee dared 'raise [her] thin pretentious voice in support of the enemy of [her] country'.[80] During the conflict and its aftermath, Lee wrote pacifist satire and polemic; afterwards, she threw herself once more into the study of art, literature, and music, most notably in the insightful *The Handling of Words* (1923) and *Music and Its Lovers* (1932). When she died in 1935 Vernon Lee had authored a good-sized library shelf's worth of books, of which Gothic and fantastic stories make up only a small fraction. Well might readers today wish that she had written more in this vein. But what she has left us—a small collection of richly ambiguous, deeply learned, and yes, haunting tales—is, to use a much-abused epithet, truly unique.

[80] Quoted in Gunn, *Vernon Lee*, 205. The writer is the novelist and journalist Augustine Bulteau.

NOTE ON THE TEXT

NEARLY all of Vernon Lee's fantastic fiction was written before 1900, though the delayed appearance of several tales in book form gives the impression of a longer period of activity: for instance, her first supernatural story, 'A Culture-Ghost', was written in the 1870s and published in 1881 in *Fraser's Magazine*, only to wait until 1927 to reappear, as 'Winthrop's Adventure', as one of the 'five unlikely tales' in *For Maurice*. Moreover, the original periodical appearances of some stories were unknown until comparatively recently (even now, some such appearance, probably *c.*1900, is only suspected, not definitely traced, in the case of 'Marsyas in Flanders'), and some of Lee's stories originally appeared in French (sometimes simultaneously with English versions, sometimes not). Despite their sometimes tangled histories, however, the stories themselves show, for the most part, little variation over time. For the present edition, texts have been taken from Lee's collections: *Hauntings: Fantastic Stories* (1890), *Vanitas: Polite Stories* (1892), *Pope Jacynth and Other Fantastic Tales* (1904), and *For Maurice: Five Unlikely Stories* (1927), with significant variations and omissions noted in the Explanatory Notes; the essay 'Faustus and Helena: Notes on the Supernatural in Art', originally published in *Cornhill Magazine*, is reproduced from the collection *Belcaro* (1881).

SELECT BIBLIOGRAPHY

Biography and Letters

Colby, Vineta, *Vernon Lee: A Literary Biography* (Charlottesville and London, 2003).

Gagel, Amanda, ed., *Selected Letters of Vernon Lee, 1856–1935*, vol. I, *1865–1884* (London and New York, 2016).

Geoffroy, Sophie, ed., *Selected Letters of Vernon Lee, 1856–1935*, vol. II, *1885–1889* (London and New York, 2021).

Gunn, Peter, *Vernon Lee: Violet Paget, 1856–1935* (Oxford, 1964).

Critical Studies

Blumberg, Angie, 'Strata of the Soul: The Queer Archaeologies of Vernon Lee and Oscar Wilde', *Victoriographies—A Journal of Nineteenth-Century Writing, 1790–1914*, 7(3) (2017), n.p.

Bristow, Joseph, 'Vernon Lee's Art of Feeling', *Tulsa Studies in Women's Literature*, 25(1) (2006), 117–39.

Caballero, Carlo, ' "A Wicked Voice": On Vernon Lee, Wagner, and the Effects of Music', *Victorian Studies*, 35(4) (1992), 385–408.

Dellamora, Richard, 'Productive Decadence: "The Queer Comradeship of Outlawed Thought": Vernon Lee, Max Nordau, and Oscar Wilde', *New Literary History*, 35(4) (2004), 529–46.

Denisoff, Dennis, 'Vernon Lee, Decadent Contamination and the Productivist Ethos', in Catherine Maxwell and Patricia Pulham (eds), *Vernon Lee: Decadence, Ethics, Aesthetics* (Basingstoke, 2006), 75–90.

Dytor, Frankie, ' "The Eyes of an Intellectual Vampire": Michael Field, Vernon Lee and Female Masculinities in Late Victorian Aestheticism', *Journal of Victorian Culture* (2021), n.p.

Evangelista, Stefano, 'Vernon Lee in the Vatican: The Uneasy Alliance of Aestheticism and Archaeology', *Victorian Studies*, 52(1) (2009), 31–41.

Evangelista, Stefano, 'Vernon Lee and the Gender of Aestheticism', in Catherine Maxwell and Patricia Pulham (eds), *Vernon Lee: Decadence, Ethics, Aesthetics* (Basingstoke, 2006), 91–111.

Fraser, Hilary, 'Writing Cosmopolis: The Cosmopolitan Aesthetics of Emilia Dilke and Vernon Lee', *19: Interdisciplinary Studies in the Long Nineteenth Century*, 28 (2019).

Haefele-Thomas, Ardel, *Queer Others in Victorian Gothic: Transgressing Monstrosity* (Cardiff, 2012).

Kandola, Sondeep, *Vernon Lee* (Horndon, 2010).

Mannocchi, Phyllis F., '"Vernon Lee": A Reintroduction and Primary Bibliography', *ELT 1880–1920*, 26 (1983).

Maxwell, Catherine, 'Sappho, Mary Wakefield, and Vernon Lee's "A Wicked Voice" ', *Modern Language Review*, 102(4) (2007), 960–74.

Maxwell, Catherine, and Patricia Pulham, Introduction, *Hauntings and Other Fantastic Tales* (Mississauga, 2006), 9–27.

Morgan, Benjamin, 'Critical Empathy: Vernon Lee's Aesthetics and the Origins of Close Reading', *Victorian Studies*, 55(1) (2012), 31–56.

Navarette, Susan Jennifer, *The Shape of Fear: Horror and the Fin de Siècle Culture of Decadence* (Lexington, KY, 1997).

Ní Bheacháin, Caoilfhionn, and Angus Mitchell, 'Alice Stopford Green and Vernon Lee: Salon Culture and Intellectual Exchange', *Journal of Victorian Culture* (2020), n.p.

Pulham, Patricia, *Art and the Transitional Object in Vernon Lee's Supernatural Tales* (London and New York, 2008).

Smith, Andrew, *The Ghost Story 1840–1920: A Cultural History* (Manchester and New York, 2010).

Tearle, Oliver, *Bewilderments of Vision: Hallucination and Literature, 1880–1914* (Brighton, 2013).

Towheed, Shafquat, 'The Creative Evolution of Scientific Paradigms: Vernon Lee and the Debate over the Hereditary Transmission of Acquired Characteristics', *Victorian Studies*, 49(1) (2006), 33–61.

Vicinus, Martha, ' "A Legion of Ghosts": Vernon Lee and the Art of Nostalgia', *GLQ*, 10(4) (2004), 599–616.

Zorn, Christa, *Vernon Lee: Aesthetics, History, & the Victorian Female Intellectual* (Athens, OH, 2003).

Further Reading in Oxford World's Classics

James, Henry, *The Turn of the Screw and Other Stories*, ed. T. J. Lustig.

James, M. R., *Collected Ghost Stories*, ed. Darryl Jones.

Le Fanu, Sheridan, *Green Tea and Other Weird Stories*, ed. Aaron Worth.

Machen, Arthur, *The Great God Pan and Other Horror Stories*, ed. Aaron Worth.

Wilde, Oscar, *The Major Works (including The Picture of Dorian Gray)*, ed. Isobel Murray.

A CHRONOLOGY OF VERNON LEE

1856 (14 Oct.) Violet Paget is born near Boulogne-sur-Mer, France, to Henry Ferguson Paget and Matilda Paget. Throughout her childhood the family moves regularly, with periods of residence in France, Switzerland, Germany, and Italy.

1864 Lee's half-brother, Eugene Lee-Hamilton, enters Oriel College at Oxford.

1866 The Pagets meet the family of John Singer Sargent in Nice.

1870 A 14-year-old Lee publishes her first work of fiction, the serialized *Les aventures d'une pièce de monnaie*, in the Lausanne periodical *La Famille*.

1873 Eugene succumbs to a psychosomatic condition which renders him semi-paralytic for over twenty years. The Pagets settle in Florence.

1875 Lee writes to her friend and mentor, the novelist Henrietta Jenkin, of her plan to use the pseudonym 'H. P. Vernon-Lee', formed by blending her own, her father's, and her stepbrother's names.

1880 Publication of Lee's first two books, both by W. Satchell & Co.: *Studies of the Eighteenth Century in Italy* and *Tuscan Fairy Tales: Taken from the Mouths of the People*. Lee meets the poet Mary Robinson, who will become her romantic partner.

1881 W. Satchell publishes Lee's *Belcaro: Being Essays on Sundry Aesthetical Questions*. The Gothic story 'A Culture-Ghost; or, Winthrop's Adventure' appears in *Fraser's Magazine* and *Appletons' Journal*. Lee visits England in the company of Mary Robinson, meeting, among other literary and intellectual celebrities, Walter Pater, Oscar Wilde, and Robert Browning.

1883 Publication of *The Prince of the Hundred Soups: A Puppet-Show in Narrative* and *Ottilie: An Eighteenth-Century Idyll*.

1884 Blackwood publishes Lee's three-volume novel *Miss Brown*, which she dedicates to Henry James (privately James will call the book 'a deplorable mistake'). Lee also publishes *Euphorion: Being Studies of the Antique and the Mediaeval in the Renaissance* and *The Countess of Albany*. Publication of Eugene's *Apollo and Marsyas, and Other Poems*.

1886 Blackwood publishes 'A Phantom Lover: A Fantastic Story' as a 'shilling dreadful'; *Baldwin: Being Dialogues on Views and Aspirations* also appears.

1887 Publication of *Juvenilia: Being a Second Series of Essays on Sundry Aesthetical Questions*; Lee meets Clementina 'Kit' Anstruther-Thomson.

1888 To the surprise and consternation of her own family as well as the Pagets', Mary Robinson marries the Jewish orientalist James Darmesteter; Lee suffers a nervous breakdown.

1889 Lee meets the American art historian Bernard Berenson, who in 1897 will accuse Lee and Anstruther-Thomson of plagiarism. The Pagets move to the Villa Il Palmerino outside Florence; this will be Vernon Lee's home until her death.

1890 Publication of *Hauntings: Fantastic Stories*, Lee's first and greatest collection of short fiction; it includes 'Amour Dure', 'Dionea', 'Oke of Okehurst' ('A Phantom Lover'), and 'A Wicked Voice'.

1892 A second collection, *Vanitas: Polite Stories*, appears; it includes 'Lady Tal', whose unflattering, thinly fictionalized portrait of Henry James sours their friendship.

1893 Publication of *Althea: A Second Book of Dialogues on Aspirations and Duties*.

1894 Death of Lee's father, Henry Ferguson Paget (November). Lee meets Edith Wharton in Florence.

1895 Publication of *Renaissance Fancies and Studies*.

1896 Lee's mother, Matilda Paget, dies (March). 'Prince Alberic and the Snake Lady' appears in *The Yellow Book*.

1897 Publication of *Limbo and Other Essays*.

1898 Eugene, now recovered from his illness, marries the Anglo-Caribbean novelist Annie E. Holdsworth.

1899 Lee publishes *Genius Loci: Notes on Places*.

1900 Mary Darmesteter marries again, to French microbiologist and chemist Émile Duclaux.

1903 Lee publishes a verse drama, *Ariadne in Mantua*, and a novel, *Penelope Brandling*.

1904 Publication of *Pope Jacynth and Other Fantastic Tales*, which includes 'Prince Alberic and the Snake Lady', and *Hortus Vitae: Essays on the Gardening of Life*.

1905 *The Enchanted Woods, and Other Essays* and 'Sister Benvenuta and the Christ Child'.

1906 *The Spirit of Rome: Leaves from a Diary*.

1907 Death of Eugene (September).

1908 *The Sentimental Traveller: Notes on Places and Gospels of Anarchy and Other Contemporary Studies.*

1909 *Laurus Nobilis: Chapters on Life and Art.*

1912 *Vital Lies: Studies of Some Varieties of Recent Obscurantism and Beauty and Ugliness and Other Studies in Psychological Aesthetics* (with Anstruther-Thomson).

1913 *The Beautiful: An Introduction to Psychological Aesthetics.*

1914 Outbreak of the First World War; Lee's pacifist position is unpopular. Publication of *Louis Norbert: A Two-Fold Romance* and *The Tower of Mirrors and Other Essays in the Spirit of Places.*

1915 *The Ballet of the Nations: A Present-Day Morality.*

1920 *Satan the Waster: A Philosophical War Trilogy.*

1921 Death of Kit Anstruther-Thomson.

1923 *The Handling of Words and Other Studies in Literary Psychology.*

1924 Lee publishes Anstruther-Thomson's posthumous *Art and Man: Essays and Fragments*, with an introduction by Lee.

1925 Publication of *The Golden Keys and Other Essays on the Genius Loci* and *Proteus; or the Future of Intelligence.*

1927 Lee's final collection of stories, *For Maurice: Five Unlikely Stories*, is published by John Lane; it includes 'Winthrop's Adventure', 'The Virgin of the Seven Daggers', 'The Gods and Ritter Tanhûser', 'Marsyas in Flanders', and 'The Doll', all written years earlier.

1929 With Lee's approval, Irene Cooper Willis prepares *A Vernon Lee Anthology.*

1932 Publication of *Music and Its Lovers: An Empirical Study of Emotional and Imaginative Responses to Music.*

1935 (13 Feb.) Death of Lee from heart failure, aged 78, at Il Palmerino.

1937 Irene Cooper Willis privately prints a heavily edited selection of Lee's correspondence.

THE TALES

WINTHROP'S ADVENTURE

I

ALL the intimates at the villa S—— knew Julian Winthrop* to be an odd sort of creature, but I am sure no one ever expected from him such an eccentric scene as that which took place on the first Wednesday of last September.

Winthrop had been a constant visitor at the Countess S——'s villa ever since his arrival in Florence, and the better we knew, the more we liked, his fantastic character. Although quite young, he had shown very considerable talent for painting, but every one seemed to agree that this talent would never come to anything. His nature was too impressionable, too mobile, for steady work; and he cared too much for all kinds of art to devote himself exclusively to any one; above all, he had too ungovernable a fancy, and too uncontrollable a love of detail, to fix and complete any impression in an artistic shape; his ideas and fancies were constantly shifting and changing like the shapes in a kaleidoscope, and their instability and variety were the chief sources of his pleasure. All that he did and thought and said had an irresistible tendency to become arabesque, feelings and moods gliding strangely into each other, thoughts and images growing into inextricable tangles, just as when he played he passed insensibly from one fragment to another totally incongruous, and when he drew one form merged into another beneath his pencil. His head was like his sketch-book—full of delightful scraps of colour and quaint, graceful forms, none finished, one on the top of the other: leaves growing out of heads, houses astride on animals, scraps of melodies noted down across scraps of verse, gleanings from all quarters—all pleasing, and all jumbled into a fantastic, useless, but very delightful whole. In short, Winthrop's artistic talent was frittered away by his love of the picturesque, and his career was spoilt by his love of adventure; but such as he was, he was almost a work of art, a living arabesque himself.

On this particular Wednesday we were all seated out on the terrace of the villa S—— at Bellosguardo,* enjoying the beautiful serene yellow moonlight and the delightful coolness after an intensely hot day. The Countess S——, who was a great musician, was trying over a violin sonata with one of her friends in the drawing room, of which the doors opened on to the terrace. Winthrop, who had been particularly gay all the evening, had cleared away the plates and cups from the tea-table, had pulled out his sketch-book and begun drawing in his drowsy, irrelevant fashion—acanthus leaves uncurling into sirens' tails, satyrs growing out of passion flowers, little Dutch manikins in tail coats and pigtails peeping out of tulip leaves under his whimsical pencil, while he listened partly to the music within, partly to the conversation without.

When the violin sonata had been tried over, passage by passage, sufficiently often, the Countess, instead of returning to us on the terrace, addressed us from the drawing-room—

"Remain where you are," she said; "I want you to hear an old air which I discovered last week among a heap of rubbish in my father-in-law's lumber room. I think it quite a treasure, as good as a wrought-iron ornament found among a heap of old rusty nails, or a piece of Gubbio majolica* found among cracked coffee cups. It is very beautiful to my mind. Just listen."

The Countess was an uncommonly fine singer, without much voice, and not at all emotional, but highly delicate and refined in execution, and with a great knowledge of music. The air which she deemed beautiful could not fail really to be so; but it was so totally different from all we moderns are accustomed to, that it seemed, with its exquisitely-finished phrases, its delicate vocal twirls and spirals, its symmetrically ordered ornaments, to take one into quite another world of musical feeling, of feeling too subdued and artistic, too subtly and cunningly balanced, to move us more than superficially—indeed, it could not move at all, for it expressed no particular state of feeling; it was difficult to say whether it was sad or cheerful; all that could be said was that it was singularly graceful and delicate.

This is how the piece affected me, and I believe, in less degree, all the rest of our party; but, turning towards Winthrop, I was surprised at seeing how very strong an impression its very first bars had made on him. He was seated at the table, his back turned towards me, but I could see that he had suddenly stopped drawing and was listening with intense eagerness. At one moment I almost fancied I saw his hand tremble as it lay on his sketch-book, as if he were breathing spasmodically. I pulled my chair near his; there could be no doubt, his whole frame was quivering.

"Winthrop," I whispered.

He paid no attention to me, but continued listening intently, and his hand unconsciously crumpled up the sheet he had drawn on.

"Winthrop," I repeated, touching his shoulder.

"Be quiet," he answered quickly, as if shaking me off; "let me listen."

There was something almost fierce in his manner; and this intense emotion caused by a piece which did not move any of the rest of us, struck me as being very odd.

He remained with his head between his hands till the end. The piece concluded with a very intricate and beautiful passage of execution, and with a curious sort of sighing fall from a high note on to a lower one, short and repeated at various intervals, with lovely effect.

"Bravo! beautiful!" cried every one. "A real treasure; so quaint and so elegant, and so admirably sung!"

I looked at Winthrop. He had turned round; his face was flushed, and he leaned against his chair as if oppressed by emotion.

The Countess returned to the terrace. "I am glad you like the piece," she said; "it is a graceful thing. Good heavens! Mr. Winthrop!" she suddenly interrupted herself; "what is the matter? are you ill?"

For ill he certainly did look.

He rose and, making an effort, answered in a husky, uncertain voice—

"It's nothing; I suddenly felt cold. I think I'll go in—or rather, no, I'll stay. What is—what is that air you have just sung?"

"That air?" she answered absently, for the sudden change in Winthrop's manner put everything else out of her thoughts. "That air? Oh! it is by a very forgotten composer of the name of Barbella,* who lived somewhere about the year 1780." It was evident that she considered this question as a sort of mask to his sudden emotion.

"Would you let me see the score?" he asked quickly.

"Certainly. Will you come into the drawing-room? I left it on the piano."

The piano candles were still lit; and as they stood there she watched his face with as much curiosity as myself. But Winthrop took no notice of either of us; he had eagerly snatched the score, and was looking at it in a fixed, vacant way. When he looked up his face was ashy; he handed me the score mechanically. It was an old yellow, blurred manuscript, in some now disused clef,* and the initial words, written in a grand, florid style, were: "Sei Regina, io son pastore."*

The Countess was still under the impression that Winthrop was trying to hide his agitation by pretending great interest in the song; but I, having seen his extraordinary emotion during its performance, could not doubt of the connection between them.

"You say the piece is very rare," said Winthrop; "do you—do you then think that no one besides yourself is acquainted with it at present?"

"Of course I can't affirm that," answered the Countess, "but this much I know, that Professor G——, who is one of the most learned of musical authorities, and to whom I showed the piece, had heard neither of it nor of its composer, and that he positively says it exists in no musical archives in Italy or in Paris."

"Then how," I asked, "do you know that it is of about the year 1780?"

"By the style; Professor G—— compared it at my request with some compositions of that day, and the style perfectly coincides."

"You think, then," continued Winthrop slowly, but eagerly—"you think, then, that no one else sings it at present?"

"I should say not; at least it seems highly unlikely."

Winthrop was silent, and continued looking at the score, but, as it seemed to me, mechanically.

Some of the rest of the party had meanwhile entered the drawing-room.

"Did you notice Mr. Winthrop's extraordinary behaviour?" whispered a lady to the Countess. "What *has* happened to him?"

"I can't conceive. He is excessively impressionable, but I don't see how that piece could impress him at all; it is a sweet thing, but so unemotional," I answered.

"That piece!" replied the Countess: "you don't suppose that piece has anything to do with it?"

"Indeed I do; it has everything to do with it. In short, I noticed that from the very first notes it violently affected him."

"Then all these inquiries about it?"

"Are perfectly genuine."

"It cannot be the piece itself which has moved him, and he can scarcely have heard it before. It's very odd. There certainly is something the matter with him."

There certainly was; Winthrop was excessively pale and agitated, all the more so as he perceived that he had become an object of universal curiosity. He evidently wished to make his escape, but was afraid of doing so too suddenly. He was standing behind the piano, looking mechanically at the old score.

"Have you ever heard that piece before, Mr. Winthrop?" asked the Countess, unable to restrain her curiosity.

He looked up, much discomposed, and answered after a moment's hesitation: "How can I have heard it, since you are the sole possessor of it?"

"The sole possessor? Oh I never said that. I thought it unlikely, but perhaps there is some other. Tell me, is there another? Where did you hear that piece before?"

"I did not say I had heard it before," he rejoined hurriedly.

"But have you, or have you not?" persisted the Countess.

"I never have," he answered decidedly, but immediately reddened as if conscious of prevarication. "Don't ask me any questions," he added quickly; "it worries me," and in a minute he was off.

We looked at each other in mute astonishment. This astonishing behaviour, this mixture of concealment and rudeness, above all, the violent excitement in which Winthrop had evidently been, and his unaccountable eagerness respecting the piece which the Countess had sung, all this entirely baffled our efforts at discovery.

"There is some mystery at the bottom of it," we said, and further we could not get.

Next evening, as we were seated once more in the Countess's drawing-room, we of course reverted to Winthrop's extraordinary behaviour.

"Do you think he will return soon?" asked one of us.

"I should think he would rather let the matter blow over, and wait till we had forgotten his absurdity," answered the Countess.

At that moment the door opened, and Winthrop entered.

He seemed confused and at a loss what to say; he did not answer our trivial remarks, but suddenly burst out, as if with a great effort:

"I have come to beg you to forgive my last night's behaviour. Forgive my rudeness and my want of openness; but I could not have explained anything then: that piece, you must know, had given me a great shock."

"A great shock? And how could it give you a shock?" we all exclaimed.

"You surely don't mean that so prim a piece as that could have affected you?" asked the Countess's sister.

"If it did," added the Countess, "it is the greatest miracle music ever worked."

"It is difficult to explain the matter," hesitated Winthrop; "but—in short—that piece gave me a shock because as soon as I heard the first bars I recognized it."

"And you told me you had never heard it before!" exclaimed the Countess indignantly.

"I know I did; it was not true, but neither was it quite false. All I can say is that I knew the piece; whether I had heard it before, or not, I knew it—in fact," he dashed out, "you will think me mad, but I had long doubted whether the piece existed at all, and I was so moved just because your performance proved that it *did* exist. Look here," and pulling a sketch-book from his pocket he was just about to open it when he stopped—"Have you got the notes of that piece?" he asked hurriedly.

"Here they are," and the Countess handed him the old roll of music.

He did not look at it, but turned over the leaves of his sketch-book. "See," he said after a minute; "look at this," and he pushed the open sketch-book across the table to us. On it, among a lot of sketches, were some roughly ruled lines, with some notes scrawled in pencil, and the words "Sei Regina, io Pastor sono."

"Why, this is the beginning of the very air!" exclaimed the Countess. "How did you get this?"

We compared the notes in the sketch-book with those on the score; they were the same, but in another clef and tone.

Winthrop sat opposite, looking doggedly at us. After a moment he remarked—

"They are the same notes, are they not? Well, this pencil scrawl was done in July of last year, while the ink of this score has been dry ninety years; yet when I wrote down these notes, I swear I did not know that any such score existed, and until yesterday I disbelieved it."

"Then," remarked one of the party, "there are only two explanations: either you composed this melody yourself, not knowing that some one else had done so ninety years ago; or, you heard that piece without knowing what it was."

"Explanation!" cried Winthrop contemptuously; "why, don't you see, that it is just what needs explaining! Of course, I either composed it myself or heard it, but which of the two was it?"

We remained much humbled and silenced.

"This is a very astonishing puzzle," remarked the Countess, "and I think it useless to rack our brains about it since Mr. Winthrop is the only person who can explain it. We don't and can't understand; he can and must explain it himself. I don't know," she added, "whether there is any reason for not explaining the mystery to us; but if not, I wish you would."

"There is no reason," he answered, "except that you would set me down as a maniac. The story is so absurd a one—you will never believe me—and yet . . ."

"Then there is a story at the bottom of it!" exclaimed the Countess. "What is it? Can't you tell it us?"

Winthrop gave a sort of deprecatory shrug, and trifled with the paper cutters and dog's-eared the books on the table. "Well," he said at last, "if you really wish to know—why—perhaps I might as well tell it you; only don't tell me afterwards that I am mad. Nothing can alter the fact of the real existence of that piece; and, as long as you continue to regard it as unique, I cannot but regard my adventure as being true."

We were afraid lest he might slip away through all these deprecatory premisings, and that after all we might hear no story whatever; so we summoned him to begin at once, and he, keeping his head well in the shadow of the lamp-shade, and scribbling as usual on his sketch-book, began his narrative, at first slowly and hesitatingly, with plentiful interruptions, but, as he grew more interested in it, becoming extremely rapid and dramatic, and exceedingly minute in details.

II

You must know (said Winthrop), that about a year and a half ago I spent the autumn with some cousins of mine, rambling about Lombardy.* In poking into all sorts of odd nooks and corners, we made the acquaintance at M—— of a highly learned and highly snuffy* old gentleman (I believe he was a count or a marchese), who went by the nickname of Maestro Fa Diesis (Master F-Sharp), and who possessed a very fine collection of things musical, a perfect museum. He had a handsome old palace, which was literally tumbling to pieces, and of which the whole first floor was taken up by his collections. His old MSS., his precious missals, his papyri, his autographs, his black-letter books, his prints and pictures, his innumerable ivory inlaid harpsichords and ebony fretted lutes and viols, lived in fine, spacious rooms, with carved oaken ceilings and painted window frames, while he lived in some miserable little garret to the back, on what I can't say, but I should judge, by the spectral appearance of his old woman servant and of a half-imbecile boy who served him, on nothing more substantial than bean husks and warm water. They seemed to suffer from this diet; but I suspect that their master must have absorbed some mysterious vivifying fluid from his MSS. and old instruments, for he seemed to be made of steel, and was the most provokingly active old fellow, keeping one's nerves in perpetual irritation by his friskiness* and volubility. He cared for nothing in the wide world save his collections; he had cut down tree after tree, he had sold field after field and farm after farm; he had sold his furniture, his tapestries, his plate, his family papers, his own clothes. He would have taken the tiles off his roof and the glass out of his windows to buy some score of the sixteenth century, some illuminated mass book or some Cremonese fiddle.* For music itself I firmly believe he cared not a jot, and regarded it as useful only inasmuch as it had produced the objects of his passion, the things which he could spend all his life in dusting, labelling, counting, and cataloguing, for not a chord, not a note was ever heard in his house, and he would have died rather than spend a soldino* on going to the opera.

My cousin, who is music mad after a fashion, quickly secured the old gentleman's good will by accepting a hundred commissions for the obtaining of catalogues and the attending of sales, and we were consequently permitted daily to enter that strange, silent house full of musical things, and to examine its contents at our leisure, always, however, under old Fa Diesis's vigilant supervision. The house, its contents, and proprietor formed a grotesque whole, which had a certain charm for me. I used often to fancy that the silence could be only apparent; that, as soon as the master had drawn his bolts and gone off to bed, all this slumbering music would awake, that the pictures of dead musicians would slip out of their frames, the glass cases fly open, the big paunched inlaid lutes turn into stately Flemish burghers, with brocaded doublets; the yellow, faded sides of the Cremonese bass viols expand into the stiff satin hoops of powdered ladies; and the little ribbed mandolins put forth a parti-coloured leg and a bushy-haired head, and hop about as Provençal Court dwarfs or Renaissance pages, while the Egyptian sistrum and fife players would slip from off the hieroglyphics of the papyrus, and all the parchment palimpsests of Greek musicians turn into chlamys-robed auletes, and citharœdi;* then the kettledrums and tamtams* would strike up, the organ tubes would suddenly be filled with sound, the old gilded harpsichords would jingle like fury, the old chapel-master yonder, in his peruke and furred robe, would beat time on his picture frame, and the whole motley company set to dancing; until all of a sudden old Fa Diesis, awakened by the noise, and suspecting thieves, would rush in wildly in his dressing gown, a three-wicked kitchen lamp in one hand and his great-grandfather's court sword in the other, when all the dancers and players would start and slide back into their frames and cases. I should not, however, have gone so often to the old gentleman's museum had not my cousin extorted from me the promise of a water-colour sketch of a picture of Palestrina,* which, for some reason or other, she (for the cousin was a lady, which explains my docility) chose to consider as particularly authentic. It was a monster, a daub, which I shuddered at, and my admiration for Palestrina would have rather induced me to burn the hideous, blear-eyed, shoulderless thing; but musical folk have their whims, and hers was to hang a copy of this monstrosity over her grand piano. So I acceded, took my drawing block and easel, and set off for Fa Diesis's palace. This palace was a queer old place, full of ups and downs and twistings and turnings, and in going to the only tolerably lighted room of the house, whither the delightful subject for my brush had been transported for my convenience, we had to pass through a narrow and wriggling corridor somewhere in the heart of the building. In doing so we passed by a door up some steps.

"By the way," exclaimed old Fa Diesis, "have I shown you this? 'Tis of no great value, but still, as a painter, it may interest you." He mounted the steps, pushed open the door, which was ajar, and ushered me into a small, bleak, whitewashed lumber-room, peopled with broken book-shelves, crazy music desks, and unsteady chairs and tables, the whole covered by a goodly layer of dust. On the walls were a few time-stained portraits in corslets and bobwigs, the senatorial ancestors of Fa Diesis, who had had to make room for the bookshelves and instrument-cases filling the state rooms. The old gentleman opened a shutter, and threw the full light upon another old picture, from whose cracked surface he deliberately swept away the dust with the rusty sleeve of his fur-lined coat.

I approached it. "This is not a bad picture," I said at once; "by no means a bad picture."

"Indeed," exclaimed Fa Diesis. "Oh, then, perhaps, I may sell it. What do you think? Is it worth much?"

I smiled. "Well, it is not a Raphael,"* I answered; "but, considering its date and the way people then smeared, it is quite creditable."

"Ah!" sighed the old fellow, much disappointed.

It was a half-length, life-size portrait of a man in the costume of the latter part of the last century—a pale lilac silk coat, a pale pea-green satin waistcoat, both extremely delicate in tint, and a deep warm-tinted amber cloak; the voluminous cravat was loosened, the large collar flapped back, the body slightly turned, and the head somewhat looking over the shoulder, Cenci fashion.*

The painting was uncommonly good for an Italian portrait of the eighteenth century, and had much that reminded me, though of course vastly inferior technically, of Greuze*—a painter I detest, and who yet fascinates me. The features were irregular and small, with intensely red lips and a crimson flush beneath the transparent bronzed skin; the eyes were slightly upturned and looking sidewards, in harmony with the turn of the head and the parted lips, and they were beautiful, brown, soft, like those of some animals, with a vague, wistful depth of look. The whole had the clear greyness, the hazy, downy touch of Greuze, and left that strange mixed impression which all the portraits of his school do. The face was not beautiful; it had something at once sullen and effeminate, something odd and not entirely agreeable; yet it attracted and riveted your attention with its dark, warm colour, rendered all the more striking for the light, pearly, powdered locks, and the general lightness and haziness of touch.

"It is a very good portrait in its way," I said, "though not of the sort that people buy. There are faults of drawing here and there, but the colour and touch are good. By whom is it?"

Old Fa Diesis, whose vision of heaps of banknotes to be obtained in exchange for the picture had been rudely cut short, seemed rather sulky.

"I don't know by whom it is," he grumbled. "If it's bad it's bad, and may remain here."

"And whom does it represent?"

"A singer. You see he has got a score in his hand. A certain Rinaldi,* who lived about a hundred years ago."

Fa Diesis had rather a contempt for singers, regarding them as poor creatures, who were of no good, since they left nothing behind them that could be collected, except indeed in the case of Madame Banti,* one of whose lungs he possessed in spirits of wine.

We went out of the room, and I set about my copy of that abominable old portrait of Palestrina. At dinner that day I mentioned the portrait of the singer to my cousins, and somehow or other I caught myself using expressions about it which I should not have used in the morning. In trying to describe the picture my recollection of it seemed to differ from the original impression. It returned to my mind as something strange and striking. My cousin wished to see it, so the next morning she accompanied me to old Fa Diesis's palace. How it affected her I don't know; but for me it had a queer sort of interest, quite apart from that in the technical execution. There was something peculiar and unaccountable in the look of that face, a yearning, half-pained look, which I could not well define to myself. I became gradually aware that the portrait was, so to speak, haunting me. Those strange red lips and wistful eyes rose up in my mind. I instinctively and without well knowing why reverted to it in our conversation.

"I wonder who he was," I said, as we sat in the square behind the cathedral apse, eating our ices in the cool autumn evening.

"Who?" asked my cousin.

"Why, the original of that portrait at old Fa Diesis's; such a weird face. I wonder who he was?"

My cousins paid no attention to my speech, for they did not share that vague, unaccountable feeling with which the picture had inspired me, but as we walked along the silent porticoed streets, where only the illuminated sign of an inn or the chestnut-roasting brazier of a fruit stall flickered in the gloom, and crossed the vast desolate square, surrounded by Oriental-like cupolas and minarets, where the green bronze condottiere rode on his green bronze charger*—during our evening ramble through the quaint Lombard city my thoughts kept reverting to the picture, with its hazy, downy colour and curious, unfathomed expression.

The next day was the last of our stay at M——, and I went to Fa Diesis's palace to finish my sketch, to take leave, present thanks for his civility towards us, and inquire whether we could execute any commission for him. In going to the room where I had left my easel and painting things, I passed through the dark, wriggling lobby and by the door up the three steps. The door was ajar, and I entered the room where the portrait was. I approached and examined it carefully. The man was apparently singing, or rather about to sing, for the red, well-cut lips were parted; and in his hand—a beautiful plump, white, blue-veined hand, strangely out of keeping with the brown, irregular face—he held an open roll of notes. The notes were mere unintelligible blotches, but I made out, written on the score, the name—Ferdinando Rinaldi, 1782; and above, the words—"Sei Regina, io pastor sono." The face had a beauty, a curious, irregular beauty, and in those deep, soft eyes there was something like a magnetic power, which I felt, and which others must have felt before me. I finished my sketch, strapped up my easel and paint-box, gave a parting snarl at the horrible blear-eyed, shoulderless Palestrina, and prepared to leave. Fa Diesis, who, in his snuffy fur-lined coat, the tassel of his tarnished blue skull-cap bobbing over his formidable nose, was seated at a desk hard by, rose also, and politely escorted me through the passage.

"By the way," I asked, "do you know an air called, 'Sei Regina, io Pastor sono'?"

" 'Sei Regina, io Pastor sono?' No, such an air doesn't exist." All airs not in his library had no business to exist, even if they did.

"It must exist," I persisted; "those words are written on the score held by the singer on that picture of yours."

"That's no proof," he cried peevishly; "it may be merely some fancy title, or else—or else it may be some rubbishy *trunk air* (aria di baule)."

"What is a *trunk air?*" I asked in amazement.

"A *trunk air*," he explained, "was a wretched air—merely a few trumpery notes and lots of pauses, on to which great singers used formerly to make their own variations. They used to insert them in every opera they sang in, and drag them all over the world; that was why they were called trunk airs. They had no merit of their own—no one ever cared to sing them except the singer to whom they belonged—no one ever kept such rubbish as that! It all went to wrap up sausages or make curl-papers." And old Fa Dieses laughed his grim little cackling laugh.

He then dropped the subject, and said—

"If I had an opportunity, or one of my illustrious family, of obtaining any catalogues of musical curiosities or attending any sales"—he was still searching for the first printed copy of Guido of Arezzo's "Micrologus"*—he had copies of all the other editions, a unique collection; there was also one specimen wanting to complete his set of Amati's fiddles,* one with *fleurs-de-lys* on the sounding board, constructed for Charles IX of France—alas! he had spent years looking for that instrument—he would pay—yes, he, as I saw him there, he standing before me, would pay five hundred golden *marenghi** for that violin with the *fleurs-de-lys* . . . .

"Pardon me," I interrupted rather rudely; "may I see this picture again?"

We had come to the door up the three steps.

"Certainly," he answered, and continued his speech about the Amati violin with the *fleurs-de-lys*, getting more and more frisky and skippery every moment.

That strange face with its weird, yearning look! I remained motionless before it while the old fellow jabbered and gesticulated like a maniac. What a deep incomprehensible look in those eyes!

"Was he a very famous singer?" I asked, by way of saying something.

"He? *Eh altro!* I should think so! Do you think perhaps the singers of that day were like ours? Pooh! Look at all they did in that day. Their paper made of linen rag, no tearing *that*; and how they built their violins! Oh, what times those were!"

"Do you know anything about this man?" I asked.

"About this singer, this Rinaldi? Oh, yes; he was a very great singer, but he ended badly."

"Badly? in what way?"

"Why—you know what such people are, and then youth! we have all been young, all young!" and old Fa Diesis shrugged his shrivelled person.

"What happened to him?" I persisted, continuing to look at the portrait; it seemed as if there were life in those soft, velvety eyes, and as if those red lips were parting in a sigh—a long, weary sigh.

"Well," answered Fa Diesis, "this Ferdinando Rinaldi was a very great singer. About the year 1780 he took service with the Court of Parma. There, it is said, he obtained too great notice from a lady in high favour at Court, and was consequently dismissed. Instead of going to a distance, he kept hanging about the frontier of Parma, now here, now there, for he had many friends among the nobility. Whether he was suspected of attempting to return to Parma, or whether he spoke with less reserve than he should, I don't know. *Basta!** one fine morning he was found lying on the staircase landing of our Senator Negri's house, stabbed."

Old Fa Diesis pulled out his horn snuff-box.

"Who had done it, no one ever knew or cared to know. A packet of letters, which his valet said he always carried on his person, was all that was found missing. The lady left Parma and entered the Convent of the Clarisse* here; she was my father's aunt, and this portrait belonged to her. A common story, a common story in those days."

And the old gentleman rammed his long nose with snuff.

"You really don't think I could sell the picture?" he asked.

"No!" I answered very decidedly, for I felt a sort of shudder. I took leave, and that evening we set off for Rome.

Winthrop paused, and asked for a cup of tea. He was flushed and seemed excited, but at the same time anxious to end his story. When he had taken his tea, he pushed back his irregular hair with both hands, gave a little sigh of recollection, and began again as follows:—

III

I returned to M—— the next year, on my way to Venice, and stopped a couple of days in the old place, having to bargain for certain Renaissance carved work, which a friend wished to buy. It was midsummer; the fields which I had left planted with cabbages and covered with white frost were tawny with ripe corn, and the vine garlands drooped down to kiss the tall, compact green hemp; the dark streets were reeking with heat, the people were all sprawling about under colonnade and awning; it was the end of June in Lombardy, God's own orchard on earth. I went to old Fa Diesis's palace to ask whether he had any commissions for Venice; he might, indeed, be in the country, but the picture, *the* portrait was at his palace, and that was enough for me. I had often thought of it in the winter, and I wondered whether now, with the sun blazing through every chink, I should still be impressed by it as I had been in the gloomy autumn. Fa Diesis was at home, and overjoyed to see me; he jumped and frisked about like a figure in the Dance of Death* in intense excitement about certain MSS. he had lately seen. He narrated, or rather acted, for it was all in the present tense and accompanied by appropriate gestures, a journey he had recently made to Guastalla* to see a psaltery at a monastery; how he had bargained for a postchaise; how the postchaise had upset halfway; how he had sworn at the driver; how he had rung—drling, drling—at the monastery door; how he cunningly pretended to be in quest of an old, valueless crucifix; how the monks had had the impudence to ask a hundred and fifty francs for it. How he had hummed and hah'd, and, pretending suddenly to notice the psaltery, had asked what it was, etc., as if he did not know; and finally struck the bargain for both crucifix and psaltery for a hundred and fifty francs—a psaltery of the year 1310 for a hundred and fifty francs! And those idiots of monks were quite overjoyed! They thought they had cheated me—cheated me! And he frisked about in an ecstasy of pride and triumph. We had got to the well-known door; it was open; I could see the portrait. The sun streamed brightly on the brown face and light powdered locks. I know not how; I felt a momentary giddiness and sickness, as if of long desired, unexpected pleasure; it lasted but an instant, and I was ashamed of myself.

Fa Diesis was in splendid spirits.

"Do you see that?" he said, forgetting all he had previously told me—"that is a certain Ferdinando Rinaldi, a singer, who was assassinated for making love to my great-aunt"; and he stalked about in great glee, thinking of the psaltery at Guastalla, and fanning himself complacently with a large green fan.

A thought suddenly struck me—

"It happened here at M——, did it not?"

"To be sure."

And Fa Diesis continued shuffling to and fro in his old red and blue dressing-gown, with parrots and cherry branches on it.

"Did you never know anyone who had seen him—heard him?"

"I? Never. How could I? He was killed ninety-four years ago."

Ninety-four years ago! I looked up at the portrait; ninety-four years ago! and yet——The eyes seemed to me to have a strange, fixed, intent look.

"And where——" I hesitated despite myself, "where did it happen?"

"That few people know; no one, probably, except me, nowadays," he answered with satisfaction. "But my father pointed out the house to me when I was little; it had belonged to a Marchese Negri, but somehow or other, after that affair, no one would live there any longer, and it was left to rot; already, when I was a child, it was all deserted and falling to pieces. A fine house, though! A fine house! and one which ought to have been worth something. I saw it again some years ago—I rarely go outside the gates now—outside Porta San Vitale—about a mile."

"Outside Porta San Vitale? the house where this Rinaldi was—it is still there?"

Fa Diesis looked at me with intense contempt.

"Bagatella!" (fiddlestick) he exclaimed. "Do you think a villa flies away like that?"

"You are sure?"

"Per Bacco!* as sure as that I see you—outside Porta San Vitale, an old tumbledown place with obelisks and vases, and that sort of thing."

We had come to the head of the staircase. "Good-bye," I said; "I'll return to-morrow for your parcels for Venice," and I ran down the stair. "Outside Porta San Vitale!" I said to myself; "outside Porta San Vitale!" It was six in the afternoon and the heat still intense; I hailed a crazy old cab, a sky-blue carriage of the year '20, with a cracked hood and emblazoned panels. "Dove commanda?" (whither do you command?) asked the sleepy driver. "Outside Porta San Vitale," I cried. He touched his bony, long-maned white horse, and off we jolted over the uneven pavement, past the red Lombard cathedral and baptistery, through the long, dark Via San Vitale, with its grand old palaces; under the red gate with the old word "Libertas"* still on it, along a dusty road bordered by acacias out into the rich Lombard plain. On we rattled through the fields of corn, hemp, and glossy dark maize, ripening under the rich evening sun. In the distance the purple walls and belfries and shining cupolas gleaming in the light; beyond, the vast blue and gold and hazy plain, bounded by the far-off Alps. The air was warm and serene, everything quiet and solemn. But I was excited. I sought out every large country house; I went wherever a tall belvedere tower peeped from behind the elms and poplars; I crossed and recrossed the plain, taking one lane after another, as far as where the road branched off to Crevalcuore;* passed villa after villa, but found none with vases and obelisks, none crumbling and falling, none that could have been *the* villa. What wonder, indeed? Fa Diesis had seen it, but Fa Diesis was seventy, and that—that had happened ninety-four years ago! Still I might be mistaken; I might have gone too far or not far enough—there was lane within lane and road within road. Perhaps the house was screened by trees, or perhaps it lay towards the next gate. So I went again, through the cyclamen-lined lanes, overhung by gnarled mulberries and oaks; I looked up at one house after another: all were old, many dilapidated, some seeming old churches with walled-up colonnades, others built up against old watch-towers; but of what old Fa Diesis had described I could see nothing. I asked the driver, and the driver asked the old women and the fair-haired children who crowded out of the little farms. Did anyone know of a large deserted house with obelisks and vases—a house that had once belonged to a Marchese Negri? Not in that neighbourhood; there was the Villa Monte-casignoli with the tower and the sundial, which was dilapidated enough, and the Casino Fava crumbling in yonder cabbage-field, but neither had vases nor obelisks, neither had ever belonged to a Marchese Negri.

At last I gave it up in despair. Ninety-four years ago! The house no longer existed; so I returned to my inn, where the three jolly mediæval pilgrims swung over the door lamp; took my supper and tried to forget the whole matter.

Next day I went and finally settled with the owner of the carved work I had been commissioned to buy, and then I sauntered lazily about the old town. The day after there was to be a great fair, and preparations were being made for it; baskets and hampers being unloaded, and stalls put up everywhere in the great square; festoons of tinware and garlands of onions were slung across the Gothic arches of the Town Hall and to its massive bronze torch-holders; there was a quack already holding forth on the top of his stage coach, with a skull and many bottles before him, and a little bespangled page handing about his bills; there was a puppet-show at a corner, with a circle of empty chairs round it, just under the stone pulpit where the monks of the Middle Ages had once exhorted the Montagus and Capulets* of M—— to make peace and embrace. I sauntered about among the crockery and glassware, picking my way among the packing-cases and hay, and among the vociferating peasants and townsfolk. I looked at the figs and cherries and red peppers in the baskets, at the old ironwork, rusty keys, nails, chains, bits of ornament on the stalls; at the vast blue and green glazed umbrellas, at the old prints and images of saints tied against the church bench, at the whole moving, quarrelling, gesticulating crowd. I bought an old silver death's-head trinket at the table of a perambulating watch-maker, and some fresh sweet peas and roses from a peasant woman selling fowls and turkeys; then I turned into the maze of quaint little paved streets, protected by chains from carts and carriages, and named after mediæval hostelries and labelled on little slabs, "Scimmia" (monkey), "Alemagna" (Germany), "Venetia," and, most singular of all, "Brocca in dosso" (Jug on the Back). Behind the great, red, time-stained, castle-like Town Hall were a number of tinkers' dens; and beneath its arches hung caldrons, pitchers, saucepans, and immense pudding moulds with the imperial eagle of Austria on them, capacious and ancient enough to have contained the puddings of generations of German Cæsars.* Then I poked into some of those wondrous curiosity-shops of M——, little black dens, where oaken presses contain heaps and heaps of brocaded dresses and embroidered waistcoats, and yards of lace, and splendid chasubles, the spoils of centuries of magnificence. I walked down the main street and saw a crowd collected round a man with an immense white crested owl; the creature was such a splendid one, I determined to buy him and keep him in my studio at Venice, but when I approached him he flew at me, shaking his wings and screeching so that I beat an ignominious retreat. At length I returned to the square and sat down beneath an awning, where two bare-legged urchins served me excellent snow and lemon juice, at the price of a sou the glass. In short, I enjoyed my last day at M—— amazingly; and, in this bright, sunny square, with all the bustle about me, I wondered whether the person who the previous evening had scoured the country in search of a crazy villa where a man had been assassinated ninety-four years ago, could really and truly have been myself.

So I spent the morning; and the afternoon I passed indoors, packing up the delicate carved work with my own hands, although the perspiration ran down my face, and I gasped for air. At length, when evening and coolness were approaching, I took my hat and went once more to Fa Diesis's palace.

I found the old fellow in his many-coloured dressing-gown, seated in his cool, dusky room, among his inlaid lutes and Cremonese viols, carefully mending the torn pages of an illuminated missal, while his old, witchlike housekeeper was cutting out and pasting labels on to a heap of manuscript scores on the table. Fa Diesis got up, jumped about ecstatically, made magnificent speeches, and said that since I insisted on being of use to him, he had prepared half a dozen letters, which I might kindly leave on various correspondents of his at Venice, in order to save the twopenny stamp for each. The grim, lank, old fellow, with his astounding dressing-gown and cap, his lantern-jawed housekeeper, his old, morose grey cat, and his splendid harpsichords and lutes and missals, amused me more than usual. I sat with him for some time while he patched away at his missal. Mechanically I turned over the yellow pages of a music book that lay, waiting for a label, under my hand, and mechanically my eye fell on the words, in faded, yellow ink, at the top of one of the pieces, the indication of its performer:—

Rondò di Cajo Gracco, "Mille pene mio tesoro," per il Signor Ferdinando Rinaldi. Parma, 1782.

I positively started, for somehow that whole business had gone out of my mind.

"What have you got there?" asked Fa Diesis, perhaps a little suspiciously, and leaning across the table, he twitched the notes towards him—

"Oh, only that old opera of Cimarosa's*——Ah, by the way, per Bacco, how could I have made such a mistake yesterday? Didn't I tell you that Rinaldi had been stabbed in a villa outside Porta San Vitale?"

"Yes," I cried eagerly. "Why?"

"Why, I can't conceive how, but I must have been thinking about that blessed psaltery at San Vitale, at Guastalla. The villa where Rinaldi was killed is outside Porta San Zaccaria, in the direction of the river, near that old monastery where there are those frescoes by—I forget the fellow's name, that all the foreigners go to see. Don't you know?"

"Ah," I exclaimed, "I understand." And I did understand, for Porta San Zaccaria happens to be at exactly the opposite end of the town to Porta San Vitale, and here was the explanation of my unsuccessful search of the previous evening. So after all the house might still be standing; and the desire to see it again seized hold of me. I rose, took the letters, which I strongly suspected contained other letters whose postage was to be saved in the same way, by being delivered by the original correspondent, and prepared to depart.

"Good-bye, good-bye," said old Fa Diesis, with effusion, as we passed through the dark passage in order to get to the staircase. "Continue, my dear friend, in those paths of wisdom and culture which the youth of our days has so miserably abandoned, in order that the sweet promise of your happy silver youth be worthily accomplished in your riper——Ah, by the way," he interrupted himself, "I have forgotten to give you a little pamphlet of mine on the manufacture of violin strings which I wish to send as an act of reverence to my old friend the Commander of the garrison of Venice"; and off he scuddled. I was near the door up the three steps and could not resist the temptation of seeing the picture once more. I pushed open the door and entered; a long ray of the declining sunlight, reflected from the neighbouring red church tower, fell across the face of the portrait, playing in the light, powdered hair and on the downy, well-cut lips, and ending in a tremulous crimson stain on the boarded floor. I went close up to the picture; there was the name "Ferdinando Rinaldi, 1782," on the roll of music he was holding; but the notes themselves were mere imitative, meaningless smears and blotches, although the title of the piece stood distinct and legible—"Sei Regina, io Pastor sono."

"Why, where is he?" cried Fa Diesis's shrill voice in the passage. "Ah, here you are"; and he handed me the pamphlet, pompously addressed to the illustrious General S——, at Venice. I put it in my pocket.

"You won't forget to deliver it?" he asked, and then went on with the speech he had before begun: "Let the promise of your happy silver youth be fulfilled in a golden manhood, in order that the world may mark down your name *albo lapillo*.* Ah," he continued, "perhaps we shall never meet again. I am old, my dear friend, I am old!" and he smacked his lips. "Perhaps, when you return to M——, I may have gone to rest with my immortal ancestors, who, as you know, intermarried with the Ducal family of Sforza,* A.D. 1490!"

The last time! This might be the last time I saw the picture! What would become of it after old Fa Diesis's death? I turned once more towards it, in leaving the room; the last flicker of light fell on the dark, yearning face, and it seemed, in the trembling sunbeam, as if the head turned and looked towards me. I never saw the portrait again.

I walked along quickly through the darkening streets, on through the crowd of loiterers and pleasure seekers, on towards Porta San Zaccaria. It was late, but if I hastened, I might still have an hour of twilight; and next morning I had to leave M——. This was my last opportunity, I could not relinquish it; so on I went, heedless of the ominous puffs of warm, damp air, and of the rapidly clouding sky.

It was St. John's Eve,* and bonfires began to appear on the little hills round the town; fire-balloons were sent up, and the great bell of the cathedral boomed out in honour of the coming holiday. I threaded my way through the dusty streets and out by Porta San Zaccaria.

I walked smartly along the avenues of poplars along the walls, and then cut across into the fields by a lane leading towards the river. Behind me were the city walls, all crenelated and jagged; in front the tall belfry and cypresses of the Carthusian monastery;* above, the starless, moonless sky, overhung by heavy clouds. The air was mild and relaxing; every now and then there came a gust of hot, damp wind, making a shudder run across the silver poplars and trailed vines; a few heavy drops fell, admonishing me of the coming storm, and every moment some of the light faded away. But I was determined; was not this my last opportunity? So on I stumbled through the rough lane, on through the fields of corn and sweet, fresh-scented hemp, the fireflies dancing in fantastic spirals before me. Something dark wriggled across my path; I caught it on my stick: it was a long, slimy snake which slipped quickly off. The frogs roared for rain, the crickets sawed with ominous loudness, the fireflies crossed and recrossed before me; yet on I went, quicker and quicker in the fast increasing darkness. A broad sheet of pink lightning and a distant rumble: more drops fell; the frogs roared louder, the crickets sawed faster and faster, the air got heavier and the sky yellow and lurid where the sun had set; yet on I went towards the river. Suddenly down came a tremendous stream of rain, as if the heavens had opened, and with it down came the darkness, complete though sudden; the storm had changed evening into the deepest night. What should I do? Return? How? I saw a light glimmering behind a dark mass of trees; I would go on; there must be a house out there, where I could take shelter till the storm was over; I was too far to get back to the town. So on I went in the pelting rain. The lane made a sudden bend, and I found myself in an open space in the midst of the fields, before an iron gate, behind which, surrounded by trees, rose a dark, vast mass; a rent in the clouds permitted me to distinguish a gaunt, grey villa, with broken obelisks on its triangular front. My heart gave a great thump; I stopped, the rain continuing to stream down. A dog began to bark furiously from a little peasant's house on the other side of the road, whence issued the light I had perceived. The door opened and a man appeared holding a lamp.

"Who's there?" he cried.

I went up to him. He held up the light and surveyed me.

"Ah!" he said immediately, "a stranger— a foreigner. Pray enter, illustrissimo."* My dress and my sketch-book had immediately revealed what I was; he took me for an artist, one of the many who visited the neighbouring Carthusian Abbey, who had lost his way in the maze of little lanes.

I shook the rain off me and entered the low room, whose white-washed walls were lit yellow by the kitchen fire. A picturesque group of peasants stood out in black outline on the luminous background: an old woman was spinning on her classic distaff,* a young one was unravelling skeins of thread on a sort of rotating star; another was cracking pea pods; an old, close-shaven man sat smoking with his elbows on the table, and opposite to him sat a portly priest in three-cornered hat, knee-breeches, and short coat. They rose and looked at me, and welcomed me with the familiar courtesy of their class; the priest offered me his seat, the girl took my soaking coat and hat, and hung them over the fire, the young man brought an immense hempen towel, and proceeded to dry me, much to the general hilarity. They had been reading their usual stories of Charlemagne in their well-thumbed "Reali di Francia,"* that encyclopædia of Italian peasants; but they put by their books on my entrance and began talking, questioning me on every possible and impossible subject. Was it true that it always rained in England? (at that rate, remarked the old man shrewdly, how could the English grow grapes; and if they did not make wine, what could they live on?) Was it true that one could pick up lumps of gold somewhere in England? Was there any town as large as M—— in that country? etc., etc. The priest thought these questions foolish, and inquired with much gravity after the health of Milord Vellingtone,* who, he understood, had been seriously unwell of late. I scarcely listened; I was absent and pre-occupied. I gave the women my sketch-book to look over; they were delighted with its contents; mistook all the horses for oxen and all the men for women, and exclaimed and tittered with much glee. The priest, who prided himself on superior education, gave me the blandest encouragement; asked me whether I had been to the picture gallery, whether I had been to the neighbouring Bologna (he was very proud of having been there last St. Petronius's day); informed me that that city was the mother of all art, and that the Caracci* especially were her most glorious sons, etc., etc. Meanwhile, the rain continued coming down in a steady pour.

"I don't think I shall be able to get home to-night," said the priest, looking through the window into the darkness. "My donkey is the most wonderful donkey in the world—quite a human being. When you say 'Leone, Leone' to him, he kicks up his heels and stands on his hind legs like an acrobat; indeed he does, upon my honour; but I don't believe even he could find his way through this darkness, and the wheels of my gig would infallibly stick in some rut, and where should I be then? I must stay here overnight, no help for that; but I'm sorry for the Signore here, who will find these very poor quarters."

"Indeed," I said, "I shall be but too happy to stay, if I be sure that I shall be in no one's way."

"In our way! What a notion!" they all cried.

"That's it," said the priest, particularly proud of the little vehicle he drove, after the droll fashion of Lombard clergymen. "And I'll drive the Signore into town to-morrow morning, and you can bring your cart with the vegetables for the fair."

I paid but little attention to all this; I felt sure I had at length found the object of my search; there, over the way, was the villa; but I seemed almost as far from it as ever, seated in this bright, whitewashed kitchen, among these country folk. The young man asked me timidly, and as a special favour, to make a picture of the girl who was his bride, and very pretty, with laughing, irregular features, and curly crisp golden hair. I took out my pencil and began, I fear not as conscientiously as these good people deserved; but they were enchanted, and stood in a circle round me, exchanging whispered remarks, while the girl sat all giggling and restless on the large wooden settle.

"What a night!" exclaimed the old man. "What a bad night, and St. John's Eve too!"

"What has that to do with it?" I asked.

"Why," he answered, "they say that on St. John's night they permit dead people to walk about."

"What rubbish!" cried the priest indignantly; "who ever told you that? What is there about ghosts in the mass book, or in the Archbishop's pastorals, or in the Holy Fathers of the Church?" and he raised his voice to inquisitorial dignity.

"You may say what you like," answered the old man doggedly; "it's true none the less. I've never seen anything myself, and perhaps the Archbishop hasn't either, but I know people who have."

The priest was about to fall upon him with a deluge of arguments in dialect, when I interrupted,

"To whom does that large house over the way belong?" I waited with anxiety for an answer.

"It belongs to the Avvocato* Bargellini," said the woman with great deference, and they proceeded to inform me that they were his tenants, his *contadini* having charge of all the property belonging to the house; that the Avvocato Bargellini was immensely rich and immensely learned.

"An encyclopædic man!" burst out the priest; "he knows everything, law, art, geography, mathematics, numismatics, gymnastics!"

And he waved his hand between each branch of knowledge. I was disappointed.

"Is it inhabited?" I asked.

"No," they answered, no one has ever lived in it. "The Avvocato bought it twenty years ago from the heir of a certain Marchese Negri who died very poor."

"A Marchese Negri?" I exclaimed; then, after all, I was right.

"But why is it not inhabited, and since when?"

"Oh, since—since always—no one has ever lived in it since the Marchese Negri's grand-father. It is all going to pieces; we keep our garden tools and a few sacks there, but there is no living there—there are no windows or shutters."

"But why doesn't the Avvocato patch it up?"

I persisted. "It seems a very fine house."

The old man was going to answer, but the priest glanced at him and answered quickly—

"The position in these fields is unhealthy."

"Unhealthy!" cried the old man angrily, much annoyed at the priest's interference. "Un-healthy! why, haven't I lived here these sixty years, and not one of us has had a headache? Unhealthy, indeed! No, the house is a bad house to live in, that's what it is!"

"This is very odd," I said, "surely there must be ghosts?" and I tried to laugh.

The word *ghosts* acted like magic; like all Italian peasants, they loudly disclaimed such a thing when questioned, although they would accidentally refer to it themselves.

"Ghosts! Ghosts!" they cried, "surely the Signore does not believe in such trash? Rats there are and in plenty. Do ghosts gnaw the chestnuts, and steal the Indian corn?"

Even the old man, who had seemed inclined to be ghostly from rebellion to the priest, was now thoroughly on his guard, and not a word on the subject could be extracted from him. They did not wish to talk about ghosts, and I for my part did not want to hear about them; for in my present highly wrought, imaginative mood, an apparition in a winding sheet, a clanking of chains, and all the authorised ghostly manifestations seemed in the highest degree disgusting; my mind was too much haunted to be intruded on by vulgar spectres, and as I mechanically sketched the giggling, blushing little peasant girl, and looked up in her healthy, rosy, sunburnt face, peeping from beneath a gaudy silk kerchief, my mental eyes were fixed on a very different face, which I saw as distinctly as hers—that dark yearning face with the strange red lips and the lightly powdered locks. The peasants and the priest went on chattering gaily, running from one topic to another—the harvest, the vines, the next day's fair; politics the most fantastic, scraps of historical lore even more astounding, rattling on unceasingly, with much good humour, the most astonishing ignorance of facts, infantine absurdity, perfect seriousness, and much shrewd sceptical humour. I did my best to join in this conversation, and laughed and joked to the best of my power. The fact is I felt quite happy and serene, for I had little by little made up my mind to an absurd step, either babyish in the extreme or foolhardy to the utmost, but which I contemplated with perfect coolness and assurance, as one sometimes does hazardous or foolish courses which gratify a momentary whim. I had at length found the house; I would pass the night there.

I must have been in violent mental excitement, but the excitement was so uniform and unimpeded as to seem almost regular; I felt as if it were quite natural to live in an atmosphere of weirdness and adventure, and I was firm in my purpose. At length came the moment for action: the women put by their work, the old man shook the ashes out of his pipe; they looked at each other as if not knowing how to begin. The priest, who had just re-entered from giving his wondrous donkey some hay, made himself their spokesman—

"Ahem!" he cleared his throat; "the Signore must excuse the extreme simplicity of these uneducated rustics, and bear in mind that as they are unaccustomed to the luxuries of cities, and have, moreover, to be up by daybreak in order to attend to their agricultural——"

"Yes, yes," I answered, smiling; "I understand. They want to go to bed, and they are quite right. I must beg you all to forgive my having thoughtlessly kept you up so late." How was I now to proceed? I scarcely understood.

"Keep them up late? Oh, not at all; they had been but too much honoured," they cried.

"Well," said the priest, who was growing sleepy, "of course there is no returning through this rain; the lanes are too unsafe; besides, the city gates are locked. Come, what can we do for the Signore? Can we make him up a bed here? I will go and sleep with our old Maso," and he tapped the young man's shoulder.

The women were already starting off for pillows, and mattresses, and what not; but I stopped them.

"On no account," I said. "I will not encroach upon your hospitality. I can sleep quite comfortably over the way—in the large house."

"Over the way? In the big house?" they cried, all together. "The Signore sleep in the big house? Oh, never, never! Impossible."

"Rather than that, I'll harness my donkey and drive the Signore through the mud and rain and darkness; that I will, corpo di Bacco,"* cried the little, red-faced priest.

"But why not?" I answered, determined not to be baulked. "I can get a splendid night's rest over the way. Why shouldn't I?"

"Never, never!" they answered in a chorus of expostulation.

"But since there are no ghosts there," I protested, trying to laugh, "what reason is there against it?"

"Oh, as to ghosts," put in the priest, "I promise you there are none. I snap my fingers at ghosts!"

"Well," I persisted, "you won't tell me that the rats will mistake me for a sack of chestnuts and eat me up, will you? Come, give me the key." I was beginning to believe in the use of a little violence. "Which is it? I asked, seeing a bunch hanging on a nail; "is it this one?—or this one? *Via*!* tell me which it is."

The old man seized hold of the keys. "You must not sleep there," he said, very positively. "It's no use trying to hide it. That house is no house for a Christian to sleep in. A bad thing happened there once—some one was murdered; that is why no one will live in it. It's no use to say *No*, Abate,"* and he turned contemptuously towards the priest. "There are evil things in that house."

"Ghosts?" I cried, laughing, and trying to force the keys from him.

"Not exactly ghosts," he answered; "but—the devil is sometimes in that house."

"Indeed!" I exclaimed, quite desperate. "That is just what I want. I have to paint a picture of him fighting with a saint of ours who once pulled his nose with a pair of tongs,* and I am overjoyed to do his portrait from the life."

They did not well understand; they suspected I was mad, and so, truly, I was.

"Let him have his way," grumbled the old man; "he is a headstrong boy—let him go and see and hear all he will."

"For heaven's sake, Signore!" entreated the women.

"Is it possible, Signor Forestiere,* that you can be serious?" protested the priest, with his hand on my arm.

"Indeed I am," I answered; "you shall hear all I have seen tomorrow morning. I'll throw my black paint at the devil if he won't sit still while I paint him."

"Paint the devil! is he mad?" whispered the women, aghast.

I had got hold of the keys. "Is this it?" I asked, pointing to a heavy, handsomely-wrought, but very rusty key.

The old man nodded.

I took it off the ring. The women, although extremely terrified by my daring, were secretly delighted at the prospect of a good story the next morning. One of them gave me a large, two-wicked kitchen lamp, with snuffers and tweezers chained to its tall stand; another brought an immense rose-coloured umbrella; the young man produced a large mantle lined with green and a thick horsecloth; they would have brought a mattress and blankets if I had let them.

"You insist on going?" asked the priest. "Think how wretchedly cold and damp it must be over there!"

"Do, pray, reflect, Signore!" entreated the young woman.

"Haven't I told you I am engaged to paint the devil's portrait?" I answered, and, drawing the bolt, and opening the umbrella, I dashed out of the cottage.

"Gesu Maria!" cried the women; "to go there on such a night as this!"

"To sleep on the floor!" exclaimed the priest; "what a man, what a man!"

"È matto, è matto! he is mad!" they all joined, and shut the door.

I dashed across the flood before the door, unlocked the iron gate, walked quickly through the dark and wet up the avenue of moaning poplars. A sudden flash of lightning, broad, pink, and enduring, permitted me to see the house, like an immense stranded ship or huge grim skeleton, looming in the darkness,

I ran up the steps, unlocked the door, and gave it a violent shake.

IV

I gave a vigorous push to the old, rotten door; it opened, creaking, and I entered a vast, lofty hall, the entrance saloon of the noble old villa. As I stepped forward cautiously, I heard a cutting, hissing sound, and something soft and velvety brushed against my cheek. I stepped backwards and held up the lamp: it was only an owl whom the light had scared; it hooted dismally as it regained its perch. The rain fell sullen and monotonous; the only other sound was that of my footsteps waking the echoes of the huge room. I looked about as much as the uncertain light of my two-wicked lamp permitted; the shiny marble pavement was visible only in a few places; dust had formed a thick crust over it, and everywhere yellow maize seed was strewn about. In the middle were some broken chairs—tall, gaunt chairs, with remains of gilding and brocade, and some small wooden ones with their ragged straw half pushed out. Against a large oaken table rested some sacks of corn; in the corners were heaps of chestnuts and of green and yellow silkworm cocoons, hoes, spades, and other garden implements; roots and bulbs strewed the floor; the whole place was full of a vague, musty smell of decaying wood and plaster, of earth, of drying fruit and silkworms.* I looked up; the rain battered in through the unglazed windows and poured in a stream over some remains of tracery and fresco; I looked higher, at the bare mouldering rafters. Thus I stood while the rain fell heavy and sullen, and the water splashed down outside from the roof; there I stood in the desolate room, in a stupid, unthinking condition. All this solemn, silent decay impressed me deeply, far more than I had expected; all my excitement seemed over, all my whims seemed to have fled.

I almost forgot why I had wished to be here; indeed, why had I? That mad infatuation seemed wholly aimless and inexplicable; this strange, solemn scene was enough in itself. I felt at a loss what to do, or even how to feel; I had the object of my wish, all was over. I was in the house; further I neither ventured to go nor dared to think of; all the dare-devil courting of the picturesque and the supernatural which had hitherto filled me was gone; I felt like an intruder, timid and humble—an intruder on solitude and ruin.

I spread the horse-cloth on the floor, placed the lamp by my side, wrapped myself in the peasant's cloak, leaned my head on a broken chair and looked up listlessly at the bare rafters, listening to the dull falling rain and to the water splashing from the roof; thoughts or feelings I appeared to have none.

How long I remained thus I cannot tell; the minutes seemed hours in this vigil, with nothing but the spluttering and flickering of the lamp within, the monotonous splash without; lying all alone, awake but vacant, in the vast crumbling hall.

I can scarcely tell whether suddenly or gradually I began to perceive, or thought I perceived, faint and confused sounds issuing I knew not whence. What they were I could not distinguish; all I knew was that they were distinct from the drop and splash of the rain. I raised myself on my elbow and listened; I took out my watch and pressed the repeater* to assure myself I was awake: one, two, three, four, five, six, seven, eight, nine, ten, eleven, twelve tremulous ticks. I sat up and listened more intently, trying to separate the sounds from those of the rain outside. The sounds—silvery, sharp, but faint—seemed to become more distinct. Were they approaching, or was I awaking? I rose and listened, holding my breath. I trembled; I took up the lamp and stepped forward; I waited a moment, listening again. There could be no doubt the light, metallic sounds proceeded from the interior of the house; they were notes, the notes of some instrument. I went on cautiously. At the end of the hall was a crazy, gilded, battered door up some steps; I hesitated before opening it, for I had a vague, horrible fear of what might be behind it. I pushed it open gently and by degrees, and stood on the threshold, trembling and breathless. There was nothing save a dark, empty room, and then another; they had the cold, damp feeling and smell of a crypt. I passed through them slowly, startling the bats with my light; and the sounds, the sharp, metallic chords became more and more distinct; and as they did so, the vague, numbing terror seemed to gain more and more hold on me. I came to a broad spiral staircase, of which the top was lost in the darkness, my lamp shedding a flickering light on the lower steps. The sounds were now quite distinct, the light, sharp, silvery sounds of a harpsichord or spinet; they fell clear and vibrating into the silence of the crypt-like house. A cold perspiration covered my forehead; I seized hold of the banisters of the stairs, and little by little dragged myself up them like an inert mass. There came a chord, and delicately, insensibly there glided into the modulations of the instrument the notes of a strange, exquisite voice. It was of a wondrous sweet, thick, downy quality, neither limpid nor penetrating, but with a vague, drowsy charm, that seemed to steep the soul in enervating bliss; but, together with this charm, a terrible cold seemed to sink into my heart. I crept up the stairs, listening and panting. On the broad landing was a folding, gilded door, through whose interstices issued a faint glimmer of light, and from behind it proceeded the sounds. By the side of the door, but higher up, was one of those oval, ornamental windows called in French "œil de bœuf";* an old broken table stood beneath it. I summoned up my courage and, clambering on to the unsteady table, raised myself on tiptoe to the level of the window and, trembling, peeped though its dust-dimmed glass. I saw into a large, lofty room, the greater part of which was hidden in darkness, so that I could distinguish only the outline of the heavily-curtained windows, and of a screen, and of one or two ponderous chairs. In the middle was a small, inlaid harpsichord, on which stood two wax lights, shedding a bright reflection on the shining marble floor, and forming a pale, yellowish mass of light in the dark room. At the harpsichord, turned slightly away from me, sat a figure in the dress of the end of the last century—a long, pale lilac coat, and pale green waistcoat, and lightly-powdered hair gathered into a black silk bag;* a deep amber-coloured silk cloak was thrown over the chairback. He was singing intently, and accompanying himself on the harpsichord, his back turned towards the window at which I was. I stood spellbound, incapable of moving, as if all my blood were frozen and my limbs paralysed, almost insensible, save that I saw and I heard, saw and heard him alone. The wonderful sweet, downy voice glided lightly and dexterously through the complicated mazes of the song; it rounded off ornament after ornament, it swelled imperceptibly into glorious, hazy magnitude, and diminished, dying gently away from a high note to a lower one, like a weird, mysterious sigh; then it leaped into a high, clear, triumphant note, and burst out into a rapid, luminous shake.

For a moment he took his hands off the keys, and turned partially round. My eyes caught his: they were the deep, soft, yearning eyes of the portrait at Fa Diesis's.

At that moment a shadow was interposed between me and the lights, and instantly, by whom or how I know not, they were extinguished, and the room left in complete darkness; at the same instant the modulation was broken off unfinished; the last notes of the piece changed into a long, shrill, quivering cry; there was a sound of scuffling and suppressed voices, the heavy dead thud of a falling body, a tremendous crash, and another long, vibrating, terrible cry. The spell was broken, I started up, leaped from the table, and rushed to the closed door of the room; I shook its gilded panels twice and thrice in vain; I wrenched them asunder with a tremendous effort, and entered.

The moonlight fell in a broad, white sheet through a hole in the broken roof, filling the desolate room with a vague, greenish light. It was empty. Heaps of broken tiles and plaster lay on the floor; the water trickled down the stained wall and stagnated on the pavement; a broken fallen beam lay across the middle; and there, solitary and abandoned in the midst of the room, stood an open harpsichord, its cover incrusted with dust and split from end to end, its strings rusty and broken, its yellow keyboard thick with cobweb; the greenish-white light falling straight upon it.

I was seized with an irresistible panic; I rushed out, caught up the lamp which I had left on the landing, and dashed down the staircase, never daring to look behind me, nor to the right or the left, as if something horrible and undefinable were pursuing me, that long, agonized cry continually ringing in my ears. I rushed on through the empty, echoing rooms and tore open the door of the large entrance hall—there, at least, I might be safe—when, just as I entered it, I slipped, my lamp fell and was extinguished, and I fell down, down, I knew not where, and lost consciousness.

When I came to my senses, gradually and vaguely, I was lying at the extremity of the vast entrance hall of the crumbling villa, at the foot of some steps, the fallen lamp by my side. I looked round all dazed and astonished; the white morning light was streaming into the hall. How had I come there? what had happened to me? Little by little I recollected, and as the recollection returned, so also returned my fear, and I rose quickly. I pressed my hand to my aching head, and drew it back stained with a little blood. I must, in my panic, have forgotten the steps and fallen, so that my head had struck against the sharp base of a column. I wiped off the blood, took the lamp and the cloak and horse-cloth, which lay where I had left them, spread on the dust-encrusted marble floor, amidst the sacks of flour and the heaps of chestnuts, and staggered through the room, not well aware whether I was really awake. At the doorway I paused and looked back once more on the great bare hall, with its mouldering rafters and decaying frescoes, the heaps of rubbish and garden implements, its sad, solemn ruin. I opened the door and went out on to the long flight of steps before the house, and looked wonderingly at the serenely lovely scene. The storm had passed away, leaving only a few hazy white clouds in the blue sky; the soaking earth steamed beneath the already strong sun; the yellow corn was beaten down and drenched, the maize and vine leaves sparkled with rain drops, the tall green hemp gave out its sweet, fresh scent. Before me lay the broken-up garden, with its overgrown box hedges, its immense decorated lemon vases, its spread out silkworm mats, its tangle of weeds and vegetables and flowers; further, the waving green plain with its avenues of tall poplars stretching in all directions, and from its midst rose the purple and grey walls and roofs and towers of the old town; hens were cackling about in search of worms in the soft moist earth, and the deep, clear sounds of the great cathedral bell floated across the fields. Looking down on all this fresh, lovely scene, it struck me, more vividly than ever before, how terrible it must be to be cut off for ever from all this, to lie blind and deaf and motionless mouldering underground. The idea made me shudder and shrink from the decaying house; I ran down to the road; the peasants were there, dressed in their gayest clothes, red, blue, cinnamon, and pea-green, busy piling vegetables into a light cart, painted with vine wreaths and souls in the flames of purgatory. A little further, at the door of the white, arcaded farmhouse, with its sundial and vine trellis, the jolly little priest was buckling the harness of his wonderful donkey, while one of the girls, mounted on a chair, was placing a fresh wreath of berries and a fresh dripping nosegay before the little faded Madonna shrine.

When they saw me, they all cried out and came eagerly to meet me.

"Well!" asked the priest, "did you see any ghosts?"

"Did you do the devil's picture?" laughed the girl.

I shook my head with a forced smile.

"Why!" exclaimed the lad, "the Signore has hurt his forehead. How could that have happened?"

"The lamp went out and I stumbled against a sharp corner," I answered hastily.

They noticed that I seemed pale and ill, and attributed it to my fall. One of the women ran into the house and returned with a tiny, bulb-shaped glass bottle, filled with some greenish fluid.

"Rub some of this into the cut," she directed; "this is infallible, it will cure any wound. It is some holy oil more than a hundred years old, left us by our grandmother."

I shook my head, but obeyed and rubbed some of the queer smelling green staff on to the cut, without noticing any particularly miraculous effect.

They were going to the fair; when the cart was well stocked, they all mounted on to its benches, till it tilted upwards with the weight; the lad touched the shaggy old horse and off they rattled, waving their hats and handkerchiefs at me. The priest courteously offered me a seat beside him in his gig; I accepted mechanically, and off we went, behind the jingling cart of the peasants, through the muddy lanes, where the wet boughs bent over us, and we brushed the drops off the green hedges. The priest was highly talkative, but I scarcely heard what he said, for my head ached and reeled. I looked back at the deserted villa, a huge dark mass in the shining green fields of hemp and maize, and shuddered.

"You are unwell," said the priest; "you must have taken cold in that confounded damp old hole."

We entered the town, crowded with carts and peasants, passed through the market place, with its grand old buildings all festooned with tin ware and onions and coloured stuffs, and what not; and he set me down at my inn, where the sign of the three pilgrims swings over the door.

"Good-bye, good-bye! *a rivederci!* to our next meeting!" he cried.

"*A rivederci!*" I answered faintly. I felt numb and sick; I paid my bill and sent off my luggage at once. I longed to be out of M——; I knew instinctively that I was on the eve of a bad illness, and my only thought was to reach Venice while I yet could.

I proved right; the day after my arrival at Venice the fever seized me and kept fast hold of me many a week.

"That's what comes of remaining in Rome until July!" cried all my friends, and I let them continue in their opinion.

Winthrop paused, and remained for a moment with his head between his hands; none of us made any remark, for we were at a loss what to say.

"That air—the one I had heard that night," he added after a moment, "and its opening words, those on the portrait, 'Sei Regina, io Pastor sono,' remained deep in my memory. I took every opportunity of discovering whether such an air really existed; I asked lots of people, and ransacked half a dozen musical archives. I did find an air, even more than one, with those words, which appear to have been set by several composers; but on trying them over at the piano they proved totally different from the one in my mind. The consequence naturally was that, as the impression or the adventure grew fainter, I began to doubt whether it had not been all a delusion, a nightmare phantasm, due to over-excitement and fever, due to the morbid, vague desire for something strange and supernatural. Little by little I settled down in this idea, regarding the whole story as an hallucination. As to the air, I couldn't explain that, I shuffled it off half unexplained and tried to forget it. But now, on suddenly hearing that very same air from you—on being assured of its existence outside my imagination—the whole scene has returned to me in all its vividness, and I feel compelled to believe. Can I do otherwise? Tell me? Is it reality or fiction? At any rate," he added, rising and taking his hat, and trying to speak more lightly, "will you forgive my begging you never to let me hear that piece again?"

"Be assured you shall not," answered the Countess, pressing his hand; "it makes even me feel a little uncomfortable now; besides, the comparison would be too much to my disadvantage. Ah! my dear Mr. Winthrop, do you know, I think I would almost spend a night in the Villa Negri, in order to hear a song of Cimarosa's time sung by a singer of the last century."

"I knew you wouldn't believe a word of it," was Winthrop's only reply.

Oke of Okehurst;

OR,

THE PHANTOM LOVER.

To COUNT PETER BOUTOURLINE,*

AT TAGANTCHA,

GOVERNMENT OF KIEW, RUSSIA.

My dear Boutourline,—Do you remember my telling you, one afternoon that you sat upon the hearthstool at Florence, the story of Mrs. Oke of Okehurst?

You thought it a fantastic tale, you lover of fantastic things, and urged me to write it out at once, although I protested that, in such matters, to write is to exorcise, to dispel the charm; and that printers' ink chases away the ghosts that may pleasantly haunt us, as efficaciously as gallons of holy water.

But if, as I suspect, you will now put down any charm that story may have possessed to the way in which we had been working ourselves up, that firelight evening, with all manner of fantastic stuff—if, as I fear, the story of Mrs. Oke of Okehurst will strike you as stale and unprofitable—the sight of this little book will serve at least to remind you, in the middle of your Russian summer, that there is such a season as winter, such a place as Florence, and such a person as your friend,

VERNON LEE.

Kensington, *July* 1886.

OKE OF OKEHURST;

OR,

THE PHANTOM LOVER

I

THAT sketch up there with the boy's cap? Yes; that's the same woman. I wonder whether you could guess who she was. A singular being, is she not? The most marvellous creature, quite, that I have ever met: a wonderful elegance, exotic, far-fetched, poignant; an artificial perverse sort of grace and research in every outline and movement and arrangement of head and neck, and hands and fingers. Here are a lot of pencil-sketches I made while I was preparing to paint her portrait. Yes; there's nothing but her in the whole sketch-book. Mere scratches, but they may give some idea of her marvellous, fantastic kind of grace. Here she is leaning over the staircase, and here sitting in the swing. Here she is walking quickly out of the room. That's her head. You see she isn't really handsome; her forehead is too big, and her nose too short. This gives no idea of her. It was altogether a question of movement. Look at the strange cheeks, hollow and rather flat; well, when she smiled she had the most marvellous dimples here. There was something exquisite and uncanny about it. Yes; I began the picture, but it was never finished. I did the husband first. I wonder who has his likeness now? Help me to move these pictures away from the wall. Thanks. This is her portrait; a huge wreck. I don't suppose you can make much of it; it is merely blocked in, and seems quite mad. You see my idea was to make her leaning against a wall—there was one hung with yellow that seemed almost brown—so as to bring out the silhouette.

It was very singular I should have chosen that particular wall. It does look rather insane in this condition, but I like it; it has something of her. I would frame it and hang it up, only people would ask questions. Yes; you have guessed quite right—it is Mrs. Oke of Okehurst. I forgot you had relations in that part of the country; besides, I suppose the newspapers were full of it at the time. You didn't know that it all took place under my eyes? I can scarcely believe now that it did: it all seems so distant, vivid but unreal, like a thing of my own invention. It really was much stranger than any one guessed. People could no more understand it than they could understand her. I doubt whether any one ever understood Alice Oke besides myself. You mustn't think me unfeeling. She was a marvellous, weird, exquisite creature, but one couldn't feel sorry for her. I felt much sorrier for the wretched creature of a husband. It seemed such an appropriate end for her; I fancy she would have liked it could she have known. Ah! I shall never have another chance of painting such a portrait as I wanted. She seemed sent me from heaven or the other place. You have never heard the story in detail? Well, I don't usually mention it, because people are so brutally stupid or sentimental; but I'll tell it you. Let me see. It's too dark to paint any more to-day, so I can tell it you now. Wait; I must turn her face to the wall. Ah, she was a marvellous creature!

II

You remember, three years ago, my telling you I had let myself in for painting a couple of Kentish squireen? I really could not understand what had possessed me to say yes to that man. A friend of mine had brought him one day to my studio—Mr. Oke of Okehurst, that was the name on his card. He was a very tall, very well-made, very good-looking young man, with a beautiful fair complexion, beautiful fair moustache, and beautifully fitting clothes; absolutely like a hundred other young men you can see any day in the Park,* and absolutely uninteresting from the crown of his head to the tip of his boots. Mr. Oke, who had been a lieutenant in the Blues* before his marriage, was evidently extremely uncomfortable on finding himself in a studio. He felt misgivings about a man who could wear a velvet coat* in town, but at the same time he was nervously anxious not to treat me in the very least like a tradesman. He walked round my place, looked at everything with the most scrupulous attention, stammered out a few complimentary phrases, and then, looking at his friend for assistance, tried to come to the point, but failed. The point, which the friend kindly explained, was that Mr. Oke was desirous to know whether my engagements would allow of my painting him and his wife, and what my terms would be. The poor man blushed perfectly crimson during this explanation, as if he had come with the most improper proposal; and I noticed—the only interesting thing about him—a very odd nervous frown between his eyebrows, a perfect double gash,—a thing which usually means something abnormal: a mad-doctor of my acquaintance calls it the maniac-frown. When I had answered, he suddenly burst out into rather confused explanations: his wife—Mrs. Oke—had seen some of my—pictures—paintings—portraits—at the—the—what d'you call it?—Academy.* She had—in short, they had made a very great impression upon her. Mrs. Oke had a great taste for art; she was, in short, extremely desirous of having her portrait and his painted by me, *etcetera.*

"My wife," he suddenly added, "is a remarkable woman. I don't know whether you will think her handsome,—she isn't exactly, you know. But she's awfully strange," and Mr. Oke of Okehurst gave a little sigh and frowned that curious frown, as if so long a speech and so decided an expression of opinion had cost him a great deal.

It was a rather unfortunate moment in my career. A very influential sitter of mine—you remember the fat lady with the crimson curtain behind her?—had come to the conclusion or been persuaded that I had painted her old and vulgar, which, in fact, she was. Her whole clique had turned against me, the newspapers had taken up the matter, and for the moment I was considered as a painter to whose brushes no woman would trust her reputation. Things were going badly. So I snapped but too gladly at Mr. Oke's offer, and settled to go down to Okehurst at the end of a fortnight. But the door had scarcely closed upon my future sitter when I began to regret my rashness; and my disgust at the thought of wasting a whole summer upon the portrait of a totally uninteresting Kentish squire, and his doubtless equally uninteresting wife, grew greater and greater as the time for execution approached. I remember so well the frightful temper in which I got into the train for Kent, and the even more frightful temper in which I got out of it at the little station nearest to Okehurst. It was pouring floods. I felt a comfortable fury at the thought that my canvases would get nicely wetted before Mr. Oke's coachman had packed them on the top of the waggonette. It was just what served me right for coming to this confounded place to paint these confounded people. We drove off in the steady downpour. The roads were a mass of yellow mud; the endless flat grazing-grounds under the oak-trees, after having been burnt to cinders in a long drought, were turned into a hideous brown sop; the country seemed intolerably monotonous.

My spirits sank lower and lower. I began to meditate upon the modern Gothic country-house, with the usual amount of Morris furniture, Liberty rugs, and Mudie novels,* to which I was doubtless being taken. My fancy pictured very vividly the five or six little Okes—that man certainly must have at least five children—the aunts, and sisters-in-law, and cousins; the eternal routine of afternoon tea and lawn-tennis; above all, it pictured Mrs. Oke, the bouncing, well-informed, model housekeeper, electioneering, charity-organising young lady, whom such an individual as Mr. Oke would regard in the light of a remarkable woman. And my spirit sank within me, and I cursed my avarice in accepting the commission, my spiritlessness in not throwing it over while yet there was time. We had meanwhile driven into a large park, or rather a long succession of grazing-grounds, dotted about with large oaks, under which the sheep were huddled together for shelter from the rain. In the distance, blurred by the sheets of rain, was a line of low hills, with a jagged fringe of bluish firs and a solitary windmill. It must be a good mile and a half since we had passed a house, and there was none to be seen in the distance—nothing but the undulation of sere grass, sopped brown beneath the huge blackish oak-trees, and whence arose, from all sides, a vague disconsolate bleating. At last the road made a sudden bend, and disclosed what was evidently the home of my sitter. It was not what I had expected. In a dip in the ground a large red-brick house, with the rounded gables and high chimney-stacks of the time of James I.,*—a forlorn, vast place, set in the midst of the pasture-land, with no trace of garden before it, and only a few large trees indicating the possibility of one to the back; no lawn either, but on the other side of the sandy dip, which suggested a filled-up moat, a huge oak, short, hollow, with wreathing, blasted, black branches, upon which only a handful of leaves shook in the rain. It was not at all what I had pictured to myself the home of Mr. Oke of Okehurst.

My host received me in the hall, a large place, panelled and carved, hung round with portraits up to its curious ceiling—vaulted and ribbed like the inside of a ship's hull.* He looked even more blond and pink and white, more absolutely mediocre in his tweed suit; and also, I thought, even more good-natured and duller. He took me into his study, a room hung round with whips and fishing-tackle in place of books, while my things were being carried upstairs. It was very damp, and a fire was smouldering. He gave the embers a nervous kick with his foot, and said, as he offered me a cigar—

"You must excuse my not introducing you at once to Mrs. Oke. My wife—in short, I believe my wife is asleep."

"Is Mrs. Oke unwell?" I asked, a sudden hope flashing across me that I might be off the whole matter.

"Oh no! Alice is quite well; at least, quite as well as she usually is. My wife," he added, after a minute, and in a very decided tone, "does not enjoy very good health—a nervous constitution. Oh no! not at all ill, nothing at all serious, you know. Only nervous, the doctors say; mustn't be worried or excited, the doctors say; requires lots of repose,—that sort of thing."

There was a dead pause. This man depressed me, I knew not why. He had a listless, puzzled look, very much out of keeping with his evident admirable health and strength.

"I suppose you are a great sportsman?" I asked from sheer despair, nodding in the direction of the whips and guns and fishing-rods.

"Oh no! not now. I was once. I have given up all that," he answered, standing with his back to the fire, and staring at the polar bear beneath his feet. "I—I have no time for all that now," he added, as if an explanation were due. "A married man—you know. Would you like to come up to your rooms?" he suddenly interrupted himself. "I have had one arranged for you to paint in. My wife said you would prefer a north light. If that one doesn't suit, you can have your choice of any other."

I followed him out of the study, through the vast entrance-hall. In less than a minute I was no longer thinking of Mr. and Mrs. Oke and the boredom of doing their likeness; I was simply overcome by the beauty of this house, which I had pictured modern and philistine. It was, without exception, the most perfect example of an old English manor-house that I had ever seen; the most magnificent intrinsically, and the most admirably preserved. Out of the huge hall, with its immense fireplace of delicately carved and inlaid grey and black stone, and its rows of family portraits, reaching from the wainscoting to the oaken ceiling, vaulted and ribbed like a ship's hull, opened the wide, flat-stepped staircase, the parapet surmounted at intervals by heraldic monsters, the wall covered with oak carvings of coats-of-arms, leafage, and little mythological scenes, painted a faded red and blue, and picked out with tarnished gold, which harmonised with the tarnished blue and gold of the stamped leather that reached to the oak cornice, again delicately tinted and gilded. The beautifully damascened* suits of court armour looked, without being at all rusty, as if no modern hand had ever touched them; the very rugs under foot were of sixteenth-century Persian make; the only things of to-day were the big bunches of flowers and ferns, arranged in majolica* dishes upon the landings. Everything was perfectly silent; only from below came the chimes, silvery like an Italian palace fountain, of an old-fashioned clock.

It seemed to me that I was being led through the palace of the Sleeping Beauty.*

"What a magnificent house!" I exclaimed as I followed my host through a long corridor, also hung with leather, wainscoted with carvings, and furnished with big wedding coffers, and chairs that looked as if they came out of some Vandyck* portrait. In my mind was the strong impression that all this was natural, spontaneous—that it had about it nothing of the picturesqueness which swell studios have taught to rich and æsthetic houses. Mr. Oke misunderstood me.

"It is a nice old place," he said, "but it's too large for us. You see, my wife's health does not allow of our having many guests; and there are no children."

I thought I noticed a vague complaint in his voice; and he evidently was afraid there might have seemed something of the kind, for he added immediately—

"I don't care for children one jackstraw, you know, myself; can't understand how any one can, for my part."

If ever a man went out of his way to tell a lie, I said to myself, Mr. Oke of Okehurst was doing so at the present moment.

When he had left me in one of the two enormous rooms that were allotted to me, I threw myself into an arm-chair and tried to focus the extraordinary imaginative impression which this house had given me.

I am very susceptible to such impressions; and besides the sort of spasm of imaginative interest sometimes given to me by certain rare and eccentric personalities, I know nothing more subduing than the charm, quieter and less analytic, of any sort of complete and out-of-the-common-run sort of house. To sit in a room like the one I was sitting in, with the figures of the tapestry glimmering grey and lilac and purple in the twilight, the great bed, columned and curtained, looming in the middle, and the embers reddening beneath the overhanging mantelpiece of inlaid Italian stonework, a vague scent of rose-leaves and spices, put into the china bowls by the hands of ladies long since dead, while the clock downstairs sent up, every now and then, its faint silvery tune of forgotten days, filled the room;—to do this is a special kind of voluptuousness, peculiar and complex and indescribable, like the half-drunkenness of opium or haschisch, and which, to be conveyed to others in any sense as I feel it, would require a genius, subtle and heady, like that of Baudelaire.*

After I had dressed for dinner I resumed my place in the arm-chair, and resumed also my reverie, letting all these impressions of the past—which seemed faded like the figures in the arras, but still warm like the embers in the fireplace, still sweet and subtle like the perfume of the dead rose-leaves and broken spices in the china bowls—permeate me and go to my head. Of Oke and Oke's wife I did not think; I seemed quite alone, isolated from the world, separated from it in this exotic enjoyment.

Gradually the embers grew paler; the figures in the tapestry more shadowy; the columned and curtained bed loomed out vaguer; the room seemed to fill with greyness; and my eyes wandered to the mullioned bow-window, beyond whose panes, between whose heavy stone-work, stretched a greyish-brown expanse of sere and sodden park grass, dotted with big oaks; while far off, behind a jagged fringe of dark Scotch firs, the wet sky was suffused with the blood-red of the sunset. Between the falling of the raindrops from the ivy outside, there came, fainter or sharper, the recurring bleating of the lambs separated from their mothers, a forlorn, quavering, eerie little cry.

I started up at a sudden rap at my door.

"Haven't you heard the gong for dinner?" asked Mr. Oke's voice.

I had completely forgotten his existence.

III

I feel that I cannot possibly reconstruct my earliest impressions of Mrs. Oke. My recollection of them would be entirely coloured by my subsequent knowledge of her; whence I conclude that I could not at first have experienced the strange interest and admiration which that extraordinary woman very soon excited in me. Interest and admiration, be it well understood, of a very unusual kind, as she was herself a very unusual kind of woman; and I, if you choose, am a rather unusual kind of man. But I can explain that better anon.

This much is certain, that I must have been immeasurably surprised at finding my hostess and future sitter so completely unlike everything I had anticipated. Or no—now I come to think of it, I scarcely felt surprised at all; or if I did, that shock of surprise could have lasted but an infinitesimal part of a minute. The fact is, that, having once seen Alice Oke in the reality, it was quite impossible to remember that one could have fancied her at all different: there was something so complete, so completely unlike every one else, in her personality, that she seemed always to have been present in one's consciousness, although present, perhaps, as an enigma.

Let me try and give you some notion of her: not that first impression, whatever it may have been, but the absolute reality of her as I gradually learned to see it. To begin with, I must repeat and reiterate over and over again, that she was, beyond all comparison, the most graceful and exquisite woman I have ever seen, but with a grace and an exquisiteness that had nothing to do with any preconceived notion or previous experience of what goes by these names: grace and exquisiteness recognised at once as perfect, but which were seen in her for the first, and probably, I do believe, for the last time. It is conceivable, is it not, that once in a thousand years there may arise a combination of lines, a system of movements, an outline, a gesture, which is new, unprecedented, and yet hits off exactly our desires for beauty and rareness? She was very tall; and I suppose people would have called her thin. I don't know, for I never thought about her as a body—bones, flesh, that sort of thing; but merely as a wonderful series of lines, and a wonderful strangeness of personality. Tall and slender, certainly, and with not one item of what makes up our notion of a well-built woman. She was as straight—I mean she had as little of what people call figure—as a bamboo; her shoulders were a trifle high, and she had a decided stoop; her arms and her shoulders she never once wore uncovered. But this bamboo figure of hers had a suppleness and a stateliness, a play of outline with every step she took, that I can't compare to anything else; there was in it something of the peacock and something also of the stag; but, above all, it was her own. I wish I could describe her. I wish, alas!—I wish, I wish, I have wished a hundred thousand times—I could paint her, as I see her now, if I shut my eyes—even if it were only a silhouette. There! I see her so plainly, walking slowly up and down a room, the slight highness of her shoulders just completing the exquisite arrangement of lines made by the straight supple back, the long exquisite neck, the head, with the hair cropped in short pale curls, always drooping a little, except when she would suddenly throw it back, and smile, not at me, nor at any one, nor at anything that had been said, but as if she alone had suddenly seen or heard something, with the strange dimple in her thin, pale cheeks, and the strange whiteness in her full, wide-opened eyes: the moment when she had something of the stag in her movement. But where is the use of talking about her? I don't believe, you know, that even the greatest painter can show what is the real beauty of a very beautiful woman in the ordinary sense: Titian's and Tintoretto's women* must have been miles handsomer than they have made them. Something—and that the very essence—always escapes, perhaps because real beauty is as much a thing in time—a thing like music, a succession, a series—as in space. Mind you, I am speaking of a woman beautiful in the conventional sense. Imagine, then, how much more so in the case of a woman like Alice Oke; and if the pencil and brush, imitating each line and tint, can't succeed, how is it possible to give even the vaguest notion with mere wretched words—words possessing only a wretched abstract meaning, an impotent conventional association? To make a long story short, Mrs. Oke of Okehurst was, in my opinion, to the highest degree exquisite and strange,—an exotic creature, whose charm you can no more describe than you could bring home the perfume of some newly discovered tropical flower by comparing it with the scent of a cabbage-rose or a lily.

That first dinner was gloomy enough. Mr. Oke—Oke of Okehurst, as the people down there called him—was horribly shy, consumed with a fear of making a fool of himself before me and his wife, I then thought. But that sort of shyness did not wear off; and I soon discovered that, although it was doubtless increased by the presence of a total stranger, it was inspired in Oke, not by me, but by his wife. He would look every now and then as if he were going to make a remark, and then evidently restrain himself, and remain silent. It was very curious to see this big, handsome, manly young fellow, who ought to have had any amount of success with women, suddenly stammer and grow crimson in the presence of his own wife. Nor was it the consciousness of stupidity; for when you got him alone, Oke, although always slow and timid, had a certain amount of ideas, and very defined political and social views, and a certain childlike earnestness and desire to attain certainty and truth which was rather touching. On the other hand, Oke's singular shyness was not, so far as I could see, the result of any kind of bullying on his wife's part. You can always detect, if you have any observation, the husband or the wife who is accustomed to be snubbed, to be corrected, by his or her better-half: there is a self-consciousness in both parties, a habit of watching and fault-finding, of being watched and found fault with. This was clearly not the case at Okehurst. Mrs. Oke evidently did not trouble herself about her husband in the very least; he might say or do any amount of silly things without rebuke or even notice; and he might have done so, had he chosen, ever since his wedding-day. You felt that at once. Mrs. Oke simply passed over his existence. I cannot say she paid much attention to any one's, even to mine. At first I thought it an affectation on her part—for there was something far-fetched in her whole appearance, something suggesting study, which might lead one to tax her with affectation at first; she was dressed in a strange way, not according to any established aesthetic eccentricity, but individually, strangely, as if in the clothes of an ancestress of the seventeenth century. Well, at first I thought it a kind of pose on her part, this mixture of extreme graciousness and utter indifference which she manifested towards me. She always seemed to be thinking of something else; and although she talked quite sufficiently, and with every sign of superior intelligence, she left the impression of having been as taciturn as her husband.

In the beginning, in the first few days of my stay at Okehurst, I imagined that Mrs. Oke was a highly superior sort of flirt; and that her absent manner, her look, while speaking to you, into an invisible distance, her curious irrelevant smile, were so many means of attracting and baffling adoration. I mistook it for the somewhat similar manners of certain foreign women—it is beyond English ones—which mean, to those who can understand, "pay court to me." But I soon found I was mistaken. Mrs. Oke had not the faintest desire that I should pay court to her; indeed she did not honour me with sufficient thought for that; and I, on my part, began to be too much interested in her from another point of view to dream of such a thing. I became aware, not merely that I had before me the most marvellously rare and exquisite and baffling subject for a portrait, but also one of the most peculiar and enigmatic of characters. Now that I look back upon it, I am tempted to think that the psychological peculiarity of that woman might be summed up in an exorbitant and absorbing interest in herself—a Narcissus* attitude—curiously complicated with a fantastic imagination, a sort of morbid day-dreaming, all turned inwards, and with no outer characteristic save a certain restlessness, a perverse desire to surprise and shock, to surprise and shock more particularly her husband, and thus be revenged for the intense boredom which his want of appreciation inflicted upon her.

I got to understand this much little by little, yet I did not seem to have really penetrated the something mysterious about Mrs. Oke. There was a waywardness, a strangeness, which I felt but could not explain—a something as difficult to define as the peculiarity of her outward appearance, and perhaps very closely connected therewith. I became interested in Mrs. Oke as if I had been in love with her; and I was not in the least in love. I neither dreaded parting from her, nor felt any pleasure in her presence. I had not the smallest wish to please or to gain her notice. But I had her on the brain. I pursued her, her physical image, her psychological explanation, with a kind of passion which filled my days, and prevented my ever feeling dull. The Okes lived a remarkably solitary life. There were but few neighbours, of whom they saw but little; and they rarely had a guest in the house. Oke himself seemed every now and then seized with a sense of responsibility towards me. He would remark vaguely, during our walks and after-dinner chats, that I must find life at Okehurst horribly dull; his wife's health had accustomed him to solitude, and then also his wife thought the neighbours a bore. He never questioned his wife's judgment in these matters. He merely stated the case as if resignation were quite simple and inevitable; yet it seemed to me, sometimes, that this monotonous life of solitude, by the side of a woman who took no more heed of him than of a table or chair, was producing a vague depression and irritation in this young man, so evidently cut out for a cheerful, commonplace life. I often wondered how he could endure it at all, not having, as I had, the interest of a strange psychological riddle to solve, and of a great portrait to paint. He was, I found, extremely good,—the type of the perfectly conscientious young Englishman, the sort of man who ought to have been the Christian soldier kind of thing;* devout, pure-minded, brave, incapable of any baseness, a little intellectually dense, and puzzled by all manner of moral scruples. The condition of his tenants and of his political party—he was a regular Kentish Tory lay heavy on his mind. He spent hours every day in his study, doing the work of a land agent and a political whip, reading piles of reports and newspapers and agricultural treatises; and emerging for lunch with piles of letters in his hand, and that odd puzzled look in his good healthy face, that deep gash between his eyebrows, which my friend the mad-doctor calls the *maniac-frown*. It was with this expression of face that I should have liked to paint him; but I felt that he would not have liked it, that it was more fair to him to represent him in his mere wholesome pink and white and blond conventionality. I was perhaps rather unconscientious about the likeness of Mr. Oke; I felt satisfied to paint it no matter how, I mean as regards character, for my whole mind was swallowed up in thinking how I should paint Mrs. Oke, how I could best transport on to canvas that singular and enigmatic personality. I began with her husband, and told her frankly that I must have much longer to study her. Mr. Oke couldn't understand why it should be necessary to make a hundred and one pencil-sketches of his wife before even determining in what attitude to paint her; but I think he was rather pleased to have an opportunity of keeping me at Okehurst; my presence evidently broke the monotony of his life. Mrs. Oke seemed perfectly indifferent to my staying, as she was perfectly indifferent to my presence. Without being rude, I never saw a woman pay so little attention to a guest; she would talk with me sometimes by the hour, or rather let me talk to her, but she never seemed to be listening. She would lie back in a big seventeenth-century armchair while I played the piano, with that strange smile every now and then in her thin cheeks, that strange whiteness in her eyes; but it seemed a matter of indifference whether my music stopped or went on. In my portrait of her husband she did not take, or pretend to take, the very faintest interest; but that was nothing to me. I did not want Mrs. Oke to think me interesting; I merely wished to go on studying her.

The first time that Mrs. Oke seemed to become at all aware of my presence as distinguished from that of the chairs and tables, the dogs that lay in the porch, or the clergyman or lawyer or stray neighbour who was occasionally asked to dinner, was one day—I might have been there a week—when I chanced to remark to her upon the very singular resemblance that existed between herself and the portrait of a lady that hung in the hall with the ceiling like a ship's hull. The picture in question was a full length, neither very good nor very bad, probably done by some stray Italian of the early seventeenth century. It hung in a rather dark corner, facing the portrait, evidently painted to be its companion, of a dark man, with a somewhat unpleasant expression of resolution and efficiency, in a black Vandyck dress. The two were evidently man and wife; and in the corner of the woman's portrait were the words, "Alice Oke, daughter of Virgil Pomfret, Esq., and wife to Nicholas Oke of Okehurst," and the date 1626—"Nicholas Oke" being the name painted in the corner of the small portrait. The lady was really wonderfully like the present Mrs. Oke, at least so far as an indifferently painted portrait of the early days of Charles I. can be like a living woman of the nineteenth century. There were the same strange lines of figure and face, the same dimples in the thin cheeks, the same wide-opened eyes, the same vague eccentricity of expression, not destroyed even by the feeble painting and conventional manner of the time. One could fancy that this woman had the same walk, the same beautiful line of nape of the neck and stooping head as her descendant; for I found that Mr. and Mrs. Oke, who were first cousins, were both descended from that Nicholas Oke and that Alice, daughter of Virgil Pomfret. But the resemblance was heightened by the fact that, as I soon saw, the present Mrs. Oke distinctly made herself up to look like her ancestress, dressing in garments that had a seventeenth-century look; nay, that were sometimes absolutely copied from this portrait.

"You think I am like her," answered Mrs. Oke dreamily to my remark, and her eyes wandered off to that unseen something, and the faint smile dimpled her thin cheeks.

"You are like her, and you know it. I may even say you wish to be like her, Mrs. Oke," I answered, laughing.

"Perhaps I do."

And she looked in the direction of her husband.

I noticed that he had an expression of distinct annoyance besides that frown of his.

"Isn't it true that Mrs. Oke tries to look like that portrait?" I asked, with a perverse curiosity.

"Oh, fudge!" he exclaimed, rising from his chair and walking nervously to the window. "It's all nonsense, mere nonsense. I wish you wouldn't, Alice."

"Wouldn't what?" asked Mrs. Oke, with a sort of contemptuous indifference, "If I am like that Alice Oke, why I am; and I am very pleased any one should think so. She and her husband are just about the only two members of our family—our most flat, stale, and unprofitable* family—that ever were in the least degree interesting."

Oke grew crimson, and frowned as if in pain.

"I don't see why you should abuse our family, Alice," he said. "Thank God, our people have always been honourable and upright men and women!"

"Excepting always Nicholas Oke and Alice his wife, daughter of Virgil Pomfret, Esq.," she answered, laughing, as he strode out into the park.

"How childish he is!" she exclaimed when we were alone. "He really minds, really feels disgraced by what our ancestors did two centuries and a half ago. I do believe William would have those two portraits taken down and burned if he weren't afraid of me and ashamed of the neighbours. And as it is, these two people really are the only two members of our family that ever were in the least interesting. I will tell you the story some day."

As it was, the story was told to me by Oke himself. The next day, as we were taking our morning walk, he suddenly broke a long silence, laying about him all the time at the sere grasses with the hooked stick that he carried, like the conscientious Kentishman he was, for the purpose of cutting down his and other folk's thistles.

"I fear you must have thought me very ill-mannered towards my wife yesterday," he said shyly; "and indeed I know I was."

Oke was one of those chivalrous beings to whom every woman, every wife—and his own most of all—appeared in the light of something holy. "But—but—I have a prejudice which my wife does not enter into, about raking up ugly things in one's own family. I suppose Alice thinks that it is so long ago that it has really got no connection with us; she thinks of it merely as a picturesque story. I daresay many people feel like that; in short, I am sure they do, otherwise there wouldn't be such lots of discreditable family traditions afloat. But I feel as if it were all one whether it was long ago or not; when it's a question of one's own people, I would rather have it forgotten. I can't understand how people can talk about murders in their families, and ghosts, and so forth."

"Have you any ghosts at Okehurst, by the way?" I asked. The place seemed as if it required some to complete it.

"I hope not," answered Oke gravely.

His gravity made me smile.

"Why, would you dislike it if there were?" I asked.

"If there are such things as ghosts," he replied, "I don't think they should be taken lightly. God would not permit them to be, except as a warning or a punishment."

We walked on some time in silence, I wondering at the strange type of this commonplace young man, and half wishing I could put something into my portrait that should be the equivalent of this curious unimaginative earnestness. Then Oke told me the story of those two pictures—told it me about as badly and hesitatingly as was possible for mortal man.

He and his wife were, as I have said, cousins, and therefore descended from the same old Kentish stock. The Okes of Okehurst could trace back to Norman, almost to Saxon times, far longer than any of the titled or better-known families of the neighbourhood. I saw that William Oke, in his heart, thoroughly looked down upon all his neighbours. "We have never done anything particular, or been anything particular—never held any office," he said; "but we have always been here, and apparently always done our duty. An ancestor of ours was killed in the Scotch wars, another at Agincourt*—mere honest captains." Well, early in the seventeenth century, the family had dwindled to a single member, Nicholas Oke, the same who had rebuilt Okehurst in its present shape. This Nicholas appears to have been somewhat different from the usual run of the family. He had, in his youth, sought adventures in America, and seems, generally speaking, to have been less of a nonentity than his ancestors. He married, when no longer very young, Alice, daughter of Virgil Pomfret, a beautiful young heiress from a neighbouring county. "It was the first time an Oke married a Pomfret," my host informed me, "and the last time. The Pomfrets were quite different sort of people—restless, self-seeking; one of them had been a favourite of Henry VIII." It was clear that William Oke had no feeling of having any Pomfret blood in his veins; he spoke of these people with an evident family dislike—the dislike of an Oke, one of the old, honourable, modest stock, which had quietly done its duty, for a family of fortune-seekers and Court minions. Well, there had come to live near Okehurst, in a little house recently inherited from an uncle, a certain Christopher Lovelock, a young gallant and poet, who was in momentary disgrace at Court for some love affair. This Lovelock had struck up a great friendship with his neighbours of Okehurst—too great a friendship, apparently, with the wife, either for her husband's taste or her own. Anyhow, one evening as he was riding home alone, Lovelock had been attacked and murdered, ostensibly by highwaymen, but as was afterwards rumoured, by Nicholas Oke, accompanied by his wife dressed as a groom.

No legal evidence had been got, but the tradition had remained. "They used to tell it us when we were children," said my host, in a hoarse voice, "and to frighten my cousin—I mean my wife—and me with stories about Lovelock. It is merely a tradition, which I hope may die out, as I sincerely pray to heaven that it may be false." "Alice—Mrs. Oke—you see," he went on after some time, "doesn't feel about it as I do. Perhaps I am morbid. But I do dislike having the old story raked up."

And we said no more on the subject.

IV

From that moment I began to assume a certain interest in the eyes of Mrs. Oke; or rather, I began to perceive that I had a means of securing her attention. Perhaps it was wrong of me to do so; and I have often reproached myself very seriously later on. But after all, how was I to guess that I was making mischief merely by chiming in, for the sake of the portrait I had undertaken, and of a very harmless psychological mania, with what was merely the fad, the little romantic affectation or eccentricity, of a scatter-brained and eccentric young woman? How in the world should I have dreamed that I was handling explosive substances? A man is surely not responsible if the people with whom he is forced to deal, and whom he deals with as with all the rest of the world, are quite different from all other human creatures.

So, if indeed I did at all conduce to mischief, I really cannot blame myself. I had met in Mrs. Oke an almost unique subject for a portrait-painter of my particular sort, and a most singular, *bizarre* personality. I could not possibly do my subject justice so long as I was kept at a distance, prevented from studying the real character of the woman. I required to put her into play. And I ask you whether any more innocent way of doing so could be found than talking to a woman, and letting her talk, about an absurd fancy she had for a couple of ancestors of hers of the time of Charles I., and a poet whom they had murdered?—particularly as I studiously respected the prejudices of my host, and refrained from mentioning the matter, and tried to restrain Mrs. Oke from doing so, in the presence of William Oke himself.

I had certainly guessed correctly. To resemble the Alice Oke of the year 1626 was the caprice, the mania, the pose, the whatever you may call it, of the Alice Oke of 1880; and to perceive this resemblance was the sure way of gaining her good graces. It was the most extraordinary craze, of all the extraordinary crazes of childless and idle women, that I had ever met; but it was more than that, it was admirably characteristic. It finished off the strange figure of Mrs. Oke, as I saw it in my imagination—this *bizarre* creature of enigmatic, far-fetched exquisiteness—that she should have no interest in the present, but only an eccentric passion in the past. It seemed to give the meaning to the absent look in her eyes, to her irrelevant and far-off smile. It was like the words to a weird piece of gipsy music, this that she, who was so different, so distant from all women of her own time, should try and identify herself with a woman of the past—that she should have a kind of flirtation. But of this anon.

I told Mrs. Oke that I had learnt from her husband the outline of the tragedy, or mystery, whichever it was, of Alice Oke, daughter of Virgil Pomfret, and the poet Christopher Lovelock. That look of vague contempt, of a desire to shock, which I had noticed before, came into her beautiful, pale, diaphanous face.

"I suppose my husband was very shocked at the whole matter," she said—"told it you with as little detail as possible, and assured you very solemnly that he hoped the whole story might be a mere dreadful calumny? Poor Willie! I remember already when we were children, and I used to come with my mother to spend Christmas at Okehurst, and my cousin was down here for his holidays, how I used to horrify him by insisting upon dressing up in shawls and waterproofs, and playing the story of the wicked Mrs. Oke; and he always piously refused to do the part of Nicholas, when I wanted to have the scene on Cotes Common. I didn't know then that I was like the original Alice Oke; I found it out only after our marriage. You really think that I am?"

She certainly was, particularly at that moment, as she stood in a white Vandyck dress, with the green of the park-land rising up behind her, and the low sun catching her short locks and surrounding her head, her exquisitely bowed head, with a pale-yellow halo. But I confess I thought the original Alice Oke, siren and murderess though she might be, very uninteresting compared with this wayward and exquisite creature whom I had rashly promised myself to send down to posterity in all her unlikely wayward exquisiteness.

One morning while Mr. Oke was despatching his Saturday heap of Conservative manifestoes and rural decisions—he was justice of the peace in a most literal sense, penetrating into cottages and huts, defending the weak and admonishing the ill-conducted—one morning while I was making one of my many pencil-sketches (alas, they are all that remain to me now!) of my future sitter, Mrs. Oke gave me her version of the story of Alice Oke and Christopher Lovelock.

"Do you suppose there was anything between them?" I asked—"that she was ever in love with him? How do you explain the part which tradition ascribes to her in the supposed murder? One has heard of women and their lovers who have killed the husband; but a woman who combines with her husband to kill her lover, or at least the man who is in love with her—that is surely very singular." I was absorbed in my drawing, and really thinking very little of what I was saying.

"I don't know," she answered pensively, with that distant look in her eyes. "Alice Oke was very proud, I am sure. She may have loved the poet very much, and yet been indignant with him, hated having to love him. She may have felt that she had a right to rid herself of him, and to call upon her husband to help her to do so."

"Good heavens! what a fearful idea!" I exclaimed, half laughing. "Don't you think, after all, that Mr. Oke may be right in saying that it is easier and more comfortable to take the whole story as a pure invention?"

"I cannot take it as an invention," answered Mrs. Oke contemptuously, "because I happen to know that it is true."

"Indeed!" I answered, working away at my sketch, and enjoying putting this strange creature, as I said to myself, through her paces; "how is that?"

"How does one know that anything is true in this world?" she replied evasively; "because one does, because one feels it to be true, I suppose."

And, with that far-off look in her light eyes, she relapsed into silence.

"Have you ever read any of Lovelock's poetry?" she asked me suddenly the next day.

"Lovelock?" I answered, for I had forgotten the name. "Lovelock, who"—— But I stopped, remembering the prejudices of my host, who was seated next to me at table.

"Lovelock who was killed by Mr. Oke's and my ancestors."

And she looked full at her husband, as if in perverse enjoyment of the evident annoyance which it caused him.

"Alice," he entreated in a low voice, his whole face crimson, "for mercy's sake, don't talk about such things before the servants."

Mrs. Oke burst into a high, light, rather hysterical laugh, the laugh of a naughty child.

"The servants! Gracious heavens! do you suppose they haven't heard the story? Why, it's as well known as Okehurst itself in the neighbourhood. Don't they believe that Lovelock has been seen about the house? Haven't they all heard his footsteps in the big corridor? Haven't they, my dear Willie, noticed a thousand times that you never will stay a minute alone in the yellow drawing-room—that you run out of it, like a child, if I happen to leave you there for a minute?"

True! How was it I had not noticed that? or rather, that I only now remembered having noticed it? The yellow drawing-room was one of the most charming rooms in the house: a large, bright room, hung with yellow damask and panelled with carvings, that opened straight out on to the lawn, far superior to the room in which we habitually sat, which was comparatively gloomy. This time Mr. Oke struck me as really too childish. I felt an intense desire to badger him.

"The yellow drawing-room!" I exclaimed. "Does this interesting literary character haunt the yellow drawing-room? Do tell me about it. What happened there?"

Mr. Oke made a painful effort to laugh.

"Nothing ever happened there, so far as I know," he said, and rose from the table.

"Really?" I asked incredulously.

"Nothing did happen there," answered Mrs. Oke slowly, playing mechanically with a fork, and picking out the pattern of the table-cloth. "That is just the extraordinary circumstance, that, so far as any one knows, nothing ever did happen there; and yet that room has an evil reputation. No member of our family, they say, can bear to sit there alone for more than a minute. You see, William evidently cannot."

"Have you ever seen or heard anything strange there?" I asked of my host.

He shook his head. "Nothing," he answered curtly, and lit his cigar.

"I presume you have not," I asked, half laughing, of Mrs. Oke, "since you don't mind sitting in that room for hours alone? How do you explain this uncanny reputation, since nothing ever happened there?"

"Perhaps something is destined to happen there in the future," she answered, in her absent voice. And then she suddenly added, "Suppose you paint my portrait in that room?"

Mr. Oke suddenly turned round. He was very white, and looked as if he were going to say something, but desisted.

"Why do you worry Mr. Oke like that?" I asked, when he had gone into his smoking-room with his usual bundle of papers. "It is very cruel of you, Mrs. Oke. You ought to have more consideration for people who believe in such things, although you may not be able to put yourself in their frame of mind."

"Who tells you that I don't believe in *such things*, as you call them?" she answered abruptly.

"Come," she said, after a minute, "I want to show you why I believe in Christopher Lovelock. Come with me into the yellow room."

V

What Mrs. Oke showed me in the yellow room was a large bundle of papers, some printed and some manuscript, but all of them brown with age, which she took out of an old Italian ebony inlaid cabinet. It took her some time to get them, as a complicated arrangement of double locks and false drawers had to be put in play; and while she was doing so, I looked round the room, in which I had been only three or four times before. It was certainly the most beautiful room in this beautiful house, and, as it seemed to me now, the most strange. It was long and low, with something that made you think of the cabin of a ship, with a great mullioned window that let in, as it were, a perspective of the brownish green park-land, dotted with oaks, and sloping upwards to the distant line of bluish firs against the horizon. The walls were hung with flowered damask, whose yellow, faded to brown, united with the reddish colour of the carved wainscoting and the carved oaken beams. For the rest, it reminded me more of an Italian room than an English one. The furniture was Tuscan of the early seventeenth century, inlaid and carved; there were a couple of faded allegorical pictures, by some Bolognese master,* on the walls; and in a corner, among a stack of dwarf orange-trees, a little Italian harpsichord of exquisite curve and slenderness, with flowers and landscapes painted upon its cover. In a recess was a shelf of old books, mainly English and Italian poets of the Elizabethan time; and close by it, placed upon a carved wedding-chest, a large and beautiful melon-shaped lute. The panes of the mullioned window were open, and yet the air seemed heavy, with an indescribable heady perfume, not that of any growing flower, but like that of old stuff that should have lain for years among spices.

"It is a beautiful room!" I exclaimed. "I should awfully like to paint you in it;" but I had scarcely spoken the words when I felt I had done wrong. This woman's husband could not bear the room, and it seemed to me vaguely as if he were right in detesting it.

Mrs. Oke took no notice of my exclamation, but beckoned me to the table where she was standing sorting the papers.

"Look!" she said, "these are all poems by Christopher Lovelock;" and touching the yellow papers with delicate and reverent fingers, she commenced reading some of them out loud in a slow, half-audible voice. They were songs in the style of those of Herrick, Waller, and Drayton, complaining for the most part of the cruelty of a lady called Dryope,* in whose name was evidently concealed a reference to that of the mistress of Okehurst. The songs were graceful, and not without a certain faded passion: but I was thinking not of them, but of the woman who was reading them to me.

Mrs. Oke was standing with the brownish yellow wall as a background to her white brocade dress, which, in its stiff seventeenth-century make, seemed but to bring out more clearly the slightness, the exquisite suppleness, of her tall figure. She held the papers in one hand, and leaned the other, as if for support, on the inlaid cabinet by her side. Her voice, which was delicate, shadowy, like her person, had a curious throbbing cadence, as if she were reading the words of a melody, and restraining herself with difficulty from singing it; and as she read, her long slender throat throbbed slightly, and a faint redness came into her thin face. She evidently knew the verses by heart, and her eyes were mostly fixed with that distant smile in them, with which harmonised a constant tremulous little smile in her lips.

"That is how I would wish to paint her!" I exclaimed within myself; and scarcely noticed, what struck me on thinking over the scene, that this strange being read these verses as one might fancy a woman would read love-verses addressed to herself.

"Those are all written for Alice Oke—Alice the daughter of Virgil Pomfret," she said slowly, folding up the papers. "I found them at the bottom of this cabinet. Can you doubt of the reality of Christopher Lovelock now?"

The question was an illogical one, for to doubt of the existence of Christopher Lovelock was one thing, and to doubt of the mode of his death was another; but somehow I did feel convinced.

"Look!" she said, when she had replaced the poems, "I will show you something else." Among the flowers that stood on the upper storey of her writing-table—for I found that Mrs. Oke had a writing-table in the yellow room—stood, as on an altar, a small black carved frame, with a silk curtain drawn over it: the sort of thing behind which you would have expected to find a head of Christ or of the Virgin Mary. She drew the curtain and displayed a large-sized miniature, representing a young man, with auburn curls and a peaked auburn beard, dressed in black, but with lace about his neck, and large pear-shaped pearls in his ears: a wistful, melancholy face. Mrs. Oke took the miniature religiously off its stand, and showed me, written in faded characters upon the back, the name "Christopher Lovelock," and the date 1626.

"I found this in the secret drawer of that cabinet, together with the heap of poems," she said, taking the miniature out of my hand.

I was silent for a minute.

"Does—does Mr. Oke know that you have got it here?" I asked; and then wondered what in the world had impelled me to put such a question.

Mrs. Oke smiled that smile of contemptuous indifference. "I have never hidden it from any one. If my husband disliked my having it, he might have taken it away, I suppose. It belongs to him, since it was found in his house."

I did not answer, but walked mechanically towards the door. There was something heady and oppressive in this beautiful room; something, I thought, almost repulsive in this exquisite woman. She seemed to me, suddenly, perverse and dangerous.

I scarcely know why, but I neglected Mrs. Oke that afternoon. I went to Mr. Oke's study, and sat opposite to him smoking while he was engrossed in his accounts, his reports, and electioneering papers. On the table, above the heap of paper-bound volumes and pigeon-holed documents, was, as sole ornament of his den, a little photograph of his wife, done some years before. I don't know why, but as I sat and watched him, with his florid, honest, manly beauty, working away conscientiously, with that little perplexed frown of his, I felt intensely sorry for this man.

But this feeling did not last. There was no help for it: Oke was not as interesting as Mrs. Oke; and it required too great an effort to pump up sympathy for this normal, excellent, exemplary young squire, in the presence of so wonderful a creature as his wife. So I let myself go to the habit of allowing Mrs. Oke daily to talk over her strange craze, or rather of drawing her out about it. I confess that I derived a morbid and exquisite pleasure in doing so: it was so characteristic in her, so appropriate to the house! It completed her personality so perfectly, and made it so much easier to conceive a way of painting her. I made up my mind little by little, while working at William Oke's portrait (he proved a less easy subject than I had anticipated, and, despite his conscientious efforts, was a nervous, uncomfortable sitter, silent and brooding)—I made up my mind that I would paint Mrs. Oke standing by the cabinet in the yellow room, in the white Vandyck dress copied from the portrait of her ancestress. Mr. Oke might resent it, Mrs. Oke even might resent it; they might refuse to take the picture, to pay for it, to allow me to exhibit; they might force me to run my umbrella through the picture. No matter. That picture should be painted, if merely for the sake of having painted it; for I felt it was the only thing I could do, and that it would be far away my best work. I told neither of my resolution, but prepared sketch after sketch of Mrs. Oke, while continuing to paint her husband.

Mrs. Oke was a silent person, more silent even than her husband, for she did not feel bound, as he did, to attempt to entertain a guest or to show any interest in him. She seemed to spend her life—a curious, inactive, half-invalidish life, broken by sudden fits of childish cheerfulness—in an eternal day-dream, strolling about the house and grounds, arranging the quantities of flowers that always filled all the rooms, beginning to read and then throwing aside novels and books of poetry, of which she always had a large number; and, I believe, lying for hours, doing nothing, on a couch in that yellow drawing-room, which, with her sole exception, no member of the Oke family had ever been known to stay in alone. Little by little I began to suspect and to verify another eccentricity of this eccentric being, and to understand why there were stringent orders never to disturb her in that yellow room.

It had been a habit at Okehurst, as at one or two other English manor-houses, to keep a certain amount of the clothes of each generation, more particularly wedding-dresses. A certain carved oaken press, of which Mr. Oke once displayed the contents to me, was a perfect museum of costumes, male and female, from the early years of the seventeenth to the end of the eighteenth century—a thing to take away the breath of a bric-a-brac collector, an antiquary, or a genre painter;* Mr. Oke was none of these, and therefore took but little interest in the collection, save in so far as it interested his family feeling. Still he seemed well acquainted with the contents of that press.

He was turning over the clothes for my benefit, when suddenly I noticed that he frowned. I know not what impelled me to say, "By the way, have you any dresses of that Mrs. Oke whom your wife resembles so much? Have you got that particular white dress she was painted in, perhaps?"

Oke of Okehurst flushed very red.

"We have it," he answered hesitatingly, "but—it isn't here at present—I can't find it. I suppose," he blurted out with an effort, "that Alice has got it. Mrs. Oke sometimes has the fancy of having some of these old things down. I suppose she takes ideas from them."

A sudden light dawned in my mind. The white dress in which I had seen Mrs. Oke in the yellow room, the day that she showed me Lovelock's verses, was not, as I had thought, a modern copy; it was the original dress of Alice Oke, the daughter of Virgil Pomfret—the dress in which, perhaps, Christopher Lovelock had seen her in that very room.

The idea gave me a delightful picturesque shudder. I said nothing. But I pictured to myself Mrs. Oke sitting in that yellow room—that room which no Oke of Okehurst save herself ventured to remain in alone, in the dress of her ancestress, confronting, as it were, that vague, haunting something that seemed to fill the place—that vague presence, it seemed to me, of the murdered cavalier poet.

Mrs. Oke, as I have said, was extremely silent, as a result of being extremely indifferent. She really did not care in the least about anything except her own ideas and day-dreams, except when, every now and then, she was seized with a sudden desire to shock the prejudices or superstitions of her husband. Very soon she got into the way of never talking to me at all, save about Alice and Nicholas Oke and Christopher Lovelock; and then, when the fit seized her, she would go on by the hour, never asking herself whether I was or was not equally interested in the strange craze that fascinated her. It so happened that I was. I loved to listen to her, going on discussing by the hour the merits of Lovelock's poems, and analysing her feelings and those of her two ancestors. It was quite wonderful to watch the exquisite, exotic creature in one of these moods, with the distant look in her grey eyes and the absent-looking smile in her thin cheeks, talking as if she had intimately known these people of the seventeenth century, discussing every minute mood of theirs, detailing every scene between them and their victim, talking of Alice, and Nicholas, and Lovelock as she might of her most intimate friends. Of Alice particularly, and of Lovelock. She seemed to know every word that Alice had spoken, every idea that had crossed her mind. It sometimes struck me as if she were telling me, speaking of herself in the third person, of her own feelings—as if I were listening to a woman's confidences, the recital of her doubts, scruples, and agonies about a living lover. For Mrs. Oke, who seemed the most self-absorbed of creatures in all other matters, and utterly incapable of understanding or sympathising with the feelings of other persons, entered completely and passionately into the feelings of this woman, this Alice, who, at some moments, seemed to be not another woman, but herself.

"But how could she do it—how could she kill the man she cared for?" I once asked her.

"Because she loved him more than the whole world!" she exclaimed, and rising suddenly from her chair, walked towards the window, covering her face with her hands.

I could see, from the movement of her neck, that she was sobbing. She did not turn round, but motioned me to go away.

"Don't let us talk any more about it," she said. "I am ill to-day, and silly."

I closed the door gently behind me. What mystery was there in this woman's life? This listlessness, this strange self-engrossment and stranger mania about people long dead, this indifference and desire to annoy towards her husband—did it all mean that Alice Oke had loved or still loved some one who was not the master of Okehurst? And his melancholy, his preoccupation, the something about him that told of a broken youth—did it mean that he knew it?

VI

The following days Mrs. Oke was in a condition of quite unusual good spirits. Some visitors—distant relatives—were expected, and although she had expressed the utmost annoyance at the idea of their coming, she was now seized with a fit of housekeeping activity, and was perpetually about arranging things and giving orders, although all arrangements, as usual, had been made, and all orders given, by her husband.

William Oke was quite radiant.

"If only Alice were always well like this!" he exclaimed; "if only she would take, or could take, an interest in life, how different things would be! But," he added, as if fearful lest he should be supposed to accuse her in any way, "how can she, usually, with her wretched health? Still, it does make me awfully happy to see her like this."

I nodded. But I cannot say that I really acquiesced in his views. It seemed to me, particularly with the recollection of yesterday's extraordinary scene, that Mrs. Oke's high spirits were anything but normal. There was something in her unusual activity and still more unusual cheerfulness that was merely nervous and feverish; and I had, the whole day, the impression of dealing with a woman who was ill and who would very speedily collapse.

Mrs. Oke spent her day wandering from one room to another, and from the garden to the greenhouse, seeing whether all was in order, when, as a matter of fact, all was always in order at Okehurst. She did not give me any sitting, and not a word was spoken about Alice Oke or Christopher Lovelock. Indeed, to a casual observer, it might have seemed as if all that craze about Lovelock had completely departed, or never existed. About five o'clock, as I was strolling among the red-brick round-gabled outhouses—each with its armorial oak—and the old-fashioned spalliered* kitchen and fruit garden, I saw Mrs. Oke standing, her hands full of York and Lancaster roses, upon the steps facing the stables. A groom was currycombing a horse, and outside the coach-house was Mr. Oke's little high-wheeled cart.

"Let us have a drive!" suddenly exclaimed Mrs. Oke, on seeing me. "Look what a beautiful evening—and look at that dear little cart! It is so long since I have driven, and I feel as if I must drive again. Come with me. And you, harness Jim at once and come round to the door."

I was quite amazed; and still more so when the cart drove up before the door, and Mrs. Oke called to me to accompany her. She sent away the groom, and in a minute we were rolling along, at a tremendous pace, along the yellow-sand road, with the sere pasture-lands, the big oaks, on either side.

I could scarcely believe my senses. This woman, in her mannish little coat and hat, driving a powerful young horse with the utmost skill, and chattering like a school-girl of sixteen, could not be the delicate, morbid, exotic, hot-house creature, unable to walk or to do anything, who spent her days lying about on couches in the heavy atmosphere, redolent with strange scents and associations, of the yellow drawing-room. The movement of the light carriage, the cool draught, the very grind of the wheels upon the gravel, seemed to go to her head like wine.

"It is so long since I have done this sort of thing," she kept repeating; "so long, so long. Oh, don't you think it delightful, going at this pace, with the idea that any moment the horse may come down and we two be killed?" and she laughed her childish laugh, and turned her face, no longer pale, but flushed with the movement and the excitement, towards me.

The cart rolled on quicker and quicker, one gate after another swinging to behind us, as we flew up and down the little hills, across the pasture lands, through the little red-brick gabled villages, where the people came out to see us pass, past the rows of willows along the streams, and the dark-green compact hop-fields, with the blue and hazy tree-tops of the horizon getting bluer and more hazy as the yellow light began to graze the ground. At last we got to an open space, a high-lying piece of common-land, such as is rare in that ruthlessly utilised country of grazing-grounds and hop-gardens. Among the low hills of the Weald, it seemed quite preternaturally high up, giving a sense that its extent of flat heather and gorse, bound by distant firs, was really on the top of the world. The sun was setting just opposite, and its lights lay flat on the ground, staining it with the red and black of the heather, or rather turning it into the surface of a purple sea, canopied over by a bank of dark-purple clouds—the jet-like sparkle of the dry ling* and gorse tipping the purple like sunlit wavelets. A cold wind swept in our faces.

"What is the name of this place?" I asked. It was the only bit of impressive scenery that I had met in the neighbourhood of Okehurst.

"It is called Cotes Common," answered Mrs. Oke, who had slackened the pace of the horse, and let the reins hang loose about his neck. "It was here that Christopher Lovelock was killed."

There was a moment's pause; and then she proceeded, tickling the flies from the horse's ears with the end of her whip, and looking straight into the sunset, which now rolled, a deep purple stream, across the heath to our feet—

"Lovelock was riding home one summer evening from Appledore,* when, as he had got half-way across Cotes Common, somewhere about here—for I have always heard them mention the pond in the old gravel-pits as about the place—he saw two men riding towards him, in whom he presently recognised Nicholas Oke of Okehurst accompanied by a groom. Oke of Okehurst hailed him; and Lovelock rode up to meet him. 'I am glad to have met you, Mr. Lovelock,' said Nicholas, 'because I have some important news for you;' and so saying, he brought his horse close to the one that Lovelock was riding, and suddenly turning round, fired off a pistol at his head. Lovelock had time to move, and the bullet, instead of striking him, went straight into the head of his horse, which fell beneath him. Lovelock, however, had fallen in such a way as to be able to extricate himself easily from his horse; and drawing his sword, he rushed upon Oke, and seized his horse by the bridle. Oke quickly jumped off and drew his sword; and in a minute, Lovelock, who was much the better swordsman of the two, was having the better of him. Lovelock had completely disarmed him, and got his sword at Oke's throat, crying out to him that if he would ask forgiveness he should be spared for the sake of their old friendship, when the groom suddenly rode up from behind and shot Lovelock through the back. Lovelock fell, and Oke immediately tried to finish him with his sword, while the groom drew up and held the bridle of Oke's horse. At that moment the sunlight fell upon the groom's face, and Lovelock recognised Mrs. Oke. He cried out, 'Alice, Alice! it is you who have murdered me!' and died. Then Nicholas Oke sprang into his saddle and rode off with his wife, leaving Lovelock dead by the side of his fallen horse. Nicholas Oke had taken the precaution of removing Lovelock's purse and throwing it into the pond, so the murder was put down to certain highwaymen who were about in that part of the country. Alice Oke died many years afterwards, quite an old woman, in the reign of Charles II.; but Nicholas did not live very long, and shortly before his death got into a very strange condition, always brooding, and sometimes threatening to kill his wife. They say that in one of these fits, just shortly before his death, he told the whole story of the murder, and made a prophecy that when the head of his house and master of Okehurst should marry another Alice Oke, descended from himself and his wife, there should be an end of the Okes of Okehurst. You see, it seems to be coming true. We have no children, and I don't suppose we shall ever have any. I, at least, have never wished for them."

Mrs. Oke paused, and turned her face towards me with the absent smile in her thin cheeks: her eyes no longer had that distant look; they were strangely eager and fixed. I did not know what to answer; this woman positively frightened me. We remained for a moment in that same place, with the sunlight dying away in crimson ripples on the heather, gilding the yellow banks, the black waters of the pond, surrounded by thin rushes, and the yellow gravel-pits; while the wind blew in our faces and bent the ragged warped bluish tops of the firs. Then Mrs. Oke touched the horse, and off we went at a furious pace. We did not exchange a single word, I think, on the way home. Mrs. Oke sat with her eyes fixed on the reins, breaking the silence now and then only by a word to the horse, urging him to an even more furious pace. The people we met along the roads must have thought that the horse was running away, unless they noticed Mrs. Oke's calm manner and the look of excited enjoyment in her face. To me it seemed that I was in the hands of a madwoman, and I quietly prepared myself for being upset or dashed against a cart. It had turned cold, and the draught was icy in our faces when we got within sight of the red gables and high chimney-stacks of Okehurst. Mr. Oke was standing before the door. On our approach I saw a look of relieved suspense, of keen pleasure come into his face.

He lifted his wife out of the cart in his strong arms with a kind of chivalrous tenderness.

"I am so glad to have you back, darling," he exclaimed—"so glad! I was delighted to hear you had gone out with the cart, but as you have not driven for so long, I was beginning to be frightfully anxious, dearest. Where have you been all this time?"

Mrs. Oke had quickly extricated herself from her husband, who had remained holding her, as one might hold a delicate child who has been causing anxiety. The gentleness and affection of the poor fellow had evidently not touched her—she seemed almost to recoil from it.

"I have taken him to Cotes Common," she said, with that perverse look which I had noticed before, as she pulled off her driving-gloves. "It is such a splendid old place."

Mr. Oke flushed as if he had bitten upon a sore tooth, and the double gash painted itself scarlet between his eyebrows.

Outside, the mists were beginning to rise, veiling the park-land dotted with big black oaks, and from which, in the watery moonlight, rose on all sides the eerie little cry of the lambs separated from their mothers. It was damp and cold, and I shivered.

VII

The next day Okehurst was full of people, and Mrs. Oke, to my amazement, was doing the honours of it as if a house full of commonplace, noisy young creatures, bent upon flirting and tennis, were her usual idea of felicity.

The afternoon of the third day—they had come for an electioneering ball, and stayed three nights—the weather changed; it turned suddenly very cold and began to pour. Every one was sent indoors, and there was a general gloom suddenly over the company. Mrs. Oke seemed to have got sick of her guests, and was listlessly lying back on a couch, paying not the slightest attention to the chattering and piano-strumming in the room, when one of the guests suddenly proposed that they should play charades. He was a distant cousin of the Okes, a sort of fashionable artistic Bohemian, swelled out to intolerable conceit by the amateur-actor vogue of a season.

"It would be lovely in this marvellous old place," he cried, "just to dress up, and parade about, and feel as if we belonged to the past. I have heard you have a marvellous collection of old costumes, more or less ever since the days of Noah, somewhere, Cousin Bill."

The whole party exclaimed in joy at this proposal. William Oke looked puzzled for a moment, and glanced at his wife, who continued to lie listless on her sofa.

"There is a press full of clothes belonging to the family," he answered dubiously, apparently overwhelmed by the desire to please his guests; "but—but—I don't know whether it's quite respectful to dress up in the clothes of dead people."

"Oh, fiddlestick!" cried the cousin. "What do the dead people know about it? Besides," he added, with mock seriousness, "I assure you we shall behave in the most reverent way and feel quite solemn about it all, if only you will give us the key, old man."

Again Mr. Oke looked towards his wife, and again met only her vague, absent glance.

"Very well," he said, and led his guests upstairs.

An hour later the house was filled with the strangest crew and the strangest noises. I had entered, to a certain extent, into William Oke's feeling of unwillingness to let his ancestors' clothes and personality be taken in vain; but when the masquerade was complete, I must say that the effect was quite magnificent. A dozen youngish men and women—those who were staying in the house and some neighbours who had come for lawn-tennis and dinner—were rigged out, under the direction of the theatrical cousin, in the contents of that oaken press: and I have never seen a more beautiful sight than the panelled corridors, the carved and escutcheoned staircase, the dim drawing-rooms with their faded tapestries, the great hall with its vaulted and ribbed ceiling, dotted about with groups or single figures that seemed to have come straight from the past. Even William Oke, who, besides myself and a few elderly people, was the only man not masqueraded, seemed delighted and fired by the sight. A certain schoolboy character suddenly came out in him; and finding that there was no costume left for him, he rushed upstairs and presently returned in the uniform he had worn before his marriage. I thought I had really never seen so magnificent a specimen of the handsome Englishman; he looked, despite all the modern associations of his costume, more genuinely old-world than all the rest, a knight for the Black Prince or Sidney,* with his admirably regular features and beautiful fair hair and complexion. After a minute, even the elderly people had got costumes of some sort—dominoes arranged at the moment, and hoods and all manner of disguises made out of pieces of old embroidery and Oriental stuffs and furs; and very soon this rabble of masquers had become, so to speak, completely drunk with its own amusement—with the childishness, and, if I may say so, the barbarism, the vulgarity underlying the majority even of well-bred English men and women—Mr. Oke himself doing the mountebank like a schoolboy at Christmas.

"Where is Mrs. Oke? Where is Alice?" some one suddenly asked.

Mrs. Oke had vanished. I could fully understand that to this eccentric being, with her fantastic, imaginative, morbid passion for the past, such a carnival as this must be positively revolting; and, absolutely indifferent as she was to giving offence, I could imagine how she would have retired, disgusted and outraged, to dream her strange day-dreams in the yellow room.

But a moment later, as we were all noisily preparing to go in to dinner, the door opened and a strange figure entered, stranger than any of these others who were profaning the clothes of the dead: a boy, slight and tall, in a brown riding-coat, leathern belt, and big buff boots, a little grey cloak over one shoulder, a large grey hat slouched over the eyes, a dagger and pistol at the waist. It was Mrs. Oke, her eyes preternaturally bright, and her whole face lit up with a bold, perverse smile.

Every one exclaimed, and stood aside. Then there was a moment's silence, broken by faint applause. Even to a crew of noisy boys and girls playing the fool in the garments of men and women long dead and buried, there is something questionable in the sudden appearance of a young married woman, the mistress of the house, in a riding-coat and jack-boots; and Mrs. Oke's expression did not make the jest seem any the less questionable.

"What is that costume?" asked the theatrical cousin, who, after a second, had come to the conclusion that Mrs. Oke was merely a woman of marvellous talent whom he must try and secure for his amateur troop next season.

"It is the dress in which an ancestress of ours, my namesake Alice Oke, used to go out riding with her husband in the days of Charles I.," she answered, and took her seat at the head of the table. Involuntarily my eyes sought those of Oke of Okehurst. He, who blushed as easily as a girl of sixteen, was now as white as ashes, and I noticed that he pressed his hand almost convulsively to his mouth.

"Don't you recognise my dress, William?" asked Mrs. Oke, fixing her eyes upon him with a cruel smile.

He did not answer, and there was a moment's silence, which the theatrical cousin had the happy thought of breaking by jumping upon his seat and emptying off his glass with the exclamation—

"To the health of the two Alice Okes, of the past and the present!"

Mrs. Oke nodded, and with an expression I had never seen in her face before, answered in a loud and aggressive tone—

"To the health of the poet, Mr. Christopher Lovelock, if his ghost be honouring this house with its presence!"

I felt suddenly as if I were in a madhouse. Across the table, in the midst of this room full of noisy wretches, tricked out red, blue, purple, and parti-coloured, as men and women of the sixteenth, seventeenth, and eighteenth centuries, as improvised Turks and Eskimos, and dominoes, and clowns, with faces painted and corked and floured over, I seemed to see that sanguine sunset, washing like a sea of blood over the heather, to where, by the black pond and the wind-warped firs, there lay the body of Christopher Lovelock, with his dead horse near him, the yellow gravel and lilac ling soaked crimson all around; and above emerged, as out of the redness, the pale blond head covered with the grey hat, the absent eyes, and strange smile of Mrs. Oke. It seemed to me horrible, vulgar, abominable, as if I had got inside a madhouse.

VIII

From that moment I noticed a change in William Oke; or rather, a change that had probably been coming on for some time got to the stage of being noticeable.

I don't know whether he had any words with his wife about her masquerade of that unlucky evening. On the whole I decidedly think not. Oke was with every one a diffident and reserved man, and most of all so with his wife; besides, I can fancy that he would experience a positive impossibility of putting into words any strong feeling of disapprobation towards her, that his disgust would necessarily be silent. But be this as it may, I perceived very soon that the relations between my host and hostess had become exceedingly strained. Mrs. Oke, indeed, had never paid much attention to her husband, and seemed merely a trifle more indifferent to his presence than she had been before. But Oke himself, although he affected to address her at meals from a desire to conceal his feeling, and a fear of making the position disagreeable to me, very clearly could scarcely bear to speak to or even see his wife. The poor fellow's honest soul was quite brimful of pain, which he was determined not to allow to overflow, and which seemed to filter into his whole nature and poison it. This woman had shocked and pained him more than was possible to say, and yet it was evident that he could neither cease loving her nor commence comprehending her real nature. I sometimes felt, as we took our long walks through the monotonous country, across the oak-dotted grazing-grounds, and by the brink of the dull-green, serried hop-rows, talking at rare intervals about the value of the crops, the drainage of the estate, the village schools, the Primrose League, and the iniquities of Mr. Gladstone,* while Oke of Okehurst carefully cut down every tall thistle that caught his eye—I sometimes felt, I say, an intense and impotent desire to enlighten this man about his wife's character.

I seemed to understand it so well, and to understand it well seemed to imply such a comfortable acquiescence; and it seemed so unfair that just he should be condemned to puzzle for ever over this enigma, and wear out his soul trying to comprehend what now seemed so plain to me. But how would it ever be possible to get this serious, conscientious, slow-brained representative of English simplicity and honesty and thoroughness to understand the mixture of self-engrossed vanity, of shallowness, of poetic vision, of love of morbid excitement, that walked this earth under the name of Alice Oke?

So Oke of Okehurst was condemned never to understand; but he was condemned also to suffer from his inability to do so. The poor fellow was constantly straining after an explanation of his wife's peculiarities; and although the effort was probably unconscious, it caused him a great deal of pain. The gash—the maniac-frown, as my friend calls it—between his eyebrows, seemed to have grown a permanent feature of his face.

Mrs. Oke, on her side, was making the very worst of the situation. Perhaps she resented her husband's tacit reproval of that masquerade night's freak, and determined to make him swallow more of the same stuff, for she clearly thought that one of William's peculiarities, and one for which she despised him, was that he could never be goaded into an outspoken expression of disapprobation; that from her he would swallow any amount of bitterness without complaining. At any rate she now adopted a perfect policy of teasing and shocking her husband about the murder of Lovelock. She was perpetually alluding to it in her conversation, discussing in his presence what had or had not been the feelings of the various actors in the tragedy of 1626, and insisting upon her resemblance and almost identity with the original Alice Oke. Something had suggested to her eccentric mind that it would be delightful to perform in the garden at Okehurst, under the huge ilexes and elms, a little masque which she had discovered among Christopher Lovelock's works; and she began to scour the country and enter into vast correspondence for the purpose of effectuating this scheme. Letters arrived every other day from the theatrical cousin, whose only objection was that Okehurst was too remote a locality for an entertainment in which he foresaw great glory to himself. And every now and then there would arrive some young gentleman or lady, whom Alice Oke had sent for to see whether they would do.

I saw very plainly that the performance would never take place, and that Mrs. Oke herself had no intention that it ever should. She was one of those creatures to whom realisation of a project is nothing, and who enjoy plan-making almost the more for knowing that all will stop short at the plan. Meanwhile, this perpetual talk about the pastoral, about Lovelock, this continual attitudinising as the wife of Nicholas Oke, had the further attraction to Mrs. Oke of putting her husband into a condition of frightful though suppressed irritation, which she enjoyed with the enjoyment of a perverse child. You must not think that I looked on indifferent, although I admit that this was a perfect treat to an amateur student of character like myself. I really did feel most sorry for poor Oke, and frequently quite indignant with his wife. I was several times on the point of begging her to have more consideration for him, even of suggesting that this kind of behaviour, particularly before a comparative stranger like me, was very poor taste. But there was something elusive about Mrs. Oke, which made it next to impossible to speak seriously with her; and besides, I was by no means sure that any interference on my part would not merely animate her perversity.

One evening a curious incident took place. We had just sat down to dinner, the Okes, the theatrical cousin, who was down for a couple of days, and three or four neighbours. It was dusk, and the yellow light of the candles mingled charmingly with the greyness of the evening. Mrs. Oke was not well, and had been remarkably quiet all day, more diaphanous, strange, and far-away than ever; and her husband seemed to have felt a sudden return of tenderness, almost of compassion, for this delicate, fragile creature. We had been talking of quite indifferent matters, when I saw Mr. Oke suddenly turn very white, and look fixedly for a moment at the window opposite to his seat.

"Who's that fellow looking in at the window, and making signs to you, Alice? Damn his impudence!" he cried, and jumping up, ran to the window, opened it, and passed out into the twilight. We all looked at each other in surprise; some of the party remarked upon the carelessness of servants in letting nasty-looking fellows hang about the kitchen, others told stories of tramps and burglars. Mrs. Oke did not speak; but I noticed the curious, distant-looking smile in her thin cheeks.

After a minute William Oke came in, his napkin in his hand. He shut the window behind him and silently resumed his place.

"Well, who was it?" we all asked.

"Nobody. I—I must have made a mistake," he answered, and turned crimson, while he busily peeled a pear.

"It was probably Lovelock," remarked Mrs. Oke, just as she might have said, "It was probably the gardener," but with that faint smile of pleasure still in her face. Except the theatrical cousin, who burst into a loud laugh, none of the company had ever heard Lovelock's name, and, doubtless imagining him to be some natural appanage of the Oke family, groom or farmer, said nothing, so the subject dropped.

From that evening onwards things began to assume a different aspect. That incident was the beginning of a perfect system—a system of what? I scarcely know how to call it. A system of grim jokes on the part of Mrs. Oke, of superstitious fancies on the part of her husband—a system of mysterious persecutions on the part of some less earthly tenant of Okehurst. Well, yes, after all, why not? We have all heard of ghosts, had uncles, cousins, grandmothers, nurses, who have seen them; we are all a bit afraid of them at the bottom of our soul; so why shouldn't they be? I am too sceptical to believe in the impossibility of anything, for my part! Besides, when a man has lived throughout a summer in the same house with a woman like Mrs. Oke of Okehurst, he gets to believe in the possibility of a great many improbable things, I assure you, as a mere result of believing in her. And when you come to think of it, why not? That a weird creature, visibly not of this earth, a reincarnation of a woman who murdered her lover two centuries and a half ago, that such a creature should have the power of attracting about her (being altogether superior to earthly lovers) the man who loved her in that previous existence, whose love for her was his death—what is there astonishing in that? Mrs. Oke herself, I feel quite persuaded, believed or half believed it; indeed she very seriously admitted the possibility thereof, one day that I made the suggestion half in jest. At all events, it rather pleased me to think so; it fitted in so well with the woman's whole personality; it explained those hours and hours spent all alone in the yellow room, where the very air, with its scent of heady flowers and old perfumed stuffs, seemed redolent of ghosts. It explained that strange smile which was not for any of us, and yet was not merely for herself—that strange, far-off look in the wide pale eyes. I liked the idea, and I liked to tease, or rather to delight her with it. How should I know that the wretched husband would take such matters seriously?

He became day by day more silent and perplexed-looking; and, as a result, worked harder, and probably with less effect, at his land-improving schemes and political canvassing. It seemed to me that he was perpetually listening, watching, waiting for something to happen: a word spoken suddenly, the sharp opening of a door, would make him start, turn crimson, and almost tremble; the mention of Lovelock brought a helpless look, half a convulsion, like that of a man overcome by great heat, into his face. And his wife, so far from taking any interest in his altered looks, went on irritating him more and more. Every time that the poor fellow gave one of those starts of his, or turned crimson at the sudden sound of a footstep, Mrs. Oke would ask him, with her contemptuous indifference, whether he had seen Lovelock. I soon began to perceive that my host was getting perfectly ill. He would sit at meals never saying a word, with his eyes fixed scrutinisingly on his wife, as if vainly trying to solve some dreadful mystery; while his wife, ethereal, exquisite, went on talking in her listless way about the masque, about Lovelock, always about Lovelock. During our walks and rides, which we continued pretty regularly, he would start whenever in the roads or lanes surrounding Okehurst, or in its grounds, we perceived a figure in the distance, I have seen him tremble at what, on nearer approach, I could scarcely restrain my laughter on discovering to be some well-known farmer or neighbour or servant. Once, as we were returning home at dusk, he suddenly caught my arm and pointed across the oak-dotted pastures in the direction of the garden, then started off almost at a run, with his dog behind him, as if in pursuit of some intruder.

"Who was it?" I asked. And Mr. Oke merely shook his head mournfully. Sometimes in the early autumn twilights, when the white mists rose from the park-land, and the rooks formed long black lines on the palings, I almost fancied I saw him start at the very trees and bushes, the outlines of the distant oast-houses,* with their conical roofs and projecting vanes, like gibing fingers in the half light.

"Your husband is ill," I once ventured to remark to Mrs. Oke, as she sat for the hundred-and-thirtieth of my preparatory sketches (I somehow could never get beyond preparatory sketches with her). She raised her beautiful, wide, pale eyes, making as she did so that exquisite curve of shoulders and neck and delicate pale head that I so vainly longed to reproduce.

"I don't see it," she answered quietly. "If he is, why doesn't he go up to town and see the doctor? It's merely one of his glum fits."

"You should not tease him about Lovelock," I added, very seriously. "He will get to believe in him."

"Why not? If he sees him, why he sees him. He would not be the only person that has done so;" and she smiled faintly and half perversely, as her eyes sought that usual distant indefinable something.

But Oke got worse. He was growing perfectly unstrung, like a hysterical woman. One evening that we were sitting alone in the smoking-room, he began unexpectedly a rambling discourse about his wife; how he had first known her when they were children, and they had gone to the same dancing-school near Portland Place; how her mother, his aunt-in-law, had brought her for Christmas to Okehurst while he was on his holidays; how finally, thirteen years ago, when he was twenty-three and she was eighteen, they had been married; how terribly he had suffered when they had been disappointed of their baby, and she had nearly died of the illness.

"I did not mind about the child, you know," he said in an excited voice; "although there will be an end of us now, and Okehurst will go to the Curtises. I minded only about Alice." It was next to inconceivable that this poor excited creature, speaking almost with tears in his voice and in his eyes, was the quiet, well-got-up, irreproachable young ex-Guardsman who had walked into my studio a couple of months before.

Oke was silent for a moment, looking fixedly at the rug at his feet, when he suddenly burst out in a scarce audible voice—

"If you knew how I cared for Alice—how I still care for her. I could kiss the ground she walks upon. I would give anything—my life any day—if only she would look for two minutes as if she liked me a little—as if she didn't utterly despise me;" and the poor fellow burst into a hysterical laugh, which was almost a sob. Then he suddenly began to laugh outright, exclaiming, with a sort of vulgarity of intonation which was extremely foreign to him—

"Damn it, old fellow, this is a queer world we live in!" and rang for more brandy and soda, which he was beginning, I noticed, to take pretty freely now, although he had been almost a blue-ribbon man*—as much so as is possible for a hospitable country gentleman—when I first arrived.

IX

It became clear to me now that, incredible as it might seem, the thing that ailed William Oke was jealousy. He was simply madly in love with his wife, and madly jealous of her. Jealous—but of whom? He himself would probably have been quite unable to say. In the first place—to clear off any possible suspicion—certainly not of me. Besides the fact that Mrs. Oke took only just a very little more interest in me than in the butler or the upper housemaid, I think that Oke himself was the sort of man whose imagination would recoil from realising any definite object of jealousy, even though jealousy might be killing him inch by inch. It remained a vague, permeating, continuous feeling—the feeling that he loved her, and she did not care a jackstraw about him, and that every thing with which she came into contact was receiving some of that notice which was refused to him—every person, or thing, or tree, or stone: it was the recognition of that strange far-off look in Mrs. Oke's eyes, of that strange absent smile on Mrs. Oke's lips—eyes and lips that had no look and no smile for him.

Gradually his nervousness, his watchfulness, suspiciousness, tendency to start, took a definite shape. Mr. Oke was for ever alluding to steps or voices he had heard, to figures he had seen sneaking round the house. The sudden bark of one of the dogs would make him jump up. He cleaned and loaded very carefully all the guns and revolvers in his study, and even some of the old fowling-pieces and holster-pistols in the hall. The servants and tenants thought that Oke of Okehurst had been seized with a terror of tramps and burglars. Mrs. Oke smiled contemptuously at all these doings.

"My dear William," she said one day, "the persons who worry you have just as good a right to walk up and down the passages and staircase, and to hang about the house, as you or I. They were there, in all probability, long before either of us was born, and are greatly amused by your preposterous notions of privacy."

Mr. Oke laughed angrily. "I suppose you will tell me it is Lovelock—your eternal Lovelock—whose steps I hear on the gravel every night. I suppose he has as good a right to be here as you or I." And he strode out of the room.

"Lovelock—Lovelock! Why will she always go on like that about Lovelock?" Mr. Oke asked me that evening, suddenly staring me in the face.

I merely laughed.

"It's only because she has that play of his on the brain," I answered; "and because she thinks you superstitious, and likes to tease you."

"I don't understand," sighed Oke.

How could he? And if I had tried to make him do so, he would merely have thought I was insulting his wife, and have perhaps kicked me out of the room. So I made no attempt to explain psychological problems to him, and he asked me no more questions until once—But I must first mention a curious incident that happened.

The incident was simply this. Returning one afternoon from our usual walk, Mr. Oke suddenly asked the servant whether any one had come. The answer was in the negative; but Oke did not seem satisfied. We had hardly sat down to dinner when he turned to his wife and asked, in a strange voice which I scarcely recognised as his own, who had called that afternoon.

"No one," answered Mrs. Oke; "at least to the best of my knowledge."

William Oke looked at her fixedly.

"No one?" he repeated, in a scrutinising tone; "no one, Alice?"

Mrs. Oke shook her head. "No one," she replied.

There was a pause.

"Who was it, then, that was walking with you near the pond, about five o'clock?" asked Oke slowly.

His wife lifted her eyes straight to his and answered contemptuously—

"No one was walking with me near the pond, at five o'clock or any other hour."

Mr. Oke turned purple, and made a curious hoarse noise like a man choking.

"I—I thought I saw you walking with a man this afternoon, Alice," he brought out with an effort; adding, for the sake of appearances before me, "I thought it might have been the curate come with that report for me."

Mrs. Oke smiled.

"I can only repeat that no living creature has been near me this afternoon," she said slowly. "If you saw any one with me, it must have been Lovelock, for there certainly was no one else."

And she gave a little sigh, like a person trying to reproduce in her mind some delightful but too evanescent impression.

I looked at my host; from crimson his face had turned perfectly livid, and he breathed as if some one were squeezing his windpipe.

No more was said about the matter. I vaguely felt that a great danger was threatening. To Oke or to Mrs. Oke? I could not tell which; but I was aware of an imperious inner call to avert some dreadful evil, to exert myself, to explain, to interpose. I determined to speak to Oke the following day, for I trusted him to give me a quiet hearing, and I did not trust Mrs. Oke. That woman would slip through my fingers like a snake if I attempted to grasp her elusive character.

I asked Oke whether he would take a walk with me the next afternoon, and he accepted to do so with a curious eagerness. We started about three o'clock. It was a stormy, chilly afternoon, with great balls of white clouds rolling rapidly in the cold blue sky, and occasional lurid gleams of sunlight, broad and yellow, which made the black ridge of the storm, gathered on the horizon, look blue-black like ink.

We walked quickly across the sere and sodden grass of the park, and on to the highroad that led over the low hills, I don't know why, in the direction of Cotes Common. Both of us were silent, for both of us had something to say, and did not know how to begin. For my part, I recognised the impossibility of starting the subject: an uncalled-for interference from me would merely indispose Mr. Oke, and make him doubly dense of comprehension. So, if Oke had something to say, which he evidently had, it was better to wait for him.

Oke, however, broke the silence only by pointing out to me the condition of the hops, as we passed one of his many hop gardens. "It will be a poor year," he said, stopping short and looking intently before him—"no hops at all. No hops this autumn."

I looked at him. It was clear that he had no notion what he was saying. The dark-green vines were covered with fruit; and only yesterday he himself had informed me that he had not seen such a profusion of hops for many years.

I did not answer, and we walked on. A cart met us in a dip of the road, and the carter touched his hat and greeted Mr. Oke. But Oke took no heed; he did not seem to be aware of the man's presence.

The clouds were collecting all round; black domes, among which coursed the round grey masses of fleecy stuff.

"I think we shall be caught in a tremendous storm," I said; "hadn't we better be turning?" He nodded, and turned sharp round.

The sunlight lay in yellow patches under the oaks of the pasture-lands, and burnished the green hedges, The air was heavy and yet cold, and everything seemed preparing for a great storm. The rooks whirled in black clouds round the trees and the conical red caps of the oast-houses which give that country the look of being studded with turreted castles; then they descended—a black line—upon the fields, with what seemed an unearthly loudness of caw. And all round there arose a shrill quavering bleating of lambs and calling of sheep, while the wind began to catch the topmost branches of the trees.

Suddenly Mr. Oke broke the silence.

"I don't know you very well," he began hurriedly, and without turning his face towards me; "but I think you are honest, and you have seen a good deal of the world—much more than I. I want you to tell me—but truly, please—what do you think a man should do if"——and he stopped for some minutes.

"Imagine," he went on quickly, "that a man cares a great deal—a very great deal for his wife, and that he find out that she—well, that—that she is deceiving him. No—don't misunderstand me; I mean—that she is constantly surrounded by some one else and will not admit it—some one whom she hides away. Do you understand? Perhaps she does not know all the risk she is running, you know, but she will not draw back—she will not avow it to her husband"——

"My dear Oke," I interrupted, attempting to take the matter lightly, "these are questions that can't be solved in the abstract, or by people to whom the thing has not happened. And it certainly has not happened to you or me."

Oke took no notice of my interruption. "You see," he went on, "the man doesn't expect his wife to care much about him. It's not that; he isn't merely jealous, you know. But he feels that she is on the brink of dishonouring herself—because I don't think a woman can really dishonour her husband; dishonour is in our own hands, and depends only on our own acts. He ought to save her, do you see? He must, must save her, in one way or another. But if she will not listen to him, what can he do? Must he seek out the other one, and try and get him out of the way? You see it's all the fault of the other—not hers, not hers. If only she would trust in her husband, she would be safe. But that other one won't let her."

"Look here, Oke," I said boldly, but feeling rather frightened; "I know quite well what you are talking about. And I see you don't understand the matter in the very least. I do. I have watched you and watched Mrs. Oke these six weeks, and I see what is the matter. Will you listen to me?"

And taking his arm, I tried to explain to him my view of the situation—that his wife was merely eccentric, and a little theatrical and imaginative, and that she took a pleasure in teasing him. That he, on the other hand, was letting himself get into a morbid state; that he was ill, and ought to see a good doctor. I even offered to take him to town with me.

I poured out volumes of psychological explanations. I dissected Mrs. Oke's character twenty times over, and tried to show him that there was absolutely nothing at the bottom of his suspicions beyond an imaginative pose and a garden-play on the brain. I adduced twenty instances, mostly invented for the nonce, of ladies of my acquaintance who had suffered from similar fads. I pointed out to him that his wife ought to have an outlet for her imaginative and theatrical over-energy. I advised him to take her to London and plunge her into some set where every one should be more or less in a similar condition. I laughed at the notion of there being any hidden individual about the house. I explained to Oke that he was suffering from delusions, and called upon so conscientious and religious a man to take every step to rid himself of them, adding innumerable examples of people who had cured themselves of seeing visions and of brooding over morbid fancies. I struggled and wrestled, like Jacob with the angel,* and I really hoped I had made some impression. At first, indeed, I felt that not one of my words went into the man's brain—that, though silent, he was not listening. It seemed almost hopeless to present my views in such a light that he could grasp them. I felt as if I were expounding and arguing at a rock. But when I got on to the tack of his duty towards his wife and himself, and appealed to his moral and religious notions, I felt that I was making an impression.

"I daresay you are right," he said, taking my hand as we came in sight of the red gables of Okehurst, and speaking in a weak, tired, humble voice. "I don't understand you quite, but I am sure what you say is true. I daresay it is all that I'm seedy.* I feel sometimes as if

I were mad, and just fit to be locked up. But don't think I don't struggle against it. I do, I do continually, only sometimes it seems too strong for me. I pray God night and morning to give me the strength to overcome my suspicions, or to remove these dreadful thoughts from me. God knows, I know what a wretched creature I am, and how unfit to take care of that poor girl."

And Oke again pressed my hand. As we entered the garden, he turned to me once more.

"I am very, very grateful to you," he said, "and, indeed, I will do my best to try and be stronger. If only," he added, with a sigh, "if only Alice would give me a moment's breathing-time, and not go on day after day mocking me with her Lovelock."

X

I had begun Mrs. Oke's portrait, and she was giving me a sitting. She was unusually quiet that morning; but, it seemed to me, with the quietness of a woman who is expecting something, and she gave me the impression of being extremely happy. She had been reading, at my suggestion, the "Vita Nuova,"* which she did not know before, and the conversation came to roll upon that, and upon the question whether love so abstract and so enduring was a possibility. Such a discussion, which might have savoured of flirtation in the case of almost any other young and beautiful woman, became in the case of Mrs. Oke something quite different; it seemed distant, intangible, not of this earth, like her smile and the look in her eyes.

"Such love as that," she said, looking into the far distance of the oak-dotted park-land, "is very rare, but it can exist. It becomes a person's whole existence, his whole soul; and it can survive the death, not merely of the beloved, but of the lover. It is unextinguishable, and goes on in the spiritual world until it meet a reincarnation of the beloved; and when this happens, it jets out and draws to it all that may remain of that lover's soul, and takes shape and surrounds the beloved one once more."

Mrs. Oke was speaking slowly, almost to herself, and I had never, I think, seen her look so strange and so beautiful, the stiff white dress bringing out but the more the exotic exquisiteness and incorporealness of her person.

I did not know what to answer, so I said half in jest—

"I fear you have been reading too much Buddhist literature, Mrs. Oke. There is something dreadfully esoteric* in all you say."

She smiled contemptuously.

"I know people can't understand such matters," she replied, and was silent for some time. But, through her quietness and silence, I felt, as it were, the throb of a strange excitement in this woman, almost as if I had been holding her pulse.

Still, I was in hopes that things might be beginning to go better in consequence of my interference. Mrs. Oke had scarcely once alluded to Lovelock in the last two or three days; and Oke had been much more cheerful and natural since our conversation. He no longer seemed so worried; and once or twice I had caught in him a look of great gentleness and loving-kindness, almost of pity, as towards some young and very frail thing, as he sat opposite his wife.

But the end had come. After that sitting Mrs. Oke had complained of fatigue and retired to her room, and Oke had driven off on some business to the nearest town. I felt all alone in the big house, and after having worked a little at a sketch I was making in the park, I amused myself rambling about the house.

It was a warm, enervating, autumn afternoon: the kind of weather that brings the perfume out of everything, the damp ground and fallen leaves, the flowers in the jars, the old woodwork and stuffs; that seems to bring on to the surface of one's consciousness all manner of vague recollections and expectations, a something half pleasurable, half painful, that makes it impossible to do or to think. I was the prey of this particular, not at all unpleasurable, restlessness. I wandered up and down the corridors, stopping to look at the pictures, which I knew already in every detail, to follow the pattern of the carvings and old stuffs, to stare at the autumn flowers, arranged in magnificent masses of colour in the big china bowls and jars. I took up one book after another and threw it aside; then I sat down to the piano and began to play irrelevant fragments. I felt quite alone, although I had heard the grind of the wheels on the gravel, which meant that my host had returned. I was lazily turning over a book of verses—I remember it perfectly well, it was Morris's 'Love is Enough'*—in a corner of the drawing-room, when the door suddenly opened and William Oke showed himself. He did not enter, but beckoned to me to come out to him. There was something in his face that made me start up and follow him at once. He was extremely quiet, even stiff, not a muscle of his face moving, but very pale.

"I have something to show you," he said, leading me through the vaulted hall, hung round with ancestral pictures, into the gravelled space that looked like a filled-up moat, where stood the big blasted oak, with its twisted, pointing branches. I followed him on to the lawn, or rather the piece of park-land that ran up to the house. We walked quickly, he in front, without exchanging a word. Suddenly he stopped, just where there jutted out the bow-window of the yellow drawing-room, and I felt Oke's hand tight upon my arm.

"I have brought you here to see something," he whispered hoarsely; and he led me to the window.

I looked in. The room, compared with the out door, was rather dark; but against the yellow wall I saw Mrs. Oke sitting alone on a couch in her white dress, her head slightly thrown back, a large red rose in her hand.

"Do you believe now?" whispered Oke's voice hot at my ear. "Do you believe, now? Was it all my fancy? But I will have him this time. I have locked the door inside, and, by God! he shan't escape."

The words were not out of Oke's mouth. I felt myself struggling with him silently outside that window. But he broke loose, pulled open the window, and leapt into the room, and I after him. As I crossed the threshold, something flashed in my eyes; there was a loud report, a sharp cry, and the thud of a body on the ground.

Oke was standing in the middle of the room, with a faint smoke about him; and at his feet, sunk down from the sofa, with her blond head resting on its seat, lay Mrs. Oke, a pool of red forming in her white dress. Her mouth was convulsed, as if in that automatic shriek, but her wide-open white eyes seemed to smile vaguely and distantly.

I know nothing of time. It all seemed to be one second, but a second that lasted hours. Oke stared, then turned round and laughed.

"The damned rascal has given me the slip again!" he cried; and quickly unlocking the door, rushed out of the house with dreadful cries.

That is the end of the story. Oke tried to shoot himself that evening, but merely fractured his jaw, and died a few days later, raving. There were all sorts of legal inquiries, through which I went as through a dream; and whence it resulted that Mr. Oke had killed his wife in a fit of momentary madness. That was the end of Alice Oke. By the way, her maid brought me a locket which was found round her neck, all stained with blood. It contained some very dark auburn hair, not at all the colour of William Oke's. I am quite sure it was Lovelock's.

AMOUR DURE:

PASSAGES FROM THE DIARY OF SPIRIDION* TREPKA

PART I

Urbania,* *August 20th*, 1885.—I had longed, these years and years, to be in Italy, to come face to face with the Past; and was this Italy, was this the Past? I could have cried, yes cried, for disappointment when I first wandered about Rome, with an invitation to dine at the German Embassy in my pocket, and three or four Berlin and Munich Vandals* at my heels, telling me where the best beer and sauerkraut could be had, and what the last article by Grimm or Mommsen* was about.

Is this folly? Is it falsehood? Am I not myself a product of modern, northern civilisation; is not my coming to Italy due to this very modern scientific vandalism, which has given me a travelling scholarship because I have written a book like all those other atrocious books of erudition and art-criticism? Nay, am I not here at Urbania on the express understanding that, in a certain number of months, I shall produce just another such book? Dost thou imagine, thou miserable Spiridion, thou Pole grown into the semblance of a German pedant, doctor of philosophy, professor even, author of a prize essay on the despots of the fifteenth century, dost thou imagine that thou, with thy ministerial letters and proof-sheets in thy black professorial coat-pocket, canst ever come in spirit into the presence of the Past?

Too true, alas! But let me forget it, at least, every now and then; as I forgot it this afternoon, while the white bullocks dragged my gig slowly winding along interminable valleys, crawling along interminable hill-sides, with the invisible droning torrent far below, and only the bare grey and reddish peaks all around, up to this town of Urbania, forgotten of mankind, towered and battlemented on the high Apennine ridge. Sigillo, Penna, Fossombrone, Mercatello, Montemurlo*—each single village name, as the driver pointed it out, brought to my mind the recollection of some battle or some great act of treachery of former days. And as the huge mountains shut out the setting sun, and the valleys filled with bluish shadow and mist, only a band of threatening smoke-red remaining behind the towers and cupolas of the city on its mountain-top, and the sound of church bells floated across the precipice from Urbania, I almost expected, at every turning of the road, that a troop of horsemen, with beaked helmets and clawed shoes, would emerge, with armour glittering and pennons waving in the sunset. And then, not two hours ago, entering the town at dusk, passing along the deserted streets, with only a smoky light here and there under a shrine or in front of a fruit-stall, or a fire reddening the blackness of a smithy; passing beneath the battlements and turrets of the palace. . . . Ah, that was Italy, it was the Past!

August 21st.—And this is the Present! Four letters of introduction to deliver, and an hour's polite conversation to endure with the Vice-Prefect, the Syndic, the Director of the Archives, and the good man to whom my friend Max had sent me for lodgings. . . .

August 22nd–27th.—Spent the greater part of the day in the Archives, and the greater part of my time there in being bored to extinction by the Director thereof, who to-day spouted Æneas Sylvius' Commentaries* for three-quarters of an hour without taking breath. From this sort of martyrdom (what are the sensations of a former racehorse being driven in a cab? If you can conceive them, they are those of a Pole turned Prussian professor) I take refuge in long rambles through the town. This town is a handful of tall black houses huddled on to the top of an Alp, long narrow lanes trickling down its sides, like the slides we made on hillocks in our boyhood, and in the middle the superb red brick structure, turreted and battlemented, of Duke Ottobuono's palace, from whose windows you look down upon a sea, a kind of whirlpool, of melancholy grey mountains. Then there are the people, dark, bushy-bearded men, riding about like brigands, wrapped in green-lined cloaks upon their shaggy pack-mules; or loitering about, great, brawny, low-headed youngsters, like the parti-coloured bravos in Signorelli's frescoes; the beautiful boys, like so many young Raphaels, with eyes like the eyes of bullocks, and the huge women, Madonnas or St. Elizabeths, as the case may be, with their clogs firmly poised on their toes and their brass pitchers on their heads, as they go up and down the steep black alleys. I do not talk much to these people; I fear my illusions being dispelled. At the corner of a street, opposite Francesco di Giorgio's beautiful little portico, is a great blue and red advertisement, representing an angel descending to crown Elias Howe, on account of his sewing-machines; and the clerks of the Vice-Prefecture, who dine at the place where I get my dinner, yell politics, Minghetti, Cairoli, Tunis, ironclads, &c., at each other, and sing snatches of *La Fille de Mme. Angot*,* which I imagine they have been performing here recently.

No; talking to the natives is evidently a dangerous experiment. Except indeed, perhaps, to my good landlord, Signor Notaro Porri, who is just as learned, and takes considerably less snuff (or rather brushes it off his coat more often) than the Director of the Archives. I forgot to jot down (and I feel I must jot down, in the vain belief that some day these scraps will help, like a withered twig of olive or a three-wicked Tuscan lamp on my table, to bring to my mind, in that hateful Babylon of Berlin, these happy Italian days)—I forgot to record that I am lodging in the house of a dealer in antiquities. My window looks up the principal street to where the little column with Mercury* on the top rises in the midst of the awnings and porticoes of the market-place. Bending over the chipped ewers and tubs full of sweet basil, clove pinks, and marigolds, I can just see a corner of the palace turret, and the vague ultramarine of the hills beyond. The house, whose back goes sharp down into the ravine, is a queer up-and-down black place, whitewashed rooms, hung with the Raphaels and Francias and Peruginos,* whom mine host regularly carries to the chief inn whenever a stranger is expected; and surrounded by old carved chairs, sofas of the Empire,* embossed and gilded wedding-chests, and the cupboards which contain bits of old damask and embroidered altar-cloths scenting the place with the smell of old incense and mustiness; all of which are presided over by Signor Porri's three maiden sisters—Sora Serafina, Sora Lodovica, and Sora Adalgisa—the three Fates* in person, even to the distaffs and their black cats.

Sor Asdrubale,* as they call my landlord, is also a notary. He regrets the Pontifical Government,* having had a cousin who was a Cardinal's train-bearer, and believes that if only you lay a table for two, light four candles made of dead men's fat, and perform certain rites about which he is not very precise, you can, on Christmas Eve and similar nights, summon up San Pasquale Baylon,* who will write you the winning numbers of the lottery upon the smoked back of a plate, if you have previously slapped him on both cheeks and repeated three Ave Marias. The difficulty consists in obtaining the dead men's fat for the candles, and also in slapping the saint before he have time to vanish.

"If it were not for that," says Sor Asdrubale, "the Government would have had to suppress the lottery ages ago—eh!"

Sept. 9th.—This history of Urbania is not without its romance, although that romance (as usual) has been overlooked by our Dryasdusts.* Even before coming here I felt attracted by the strange figure of a woman, which appeared from out of the dry pages of Gualterio's and Padre de Sanctis' histories* of this place. This woman is Medea, daughter of Galeazzo IV. Malatesta, Lord of Carpi,* wife first of Pierluigi Orsini, Duke of Stimigliano, and subsequently of Guidalfonso II., Duke of Urbania, predecessor of the great Duke Robert II.

This woman's history and character remind one of that of Bianca Cappello, and at the same time of Lucrezia Borgia.* Born in 1556, she was affianced at the age of twelve to a cousin, a Malatesta of the Rimini family.* This family having greatly gone down in the world, her engagement was broken, and she was betrothed a year later to a member of the Pico family,* and married to him by proxy at the age of fourteen. But this match not satisfying her own or her father's ambition, the marriage by proxy was, upon some pretext, declared null, and the suit encouraged of the Duke of Stimigliano,* a great Umbrian feudatory of the Orsini family.* But the bridegroom, Giovanfrancesco Pico, refused to submit, pleaded his case before the Pope, and tried to carry off by force his bride, with whom he was madly in love, as the lady was most lovely and of most cheerful and amiable manner, says an old anonymous chronicle. Pico waylaid her litter as she was going to a villa of her father's, and carried her to his castle near Mirandola, where he respectfully pressed his suit; insisting that he had a right to consider her as his wife. But the lady escaped by letting herself into the moat by a rope of sheets, and Giovanfrancesco Pico was discovered stabbed in the chest, by the hand of Madonna Medea da Carpi. He was a handsome youth only eighteen years old.

The Pico having been settled, and the marriage with him declared null by the Pope, Medea da Carpi was solemnly married to the Duke of Stimigliano, and went to live upon his domains near Rome.

Two years later, Pierluigi Orsini was stabbed by one of his grooms at his castle of Stimigliano, near Orvieto;* and suspicion fell upon his widow, more especially as, immediately after the event, she caused the murderer to be cut down by two servants in her own chamber; but not before he had declared that she had induced him to assassinate his master by a promise of her love. Things became so hot for Medea da

Carpi that she fled to Urbania and threw herself at the feet of Duke Guidalfonso II., declaring that she had caused the groom to be killed merely to avenge her good fame, which he had slandered, and that she was absolutely guiltless of the death of her husband. The marvellous beauty of the widowed Duchess of Stimigliano, who was only nineteen, entirely turned the head of the Duke of Urbania. He affected implicit belief in her innocence, refused to give her up to the Orsinis, kinsmen of her late husband, and assigned to her magnificent apartments in the left wing of the palace, among which the room containing the famous fireplace ornamented with marble Cupids* on a blue ground. Guidalfonso fell madly in love with his beautiful guest. Hitherto timid and domestic in character, he began publicly to neglect his wife, Maddalena Varano of Camerino,* with whom, although childless, he had hitherto lived on excellent terms; he not only treated with contempt the admonitions of his advisers and of his suzerain the Pope, but went so far as to take measures to repudiate his wife, on the score of quite imaginary ill-conduct. The Duchess Maddalena, unable to bear this treatment, fled to the convent of the barefooted sisters at Pesaro,* where she pined away, while Medea da Carpi reigned in her place at Urbania, embroiling Duke Guidalfonso in quarrels both with the powerful Orsinis, who continued to accuse her of Stimigliano's murder, and with the Varanos, kinsmen of the injured Duchess Maddalena; until at length, in the year 1576, the Duke of Urbania, having become suddenly, and not without suspicious circumstances, a widower, publicly married Medea da Carpi two days after the decease of his unhappy wife. No child was born of this marriage; but such was the infatuation of Duke Guidalfonso, that the new Duchess induced him to settle the inheritance of the Duchy (having, with great difficulty, obtained the consent of the Pope) on the boy Bartolommeo, her son by Stimigliano, but whom the Orsinis refused to acknowledge as such, declaring him to be the child of that Giovanfrancesco Pico to whom Medea had been married by proxy, and whom, in defence, as she had said, of her honour, she had assassinated; and this investiture of the Duchy of Urbania on to a stranger and a bastard was at the expense of the obvious rights of the Cardinal Robert, Guidalfonso's younger brother.

In May 1579 Duke Guidalfonso died suddenly and mysteriously, Medea having forbidden all access to his chamber, lest, on his deathbed, he might repent and reinstate his brother in his rights. The Duchess immediately caused her son, Bartolommeo Orsini, to be proclaimed Duke of Urbania, and herself regent; and, with the help of two or three unscrupulous young men, particularly a certain Captain Oliverotto da Narni,* who was rumoured to be her lover, seized the reins of government with extraordinary and terrible vigour, marching an army against the Varanos and Orsinis, who were defeated at Sigillo, and ruthlessly exterminating every person who dared question the lawfulness of the succession; while, all the time, Cardinal Robert, who had flung aside his priest's garb and vows, went about in Rome, Tuscany, Venice—nay, even to the Emperor and the King of Spain, imploring help against the usurper. In a few months he had turned the tide of sympathy against the Duchess-Regent; the Pope solemnly declared the investiture of Bartolommeo Orsini worthless, and published the accession of Robert II., Duke of Urbania and Count of Montemurlo; the Grand Duke of Tuscany and the Venetians secretly promised assistance, but only if Robert were able to assert his rights by main force. Little by little, one town after the other of the Duchy went over to Robert, and Medea da Carpi found herself surrounded in the mountain citadel of Urbania like a scorpion surrounded by flames. (This simile is not mine, but belongs to Raffaello Gualterio, historiographer to Robert II.) But, unlike the scorpion, Medea refused to commit suicide. It is perfectly marvellous how, without money or allies, she could so long keep her enemies at bay; and Gualterio attributes this to those fatal fascinations which had brought Pico and Stimigliano to their deaths, which had turned the once honest Guidalfonso into a villain, and which were such that, of all her lovers, not one but preferred dying for her, even after he had been treated with ingratitude and ousted by a rival; a faculty which Messer Raffaello Gualterio clearly attributed to hellish connivance.

At last the ex-Cardinal Robert succeeded, and triumphantly entered Urbania in November 1579. His accession was marked by moderation and clemency. Not a man was put to death, save Oliverotto da Narni, who threw himself on the new Duke, tried to stab him as he alighted at the palace, and who was cut down by the Duke's men, crying, "Orsini, Orsini! Medea, Medea! Long live Duke Bartolommeo!" with his dying breath, although it is said that the Duchess had treated him with ignominy. The little Bartolommeo was sent to Rome to the Orsinis; the Duchess, respectfully confined in the left wing of the palace.

It is said that she haughtily requested to see the new Duke, but that he shook his head, and, in his priest's fashion, quoted a verse about

Ulysses and the Sirens;* and it is remarkable that he persistently refused to see her, abruptly leaving his chamber one day that she had entered it by stealth. After a few months a conspiracy was discovered to murder Duke Robert, which had obviously been set on foot by Medea. But the young man, one Marcantonio Frangipani* of Rome, denied, even under the severest torture, any complicity of hers; so that Duke Robert, who wished to do nothing violent, merely transferred the Duchess from his villa at Sant' Elmo to the convent of the Clarisse* in town, where she was guarded and watched in the closest manner. It seemed impossible that Medea should intrigue any further, for she certainly saw and could be seen by no one. Yet she contrived to send a letter and her portrait to one Prinzivalle degli Ordelaffi, a youth, only nineteen years old, of noble Romagnole family,* and who was betrothed to one of the most beautiful girls of Urbania. He immediately broke off his engagement, and, shortly afterwards, attempted to shoot Duke Robert with a holster-pistol as he knelt at mass on the festival of Easter Day. This time Duke Robert was determined to obtain proofs against Medea. Prinzivalle degli Ordelaffi was kept some days without food, then submitted to the most violent tortures, and finally condemned. When he was going to be flayed with red-hot pincers and quartered by horses, he was told that he might obtain the grace of immediate death by confessing the complicity of the Duchess; and the confessor and nuns of the convent, which stood in the place of execution outside Porta San Romano, pressed Medea to save the wretch, whose screams reached her, by confessing her own guilt. Medea asked permission to go to a balcony, where she could see Prinzivalle and be seen by him. She looked on coldly, then threw down her embroidered kerchief to the poor mangled creature. He asked the executioner to wipe his mouth with it, kissed it, and cried out that Medea was innocent. Then, after several hours of torments, he died. This was too much for the patience even of Duke Robert. Seeing that as long as Medea lived his life would be in perpetual danger, but unwilling to cause a scandal (somewhat of the priest-nature remaining), he had Medea strangled in the convent, and, what is remarkable, insisted that only women—two infanticides to whom he remitted their sentence—should be employed for the deed.

"This clement prince," writes Don Arcangelo Zappi* in his life of him, published in 1725, "can be blamed only for one act of cruelty, the more odious as he had himself, until released from his vows by the Pope, been in holy orders. It is said that when he caused the death of the infamous Medea da Carpi, his fear lest her extraordinary charms should seduce any man was such, that he not only employed women as executioners, but refused to permit her a priest or monk, thus forcing her to die unshriven, and refusing her the benefit of any penitence that may have lurked in her adamantine heart."

Such is the story of Medea da Carpi, Duchess of Stimigliano Orsini, and then wife of Duke Guidalfonso II. of Urbania. She was put to death just two hundred and ninety-seven years ago, December 1582, at the age of barely seven-and twenty, and having, in the course of her short life, brought to a violent end five of her lovers, from Giovanfrancesco Pico to Prinzivalle degli Ordelaffi.

Sept. 20th.—A grand illumination of the town in honour of the taking of Rome fifteen years ago. Except Sor Asdrubale, my landlord, who shakes his head at the Piedmontese, as he calls them, the people here are all Italianissimi.* The Popes kept them very much down since Urbania lapsed to the Holy See in 1645.

Sept. 28th.—I have for some time been hunting for portraits of the Duchess Medea. Most of them, I imagine, must have been destroyed, perhaps by Duke Robert II.'s fear lest even after her death this terrible beauty should play him a trick. Three or four I have, however, been able to find—one a miniature in the Archives, said to be that which she sent to poor Prinzivalle degli Ordelaffi in order to turn his head; one a marble bust in the palace lumber-room; one in a large composition, possibly by Baroccio, representing Cleopatra at the feet of Augustus.* Augustus is the idealised portrait of Robert II., round cropped head, nose a little awry, clipped beard and scar as usual, but in Roman dress. Cleopatra seems to me, for all her Oriental dress, and although she wears a black wig, to be meant for Medea da Carpi; she is kneeling, baring her breast for the victor to strike, but in reality to captivate him, and he turns away with an awkward gesture of loathing. None of these portraits seem very good, save the miniature, but that is an exquisite work, and with it, and the suggestions of the bust, it is easy to reconstruct the beauty of this terrible being. The type is that most admired by the late Renaissance, and, in some measure, immortalised by Jean Goujon* and the French. The face is a perfect oval, the forehead somewhat over-round, with minute curls, like a fleece, of bright auburn hair; the nose a trifle over-aquiline, and the cheek-bones a trifle too low; the eyes grey, large, prominent, beneath exquisitely curved brows and lids just a little too tight at the corners; the mouth also, brilliantly red and most delicately designed, is a little too tight, the lips strained a trifle over the teeth. Tight eyelids and tight lips give a strange refinement, and, at the same time, an air of mystery, a somewhat sinister seductiveness; they seem to take, but not to give. The mouth with a kind of childish pout, looks as if it could bite or suck like a leech. The complexion is dazzlingly fair, the perfect transparent roset lily of a red-haired beauty; the head, with hair elaborately curled and plaited close to it, and adorned with pearls, sits like that of the antique Arethusa* on a long, supple, swan-like neck. A curious, at first rather conventional, artificial-looking sort of beauty, voluptuous yet cold, which, the more it is contemplated, the more it troubles and haunts the mind. Round the lady's neck is a gold chain with little gold lozenges at intervals, on which is engraved the posy* or pun (the fashion of French devices is common in those days), "Amour Dure—Dure Amour." The same posy is inscribed in the hollow of the bust, and, thanks to it, I have been able to identify the latter as Medea's portrait. I often examine these tragic portraits, wondering what this face, which led so many men to their death, may have been like when it spoke or smiled, what at the moment when Medea da Carpi fascinated her victims into love unto death—"Amour Dure—Dure Amour," as runs her device—love that lasts, cruel love—yes indeed, when one thinks of the fidelity and fate of her lovers.

Oct. 13th.—I have literally not had time to write a line of my diary all these days. My whole mornings have gone in those Archives, my afternoons taking long walks in this lovely autumn weather (the highest hills are just tipped with snow). My evenings go in writing that confounded account of the Palace of Urbania which Government requires, merely to keep me at work at something useless. Of my history I have not yet been able to write a word. . . . By the way, I must note down a curious circumstance mentioned in an anonymous MS. life of Duke Robert, which I fell upon to-day. When this prince had the equestrian statue of himself by Antonio Tassi, Gianbologna's pupil,* erected in the square of the *Corte*, he secretly caused to be made, says my anonymous MS., a silver statuette of his familiar genius or angel—"familiaris ejus angelus seu genius, quod a vulgo dicitur *idolino*"—which statuette or idol, after having been consecrated by the astrologers—"at astrologis quibusdam ritibus sacrato"*—was placed in the cavity of the chest of the effigy by Tassi, in order, says the MS., that his soul might rest until the general Resurrection. This passage is curious, and to me somewhat puzzling; how could the soul of Duke Robert await the general Resurrection, when, as a Catholic, he ought to have believed that it must, as soon as separated from his body, go to Purgatory? Or is there some semi-pagan superstition of the Renaissance (most strange, certainly, in a man who had been a Cardinal) connecting the soul with a guardian genius, who could be compelled, by magic rites ("ab astrologis sacrato," the MS. says of the little idol), to remain fixed to earth, so that the soul should sleep in the body until the Day of Judgment? I confess this story baffles me. I wonder whether such an idol ever existed, or exists nowadays, in the body of Tassi's bronze effigy?

Oct. 20th.—I have been seeing a good deal of late of the Vice-Prefect's son: an amiable young man with a love-sick face and a languid interest in Urbanian history and archæology, of which he is profoundly ignorant. This young man, who has lived at Siena and Lucca* before his father was promoted here, wears extremely long and tight trousers, which almost preclude his bending his knees, a stick-up collar and an eyeglass, and a pair of fresh kid gloves stuck in the breast of his coat, speaks of Urbania as Ovid might have spoken of Pontus,* and complains (as well he may) of the barbarism of the young men, the officials who dine at my inn and howl and sing like madmen, and the nobles who drive gigs, showing almost as much throat as a lady at a ball. This person frequently entertains me with his *amori*,* past, present, and future; he evidently thinks me very odd for having none to entertain him with in return; he points out to me the pretty (or ugly) servant-girls and dressmakers as we walk in the street, sighs deeply or sings in falsetto behind every tolerably young-looking woman, and has finally taken me to the house of the lady of his heart, a great black-moustachioed countess, with a voice like a fish-crier; here, he says, I shall meet all the best company in Urbania and some beautiful women—ah, too beautiful, alas! I find three huge half-furnished rooms, with bare brick floors, petroleum lamps, and horribly bad pictures on bright wash ball-blue and gamboge walls,* and in the midst of it all, every evening, a dozen ladies and gentlemen seated in a circle, vociferating at each other the same news a year old; the younger ladies in bright yellows and greens, fanning themselves while my teeth chatter, and having sweet things whispered behind their fans by officers with hair brushed up like a hedgehog. And these are the women my friend expects me to fall in love with! I vainly wait for tea or supper which does not come, and rush home, determined to leave alone the Urbanian *beau monde*.*

It is quite true that I have no *amori*, although my friend does not believe it. When I came to Italy first, I looked out for romance; I sighed, like Goethe in Rome, for a window to open and a wondrous creature to appear, "welch mich versengend erquickt." Perhaps it is because Goethe was a German, accustomed to German *Fraus*, and I am, after all, a Pole, accustomed to something very different from *Fraus*;* but anyhow, for all my efforts, in Rome, Florence, and Siena, I never could find a woman to go mad about, either among the ladies, chattering bad French, or among the lower classes, as 'cute* and cold as money-lenders; so I steer clear of Italian womankind, its shrill voice and gaudy toilettes. I am wedded to history, to the Past, to women like Lucrezia Borgia, Vittoria Accoramboni,* or that Medea da Carpi, for the present; some day I shall perhaps find a grand passion, a woman to play the Don Quixote* about, like the Pole that I am; a woman out of whose slipper to drink, and for whose pleasure to die; but not here! Few things strike me so much as the degeneracy of Italian women. What has become of the race of Faustinas, Marozias, Bianca Cappellos?* Where discover nowadays (I confess she haunts me) another Medea da Carpi? Were it only possible to meet a woman of that extreme distinction of beauty, of that terribleness of nature, even if only potential, I do believe I could love her, even to the Day of Judgment, like any Oliverotto da Narni, or Frangipani or Prinzivalle.

Oct. 27th.—Fine sentiments the above are for a professor, a learned man! I thought the young artists of Rome childish because they played practical jokes and yelled at night in the streets, returning from the Caffé Greco or the cellar in the Via Palombella;* but am I not as childish to the full—I, melancholy wretch, whom they called Hamlet and the Knight of the Doleful Countenance?*

Nov. 5th.—I can't free myself from the thought of this Medea da Carpi. In my walks, my mornings in the Archives, my solitary evenings, I catch myself thinking over the woman. Am I turning novelist instead of historian? And still it seems to me that I understand her so well; so much better than my facts warrant. First, we must put aside all pedantic modern ideas of right and wrong. Right and wrong in a century of violence and treachery does not exist, least of all for creatures like Medea. Go preach right and wrong to a tigress, my dear sir! Yet is there in the world anything nobler than the huge creature, steel when she springs, velvet when she treads, as she stretches her supple body, or smooths her beautiful skin, or fastens her strong claws into her victim?

Yes; I can understand Medea. Fancy a woman of superlative beauty, of the highest courage and calmness, a woman of many resources, of genius, brought up by a petty princelet of a father, upon Tacitus and Sallust, and the tales of the great Malatestas, of Cæsar Borgia* and such-like!—a woman whose one passion is conquest and empire—fancy her, on the eve of being wedded to a man of the power of the Duke of Stimigliano, claimed, carried off by a small fry of a Pico, locked up in his hereditary brigand's castle, and having to receive the young fool's red-hot love as an honour and a necessity! The mere thought of any violence to such a nature is an abominable outrage; and if Pico chooses to embrace such a woman at the risk of meeting a sharp piece of steel in her arms, why, it is a fair bargain. Young hound—or, if you prefer, young hero—to think to treat a woman like this as if she were any village wench! Medea marries her Orsini. A marriage, let it be noted, between an old soldier of fifty and a girl of sixteen. Reflect what that means: it means that this imperious woman is soon treated like a chattel, made roughly to understand that her business is to give the Duke an heir, not advice; that she must never ask "wherefore this or that?" that she must courtesy before the Duke's counsellors, his captains, his mistresses; that, at the least suspicion of rebelliousness, she is subject to his foul words and blows; at the least suspicion of infidelity, to be strangled or starved to death, or thrown down an oubliette.* Suppose that she know that her husband has taken it into his head that she has looked too hard at this man or that, that one of his lieutenants or one of his women have whispered that, after all, the boy Bartolommeo might as soon be a Pico as an Orsini. Suppose she know that she must strike or be struck? Why, she strikes, or gets some one to strike for her. At what price? A promise of love, of love to a groom, the son of a serf! Why, the dog must be mad or drunk to believe such a thing possible; his very belief in anything so monstrous makes him worthy of death. And then he dares to blab! This is much worse than Pico. Medea is bound to defend her honour a second time; if she could stab Pico, she can certainly stab this fellow, or have him stabbed.

Hounded by her husband's kinsmen, she takes refuge at Urbania. The Duke, like every other man, falls wildly in love with Medea, and neglects his wife; let us even go so far as to say, breaks his wife's heart. Is this Medea's fault? Is it her fault that every stone that comes beneath her chariot-wheels is crushed? Certainly not. Do you suppose that a woman like Medea feels the smallest ill-will against a poor, craven Duchess Maddalena? Why, she ignores her very existence. To suppose Medea a cruel woman is as grotesque as to call her an immoral woman. Her fate is, sooner or later, to triumph over her enemies, at all events to make their victory almost a defeat; her magic faculty is to enslave all the men who come across her path; all those who see her, love her, become her slaves; and it is the destiny of all her slaves to perish. Her lovers, with the exception of Duke Guidalfonso, all come to an untimely end; and in this there is nothing unjust. The possession of a woman like Medea is a happiness too great for a mortal man; it would turn his head, make him forget even what he owed her; no man must survive long who conceives himself to have a right over her; it is a kind of sacrilege. And only death, the willingness to pay for such happiness by death, can at all make a man worthy of being her lover; he must be willing to love and suffer and die. This is the meaning of her device—"Amour Dure—Dure Amour." The love of Medea da Carpi cannot fade, but the lover can die; it is a constant and a cruel love.

Nov. 11th.—I was right, quite right in my idea. I have found—Oh, joy! I treated the Vice-Prefect's son to a dinner of five courses at the Trattoria La Stella d'Italia* out of sheer jubilation—I have found in the Archives, unknown, of course, to the Director, a heap of letters—letters of Duke Robert about Medea da Carpi, letters of Medea herself! Yes, Medea's own handwriting—a round, scholarly character, full of abbreviations, with a Greek look about it, as befits a learned princess who could read Plato as well as Petrarch.* The letters are of little importance, mere drafts of business letters for her secretary to copy, during the time that she governed the poor weak Guidalfonso. But they are her letters, and I can imagine almost that there hangs about these mouldering pieces of paper a scent as of a woman's hair.

The few letters of Duke Robert show him in a new light. A cunning, cold, but craven priest. He trembles at the bare thought of Medea—"la pessima Medea"—worse than her namesake of Colchis,* as he calls her. His long clemency is a result of mere fear of laying violent hands upon her. He fears her as something almost supernatural; he would have enjoyed having had her burnt as a witch. After letter on letter, telling his crony, Cardinal Sanseverino, at Rome his various precautions during her lifetime—how he wears a jacket of mail under his coat; how he drinks only milk from a cow which he has milked in his presence; how he tries his dog with morsels of his food, lest it be poisoned; how he suspects the wax-candles because of their peculiar smell; how he fears riding out lest some one should frighten his horse and cause him to break his neck—after all this, and when Medea has been in her grave two years, he tells his correspondent of his fear of meeting the soul of Medea after his own death, and chuckles over the ingenious device (concocted by his astrologer and a certain Fra Gaudenzio, a Capuchin*) by which he shall secure the absolute peace of his soul until that of the wicked Medea be finally "chained up in hell among the lakes of boiling pitch and the ice of Caina described by the immortal bard"*—old pedant! Here, then, is the explanation of that silver image—*quod vulgo dicitur idolino*—which he caused to be soldered into his effigy by Tassi. As long as the image of his soul was attached to the image of his body, he should sleep awaiting the Day of Judgment, fully convinced that Medea's soul will then be properly tarred and feathered, while his—honest man!—will fly straight to Paradise. And to think that, two weeks ago, I believed this man to be a hero! Aha! my good Duke Robert, you shall be shown up in my history; and no amount of silver idolinos shall save you from being heartily laughed at!

Nov. 15th.—Strange! That idiot of a Prefect's son, who has heard me talk a hundred times of Medea da Carpi, suddenly recollects that, when he was a child at Urbania, his nurse used to threaten him with a visit from Madonna Medea, who rode in the sky on a black he-goat. My Duchess Medea turned into a bogey for naughty little boys!

Nov. 20th.—I have been going about with a Bavarian Professor of mediæval history, showing him all over the country. Among other places we went to Rocca Sant' Elmo, to see the former villa of the Dukes of Urbania, the villa where Medea was confined between the accession of Duke Robert and the conspiracy of Marcantonio Frangipani, which caused her removal to the nunnery immediately outside the town. A long ride up the desolate Apennine valleys, bleak beyond words just now with their thin fringe of oak scrub turned russet, thin patches of grass sered by the frost, the last few yellow leaves of the poplars by the torrents shaking and fluttering about in the chill Tramontana;* the mountain-tops are wrapped in thick grey cloud; to-morrow, if the wind continues, we shall see them round masses of snow against the cold blue sky. Sant' Elmo is a wretched hamlet high on the Apennine ridge, where the Italian vegetation is already replaced by that of the North. You ride for miles through leafless chestnut woods, the scent of the soaking brown leaves filling the air, the roar of the torrent, turbid with autumn rains, rising from the precipice below; then suddenly the leafless chestnut woods are replaced, as at Vallombrosa,* by a belt of black, dense fir plantations. Emerging from these, you come to an open space, frozen blasted meadows, the rocks of snow clad peak, the newly fallen snow, close above you; and in the midst, on a knoll, with a gnarled larch on either side, the ducal villa of Sant' Elmo, a big black stone box with a stone escutcheon, grated windows, and a double flight of steps in front. It is now let out to the proprietor of the neighbouring woods, who uses it for the storage of chestnuts, faggots, and charcoal from the neighbouring ovens. We tied our horses to the iron rings and entered: an old woman, with dishevelled hair, was alone in the house. The villa is a mere hunting-lodge, built by Ottobuono IV., the father of Dukes Guidalfonso and Robert, about 1530. Some of the rooms have at one time been frescoed and panelled with oak carvings, but all this has disappeared. Only, in one of the big rooms, there remains a large marble fireplace, similar to those in the palace at Urbania, beautifully carved with Cupids on a blue ground; a charming naked boy sustains a jar on either side, one containing clove pinks, the other roses. The room was filled with stacks of faggots.

We returned home late, my companion in excessively bad humour at the fruitlessness of the expedition. We were caught in the skirt of a snowstorm as we got into the chestnut woods. The sight of the snow falling gently, of the earth and bushes whitened all round, made me feel back at Posen, once more a child. I sang and shouted, to my companion's horror. This will be a bad point against me if reported at Berlin. A historian of twenty-four who shouts and sings, and that when another historian is cursing at the snow and the bad roads! All night I lay awake watching the embers of my wood fire, and thinking of Medea da Carpi mewed up,* in winter, in that solitude of Sant' Elmo, the firs groaning, the torrent roaring, the snow falling all round; miles and miles away from human creatures. I fancied I saw it all, and that I, somehow, was Marcantonio Frangipani come to liberate her—or was it Prinzivalle degli Ordelaffi? I suppose it was because of the long ride, the unaccustomed pricking feeling of the snow in the air; or perhaps the punch which my professor insisted on drinking after dinner.

Nov. 23rd.—Thank goodness, that Bavarian professor has finally departed! Those days he spent here drove me nearly crazy. Talking over my work, I told him one day my views on Medea da Carpi; whereupon he condescended to answer that those were the usual tales due to the mythopœic (old idiot!) tendency of the Renaissance; that research would disprove the greater part of them, as it had disproved the stories current about the Borgias, &c.; that, moreover, such a woman as I made out was psychologically and physiologically impossible. Would that one could say as much of such professors as he and his fellows!

Nov. 24th.—I cannot get over my pleasure in being rid of that imbecile; I felt as if I could have throttled him every time he spoke of the Lady of my thoughts—for such she has become—*Metea*, as the animal called her!

Nov. 30th.—I feel quite shaken at what has just happened; I am beginning to fear that that old pedant was right in saying that it was bad for me to live all alone in a strange country, that it would make me morbid. It is ridiculous that I should be put into such a state of excitement merely by the chance discovery of a portrait of a woman dead these three hundred years. With the case of my uncle Ladislas, and other suspicions of insanity in my family, I ought really to guard against such foolish excitement.

Yet the incident was really dramatic, uncanny. I could have sworn that I knew every picture in the palace here; and particularly every picture of Her. Anyhow, this morning, as I was leaving the Archives, I passed through one of the many small rooms—irregular-shaped closets—which fill up the ins and outs of this curious palace, turreted like a French château. I must have passed through that closet before, for the view was so familiar out of its window; just the particular bit of round tower in front, the cypress on the other side of the ravine, the belfry beyond, and the piece of the line of Monte Sant' Agata and the Leonessa, covered with snow, against the sky. I suppose there must be twin rooms, and that I had got into the wrong one; or rather, perhaps some shutter had been opened or curtain withdrawn. As I was passing, my eye was caught by a very beautiful old mirror-frame let into the brown and yellow inlaid wall. I approached, and looking at the frame, looked also, mechanically, into the glass. I gave a great start, and almost shrieked, I do believe—(it's lucky the Munich professor is safe out of Urbania!). Behind my own image stood another, a figure close to my shoulder, a face close to mine; and that figure, that face, hers! Medea da Carpi's! I turned sharp round, as white, I think, as the ghost I expected to see. On the wall opposite the mirror, just a pace or two behind where I had been standing, hung a portrait. And such a portrait!—Bronzino* never painted a grander one. Against a background of harsh, dark blue, there stands out the figure of the Duchess (for it is Medea, the real Medea, a thousand times more real, individual, and powerful than in the other portraits), seated stiffly in a high-backed chair, sustained, as it were, almost rigid, by the stiff brocade of skirts and stomacher,* stiffer for plaques of embroidered silver flowers and rows of seed pearl. The dress is, with its mixture of silver and pearl, of a strange dull red, a wicked poppy-juice colour, against which the flesh of the long, narrow hands with fringe-like fingers; of the long slender neck, and the face with bared forehead, looks white and hard, like alabaster. The face is the same as in the other portraits: the same rounded forehead, with the short fleece-like, yellowish-red curls; the same beautifully curved eyebrows, just barely marked; the same eyelids, a little tight across the eyes; the same lips, a little tight across the mouth; but with a purity of line, a dazzling splendour of skin, and intensity of look immeasurably superior to all the other portraits.

She looks out of the frame with a cold, level glance; yet the lips smile. One hand holds a dull-red rose; the other, long, narrow, tapering, plays with a thick rope of silk and gold and jewels hanging from the waist; round the throat, white as marble, partially confined in the tight dull-red bodice, hangs a gold collar, with the device on alternate enamelled medallions, "AMOUR DURE—DURE AMOUR."

On reflection, I see that I simply could never have been in that room or closet before; I must have mistaken the door. But, although the explanation is so simple, I still, after several hours, feel terribly shaken in all my being. If I grow so excitable I shall have to go to Rome at Christmas for a holiday. I feel as if some danger pursued me here (can it be fever?); and yet, and yet, I don't see how I shall ever tear myself away.

Dec. 10th.—I have made an effort, and accepted the Vice-Prefect's son's invitation to see the oil-making at a villa of theirs near the coast.

The villa, or farm, is an old fortified, towered place, standing on a hillside among olive-trees and little osier-bushes, which look like a bright orange flame. The olives are squeezed in a tremendous black cellar, like a prison: you see, by the faint white daylight, and the smoky yellow flare of resin burning in pans, great white bullocks moving round a huge millstone; vague figures working at pulleys and handles: it looks, to my fancy, like some scene of the Inquisition.* The Cavaliere regaled me with his best wine and rusks.* I took some long walks by the seaside; I had left Urbania wrapped in snow-clouds; down on the coast there was a bright sun; the sunshine, the sea, the bustle of the little port on the Adriatic seemed to do me good. I came back to Urbania another man. Sor Asdrubale, my landlord, poking about in slippers among the gilded chests, the Empire sofas, the old cups and saucers and pictures which no one will buy, congratulated me upon the improvement in my looks. "You work too much," he says; "youth requires amusement, theatres, promenades, *amori*—it is time enough to be serious when one is bald"—and he took off his greasy red cap. Yes, I am better! and, as a result, I take to my work with delight again. I will cut them out still, those wiseacres at Berlin!

Dec. 14th.—I don't think I have ever felt so happy about my work. I see it all so well—that crafty, cowardly Duke Robert; that melancholy Duchess Maddalena; that weak, showy, would-be chivalrous Duke Guidalfonso; and above all, the splendid figure of Medea. I feel as if I were the greatest historian of the age; and, at the same time, as if I were a boy of twelve. It snowed yesterday for the first time in the city, for two good hours. When it had done, I actually went into the square and taught the ragamuffins to make a snow-man; no, a snow-woman; and I had the fancy to call her Medea. "La pessima Medea!" cried one of the boys—"the one who used to ride through the air on a goat?" "No, no," I said; "she was a beautiful lady, the Duchess of Urbania, the most beautiful woman that ever lived." I made her a crown of tinsel, and taught the boys to cry "Evviva, Medea!"* But one of them said, "She is a witch! She must be burnt!" At which they all rushed to fetch burning faggots and tow; in a minute the yelling demons had melted her down.

Dec. 15th.—What a goose I am, and to think I am twenty-four, and known in literature! In my long walks I have composed to a tune (I don't know what it is) which all the people are singing and whistling in the street at present, a poem in frightful Italian, beginning "Medea, mia dea," calling on her in the name of her various lovers. I go about humming between my teeth, "Why am I not Marcantonio? or Prinzivalle? or he of Narni? or the good Duke Alfonso? that I might be beloved by thee, Medea, mia dea," &c. &c. Awful rubbish! My landlord, I think, suspects that Medea must be some lady I met while I was staying by the seaside. I am sure Sora Serafina, Sora Lodovica, and Sora Adalgisa—the three Parcæ or *Norns*,* as I call them—have some such notion. This afternoon, at dusk, while tidying my room, Sora Lodovica said to me, "How beautifully the Signorino has taken to singing!" I was scarcely aware that I had been vociferating, "Vieni, Medea, mia dea," while the old lady bobbed about making up my fire. I stopped; a nice reputation I shall get! I thought, and all this will somehow get to Rome, and thence to Berlin. Sora Lodovica was leaning out of the window, pulling in the iron hook of the shrine-lamp which marks Sor Asdrubale's house. As she was trimming the lamp previous to swinging it out again, she said in her odd, prudish little way, "You are wrong to stop singing, my son" (she varies between calling me Signor Professore and such terms of affection as "Nino," "Viscere mie,"* &c.); "you are wrong to stop singing, for there is a young lady there in the street who has actually stopped to listen to you."

I ran to the window. A woman, wrapped in a black shawl, was standing in an archway, looking up to the window.

"Eh, eh! the Signor Professore has admirers," said Sora Lodovica.

"Medea, mia dea!" I burst out as loud as I could, with a boy's pleasure in disconcerting the inquisitive passer-by. She turned suddenly round to go away, waving her hand at me; at that moment Sora Lodovica swung the shrine-lamp back into its place. A stream of light fell across the street. I felt myself grow quite cold; the face of the woman outside was that of Medea da Carpi!

What a fool I am, to be sure!

PART II.

Dec. 17th.—I fear that my craze about Medea da Carpi has become well known, thanks to my silly talk and idiotic songs. That Vice-Prefect's son—or the assistant at the Archives, or perhaps some of the company at the Contessa's, is trying to play me a trick! But take care, my good ladies and gentlemen, I shall pay you out in your own coin! Imagine my feelings when, this morning, I found on my desk a folded letter addressed to me in a curious handwriting which seemed strangely familiar to me, and which, after a moment, I recognised as that of the letters of Medea da Carpi at the Archives. It gave me a horrible shock. My next idea was that it must be a present from some one who knew my interest in Medea—a genuine letter of hers on which some idiot had written my address instead of putting it into an envelope. But it was addressed to me, written to me, no old letter; merely four lines, which ran as follows:—

"To Spiridion.—A person who knows the interest you bear her will be at the Church of San Giovanni Decollato* this evening at nine. Look out, in the left aisle, for a lady wearing a black mantle, and holding a rose."

By this time I understood that I was the object of a conspiracy, the victim of a hoax. I turned the letter round and round. It was written on paper such as was made in the sixteenth century, and in an extraordinarily precise imitation of Medea da Carpi's characters. Who had written it? I thought over all the possible people. On the whole, it must be the Vice-Prefect's son, perhaps in combination with his lady-love, the Countess. They must have torn a blank page off some old letter; but that either of them should have had the ingenuity of inventing such a hoax, or the power of committing such a forgery, astounds me beyond measure. There is more in these people than I should have guessed. How pay them off? By taking no notice of the letter? Dignified, but dull. No, I will go; perhaps some one will be there, and I will mystify them in their turn. Or, if no one is there, how I shall crow over them for their imperfectly carried out plot! Perhaps this is some folly of the Cavalier Muzio's to bring me into the presence of some lady whom he destines to be the flame of my future *amori*. That is likely enough. And it would be too idiotic and professorial to refuse such an invitation; the lady must be worth knowing who can forge sixteenth-century letters like this, for I am sure that languid swell Muzio never could. I will go! By Heaven! I'll pay them back in their own coin! It is now five—how long these days are!

Dec. 18th.—Am I mad? Or are there really ghosts? That adventure of last night has shaken me to the very depth of my soul.

I went at nine, as the mysterious letter had bid me. It was bitterly cold, and the air full of fog and sleet; not a shop open, not a window unshuttered, not a creature visible; the narrow black streets, precipitous between their high walls and under their lofty archways, were only the blacker for the dull light of an oil-lamp here and there, with its flickering yellow reflection on the wet flags. San Giovanni Decollato is a little church, or rather oratory,* which I have always hitherto seen shut up (as so many churches here are shut up except on great festivals); and situate behind the ducal palace, on a sharp ascent, and forming the bifurcation of two steep paved lanes. I have passed by the place a hundred times, and scarcely noticed the little church, except for the marble high relief over the door, showing the grizzly head of the Baptist in the charger, and for the iron cage close by, in which were formerly exposed the heads of criminals; the decapitated, or, as they call him here, decollated, John the Baptist, being apparently the patron of axe and block.

A few strides took me from my lodgings to San Giovanni Decollato. I confess I was excited; one is not twenty-four and a Pole for nothing. On getting to the kind of little platform at the bifurcation of the two precipitous streets, I found, to my surprise, that the windows of the church or oratory were not lighted, and that the door was locked! So this was the precious joke that had been played upon me; to send me on a bitter cold, sleety night, to a church which was shut up and had perhaps been shut up for years! I don't know what I couldn't have done in that moment of rage; I felt inclined to break open the church door, or to go and pull the Vice-Prefect's son out of bed (for I felt sure that the joke was his). I determined upon the latter course; and was walking towards his door, along the black alley to the left of the church, when I was suddenly stopped by the sound as of an organ close by; an organ, yes, quite plainly, and the voice of choristers and the drone of a litany. So the church was not shut, after all! I retraced my steps to the top of the lane. All was dark and in complete silence. Suddenly there came again a faint gust of organ and voices. I listened; it clearly came from the other lane, the one on the right-hand side. Was there, perhaps, another door there? I passed beneath the archway, and descended a little way in the direction whence the sounds seemed to come. But no door, no light, only the black walls, the black wet flags, with their faint yellow reflections of flickering oil-lamps; moreover, complete silence. I stopped a minute, and then the chant rose again; this time it seemed to me most certainly from the lane I had just left. I went back—nothing. Thus backwards and forwards, the sounds always beckoning, as it were, one way, only to beckon me back, vainly, to the other.

At last I lost patience; and I felt a sort of creeping terror, which only a violent action could dispel. If the mysterious sounds came neither from the street to the right, nor from the street to the left, they could come only from the church. Half-maddened, I rushed up the two or three steps, and prepared to wrench the door open with a tremendous effort. To my amazement, it opened with the greatest ease. I entered, and the sounds of the litany met me louder than before, as I paused a moment between the outer door and the heavy leathern curtain. I raised the latter and crept in. The altar was brilliantly illuminated with tapers and garlands of chandeliers; this was evidently some evening service connected with Christmas. The nave and aisles were comparatively dark, and about half-full. I elbowed my way along the right aisle towards the altar. When my eyes had got accustomed to the unexpected light, I began to look round me, and with a beating heart. The idea that all this was a hoax, that I should meet merely some acquaintance of my friend the Cavaliere's, had somehow departed: I looked about. The people were all wrapped up, the men in big cloaks, the women in woollen veils and mantles. The body of the church was comparatively dark, and I could not make out anything very clearly, but it seemed to me, somehow, as if, under the cloaks and veils, these people were dressed in a rather extraordinary fashion. The man in front of me, I remarked, showed yellow stockings beneath his cloak; a woman, hard by, a red bodice, laced behind with gold tags. Could these be peasants from some remote part come for the Christmas festivities, or did the inhabitants of Urbania don some old-fashioned garb in honour of Christmas?

As I was wondering, my eye suddenly caught that of a woman standing in the opposite aisle, close to the altar, and in the full blaze of its lights. She was wrapped in black, but held, in a very conspicuous way, a red rose, an unknown luxury at this time of the year in a place like Urbania. She evidently saw me, and turning even more fully into the light, she loosened her heavy black cloak, displaying a dress of deep red, with gleams of silver and gold embroideries; she turned her face towards me; the full blaze of the chandeliers and tapers fell upon it. It was the face of Medea da Carpi! I dashed across the nave, pushing people roughly aside, or rather, it seemed to me, passing through impalpable bodies. But the lady turned and walked rapidly down the aisle towards the door. I followed close upon her, but somehow I could not get up with her. Once, at the curtain, she turned round again. She was within a few paces of me. Yes, it was Medea. Medea herself, no mistake, no delusion, no sham; the oval face, the lips tightened over the mouth, the eyelids tight over the corner of the eyes, the exquisite alabaster complexion! She raised the curtain and glided out. I followed; the curtain alone separated me from her. I saw the wooden door swing to behind her. One step ahead of me! I tore open the door; she must be on the steps, within reach of my arm!

I stood outside the church. All was empty, merely the wet pavement and the yellow reflections in the pools: a sudden cold seized me; I could not go on. I tried to re-enter the church; it was shut. I rushed home, my hair standing on end, and trembling in all my limbs, and remained for an hour like a maniac. Is it a delusion? Am I too going mad? O God, God! am I going mad?

Dec. 19th.—A brilliant, sunny day; all the black snow-slush has disappeared out of the town, off the bushes and trees. The snow-clad mountains sparkle against the bright blue sky. A Sunday, and Sunday weather; all the bells are ringing for the approach of Christmas. They are preparing for a kind of fair in the square with the colonnade, putting up booths filled with coloured cotton and woollen ware, bright shawls and kerchiefs, mirrors, ribbons, brilliant pewter lamps; the whole turn-out of the pedlar in "Winter's Tale."* The pork-shops are all garlanded with green and with paper flowers, the hams and cheeses stuck full of little flags and green twigs. I strolled out to see the cattle-fair outside the gate; a forest of interlacing horns, an ocean of lowing and stamping: hundreds of immense white bullocks, with horns a yard long and red tassels, packed close together on the little piazza d'armi under the city walls. Bah! why do I write this trash? What's the use of it all? While I am forcing myself to write about bells, and Christmas festivities, and cattle-fairs, one idea goes on like a bell within me: Medea, Medea! Have I really seen her, or am I mad?

Two hours later.—That Church of San Giovanni Decollato—so my landlord informs me—has not been made use of within the memory of man. Could it have been all a hallucination or a dream—perhaps a dream dreamed that night? I have been out again to look at that church. There it is, at the bifurcation of the two steep lanes, with its bas-relief of the Baptist's head over the door. The door does look as if it had not been opened for years. I can see the cobwebs in the window-panes; it does look as if, as Sor Asdrubale says, only rats and spiders congregated within it. And yet—and yet; I have so clear a remembrance, so distinct a consciousness of it all. There was a picture of the daughter of Herodias* dancing, upon the altar; I remember her white turban with a scarlet tuft of feathers, and Herod's blue caftan; I remember the shape of the central chandelier; it swung round slowly, and one of the wax lights had got bent almost in two by the heat and draught.

Things, all these, which I may have seen elsewhere, stored unawares in my brain, and which may have come out, somehow, in a dream; I have heard physiologists allude to such things. I will go again: if the church be shut, why then it must have been a dream, a vision, the result of over-excitement. I must leave at once for Rome and see doctors, for I am afraid of going mad. If, on the other hand—pshaw! there *is no other hand* in such a case. Yet if there were—why then, I should really have seen Medea; I might see her again; speak to her. The mere thought sets my blood in a whirl, not with horror, but with . . . I know not what to call it. The feeling terrifies me, but it is delicious. Idiot! There is some little coil of my brain, the twentieth of a hair's-breadth out of order—that's all!

Dec. 20th.—I have been again; I have heard the music; I have been inside the church; I have seen Her! I can no longer doubt my senses. Why should I? Those pedants say that the dead are dead, the past is past. For them, yes; but why for me?—why for a man who loves, who is consumed with the love of a woman?—a woman who, indeed—yes, let me finish the sentence. Why should there not be ghosts to such as can see them? Why should she not return to the earth, if she knows that it contains a man who thinks of, desires, only her?

A hallucination? Why, I saw her, as I see this paper that I write upon; standing there, in the full blaze of the altar. Why, I heard the rustle of her skirts, I smelt the scent of her hair, I raised the curtain which was shaking from her touch. Again I missed her. But this time, as I rushed out into the empty moonlit street, I found upon the church steps a rose—the rose which I had seen in her hand the moment before—I felt it, smelt it; a rose, a real, living rose, dark red and only just plucked. I put it into water when I returned, after having kissed it, who knows how many times? I placed it on the top of the cupboard; I determined not to look at it for twenty-four hours lest it should be a delusion. But I must see it again; I must. . . . Good Heavens! this is horrible, horrible; if I had found a skeleton it could not have been worse! The rose, which last night seemed freshly plucked, full of colour and perfume, is brown, dry—a thing kept for centuries between the leaves of a book—it has crumbled into dust between my fingers. Horrible, horrible! But why so, pray? Did I not know that I was in love with a woman dead three hundred years? If I wanted fresh roses which bloomed yesterday, the Countess Fiammetta or any little sempstress in Urbania might have given them me. What if the rose has fallen to dust? If only I could hold Medea in my arms as I held it in my fingers, kiss her lips as I kissed its petals, should I not be satisfied if she too were to fall to dust the next moment, if I were to fall to dust myself?

Dec. 22nd, Eleven at night.—I have seen her once more!—almost spoken to her. I have been promised her love! Ah, Spiridion! you were right when you felt that you were not made for any earthly *amori*. At the usual hour I betook myself this evening to San Giovanni Decollato. A bright winter night; the high houses and belfries standing out against a deep blue heaven luminous, shimmering like steel with myriads of stars; the moon has not yet risen. There was no light in the windows; but, after a little effort, the door opened and I entered the church, the altar, as usual, brilliantly illuminated. It struck me suddenly that all this crowd of men and women standing all round, these priests chanting and moving about the altar, were dead—that they did not exist for any man save me. I touched, as if by accident, the hand of my neighbour; it was cold, like wet clay. He turned round, but did not seem to see me: his face was ashy, and his eyes staring, fixed, like those of a blind man or a corpse. I felt as if I must rush out. But at that moment my eye fell upon Her, standing as usual by the altar steps, wrapped in a black mantle, in the full blaze of the lights. She turned round; the light fell straight upon her face, the face with the delicate features, the eyelids and lips a little tight, the alabaster skin faintly tinged with pale pink. Our eyes met.

I pushed my way across the nave towards where she stood by the altar steps; she turned quickly down the aisle, and I after her. Once or twice she lingered, and I thought I should overtake her; but again, when, not a second after the door had closed upon her, I stepped out into the street, she had vanished. On the church step lay something white. It was not a flower this time, but a letter. I rushed back to the church to read it; but the church was fast shut, as if it had not been opened for years. I could not see by the flickering shrine-lamps—I rushed home, lit my lamp, pulled the letter from my breast. I have it before me. The handwriting is hers; the same as in the Archives, the same as in that first letter:—

"To Spiridion.—Let thy courage be equal to thy love, and thy love shall be rewarded. On the night preceding Christmas, take a hatchet and saw; cut boldly into the body of the bronze rider who stands in the Corte, on the left side, near the waist. Saw open the body, and within it thou wilt find the silver effigy of a winged genius. Take it out, hack it into a hundred pieces, and fling them in all directions, so that the winds may sweep them away. That night she whom thou lovest will come to reward thy fidelity."

On the brownish wax is the device—

"Amour Dure—Dure Amour."

Dec. 23rd.—So it is true! I was reserved for something wonderful in this world. I have at last found that after which my soul has been straining. Ambition, love of art, love of Italy, these things which have occupied my spirit, and have yet left me continually unsatisfied, these were none of them my real destiny. I have sought for life, thirsting for it as a man in the desert thirsts for a well; but the life of the senses of other youths, the life of the intellect of other men, have never slaked that thirst. Shall life for me mean the love of a dead woman? We smile at what we choose to call the superstition of the past, forgetting that all our vaunted science of to-day may seem just such another superstition to the men of the future; but why should the present be right and the past wrong? The men who painted the pictures and built the palaces of three hundred years ago were certainly of as delicate fibre, of as keen reason, as ourselves, who merely print calico and build locomotives. What makes me think this, is that I have been calculating my nativity by help of an old book belonging to Sor Asdrubale—and see, my horoscope tallies almost exactly with that of Medea da Carpi, as given by a chronicler. May this explain? No, no; all is explained by the fact that the first time I read of this woman's career, the first time I saw her portrait, I loved her, though I hid my love to myself in the garb of historical interest. Historical interest indeed!

I have got the hatchet and the saw. I bought the saw of a poor joiner, in a village some miles off; he did not understand at first what I meant, and I think he thought me mad; perhaps I am. But if madness means the happiness of one's life, what of it? The hatchet I saw lying in a timber-yard, where they prepare the great trunks of the fir-trees which grow high on the Apennines of Sant' Elmo. There was no one in the yard, and I could not resist the temptation; I handled the thing, tried its edge, and stole it. This is the first time in my life that I have been a thief; why did I not go into a shop and buy a hatchet? I don't know; I seemed unable to resist the sight of the shining blade. What I am going to do is, I suppose, an act of vandalism; and certainly I have no right to spoil the property of this city of Urbania. But I wish no harm either to the statue or the city; if I could plaster up the bronze, I would do so willingly. But I must obey Her; I must avenge Her; I must get at that silver image which Robert of Montemurlo had made and consecrated in order that his cowardly soul might sleep in peace, and not encounter that of the being whom he dreaded most in the world. Aha! Duke Robert, you forced her to die unshriven, and you stuck the image of your soul into the image of your body, thinking thereby that, while she suffered the tortures of Hell, you would rest in peace, until your well-scoured little soul might fly straight up to Paradise;—you were afraid of Her when both of you should be dead, and thought yourself very clever to have prepared for all emergencies! Not so, Serene Highness. You too shall taste what it is to wander after death, and to meet the dead whom one has injured.

What an interminable day! But I shall see her again to-night.

Eleven o'clock.—No; the church was fast closed; the spell had ceased. Until to-morrow I shall not see her. But to-morrow! Ah, Medea! did any of thy lovers love thee as I do?

Twenty-four hours more till the moment of happiness—the moment for which I seem to have been waiting all my life. And after that, what next? Yes, I see it plainer every minute; after that, nothing more. All those who loved Medea da Carpi, who loved and who served her, died: Giovanfrancesco Pico, her first husband, whom she left stabbed in the castle from which she fled; Stimigliano, who died of poison; the groom who gave him the poison, cut down by her orders; Oliverotto da Narni, Marcantonio Frangipani, and that poor boy of the Ordelaffi, who had never even looked upon her face, and whose only reward was that handkerchief with which the hangman wiped the sweat off his face, when he was one mass of broken limbs and torn flesh: all had to die, and I shall die also.

The love of such a woman is enough, and is fatal—"Amour Dure," as her device says. I shall die also. But why not? Would it be possible to live in order to love another woman? Nay, would it be possible to drag on a life like this one after the happiness of to-morrow? Impossible; the others died, and I must die. I always felt that I should not live long; a gipsy in Poland told me once that I had in my hand the cut-line which signifies a violent death. I might have ended in a duel with some brother-student, or in a railway accident. No, no; my death will not be of that sort! Death—and is not she also dead? What strange vistas does such a thought not open! Then the others—Pico, the Groom, Stimigliano, Oliverotto, Frangipani, Prinzivalle degli Ordelaffi—will they all be *there?* But she shall love me best—me by whom she has been loved after she has been three hundred years in the grave!

Dec. 24th.—I have made all my arrangements. To-night at eleven I slip out; Sor Asdrubale and his sisters will be sound asleep. I have questioned them; their fear of rheumatism prevents their attending midnight mass. Luckily there are no churches between this and the Corte; whatever movement Christmas night may entail will be a good way off. The Vice-Prefect's rooms are on the other side of the palace; the rest of the square is taken up with state-rooms, archives, and empty stables and coach-houses of the palace. Besides, I shall be quick at my work.

I have tried my saw on a stout bronze vase I bought of Sor Asdrubale; and the bronze of the statue, hollow and worn away by rust (I have even noticed holes), cannot resist very much, especially after a blow with the sharp hatchet. I have put my papers in order, for the benefit of the Government which has sent me hither. I am sorry to have defrauded them of their "History of Urbania." To pass the endless day and calm the fever of impatience, I have just taken a long walk. This is the coldest day we have had. The bright sun does not warm in the least, but seems only to increase the impression of cold, to make the snow on the mountains glitter, the blue air to sparkle like steel. The few people who are out are muffled to the nose, and carry earthenware braziers beneath their cloaks; long icicles hang from the fountain with the figure of Mercury upon it; one can imagine the wolves trooping down through the dry scrub and beleaguering this town. Somehow this cold makes me feel wonderfully calm—it seems to bring back to me my boyhood.

As I walked up the rough, steep, paved alleys, slippery with frost, and with their vista of snow mountains against the sky, and passed by the church steps strewn with box and laurel, with the faint smell of incense coming out, there returned to me—I know not why—the recollection, almost the sensation, of those Christmas Eves long ago at Posen and Breslau,* when I walked as a child along the wide streets, peeping into the windows where they were beginning to light the tapers of the Christmas-trees, and wondering whether I too, on returning home, should be let into a wonderful room all blazing with lights and gilded nuts and glass beads. They are hanging the last strings of those blue and red metallic beads, fastening on the last gilded and silvered walnuts on the trees out there at home in the North; they are lighting the blue and red tapers; the wax is beginning to run on to the beautiful spruce green branches; the children are waiting with beating hearts behind the door, to be told that the Christ-Child has been. And I, for what am I waiting? I don't know; all seems a dream; everything vague and unsubstantial about me, as if time had ceased, nothing could happen, my own desires and hopes were all dead, myself absorbed into I know not what passive dreamland. Do I long for to-night? Do I dread it? Will to-night ever come? Do I feel anything, does anything exist all round me? I sit and seem to see that street at Posen, the wide street with the windows illuminated by the Christmas lights, the green fir-branches grazing the window-panes.

Christmas Eve, Midnight.—I have done it. I slipped out noiselessly. Sor Asdrubale and his sisters were fast asleep. I feared I had waked them, for my hatchet fell as I was passing through the principal room where my landlord keeps his curiosities for sale; it struck against some old armour which he has been piecing. I heard him exclaim, half in his sleep; and blew out my light and hid in the stairs. He came out in his dressing-gown, but finding no one, went back to bed again. "Some cat, no doubt!" he said. I closed the house door softly behind me. The sky had become stormy since the afternoon, luminous with the full moon, but strewn with grey and buff-coloured vapours; every now and then the moon disappeared entirely. Not a creature abroad; the tall gaunt houses staring in the moonlight.

I know not why, I took a roundabout way to the Corte, past one or two church doors, whence issued the faint flicker of midnight mass. For a moment I felt a temptation to enter one of them; but something seemed to restrain me. I caught snatches of the Christmas hymn. I felt myself beginning to be unnerved, and hastened towards the Corte. As I passed under the portico at San Francesco I heard steps behind me; it seemed to me that I was followed. I stopped to let the other pass.

As he approached his pace flagged; he passed close by me and murmured, "Do not go: I am Giovanfrancesco Pico." I turned round; he was gone. A coldness numbed me; but I hastened on.

Behind the cathedral apse, in a narrow lane, I saw a man leaning against a wall. The moonlight was full upon him; it seemed to me that his face, with a thin pointed beard, was streaming with blood. I quickened my pace; but as I grazed by him he whispered, "Do not obey her; return home: I am Marcantonio Frangipani." My teeth chattered, but I hurried along the narrow lane, with the moonlight blue upon the white walls.

At last I saw the Corte before me: the square was flooded with moonlight, the windows of the palace seemed brightly illuminated, and the statue of Duke Robert, shimmering green, seemed advancing towards me on its horse. I came into the shadow. I had to pass beneath an archway. There started a figure as if out of the wall, and barred my passage with his outstretched cloaked arm. I tried to pass. He seized me by the arm, and his grasp was like a weight of ice. "You shall not pass!" he cried, and, as the moon came out once more, I saw his face, ghastly white and bound with an embroidered kerchief; he seemed almost a child. "You shall not pass!" he cried; "you shall not have her! She is mine, and mine alone! I am Prinzivalle degli Ordelaffi." I felt his ice-cold clutch, but with my other arm I laid about me wildly with the hatchet which I carried beneath my cloak. The hatchet struck the wall and rang upon the stone. He had vanished.

I hurried on. I did it. I cut open the bronze; I sawed it into a wider gash. I tore out the silver image, and hacked it into innumerable pieces. As I scattered the last fragments about, the moon was suddenly veiled; a great wind arose, howling down the square; it seemed to me that the earth shook. I threw down the hatchet and the saw, and fled home. I felt pursued, as if by the tramp of hundreds of invisible horsemen.

Now I am calm. It is midnight; another moment and she will be here! Patience, my heart! I hear it beating loud. I trust that no one will accuse poor Sor Asdrubale. I will write a letter to the authorities to declare his innocence should anything happen. . . . One! the clock in the palace tower has just struck. . . . "I hereby certify that, should anything happen this night to me, Spiridion Trepka, no one but myself is to be held . . ." A step on the staircase! It is she! it is she! At last, Medea, Medea! Ah! AMOUR DURE—DURE AMOUR!

NOTE.—Here ends the diary of the late Spiridion Trepka. The chief newspapers of the province of Umbria informed the public that, on Christmas morning of the year 1885, the bronze equestrian statue of Robert II. had been found grievously mutilated; and that Professor Spiridion Trepka of Posen, in the German Empire, had been discovered dead of a stab in the region of the heart, given by an unknown hand.

DIONEA

FROM the Letters of Doctor Alessandro De Rosis to the Lady Evelyn Savelli, Princess of Sabina.*

MONTEMIRTO LIGURE,* *June* 29, 1873.

I TAKE immediate advantage of the generous offer of your Excellency (allow an old Republican* who has held you on his knees to address you by that title sometimes, 'tis so appropriate) to help our poor people. I never expected to come a-begging so soon. For the olive crop has been unusually plenteous. We semi-Genoese don't pick the olives unripe, like our Tuscan neighbours, but let them grow big and black, when the young fellows go into the trees with long reeds and shake them down on the grass for the women to collect—a pretty sight which your Excellency must see some day: the grey trees with the brown, barefoot lads craning, balanced in the branches, and the turquoise sea as background just beneath. . . . That sea of ours—it is all along of it that I wish to ask for money. Looking up from my desk, I see the sea through the window, deep below and beyond the olive woods, bluish-green in the sunshine and veined with violet under the cloud-bars, like one of your Ravenna mosaics spread out as pavement for the world: a wicked sea, wicked in its loveliness, wickeder than your grey northern ones, and from which must have arisen in times gone by (when Phœnicians or Greeks built the temples at Lerici and Porto Venere*) a baleful goddess of beauty, a Venus Verticordia,* but in the bad sense of the word, overwhelming men's lives in sudden darkness like that squall of last week.

To come to the point. I want you, dear Lady Evelyn, to promise me some money, a great deal of money, as much as would buy you a little mannish cloth frock—for the complete bringing-up, until years of discretion, of a young stranger whom the sea has laid upon our shore. Our people, kind as they are, are very poor, and overburdened with children; besides, they have got a certain repugnance for this poor little waif, cast up by that dreadful storm, and who is doubtless a heathen, for she had no little crosses or scapulars* on, like proper Christian children. So, being unable to get any of our women to adopt the child, and having an old bachelor's terror of my housekeeper,

I have bethought me of certain nuns, holy women, who teach little girls to say their prayers and make lace close by here; and of your dear Excellency to pay for the whole business.

Poor little brown mite! She was picked up after the storm (such a set-out of ship-models and votive candles as that storm must have brought the Madonna at Porto Venere!) on a strip of sand between the rocks of our castle: the thing was really miraculous, for this coast is like a shark's jaw, and the bits of sand are tiny and far between. She was lashed to a plank, swaddled up close in outlandish garments; and when they brought her to me they thought she must certainly be dead: a little girl of four or five, decidedly pretty, and as brown as a berry, who, when she came to, shook her head to show she understood no kind of Italian, and jabbered some half-intelligible Eastern jabber, a few Greek words embedded in I know not what; the Superior of the College De Propagandâ Fidē* would be puzzled to know. The child appears to be the only survivor from a ship which must have gone down in the great squall, and whose timbers have been strewing the bay for some days past; no one at Spezia or in any of our ports knows anything about her, but she was seen, apparently making for Porto Venere, by some of our sardine-fishers: a big, lumbering craft, with eyes painted on each side of the prow, which, as you know, is a peculiarity of Greek boats. She was sighted for the last time off the island of Palmaria, entering, with all sails spread, right into the thick of the storm-darkness. No bodies, strangely enough, have been washed ashore.

July 10.

I have received the money, dear Donna Evelina. There was tremendous excitement down at San Massimo when the carrier came in with a registered letter, and I was sent for, in presence of all the village authorities, to sign my name on the postal register.

The child has already been settled some days with the nuns; such dear little nuns (nuns always go straight to the heart of an old priest-hater and conspirator against the Pope, you know), dressed in brown robes and close, white caps, with an immense round straw-hat flapping behind their heads like a nimbus: they are called Sisters of the Stigmata, and have a convent and school at San Massimo, a little way inland, with an untidy garden full of lavender and cherry-trees. Your *protégée* has already half set the convent, the village, the

Episcopal See, the Order of St. Francis, by the ears. First, because nobody could make out whether or not she had been christened. The question was a grave one, for it appears (as your uncle-in-law, the Cardinal, will tell you) that it is almost equally undesirable to be christened twice over as not to be christened at all. The first danger was finally decided upon as the less terrible; but the child, they say, had evidently been baptized before, and knew that the operation ought not to be repeated, for she kicked and plunged and yelled like twenty little devils, and positively would not let the holy water touch her. The Mother Superior, who always took for granted that the baptism had taken place before, says that the child was quite right, and that Heaven was trying to prevent a sacrilege; but the priest and the barber's wife, who had to hold her, think the occurrence fearful, and suspect the little girl of being a Protestant. Then the question of the name. Pinned to her clothes—striped Eastern things, and that kind of crinkled silk stuff they weave in Crete and Cyprus—was a piece of parchment, a scapular we thought at first, but which was found to contain only the name *Διονεα*—Dionea,* as they pronounce it here. The question was, Could such a name be fitly borne by a young lady at the Convent of the Stigmata? Half the population here have names as unchristian quite—Norma, Odoacer, Archimedes—my housemaid is called Themis*—but Dionea seemed to scandalise every one, perhaps because these good folk had a mysterious instinct that the name is derived from Dione, one of the loves of Father Zeus, and mother of no less a lady than the goddess Venus. The child was very near being called Maria, although there are already twenty-three other Marias, Mariettas, Mariuccias, and so forth at the convent. But the sister-book-keeper, who apparently detests monotony, bethought her to look out Dionea first in the Calendar,* which proved useless; and then in a big vellum-bound book, printed at Venice in 1625, called "Flos Sanctorum, or Lives of the Saints, by Father Ribadeneira, S.J., with the addition of such Saints as have no assigned place in the Almanack, otherwise called the Movable or Extravagant Saints."* The zeal of Sister Anna Maddalena has been rewarded, for there, among the Extravagant Saints, sure enough, with a border of palm-branches and hour-glasses, stands the name of Saint Dionea, Virgin and Martyr, a lady of Antioch, put to death by the Emperor Decius.* I know your Excellency's taste for historical information, so I forward this item.

But I fear, dear Lady Evelyn, I fear that the heavenly patroness of your little sea-waif was a much more extravagant saint than that.

December 21, 1879.

Many thanks, dear Donna Evelina, for the money for Dionea's schooling. Indeed, it was not wanted yet: the accomplishments of young ladies are taught at a very moderate rate at Montemirto: and as to clothes, which you mention, a pair of wooden clogs, with pretty red tips, costs sixty-five centimes, and ought to last three years, if the owner is careful to carry them on her head in a neat parcel when out walking, and to put them on again only on entering the village. The Mother Superior is greatly overcome by your Excellency's munificence towards the convent, and much perturbed at being unable to send you a specimen of your *protégée*'s skill, exemplified in an embroidered pocket-handkerchief or a pair of mittens; but the fact is that poor Dionea *has* no skill. "We will pray to the Madonna and St. Francis to make her more worthy," remarked the Superior. Perhaps, however, your Excellency, who is, I fear but a Pagan woman (for all the Savelli Popes and St. Andrew Savelli's miracles*), and insufficiently appreciative of embroidered pocket-handkerchiefs, will be quite as satisfied to hear that Dionea, instead of skill, has got the prettiest face of any little girl in Montemirto. She is tall, for her age (she is eleven) quite wonderfully well proportioned and extremely strong: of all the convent-full, she is the only one for whom I have never been called in. The features are very regular, the hair black, and despite all the good Sisters' efforts to keep it smooth like a Chinaman's, beautifully curly. I am glad she should be pretty, for she will more easily find a husband; and also because it seems fitting that your *protégée* should be beautiful. Unfortunately her character is not so satisfactory: she hates learning, sewing, washing up the dishes, all equally. I am sorry to say she shows no natural piety. Her companions detest her, and the nuns, although they admit that she is not exactly naughty, seem to feel her as a dreadful thorn in the flesh. She spends hours and hours on the terrace overlooking the sea (her great desire, she confided to me, is to get to the sea—to get *back to the sea*, as she expressed it), and lying in the garden, under the big myrtle-bushes, and, in spring and summer, under the rose-hedge. The nuns say that rose-hedge and that myrtle-bush are growing a great deal too big, one would think from Dionea's lying under them; the fact, I suppose, has drawn attention to them.

"That child makes all the useless weeds grow," remarked Sister Reparata. Another of Dionea's amusements is playing with pigeons.* The number of pigeons she collects about her is quite amazing; you would never have thought that San Massimo or the neighbouring hills contained as many. They flutter down like snowflakes, and strut and swell themselves out, and furl and unfurl their tails, and peck; with little sharp movements of their silly, sensual heads and a little throb and gurgle in their throats, while Dionea lies stretched out full length in the sun, putting out her lips, which they come to kiss, and uttering strange, cooing sounds; or hopping about, flapping her arms slowly like wings, and raising her little head with much the same odd gesture as they;—'tis a lovely sight, a thing fit for one of your painters, Burne Jones or Tadema,* with the myrtle-bushes all round, the bright, white-washed convent walls behind, the white marble chapel steps (all steps are marble in this Carrara* country), and the enamel blue sea through the ilex-branches beyond. But the good Sisters abominate these pigeons, who, it appears, are messy little creatures, and they complain that, were it not that the Reverend Director likes a pigeon in his pot on a holiday, they could not stand the bother of perpetually sweeping the chapel steps and the kitchen threshold all along of those dirty birds. . . .

August 6, 1882.

Do not tempt me, dearest Excellency, with your invitations to Rome. I should not be happy there, and do but little honour to your friendship. My many years of exile, of wanderings in northern countries, have made me a little bit into a northern man: I cannot quite get on with my own fellow-countrymen, except with the good peasants and fishermen all round. Besides—forgive the vanity of an old man, who has learned to make triple acrostic sonnets to cheat the days and months at Theresienstadt and Spielberg*—I have suffered too much for Italy to endure patiently the sight of little parliamentary cabals and municipal wranglings, although they also are necessary in this day as conspiracies and battles were in mine. I am not fit for your roomful of ministers and learned men and pretty women: the former would think me an ignoramus, and the latter—what would afflict me much more—a pedant. . . . Rather, if your Excellency really wants to show yourself and your children to your father's old *protégé* of Mazzinian times,* find a few days to come here next spring. You shall have some very bare rooms with brick floors and white curtains opening out on my terrace; and a dinner of all manner of fish and milk (the white garlic flowers shall be mown away from under the olives lest my cow should eat it) and eggs cooked in herbs plucked in the hedges. Your boys can go and see the big ironclads at Spezia;* and you shall come with me up our lanes fringed with delicate ferns and overhung by big olives, and into the fields where the cherry-trees shed their blossoms on to the budding vines, the fig-trees stretching out their little green gloves, where the goats nibble perched on their hind legs, and the cows low in the huts of reeds; and there rise from the ravines, with the gurgle of the brooks, from the cliffs with the boom of the surf, the voices of unseen boys and girls, singing about love and flowers and death, just as in the days of Theocritus, whom your learned Excellency does well to read. Has your Excellency ever read Longus, a Greek pastoral novelist? He is a trifle free, a trifle nude for us readers of Zola; but the old French of Amyot* has a wonderful charm, and he gives one an idea, as no one else does, how folk lived in such valleys, by such sea-boards, as these in the days when daisy-chains and garlands of roses were still hung on the olive-trees for the nymphs of the grove; when across the bay, at the end of the narrow neck of blue sea, there clung to the marble rocks not a church of Saint Laurence, with the sculptured martyr on his gridiron, but the temple of Venus, protecting her harbour. . . . Yes, dear Lady Evelyn, you have guessed aright. Your old friend has returned to his sins, and is scribbling once more. But no longer at verses or political pamphlets. I am enthralled by a tragic history, the history of the fall of the Pagan Gods. . . . Have you ever read of their wanderings and disguises, in my friend Heine's little book?*

And if you come to Montemirto, you shall see also your *protégée*, of whom you ask for news. It has just missed being disastrous. Poor Dionea! I fear that early voyage tied to the spar did no good to her wits, poor little waif! There has been a fearful row; and it has required all my influence, and all the awfulness of your Excellency's name, and the Papacy, and the Holy Roman Empire, to prevent her expulsion by the Sisters of the Stigmata. It appears that this mad creature very nearly committed a sacrilege: she was discovered handling in a suspicious manner the Madonna's gala frock and her best veil of *pizzo di Cantù*,* a gift of the late Marchioness Violante Vigalena of Fornovo. One of the orphans, Zaira Barsanti, whom they call the Rossaccia, even pretends to have surprised Dionea as she was about to adorn her wicked little person with these sacred garments; and, on another occasion, when Dionea had been sent to pass some oil and sawdust over the chapel floor (it was the eve of Easter of the Roses*), to have discovered her seated on the edge of the altar, in the very place of the Most Holy Sacrament. I was sent for in hot haste, and had to assist at an ecclesiastical council in the convent parlour, where Dionea appeared, rather out of place, an amazing little beauty, dark, lithe, with an odd, ferocious gleam in her eyes, and a still odder smile, tortuous, serpentine, like that of Leonardo da Vinci's women,* among the plaster images of St. Francis, and the glazed and framed samplers before the little statue of the Virgin, which wears in summer a kind of mosquito-curtain to guard it from the flies, who, as you know, are creatures of Satan.*

Speaking of Satan, does your Excellency know that on the inside of our little convent door, just above the little perforated plate of metal (like the rose of a watering-pot) through which the Sister-portress peeps and talks, is pasted a printed form, an arrangement of holy names and texts in triangles, and the stigmatised hands of St. Francis, and a variety of other devices, for the purpose, as is explained in a special notice, of baffling the Evil One, and preventing his entrance into that building? Had you seen Dionea, and the stolid, contemptuous way in which she took, without attempting to refute, the various shocking allegations against her, your Excellency would have reflected, as I did, that the door in question must have been accidentally absent from the premises, perhaps at the joiner's for repair, the day that your *protégée* first penetrated into the convent. The ecclesiastical tribunal, consisting of the Mother Superior, three Sisters, the Capuchin Director, and your humble servant (who vainly attempted to be Devil's advocate), sentenced Dionea, among other things, to make the sign of the cross twenty-six times on the bare floor with her tongue. Poor little child! One might almost expect that, as happened when Dame Venus scratched her hand on the thorn-bush, red roses should sprout up between the fissures of the dirty old bricks.

October 14, 1883.

You ask whether, now that the Sisters let Dionea go and do half a day's service now and then in the village, and that Dionea is a grown-up creature, she does not set the place by the ears with her beauty. The people here are quite aware of its existence. She is already dubbed *La bella Dionea*; but that does not bring her any nearer getting a husband, although your Excellency's generous offer of a wedding-portion is well known throughout the district of San Massimo and Montemirto. None of our boys, peasants or fishermen, seem to hang on her steps; and if they turn round to stare and whisper as she goes by straight and dainty in her wooden clogs, with the pitcher of water or the basket of linen on her beautiful crisp dark head, it is, I remark, with an expression rather of fear than of love. The women, on their side, make horns with their fingers as she passes, and as they sit by her side in the convent chapel; but that seems natural. My housekeeper tells me that down in the village she is regarded as possessing the evil eye and bringing love misery. "You mean," I said, "that a glance from her is too much for our lads' peace of mind." Veneranda shook her head, and explained, with the deference and contempt with which she always mentions any of her countryfolk's superstitions to me, that the matter is different: it's not with her they are in love (they would be afraid of her eye), but wherever she goes the young people must needs fall in love with each other, and usually where it is far from desirable. "You know Sora Luisa, the blacksmith's widow? Well, Dionea did a *half-service* for her last month, to prepare for the wedding of Luisa's daughter. Well, now, the girl must say, forsooth! that she won't have Pieriho of Lerici any longer, but will have that raggamuffin Wooden Pipe from Solaro, or go into a convent. And the girl changed her mind the very day that Dionea had come into the house. Then there is the wife of Pippo, the coffee-house keeper; they say she is carrying on with one of the coastguards, and Dionea helped her to do her washing six weeks ago. The son of Sor Temistocle has just cut off a finger to avoid the conscription, because he is mad about his cousin and afraid of being taken for a soldier; and it is a fact that some of the shirts which were made for him at the Stigmata had been sewn by Dionea;" . . . and thus a perfect string of love misfortunes, enough to make a little "Decameron,"* I assure you, and all laid to Dionea's account. Certain it is that the people of San Massimo are terribly afraid of Dionea. . . .

July 17, 1884.

Dionea's strange influence seems to be extending in a terrible way. I am almost beginning to think that our folk are correct in their fear of the young witch. I used to think, as physician to a convent, that nothing was more erroneous than all the romancings of Diderot and Schubert* (your Excellency sang me his "Young Nun" once: do you recollect, just before your marriage?), and that no more humdrum creature existed than one of our little nuns, with their pink baby faces under their tight white caps. It appeared the romancing was more correct than the prose. Unknown things have sprung up in these good Sisters' hearts, as unknown flowers have sprung up among the myrtle-bushes and the rose-hedge which Dionea lies under. Did I ever mention to you a certain little Sister Giuliana, who professed only two years ago?—a funny rose and white little creature presiding over the infirmary, as prosaic a little saint as ever kissed a crucifix or scoured a saucepan. Well, Sister Giuliana has disappeared, and the same day has disappeared also a sailor-boy from the port.

August 20, 1884.

The case of Sister Giuliana seems to have been but the beginning of an extraordinary love epidemic at the Convent of the Stigmata: the elder schoolgirls have to be kept under lock and key lest they should talk over the wall in the moon-light, or steal out to the little hunchback who writes love-letters at a penny a-piece, beautiful flourishes and all, under the portico by the Fish-market. I wonder does that wicked little Dionea, whom no one pays court to, smile (her lips like a Cupid's bow or a tiny snake's curves) as she calls the pigeons down around her, or lies fondling the cats under the myrtle-bush, when she sees the pupils going about with swollen, red eyes; the poor little nuns taking fresh penances on the cold chapel flags; and hears the long-drawn guttural vowels, *amore* and *morte* and *mio bene*,* which rise up of an evening, with the boom of the surf and the scent of the lemon-flowers, as the young men wander up and down, arm-in-arm, twanging their guitars along the moonlit lanes under the olives?

October 20, 1885.

A terrible, terrible thing has happened! I write to your Excellency with hands all a-tremble; and yet I *must* write, I must speak, or else I shall cry out. Did I ever mention to you Father Domenico of Casoria, the confessor of our Convent of the Stigmata? A young man, tall, emaciated with fasts and vigils, but handsome like the monk playing the virginal in Giorgione's "Concert,"* and under his brown serge still the most stalwart fellow of the country all round? One has heard of men struggling with the tempter. Well, well, Father Domenico had struggled as hard as any of the Anchorites recorded by St. Jerome,* and he had conquered. I never knew anything comparable to the angelic serenity of gentleness of this victorious soul. I don't like monks, but I loved Father Domenico. I might have been his father, easily, yet I always felt a certain shyness and awe of him; and yet men have accounted me a clean-lived man in my generation; but I felt, whenever I approached him, a poor worldly creature, debased by the knowledge of so many mean and ugly things. Of late Father Domenico had seemed to me less calm than usual: his eyes had grown strangely bright, and red spots had formed on his salient cheekbones. One day last week, taking his hand, I felt his pulse flutter, and all his strength as it were, liquefy under my touch. "You are ill," I said. "You have fever, Father Domenico. You have been overdoing yourself—some new privation, some new penance. Take care and do not tempt Heaven; remember the flesh is weak." Father Domenico withdrew his hand quickly. "Do not say that," he cried; "the flesh is strong!" and turned away his face. His eyes were glistening and he shook all over. "Some quinine," I ordered. But I felt it was no case for quinine. Prayers might be more useful, and could I have given them he should not have wanted. Last night I was suddenly sent for to Father Domenico's monastery above Montemirto: they told me he was ill. I ran up through the dim twilight of moonbeams and olives with a sinking heart. Something told me my monk was dead. He was lying in a little low whitewashed room; they had carried him there from his own cell in hopes he might still be alive. The windows were wide open; they framed some olive-branches, glistening in the moonlight, and far below, a strip of moonlit sea. When I told them that he was really dead, they brought some tapers and lit them at his head and feet, and placed a crucifix between his hands. "The Lord has been pleased to call our poor brother to Him," said the Superior. "A case of apoplexy, my dear Doctor—a case of apoplexy. You will make out the certificate for the authorities." I made out the certificate. It was weak of me. But, after all, why make a scandal? He certainly had no wish to injure the poor monks.

Next day I found the little nuns all in tears. They were gathering flowers to send as a last gift to their confessor. In the convent garden I found Dionea, standing by the side of a big basket of roses, one of the white pigeons perched on her shoulder.

"So," she said, "he has killed himself with charcoal,* poor Padre Domenico!"

Something in her tone, her eyes, shocked me.

"God has called to Himself one of His most faithful servants," I said gravely.

Standing opposite this girl, magnificent, radiant in her beauty, before the rose-hedge, with the white pigeons furling and unfurling, strutting and pecking all round, I seemed to see suddenly the whitewashed room of last night, the big crucifix, that poor thin face under the yellow wax-light. I felt glad for Father Domenico; his battle was over.

"Take this to Father Domenico from me," said Dionea, breaking off a twig of myrtle starred over with white blossom; and raising her head with that smile like the twist of a young snake, she sang out in a high guttural voice a strange chaunt, consisting of the word *Amor—amor—amor*. I took the branch of myrtle and threw it in her face.

January 3, 1886.

It will be difficult to find a place for Dionea, and in this neighbourhood well-nigh impossible. The people associate her somehow with the death of Father Domenico, which has confirmed her reputation of having the evil eye. She left the convent (being now seventeen) some two months back, and is at present gaining her bread working with the masons at our notary's new house at Lerici: the work is hard, but our women often do it, and it is magnificent to see Dionea, in her short white skirt and tight white bodice, mixing the smoking lime with her beautiful strong arms; or, an empty sack drawn over her head and shoulders, walking majestically up the cliff, up the scaffoldings with her load of bricks. . . . I am, however, very anxious to get Dionea out of the neighbourhood, because I cannot help dreading the annoyances to which her reputation for the evil eye exposes her, and even some explosion of rage if ever she should lose the indifferent contempt with which she treats them. I hear that one of the rich men of our part of the world, a certain Sor Agostino of Sarzana, who owns a whole flank of marble mountain, is looking out for a maid for his daughter, who is about to be married; kind people and patriarchal in their riches, the old man still sitting down to table with all his servants; and his nephew, who is going to be his son-in-law, a splendid young fellow, who has worked like Jacob,* in the quarry and at the saw-mill, for love of his pretty cousin. That whole house is so good, simple, and peaceful, that I hope it may tame down even Dionea. If I do not succeed in getting Dionea this place (and all your Excellency's illustriousness and all my poor eloquence will be needed to counteract the sinister reports attaching to our poor little waif), it will be best to accept your suggestion of taking the girl into your household at Rome, since you are curious to see what you call our baleful beauty. I am amused, and a little indignant at what you say about your footmen being handsome: Don Juan* himself, my dear Lady Evelyn, would be cowed by Dionea. . . .

May 29, 1886.

Here is Dionea back upon our hands once more! but I cannot send her to your Excellency. Is it from living among these peasants and fishing-folk, or is it because, as people pretend, a sceptic is always superstitious? I could not muster courage to send you Dionea, although your boys are still in sailor-clothes and your uncle, the Cardinal, is eighty-four; and as to the Prince, why, he bears the most potent amulet against Dionea's terrible powers in your own dear capricious person. Seriously, there is something eerie in this coincidence. Poor Dionea! I feel sorry for her, exposed to the passion of a once patriarchally respectable old man. I feel even more abashed at the incredible audacity, I should almost say sacrilegious madness, of the vile old creature. But still the coincidence is strange and uncomfortable. Last week the lightning struck a huge olive in the orchard of Sor Agostino's house above Sarzana. Under the olive was Sor Agostino himself, who was killed on the spot; and opposite, not twenty paces off, drawing water from the well, unhurt and calm, was Dionea. It was the end of a sultry afternoon: I was on a terrace in one of those villages of ours, jammed, like some hardy bush, in the gash of a hill-side. I saw the storm rush down the valley, a sudden blackness, and then, like a curse, a flash, a tremendous crash, re-echoed by a dozen hills. "I told him," Dionea said very quietly, when she came to stay with me the next day (for Sor Agostino's family would not have her for another half-minute), "that if he did not leave me alone Heaven would send him an accident."

July 15, 1886.

My book? Oh, dear Donna Evelina, do not make me blush by talking of my book! Do not make an old man, respectable, a Government functionary (communal physician of the district of San Massimo and

Montemirto Ligure), confess that he is but a lazy unprofitable dreamer, collecting materials as a child picks hips out of a hedge, only to throw them away, liking them merely for the little occupation of scratching his hands and standing on tiptoe, for their pretty redness. . . . You remember what Balzac says about projecting any piece of work?—"*C'est fumer des cigarettes enchantées.*"* . . . Well, well! The data obtainable about the ancient gods in their days of adversity are few and far between: a quotation here and there from the Fathers; two or three legends; Venus reappearing; the persecutions of Apollo in Styria; Proserpina going, in Chaucer, to reign over the fairies; a few obscure religious persecutions in the Middle Ages on the score of Paganism; some strange rites practised till lately in the depths of a Breton forest near Lannion. . . . As to Tannhäuser, he was a real knight, and a sorry one, and a real Minnesinger not of the best. Your Excellency will find some of his poems in Von der Hagen's four immense volumes, but I recommend you to take your notions of Ritter Tannhäuser's poetry rather from Wagner.* Certain it is that the Pagan divinities lasted much longer than we suspect, sometimes in their own nakedness, sometimes in the stolen garb of the Madonna or the saints. Who knows whether they do not exist to this day? And, indeed, is it possible they should not? For the awfulness of the deep woods, with their filtered green light, the creak of the swaying, solitary reeds, exists, and is Pan;* and the blue, starry May night exists, the sough of the waves, the warm wind carrying the sweetness of the lemon-blossoms, the bitterness of the myrtle on our rocks, the distant chaunt of the boys cleaning out their nets, of the girls sickling the grass under the olives, *Amor—amor—amor*, and all this is the great goddess Venus. And opposite to me, as I write, between the branches of the ilexes, across the blue sea, streaked like a Ravenna mosaic with purple and green, shimmer the white houses and walls, the steeple and towers, an enchanted Fata Morgana* city, of dim Porto Venere; . . . and I mumble to myself the verse of Catullus, but addressing a greater and more terrible goddess than he did:—

"Procul a mea sit furor omnis, Hera, domo; alios age incitatos, alios age rabidos."*

March 25, 1887.

Yes; I will do everything in my power for your friends. Are you well-bred folk as well bred as we, Republican *bourgeois*, with the coarse hands (though you once told me mine were psychic hands when the mania of palmistry had not yet been succeeded by that of the Reconciliation between Church and State), I wonder, that you should apologise, you whose father fed me and housed me and clothed me in my exile, for giving me the horrid trouble of hunting for lodgings? It is like you, dear Donna Evelina, to have sent me photographs of my future friend Waldemar's statue. . . . I have no love for modern sculpture, for all the hours I have spent in Gibson's and Dupré's studio:* 'tis a dead art we should do better to bury. But your Waldemar has something of the old spirit: he seems to feel the divineness of the mere body, the spirituality of a limpid stream of mere physical life. But why among these statues only men and boys, athletes and fauns? Why only the bust of that thin, delicate-lipped little Madonna wife of his? Why no wide-shouldered Amazon* or broad-flanked Aphrodite?

April 10, 1887.

You ask me how poor Dionea is getting on. Not as your Excellency and I ought to have expected when we placed her with the good Sisters of the Stigmata: although I wager that, fantastic and capricious as you are, you would be better pleased (hiding it carefully from that grave side of you which bestows devout little books and carbolic acid upon the indigent) that your *protégée* should be a witch than a serving-maid, a maker of philters rather than a knitter of stockings and sewer of shirts.

A maker of philters. Roughly speaking, that is Dionea's profession. She lives upon the money which I dole out to her (with many useless objurgations) on behalf of your Excellency; and her ostensible employment is mending nets, collecting olives, carrying bricks, and other miscellaneous jobs; but her real status is that of village sorceress. You think our peasants are sceptical? Perhaps they do not believe in thought-reading, mesmerism, and ghosts, like you, dear Lady Evelyn. But they believe very firmly in the evil eye, in magic, and in love-potions. Every one has his little story of this or that which happened to his brother or cousin or neighbour. My stable-boy and male factotum's brother-in-law, living some years ago in Corsica, was seized with a longing for a dance with his beloved at one of those balls which our peasants give in the winter, when the snow makes leisure in the mountains. A wizard anointed him for money, and straightway he turned into a black cat, and in three bounds was over the seas, at the door of his uncle's cottage, and among the dancers. He caught his beloved by the skirt to draw her attention; but she replied with a kick which sent him squealing back to Corsica. When he returned in summer he refused to marry the lady, and carried his left arm in a sling. "You broke it when I came to the Veglia!"* he said, and all seemed explained. Another lad, returning from working in the vineyards near Marseilles, was walking up to his native village, high in our hills, one moonlight night. He heard sounds of fiddle and fife from a roadside barn, and saw yellow light from its chinks; and then entering, he found many women dancing, old and young, and among them his affianced. He tried to snatch her round the waist for a waltz (they play *Mme. Angot** at our rustic balls), but the girl was unclutchable, and whispered, "Go; for these are witches, who will kill thee; and I am a witch also. Alas! I shall go to hell when I die."

I could tell your Excellency dozens of such stories. But love-philters are among the commonest things to sell and buy. Do you remember the sad little story of Cervantes' Licentiate,* who, instead of a love-potion, drank a philter which made him think he was made of glass, fit emblem of a poor mad poet? . . . It is love-philters that Dionea prepares. No; do not misunderstand; they do not give love of her, still less her love. Your seller of love-charms is as cold as ice, as pure as snow. The priest has crusaded against her, and stones have flown at her as she went by from dissatisfied lovers; and the very children, paddling in the sea and making mud-pies in the sand, have put out forefinger and little finger and screamed, "Witch, witch! ugly witch!" as she passed with basket or brick load; but Dionea has only smiled, that snake-like, amused smile, but more ominous than of yore. The other day I determined to seek her and argue with her on the subject of her evil trade. Dionea has a certain regard for me; not, I fancy, a result of gratitude, but rather the recognition of a certain admiration and awe which she inspires in your Excellency's foolish old servant. She has taken up her abode in a deserted hut, built of dried reeds and thatch, such as they keep cows in, among the olives on the cliffs. She was not there, but about the hut pecked some white pigeons, and from it, startling me foolishly with its unexpected sound, came the eerie bleat of her pet goat. . . . Among the olives it was twilight already, with streakings of faded rose in the sky, and faded rose, like long trails of petals, on the distant sea. I clambered down among the myrtle-bushes and came to a little semicircle of yellow sand, between two high and jagged rocks, the place where the sea had deposited Dionea after the wreck. She was seated there on the sand, her bare foot dabbling in the waves; she had twisted a wreath of myrtle and wild roses on her black, crisp hair. Near her was one of our prettiest girls, the Lena of Sor Tullio the blacksmith, with ashy, terrified face under her flowered kerchief. I determined to speak to the child, but without startling her now, for she is a nervous, hysteric little thing. So I sat on the rocks, screened by the myrtle-bushes, waiting till the girl had gone. Dionea, seated listless on the sands, leaned over the sea and took some of its water in the hollow of her hand. "Here," she said to the Lena of Sor Tullio, "fill your bottle with this and give it to drink to Tommasino the Rosebud." Then she set to singing:—

"Love is salt, like sea-water—I drink and I die of thirst. . . . Water! water! Yet the more I drink, the more I burn. Love! thou art bitter as the seaweed."

April 20, 1887.

Your friends are settled here, dear Lady Evelyn. The house is built in what was once a Genoese fort, growing like a grey spiked aloes out of the marble rocks of our bay; rock and wall (the walls existed long before Genoa was ever heard of) grown almost into a homogeneous mass, delicate grey, stained with black and yellow lichen, and dotted here and there with myrtle-shoots and crimson snapdragon. In what was once the highest enclosure of the fort, where your friend Gertrude watches the maids hanging out the fine white sheets and pillow-cases to dry (a bit of the North, of Hermann and Dorothea* transferred to the South), a great twisted fig-tree juts out like an eccentric gargoyle over the sea, and drops its ripe fruit into the deep blue pools. There is but scant furniture in the house, but a great oleander overhangs it, presently to burst into pink splendour; and on all the window-sills, even that of the kitchen (such a background of shining brass saucepans Waldemar's wife has made of it!) are pipkins and tubs full of trailing carnations, and tufts of sweet basil and thyme and mignonette. She pleases me most, your Gertrude, although you foretold I should prefer the husband; with her thin white face, a Memling Madonna* finished by some Tuscan sculptor, and her long, delicate white hands ever busy, like those of a mediæval lady, with some delicate piece of work; and the strange blue, more limpid than the sky and deeper than the sea, of her rarely lifted glance.

It is in her company that I like Waldemar best; I prefer to the genius that infinitely tender and respectful, I would not say *lover*—yet I have no other word—of his pale wife. He seems to me, when with her, like some fierce, generous, wild thing from the woods, like the lion of Una,* tame and submissive to this saint. . . . This tenderness is really very beautiful on the part of that big lion Waldemar, with his odd eyes, as of some wild animal—odd, and, your Excellency remarks, not without a gleam of latent ferocity. I think that hereby hangs the explanation of his never doing any but male figures: the female figure, he says (and your Excellency must hold him responsible, not me, for such profanity), is almost inevitably inferior in strength and beauty; woman is not form, but expression, and therefore suits painting, but not sculpture. The point of a woman is not her body, but (and here his eyes rested very tenderly upon the thin white profile of his wife) her soul. "Still," I answered, "the ancients, who understood such matters, did manufacture some tolerable female statues: the Fates of the Parthenon, the Phidian Pallas, the Venus of Milo." . . .

"Ah! yes," exclaimed Waldemar, smiling, with that savage gleam of his eyes; "but those are not women, and the people who made them have left us the tales of Endymion, Adonis, Anchises:* a goddess might sit for them." . . .

May 5, 1887.

Has it ever struck your Excellency in one of your La Rochefoucauld* fits (in Lent say, after too many balls) that not merely maternal but conjugal unselfishness may be a very selfish thing? There! you toss your little head at my words; yet I wager I have heard you say that *other* women may think it right to humour their husbands, but as to you, the Prince must learn that a wife's duty is as much to chasten her husband's whims as to satisfy them. I really do feel indignant that such a snow-white saint should wish another woman to part with all instincts of modesty merely because that other woman would be a good model for her husband; really it is intolerable. "Leave the girl alone," Waldemar said, laughing. "What do I want with the unæsthetic sex, as Schopenhauer calls it?"* But Gertrude has set her heart on his doing a female figure; it seems that folk have twitted him with never having produced one. She has long been on the look-out for a model for him. It is odd to see this pale, demure, diaphanous creature, not the more earthly for approaching motherhood, scanning the girls of our village with the eyes of a slave-dealer.

"If you insist on speaking to Dionea," I said, "I shall insist on speaking to her at the same time, to urge her to refuse your proposal." But Waldemar's pale wife was indifferent to all my speeches about modesty being a poor girl's only dowry. "She will do for a Venus," she merely answered.

We went up to the cliffs together, after some sharp words, Waldemar's wife hanging on my arm as we slowly clambered up the stony path among the olives. We found Dionea at the door of her hut, making faggots of myrtle-branches. She listened sullenly to Gertrude's offer and explanations; indifferently to my admonitions not to accept. The thought of stripping for the view of a man, which would send a shudder through our most brazen village girls, seemed not to startle her, immaculate and savage as she is accounted. She did not answer, but sat under the olives, looking vaguely across the sea. At that moment Waldemar came up to us; he had followed with the intention of putting an end to these wranglings.

"Gertrude," he said, "do leave her alone. I have found a model—a fisher-boy, whom I much prefer to any woman."

Dionea raised her head with that serpentine smile. "I will come," she said.

Waldemar stood silent; his eyes were fixed on her, where she stood under the olives, her white shift loose about her splendid throat, her shining feet bare in the grass. Vaguely, as if not knowing what he said, he asked her name. She answered that her name was Dionea; for the rest, she was an Innocentina, that is to say, a foundling; then she began to sing:—

> "Flower of the myrtle!
> My father is the starry sky;
> The mother that made me is the sea."*

June 22, 1887.

I confess I was an old fool to have grudged Waldemar his model. As I watch him gradually building up his statue, watch the goddess gradually emerging from the clay heap, I ask myself—and the case might trouble a more subtle moralist than me—whether a village girl, an obscure, useless life within the bounds of what we choose to call right and wrong, can be weighed against the possession by mankind of a great work of art, a Venus immortally beautiful? Still, I am glad that the two alternatives need not be weighed against each other. Nothing can equal the kindness of Gertrude, now that Dionea has consented to sit to her husband; the girl is ostensibly merely a servant like any other; and, lest any report of her real functions should get abroad and discredit her at San Massimo or Montemirto, she is to be taken to Rome, where no one will be the wiser, and where, by the way, your Excellency will have an opportunity of comparing Waldemar's goddess of love with our little orphan of the Convent of the Stigmata. What reassures me still more is the curious attitude of Waldemar towards the girl. I could never have believed that an artist could regard a woman so utterly as a mere inanimate thing, a form to copy, like a tree or flower. Truly he carries out his theory that sculpture knows only the body, and the body scarcely considered as human. The way in which he speaks to Dionea after hours of the most rapt contemplation of her is almost brutal in its coldness. And yet to hear him exclaim, "How beautiful she is! Good God, how beautiful!" No love of mere woman was ever so violent as this love of woman's mere shape.

June 27, 1887.

You asked me once, dearest Excellency, whether there survived among our people (you had evidently added a volume on folk-lore to that heap of half-cut, dog's-eared books that litter about among the Chineseries* and mediæval brocades of your rooms) any trace of Pagan myths. I explained to you then that all our fairy mythology, classic gods, and demons and heroes, teemed with fairies, ogres, and princes. Last night I had a curious proof of this. Going to see the Waldemar, I found Dionea seated under the oleander at the top of the old Genoese fort, telling stories to the two little blonde children who were making the falling pink blossoms into necklaces at her feet; the pigeons, Dionea's white pigeons, which never leave her, strutting and pecking among the basil pots, and the white gulls flying round the rocks overhead. This is what I heard. . . . "And the three fairies said to the youngest son of the King, to the one who had been brought up as a shepherd, 'Take this apple, and give it to her among us who is most beautiful.' And the first fairy said, 'If thou give it to me thou shalt be Emperor of Rome, and have purple clothes, and have a gold crown and gold armour, and horses and courtiers;' and the second said, 'If thou give it to me thou shalt be Pope, and wear a mitre, and have the keys of heaven and hell;' and the third fairy said, 'Give the apple to me, for I will give thee the most beautiful lady to wife.' And the youngest son of the King sat in the green meadow and thought about it a little, and then said, 'What use is there in being Emperor or Pope? Give me the beautiful lady to wife, since I am young myself.' And he gave the apple to the third of the three fairies."* . . .

Dionea droned out the story in her half-Genoese dialect, her eyes looking far away across the blue sea, dotted with sails like white sea-gulls, that strange serpentine smile on her lips.

"Who told thee that fable?" I asked.

She took a handful of oleander-blossoms from the ground, and throwing them in the air, answered listlessly, as she watched the little shower of rosy petals descend on her black hair and pale breast—

"Who knows?"

July 6, 1887.

How strange is the power of art! Has Waldemar's statue shown me the real Dionea, or has Dionea really grown more strangely beautiful than before? Your Excellency will laugh; but when I meet her I cast down my eyes after the first glimpse of her loveliness; not with the shyness of a ridiculous old pursuer of the Eternal Feminine,* but with a sort of religious awe—the feeling with which, as a child kneeling by my mother's side, I looked down on the church flags when the Mass bell told the elevation of the Host. . . . Do you remember the story of Zeuxis and the ladies of Crotona, five of the fairest not being too much for his Juno?* Do you remember—you, who have read everything—all the bosh of our writers about the Ideal in Art? Why, here is a girl who disproves all this nonsense in a minute; she is far, far more beautiful than Waldemar's statue of her. He said so angrily, only yesterday, when his wife took me into his studio (he has made a studio of the long-desecrated chapel of the old Genoese fort, itself, they say, occupying the site of the temple of Venus).

As he spoke that odd spark of ferocity dilated in his eyes, and seizing the largest of his modelling tools, he obliterated at one swoop the whole exquisite face. Poor Gertrude turned ashy white, and a convulsion passed over her face. . . .

July 15.

I wish I could make Gertrude understand, and yet I could never, never bring myself to say a word. As a matter of fact, what is there to be said? Surely she knows best that her husband will never love any woman but herself. Yet ill, nervous as she is, I quite understand that she must loathe this unceasing talk of Dionea, of the superiority of the model over the statue. Cursed statue! I wish it were finished, or else that it had never been begun.

July 20.

This morning Waldemar came to me. He seemed strangely agitated: I guessed he had something to tell me, and yet I could never ask. Was it cowardice on my part? He sat in my shuttered room, the sunshine making pools on the red bricks and tremulous stars on the ceiling, talking of many things at random, and mechanically turning over the manuscript, the heap of notes of my poor, never-finished book on the Exiled Gods. Then he rose, and walking nervously round my study, talking disconnectedly about his work, his eye suddenly fell upon a little altar, one of my few antiquities, a little block of marble with a carved garland and rams' heads, and a half-effaced inscription dedicating it to Venus, the mother of Love.

"It was found," I explained, "in the ruins of the temple, somewhere on the site of your studio: so, at least, the man said from whom I bought it."

Waldemar looked at it long. "So," he said, "this little cavity was to burn the incense in; or rather, I suppose, since it has two little gutters running into it, for collecting the blood of the victim? Well, well! they were wiser in that day, to wring the neck of a pigeon or burn a pinch of incense than to eat their own hearts out, as we do, all along of Dame Venus;" and he laughed, and left me with that odd ferocious lighting-up of his face. Presently there came a knock at my door. It was Waldemar. "Doctor," he said very quietly, "will you do me a favour? Lend me your little Venus altar—only for a few days, only till the day after to-morrow. I want to copy the design of it for the pedestal of my statue: it is appropriate." I sent the altar to him: the lad who carried it told me that Waldemar had set it up in the studio, and calling for a flask of wine, poured out two glasses. One he had given to my messenger for his pains; of the other he had drunk a mouthful, and thrown the rest over the altar, saying some unknown words. "It must be some German habit," said my servant. What odd fancies this man has!

July 25.

You ask me, dearest Excellency, to send you some sheets of my book: you want to know what I have discovered. Alas! dear Donna Evelina,

I have discovered, I fear, that there is nothing to discover; that Apollo was never in Styria; that Chaucer, when he called the Queen of the Fairies Proserpine, meant nothing more than an eighteenth century poet when he called Dolly or Betty Cynthia or Amaryllis; that the lady who damned poor Tannhäuser was not Venus, but a mere little Suabian mountain sprite;* in fact, that poetry is only the invention of poets, and that that rogue, Heinrich Heine, is entirely responsible for the existence of *Dieux en Exil*. . . . My poor manuscript can only tell you what St. Augustine, Tertullian, and sundry morose old Bishops thought about the loves of Father Zeus and the miracles of the Lady Isis,* none of which is much worth your attention. . . . Reality, my dear Lady Evelyn, is always prosaic: at least when investigated into by bald old gentlemen like me.

And yet, it does not look so. The world, at times, seems to be playing at being poetic, mysterious, full of wonder and romance. I am writing as usual, by my window, the moonlight brighter in its whiteness than my mean little yellow-shining lamp. From the mysterious greyness, the olive groves and lanes beneath my terrace, rises a confused quaver of frogs, and buzz and whirr of insects: something, in sound, like the vague trails of countless stars, the galaxies on galaxies blurred into mere blue shimmer by the moon, which rides slowly across the highest heaven. The olive twigs glisten in the rays: the flowers of the pomegranate and oleander are only veiled as with bluish mist in their scarlet and rose. In the sea is another sea, of molten, rippled silver, or a magic causeway leading to the shining vague offing, the luminous pale sky-line, where the islands of Palmaria and Tino float like unsubstantial, shadowy dolphins. The roofs of Montemirto glimmer among the black, pointing cypresses: farther below, at the end of that half-moon of land, is San Massimo: the Genoese fort inhabited by our friends is profiled black against the sky. All is dark: our fisher-folk go to bed early; Gertrude and the little ones are asleep: they at least are, for I can imagine Gertrude lying awake, the moonbeams on her thin Madonna face, smiling as she thinks of the little ones around her, of the other tiny thing that will soon lie on her breast. . . . There is a light in the old desecrated chapel, the thing that was once the temple of Venus, they say, and is now Waldemar's workshop, its broken roof mended with reeds and thatch. Waldemar has stolen in, no doubt to see his statue again. But he will return, more peaceful for the peacefulness of the night, to his sleeping wife and children. God bless and watch over them! Good-night, dearest Excellency.

July 26.

I have your Excellency's telegram in answer to mine. Many thanks for sending the Prince. I await his coming with feverish longing; it is still something to look forward to. All does not seem over. And yet what can he do?

The children are safe: we fetched them out of their bed and brought them up here. They are still a little shaken by the fire, the bustle, and by finding themselves in a strange house; also, they want to know where their mother is; but they have found a tame cat, and I hear them chirping on the stairs.

It was only the roof of the studio, the reeds and thatch, that burned, and a few old pieces of timber. Waldemar must have set fire to it with great care; he had brought armfuls of faggots of dry myrtle and heather from the bakehouse close by, and thrown into the blaze quantities of pine-cones, and of some resin, I know not what, that smelt like incense. When we made our way, early this morning, through the smouldering studio, we were stifled with a hot church-like perfume: my brain swam, and I suddenly remembered going into St. Peter's on Easter Day as a child.

It happened last night, while I was writing to you. Gertrude had gone to bed, leaving her husband in the studio. About eleven the maids heard him come out and call to Dionea to get up and come and sit to him. He had had this craze once before, of seeing her and his statue by an artificial light: you remember he had theories about the way in which the ancients lit up the statues in their temples. Gertrude, the servants say, was heard creeping downstairs a little later.

Do you see it? I have seen nothing else these hours, which have seemed weeks and months. He had placed Dionea on the big marble block behind the altar, a great curtain of dull red brocade—you know that Venetian brocade with the gold pomegranate pattern—behind her, like a Madonna of Van Eyck's.* He showed her to me once before like this, the whiteness of her neck and breast, the whiteness of the drapery round her flanks, toned to the colour of old marble by the light of the resin burning in pans all round. . . . Before Dionea was the altar—the altar of Venus which he had borrowed from me. He must have collected all the roses about it, and thrown the incense upon the embers when Gertrude suddenly entered. And then, and then . . .

We found her lying across the altar, her pale hair among the ashes of the incense, her blood—she had but little to give, poor white ghost!—trickling among the carved garlands and rams' heads, blackening the heaped-up roses. The body of Waldemar was found at the foot of the castle cliff. Had he hoped, by setting the place on fire, to bury himself among its ruins, or had he not rather wished to complete in this way the sacrifice, to make the whole temple an immense votive pyre? It looked like one, as we hurried down the hills to San Massimo: the whole hillside, dry grass, myrtle, and heather, all burning, the pale short flames waving against the blue moonlit sky, and the old fortress outlined black against the blaze.

August 30.

Of Dionea I can tell you nothing certain. We speak of her as little as we can. Some say they have seen her, on stormy nights, wandering among the cliffs: but a sailor-boy assures me, by all the holy things, that the day after the burning of the Castle Chapel—we never call it anything else—he met at dawn, off the island of Palmaria, beyond the Strait of Porto Venere, a Greek boat, with eyes painted on the prow, going full sail to sea, the men singing as she went. And against the mast, a robe of purple and gold about her, and a myrtle-wreath on her head, leaned Dionea, singing words in an unknown tongue, the white pigeons circling around her.

A WICKED VOICE

To M. W.,

IN REMEMBRANCE OF THE LAST SONG AT PALAZZO BARBARO.

*Chi ha inteso, intenda.**

THEY have been congratulating me again today upon being the only composer of our days—of these days of deafening orchestral effects and poetical quackery—who has despised the new-fangled nonsense of Wagner, and returned boldly to the traditions of Handel and Gluck and the divine Mozart,* to the supremacy of melody and the respect of the human voice.

O cursed human voice, violin of flesh and blood, fashioned with the subtle tools, the cunning hands, of Satan!* O execrable art of singing, have you not wrought mischief enough in the past, degrading so much noble genius, corrupting the purity of Mozart, reducing Handel to a writer of high-class singing-exercises, and defrauding the world of the only inspiration worthy of Sophocles and Euripides,* the poetry of the great poet Gluck? Is it not enough to have dishonoured a whole century in idolatry of that wicked and contemptible wretch the singer, without persecuting an obscure young composer of our days, whose only wealth is his love of nobility in art, and perhaps some few grains of genius?

And then they compliment me upon the perfection with which I imitate the style of the great dead masters; or ask me very seriously whether, even if I could gain over the modern public to this bygone style of music, I could hope to find singers to perform it. Sometimes, when people talk as they have been talking to-day, and laugh when I declare myself a follower of Wagner, I burst into a paroxysm of unintelligible, childish rage, and exclaim, "We shall see that some day!"

Yes; some day we shall see! For, after all, may I not recover from this strangest of maladies? It is still possible that the day may come when all these things shall seem but an incredible nightmare; the day when *Ogier the Dane** shall be completed, and men shall know whether I am a follower of the great master of the Future or the miserable singing-masters of the Past. I am but half-bewitched, since I am conscious of the spell that binds me. My old nurse, far off in Norway, used to tell me that were-wolves* are ordinary men and women half their days, and that if, during that period, they become aware of their horrid transformation they may find the means to forestall it. May this not be the case with me? My reason, after all, is free, although my artistic inspiration be enslaved; and I can despise and loathe the music I am forced to compose, and the execrable power that forces me.

Nay, is it not because I have studied with the doggedness of hatred this corrupt and corrupting music of the Past, seeking for every little peculiarity of style and every biographical trifle merely to display its vileness, is it not for this presumptuous courage that I have been overtaken by such mysterious, incredible vengeance?

And meanwhile, my only relief consists in going over and over again in my mind the tale of my miseries. This time I will write it, writing only to tear up, to throw the manuscript unread into the fire. And yet, who knows? As the last charred pages shall crackle and slowly sink into the red embers, perhaps the spell may be broken, and I may possess once more my long-lost liberty, my vanished genius.

It was a breathless evening under the full moon, that implacable full moon beneath which, even more than beneath the dreamy splendour of noon-tide, Venice seemed to swelter in the midst of the waters, exhaling, like some great lily, mysterious influences, which make the brain swim and the heart faint—a moral malaria, distilled, as I thought, from those languishing melodies, those cooing vocalisations which I had found in the musty music-books of a century ago. I see that moon-light evening as if it were present. I see my fellow-lodgers of that little artists' boarding-house. The table on which they lean after supper is strewn with bits of bread, with napkins rolled in tapestry rollers, spots of wine here and there, and at regular intervals chipped pepper-pots, stands of toothpicks, and heaps of those huge hard peaches which nature imitates from the marble-shops of Pisa. The whole *pension*-full is assembled, and examining stupidly the engraving which the American etcher has just brought for me, knowing me to be mad about eighteenth century music and musicians, and having noticed, as he turned over the heaps of penny prints in the square of San Polo,* that the portrait is that of a singer of those days.

Singer, thing of evil, stupid and wicked slave of the voice, of that instrument which was not invented by the human intellect, but begotten of the body, and which, instead of moving the soul, merely stirs up the dregs of our nature! For what is the voice but the Beast calling, awakening that other Beast sleeping in the depths of mankind, the Beast which all great art has ever sought to chain up, as the archangel chains up, in old pictures, the demon with his woman's face? How could the creature attached to this voice, its owner and its victim, the singer, the great, the real singer who once ruled over every heart, be otherwise than wicked and contemptible? But let me try and get on with my story.

I can see all my fellow-boarders, leaning on the table, contemplating the print, this effeminate beau, his hair curled into *ailes de pigeon*,* his sword passed through his embroidered pocket, seated under a triumphal arch somewhere among the clouds, surrounded by puffy Cupids and crowned with laurels by a bouncing goddess of fame. I hear again all the insipid exclamations, the insipid questions about this singer:—"When did he live? Was he very famous? Are you sure, Magnus, that this is really a portrait," &c. &c. And I hear my own voice, as if in the far distance, giving them all sorts of information, biographical and critical, out of a battered little volume called *The Theatre of Musical Glory; or, Opinions upon the most Famous Chapel-masters and Virtuosi of this Century*, by Father Prosdocimo Sabatelli, Barnalite, Professor of Eloquence at the College of Modena, and Member of the Arcadian Academy,* under the pastoral name of Evander Lilybæan, Venice, 1785, with the approbation of the Superiors. I tell them all how this singer, this Balthasar Cesari, was nicknamed Zaffirino* because of a sapphire engraved with cabalistic signs presented to him one evening by a masked stranger, in whom wise folk recognised that great cultivator of the human voice, the devil; how much more wonderful had been this Zaffirino's vocal gifts than those of any singer of ancient or modern times; how his brief life had been but a series of triumphs, petted by the greatest kings, sung by the most famous poets, and finally, adds Father Prosdocimo, "courted (if the grave Muse of history may incline her ear to the gossip of gallantry) by the most charming nymphs, even of the very highest quality."

My friends glance once more at the engraving; more insipid remarks are made; I am requested—especially by the American young ladies—to play or sing one of this Zaffirino's favourite songs—"For of course you know them, dear Maestro Magnus, you who have such a passion for all old music. Do be good, and sit down to the piano."

I refuse, rudely enough, rolling the print in my fingers. How fearfully this cursed heat, these cursed moon-light nights, must have unstrung me! This Venice would certainly kill me in the long-run! Why, the sight of this idiotic engraving, the mere name of that coxcomb of a singer, have made my heart beat and my limbs turn to water like a love-sick hobbledehoy.

After my gruff refusal, the company begins to disperse; they prepare to go out, some to have a row on the lagoon, others to saunter before the *cafés* at St. Mark's; family discussions arise, gruntings of fathers, murmurs of mothers, peals of laughing from young girls and young men. And the moon, pouring in by the wide-open windows, turns this old palace ballroom, nowadays an inn dining-room, into a lagoon, scintillating, undulating like the other lagoon, the real one, which stretches out yonder furrowed by invisible gondolas betrayed by the red prow-lights. At last the whole lot of them are on the move. I shall be able to get some quiet in my room, and to work a little at my opera of *Ogier the Dane*. But no! Conversation revives, and, of all things, about that singer, that Zaffirino, whose absurd portrait I am crunching in my fingers.

The principal speaker is Count Alvise, an old Venetian with dyed whiskers, a great check tie fastened with two pins and a chain; a threadbare patrician who is dying to secure for his lanky son that pretty American girl, whose mother is intoxicated by all his mooning anecdotes about the past glories of Venice in general, and of his illustrious family in particular. Why, in Heaven's name, must he pitch upon Zaffirino for his mooning, this old duffer of a patrician?

"Zaffirino,—ah yes, to be sure! Balthasar Cesari, called Zaffirino," snuffles the voice of Count Alvise, who always repeats the last word of every sentence at least three times. "Yes, Zaffirino, to be sure! A famous singer of the days of my forefathers; yes, of my forefathers, dear lady!" Then a lot of rubbish about the former greatness of Venice, the glories of old music, the former Conservatoires, all mixed up with anecdotes of Rossini and Donizetti,* whom he pretends to have known intimately. Finally, a story, of course containing plenty about his illustrious family:—"My great grand-aunt, the Procuratessa Vendramin, from whom we have inherited our estate of Mistrà, on the Brenta"*—a hopelessly muddled story, apparently, fully of digressions, but of which that singer Zaffirino is the hero. The narrative, little by little, becomes more intelligible, or perhaps it is I who am giving it more attention.

"It seems," says the Count, "that there was one of his songs in particular which was called the 'Husbands' Air'—*L'Aria dei Mariti*—because they didn't enjoy it quite as much as their better-halves. . . . My grand-aunt, Pisana Renier, married to the Procuratore Vendramin, was a patrician of the old school, of the style that was getting rare a hundred years ago. Her virtue and her pride rendered her unapproachable. Zaffirino, on his part, was in the habit of boasting that no woman had ever been able to resist his singing, which, it appears, had its foundation in fact—the ideal changes, my dear lady, the ideal changes a good deal from one century to another!—and that his first song could make any woman turn pale and lower her eyes, the second make her madly in love, while the third song could kill her off on the spot, kill her for love, there under his very eyes, if he only felt inclined. My grand-aunt Vendramin laughed when this story was told her, refused to go to hear this insolent dog, and added that it might be quite possible by the aid of spells and infernal pacts to kill a *gentildonna*,* but as to making her fall in love with a lackey—never! This answer was naturally reported to Zaffirino, who piqued himself upon always getting the better of any one who was wanting in deference to his voice. Like the ancient Romans, *parcere subjectis et debellare superbos*. You American ladies, who are so learned, will appreciate this little quotation from the divine Virgil.* While seeming to avoid the Procuratessa Vendramin, Zaffirino took the opportunity, one evening at a large assembly, to sing in her presence. He sang and sang and sang until the poor grand-aunt Pisana fell ill for love. The most skilful physicians were kept unable to explain the mysterious malady which was visibly killing the poor young lady; and the Procuratore Vendramin applied in vain to the most venerated Madonnas, and vainly promised an altar of silver, with massive gold candlesticks, to Saints Cosmas and Damian,* patrons of the art of healing. At last the brother-in-law of the Procuratessa, Monsignor Almorò Vendramin, Patriarch of Aquileia,* a prelate famous for the sanctity of his life, obtained in a vision of Saint Justina,* for whom he entertained a particular devotion, the information that the only thing which could benefit the strange illness of his sister-in-law was the voice of Zaffirino. Take notice that my poor grand-aunt had never condescended to such a revelation.

"The Procuratore was enchanted at this happy solution; and his lordship the Patriarch went to seek Zaffirino in person, and carried him in his own coach to the Villa of Mistrà, where the Procuratessa was residing. On being told what was about to happen, my poor grand-aunt went into fits of rage, which were succeeded immediately by equally violent fits of joy. However, she never forgot what was due to her great position. Although sick almost unto death, she had herself arrayed with the greatest pomp, caused her face to be painted, and put on all her diamonds: it would seem as if she were anxious to affirm her full dignity before this singer. Accordingly she received Zaffirino reclining on a sofa which had been placed in the great ballroom of the Villa of Mistrà, and beneath the princely canopy; for the Vendramins, who had intermarried with the house of Mantua, possessed imperial fiefs and were princes of the Holy Roman Empire. Zaffirino saluted her with the most profound respect, but not a word passed between them. Only, the singer inquired from the Procuratore whether the illustrious lady had received the Sacraments of the Church. Being told that the Procuratessa had herself asked to be given extreme unction from the hands of her brother-in-law, he declared his readiness to obey the orders of His Excellency, and sat down at once to the harpsichord.

"Never had he sung so divinely. At the end of the first song the Procuratessa Vendramin had already revived most extraordinarily; by the end of the second she appeared entirely cured and beaming with beauty and happiness; but at the third air—the *Aria dei Mariti*, no doubt—she began to change frightfully; she gave a dreadful cry, and fell into the convulsions of death. In a quarter of an hour she was dead! Zaffirino did not wait to see her die. Having finished his song, he withdrew instantly, took post-horses, and travelled day and night as far as Munich. People remarked that he had presented himself at Mistrà dressed in mourning, although he had mentioned no death among his relatives; also that he had prepared everything for his departure, as if fearing the wrath of so powerful a family. Then there was also the extraordinary question he had asked before beginning to sing, about the Procuratessa having confessed and received extreme unction. . . . No, thanks, my dear lady, no cigarettes for me. But if it does not distress you or your charming daughter, may I humbly beg permission to smoke a cigar?"

And Count Alvise, enchanted with his talent for narrative, and sure of having secured for his son the heart and the dollars of his fair audience, proceeds to light a candle, and at the candle one of those long black Italian cigars which require preliminary disinfection before smoking.

. . . If this state of things goes on I shall just have to ask the doctor for a bottle; this ridiculous beating of my heart and disgusting cold perspiration have increased steadily during Count Alvise's narrative. To keep myself in countenance among the various idiotic commentaries on this cock-and-bull story of a vocal coxcomb and a vapouring great lady, I begin to unroll the engraving, and to examine stupidly the portrait of Zaffirino, once so renowned, now so forgotten. A ridiculous ass, this singer, under his triumphal arch, with his stuffed Cupids and the great fat winged kitchenmaid crowning him with laurels. How flat and vapid and vulgar it is, to be sure, all this odious eighteenth century!

But he, personally, is not so utterly vapid as I had thought. That effeminate, fat face of his is almost beautiful, with an odd smile, brazen and cruel. I have seen faces like this, if not in real life, at least in my boyish romantic dreams, when I read Swinburne and Baudelaire,* the faces of wicked, vindictive women. Oh yes! he is decidedly a beautiful creature, this Zaffirino, and his voice must have had the same sort of beauty and the same expression of wickedness. . . .

"Come on, Magnus," sound the voices of my fellow-boarders, "be a good fellow and sing us one of the old chap's songs; or at least something or other of that day, and we'll make believe it was the air with which he killed that poor lady."

"Oh yes! the *Aria dei Mariti*, the 'Husbands' Air,'" mumbles old Alvise, between the puffs at his impossible black cigar. "My poor grand-aunt, Pisana Vendramin; he went and killed her with those songs of his, with that *Aria dei Mariti*."

I feel senseless rage overcoming me. Is it that horrible palpitation (by the way, there is a Norwegian doctor, my fellow-countryman, at Venice just now) which is sending the blood to my brain and making me mad? The people round the piano, the furniture, everything together seems to get mixed and to turn into moving blobs of colour. I set to singing; the only thing which remains distinct before my eyes being the portrait of Zaffirino, on the edge of that boarding-house piano; the sensual, effeminate face, with its wicked, cynical smile, keeps appearing and disappearing as the print wavers about in the draught that makes the candles smoke and gutter. And I set to singing madly, singing I don't know what. Yes; I begin to identify it: 'tis the

Biondina in Gondoleta,* the only song of the eighteenth century which is still remembered by the Venetian people. I sing it, mimicking every old-school grace; shakes, cadences, languishingly swelled and diminished notes, and adding all manner of buffooneries, until the audience, recovering from its surprise, begins to shake with laughing; until I begin to laugh myself, madly, frantically, between the phrases of the melody, my voice finally smothered in this dull, brutal laughter. . . . And then, to crown it all, I shake my fist at this long-dead singer, looking at me with his wicked woman's face, with his mocking, fatuous smile.

"Ah! you would like to be revenged on me also!" I exclaim. "You would like me to write you nice roulades and flourishes, another nice *Aria dei Mariti*, my fine Zaffirino!"

* * * *

That night I dreamed a very strange dream. Even in the big half-furnished room the heat and closeness were stifling. The air seemed laden with the scent of all manner of white flowers, faint and heavy in their intolerable sweetness: tuberoses, gardenias, and jasmines drooping I know not where in neglected vases. The moonlight had transformed the marble floor around me into a shallow, shining pool. On account of the heat I had exchanged my bed for a big old-fashioned sofa of light wood, painted with little nosegays and sprigs, like an old silk; and I lay there, not attempting to sleep, and letting my thoughts go vaguely to my opera of *Ogier the Dane*, of which I had long finished writing the words, and for whose music I had hoped to find some inspiration in this strange Venice, floating, as it were, in the stagnant lagoon of the past. But Venice had merely put all my ideas into hopeless confusion; it was as if there arose out of its shallow waters a miasma of long-dead melodies, which sickened but intoxicated my soul. I lay on my sofa watching that pool of whitish light, which rose higher and higher, little trickles of light meeting it here and there, wherever the moon's rays struck upon some polished surface; while huge shadows waved to and fro in the draught of the open balcony.

I went over and over that old Norse story: how the Paladin, Ogier, one of the knights of Charlemagne, was decoyed during his homeward wanderings from the Holy Land by the arts of an enchantress, the same who had once held in bondage the great Emperor Cæsar and given him King Oberon for a son; how Ogier had tarried in that island only one day and one night, and yet, when he came home to his kingdom, he found all changed, his friends dead, his family dethroned, and not a man who knew his face; until at last, driven hither and thither like a beggar, a poor minstrel had taken compassion of his sufferings and given him all he could give—a song, the song of the prowess of a hero dead for hundreds of years, the Paladin Ogier the Dane.

The story of Ogier ran into a dream, as vivid as my waking thoughts had been vague. I was looking no longer at the pool of moonlight spreading round my couch, with its trickles of light and looming, waving shadows, but the frescoed walls of a great saloon. It was not, as I recognised in a second, the dining-room of that Venetian palace now turned into a boarding-house. It was a far larger room, a real ballroom, almost circular in its octagon shape, with eight huge white doors surrounded by stucco mouldings, and, high on the vault of the ceiling, eight little galleries or recesses like boxes at a theatre, intended no doubt for musicians and spectators. The place was imperfectly lighted by only one of the eight chandeliers, which revolved slowly, like huge spiders, each on its long cord. But the light struck upon the gilt stuccoes opposite me, and on a large expanse of fresco, the sacrifice of Iphigenia, with Agamemnon and Achilles in Roman helmets, lappets, and knee-breeches. It discovered also one of the oil panels let into the mouldings of the roof, a goddess in lemon and lilac draperies, foreshortened over a great green peacock.* Round the room, where the light reached, I could make out big yellow satin sofas and heavy gilded consoles; in the shadow of a corner was what looked like a piano, and farther in the shade one of those big canopies which decorate the anterooms of Roman palaces. I looked about me, wondering where I was: a heavy, sweet smell, reminding me of the flavour of a peach, filled the place.

Little by little I began to perceive sounds; little, sharp, metallic, detached notes, like those of a mandoline; and there was united to them a voice, very low and sweet, almost a whisper, which grew and grew and grew, until the whole place was filled with that exquisite vibrating note, of a strange, exotic, unique quality. The note went on, swelling and swelling. Suddenly there was a horrible piercing shriek, and the thud of a body on the floor, and all manner of smothered exclamations. There, close by the canopy, a light suddenly appeared; and I could see, among the dark figures moving to and fro in the room, a woman lying on the ground, surrounded by other women. Her blond hair, tangled, full of diamond-sparkles which cut through the half-darkness, was hanging dishevelled; the laces of her bodice had been cut, and her white breast shone among the sheen of jewelled brocade; her face was bent forwards, and a thin white arm trailed, like a broken limb, across the knees of one of the women who were endeavouring to lift her. There was a sudden splash of water against the floor, more confused exclamations, a hoarse, broken moan, and a gurgling, dreadful sound. . . . I awoke with a start and rushed to the window.

Outside, in the blue haze of the moon, the church and belfry of St. George loomed blue and hazy, with the black hull and rigging, the red lights, of a large steamer moored before them. From the lagoon rose a damp sea-breeze. What was it all? Ah! I began to understand: that story of old Count Alvise's, the death of his grand-aunt, Pisana Vendramin. Yes, it was about that I had been dreaming.

I returned to my room; I struck a light, and sat down to my writing-table. Sleep had become impossible. I tried to work at my opera. Once or twice I thought I had got hold of what I had looked for so long. . . . But as soon as I tried to lay hold of my theme, there arose in my mind the distant echo of that voice, of that long note swelled slowly by insensible degrees, that long note whose tone was so strong and so subtle.

* * * *

There are in the life of an artist moments when, still unable to seize his own inspiration, or even clearly to discern it, he becomes aware of the approach of that long-invoked idea. A mingled joy and terror warn him that before another day, another hour have passed, the inspiration shall have crossed the threshold of his soul and flooded it with its rapture. All day I had felt the need of isolation and quiet, and at nightfall I went for a row on the most solitary part of the lagoon. All things seemed to tell that I was going to meet my inspiration, and I awaited its coming as a lover awaits his beloved.

I had stopped my gondola for a moment, and as I gently swayed to and fro on the water, all paved with moonbeams, it seemed to me that I was on the confines of an imaginary world. It lay close at hand, enveloped in luminous, pale blue mist, through which the moon had cut a wide and glistening path; out to sea, the little islands, like moored black boats, only accentuated the solitude of this region of moonbeams and wavelets; while the hum of the insects in orchards hard by merely added to the impression of untroubled silence. On some such seas, I thought, must the Paladin Ogier have sailed when about to discover that during that sleep at the enchantress's knees centuries had elapsed and the heroic world had set, and the kingdom of prose had come.

While my gondola rocked stationary on that sea of moonbeams, I pondered over that twilight of the heroic world. In the soft rattle of the water on the hull I seemed to hear the rattle of all that armour, of all those swords swinging rusty on the walls, neglected by the degenerate sons of the great champions of old. I had long been in search of a theme which I called the theme of the "Prowess of Ogier;"* it was to appear from time to time in the course of my opera, to develop at last into that song of the Minstrel, which reveals to the hero that he is one of a long-dead world. And at this moment I seemed to feel the presence of that theme. Yet an instant, and my mind would be overwhelmed by that savage music, heroic, funereal.

Suddenly there came across the lagoon, cleaving, chequering, and fretting the silence with a lace-work of sound even as the moon was fretting and cleaving the water, a ripple of music, a voice breaking itself in a shower of little scales and cadences and trills.

I sank back upon my cushions. The vision of heroic days had vanished, and before my closed eyes there seemed to dance multitudes of little stars of light, chasing and interlacing like those sudden vocalisations.

"To shore! Quick!" I cried to the gondolier.

But the sounds had ceased; and there came from the orchards, with their mulberry-trees glistening in the moonlight, and their black swaying cypress-plumes, nothing save the confused hum, the monotonous chirp, of the crickets.

I looked around me: on one side empty dunes, orchards, and meadows, without house or steeple; on the other, the blue and misty sea, empty to where distant islets were profiled black on the horizon.

A faintness overcame me, and I felt myself dissolve. For all of a sudden a second ripple of voice swept over the lagoon, a shower of little notes, which seemed to form a little mocking laugh.

Then again all was still. This silence lasted so long that I fell once more to meditating on my opera. I lay in wait once more for the half-caught theme. But no. It was not that theme for which I was waiting and watching with baited breath. I realised my delusion when, on rounding the point of the Giudecca,* the murmur of a voice arose from the midst of the waters, a thread of sound slender as a moonbeam, scarce audible, but exquisite, which expanded slowly, insensibly, taking volume and body, taking flesh almost and fire, an ineffable quality, full, passionate, but veiled, as it were, in a subtle, downy wrapper. The note grew stronger and stronger, and warmer and more passionate, until it burst through that strange and charming veil, and emerged beaming, to break itself in the luminous facets of a wonderful shake, long, superb, triumphant.

There was a dead silence.

"Row to St. Mark's!"* I exclaimed. "Quick!"

The gondola glided through the long, glittering track of moonbeams, and rent the great band of yellow, reflected light, mirroring the cupolas of St. Mark's, the lace-like pinnacles of the palace, and the slender pink belfry, which rose from the lit-up water to the pale and bluish evening sky.

In the larger of the two squares the military band was blaring through the last spirals of a *crescendo* of Rossini. The crowd was dispersing in this great open-air ballroom, and the sounds arose which invariably follow upon out-of-door music. A clatter of spoons and glasses, a rustle and grating of frocks and of chairs, and the click of scabbards on the pavement. I pushed my way among the fashionable youths contemplating the ladies while sucking the knob of their sticks; through the serried ranks of respectable families, marching arm in arm with their white frocked young ladies close in front. I took a seat before Florian's,* among the customers stretching themselves before departing, and the waiters hurrying to and fro, clattering their empty cups and trays. Two imitation Neapolitans were slipping their guitar and violin under their arm, ready to leave the place.

"Stop!" I cried to them; "don't go yet. Sing me something—sing *La Camesella* or *Funiculì, funiculà**—no matter what, provided you make a row;" and as they screamed and scraped their utmost, I added, "But can't you sing louder, d—n you!—sing louder, do you understand?"

I felt the need of noise, of yells and false notes, of something vulgar and hideous to drive away that ghost-voice which was haunting me.

* * * *

Again and again I told myself that it had been some silly prank of a romantic amateur, hidden in the gardens of the shore or gliding unperceived on the lagoon; and that the sorcery of moonlight and sea mist had transfigured for my excited brain mere humdrum roulades out of exercises of Bordogni or Crescentini.*

But all the same I continued to be haunted by that voice. My work was interrupted ever and anon by the attempt to catch its imaginary echo; and the heroic harmonies of my Scandinavian legend were strangely interwoven with voluptuous phrases and florid cadences in which I seemed to hear again that same accursed voice.

To be haunted by singing-exercises! It seemed too ridiculous for a man who professedly despised the art of singing. And still, I preferred to believe in that childish amateur, amusing himself with warbling to the moon.

One day, while making these reflections the hundredth time over, my eyes chanced to light upon the portrait of Zaffirino, which my friend had pinned against the wall. I pulled it down and tore it into half a dozen shreds. Then, already ashamed of my folly, I watched the torn pieces float down from the window, wafted hither and thither by the sea-breeze. One scrap got caught in a yellow blind below me; the others fell into the canal, and were speedily lost to sight in the dark water. I was overcome with shame. My heart beat like bursting. What a miserable, unnerved worm I had become in this cursed Venice, with its languishing moonlights, its atmosphere as of some stuffy boudoir, long unused, full of old stuffs and pot-pourri!

That night, however, things seemed to be going better. I was able to settle down to my opera, and even to work at it. In the intervals my thoughts returned, not without a certain pleasure, to those scattered fragments of the torn engraving fluttering down to the water. I was disturbed at my piano by the hoarse voices and the scraping of violins which rose from one of those music-boats that station at night under the hotels of the Grand Canal. The moon had set. Under my balcony the water stretched black into the distance, its darkness cut by the still darker outlines of the flotilla of gondolas in attendance on the music-boat, where the faces of the singers, and the guitars and violins, gleamed reddish under the unsteady light of the Chinese-lanterns.

"*Jammo, jammo; jammo, jammo jà*," sang the loud, hoarse voices; then a tremendous scrape and twang, and the yelled-out burden, "*Funiculì, funiculà; funiculì, funiculà; jammo, jammo, jammo, jammo, jammo jà*."

Then came a few cries of "*Bis, Bis!*"* from a neighbouring hotel, a brief clapping of hands, the sound of a handful of coppers rattling into the boat, and the oar-stroke of some gondolier making ready to turn away.

"Sing the *Camesella*," ordered some voice with a foreign accent.

"No, no! *Santa Lucia*."*

"I want the *Camesella*."

"No! *Santa Lucia*. Hi! sing *Santa Lucia*—d'you hear?"

The musicians, under their green and yellow and red lamps, held a whispered consultation on the manner of conciliating these contradictory demands. Then, after a minute's hesitation, the violins began the prelude of that once famous air, which has remained popular in Venice—the words written, some hundred years ago, by the patrician Gritti,* the music by an unknown composer—*La Biondina in Gondoleta*.

That cursed eighteenth century! It seemed a malignant fatality that made these brutes choose just this piece to interrupt me.

At last the long prelude came to an end; and above the cracked guitars and squeaking fiddles there arose, not the expected nasal chorus, but a single voice singing below its breath.

My arteries throbbed. How well I knew that voice! It was singing, as I have said, below its breath, yet none the less it sufficed to fill all that reach of the canal with its strange quality of tone, exquisite, far-fetched.

They were long-drawn-out notes, of intense but peculiar sweetness, a man's voice which had much of a woman's, but more even of a chorister's, but a chorister's voice without its limpidity and innocence; its youthfulness was veiled, muffled, as it were, in a sort of downy vagueness, as if a passion of tears withheld.

There was a burst of applause, and the old palaces re-echoed with the clapping. "Bravo, bravo! Thank you, thank you! Sing again—please, sing again. Who can it be?"

And then a bumping of hulls, a splashing of oars, and the oaths of gondoliers trying to push each other away, as the red prow-lamps of the gondolas pressed round the gaily lit singing-boat.

But no one stirred on board. It was to none of them that this applause was due. And while every one pressed on, and clapped and vociferated, one little red prow-lamp dropped away from the fleet; for a moment a single gondola stood forth black upon the black water, and then was lost in the night.

For several days the mysterious singer was the universal topic. The people of the music-boat swore that no one besides themselves had been on board, and that they knew as little as ourselves about the owner of that voice. The gondoliers, despite their descent from the spies of the old Republic,* were equally unable to furnish any clue. No musical celebrity was known or suspected to be at Venice; and every one agreed that such a singer must be a European celebrity. The strangest thing in this strange business was, that even among those learned in music there was no agreement on the subject of this voice: it was called by all sorts of names and described by all manner of incongruous adjectives; people went so far as to dispute whether the voice belonged to a man or to a woman: every one had some new definition.

In all these musical discussions I, alone, brought forward no opinion. I felt a repugnance, an impossibility almost, of speaking about that voice; and the more or less commonplace conjectures of my friend had the invariable effect of sending me out of the room.

Meanwhile my work was becoming daily more difficult, and I soon passed from utter impotence to a state of inexplicable agitation. Every morning I arose with fine resolutions and grand projects of work; only to go to bed that night without having accomplished anything. I spent hours leaning on my balcony, or wandering through the network of lanes with their ribbon of blue sky, endeavouring vainly to expel the thought of that voice, or endeavouring in reality to reproduce it in my memory; for the more I tried to banish it from my thoughts, the more I grew to thirst for that extraordinary tone, for those mysteriously downy, veiled notes; and no sooner did I make an effort to work at my opera than my head was full of scraps of forgotten eighteenth century airs, of frivolous or languishing little phrases; and I fell to wondering with a bitter-sweet longing how those songs would have sounded if sung by that voice.

At length it became necessary to see a doctor, from whom, however, I carefully hid away all the stranger symptoms of my malady. The air of the lagoons, the great heat, he answered cheerfully, had pulled me down a little; a tonic and a month in the country, with plenty of riding and no work, would make me myself again. That old idler, Count Alvise, who had insisted on accompanying me to the physician's, immediately suggested that I should go and stay with his son, who was boring himself to death superintending the maize harvest on the mainland: he could promise me excellent air, plenty of horses, and all the peaceful surroundings and the delightful occupations of a rural life—"Be sensible, my dear Magnus, and just go quietly to Mistrà."

Mistrà—the name sent a shiver all down me. I was about to decline the invitation, when a thought suddenly loomed vaguely in my mind.

"Yes, dear Count," I answered; "I accept your invitation with gratitude and pleasure. I will start to-morrow for Mistrà."

The next day found me at Padua, on my way to the Villa of Mistrà. It seemed as if I had left an intolerable burden behind me. I was, for the first time since how long, quite light of heart. The tortuous, rough-paved streets, with their empty, gloomy porticoes; the ill-plastered palaces, with closed, discoloured shutters; the little rambling square, with meagre trees and stubborn grass; the Venetian garden-houses reflecting their crumbling graces in the muddy canal; the gardens without gates and the gates without gardens, the avenues leading nowhere; and the population of blind and legless beggars, of whining sacristans, which issued as by magic from between the flagstones and dust-heaps and weeds under the fierce August sun, all this dreariness merely amused and pleased me. My good spirits were heightened by a musical mass which I had the good fortune to hear at St. Anthony's.*

Never in all my days had I heard anything comparable, although Italy affords many strange things in the way of sacred music. Into the deep nasal chanting of the priests there had suddenly burst a chorus of children, singing absolutely independent of all time and tune; grunting of priests answered by squealing of boys, slow Gregorian modulation* interrupted by jaunty barrel-organ pipings, an insane, insanely merry jumble of bellowing and barking, mewing and cackling and braying, such as would have enlivened a witches' meeting, or rather some mediæval Feast of Fools.* And, to make the grotesqueness of such music still more fantastic and Hoffmannlike,* there was, besides, the magnificence of the piles of sculptured marbles and gilded bronzes, the tradition of the musical splendour for which St. Anthony's had been famous in days gone by. I had read in old travellers, Lalande and Burney,* that the Republic of St. Mark had squandered immense sums not merely on the monuments and decoration, but on the musical establishment of its great cathedral of Terra Firma.* In the midst of this ineffable concert of impossible voices and instruments, I tried to imagine the voice of Guadagni, the soprano for whom Gluck had written *Che farò senza Euridice*, and the fiddle of Tartini, that Tartini* with whom the devil had once come and made music. And the delight in anything so absolutely, barbarously, grotesquely, fantastically incongruous as such a performance in such a place was heightened by a sense of profanation: such were the successors of those wonderful musicians of that hated eighteenth century!

The whole thing had delighted me so much, so very much more than the most faultless performance could have done, that I determined to enjoy it once more; and towards vesper-time, after a cheerful dinner with two bagmen at the inn of the Golden Star, and a pipe over the rough sketch of a possible cantata upon the music which the devil made for Tartini, I turned my steps once more towards St. Anthony's.

The bells were ringing for sunset, and a muffled sound of organs seemed to issue from the huge, solitary church; I pushed my way under the heavy leathern curtain, expecting to be greeted by the grotesque performance of that morning.

I proved mistaken. Vespers must long have been over. A smell of stale incense, a crypt-like damp filled my mouth; it was already night in that vast cathedral. Out of the darkness glimmered the votive-lamps of the chapels, throwing wavering lights upon the red polished marble, the gilded railing, and chandeliers, and plaqueing with yellow the muscles of some sculptured figure. In a corner a burning taper put a halo about the head of a priest, burnishing his shining bald skull, his white surplice, and the open book before him. "Amen" he chanted; the book was closed with a snap, the light moved up the apse, some dark figures of women rose from their knees and passed quickly towards the door; a man saying his prayers before a chapel also got up, making a great clatter in dropping his stick.

The church was empty, and I expected every minute to be turned out by the sacristan making his evening round to close the doors. I was leaning against a pillar, looking into the greyness of the great arches, when the organ suddenly burst out into a series of chords, rolling through the echoes of the church: it seemed to be the conclusion of some service. And above the organ rose the notes of a voice; high, soft, enveloped in a kind of downiness, like a cloud of incense, and which ran through the mazes of a long cadence. The voice dropped into silence; with two thundering chords the organ closed in. All was silent. For a moment I stood leaning against one of the pillars of the nave: my hair was clammy, my knees sank beneath me, an enervating heat spread through my body; I tried to breathe more largely, to suck in the sounds with the incense-laden air. I was supremely happy, and yet as if I were dying; then suddenly a chill ran through me, and with it a vague panic. I turned away and hurried out into the open.

The evening sky lay pure and blue along the jagged line of roofs; the bats and swallows were wheeling about; and from the belfries all around, half-drowned by the deep bell of St. Anthony's, jangled the peel of the *Ave Maria*.*

* * * *

"You really don't seem well," young Count Alvise had said the previous evening, as he welcomed me, in the light of a lantern held up by a peasant, in the weedy back-garden of the Villa of Mistrà. Everything had seemed to me like a dream: the jingle of the horse's bells driving in the dark from Padua, as the lantern swept the acacia-hedges with their wide yellow light; the grating of the wheels on the gravel; the supper-table, illumined by a single petroleum lamp for fear of attracting mosquitoes, where a broken old lackey, in an old stable jacket, handed round the dishes among the fumes of onion; Alvise's fat mother gabbling dialect in a shrill, benevolent voice behind the bull-fights on her fan; the unshaven village priest, perpetually fidgeting with his glass and foot, and sticking one shoulder up above the other. And now, in the afternoon, I felt as if I had been in this long, rambling, tumble-down Villa of Mistrà—a villa three-quarters of which was given up to the storage of grain and garden tools, or to the exercise of rats, mice, scorpions, and centipedes—all my life; as if I had always sat there, in Count Alvise's study, among the pile of undusted books on agriculture, the sheaves of accounts, the samples of grain and silkworm seed, the ink-stains and the cigar-ends; as if I had never heard of anything save the cereal basis of Italian agriculture, the diseases of maize, the peronospora* of the vine, the breeds of bullocks, and the iniquities of farm labourers; with the blue cones of the Euganean hills* closing in the green shimmer of plain outside the window.

After an early dinner, again with the screaming gabble of the fat old Countess, the fidgeting and shoulder-raising of the unshaven priest, the smell of fried oil and stewed onions, Count Alvise made me get into the cart beside him, and whirled me along among clouds of dust, between the endless glister of poplars, acacias, and maples, to one of his farms.

In the burning sun some twenty or thirty girls, in coloured skirts, laced bodices, and big straw-hats, were threshing the maize on the big red brick threshing-floor, while others were winnowing the grain in great sieves. Young Alvise III. (the old one was Alvise II.: every one is Alvise, that is to say, Lewis, in that family; the name is on the house, the carts, the barrows, the very pails) picked up the maize, touched it, tasted it, said something to the girls that made them laugh, and something to the head farmer that made him look very glum; and then led me into a huge stable, where some twenty or thirty white bullocks were stamping, switching their tails, hitting their horns against the mangers in the dark. Alvise III. patted each, called him by his name, gave him some salt or a turnip, and explained which was the Mantuan breed, which the Apulian, which the Romagnolo, and so on. Then he bade me jump into the trap, and off we went again through the dust, among the hedges and ditches, till we came to some more brick farm buildings with pinkish roofs smoking against the blue sky. Here there were more young women threshing and winnowing the maize, which made a great golden Danaë cloud;* more bullocks stamping and lowing in the cool darkness; more joking, fault-finding, explaining; and thus through five farms, until I seemed to see the rhythmical rising and falling of the flails against the hot sky, the shower of golden grains, the yellow dust from the winnowing-sieves on to the bricks, the switching of innumerable tails and plunging of innumerable horns, the glistening of huge white flanks and foreheads, whenever I closed my eyes.

"A good day's work!" cried Count Alvise, stretching out his long legs with the tight trousers riding up over the Wellington boots. "Mamma, give us some aniseed-syrup after dinner; it is an excellent restorative and precaution against the fevers of this country."

"Oh! you've got fever in this part of the world, have you? Why, your father said the air was so good!"

"Nothing, nothing," soothed the old Countess. "The only thing to be dreaded are mosquitoes; take care to fasten your shutters before lighting the candle."

"Well," rejoined young Alvise, with an effort of conscience, "of course there *are* fevers. But they needn't hurt you. Only, don't go out into the garden at night, if you don't want to catch them. Papa told me that you have fancies for moonlight rambles. It won't do in this climate, my dear fellow; it won't do. If you must stalk about at night, being a genius, take a turn inside the house; you can get quite exercise enough."

After dinner the aniseed-syrup was produced, together with brandy and cigars, and they all sat in the long, narrow, half-furnished room on the first floor; the old Countess knitting a garment of uncertain shape and destination, the priest reading out the newspaper; Count Alvise puffing at his long, crooked cigar, and pulling the ears of a long, lean dog with a suspicion of mange and a stiff eye. From the dark garden outside rose the hum and whirr of countless insects, and the smell of the grapes which hung black against the starlit, blue sky, on the trellis. I went to the balcony. The garden lay dark beneath; against the twinkling horizon stood out the tall poplars. There was the sharp cry of an owl; the barking of a dog; a sudden whiff of warm, enervating perfume, a perfume that made me think of the taste of certain peaches, and suggested white, thick, wax-like petals. I seemed to have smelt that flower once before: it made me feel languid, almost faint.

"I am very tired," I said to Count Alvise. "See how feeble we city folk become!"

* * * *

But, despite my fatigue, I found it quite impossible to sleep. The night seemed perfectly stifling. I had felt nothing like it at Venice. Despite the injunctions of the Countess I opened the solid wooden shutters, hermetically closed against mosquitoes, and looked out.

The moon had risen; and beneath it lay the big lawns, the rounded tree-tops, bathed in a blue, luminous mist, every leaf glistening and trembling in what seemed a heaving sea of light. Beneath the window was the long trellis, with the white shining piece of pavement under it. It was so bright that I could distinguish the green of the vine-leaves, the dull red of the catalpa-flowers. There was in the air a vague scent of cut grass, of ripe American grapes, of that white flower (it must be white) which made me think of the taste of peaches all melting into the delicious freshness of falling dew. From the village church came the stroke of one: Heaven knows how long I had been vainly attempting to sleep. A shiver ran through me, and my head suddenly filled as with the fumes of some subtle wine; I remembered all those weedy embankments, those canals full of stagnant water, the yellow faces of the peasants; the word malaria returned to my mind. No matter! I remained leaning on the window, with a thirsty longing to plunge myself into this blue moon-mist, this dew and perfume and silence, which seemed to vibrate and quiver like the stars that strewed the depths of heaven. . . . What music, even Wagner's, or of that great singer of starry nights, the divine Schumann,* what music could ever compare with this great silence, with this great concert of voiceless things that sing within one's soul?

As I made this reflection, a note, high, vibrating, and sweet, rent the silence, which immediately closed around it. I leaned out of the window, my heart beating as though it must burst. After a brief space the silence was cloven once more by that note, as the darkness is cloven by a falling star or a firefly rising slowly like a rocket. But this time it was plain that the voice did not come, as I had imagined, from the garden, but from the house itself, from some corner of this rambling old villa of Mistrà.

Mistrà—Mistrà! The name rang in my ears, and I began at length to grasp its significance, which seems to have escaped me till then. "Yes," I said to myself, "it is quite natural." And with this odd impression of naturalness was mixed a feverish, impatient pleasure. It was as if I had come to Mistrà on purpose, and that I was about to meet the object of my long and weary hopes.

Grasping the lamp with its singed green shade, I gently opened the door and made my way through a series of long passages and of big, empty rooms, in which my steps re-echoed as in a church, and my light disturbed whole swarms of bats. I wandered at random, farther and farther from the inhabited part of the buildings.

This silence made me feel sick; I gasped as under a sudden disappointment.

All of a sudden there came a sound—chords, metallic, sharp, rather like the tone of a mandoline—close to my ear. Yes, quite close: I was separated from the sounds only by a partition. I fumbled for a door; the unsteady light of my lamp was insufficient for my eyes, which were swimming like those of a drunkard. At last I found a latch, and, after a moment's hesitation, I lifted it and gently pushed open the door. At first I could not understand what manner of place I was in. It was dark all round me, but a brilliant light blinded me, a light coming from below and striking the opposite wall. It was as if I had entered a dark box in a half-lighted theatre. I was, in fact, in something of the kind, a sort of dark hole with a high balustrade, half-hidden by an up-drawn curtain. I remembered those little galleries or recesses for the use of musicians or lookers-on which exist under the ceiling of the ballrooms in certain old Italian palaces. Yes; it must have been one like that. Opposite me was a vaulted ceiling covered with gilt mouldings, which framed great time-blackened canvases; and lower down, in the light thrown up from below, stretched a wall covered with faded frescoes. Where had I seen that goddess in lilac and lemon draperies foreshortened over a big, green peacock? For she was familiar to me, and the stucco Tritons* also who twisted their tails round her gilded frame. And that fresco, with warriors in Roman cuirasses and green and blue lappets, and knee-breeches—where could I have seen them before? I asked myself these questions without experiencing any surprise. Moreover, I was very calm, as one is calm sometimes in extraordinary dreams—could I be dreaming?

I advanced gently and leaned over the balustrade. My eyes were met at first by the darkness above me, where, like gigantic spiders, the big chandeliers rotated slowly, hanging from the ceiling. Only one of them was lit, and its Murano-glass* pendants, its carnations and roses, shone opalescent in the light of the guttering wax. This chandelier lighted up the opposite wall and that piece of ceiling with the goddess and the green peacock; it illumined, but far less well, a corner of the huge room, where, in the shadow of a kind of canopy, a little group of people were crowding round a yellow satin sofa, of the same kind as those that lined the walls. On the sofa, half-screened from me by the surrounding persons, a woman was stretched out: the silver of her embroidered dress and the rays of her diamonds gleamed and shot forth as she moved uneasily. And immediately under the chandelier, in the full light, a man stooped over a harpsichord, his head bent slightly, as if collecting his thoughts before singing.

He struck a few chords and sang. Yes, sure enough, it was the voice, the voice that had so long been persecuting me! I recognised at once that delicate, voluptuous quality, strange, exquisite, sweet beyond words, but lacking all youth and clearness. That passion veiled in tears which had troubled my brain that night on the lagoon, and again on the Grand Canal singing the *Biondina*, and yet again, only two days since, in the deserted cathedral of Padua. But I recognised now what seemed to have been hidden from me till then, that this voice was what I cared most for in all the wide world.

The voice wound and unwound itself in long, languishing phrases, in rich, voluptuous *rifiorituras*,* all fretted with tiny scales and exquisite, crisp shakes; it stopped ever and anon, swaying as if panting in languid delight. And I felt my body melt even as wax in the sunshine, and it seemed to me that I too was turning fluid and vaporous, in order to mingle with these sounds as the moon-beams mingle with the dew.

Suddenly, from the dimly lighted corner by the canopy, came a little piteous wail; then another followed, and was lost in the singer's voice. During a long phrase on the harpsichord, sharp and tinkling, the singer turned his head towards the dais, and there came a plaintive little sob. But he, instead of stopping, struck a sharp chord; and with a thread of voice so hushed as to be scarcely audible, slid softly into a long *cadenza*.* At the same moment he threw his head backwards, and the light fell full upon the handsome, effeminate face, with its ashy pallor and big, black brows, of the singer Zaffirino. At the sight of that face, sensual and sullen, of that smile which was cruel and mocking like a bad woman's, I understood—I knew not why, by what process—that his singing *must* be cut short, that the accursed phrase *must* never be finished. I understood that I was before an assassin, that he was killing this woman, and killing me also, with his wicked voice.

I rushed down the narrow stair which led down from the box, pursued, as it were, by that exquisite voice, swelling, swelling by insensible degrees. I flung myself on the door which must be that of the big saloon. I could see its light between the panels. I bruised my hands in trying to wrench the latch. The door was fastened tight, and while I was struggling with that locked door I heard the voice swelling, swelling, rending asunder that downy veil which wrapped it, leaping forth clear, resplendent, like the sharp and glittering blade of a knife that seemed to enter deep into my breast. Then, once more, a wail, a death-groan, and that dreadful noise, that hideous gurgle of breath strangled by a rush of blood. And then a long shake, acute, brilliant, triumphant.

The door gave way beneath my weight, one half crashed in. I entered. I was blinded by a flood of blue moonlight. It poured in through four great windows, peaceful and diaphanous, a pale blue mist of moonlight, and turned the huge room into a kind of submarine cave, paved with moonbeams, full of shimmers, of pools of moonlight. It was as bright as at midday, but the brightness was cold, blue, vaporous, supernatural. The room was completely empty, like a great hay-loft. Only, there hung from the ceiling the ropes which had once supported a chandelier; and in a corner, among stacks of wood and heaps of Indian-corn, whence spread a sickly smell of damp and mildew, there stood a long, thin harpsichord, with spindle-legs, and its cover cracked from end to end.

I felt, all of a sudden, very calm. The one thing that mattered was the phrase that kept moving in my head, the phrase of that unfinished cadence which I had heard but an instant before. I opened the harpsichord, and my fingers came down boldly upon its keys. A jingle-jangle of broken strings, laughable and dreadful, was the only answer.

Then an extraordinary fear overtook me. I clambered out of one of the windows; I rushed up the garden and wandered through the fields, among the canals and the embankments, until the moon had set and the dawn began to shiver, followed, pursued for ever by that jangle of broken strings.

People expressed much satisfaction at my recovery. It seems that one dies of those fevers.

Recovery? But have I recovered? I walk, and eat and drink and talk; I can even sleep. I live the life of other living creatures. But I am wasted by a strange and deadly disease. I can never lay hold of my own inspiration. My head is filled with music which is certainly by me, since I have never heard it before, but which still is not my own, which I despise and abhor: little, tripping flourishes and languishing phrases, and long-drawn, echoing cadences.

O wicked, wicked voice, violin of flesh and blood made by the Evil One's hand, may I not even execrate thee in peace; but is it necessary that, at the moment when I curse, the longing to hear thee again should parch my soul like hell-thirst? And since I have satiated thy lust for revenge, since thou hast withered my life and withered my genius, is it not time for pity? May I not hear one note, only one note of thine, O singer, O wicked and contemptible wretch?

THE LEGEND OF MADAME KRASINSKA

It is a necessary part of this story to explain how I have come by it, or rather, how it has chanced to have me for its writer.

I was very much impressed one day by a certain nun of the order calling themselves Little Sisters of the Poor.* I had been taken to these sisters to support the recommendation of a certain old lady, the former door-keeper of his studio, whom my friend Cecco Bandini wished to place in the asylum. It turned out, of course, that Cecchino* was perfectly able to plead his case without my assistance; so I left him blandishing the Mother Superior in the big, cheerful kitchen, and begged to be shown over the rest of the establishment. The sister who was told off to accompany me was the one of whom I would speak.

This lady was tall and slight; her figure, as she preceded me up the narrow stairs and through the whitewashed wards, was uncommonly elegant and charming; and she had a girlish rapidity of movement, which caused me to experience a little shock at the first real sight which I caught of her face. It was young and remarkably pretty, with a kind of refinement peculiar to American women; but it was inexpressibly, solemnly tragic; and one felt that under her tight linen cap, the hair must be snow white. The tragedy, whatever it might have been, was now over; and the lady's expression, as she spoke to the old creatures scraping the ground in the garden, ironing the sheets in the laundry, or merely huddling over their braziers in the chill winter sunshine, was pathetic only by virtue of its strange present tenderness, and by that trace of terrible past suffering.

She answered my questions very briefly, and was as taciturn as ladies of religious communities are usually loquacious. Only, when I expressed my admiration for the institution which contrived to feed scores of old paupers on broken victuals begged from private houses and inns, she turned her eyes full upon me and said, with an earnestness which was almost passionate, "Ah, the old! The old! It is so much, much worse for them than for any others. Have you ever tried to imagine what it is to be poor and forsaken and old?"

These words and the strange ring in the sister's voice, the strange light in her eyes, remained in my memory. What was not, therefore, my surprise when, on returning to the kitchen, I saw her start and lay hold of the back of the chair as soon as she caught sight of Cecco Bandini. Cecco, on his side also, was visibly startled, but only after a moment; it was clear that she recognized him long before he identified her. What little romance could there exist in common between my eccentric painter and that serene but tragic Sister of the Poor?

A week later, it became evident that Cecco Bandini had come to explain the mystery; but to explain it (as I judged by the embarrassment of his manner) by one of those astonishingly elaborate lies occasionally attempted by perfectly frank persons. It was not the case. Cecchino had come indeed to explain that little dumb scene which had passed between him and the Little Sister of the Poor. He had come, however, not to satisfy my curiosity, or to overcome my suspicions, but to execute a commission which he had greatly at heart; to help, as he expressed it, in the accomplishment of a good work by a real saint.

Of course, he explained, smiling that good smile under his black eyebrows and white moustache, he did not expect me to believe very literally the story which he had undertaken to get me to write. He only asked, and the lady only wished, me to write down her narrative without any comments, and leave to the heart of the reader the decision about its truth or falsehood.

For this reason, and the better to attain the object of appealing to the profane, rather than to the religious, reader, I have abandoned the order of narrative of the Little Sister of the Poor; and attempted to turn her pious legend into a worldly story, as follows:—

I

Cecco Bandini had just returned from the Maremma,* to whose solitary marshes and jungles he had fled in one of his fits of fury at the stupidity and wickedness of the civilised world. A great many months spent among buffaloes and wild boars, conversing only with those wild cherry-trees, of whom he used whimsically to say, "they are such good little folk," had sent him back with an extraordinary zest for civilisation, and a comic tendency to find its products, human and otherwise, extraordinary, picturesque, and suggestive. He was in this frame of mind when there came a light rap on his door-slate; and two ladies appeared on the threshold of his studio, with the shaven face and cockaded hat of a tall footman over-topping them from behind. One of them was unknown to our painter; the other was numbered among Cecchino's very few grand acquaintances.

"Why haven't you been round to me yet, you savage?" she asked, advancing quickly with a brusque hand-shake and a brusque bright gleam of eyes and teeth, well-bred but audacious and a trifle ferocious. And dropping on to a divan she added, nodding first at her companion and then at the pictures all round, "I have brought my friend, Madame Krasinska, to see your things," and she began poking with her parasol at the contents of a gaping portfolio.

The Baroness Fosca—for such was her name—was one of the cleverest and fastest* ladies of the place, with a taste for art and ferociously frank conversation. To Cecco Bandini, as she lay back among her furs on that shabby divan of his, she appeared in the light of the modern Lucretia Borgia,* the tamed panther of fashionable life. "What an interesting thing civilisation is!" he thought, watching her every movement with the eyes of the imagination; "why, you might spend years among the wild folk of the Maremma without meeting such a tremendous, terrible, picturesque, powerful creature as this!"

Cecchino was so absorbed in the Baroness Fosca, who was in reality not at all a Lucretia Borgia, but merely an impatient lady bent upon amusing and being amused, that he was scarcely conscious of the presence of her companion. He knew that she was very young, very pretty, and very smart,* and that he had made her his best bow, and offered her his least rickety chair; for the rest, he sat opposite to his Lucretia Borgia of modern life, who had meanwhile found a cigarette, and was puffing away and explaining that she was about to give a fancy ball, which should be the most *crâne*,* the only amusing thing, of the year.

"Oh," he exclaimed, kindling at the thought, "do let me design you a dress all black and white and wicked green—you shall go as Deadly Nightshade,* as Belladonna Atropa——"

"Belladonna Atropa! why, my ball is in comic costume." . . . The Baroness was answering contemptuously, when Cecchino's attention was suddenly called to the other end of the studio by an exclamation on the part of his other visitor.

"Do tell me all about her; has she a name? Is she really a lunatic?" asked the young lady who had been introduced as Madame Krasinska, keeping a portfolio open with one hand, and holding up in the other a coloured sketch she had taken from it.

"What have you got there? Oh, only the Sora Lena!" and Madame Fosca reverted to the contemplation of the smoke-rings she was making.

"Tell me about her—Sora Lena, did you say?" asked the younger lady eagerly.

She spoke French, but with a pretty little American accent, despite her Polish name. She was very charming, Cecchino said to himself, a radiant impersonation of youthful brightness and elegance as she stood there in her long, silvery furs, holding the drawing with tiny, tight-gloved hands, and shedding around her a vague, exquisite fragrance—no, not a mere literal perfume, that would be far too coarse, but something personal akin to it.

"I have noticed her so often," she went on, with that silvery young voice of hers; "she's mad, isn't she? And what did you say her name was? Please tell me again."

Cecchino was delighted. "How true it is," he reflected, "that only refinement, high-breeding, luxury can give people certain kinds of sensitiveness, of rapid intuition! No woman of another class would have picked out just that drawing, or would have been interested in it without stupid laughter."

"Do you want to know the story of poor old Sora Lena?" asked Cecchino, taking the sketch from Madame Krasinska's hand, and looking over it at the charming, eager young face.

The sketch might have passed for a caricature; but anyone who had spent so little as a week in Florence those six or seven years ago would have recognised at once that it was merely a faithful portrait. For Sora Lena—more correctly Signora Maddalena—had been for years and years one of the most conspicuous sights of the town. In all weathers you might have seen that hulking old woman, with her vague, staring, reddish face, trudging through the streets or standing before shops, in her extraordinary costume of thirty years ago, her enormous crinoline, on which the silk skirt and ragged petticoat hung limply, her gigantic coal-scuttle bonnet, shawl, prunella boots, and great muff or parasol; one of several outfits, all alike, of that distant period, all alike inexpressibly dirty and tattered. In all weathers you might have seen her stolidly going her way, indifferent to stares and jibes, of which, indeed, there were by this time comparatively few, so familiar had she grown to staring, jibing Florence. In all weathers, but most noticeably in the worst, as if the squalor of mud and rain had an affinity with that sad, draggled, soiled, battered piece of human squalor, that lamentable rag of half-witted misery.

"Do you want to know about Sora Lena?" repeated Cecco Bandini, meditatively. They formed a strange, strange contrast, these two women, the one in the sketch and the one standing before him. And there was to him a pathetic whimsicalness in the interest which the one had excited in the other. "How long has she been wandering about here? Why, as long as I can remember the streets of Florence, and that," added Cecchino sorrowfully, "is a longer while than I care to count up. It seems to me as if she must always have been there, like the olive-trees and the paving-stones; for, after all, Giotto's tower* was not there before Giotto, whereas poor old Sora Lena—But, by the way, there is a limit even to her. There is a legend about her; they say that she was once sane, and had two sons, who went as Volunteers in '59, and were killed at Solferino,* and ever since then she has sallied forth, every day, winter or summer, in her best clothes, to meet the young fellows at the station.* May be. To my mind it doesn't matter much whether the story be true or false; it is fitting," and Cecco Bandini set about dusting some canvases which had attracted the Baroness Fosca's attention. When Cecchino was helping that lady into her furs, she gave one of her little brutal smiles, and nodded in the direction of her companion.

"Madame Krasinska," she said laughing, "is very desirous of possessing one of your sketches, but she is too polite to ask you the price of it. That's what comes of our not knowing how to earn a penny for ourselves, doesn't it, Signor Cecchino?"

Madame Krasinska blushed, and looked more young, and delicate, and charming.

"I did not know whether you would consent to part with one of your drawings," she said in her silvery, child-like voice,—"it is—this one—which I should so much have liked to have—. . . to have . . . bought." Cecchino smiled at the embarrassment which the word "bought" produced in his exquisite visitor. Poor, charming young creature, he thought; the only thing she thinks people one knows can sell, is themselves, and that's called getting married. "You must explain to your friend," said Cecchino to the Baroness Fosca, as he hunted in a drawer for a piece of clean paper, "that such rubbish as this is neither bought nor sold; it is not even possible for a poor devil of a painter to offer it as a gift to a lady—but,"—and he handed the little roll to Madame Krasinska, making his very best bow as he did so—"it is possible for a lady graciously to accept it."

"Thank you so much," answered Madame Krasinska, slipping the drawing into her muff; "it is very good of you to give me such a . . . such a very interesting sketch," and she pressed his big brown fingers in her little grey-gloved hand.

"Poor Sora Lena!" exclaimed Cecchino, when there remained of the visit only a faint perfume of exquisiteness; and he thought of the hideous old draggle-tailed mad woman, reposing, rolled up in effigy, in the delicious daintiness of that delicate grey muff.

II

A fortnight later, the great event was Madame Fosca's fancy ball, to which the guests were bidden to come in what was described as comic costume. Some, however, craved leave to appear in their ordinary apparel, and among these was Cecchino Bandini, who was persuaded, moreover, that his old-fashioned swallowtails, which he donned only at weddings, constituted quite comic costume enough.

This knowledge did not interfere at all with his enjoyment. There was even, to his whimsical mind, a certain charm in being in a crowd among which he knew no one; unnoticed, or confused, perhaps, with the waiters, as he hung about the stairs and strolled through the big palace rooms. It was as good as wearing an invisible cloak,* one saw so much just because one was not seen; indeed, one was momentarily endowed (it seemed at least to his fanciful apprehension) with a faculty akin to that of understanding the talk of birds; and, as he watched and listened he became aware of innumerable charming little romances, which were concealed from more notable but less privileged persons.

Little by little the big white and gold rooms began to fill. The ladies, who had moved in gorgeous isolation, their skirts displayed as finely as a peacock's train, became gradually visible only from the waist upwards; and only the branches of the palm-trees and tree ferns detached themselves against the shining walls. Instead of wandering among variegated brocades and iridescent silks and astonishing arrangements of feathers and flowers, Cecchino's eye was forced to a higher level by the thickening crowd; it was now the constellated sparkle of diamonds on neck and head which dazzled him, and the strange, unaccustomed splendour of white arms and shoulders. And, as the room filled, the invisible cloak was also drawn closer round our friend Cecchino, and the extraordinary faculty of perceiving romantic and delicious secrets in other folks' bosoms became more and more developed. They seemed to him like exquisite children, these creatures rustling about in fantastic dresses, powdered shepherds and shepherdesses with diamonds spirting fire among their ribbons and top-knots; Japanese and Chinese embroidered with sprays of flowers; mediæval and antique beings, and beings hidden in the plumage of birds, or the petals of flowers; children, but children somehow matured, transfigured by the touch of luxury and good-breeding, children full of courtesy and kindness. There were, of course, a few costumes which might have been better conceived or better carried out, or better—not to say best—omitted altogether. One grew bored, after a little while, with people dressed as marionettes, champagne bottles, sticks of sealing-wax, or captive balloons; a young man arrayed as a female ballet dancer, and another got up as a wet nurse, with baby *obligato*,* might certainly have been dispensed with. Also, Cecchino could not help wincing a little at the daughter of the house being mummed and painted to represent her own grandmother, a respectable old lady whose picture hung in the dining-room, and whose spectacles he had frequently picked up in his boyhood. But these were mere trifling details. And, as a whole, it was beautiful, fantastic. So Cecchino moved backward and forward, invisible in his shabby black suit, and borne hither and thither by the well-bred pressure of the many-coloured crowd; pleasantly blinded by the innumerable lights, the sparkle of chandelier pendants, and the shooting flames of jewels; gently deafened by the confused murmur of innumerable voices, of crackling stuffs and soughing fans, of distant dance music; and inhaling the vague fragrance which seemed less the decoction of cunning perfumers than the exquisite and expressive emanation of this exquisite bloom of personality. Certainly, he said to himself, there is no pleasure so delicious as seeing people amusing themselves with refinement: there is a transfiguring magic, almost a moralising power, in wealth and elegance and good-breeding.

He was making this reflection, and watching between two dances, a tiny fluff of down sailing through the warm draught across the empty space, the sort of whirlpool of the ball-room—when a little burst of voices came from the entrance saloon. The multi-coloured costumes fluttered like butterflies toward a given spot, there was a little heaping together of brilliant colours and flashing jewels. There was much craning of delicate, fluffy young necks and heads, and shuffle on tip-toe, and the crowd fell automatically aside. A little gangway was cleared; and there walked into the middle of the white and gold drawing-room, a lumbering, hideous figure, with reddish, vacant face, sunk in an immense, tarnished satin bonnet; and draggled, faded, lilac silk skirts spread over a vast dislocated crinoline. The feet dabbed along in the broken prunella* boots; the mangy rabbit-skin muff bobbed loosely with the shambling gait; and then, under the big chandelier, there came a sudden pause, and the thing looked slowly round, a gaping, mooning, blear-eyed stare.

It was the Sora Lena.

There was a perfect storm of applause.

III

Cecchino Bandini did not slacken his pace till he found himself, with his thin overcoat and opera hat all drenched, among the gas reflections and puddles before his studio door; that shout of applause and that burst of clapping pursuing him down the stairs of the palace and all through the rainy streets. There were a few embers in his stove; he threw a faggot on them, lit a cigarette, and proceeded to make reflections, the wet opera hat still on his head. He had been a fool, a savage. He had behaved like a child, rushing past his hostess with that ridiculous speech in answer to her inquiries: "I am running away because bad luck has entered your house."

Why had he not guessed it at once? What on earth else could she have wanted his sketch for?

He determined to forget the matter, and, as he imagined, he forgot it. Only, when the next day's evening paper displayed two columns describing Madame Fosca's ball, and more particularly "that mask," as the reporter had it, "which among so many which were graceful and ingenious, bore off in triumph the palm for witty novelty," he threw the paper down and gave it a kick towards the wood-box. But he felt ashamed of himself, picked it up, smoothed it out, and read it all—foreign news and home news, and even the description of Madame Fosca's masked ball, conscientiously through. Last of all he perused, with dogged resolution, the column of petty casualties: a boy bit in the calf by a dog who was not mad; the frustrated burgling of a baker's shop; even to the bunches of keys and the umbrella and two cigar-cases picked up by the police, and consigned to the appropriate municipal limbo; until he came to the following lines: "This morning the *Guardians of Public Safety*, having been called by the neighbouring inhabitants, penetrated into a room on the top floor of a house situate in the Little Street of the Gravedigger (Viccolo del Beccamorto*), and discovered, hanging from a rafter, the dead body of Maddalena X. Y. Z. The deceased had long been noted throughout Florence for her eccentric habits and apparel." The paragraph was headed, in somewhat larger type: "Suicide of a female lunatic."

Cecchino's cigarette had gone out, but he continued blowing at it all the same. He could see in his mind's eye a tall, slender figure, draped in silvery plush and silvery furs, standing by the side of an open portfolio, and holding a drawing in her tiny hand, with the slender, solitary gold bangle over the grey glove.

IV

Madame Krasinska was in a very bad humour. The old Chanoinesse,* her late husband's aunt, noticed it; her guests noticed it; her maid noticed it: and she noticed it herself. For, of all human beings, Madame Krasinska—Netta,* as smart folk familiarly called her—was the least subject to bad humour. She was as uniformly cheerful as birds are supposed to be, and she certainly had none of the causes for anxiety or sorrow which even the most proverbial bird must occasionally have. She had always had money, health, good looks; and people had always told her—in New York, in London, in Paris, Rome, and St Petersburg—from her very earliest childhood, that her one business in life was to amuse herself. The old gentleman whom she had simply and cheerfully accepted as a husband, because he had given her quantities of bonbons, and was going to give her quantities of diamonds, had been kind, and had been kindest of all in dying of sudden bronchitis when away for a month, leaving his young widow with an affectionately indifferent recollection of him, no remorse of any kind, and a great deal of money, not to speak of the excellent Chanoinesse, who constituted an invaluable chaperon. And, since his happy demise, no cloud had disturbed the cheerful life or feelings of Madame Krasinska. Other women, she knew, had innumerable subjects of wretchedness; or if they had none, they were wretched from the want of them. Some had children who made them unhappy, others were unhappy for lack of children, and similarly as to lovers; but she had never had a child and never had a lover, and never experienced the smallest desire for either. Other women suffered from sleeplessness, or from sleepiness, and took morphia or abstained from morphia with equal inconvenience; other women also grew weary of amusement. But Madame Krasinska always slept beautifully, and always stayed awake cheerfully; and Madame Krasinska was never tired of amusing herself. Perhaps it was all this which culminated in the fact that Madame Krasinska had never in all her life envied or disliked anybody; and that no one, apparently, had ever envied or disliked her. She did not wish to outshine or supplant any one; she did not want to be richer, younger, more beautiful, or more adored than they. She only wanted to amuse herself, and she succeeded in so doing.

This particular day—the day after Madame Fosca's ball—Madame Krasinska was not amusing herself. She was not at all tired: she never was; besides, she had remained in bed till mid-day: neither was she unwell, for that also she never was; nor had anyone done the slightest thing to vex her. But there it was. She was not amusing herself at all. She could not tell why; and she could not tell why, also, she was vaguely miserable. When the first batch of afternoon callers had taken leave, and the following batches had been sent away from the door, she threw down her volume of Gyp,* and walked to the window. It was raining: a thin, continuous spring drizzle. Only a few cabs, with wet, shining backs, an occasional lumbering omnibus or cart, passed by with wheezing, straining, downcast horses. In one or two shops a light was appearing, looking tiny, blear, and absurd in the gray afternoon. Madame Krasinska looked out for a few minutes; then, suddenly turning round, she brushed past the big palms and azaleas, and rang the bell.

"Order the brougham* at once," she said.

She could by no means have explained what earthly reason had impelled her to go out. When the footman had inquired for orders she felt at a loss: certainly she did not want to go to see anyone, nor to buy anything, nor to inquire about anything.

What *did* she want? Madame Krasinska was not in the habit of driving out in the rain for her pleasure; still less to drive out without knowing whither. What did she want? She sat muffled in her furs, looking out on the wet, grey streets as the brougham rolled aimlessly along. She wanted—she wanted—she couldn't tell what. But she wanted it very much. That much she knew very well—she wanted. The rain, the wet streets, the muddy crossings—oh, how dismal they were! and still she wished to go on.

Instinctively, her polite coachman made for the politer streets, for the polite Lung' Arno.* The river quay was deserted, and a warm, wet wind swept lazily along its muddy flags. Madame Krasinska let down the glass. How dreary! The foundry,* on the other side, let fly a few red sparks from its tall chimney into the grey sky; the water droned over the weir; a lamplighter hurried along.

Madame Krasinska pulled the check-string.*

"I want to walk," she said.

The polite footman followed behind along the messy flags, muddy and full of pools; the brougham followed behind him. Madame Krasinska was not at all in the habit of walking on the embankment, still less walking in the rain.

After some minutes she got in again, and bade the carriage drive home. When she got into the lit streets she again pulled the check-string and ordered the brougham to proceed at a foot's pace. At a certain spot she remembered something, and bade the coachman draw up before a shop. It was the big chemist's.

"What does the Signora Contessa command?" and the footman raised his hat over his ear. Somehow she had forgotten. "Oh," she answered, "wait a minute. Now I remember, it's the next shop, the florist's. Tell them to send fresh azaleas to-morrow and fetch away the old ones."

Now the azaleas had been changed only that morning. But the polite footman obeyed. And Madame Krasinska remained for a minute, nestled in her fur rug, looking on to the wet, yellow, lit pavement, and into the big chemist's window. There were the red, heart-shaped chest protectors,* the frictioning gloves,* the bath towels, all hanging in their place. Then boxes of eau-de-Cologne, lots of bottles of all sizes, and boxes, large and small, and variosities* of indescribable nature and use, and the great glass jars, yellow, blue, green, and ruby red, with a spark from the gas lamp behind in their heart. She stared at it all, very intently, and without a notion about any of these objects. Only she knew that the glass jars were uncommonly bright, and that each had a ruby, or topaz, or emerald of gigantic size, in its heart. The footman returned.

"Drive home," ordered Madame Krasinska. As her maid was taking her out of her dress, a thought—the first since so long—flashed across her mind, at the sight of certain skirts, and an uncouth cardboard mask, lying in a corner of her dressing-room. How odd that she had not seen the Sora Lena that evening . . . She used always to be walking in the lit streets at that hour.

V

The next morning Madame Krasinska woke up quite cheerful and happy. But she began, nevertheless, to suffer, ever since the day after the Fosca ball, from the return of that quite unprecedented and inexplicable depression. Her days became streaked, as it were, with moments during which it was quite impossible to amuse herself; and these moments grew gradually into hours. People bored her for no accountable reason, and things which she had expected as pleasures brought with them a sense of vague or more distinct wretchedness. Thus she would find herself in the midst of a ball or dinner-party, invaded suddenly by a confused sadness or boding of evil, she did not know which. And once, when a box of new clothes had arrived from Paris, she was overcome, while putting on one of the frocks, with such a fit of tears that she had to be put to bed instead of going to the Tornabuoni's* party.

Of course, people began to notice this change; indeed, Madame Krasinska had ingenuously complained of the strange alteration in herself. Some persons suggested, that she might be suffering from slow blood-poisoning and urged an inquiry into the state of the drains. Others recommended arsenic, morphia, or antipyrine.* One kind friend brought her a box of peculiar cigarettes; another forwarded a parcel of still more peculiar novels; most people had some pet doctor to cry up to the skies; and one or two suggested her changing her confessor; not to mention an attempt being made to mesmerise her into cheerfulness.

When her back was turned, meanwhile, all the kind friends discussed the probability of an unhappy love affair, loss of money on the Stock Exchange, and similar other explanations. And while one devoted lady tried to worm out of her the name of her unfaithful lover and of the rival for whom he had forsaken her, another assured her that she was suffering from a lack of personal affections. It was a fine opportunity for the display of pietism, materialism, idealism, realism, psychological lore, and esoteric theosophy.

Oddly enough, all this zeal about herself did not worry Madame Krasinska, as she would certainly have expected it to worry any other woman. She took a little of each of the tonic or soporific drugs; and read a little of each of those sickly sentimental, brutal, or politely improper novels. She also let herself be accompanied to various doctors; and she got up early in the morning and stood for an hour on a chair in a crowd in order to benefit by the preaching of the famous Father Agostino.* She was quite patient even with the friends who condoled about the lover or absence of such. For all these things became, more and more, completely indifferent to Madame Krasinska—unrealities which had no weight in the presence of the painful reality.

This reality was that she was rapidly losing all power of amusing herself, and that when she did occasionally amuse herself she had to pay for what she called this *good time* by an increase of listlessness and melancholy.

It was not melancholy or listlessness such as other women complained of. They seemed, in their fits of blues, to feel that the world around them had got all wrong, or at least was going out of its way to annoy them. But Madame Krasinska saw the world quite plainly, proceeding in the usual manner, and being quite as good a world as before. It was she who was all wrong. It was, in the literal sense of the words, what she supposed people might mean when they said that So-and-so was *not himself*; only that So-and-so, on examination, appeared to be very much himself—only himself in a worse temper than usual. Whereas she . . . Why, in her case, she really did not seem to be herself any longer. Once, at a grand dinner, she suddenly ceased eating and talking to her neighbour, and surprised herself wondering who the people all were and what they had come for. Her mind would become, every now and then, a blank; a blank at least full of vague images, misty and muddled, which she was unable to grasp, but of which she knew that they were painful, weighing on her as a heavy load must weigh on the head or back. Something had happened, or was going to happen, she could not remember which, but she burst into tears none the less. In the midst of such a state of things, if visitors or a servant entered, she would ask sometimes who they were. Once a man came to call, during one of these fits; by an effort she was able to receive him and answer his small talk more or less at random, feeling the whole time as if someone else were speaking in her place. The visitor at length rose to depart, and they both stood for a moment in the midst of the drawing-room.

"This is a very pretty house; it must belong to some rich person. Do you know to whom it belongs?" suddenly remarked Madame Krasinska, looking slowly round her at the furniture, the pictures, statuettes, nicknacks, the screens and plants. "Do you know to whom it belongs?" she repeated.

"It belongs to the most charming lady in Florence," stammered out the visitor politely, and fled.

"My darling Netta," exclaimed the Chanoinesse from where she was seated crocheting benevolently futile garments by the fire; "you should not joke in that way. That poor young man was placed in a painful, in a very painful position by your nonsense."

Madame Krasinska leaned her arms on a screen, and stared her respectable relation long in the face.

"You seem a kind woman," she said at length. "You are old, but then you aren't poor, and they don't call you a mad woman. That makes all the difference."

Then she set to singing—drumming out the tune on the screen—the soldier song of '59, *Addio, mia bella, addio.**

"Netta!" cried the Chanoinesse, dropping one ball of worsted after another. "Netta!"

But Madame Krasinska passed her hand over her brow and heaved a great sigh. Then she took a cigarette off a cloisonné tray, dipped a spill in the fire and remarked,

"Would you like to have the brougham to go to see your friend at the Sacré Cœur,* Aunt Thérèse? I have promised to wait in for Molly Wolkonsky and Bice Forteguerra. We are going to dine at Doney's* with young Pomfret."

VI

Madame Krasinska had repeated her evening drives in the rain. Indeed she began also to walk about regardless of weather. Her maid asked her whether she had been ordered exercise by the doctor, and she answered yes. But why she should not walk in the Cascine* or along the Lung' Arno, and why she should always choose the muddiest thoroughfares, the maid did not inquire. As it was, Madame

Krasinska never showed any repugnance or seemly contrition for the state of draggle in which she used to return home; sometimes when the woman was unbuttoning her boots, she would remain in contemplation of their muddiness, murmuring things which Jefferies could not understand. The servants, indeed, declared that the Countess must have gone out of her mind. The footman related that she used to stop the brougham, get out and look into the lit shops, and that he had to stand behind, in order to prevent lady-killing youths of a caddish description from whispering expressions of admiration in her ear. And once, he affirmed with horror, she had stopped in front of a certain cheap eating-house, and looked in at the bundles of asparagus, at the uncooked chops displayed in the window. And then, added the footman, she had turned round to him slowly and said,

"They have good food in there."

And meanwhile, Madame Krasinska went to dinners and parties, and gave them, and organised picnics, as much as was decently possible in Lent, and indeed a great deal more.

She no longer complained of the blues; she assured everyone that she had completely got rid of them, that she had never been in such spirits in all her life. She said it so often, and in so excited a way, that judicious people declared that now that lover must really have jilted her, or gambling on the Stock Exchange have brought her to the verge of ruin.

Nay, Madame Krasinska's spirits became so obstreperous as to change her in sundry ways. Although living in the fastest set, Madame Krasinska had never been a fast woman. There was something childlike in her nature which made her modest and decorous. She had never learned to talk slang, or to take up vulgar attitudes, or to tell impossible stories; and she had never lost a silly habit of blushing at expressions and anecdotes which she did not reprove other women for using and relating. Her amusements had never been flavoured with that spice of impropriety, of curiosity of evil, which was common in her set. She liked putting on pretty frocks, arranging pretty furniture, driving in well got up carriages, eating good dinners, laughing a great deal, and dancing a great deal, and that was all.

But now Madame Krasinska suddenly altered. She became, all of a sudden, anxious for those exotic sensations which honest women may get by studying the ways, and frequenting the haunts, of women by no means honest. She made up parties to go to the low theatres and music-halls; she proposed dressing up and going, in company with sundry adventurous spirits, for evening strolls in the more dubious portions of the town. Moreover, she, who had never touched a card, began to gamble for large sums, and to surprise people by producing a folded green roulette cloth and miniature roulette rakes out of her pocket. And she became so outrageously conspicuous in her flirtations (she who had never flirted before), and so outrageously loud in her manners and remarks, that her good friends began to venture a little remonstrance. . . .

But remonstrance was all in vain; and she would toss her head and laugh cynically, and answer in a brazen, jarring voice.

For Madame Krasinska felt that she must live, live noisily, live scandalously, live her own life of wealth and dissipation, because . . .

She used to wake up at night with the horror of that suspicion. And in the middle of the day, pull at her clothes, tear down her hair, and rush to the mirror and stare at herself, and look for every feature, and clutch for every end of silk, or bit of lace, or wisp of hair, which proved that she was really herself. For gradually, slowly, she had come to understand that she was herself no longer.

Herself—well, yes, of course she was herself. Was it not herself who rushed about in such a riot of amusement; herself whose flushed cheeks and over-bright eyes, and cynically flaunted neck and bosom she saw in the glass, whose mocking loud voice and shrill laugh she listened to? Besides, did not her servants, her visitors, know her as Netta Krasinska; and did she not know how to wear her clothes, dance, make jokes, and encourage men, afterwards to discourage them? This, she often said to herself, as she lay awake the long nights, as she sat out the longer nights gambling and chaffing,* distinctly proved that she really was herself. And she repeated it all mentally when she returned, muddy, worn out, and as awakened from a ghastly dream, after one of her long rambles through the streets, her daily walks towards the station.

But still . . . What of those strange forebodings of evil, those muddled fears of some dreadful calamity . . . something which had happened, or was going to happen . . . poverty, starvation, death—whose death, her own? or someone else's? That knowledge that it was all, all over; that blinding, felling blow which used every now and then to crush her . . . Yes, she had felt that first at the railway station. At the station? but what had happened at the station? Or was it going to happen still? Since to the station her feet seemed unconsciously to carry her every day. What was it all? Ah! she knew. There was a woman, an old woman, walking to the station to meet . . . Yes, to meet a regiment on its way back. They came back, those soldiers, among a mob yelling triumph. She remembered the illuminations, the red, green, and white lanterns,* and those garlands all over the waiting-rooms. And quantities of flags. The bands played. So gaily! They played Garibaldi's hymn,* and *Addio, Mia Bella*. Those pieces always made her cry now. The station was crammed, and all the boys, in tattered, soiled uniforms, rushed into the arms of parents, wives, friends. Then there was like a blinding light, a crash . . . An officer led the old woman gently out of the place, mopping his eyes. And she, of all the crowd, was the only one to go home alone. Had it really all happened? and to whom? Had it really happened to her, had her boys. . . . But Madame Krasinska had never had any boys.

It was dreadful how much it rained in Florence; and stuff boots do wear out so quick in mud. There was such a lot of mud on the way to the station; but of course it was necessary to go to the station in order to meet the train from Lombardy—the boys must be met.

There was a place on the other side of the river where you went in and handed your watch and your brooch over the counter, and they gave you some money and a paper. Once the paper got lost. Then there was a mattress, too. But there was a kind man—a man who sold hardware—who went and fetched it back. It was dreadfully cold in winter, but the worst was the rain. And having no watch one was afraid of being late for that train, and had to dawdle so long in the muddy streets. Of course one could look in at the pretty shops. But the little boys were so rude. Oh, no, no, not that—anything rather than be shut up in an hospital. The poor old woman did no one any harm—why shut her up?

"*Faites votre jeu, messieurs*," cried Madame Krasinska, raking up the counters with the little rake she had had made of tortoise-shell, with a gold dragon's head for a handle—"*Rien ne va plus—vingt-trois—Rouge, impair et manque*."*

VII

How did she come to know about this woman? She had never been inside that house over the tobacconist's, up three pairs of stairs to the left; and yet she knew exactly the pattern of the wall-paper. It was green, with a pinkish trellis-work, in the grand sitting-room, the one which was opened only on Sunday evenings, when the friends used to drop in and discuss the news, and have a game of *tresette*.* You passed through the dining-room to get through it. The dining-room had no window, and was lit from a skylight; there was always a little smell of dinner in it, but that was appetising. The boys' rooms were to the back. There was a plaster Joan of Arc in the hall, close to the clothes-peg. She was painted to look like silver, and one of the boys had broken her arm, so that it looked like a gas-pipe. It was Momino who had done it, jumping on to the table when they were playing. Momino was always the scapegrace; he wore out so many pairs of trousers at the knees, but he was so warm-hearted! and after all, he had got all the prizes at school, and they all said he would be a first-rate engineer. Those dear boys! They never cost their mother a farthing, once they were sixteen; and Momino bought her a big, beautiful muff out of his own earnings as a pupil-teacher. Here it is! Such a comfort in the cold weather, you can't think, especially when gloves are too dear. Yes, it is rabbit-skin, but it is made to look like ermine, quite a handsome article. Assunta, the maid of all work, never would clean out that kitchen of hers—servants are such sluts! and she tore the moreen* sofa-cover, too, against a nail in the wall. She ought to have seen that nail! But one mustn't be too hard on a poor creature, who is an orphan into the bargain. Oh, God! oh, God! and they lie in the big trench at San Martino, without even a cross over them, or a bit of wood with their name. But the white coats of the Austrians were soaked red, I warrant you! And the new dye they call magenta* is made of pipe-clay—the pipe-clay the dogs clean their white coats with—and the blood of Austrians. It's a grand dye, I tell you!

Lord, Lord, how wet the poor old woman's feet are! And no fire to warm them by. The best is to go to bed when one can't dry one's clothes; and it saves lamp-oil. That was very good oil the parish priest made her a present of . . . Aï, aï, how one's bones ache on the mere boards, even with a blanket over them! That good, good mattress at the pawnshop! It's nonsense about the Italians having been beaten. The Austrians were beaten into bits, made cats'-meat of; and the volunteers are returning to-morrow. Temistocle and Momino—Momino is Girolamo, you know—will be back to-morrow; their rooms have been cleaned, and they shall have a flask of real Montepulciano* . . . The big bottles in the chemist's window are very beautiful, particularly the green one. The shop where they sell gloves and scarfs is also very pretty; but the English chemist's is the prettiest, because of those bottles. But they say the contents of them is all rubbish, and no real medicine . . . Don't speak of San Bonifazio!* I have seen it. It is where they keep the mad folk and the wretched, dirty, wicked, wicked old women. . . . There was a handsome book bound in red, with gold edges, on the best sitting-room table; the Æneid, translated by Caro.* It was one of Temistocle's prizes. And that Berlin-wool cushion.* . . . yes, the little dog with the cherries looked quite real . . . .

"I have been thinking I should like to go to Sicily, to see Etna, and Palermo, and all those places," said Madame Krasinska, leaning on the balcony by the side of Prince Mongibello,* smoking her fifth or sixth cigarette.

She could see the hateful hooked nose, like a nasty hawk's beak, over the big black beard, and the creature's leering, languishing black eyes, as he looked up into the twilight. She knew quite well what sort of man Mongibello was. No woman could approach him, or allow him to approach her; and there she was on that balcony alone with him in the dark, far from the rest of the party, who were dancing and talking within. And to talk of Sicily to him, who was a Sicilian too! But that was what she wanted—a scandal, a horror, anything that might deaden those thoughts which would go on inside her. . . . The thought of that strange, lofty whitewashed place, which she had never seen, but which she knew so well, with an altar in the middle, and rows and rows of beds, each with its set-out of bottles and baskets, and horrid slobbering and gibbering old women. Oh . . . she could hear them!

"I should like to go to Sicily," she said in a tone that was now common to her, adding slowly and with emphasis, "but I should like to have someone to show me all the sights. . . ."

"Countess," and the black beard of the creature bent over her—close to her neck—"how strange—I also feel a great longing to see Sicily once more, but not alone—those lovely, lonely valleys . . . ."

Ah!—there was one of the creatures who had sat up in her bed and was singing, singing "Casta Diva!"* "No, not alone"—she went on hurriedly, a sort of fury of satisfaction, of the satisfaction of destroying something, destroying her own fame, her own life, filling her as she felt the man's hand on her arm—"not alone, Prince—with someone to explain things—someone who knows all about it—and in this lovely spring weather. You see, I am a bad traveller—and I am afraid . . . of being alone . . . ." The last words came out of her throat loud, hoarse, and yet cracked and shrill—and just as the Prince's arm was going to clasp her, she rushed wildly into the room, exclaiming—

"Ah, I am she—I am she—I am mad!"

For in that sudden voice, so different from her own, Madame Krasinska had recognised the voice that should have issued from the cardboard mask she had once worn, the voice of Sora Lena.

VIII

Yes, Cecchino certainly recognised her now. Strolling about in that damp May twilight among the old, tortuous streets, he had mechanically watched the big black horses draw up at the posts which closed that labyrinth of black, narrow alleys; the servant in his white waterproof opened the door, and the tall, slender woman got out and walked quickly along. And mechanically, in his wool-gathering way, he had followed the lady, enjoying the charming note of delicate pink and grey which her little frock made against those black houses, and under that wet, grey sky, streaked pink with the sunset. She walked quickly along, quite alone, having left the footman with the carriage at the entrance of that condemned old heart of Florence; and she took no notice of the stares and words of the boys playing in the gutters, the pedlars housing their barrows under the black archways, and the women leaning out of window. Yes; there was no doubt. It had struck him suddenly as he watched her pass under a double arch and into a kind of large court, not unlike that of a castle, between the frowning tall houses of the old Jews' quarter;* houses escutcheoned and stanchioned,* once the abode of Ghibelline nobles,* now given over to rag-pickers, scavengers and unspeakable trades.

As soon as he recognised her he stopped, and was about to turn: what business has a man following a lady, prying into her doings when she goes out at twilight, with carriage and footman left several streets back, quite alone through unlikely streets? And Cecchino, who by this time was on the point of returning to the Maremma, and had come to the conclusion that civilisation was a boring and loathsome thing, reflected upon the errands which French novels described ladies as performing, when they left their carriage and footman round the corner. . . . But the thought was disgraceful to Cecchino, and unjust to this lady—no, no! And at this moment he stopped, for the lady had stopped a few paces before him, and was staring fixedly into the grey evening sky. There was something strange in that stare; it was not that of a woman who is hiding disgraceful proceedings. And in staring round she must have seen him; yet she stood still, like one wrapped in wild thoughts. Then suddenly she passed under the next archway, and disappeared in the dark passage of a house. Somehow Cecco Bandini could not make up his mind, as he ought to have done long ago, to turn back. He slowly passed through the oozy, ill-smelling archway, and stood before that house. It was very tall, narrow, and black as ink, with a jagged roof against the wet, pinkish sky. From the iron hook, made to hold brocades and Persian carpets on gala days of old, fluttered some rags, obscene and ill-omened in the wind. Many of the window panes were broken. It was evidently one of the houses which the municipality had condemned to destruction for sanitary reasons, and whence the inmates were gradually being evicted.

"That's a house they're going to pull down, isn't it?" he inquired in a casual tone of the man at the corner, who kept a sort of cookshop, where chestnut pudding and boiled beans steamed on a brazier in a den. Then his eye caught a half-effaced name close to the lamp-post, "Little Street of the Grave-digger." "Ah," he added, quickly, "this is the street where old Sora Lena committed suicide—and—is—is that the house?"

Then, trying to extricate some reasonable idea out of the extraordinary tangle of absurdities which had all of a sudden filled his mind, he fumbled in his pocket for a silver coin, and said hurriedly to the man with the cooking brazier,

"See here, that house, I'm sure, isn't well inhabited. That lady has gone there for a charity—but—but one doesn't know that she mayn't be annoyed in there. Here's fifty centimes for your trouble. If that lady doesn't come out again in three-quarters of an hour—there! it's striking seven—just you go round to the stone posts—you'll find her carriage there—black horses and grey liveries—and tell the footman to run upstairs to his mistress—understand?" And Cecchino Bandini fled, overwhelmed at the thought of the indiscretion he was committing, but seeing, as he turned round, those rags waving an ominous salute from the black, gaunt house with its irregular roof against the wet, twilight sky.

IX

Madame Krasinska hurried through the long, black corridor, with its slippery bricks and typhoid smell, and went slowly but resolutely up the black staircase. Its steps, constructed perhaps in the days of Dante's grandfather,* when a horn buckle and leathern belt formed the only ornaments of Florentine dames, were extraordinarily high, and worn off at the edges by innumerable generations of successive nobles and paupers. And as it twisted sharply on itself, the staircase was lighted at rare intervals by barred windows, overlooking alternately the black square outside, with its jags of overhanging roof, and a black yard, where a broken well was surrounded by a heap of half-sorted chickens' feathers and unpicked rags. On the first landing was an open door, partly screened by a line of drying tattered clothes; and whence issued shrill sounds of altercation and snatches of tipsy song. Madame Krasinska passed on heedless of it all, the front of her delicate frock brushing the unseen filth of those black steps, in whose crypt-like cold and gloom there was an ever-growing breath of charnel. Higher and higher, flight after flight, steps and steps. Nor did she look to the right or to the left, nor ever stop to take breath, but climbed upward, slowly, steadily. At length she reached the topmost landing, on to which fell a flickering beam of the setting sun. It issued from a room, whose door was standing wide open. Madame Krasinska entered. The room was completely empty, and comparatively light. There was no furniture in it, except a chair, pushed into a dark corner, and an empty bird-cage at the window. The panes were broken, and here and there had been mended with paper. Paper also hung, in blackened rags, upon the walls.

Madame Krasinska walked to the window and looked out over the neighbouring roofs, to where the bell in an old black belfry swung tolling the Ave Maria. There was a porticoed gallery on the top of a house some way off; it had a few plants growing in pipkins,* and a drying line. She knew it all so well.

On the window-sill was a cracked basin, in which stood a dead basil plant, dry, grey. She looked at it some time, moving the hardened earth with her fingers. Then she turned to the empty bird-cage. Poor solitary starling! how he had whistled to the poor old woman! Then she began to cry.

But after a few moments she roused herself. Mechanically, she went to the door and closed it carefully. Then she went straight to the dark corner, where she knew that the staved-in straw chair stood. She dragged it into the middle of the room, where the hook was in the big rafter. She stood on the chair, and measured the height of the ceiling.

It was so low that she could graze it with the palm of her hand. She took off her gloves, and then her bonnet—it was in the way of the hook. Then she unclasped her girdle, one of those narrow Russian ribbons of silver woven stuff, studded with niello.* She buckled one end firmly to the big hook. Then she unwound the strip of muslin from under her collar. She was standing on the broken chair, just under the rafter. "Pater noster qui es in cælis,"* she mumbled, as she still childishly did when putting her head on the pillow every night.

The door creaked and opened slowly. The big, hulking woman, with the vague, red face and blear stare, and the rabbit-skin muff, bobbing on her huge crinolined skirts, shambled slowly into the room. It was the Sora Lena.

X

When the man from the cook-shop under the archway and the footman entered the room, it was pitch dark. Madame Krasinska was lying in the middle of the floor, by the side of an overturned chair, and under a hook in the rafter whence hung her Russian girdle. When she awoke from her swoon, she looked slowly round the room; then rose, fastened her collar and murmured, crossing herself, "O God, thy mercy is infinite." The men said that she smiled.

Such is the legend of Madame Krasinska, known as Mother Antoinette Marie among the Little Sisters of the Poor.

THE VIRGIN OF THE SEVEN DAGGERS

A MOORISH GHOST STORY OF THE SEVENTEENTH CENTURY

DEDICATED, IN REMEMBRANCE OF THE SPANISH LEGENDS HE WAS WONT TO TELL ME, TO MY FRIEND OF FORTY YEARS BACK, JOSE FERNANDEZ GIMENEZ*

I

In a grass-grown square of the city of Grenada, with the snows of the Sierra* staring down on it all winter, and the well-nigh Africa sun* glaring on its coloured tiles all summer, stands the yellow freestone Church of Our Lady of the Seven Daggers.* Huge garlands of pears and melons hang, carved in stone, about the cupolas and windows; and monstrous heads with laurel wreaths and epaulets burst forth from all the arches. The roof shínes barbarically, green, white and brown, above the tawny stone; and on each of the two balconied and staircased belfries, pricked up like ears above the building's monstrous front, there sways a weather-vane, figuring a heart transfixed with seven long-hilted daggers. Inside, the church presents a superb example of the pompous, pedantic and contorted Spanish architecture of the reign of the later Philips.* On colonnade is hoisted colonnade, pilasters climb upon pilasters, bases and capitals jut out, double and threefold, from the ground, in mid-air and near the ceiling; jagged lines everywhere as of spikes for exhibiting the heads of traitors; dizzy ledges as of mountain precipices for dashing to bits Morisco rebels,* line warring with line and curve with curve; a place in which the mind staggers bruised and half-stunned. But the grandeur of the church is not merely terrific; it is also gallant and ceremonious: everything on which labour can be wasted is laboured, everything on which gold can be lavished is gilded; columns and architraves curl like the curls of a periwig; walls and vaultings are flowered with precious marbles and fretted with carving and gilding like a gala dress; stone and wood are woven like lace; stucco is whipped and clotted like pastry-cooks' cream and crust; everything is crammed with flourishes like a tirade by Calderon, or a sonnet by Gongora.* A golden retablo* closes the church at the end; a black and white rood screen, of jasper and alabaster, fences it in the middle; while along each aisle hang chandeliers as for a ball; and paper flowers are stacked on every altar.

Amidst all this gloomy yet festive magnificence, and surrounded, in each minor chapel, by a train of waxen Christs with bloody wounds and spangled loin-cloths, and Madonnas of lesser fame weeping beady tears and carrying bewigged Infants, thrones the great Virgin of the Seven Daggers.

Is she seated or standing? 'Tis impossible to decide. She seems, beneath the gilded canopy and between the twisted columns of jasper, to be slowly rising, or slowly sinking, in a solemn court curtsey, buoyed up by her vast farthingale.* Her skirts bulge out in melon-shaped folds, all damasked with minute heartsease,* and brocaded with silver roses; the reddish shimmer of the gold wire, the bluish shimmer of the silver floss, blending into a strange melancholy hue without a definite name. Her body is cased like a knife in its sheath, the mysterious russet and violet of the silk made less definable still by the network of seed pearl, and the veils of delicate lace falling from head to waist. Her face, which surmounts rows upon rows of pearls, is made of wax, white with black glass eyes and a tiny coral mouth. Her head is crowned with a great jewelled crown; her slippered feet rest on a crescent moon, and in her right hand she holds a lace pocket-handkerchief. She stares steadfastly forth with a sad and ceremonious smile. In her bodice, a little clearing is made among the brocade and the seed pearl, and into this are stuck seven gold-hilted knives.

Such is Our Lady of the Seven Daggers; and such her church.

One winter afternoon, more than two hundred years ago, Charles the Melancholy* being King of Spain and the New World, there chanced to be kneeling in that church, already empty and dim save for the votive lamps, and more precisely on the steps before the Virgin of the Seven Daggers, a cavalier of very great birth, fortune, magnificence, and wickedness, Don Juan Gusman del Pulgar, Count of Miramor. "O great Madonna, O Snow Peak untrodden of the Sierras, O Sea unnavigated of the tropics, O Gold Ore unhandled by the Spaniard, O New Minted Doubloon unpocketed by the Jew"—thus prayed that devout man of quality—"look down benignly on thy knight and servant, accounted judiciously one of the greatest men of this kingdom, in wealth and honours, fearing neither the vengeance of foes, nor the rigour of laws, yet content to stand foremost among thy slaves. Consider that I have committed every crime without faltering, both murder, perjury, blasphemy, and sacrilege, yet have I always respected thy name, nor suffered any man to give greater praise to other Madonnas, neither her of Good Counsel, nor her of Swift Help, nor our Lady of Mount Carmel, nor our Lady of St. Luke of Bologna in Italy, nor our Lady of the Slipper of Famagosta in Cyprus, nor our Lady of the Pillar of Saragossa, great Madonnas every one, and revered throughout the world for their powers, and by most men preferred to thee; yet has thy servant, Juan Gusman del Pulgar, ever asserted, with words and blows, their infinite inferiority to thyself. Give me, therefore, O Great Madonna of the Seven Daggers, I pray thee, the promise that thou wilt save me ever from the clutches of Satan, as thou hast wrested me ever on earth from the King's Alguazils and the Holy Officer's delators,* and let me never burn in eternal fire in punishment of my sins. Neither think that I ask too much, for I swear to be provided always with absolution in all rules, whether by employing my own private chaplain or using violence thereunto to any monk, priest, canon, dean, bishop, cardinal, or even the Holy Father himself. Grant me this boon, O Burning Water and Cooling Fire, O Sun that shineth at midnight, and Galaxy that resplendeth at noon—grant me this boon, and I will assert always with my tongue and my sword, in the face of His Majesty and at the feet of my latest love, that although I have been beloved of all the fairest women of the world, high and low, both Spanish, Italian, German, French, Dutch, Flemish, Jewish, Saracen, and Gipsy, to the number of many hundreds, and by seven ladies, Dolores, Fatma, Catalina, Elvira, Violante, Azahar, and Sister Seraphita, for each of whom I broke a commandment and took several lives (the last, moreover, being a cloistered nun, and therefore a case of inexpiable sacrilege), despite all this I will maintain before all men and all the Gods of Olympus that no lady was ever so fair as our Lady of the Seven Daggers of Grenada."

The church was filled with ineffable fragrance; exquisite music, among which Don Juan seemed to recognize the voice of Syphax,* His Majesty's own soprano singer, murmured amongst the cupolas, and the Virgin of the Seven Daggers, slowly dipped in her lace and silver brocade farthingale, rising as slowly again to her full height, and inclined her white face imperceptibly towards her jewelled bosom.

The Count of Miramor clasped his hands in ecstasy to his breast; then he arose, walked quickly down the aisle, dipped his fingers in the black marble holy water stoop, threw a sequin to the beggar who pushed open the leathern curtain, put his black hat covered with black ostrich feathers on his head, dismissed a company of bravos and guitar players who awaited him in the square, and, gathering his black cloak about him, went forth, his sword tucked under his arm, in search of Baruch, the converted Jew of the Albaycin.*

Don Juan Gusman del Pulgar, Count of Miramor, Grandee of the First Class, Knight of Calatrava, and of the Golden Fleece, and Prince of the Holy Roman Empire, was thirty-two and a great sinner. This cavalier was tall, of large bone, his forehead low and cheekbones high, chin somewhat receding, aquiline nose, white complexion and black hair; he wore no beard, but moustachios cut short over the lip and curled upwards at the corners leaving the mouth bare; and his hair flat, parted through the middle and falling nearly to his shoulders. His clothes when bent on business or pleasure, were most often of black satin, slashed with black. His portrait has been painted by Domingo Zurbaran of Seville.*

II

All the steeples of Grenada seemed agog with bell-ringing; the big bell on the tower of the Sail* clanging irregularly into the more professional tinklings and roarings, under the vigorous, but flurried pulls of the damsels, duly accompanied by their well-ruffed duennas, who were ringing themselves a husband for the newly begun year, according to the traditions of the city. Green garlands decorated the white glazed balconies, and banners with the arms of Castile and Aragon,* and the pomegranate of Grenada, waved or drooped alongside of the hallowed palm-branches over the carved escutcheons on the doors. From the barracks arose a practising of fifes and bugles; and from the little wine-shops on the outskirts of the town a sound of guitar strumming and castagnets. The coming day was a very solemn feast for the city, being the anniversary of its liberation from the rule of the Infidels.*

But although all Grenada felt festive, in anticipation of the grand bullfight of the morrow, and the grand burning of heretics and relapses in the square of Bibrambla, Don Juan Gusman del Pulgar, Count of Miramor, was fevered with intolerable impatience, not for the following day, but for the coming and tediously lagging night.

Not, however, for the reason which had made him a thousand times before upbraid the Sun God, in true poetic style, for displaying so little of the proper anxiety to hasten the happiness of one of the greatest cavaliers of Spain. The delicious heart-beating with which he had waited, sword under his cloak, for the desired rope to be lowered from a mysterious window, or the muffled figure to loom from round a corner; the fierce joy of awaiting, with a band of gallant murderers, some inconvenient father, or brother, or husband on his evening stroll; the rapture even, spiced with awful sacrilege, of stealing in amongst the lemon-trees of that cloistered court, after throwing the Sister Portress to tell-tale in the convent well—all, and even this, seemed to him trumpery and mawkish.

Don Juan sprang from the great bed, covered and curtained with dull, blood-coloured damask, on which he had been lying dressed, vainly courting sleep, beneath a painted hermit, black and white in his lantern-jawedness, fondling a handsome skull. He went to the balcony, and looked out of one of its glazed windows. Below a marble goddess shimmered among the myrtle hedges and the cypresses of the tiled garden, and the pet dwarf of the house played at cards with the chaplain, the chief bravo, and a thread-bare poet who was kept to make the odes and sonnets required in the course of his master's daily courtships.

"Get out of my sight, you lazy scoundrels, all of you!" cried Don Juan, with a threat and an oath alike terrible to repeat, which sent the party, bowing and scraping as they went, scattering their cards, and pursued by his lordship's jack-boots, guitar, and missal.

Then Don Juan stood at the window rapt in contemplation of the towers of the Alhambra,* their tips still reddened by the departing sun, their bases already lost in the encroaching mists, on the hill yon side of the river.

He could just barely see it, that Tower of the Cypresses,* where the magic hand held the key engraven on the doorway, about which, as a child, his nurse from the Morisco village of Andarax* had told such marvellous stories of hidden treasures and slumbering infantas. He stood long at the window, his lean white hands clasped on the rail as on the handle of his sword, gazing out with knit brows and clenched teeth, and that look which made men hug the wall and drop aside on his path.

Ah! how different from any of his other loves! the only one, decidedly, at all worthy of lineage as great as his, and a character as magnanimous. Catalina, indeed, had been exquisite when she danced, and Elvira was magnificent at a banquet, and each had long possessed his heart, and had cost him, one many thousands of doubloons for a husband, and the other the death of a favourite fencing-master, killed in a fray with her relations. Violante had been a Venetian worthy of Titian,* for whose sake he had been imprisoned beneath the ducal palace, escaping only by the massacre of three gaolers; for Fatma, the Sultana of the King of Fez, he had well-nigh been impaled, and for shooting the husband of Dolores he had very nearly been broken on the wheel; Azahar, who was called so because of her cheeks like white jessamine, he had carried off at the church door, out of the arms of her bridegroom; without counting that he had cut down her old father, a Grandee of the First Class. And as to Sister Seraphita—she had indeed seemed worthy of him, and Seraphita had nearly come up to his idea of an angel. But oh! what had any of these ladies cost him, compared with what he was about to risk to-night? Let alone the chance of being roasted by the Holy Office (after all, he had already run that, and the risk of more serious burning hereafter also, in the case of Sister Seraphita) what if the business proved a swindle of that Jewish hound, Baruch?—Don Juan put his hand on his dagger and his black moustachios bristled up at the bare thought; let alone the possibility of imposture (though who could be so bold as to venture to impose upon him?) the adventure was full of dreadful things. It was terrible, after all, to have to blaspheme the Holy Catholic Apostolic Church, and all her saints, and inconceivably odious to have to be civil to that dog of a Mahomet of theirs; also, he had not much enjoyed a previous experience of calling up devils, who had smelt most vilely of brimstone and assafœtida, besides using most uncivil language; and he really could not stomach that Jew Baruch, whose trade among others consisted in procuring for the Archbishop a batch of renegade Moors, who were solemnly dressed in white and baptized afresh every year. It was detestable that this fellow should even dream of obtaining the treasure buried under the Tower of the Cypresses. Then, there were the traditions of his family, descended in direct line from the Cid, and from that Fernan del Pulgar who had nailed the Ave Maria to the Mosque;* and half his other ancestors were painted with their foot on a Moor's decollated head, much resembling a hairdresser's block; and their very title, Miramor, was derived from a castle which had been built in full Moorish territory to stare the Moor out of countenance.

But after all, this only made it more magnificent, more delicious, more worthy of so magnanimous and highborn a cavalier. . . . "Ah, princess . . . more exquisite than Venus, more noble than Juno, and infinitely more agreeable than Minerva,"* . . . sighed Don Juan at his window. The sun had long since set, making a trail of blood along the distant river reach, among the sere spider-like poplars, turning the snows of Mulhacen* a livid, bluish blood-red, and leaving all along the lower slopes of the Sierra wicked russet stains, as of the rust of blood upon marble. Darkness had come over the world, save where some illuminated court-yard, or window, suggested preparations for next day's revelry; the air was piercingly cold, as if filled with minute snow-flakes from the mountains. The joyful singing had ceased; and from a neighbouring church there came only a casual death toll, executed on a cracked and lugubrious bell. A shudder ran through Don Juan. "Holy Virgin of the Seven Daggers, take me under thy benign protection," he murmured mechanically.

A discreet knock aroused him.

"The Jew Baruch—I mean his worship, Señor Don Bonaventura,"* announced the page.

III

The Tower of the Cypresses, destroyed almost in our times by the explosion of a powder magazine,* formed part of the inner defences of the Alhambra. In the middle of its horseshoe arch was engraved a huge hand holding a flag-shaped key, which was said to be that of a subterranean and enchanted palace; and the two great cypress trees, uniting their shadows into one tapering cone of black, were said to point, under a given position of the moon, to the exact spot where the wise King Yahya,* of Cordova, had judiciously buried his jewels, his plate, and his favourite daughter many hundred years ago.

At the foot of this tower, and in the shade of those cypresses, Don Juan ordered his companion to spread out his magic paraphernalia. From a neatly packed basket, beneath which he had staggered up the steep hill-side in the moon-light, the learned Jew produced a book, a variety of lamps, some packets of frankincense, a pound of dead man's fat, the bones of a stillborn child who had been boiled by the witches, a live cock that had never crowed, a very ancient toad, and sundry other rarities, all of which he proceeded to dispose in the latest necromantic fashion, while the Count of Miramor mounted guard sword in hand. But when the fire was laid, the lamps lit, and the first layer of ingredients had already been placed in the cauldron; nay, when he had even borrowed Don Juan's embroidered pocket-handkerchief to envelop the cock that had never crowed, Baruch, the Jew, suddenly flung himself down before his patron, and implored him to desist from the terrible enterprise for which they had come.

"I have come hither," wailed the Jew, "lest your Lordship should possibly entertain doubts of my obligingness. I have run the risk of being burned alive in the Square of Bibrambla tomorrow morning before the bullfight; I have imperilled my eternal soul, and laid out large sums of money in the purchase of the necessary ingredients, all of which are abomination in the eyes of a true Jew—I mean of a good Christian. But now I implore your lordship to desist. You will see things so terrible that to mention them is impossible; you will be suffocated by the vilest stenches, and shaken by earthquakes and whirlwinds, besides having to listen to imprecations of the most horrid sort; you will have to blaspheme our Holy Mother Church and invoke Mahomet—may he roast everlastingly in hell; you will infallibly go to hell yourself in due course; and all this for the sake of a paltry treasure of which it will be most difficult to dispose to the pawnbrokers; and of a lady, about whom, thanks to my former medical position in the harem of the Emperor of Tetuan,* I may assert with probability that she is fat, ill-favoured, stained with henna and most disagreeably redolent of camphor . . . ."

"Peace, villain!" cried Don Juan, snatching him by the throat and pulling him violently on to his feet; "prepare thy messes and thy stinks, begin thy antics, and never dream of offering advice to a cavalier like me. And, remember, one other word against her Royal Highness my bride, against the Princess whom her own father has been keeping three hundred years for my benefit, and, by the Virgin of the Seven Daggers, thou shalt be hurled into yonder precipice; which, by the way, will be a very good move, in any case, when thy services are no longer wanted." So saying, he snatched from Baruch's hand the paper of responses, which the necromancer had copied out from his book of magic; and began to study it by the light of a supernumerary lamp.

"Begin!" he cried. "I am ready, and thou, great Virgin of the Seven Daggers, guard me!"

"Jab, jab, jam—Credo in Grilgroth, Astaroth et Rappatun; trish, trash, trum,"* began Baruch in faltering tones, as he poked a flame-tipped reed under the cauldron.

"Patapol, Valde Patapol," answered Don Juan from his paper of responses.

The flame of the cauldron leaped up with a tremendous smell of brimstone. The moon was veiled, the place was lit up crimson, and a legion of devils with the bodies of apes, the talons of eagles, and the snouts of pigs suddenly appeared in the battlements all round.

"Credo," again began Baruch; but the blasphemies he gabbled out, and which Don Juan indignantly echoed, were such as cannot possibly be recorded. A hot wind rose, whirling a desertful of burning sand which stung like gnats; the bushes were on fire, each flame turned into a demon like a huge locust or scorpion, who uttered piercing shrieks and vanished, leaving a choking atmosphere of melted tallow.

"Fal lal Polychronicon Nebuzaradon," continued Baruch.

"Leviathan! Esto nobis!"* answered Don Juan.

The earth shook, the sound of millions of gongs filled the air, and a snowstorm enveloped everything with a shuddering cloud. A legion of demons, in the shape of white elephants, but with snakes for their trunks and tails, and the bosoms of fair women, executed a frantic dance round the cauldron, and holding hands, balanced on their hind legs.

At this moment the Jew uncovered the Black Cock who had never crowed before.

"Osiris! Apollo! Balshazar!"* he cried, and flung the cock with superb aim into the boiling cauldron. The cock disappeared; then, rose again, shaking his wings and clawing the air, and giving a fearful, piercing crow.

"O Sultan Yahya, Sultan Yahya," answered a terrible voice from the bowels of the earth.

Again the earth shook; streams of lava bubbled from beneath the cauldron, and a flame, like a sheet of green lightning, leaped up from the fire.

As it did so, a colossal shadow appeared on the high palace wall, and the great hand, shaped like a glover's sign, engraven on the outer arch of the tower gateway, extended its candle-shaped fingers, projected a wrist, an arm to the elbow, and turned slowly in a secret lock the flag-shaped key engraven on the inside vault of the portal.

The two necromancers fell on their faces, utterly stunned.

The first to revive was Don Juan, who roughly brought the Jew back to his senses. The moon made serener daylight. There was no trace of earthquake, volcano or simoon; and the devils had disappeared without traces; only the circle of lamps was broken through, and the cauldron upset among the embers. But the great horse-shoe portals of the tower stood open; and, at the bottom of a dark corridor, there shone a speck of dim light.

"My Lord," cried Baruch, suddenly grown bold, and plucking Don Juan by the cloak, "we must now, if you please, settle a trifling business matter. Remember that the treasure was to be mine provided the Infanta were yours. Remember also, that the smallest indiscretion on your part, such as may happen to a gay young cavalier, will result in our being burned, with the New Year batch of heretics and relapses, in Bibrambla to-morrow, immediately after high mass and just before people go to early dinner, on account of the bullfight."

"Business! Discretion! Bibrambla! Early dinner!" exclaimed the Count of Miramor; "thinkest thou I shall ever go back to Grenada and its frumpish women once I am married to my Infanta, or let thee handle my late father-in-law, King Yahya's, treasure? Execrable renegade, take the reward of thy blasphemies." And, having rapidly run him through the body, he pushed Baruch into the precipice hard by. Then, covering his left arm with his cloak, and swinging his bare sword horizontally in his right hand, he advanced into the darkness of the tower.

IV

Don Juan Gusman del Pulgar plunged down a narrow corridor, as black as the shaft of a mine, following the little speck of reddish light which seemed to advance before him. The air was icy damp and heavy with a vague choking mustiness, which Don Juan imagined to be the smell of dead bats. Hundreds of these creatures fluttered all around; and hundreds more, apparently hanging head downwards from the low roof, grazed his face with their claws, their damp furry coats and clammy leathern wings. Underfoot, the ground was slippery with innumerable little snakes, who, instead of being crushed, just wriggled under the feet. The corridor was rendered even more gruesome by the fact that it was a strongly inclined plane, and that one seemed to be walking straight into a pit.

Suddenly, a sound mingled itself with that of his footsteps, and of the drip-drop of water from the roof; or rather detached itself as a whisper from it.

"Don Juan, Don Juan!" it murmured.

"Don Juan, Don Juan!" murmured the walls and roof a few yards further; a different voice this time.

"Don Juan Gusman del Pulgar!" a third voice took up, clearer and more plaintive than the others.

The magnanimous cavalier's blood began to run cold, and icy perspiration to clot his hair. He walked on nevertheless.

"Don Juan," repeated a fourth voice, a little buzz close to his ear.

But the bats set up a dreadful shrieking which drowned it.

He shivered as he went; it seemed to him he had recognized the voice of the jasmin-cheeked Azahar, as she called on him from her death-bed.

The reddish speck had meanwhile grown large at the bottom of the shaft, and he had understood that it was not a flame, but the light of some place beyond. Might it be hell? he thought. But he strode on nevertheless, grasping his sword and brushing away the bats with his cloak.

"Don Juan! Don Juan!" cried the voices issuing faintly from the darkness. He began to understand that they were trying to detain him; and he thought he recognized the voices of Dolores and Fatma, his dead mistresses.

"Silence! you sluts!" he cried. But his knees were shaking and great drops of sweat fell from his hair on to his cheek.

The speck of light had now become quite large, and turned from red to white. He understood that it represented the exit from the gallery. But he could not understand why, as he advanced, the light, instead of being brighter, seemed filmed over and fainter.

"Juan, Juan," wailed a new voice at his ear. He stood still for a second; a sudden faintness came over him.

"Seraphita!" he murmured, "it is my little nun Seraphita." But he felt that she was trying to call him back.

"Abominable witch!" he cried. "Avaunt!"

The passage had grown narrower and narrower; so narrow that now he could barely squeeze along between the clammy walls, and had to bend his head lest he should hit the ceiling with its stalactites of bats.

Suddenly there was a great rustle of wings, and a long shriek. A night bird had been startled by his tread, and had whirled on before him, tearing through the veil of vagueness which dimmed the outer light. As the bird tore open its way, a stream of dazzling light entered the corridor: it was as if a curtain had suddenly been drawn.

"Too-hoo! Too-hoo!" shrieked the bird; and Don Juan, following its flight, brushed his way through the cobwebs of four centuries, and issued, blind and dizzy, into the outer world.*

V

For a long while the Count of Miramor stood dazed and dazzled, unable to see anything, save the whirling flight of the owl, which circled in what seemed a field of waving, burning red. He closed his eyes; but through the singed lids he still saw that waving red atmosphere, and the black creature whirling about him.

Then, gradually, he began to perceive and comprehend: lines and curves arose shadowy before him, and the faint plash of waters cooled his ringing ears.

He found that he was standing in a lofty colonnade, with a deep tank at his feet, surrounded by high hedges of flowering myrtles, whose jade-coloured water held the reflection of Moorish porticoes, shining orange in the sun-light, of high walls covered with shimmering blue and green tiles, and of a great red tower, raising its battlements into the cloudless blue. From the tower waved two flags, a green one and one of purple with a gold pomegranate. As he stood there, a sudden breath of air shuddered through the myrtles, wafting their fragrance towards him; a fountain began to bubble; and the reflection of the porticoes and hedges and tower to vacillate in the jade-green water, furling and unfurling like the pieces of a fan; and, above, the two banners unfolded themselves slowly, and little by little began to stream in the wind.

Don Juan advanced. At the further end of the tank a peacock was standing by the myrtle hedge, immovable as if made of precious enamels; but as Don Juan went by, the short blue-green feathers of his neck began to ruffle; he moved his tail, and swelling himself out, he slowly unfolded it in a dazzling wheel. As he did so, some blackbirds and thrushes in gilt cages hanging within an archway, began to twitter and to sing.

From the court of the tank, Don Juan entered another and smaller court, passing through a narrow archway. On its marble steps lay three warriors, clad in long embroidered surcoats of silk, beneath which gleamed their armour, and wearing on their heads strange helmets of steel mail, which hung loose on to their gorgets and were surmounted by gilded caps; beneath them—for they had seemingly leant on them in their slumbers—lay round targes or shields, and battle-axes of Damascus work.* As he passed, they began to stir and breathe heavily. He strode quickly by; but at the entrance of the smaller court, from which issued a delicious scent of full-blown Persian roses, another sentinel was leaning against a column, his hands clasped round his lance, his head bent on his breast. As Don Juan passed he slowly raised his head, and opened one eye, then the other. Don Juan rushed past, a cold sweat on his brow.

Low beams of sunlight lay upon the little inner court, in whose midst, surrounded by rose hedges, stood a great basin of alabaster, borne on four thick-set pillars; a skin, as of ice, filmed over the basin; but, as if some one should have thrown a stone on to a frozen surface, the water began to move and to trickle slowly into a second basin below.

"The waters are flowing, the nightingales singing," murmured a figure lying by the fountain, grasping, like one just awakened, a lute which lay by his side. From the little court Don Juan entered a series of arched and domed chambers, whose roofs were hung as with icicles of gold and silver, or incrusted with mother of pearl constellations which twinkled in the darkness, while the walls shone with patterns that seemed carved of ivory and pearl and beryl and amethyst where the sunbeams grazed them, or imitated some strange sea caves, filled with flitting colours, where the shadow rose fuller and higher. In these chambers Don Juan found a number of sleepers, soldiers and slaves, black and white, all of whom sprang to their feet and rubbed their eyes and made obeisance as he went. Then he entered a long passage, lined on either side by a row of sleeping eunuchs, dressed in robes of honour, each leaning, sword in hand, against the wall, and of slave-girls with stuff of striped silver about their loins, and sequins at the end of their long hair, and drums and timbrels in their hands.

At regular intervals stood great golden cressets, in which burned sweet-smelling wood, casting a reddish light over the sleeping faces. But as Don Juan approached, the slaves inclined their bodies to the ground, touching it with their turbans, and the girls thumped on their drums and jingled the brass bells of their timbrels. Thus he passed on from chamber to chamber till he came to a great door formed of stars of cedar and ivory studded with gold nails, and bolted by a huge gold bolt, on which ran mystic inscriptions. Don Juan stopped. But, as he did so, the bolt slowly moved in its socket, retreating gradually, and the immense portals swung back, each into its carved hinge column.

Behind them was disclosed a vast circular hall, so vast that you could not possibly see where it ended, and filled with a profusion of lights, wax candles held by rows and rows of white maidens, and torches held by rows and rows of white-robed eunuchs, and cressets burning upon lofty stands, and lamps dangling from the distant vault, through which here and there entered, blending strangely with the rest, great beams of white daylight. Don Juan stopped short, blinded by this magnificence, and as he did so, the fountain in the midst of the hall arose and shivered its cypress-like crest against the topmost vault; and innumerable voices of exquisite sweetness burst forth in strange wistful chants, and instruments of all kinds, both such as are blown and such as are twanged and rubbed with a bow, and such as are shaken and thumped, united with the voices and filled the hall with sound, as it was already filled with light.

Don Juan grasped his sword and advanced. At the extremity of the hall a flight of alabaster steps led up to a daïs or raised recess, overhung by an archway whose stalactites shone like beaten gold, and whose tiled walls glistened like precious stones. And on the daïs, on a throne of sandal-wood and ivory, incrusted with gems and carpeted with the work of the Chinese loom, sat the Moorish Infanta, fast asleep.

To the right and the left, but on a step beneath the princess, stood her two most intimate attendants, the Chief Duenna and the Chief Eunuch, to whom the prudent King Yahya had intrusted his only child during her sleep of four hundred years. The Chief Duenna was habited in a suit of sad-coloured violet weeds, with many modest swathings of white muslin round her yellow and wrinkled countenance. The Chief Eunuch was a portly negro, of a fine chocolate hue, with cheeks like an allegorical wind, and a complexion as shiny as a well-worn door-knocker: he was enveloped from top to toe in marigold-coloured robes, and on his head he wore a towering turban of embroidered cashmere. Both these great personages held, beside their especial insignia of office, namely, a Mecca rosary* in the hand of the Duenna, and a silver wand in the hand of the Eunuch, great fans of white peacocks' tails, wherewith to chase away from their royal charge any ill-advised fly. But at this moment all the flies in the place were fast asleep, and the Duenna and the Eunuch also. And between them, canopied by a parasol of white silk, on which were embroidered, in figures which moved like those in dreams, the histories of Jusuf and Zuleika, of Solomon and the Queen of Sheba,* and of many other famous lovers, sat the Infanta, erect, but veiled in gold-starred gauzes, as an unfinished statue is veiled in the roughness of the marble.

Don Juan walked quickly between the rows of prostrate slaves, and the singing and dancing girls, and those holding tapers and torches; and stopped only at the very foot of the throne steps.

"Awake!" he cried, "my Princess, my Bride, awake!"

A faint stir arose in the veils of the muffled form; and Don Juan felt his temples throb, and, at the same time, a deathly coldness steal over him.

"Awake!" he repeated boldly. But instead of the Infanta, it was the venerable Duenna who raised her withered countenance and looked round with a startled jerk, awakened not so much by the voices and instruments as by the tread of a masculine boot. The Chief Eunuch also awoke suddenly; but with the grace of one grown old in the antechamber of kings, he quickly suppressed a yawn, and laying his hand on his embroidered vest, he made a profound obeisance.

"Verily," he remarked, "Allah (who alone possesses the secrets of the universe) is remarkably great, since he not only . . ."

"Awake, awake, Princess!" interrupted Don Juan ardently, his foot on the lowest step of the throne.

But the Chief Eunuch waved him back with his wand, continuing his speech—"since he not only gave unto his servant King Yahya (may his shadow never be less!) power and riches far exceeding that of any of the kings of the earth or even of Solomon the son of David . . ."

"Cease, fellow!" cried Don Juan, and pushing aside the wand and the negro's dimpled chocolate hand, he rushed up the steps and flung himself at the foot of the veiled Infanta, his rapier clanging strangely as he did so.

"Unveil, my Beloved, more beautiful than Oriana, for whom Amadis wept in the Black Mountain, than Gradasilia whom Felixmarte sought on the winged dragon, than Helen of Sparta who fired the towers of Troy, than Calixto whom Jove was obliged to change into a female bear, than Venus herself on whom Paris bestowed the fatal apple. Unveil and arise, like the rosy Aurora from old Tithonus' couch, and welcome the knight who has confronted every peril for thee, Juan Gusman del Pulgar, Count of Miramor, who is ready, for thee, to confront every other peril of the world or of hell; and to fix upon thee alone his affections, more roving hitherto than those of Prince Galaor or of the many-shaped god Proteus!"*

A shiver ran through the veiled princess. The Chief Eunuch gave a significant nod, and waved his white wand thrice. Immediately a concert of voices and instruments, as numerous as those of the forces of the air when mustered before King Solomon, filled the vast hall. The dancing girls raised their tambourines over their heads, and poised themselves on tip-toe. A wave of fragrant essences passed through the air filled with the spray of innumerable fountains. And the Duenna, slowly advancing to the side of the throne, took in her withered fingers the top-most fold of shimmering gauze, and slowly gathering it backwards, displayed the Infanta unveiled before Don Juan's gaze.

The breast of the princess heaved deeply; her lips opened with a little sigh, and she languidly raised her long-fringed lids; then cast down her eyes on the ground, and resumed the rigidity of a statue. She was most marvellously fair. She sat on the cushions of the throne with modestly crossed legs; her hands, with nails tinged violet with henna, demurely folded in her lap. Through the thinness of her embroidered muslins shone the magnificence of purple and orange vests, stiff with gold and gems, and all subdued into a wondrous opalescent radiance. From her head there descended on either side of her person a diaphanous veil of shimmering colours, powdered over with minute glittering spangles. Her breast was covered with rows and rows of the largest pearls, a perfect network reaching from her slender throat to her waist, among which flashed diamonds embroidered in her vest. Her face was oval, with the silver pallor of the young moon; her mouth, most subtly carmined, looked like a pomegranate flower among tuberoses, for her cheeks were painted white, and the orbits of her great long-fringed eyes were stained violet. In the middle of each cheek, however, was a delicate spot of pink, in which an exquisite art had painted a small pattern of pyramid shape, so naturally that you might have thought that a real piece of embroidered stuff was decorating the maiden's countenance. On her head she wore a high tiara of jewels, the ransom of many kings, which sparkled and blazed like a lit-up altar. The eyes of the princess were decorously fixed on the ground.

Don Juan stood silent in ravishment.

"Princess!" he at length began.

But the Chief Eunuch laid his wand gently on his shoulder.

"My Lord," he whispered, "it is not etiquette that your Magnificence should address her Highness in any direct fashion; let alone the fact that her Highness does not understand the Castilian tongue, nor your Magnificence the Arabic. But through the mediumship of this most respectable lady, her Discretion the Principal Duenna, and my unworthy self, a conversation can be carried on equally delicious and instructive to both parties."

"A plague upon the old brute!" thought Don Juan; but he reflected upon what had never struck him before, that they had indeed been conversing, or attempting to converse, in Spanish, and that the Castilian spoken by the Chief Eunuch was, although correct, quite obsolete, being that of the sainted King Ferdinand.* There was a whispered consultation between the two great dignitaries; and the Duenna approached her lips to the Infanta's ear. The princess moved her pomegranate lips in a faint smile, but without raising her eyelids, and murmured something which the ancient lady whispered to the Chief Eunuch, who bowed thrice in answer. Then turning to Don Juan with most mellifluous tones, "Her Highness the Princess," he said, bowing thrice as he mentioned her name, "is, like all princesses, but to an even more remarkable extent, endowed with the most exquisite modesty. She is curious therefore, despite the superiority of her charms—so conspicuous even to those born blind—to know whether your Magnificence does not consider her the most beautiful thing you have ever beheld."

Don Juan laid his hand upon his heart with an affirmative gesture more eloquent than any words.

Again an almost invisible smile hovered about the pomegranate mouth, and there was a murmur and a whispering consultation.

"Her Highness," pursued the Chief Eunuch blandly, "has been informed by the judicious instructors of her tender youth, that cavaliers are frequently fickle, and that your Lordship in particular has assured many ladies in succession that each was the most beautiful creature you had ever beheld. Without admitting for an instant the possibility of a parallel, she begs your Magnificence to satisfy her curiosity on the point. Does your Lordship consider her as infinitely more beautiful than the Lady Catalina?"

Now Catalina was one of the famous seven for whom Don Juan had committed a deadly crime.

He was taken aback by the exactness of the Infanta's information; he was rather sorry they should have told her about Catalina.

"Of course," he answered hastily, "pray do not mention such a name in her Highness's presence."

The princess bowed imperceptibly.

"Her Highness," pursued the Chief Eunuch, "still actuated by the curiosity due to her high birth and tender youth, is desirous of knowing whether your Lordship considers her far more beautiful than the Lady Violante?"

Don Juan made an impatient gesture. "Slave! never speak of Violante in my princess's presence!" he exclaimed, fixing his eyes upon the tuberose cheeks and the pomegranate mouth which bloomed among that shimmer of precious stones.

"Good. And may the same be said to apply to the ladies Dolores and Elvira?"

"Dolores and Elvira and Fatma and Azahar," answered Don Juan, greatly provoked at the Chief Eunuch's want of tact, "and all the rest of womankind."

"And shall we add also, than Sister Seraphita of the Convent of Santa Isabel la Real?"

"Yes," cried Don Juan, "than Sister Seraphita, for whom I committed the greatest sin which can be committed by living man."

As he said these words, Don Juan was about to fling his arms about the princess and cut short this rather too elaborate courtship.

But again he was waved back by the white wand.

"One question more, only one, my dear Lord," whispered the Chief Eunuch; "I am most concerned at your impatience, but the laws of etiquette and the caprices of young princesses *must* go before everything, as you will readily admit. Stand back, I pray you."

Don Juan felt sorely inclined to thrust his sword through the yellow bolster of the great personage's vest; but he choked his rage, and stood quietly on the throne steps, one hand on his heart, the other on his sword-hilt, the boldest cavalier in all the kingdom of Spain.

"Speak, speak!" he begged.

The princess, without moving a muscle of her exquisite face, or unclosing her flower-like mouth, murmured some words to the Duenna, who whispered them mysteriously to the Chief Eunuch.

At this moment also the Infanta raised her heavy eyelids, stained violet with henna, and fixed upon the cavalier a glance long, dark and deep, like that of the wild antelope.

"Her Highness," resumed the Chief Eunuch, with a sweet smile, "is extremely gratified with your Lordship's answers, although of course they could not possibly have been at all different. But there remains yet another lady . . ."

Don Juan shook his head impatiently.

"Another lady concerning whom the Infanta desires some information. Does your Lordship consider her more beautiful also than the Virgin of the Seven Daggers?"

The place seemed to swim about Don Juan. Before his eyes rose the throne, all vacillating in its splendour, and on the throne the Moorish Infanta with the triangular patterns painted on her tuberose cheeks, and the long look in her henna'd eyes; and the image of her was blurred, and imperceptibly it seemed to turn into the effigy, black and white in her stiff puce frock and seed-pearl stomacher,* of the Virgin of the Seven Daggers staring blankly into space.

"My Lord," remarked the Chief Eunuch, "methinks that love has made you somewhat inattentive, a great blemish in a cavalier, when answering the questions of a lovely princess. I therefore venture to repeat: do you consider her more beautiful than the Virgin of the Seven Daggers?"

"Do you consider her more beautiful than the Virgin of the Seven Daggers?" repeated the Duenna, glaring at Don Juan.

"Do you consider me more beautiful than the Virgin of the Seven Daggers?" asked the princess, speaking suddenly in Spanish, or at least in language perfectly intelligible to Don Juan. And, as she spoke the words, all the slave-girls and eunuchs and singers and players, the whole vast hall full, seemed to echo the same question.

The Count of Miramor stood silent for an instant; then raising his hand and looking round him with quiet decision, he answered in a loud voice:

"No!"

"In that case," said the Chief Eunuch with the politeness of a man desirous to cut short an embarrassing silence, "in that case I am very sorry it should be my painful duty to intimate to your Lordship that you must undergo the punishment usually allotted to cavaliers who are disobliging to young and tender princesses."

So saying, he clapped his black hands, and, as if by magic, there arose at the foot of the steps, a gigantic Berber of the Rif,* his brawny sunburnt limbs left bare by a scanty striped shirt, fastened round his waist by a wisp of rope, his head shaven blue except in the middle, where, encircled by a coronet of worsted rag, there flamed a top-knot of dreadful orange hair.

"Decapitate that gentleman," ordered the Chief Eunuch in his most obliging tones. Don Juan felt himself collared, dragged down the steps, and forced into a kneeling posture on the lowest landing, all in the twinkling of an eye.

From beneath the bronzed left arm of the ruffian he could see the milk-white of the alabaster steps, the gleam of an immense scimitar, the mingled blue and yellow of the cressets and tapers, the daylight filtering through the constellations in the dark cedar vault, the glitter of the Infanta's diamonds, and, of a sudden, the twinkle of the Chief Eunuch's eye.

Then all was black, and Don Juan felt himself, that is to say, his own head, rebound three times like a ball upon the alabaster steps.

VI

It had evidently all been a dream—perhaps a delusion induced by the vile fumigations of that filthy ruffian of a renegade Jew. The infidel dogs had certain abominable drugs which gave them visions of paradise and hell when smoked or chewed—nasty brutes that they were—and this was some of their devilry. But he should pay for it, the cursed old grey-beard, the Holy Office should keep him warm, or a Miramor was not a Miramor! For Don Juan forgot, or disbelieved, not only that he himself had been beheaded by a Rif Berber the evening before, but that he had previously run poor Baruch through the body and hurled him down the rocks near the Tower of the Cypresses.

This confusion of mind was excusable on the part of the cavalier. For, on opening his eyes, he had found himself lying in a most unlikely resting-place, considering the time and season, namely, a heap of old bricks and rubbish, half-hidden in withered reeds and sprouting weeds, on a ledge of the precipitous hillside which descends into the River Darro. Above him rose the dizzy red-brick straightness of the tallest tower of the Alhambra, pierced at its very top by an arched and pillared window, and scantily overgrown with the roots of a dead ivy-tree. Below, at the bottom of the precipice, dashed the little Darro, brown and swollen with melted snows, between its rows of leafless poplars; beyond it rose the roofs and balconies and orange-trees of the older part of Grenada; and above that, with the morning sunshine and mists fighting among its hovels, its square belfries and great masses of prickly pear and aloe, the Albaycin whose highest convent tower stood out already against a sky of winter blue. The Albaycin; that was the quarter of that villain Baruch, who dared to play practical jokes on grandees of Spain of the very first class!

This thought caused Don Juan to spring up, and, grasping his sword, to scramble through the sprouting elder-bushes and the heaps of broken masonry, down to the bridge over the river.

It was a beautiful winter morning, sunny, blue and crisp through the white mists. And Don Juan sped along as with wings to his feet; for having remembered that it was the anniversary of the Liberation, and that he, as descendant of Fernan Perez del Pulgar, would be expected to carry the banner of the city at High Mass in the cathedral, he had determined that his absence from the ceremony should raise no suspicions of his ridiculous adventure. For ridiculous it had been—and the sense of its being ridiculous filled the generous breast of the Count of Miramor with a longing to murder every man, woman or child he encountered as he sped through the streets. "Look at his Excellency the Count of Miramor; look at Don Juan Gusman del Pulgar! He's been made a fool of by old Baruch the renegade Jew!" he imagined everybody to be thinking.

But, on the contrary, no one took the smallest notice of him. The muleteers, driving along their beasts laden with heather and myrtle for the bakehouse ovens, allowed their loads to brush him, as if he had been the merest errand-boy; the stout black housewives, going to market with their brass braziers tucked under their cloaks, never once turned round as he pushed them rudely on the cobbles; nay, the very beggars, armless and legless and shameless, who were alighting from their go-carts and taking up their station at the church-doors, did not even extend a hand towards the passing cavalier. Before a popular barber's some citizens were waiting to have their top-knots plaited into tidy tails, discussing the while the olive harvest, the price of spart-grass and the chances of the bull-ring. This, Don Juan expected, would be a fatal spot, for from the barber's shop the news must go about that Don Juan del Pulgar, hatless and covered with mud, was hurrying home with a discomfited countenance, ill-befitting the hero of so many nocturnal adventures. But, although Don Juan had to make his way right in front of the barber's, not one of the clients did so much as turn his head, perhaps out of fear of displeasing so great a cavalier.

Suddenly, as Don Juan hurried along, he noticed for the first time, among the cobbles and the dry mud of the street, large drops of blood, growing larger as they went, becoming an almost uninterrupted line, then, in the puddles, a little red stream. Such were by no means uncommon vestiges in those days of duels and town brawls; besides, some early sportsman, a wild boar on his horse, might have been passing. But somehow or other, this track of blood exerted an odd attraction over Don Juan; and unconsciously to himself, instead of taking the short cut to his palace, he followed it along some of the chief streets of Grenada. The blood-stains, as was natural, led in the direction of the great hospital, founded by Saint John of God,* to which it was customary to carry the victims of accidents and street fights. Before the monumental gateway, where Saint John of God knelt in effigy before the Madonna, a large crowd was collected, above whose heads oscillated the black and white banners of a mortuary confraternity, and the flame and smoke of their torches. The street was blocked with carts, and with riders rising in their stirrups to look over the crowd, and even with gaily trapped mules and gilded coaches, in which veiled ladies were anxiously questioning their lackeys and outriders. The throng of idle and curious citizens, of monks and brothers of mercy, reached up the steps and right into the cloistered court of the hospital.

"Who is it?" asked Don Juan with his usual masterful manner, pushing his way into the crowd. The man whom he addressed, a stalwart peasant with a long tail pinned under his hat, turned round vaguely, but did not answer.

"Who is it?" repeated Don Juan louder.

But no one answered, although he accompanied the question with a good push, and even a thrust with his sheathed sword.

"Cursed idiots! Are you all deaf and dumb, that you cannot answer a cavalier?" he cried angrily, and taking a portly priest by the collar, he shook him roughly.

"Jesus Maria Joseph!" exclaimed the priest; but turning round he took no notice of Don Juan, and merely rubbed his collar, muttering, "Well, if the demons are to be allowed to take respectable canons by the collar, it *is* time that we should have a good witch-burning."

Don Juan took no heed of his words, but thrust onward, knocking over, as he did so, a young woman who was lifting her child to let it see the show. The crowd parted as the woman fell, and people ran to pick her up, but no one took any notice of Don Juan. Indeed, he himself was struck by the way in which he passed through its midst, encountering no opposition from the phalanx of robust shoulders and hips.

"Who is it?" asked Don Juan again.

He had got into a clearing of the crowd. On the lowest step of the hospital gate stood a little knot of black penitents, their black linen cowls flung back on their shoulders, and of priests and monks muttering together. Some of them were beating back the crowd, others snuffing their torches against the paving-stones, and letting the wax drip off their tapers. In the midst of them, with a standard of the Virgin at its head, was a light wooden bier, set down by its bearers. It was covered with coarse black serge, on which were embroidered in yellow braid a skull and cross-bones, and the monogram I.H.S.* Under the bier was a little red pool.

"Who is it?" asked Don Juan one last time; but instead of waiting for an answer, he stepped forward, sword in hand, and rudely pulled aside the rusty black pall.

On the bier was stretched a corpse dressed in black velvet, with lace cuffs and collar, loose boots, buff gloves, and with a blood-clotted dark matted head, lying loose half an inch above the mangled throat.

Don Juan Gusman del Pulgar stared fixedly. It was himself.

The church into which Don Juan had fled was that of the Virgin of the Seven Daggers. It was deserted, as usual, and filled with chill morning light, in which glittered the gilded cornices and altars, and gleamed, like pools of water, the many precious marbles. A sort of mist seemed to hang about it all, and dim the splendour of the high altar.

Don Juan del Pulgar sank down in the midst of the nave; not on his knees, for (Oh horror!) he felt that he had no longer any knees, nor indeed any back, any arms, or limbs of any kind, and he dared not ask himself whether he was still in possession of a head: his only sensations were such as might be experienced by a slowly trickling pool, or a snow-wreath in process of melting, or a cloud fitting itself on to a flat surface of rock.

He was disembodied. He now understood why no one had noticed him in the crowd, why he had been able to penetrate through its thickness, and why, when he struck people and pulled them by the collar and knocked them down, they had taken no more notice of him than of a blast of wind. He was a ghost. He was dead. This must be the after life; and he was infallibly within a few minutes of hell.

"O Virgin, Virgin of the Seven Daggers!" he cried with hopeless bitterness, "is this the way you recompense my faithfulness? I have died unshriven, in the midst of mortal sin, merely because I would not say you were less beautiful than the Moorish Infanta; and is this all my reward?"

But even as he spoke these words an extraordinary miracle took place. The white winter light broke into wondrous iridescences; the white mist collected into shoals of dim palm-bearing angels; the cloud of stale incense, still hanging over the high altar, gathered into fleecy balls, which became the heads and backsides of chubby celestials; and Don Juan, reeling and fainting, felt himself rise, higher and higher, as if borne up on clusters of soap-bubbles. The cupola began to rise and expand; the painted clouds to move and blush a deeper pink; the painted sky to recede and turn into deep holes of real blue. As he was borne upwards, the allegorical virtues in the lunettes began to move and brandish their attributes; the colossal stucco angels on the cornices to pelt him with flowers no longer of plaster of Paris; the place was filled with delicious fragrance of incense, and with sounds of exquisitely played lutes and viols, and of voices, among which he distinctly recognized Syphax, His Majesty's chief soprano. And, as Don Juan floated upwards through the cupola of the church, his heart suddenly filled with a consciousness of extraordinary virtue; the gold transparency at the top of the dome expanded; its rays grew redder and more golden, and there burst from it at last a golden moon crescent, on which stood, in her farthingale of puce and her stomacher of seed-pearl, her big black eyes fixed mildly upon him, the Virgin of the Seven Daggers.

* * * *

"Your story of His Excellency the late Count of Miramor, Don Juan Gusman del Pulgar," wrote Don Pedro Calderon de la Barca, in March, 1686, to his friend, the Archpriest Morales,* at Grenada, "so veraciously revealed in a vision to the holy prior of Saint Nicholas, is indeed such as must touch the heart of the most stubborn. Were it presented in the shape of a play, say in the style of my *Purgatory of St. Patrick*, it should outshine that humble work as much as the villainy of your late noble friend, and the marvel of his salvation, throw into the shade the villainy of my Ludovic Enio* and the miracle wrought in his person. And to what better use could I dedicate whatever remains in me of the Sacred Fire than setting forth and adorning wonders so calculated to inculcate virtue and magnify piety? But alas, my dear friend, the snows of age are as thick on my head as the snows of winter upon your Mulhacen; and who knows whether I shall ever be able to write again?"

The forecast of the illustrious dramatic poet proved, indeed, too true; and hence it is that unworthy modern hands have sought to frame the veracious and edifying history of Don Juan and the Virgin of the Seven Daggers.

PRINCE ALBERIC AND THE SNAKE LADY

TO HER HIGHNESS

THE RANEE OF SARÀWAK*

In the year 1701, the Duchy of Luna* became united to the Italian dominions of the Holy Roman Empire, in consequence of the extinction of its famous ducal house in the persons of Duke Balthasar Maria and of his grandson Alberic, who should have been third of the name. Under this dry historical fact lies hidden the strange story of Prince Alberic and the Snake Lady.

I

The first act of hostility of old Duke Balthasar towards the Snake Lady, in whose existence he did not, of course, believe, was connected with the arrival at Luna of certain tapestries after the designs of the famous Monsieur Le Brun, a present from his Most Christian Majesty King Lewis the XIV. These Gobelins, which represented the marriage of Alexander and Roxana,* were placed in the throne-room, and in the most gallant suite of chambers overlooking the great rockery garden, all of which had been completed by Duke Balthasar Maria in 1680; and, as a consequence, the already existing tapestries, silk hangings, and mirrors painted by Marius of the Flowers,* were transferred into other apartments, thus occasioning a general re-hanging of the Red Palace at Luna.* These magnificent operations, in which, as the court poets sang, Apollo and the Graces* lent their services to their beloved patron, aroused in Duke Balthasar's mind a sudden curiosity to see what might be made of the rooms occupied by his grandson and heir, and which he had not entered since Prince Alberic's christening. He found the apartments in a shocking state of neglect, and the youthful prince unspeakably shy and rustic; and he determined to give him at once an establishment befitting his age, to look out presently for a princess worthy to be his wife, and, somewhat earlier, for a less illustrious but more agreeable lady to fashion his manners. Meanwhile, Duke Balthasar Maria gave orders to change the tapestry in Prince Alberic's chamber. This tapestry was of old and Gothic taste, extremely worn, and represented Alberic the Blond and the Snake Lady Oriana,* as described in the Chronicles of Archbishop Turpin and the poems of Boiardo.* Duke Balthasar Maria was a prince of enlightened mind and delicate taste; the literature as well as the art of the dark ages found no grace in his sight; he reproved the folly of feeding the thoughts of youth on improbable events; besides, he disliked snakes and was afraid of the devil. So he ordered the tapestry to be removed and another, representing Susanna and the Elders,* to be put in its stead. But when Prince Alberic discovered the change, he cut Susanna and the Elders into strips with a knife he had stolen out of the ducal kitchens (no dangerous instruments being allowed to young princes before they were of an age to learn to fence) and refused to touch his food for three days.

The tapestry over which little Prince Alberic mourned so deeply had indeed been both tattered and Gothic. But for the boy it possessed an inexhaustible charm. It was quite full of things, and they were all delightful. The sorely-frayed borders consisted of wonderful garlands of leaves and fruits and flowers, tied at intervals with ribbons, although they seemed all to grow like tall narrow bushes, each from a big vase in the bottom corner, and made of all manner of different plants. There were bunches of spiky bays, and of acorned oak leaves; sheaves of lilies and heads of poppies, gourds, and apples and pears, and hazelnuts and mulberries, wheat ears, and beans, and pine tufts. And in each of these plants, of which those above named are only a very few, there were curious live creatures of some sort—various birds, big and little, butterflies on the lilies, snails, squirrels, mice, and rabbits, and even a hare, with such pointed ears, darting among the spruce fir. Alberic learned the names of most of these plants and creatures from his nurse, who had been a peasant, and he spent much ingenuity seeking for them in the palace gardens and terraces; but there were no live creatures there, except snails and toads, which the gardeners killed, and carp swimming about in the big tank, whom Alberic did not like, and who were not in the tapestry; and he had to supplement his nurse's information by that of the grooms and scullions, when he could visit them secretly. He was even promised a sight, one day, of a dead rabbit—the rabbit was the most fascinating of the inhabitants of the tapestry border—but he came to the kitchen too late, and saw it with its pretty fur pulled off, and looking so sad and naked that it made him cry. But Alberic had grown so accustomed to never quitting the Red Palace and its gardens, that he was usually satisfied with seeing the plants and animals in the tapestry, and looked forward to seeing the real things only when he should be grown up. "When I am a man," he would say to himself—for his nurse scolded him for saying it to her—"I will have a live rabbit of my own."

The border of the tapestry interested Prince Alberic most when he was very little—indeed, his remembrance of it was older than that of the Red Palace, its terraces and gardens—but gradually he began to care more and more for the picture in the middle.

There were mountains, and the sea with ships; and these first made him care to go on to the topmost palace terrace and look at the real mountains and the sea beyond the roofs and gardens; and there were woods of all manner of tall trees, with clover and wild strawberries growing beneath them; and roads, and paths, and rivers, in and out; these were rather confused with the places where the tapestry was worn out, and with the patches and mendings thereof, but Alberic, in the course of time, contrived to make them all out, and knew exactly whence the river came which turned the big mill-wheel, and how many bends it made before coming to the fishing-nets; and how the horsemen must cross over the bridge, then wind behind the cliff with the chapel, and pass through the wood of pines in order to get from the castle in the left-hand corner nearest the bottom to the town, over which the sun was shining with all its beams, and a wind blowing with inflated cheeks on the right hand close to the top.

The centre of the tapestry was the most worn and discoloured; and it was for this reason perhaps that little Alberic scarcely noticed it for some years, his eye and mind led away by the bright red and yellow of the border of fruit and flowers, and the still vivid green and orange of the background landscape. Red, yellow, and orange, even green, had faded in the centre into pale blue and lilac; even the green had grown an odd dusty tint; and the figures seemed like ghosts, sometimes emerging and then receding again into vagueness. Indeed, it was only as he grew bigger that Alberic began to see any figures at all; and then, for a long time he would lose sight of them. But little by little, when the light was strong, he could see them always; and even in the dark make them out with a little attention. Among the spruce firs and pines, and against a hedge of roses, on which there still lingered a remnant of redness, a knight had reined in his big white horse, and was putting one arm round the shoulder of a lady, who was leaning against the horse's flank. The knight was all dressed in armour—not at all like that of the equestrian statue of Duke Balthasar Maria in the square, but all made of plates, with plates also on the legs, instead of having them bare like Duke Balthasar's statue; and on his head he had no wig, but a helmet with big plumes. It seemed a more reasonable dress than the other, but probably Duke Balthasar was right to go to battle with bare legs and a kilt and a wig, since he did so. The lady who was looking up into his face was dressed with a high collar and long sleeves, and on her head she wore a thick circular garland, from under which the hair fell about her shoulders. She was very lovely, Alberic got to think, particularly when, having climbed upon a chest of drawers, he saw that her hair was still full of threads of gold, some of them quite loose because the tapestry was so rubbed. The knight and his horse were of course very beautiful, and he liked the way in which the knight reined in the horse with one hand, and embraced the lady with the other arm. But Alberic got to love the lady most, although she was so very pale and faded, and almost the colour of the moonbeams through the palace windows in summer. Her dress also was so beautiful and unlike those of the ladies who got out of the coaches in the Court of Honour, and who had on hoops and no clothes at all on their upper part. This lady, on the contrary, had that collar like a lily, and a beautiful gold chain, and patterns in gold (Alberic made them out little by little) all over her bodice. He got to want so much to see her skirt; it was probably very beautiful too, but it so happened that the inlaid chest of drawers before mentioned stood against the wall in that place, and on it a large ebony and ivory crucifix, which covered the lower part of the lady's body. Alberic often tried to lift off the crucifix, but it was a great deal too heavy, and there was not room on the chest of drawers to push it aside, so the lady's skirt and feet were invisible. But one day, when Alberic was eleven, his nurse suddenly took a fancy to having all the furniture shifted. It was time that the child should cease to sleep in her room, and plague her with his loud talking in his dreams. And she might as well have the handsome inlaid chest of drawers, and that nice pious crucifix for herself next door, in place of Alberic's little bed. So one morning there was a great shifting and dusting, and when Alberic came in from his walk on the terrace, there hung the tapestry entirely uncovered. He stood for a few minutes before it, riveted to the ground. Then he ran to his nurse, exclaiming: "O, nurse, dear nurse, look—the lady——!"

For where the big crucifix had stood, the lower part of the beautiful pale lady with the gold-thread hair was now exposed. But instead of a skirt, she ended off in a big snake's tail, with scales of still most vivid (the tapestry not having faded there) green and gold.

The nurse turned round.

"Holy Virgin," she cried, "why, she's a serpent!" Then, noticing the boy's violent excitement, she added, "You little ninny, it's only Duke Alberic the Blond, who was your ancestor, and the Snake Lady."

Little Prince Alberic asked no questions, feeling that he must not. Very strange it was, but he loved the beautiful lady with the thread of gold hair only the more because she ended off in the long twisting body of a snake. And that, no doubt, was why the knight was so very good to her.

II

For want of that tapestry, poor Alberic, having cut its successor to pieces, began to pine away. It had been his whole world; and now it was gone he discovered that he had no other. No one had ever cared for him except his nurse, who was very cross. Nothing had ever been taught him except the Latin catechism; he had had nothing to make a pet of except the fat carp, supposed to be four hundred years old, in the tank; he had nothing to play with except a gala coral with bells by Benvenuto Cellini,* which Duke Balthasar Maria had sent him on his eighth birthday. He had never had anything except a Grandfather, and had never been outside the Red Palace.

Now, after the loss of the tapestry, the disappearance of the plants and flowers and birds and beasts on its borders, and the departure of the kind knight on the horse and the dear golden-haired Snake Lady, Alberic became aware that he had always hated both his grandfather and the Red Palace.

The whole world, indeed, were agreed that Duke Balthasar was the most magnanimous and fascinating of monarchs, and that the Red Palace of Luna was the most magnificent and delectable of residences. But the knowledge of this universal opinion, and the consequent sense of his own extreme unworthiness, merely exasperated Alberic's detestation, which, as it grew, came to identify the Duke and the Palace as the personification and visible manifestation of each other. He knew now—oh, how well!—every time that he walked on the terrace or in the garden (at the hours when no one else ever entered them) that he had always abominated the brilliant tomato-coloured plaster which gave the palace its name: such a pleasant, gay colour, people would remark, particularly against the blue of the sky. Then there were the Twelve Cæsars*—they were the Twelve Cæsars, but multiplied over and over again—busts with flying draperies and spiky garlands, one over every first-floor window, hundreds of them, all fluttering and grimacing round the place. Alberic had always thought them uncanny; but now he positively avoided looking out of the window, lest his eye should catch the stucco eyeball of one of those Cæsars in the opposite wing of the building. But there was one thing more especially in the Red Palace, of which a bare glimpse had always filled the youthful Prince with terror, and which now kept recurring to his mind like a nightmare. This was no other than the famous grotto of the Court of Honour. Its roof was ingeniously inlaid with oyster-shells, forming elegant patterns, among which you could plainly distinguish some colossal satyrs;* the sides were built of rockery, and in its depths, disposed in a most natural and tasteful manner, was a herd of lifesize animals all carved out of various precious marbles. On holidays the water was turned on, and spurted about in a gallant fashion. On such occasions persons of taste would flock to Luna from all parts of the world to enjoy the spectacle. But ever since his earliest infancy Prince Alberic had held this grotto in abhorrence. The oyster-shell satyrs on the roof frightened him into fits, particularly when the fountains were playing; and his terror of the marble animals was such that a bare allusion to the Porphyry Rhinoceros, the Giraffe of Cipollino, and the Verde Antique Monkeys,* set him screaming for an hour. The grotto, moreover, had become associated in his mind with the other great glory of the Red Palace, to wit, the domed chapel in which Duke Balthasar Maria intended erecting monuments to his immediate ancestors, and in which he had already prepared a monument for himself. And the whole magnificent palace, grotto, chapel and all, had become mysteriously connected with Alberic's grandfather, owing to a particularly terrible dream. When the boy was eight years old, he was taken one day to see his grandfather. It was the feast of St. Balthasar, one of the Three Wise Kings from the East, as is well known.* There had been firing of mortars and ringing of bells ever since daybreak. Alberic had his hair curled, was put into new clothes (his usual raiment being somewhat tattered), a large nosegay was placed in his hand, and he and his nurse were conveyed by complicated relays of lackeys and of pages up to the ducal apartments. Here, in a crowded outer room, he was separated from his nurse and received by a gaunt person in a long black robe like a sheath, and a long shovel hat, whom Alberic identified many years later as his grandfather's Jesuit Confessor. He smiled a long smile, discovering a prodigious number of teeth, in a manner which froze the child's blood; and lifting an embroidered curtain, pushed Alberic into his grandfather's presence. Duke Balthasar Maria, called in all Italy the Ever Young Prince, was at his toilet. He was wrapped in a green Chinese wrapper, embroidered with gold pagodas, and round his head was tied an orange scarf of delicate fabric. He was listening to the performance of some fiddlers, and of a lady dressed as a nymph, who was singing the birthday ode with many shrill trills and quavers; and meanwhile his face, in the hands of a valet, was being plastered with a variety of brilliant colours. In his green and gold wrapper and orange head-dress, with the strange patches of vermilion and white on his cheeks, Duke Balthasar looked to the diseased fancy of his nephew as if he had been made of various precious metals, like the celebrated effigy he had erected of himself in the great burial-chapel. But, just as Alberic was mustering up courage and approaching his magnificent grandparent, his eye fell upon a sight so mysterious and terrible that he fled wildly out of the ducal presence. For through an open door he could see in an adjacent closet a man dressed in white, combing the long flowing locks of what he recognised as his grandfather's head, stuck on a short pole in the light of a window.

That night Alberic had seen in his dreams the Ever Young Duke Balthasar Maria descend from his niche in the burial-chapel; and, with his Roman lappets and corslet visible beneath the green bronze cloak embroidered with gold pagodas, march down the great staircase into the Court of Honour, and ascend to the empty place at the end of the rockery grotto (where, as a matter of fact, a statue of Neptune, by a pupil of Bernini,* was placed some months later), and there, raising his sceptre, receive the obeisance of all the marble animals—the Giraffe, the Rhinoceros, the Stag, the Peacock, and the Monkeys. And behold! suddenly his well-known features waxed dim, and beneath the great curly peruke there was a round blank thing—a barber's block!

Alberic, who was an intelligent child, had gradually learned to disentangle this dream from reality; but its grotesque terror never vanished from his mind, and became the core of all his feelings towards Duke Balthasar Maria and the Red Palace.

III

The news—which was kept back as long as possible—of the destruction of Susanna and the Elders threw Duke Balthasar Maria into a most violent rage with his grandson. The boy should be punished by exile, and exile to a terrible place; above all, to a place where there was no furniture to destroy. Taking due counsel with his Jesuit, his Jester, and his Dwarf, Duke Balthasar decided that in the whole Duchy of Luna there was no place more fitted for the purpose than the Castle of Sparkling Waters.

For the Castle of Sparkling Waters was little better than a ruin, and its sole inhabitants were a family of peasants. The original cradle of the House of Luna, and its principal bulwark against invasion, the castle had been ignominiously discarded and forsaken a couple of centuries before, when the dukes had built the rectangular town in the plain; after which it had been used as a quarry for ready-cut stone, and the greater part carted off to rebuild the town of Luna, and even the central portion of the Red Palace. The castle was therefore reduced to its outer circuit of walls, enclosing vineyards and orange-gardens, instead of moats and yards and towers, and to the large gate tower, which had been kept, with one or two smaller buildings, for the housing of the farmer, his cattle, and his stores.

Thither the misguided young Prince was conveyed in a carefully shuttered coach and at a late hour of the evening, as was proper in the case of an offender at once so illustrious and so criminal. Nature, moreover, had clearly shared Duke Balthasar Maria's legitimate anger, and had done her best to increase the horror of this just though terrible sentence. For that particular night the long summer broke up in a storm of fearful violence; and Alberic entered the ruined castle amid the howling of wind, the rumble of thunder, and the rush of torrents of rain.

But the young Prince showed no fear or reluctance; he saluted with dignity and sweetness the farmer and his wife and family, and took possession of his attic, where the curtains of an antique and crazy four-poster shook in the draught of the unglazed windows, as if he were taking possession of the gala chambers of a great palace. "And so," he merely remarked, looking round him with reserved satisfaction, "I am now in the castle which was built by my ancestor and name-sake, the Marquis Alberic the Blond."

He looked not unworthy of such illustrious lineage, as he stood there in the flickering light of the pine-torch: tall for his age, slender and strong, with abundant golden hair falling about his very white face.

That first night at the Castle of Sparkling Waters, Alberic dreamed without end about his dear, lost tapestry. And when, in the radiant autumn morning, he descended to explore the place of his banishment and captivity, it seemed as if those dreams were still going on. Or had the tapestry been removed to this spot, and become a reality in which he himself was running about?

The gate tower in which he had slept was still intact and chivalrous. It had battlements, a drawbridge, a great escutcheon with the arms of Luna, just like the castle in the tapestry. Some vines, quite loaded with grapes, rose on the strong cords of their fibrous wood from the ground to the very roof of the town, exactly like those borders of leaves and fruit which Alberic had loved so much. And, between the vines, all along the masonry, were strung long narrow ropes of maize, like garlands of gold. A plantation of orange-trees filled what had once been the moat; lemons were spalliered against the delicate pink brickwork. There were no lilies, indeed, but big carnations hung down from the tower windows, and a tall oleander, which Alberic mistook for a special sort of rose-tree, shed its blossoms on to the drawbridge. After the storm of the night, birds were singing all round; not indeed as they sang in spring, which Alberic, of course, did not know, but in a manner quite different from the canaries in the ducal aviaries at Luna. Moreover, other birds, wonderful white and gold creatures, some of them with brilliant tails and scarlet crests, were pecking and strutting and making curious noises in the yard. And—could it be true?—a little way further up the hill, for the castle walls climbed steeply from the seaboard, in the grass beneath the olive-trees, white creatures were running in and out—white creatures with pinkish lining to their ears, undoubtedly—as Alberic's nurse had taught him on the tapestry—undoubtedly *rabbits*.

Thus Alberic rambled on, from discovery to discovery, with the growing sense that he was in the tapestry, but that the tapestry had become the whole world. He climbed from terrace to terrace of the steep olive-yard, among the sage and the fennel tufts, the long red walls of the castle winding ever higher on the hill. And on the very top of the hill was a high terrace surrounded by towers, and a white shining house with columns and windows, which seemed to drag him upwards.

It was, indeed, the citadel of the place, the very centre of the castle.

Alberic's heart beat strangely as he passed beneath the wide arch of delicate ivy-grown brick, and clambered up the rough-paved path to the topmost terrace. And there he actually forgot the tapestry. The terrace was laid out as a vineyard, the vines trellised on the top of stone columns; at one end stood a clump of trees, pines, and a big ilex and a walnut, whose shrivelled leaves already strewed the grass. To the back stood a tiny little house all built of shining marble, with two large rounded windows divided by delicate pillars, of the sort (as Alberic later learned) which people built in the barbarous days of the Goths. Among the vines, which formed a vast arbour, were growing, in open spaces, large orange and lemon trees, and flowering bushes of rosemary, and pale pink roses. And in front of the house, under a great umbrella pine, was a well, with an arch over it and a bucket hanging to a chain.

Alberic wandered about in the vineyard, and then slowly mounted the marble staircase which flanked the white house. There was no one in it. The two or three small upper chambers stood open, and on their blackened floor were heaped sacks, and faggots, and fodder, and all manner of coloured seeds. The unglazed windows stood open, framing in between their white pillars a piece of deep blue sea. For there, below, but seen over the tops of the olive-trees and the green leaves of the oranges and lemons, stretched the sea, deep blue, speckled with white sails, bounded by pale blue capes, and arched over by a dazzling pale blue sky. From the lower story there rose faint sounds of cattle, and a fresh, sweet smell as of grass and herbs and coolness, which Alberic had never known before. How long did Alberic stand at that window? He was startled by what he took to be steps close behind him, and a rustle as of silk. But the rooms were empty, and he could see nothing moving among the stacked up fodder and seeds. Still, the sounds seemed to recur, but now outside, and he thought he heard some one in a very low voice call his name. He descended into the vineyard; he walked round every tree and every shrub, and climbed upon the broken masses of rose-coloured masonry, crushing the scented ragwort and peppermint with which they were overgrown. But all was still and empty. Only, from far, far below, there rose a stave of peasant's song.

The great gold balls of oranges, and the delicate yellow lemons, stood out among their glossy green against the deep blue of the sea; the long bunches of grapes hung, filled with sunshine, like clusters of rubies and jacinths and topazes, from the trellis which patterned the pale blue sky. But Alberic felt not hunger, but sudden thirst, and mounted the three broken marble steps of the well. By its side was a long narrow trough of marble, such as stood in the court at Luna, and which, Alberic had been told, people had used as coffins in pagan times. This one was evidently intended to receive water from the well, for it had a mark in the middle, with a spout; but it was quite dry and full of wild herbs, and even of pale, prickly roses. There were garlands carved upon it, and people with twisted snakes about them; and the carving was picked out with golden brown minute mosses. Alberic looked at it, for it pleased him greatly; and then he lowered the bucket into the deep well, and drank. The well was very, very deep. Its inner sides were covered, as far as you could see, with long delicate weeds like pale green hair, but this faded away in the darkness. At the bottom was a bright space, reflecting the sky, but looking like some subterranean country. Alberic, as he bent over, was startled by suddenly seeing what seemed a face filling up part of that shining circle; but he remembered it must be his own reflection, and felt ashamed. So, to give himself courage, he bent over again, and sang his own name to the image. But instead of his own boyish voice he was answered by wonderful tones, high and deep alternately, running through the notes of a long, long cadence, as he had heard them on holidays at the Ducal Chapel at Luna.

When he had slaked his thirst, Alberic was about to unchain the bucket, when there was a rustle hard by, and a sort of little hiss, and there rose from the carved trough, from among the weeds and roses, and glided on to the brick of the well, a long, green, glittering thing. Alberic recognised it to be a snake; only, he had no idea it had such a flat, strange little head, and such a long forked tongue, for the lady on the tapestry was a woman from the waist upwards. It sat on the opposite side of the well, moving its long neck in his direction, and fixing him with its small golden eyes. Then, slowly, it began to glide round the well circle towards him. Perhaps it wants to drink, thought Alberic, and tipped the bronze pitcher in its direction. But the creature glided past, and came around and rubbed itself against Alberic's hand. The boy was not afraid, for he knew nothing about snakes; but he started, for, on this hot day, the creature was icy cold. But then he felt sorry. "It must be dreadful to be always so cold," he said; "come, try and get warm in my pocket."

But the snake merely rubbed itself against his coat, and then disappeared back into the carved sarcophagus.

IV

Duke Balthasar Maria, as we have seen, was famous for his unfading youth, and much of his happiness and pride was due to this delightful peculiarity. Any comparison, therefore, which might diminish it, was distasteful to the Ever Young sovereign of Luna; and when his son had died with mysterious suddenness, Duke Balthasar Maria's grief had been tempered by the consolatory fact that he was now the youngest man at his own court. This very natural feeling explains why the Duke of Luna had put behind him for several years the fact of having a grandson, painful because implying that he was of an age to be a grandfather. He had done his best, and succeeded not badly, to forget Alberic while the latter abode under his own roof; and now that the boy had been sent away to a distance, he forgot him entirely for the space of several years.

But Balthasar Maria's three chief counsellors had no such reason for forgetfulness; and so, in turn, each unknown to the other, the Jesuit, the Dwarf, and the Jester sent spies to the Castle of Sparkling Waters, and even secretly visited that place in person. For by the coincidence of genius, the mind of each of these profound politicians, had been illuminated by the same remarkable thought, to wit: that Duke Balthasar Maria, unnatural as it seemed, would some day have to die, and Prince Alberic, if still alive, become duke in his stead. Those were the times of subtle statecraft; and the Jesuit, the Dwarf, and the Jester were notable statesmen even in their day. So each of them had provided himself with a scheme, which, in order to be thoroughly artistic, was twofold and, so to speak, double-barrelled. Alberic might live or he might die, and therefore Alberic must be turned to profit in either case. If, to invert the chances, Alberic should die before coming to the throne, the Jesuit, the Dwarf, and the Jester had each privately determined to represent this death as purposely brought about by himself for the benefit of one of the three Powers which would claim the duchy in case of extinction of the male line. The Jesuit had chosen to attribute the murder to devotion to the Holy See; the Dwarf had preferred to appear active in favour of the King of Spain; and the Jester had decided that he would lay claim to the gratitude of the Emperor. The very means which each would pretend to have used had been thought out: poison in each case, only while the Dwarf had selected henbane, taken through a pair of perfumed gloves, and the Jester pounded diamonds mixed in champagne, the Jesuit had modestly adhered to the humble cup of chocolate, which, whether real or fictitious, had always stood his order in such good stead. Thus did each of these wily courtiers dispose of Alberic in case he should die.

There remained the alternative of Alberic continuing to live; and for this the three rival statesmen were also prepared. If Alberic lived, it was obvious that he must be made to select one of the three as his sole minister, and banish, imprison, or put to death the other two. For this purpose it was necessary to secure his affection by gifts, until he should be old enough to understand that he had actually owed his life to the passionate loyalty of the Jesuit, or the Dwarf, or the Jester, each of whom had saved him from the atrocious enterprises of the other two counsellors of Balthasar Maria—nay, who knows? perhaps from the malignity of Balthasar Maria himself.

In accordance with these subtle machinations, each of the three statesmen determined to outwit his rivals by sending young Alberic such things as would appeal most strongly to a poor young Prince living in banishment among peasants, and wholly unsupplied with pocket-money. The Jesuit expended a considerable sum on books, magnificently bound with the arms of Luna; the Dwarf prepared several suits of tasteful clothes; and the Jester selected, with infinite care, a horse of equal and perfect gentleness and mettle. And, unknown to one another, but much about the same period, each of the statesmen sent his present most secretly to Alberic. Imagine the astonishment and wrath of the Jesuit, the Dwarf, and the Jester, when each saw his messenger come back from Sparkling Waters with his gift returned, and the news that Prince Alberic was already supplied with a complete library, a handsome wardrobe, and not one, but two horses of the finest breed and training; nay, more unexpected still, that while returning the gifts to their respective donors, he had rewarded the messengers with splendid liberality.

The result of this amazing discovery was much the same in the mind of the Jesuit, the Dwarf, and the Jester. Each instantly suspected one or both of his rivals; then, on second thoughts, determined to change the present to one of the other items (horse, clothes, or books, as the case might be), little suspecting that each of them had been supplied already; and, on further reflection, began to doubt the reality of the whole business, to suspect connivance of the messengers, intended insult on the part of the Prince; and, therefore, decided to trust only to the evidence of his own eyes in the matter.

Accordingly, within the same few months, the Jesuit, the Dwarf, and the Jester feigned grievous illness to their Ducal Master, and while everybody thought them safe in bed in the Red Palace at Luna, hurried, on horseback, or in a litter, or in a coach, to the Castle of Sparkling Waters.

The scene with the peasant and his family, young Alberic's host, was identical on the three occasions; and, as the farmer saw that each of these personages was willing to pay liberally for absolute secrecy, he very consistently swore to supply that desideratum to each of the three great functionaries. And similarly, in all three cases, it was deemed preferable to see the young Prince first from a hiding-place, before asking leave to pay their respects.

The Dwarf, who was the first in the field, was able to hide very conveniently in one of the cut velvet plumes which surmounted Alberic's four-post bedstead, and to observe the young Prince as he changed his apparel. But he scarcely recognised the Duke's grandson. Alberic was sixteen, but far taller and stronger than his age would warrant. His figure was at once manly and delicate, and full of grace and vigour of movement. His long hair, the colour of floss silk, fell in wavy curls, which seemed to imply almost a woman's care and coquetry. His hands also, though powerful, were, as the Dwarf took note, of princely form and whiteness. As to his garments, the open doors of his wardrobe displayed every variety that a young Prince could need; and, while the Dwarf was watching, he was exchanging a russet and purple hunting-dress, cut after the Hungarian fashion with cape and hood, and accompanied by a cap crowned with peacock's feathers, for a habit of white and silver, trimmed with Venetian lace, in which he intended to honour the wedding of one of the farmer's daughters. Never, in his most genuine youth, had Balthasar Maria, the ever young and handsome, been one-quarter as beautiful in person or as delicate in apparel as his grandson in exile among poor country folk.

The Jesuit, in his turn, came to verify his messenger's extraordinary statements. Through the gap between two rafters he was enabled to look down on to Prince Alberic in his study. Magnificently bound books lined the walls of the closet, and in their gaps hung valuable prints and maps. On the table were heaped several open volumes, among globes both terrestrial and celestial; and Alberic himself was leaning on the arm of a great chair, reciting the verses of Virgil* in a most graceful chant. Never had the Jesuit seen a better-appointed study nor a more precocious young scholar.

As regards the Jester, he came at the very moment that Alberic was returning from a ride; and, having begun life as an acrobat, he was able to climb into a large ilex which commanded an excellent view of the Castle yard.

Alberic was mounted on a splendid jet-black barb, magnificently caparisoned in crimson and gold Spanish trappings. His groom—for he had even a groom—was riding a horse only a shade less perfect: it was white and he was black—a splendid negro such as only great princes own. When Alberic came in sight of the farmer's wife, who stood shelling peas on the doorstep, he waved his hat with infinite grace, caused his horse to caracole* and rear three times in salutation, picked an apple up while cantering round the Castle yard, threw it in the air with his sword and cut it in two as it descended, and did a number of similar feats such as are taught only to the most brilliant cavaliers. Now, as he was going to dismount, a branch of the ilex cracked, the black barb reared, and Alberic, looking up, perceived the Jester moving in the tree.

"A wonderful parti-coloured bird!" he exclaimed, and seized the fowling-piece that hung to his saddle. But before he had time to fire the Jester had thrown himself down and alighted, making three somersaults, on the ground.

"My Lord," said the Jester, 'you see before you a faithful subject who, braving the threats and traps of your enemies, and, I am bound to add, risking also your Highness's sovereign displeasure, has been determined to see his Prince once more, to have the supreme happiness of seeing him at last clad and equipped and mounted——'

"Enough!" interrupted Alberic sternly. "You need say no more. You would have me believe that it is to you I owe my horses and books and clothes, even as the Dwarf and the Jesuit tried to make me believe about themselves last month. Know, then, that Alberic of Luna requires gifts from none of you. And now, most miserable counsellor of my unhappy grandfather, begone!"

The Jester checked his rage, and tried, all the way back to Luna, to get at some solution of this intolerable riddle. The Jesuit and the Dwarf—the scoundrels—had been trying *their* hand then! Perhaps, indeed, it was their blundering which had ruined his own perfectly-concocted scheme. But for their having come and claimed gratitude for gifts they had not made, Alberic would perhaps have believed that the Jester had not merely offered the horse which was refused, but had actually given the two which had been accepted, and the books and clothes (since there had been books and clothes given) into the bargain. But then, had not Alberic spoken as if he were perfectly sure from what quarter all his possessions had come? This reminded the Jester of the allusion to the Duke Balthasar Maria; Alberic had spoken of him as unhappy. Was it, could it be, possible that the treacherous old wretch had been keeping up relations with his grandson in secret, afraid—for he was a miserable old coward at bottom—both of the wrath of his three counsellors, and of the hatred of his grandson? Was it possible, thought the Jester, that not only the Jesuit and the Dwarf, but the Duke of Luna also, had been intriguing against him round young Prince Alberic? Balthasar Maria was quite capable of it; he might be enjoying the trick he was playing his three masters—for they were his masters; he might be preparing to turn suddenly upon them with his long neglected grandson like a sword to smite them. On the other hand, might this not be a mere mistaken supposition on the part of Prince Alberic, who, in his silly dignity, preferred to believe in the liberality of his ducal grandfather than in that of his grandfather's servants? Might the horses, and all the rest, not really be the gift of either the Dwarf or the Jesuit, although neither had got the credit for it? "No, no," exclaimed the Jester, for he hated his fellow-servants worse than his master, "anything better than that! Rather a thousand times that it were the Duke himself who had outwitted them."

Then, in his bitterness, having gone over the old arguments again and again, some additional circumstances returned to his memory. The black groom was deaf and dumb, and the peasants, it appeared, had been quite unable to extract any information from him. But he had arrived with those particular horses only a few months ago; a gift, the peasants had thought, from the old Duke of Luna. But Alberic, they had said, had possessed other horses before, which they had also taken for granted had come from the Red Palace. And the clothes and books had been accumulating, it appeared, ever since the Prince's arrival in his place of banishment. Since this was the case, the plot, whether on the part of the Jesuit or the Dwarf, or on that of the Duke himself, had been going on for years before the Jester had bestirred himself! Moreover, the Prince not only possessed horses, but he learned to ride, he not only had books, but he had learned to read, and even to read various tongues; and finally, the Prince was not only clad in princely garments, but he was every inch of him a Prince. He had then been consorting with other people than the peasants at Sparkling Waters. He must have been away—or—some one must have come. He had not been living in solitude.

But when—how—and above all, who?

And again the baffled Jester revolved the probabilities concerning the Dwarf, the Jesuit, and the Duke. It must be—it could be no other—it evidently could only be——.

"Ah!" exclaimed the unhappy diplomatist; "if only one could believe in magic!"

And it suddenly struck him, with terror and mingled relief, "Was it magic?"

But the Jester, like the Dwarf and the Jesuit, and the Duke of Luna himself, was altogether superior to such foolish beliefs.

V

The young Prince of Luna had never attempted to learn the story of Alberic the Blond and the Snake Lady. Children sometimes conceive an inexplicable shyness, almost a dread, of knowing more on some subject which is uppermost in their thoughts; and such had been the case of Duke Balthasar Maria's grandson. Ever since the memorable morning when the ebony crucifix had been removed from in front of the faded tapestry, and the whole figure of the Snake Lady had been for the first time revealed, scarcely a day had passed without their coming to the boy's mind: his nurse's words about his ancestors Alberic and the Snake Lady Oriana. But, even as he had asked no questions then, so he had asked no questions since; shrinking more and more from all further knowledge of the matter. He had never questioned his nurse; he had never questioned the peasants of Sparkling Waters, although the story, he felt quite sure, must be well known among the ruins of Alberic the Blond's own castle. Nay, stranger still, he had never mentioned the subject to his dear Godmother, to whom he had learned to open his heart about all things, and who had taught him all that he knew.

For the Duke's Jester had guessed rightly that, during these years at Sparkling Waters, the young Prince had not consorted solely with peasants. The very evening after his arrival, as he was sitting by the marble well in the vineyard, looking towards the sea, he had felt a hand placed lightly on his shoulder, and looked up into the face of a beautiful lady dressed in green.

"Do not be afraid," she had said, smiling at his terror. "I am not a ghost, but alive like you; and I am, though you do not know it, your Godmother. My dwelling is close to this castle, and I shall come every evening to play and talk with you, here by the little white palace with the pillars, where the fodder is stacked. Only, you must remember that I do so against the wishes of your grandfather and all his friends, and that if ever you mention me to any one, or allude in any way to our meetings, I shall be obliged to leave the neighbourhood, and you will never see me again. Some day when you are big you will learn why; till then you must take me on trust. And now what shall we play at?"

And thus his Godmother had come every evening at sunset, just for an hour and no more, and had taught the poor solitary little Prince to play (for he had never played) and to read, and to manage a horse, and, above all, to love: for, except the old tapestry in the Red Palace, he had never loved anything in the world.

Alberic told his dear Godmother everything, beginning with the story of the two pieces of tapestry, the one they had taken away and the one he had cut to pieces; and he asked her about all the things he ever wanted to know, and she was always able to answer. Only about two things they were silent: she never told him her name nor where she lived, nor whether Duke Balthasar Maria knew her (the boy guessed that she had been a friend of his father's); and Alberic never revealed the fact that the tapestry had represented his ancestor and the beautiful Oriana; for, even to his dear Godmother, and most perhaps to her, he found it impossible even to mention Alberic the Blond and the Snake Lady.

But the story, or rather the name of the story he did not know, never loosened its hold on Alberic's mind. Little by little, as he grew up, it came to add to his life two friends, of whom he never told his Godmother. They were, to be sure, of such sort, however different, that a boy might find it difficult to speak about without feeling foolish. The first of the two friends was his own ancestor, Alberic the Blond; and the second that large tame grass snake whose acquaintance he had made the day after his arrival at the castle. About Alberic the Blond he knew indeed but little, save that he had reigned in Luna many hundreds of years ago, and that he had been a very brave and glorious Prince indeed, who had helped to conquer the Holy Sepulchre with Godfrey and Tancred and the other heroes of Tasso.* But, perhaps in proportion to this vagueness, Alberic the Blond served to personify all the notions of chivalry which the boy had learned from his Godmother, and those which bubbled up in his own breast. Nay, little by little the young Prince began to take his unknown ancestor as a model, and in a confused way, to identify himself with him. For was he not fair-haired too, and Prince of Luna, *Alberic*, third of the name, as the other had been first? Perhaps for this reason he could never speak of this ancestor with his Godmother. She might think it presumptuous and foolish; besides, she might perhaps tell him things about Alberic the Blond which would hurt him; the poor young Prince, who had compared the splendid reputation of his own grandfather with the miserable reality, had grown up precociously sceptical. As to the Snake, with whom he played every day in the grass, and who was his only companion during the many hours of his Godmother's absence, he would willingly have spoken of her, and had once been on the point of doing so, but he had noticed that the mere name of such creatures seemed to be odious to his Godmother. Whenever, in their readings, they came across any mention of serpents, his Godmother would exclaim, "Let us skip that," with a look of intense pain in her usually cheerful countenance. It was a pity, Alberic thought, that so lovely and dear a lady should feel such hatred towards any living creature, particularly towards a kind which, like his own tame grass snake, was perfectly harmless. But he loved her too much to dream of thwarting her; and he was very grateful to his tame snake for having the tact never to show herself at the hour of his Godmother's visits.

But to return to the story represented on the dear, faded tapestry in the Red Palace.

When Prince Alberic, unconscious to himself, was beginning to turn into a full-grown and gallant-looking youth, a change began to take place in him, and it was about the story of his ancestor and the Lady Oriana. He thought of it more than ever, and it began to haunt his dreams; only it was now a vaguely painful thought; and, while dreading still to know more, he began to experience a restless, miserable craving to know all. His curiosity was like a thorn in his flesh, working its way in and in; and it seemed something almost more than curiosity. And yet, he was still shy and frightened of the subject; nay, the greater his craving to know, the greater grew a strange certainty that the knowing would be accompanied by evil. So, although many people could have answered—the very peasants, the fishermen of the coast, and first and foremost, his Godmother—he let months pass before he asked the question.

It, and the answer, came of a sudden.

There came occasionally to Sparkling Waters an old man, who united in his tattered person the trades of mending crockery and reciting fairy tales. He would seat himself in summer, under the spreading fig-tree in the Castle yard, and in winter by the peasants' deep, black chimney, alternately boring holes in pipkins,* or gluing plate edges, and singing, in a cracked, nasal voice, but not without dignity and charm of manner, the stories of the King of Portugal's Cowherd, of the Feathers of the Griffin, or some of the many stanzas of *Orlando* or *Jerusalem Delivered** which he knew by heart. Our young Prince had always avoided him, partly from a vague fear of a mention of his ancestor and the Snake Lady, and partly because of something vaguely sinister in the old man's eye. But now he awaited with impatience the vagrant's periodical return, and on one occasion, summoned him to his own chamber.

"Sing me," he commanded, "the story of Alberic the Blond and the Snake Lady."

The old man hesitated, and answered with a strange look—

"My Lord, I do not know it."

A sudden feeling, such as the youth had never experienced before, seized hold of Alberic. He did not recognise himself. He saw and heard himself, as if it were some one else, nod first at some pieces of gold, of those his Godmother had given him, and then at his fowling-piece hung on the wall; and as he did so he had a strange thought: "I must be mad." But he merely said, sternly—

"Old man, that is not true. Sing that story at once, if you value my money and your safety."

The vagrant took his white-bearded chin in his hand, mused, and then, fumbling among the files and drills and pieces of wire in his tool-basket, which made a faint metallic accompaniment, he slowly began to chant the following stanzas:—

VI

Now listen, courteous Prince, to what befell your ancestor, the valorous Alberic, returning from the Holy Land.

Already a year had passed since the strong-holds of Jerusalem had fallen beneath the blows of the faithful, and since the Sepulchre of Christ had been delivered from the worshippers of Macomet. The great Godfrey was enthroned as its guardian, and the mighty barons, his companions, were wending their way homewards—Tancred, and Bohemund, and Reynold, and the rest.*

The valorous Alberic, the honour of Luna, after many perilous adventures, brought by the anger of the Wizard Macomet, whom he had offended, was shipwrecked on his homeward way, and cast, alone of all his great army, upon the rocky shore of an unknown island. He wandered long about, among woods and pleasant pastures, but without ever seeing any signs of habitation; nourishing himself solely on berries and clear water, and taking his rest in the green grass beneath the trees. At length, after some days of wandering, he came to a dense forest, the like of which he had never seen before, so deep was its shade and so tangled were its boughs. He broke the branches with his iron-gloved hand, and the air became filled with the croaking and screeching of dreadful night-birds. He pushed his way with shoulder and knee, trampling the broken leafage under foot, and the air was filled with the roaring of monstrous lions and tigers. He grasped his sharp double-edged sword and hewed through the interlaced branches, and the air was filled with the shrieks and sobs of a vanquished city. But the Knight of Luna went on, undaunted, cutting his way through the enchanted wood. And behold! as he issued thence, there was before him a lordly castle, as of some great Prince, situate in a pleasant meadow among running streams. And as Alberic approached, the portcullis was raised, and the drawbridge lowered; and there arose sounds of fifes and bugles, but nowhere could he descry any living wight around. And Alberic entered the castle, and found therein guardrooms full of shining arms, and chambers spread with rich stuffs, and a banqueting-hall, with a great table laid and a chair of state at the end. And as he entered a concert of invisible voices and instruments greeted him sweetly, and called him by name, and bid him be welcome; but not a living soul did he see. So he sat him down at the table, and as he did so, invisible hands filled his cup and his plate, and ministered to him with delicacies of all sorts. Now, when the good knight had eaten and drunken his fill, he drank to the health of his unknown host, declaring himself the servant thereof with his sword and heart. After which, weary with wandering, he prepared to take rest on the carpets which strewed the ground; but invisible hands unbuckled his armour, and clad him in silken robes, and led him to a couch all covered with rose-leaves. And when he had lain himself down, the concert of invisible singers and players put him to sleep with their melodies.

It was the hour of sunset when the valorous Baron awoke, and buckled on his armour, and hung on his thigh the great sword Brillamorte;* and invisible hands helped him once more.

The Knight of Luna went all over the enchanted castle, and found all manner of rarities, treasures of precious stones, such as great kings possess, and stores of gold and silver vessels, and rich stuffs, and stables full of fiery coursers ready caparisoned; but never a human creature anywhere. And, wondering more and more, he went forth into the orchard, which lay within the castle walls. And such another orchard, sure, was never seen, since that in which the hero Hercules found the three golden apples and slew the great dragon.* For you might see in this place fruit-trees of all kinds, apples and pears, and peaches and plums, and the goodly orange, which bore at the same time fruit and delicate and scented blossom. And all around were set hedges of roses, whose scent was even like heaven; and there were other flowers of all kinds, those into which the vain Narcissus turned through love of himself, and those which grew, they tell us, from the blood-drops of fair Venus's minion; and lilies of which that Messenger carried a sheaf who saluted the Meek Damsel,* glorious above all womankind. And in the trees sang innumerable birds; and others, of unknown breed, joined melody in hanging cages and aviaries. And in the orchard's midst was set a fountain, the most wonderful e'er made, its waters running in green channels among the flowered grass. For that fountain was made in the likeness of twin naked maidens, dancing together, and pouring water out of pitchers as they did so; and the maidens were of fine silver, and the pitchers of wrought gold, and the whole so cunningly contrived by magic art that the maidens really moved and danced with the waters they were pouring out—a wonderful work, most truly. And when the Knight of Luna had feasted his eyes upon this marvel, he saw among the grass, beneath a flowering almond-tree, a sepulchre of marble, cunningly carved and gilded, on which was written, "Here is imprisoned the Fairy Oriana, most miserable of all fairies, condemned for no fault, but by envious powers, to a dreadful fate,"—and as he read, the inscription changed, and the sepulchre showed these words: "O Knight of Luna, valorous Alberic, if thou wouldst show thy gratitude to the hapless mistress of this castle, summon up thy redoubtable courage, and, whatsoever creature issue from my marble heart, swear thou to kiss it three times on the mouth, that Oriana may be released."

And Alberic drew his great sword, and on its hilt, shaped like a cross, he swore.

Then wouldst thou have heard a terrible sound of thunder, and seen the castle walls rock. But Alberic, nothing daunted, repeats in a loud voice, "I swear," and instantly that sepulchre's lid upheaves, and there issues thence and rises up a great green snake, wearing a golden crown, and raises itself and fawns towards the valorous Knight of Luna. And Alberic starts and recoils in terror. For rather, a thousand times, confront alone the armed hosts of all the heathen, than put his lips to that cold, creeping beast! And the serpent looks at Alberic with great gold eyes, and big tears issue thence, and it drops prostrate on the grass; and Alberic summons courage and approaches; but when the serpent glides along his arm, a horror takes him, and he falls back, unable. And the tears stream from the snake's golden eyes, and moans come from its mouth.

And Alberic runs forward, and seizes the serpent in both arms, and lifts it up, and three times presses his warm lips against its cold and slippery skin, shutting his eyes in horror. And when the Knight of Luna opens them again, behold! O wonder! in his arms no longer a dreadful snake, but a damsel, richly dressed and beautiful beyond compare.

VII

Young Alberic sickened that very night, and lay for many days raging with fever. The peasant's wife and a good neighbouring priest nursed him unhelped, for when the messenger they sent arrived at Luna, Duke Balthasar was busy rehearsing a grand ballet in which he himself danced the part of Phœbus Apollo;* and the ducal physician was therefore despatched to Sparkling Waters only when the young Prince was already recovering.

Prince Alberic undoubtedly passed through a very bad illness, and went fairly out of his mind for fever and ague.

He raved so dreadfully in his delirium about enchanted tapestries and terrible grottoes, Twelve Cæsars with rolling eyeballs, barbers' blocks with perukes on them, monkeys of verde antique, and porphyry rhinoceroses, and all manner of hellish creatures, that the good priest began to suspect a case of demoniac possession, and caused candles to be kept lighted all day and all night, and holy water to be sprinkled, and a printed form of exorcism, absolutely sovereign in such trouble, to be nailed against the bed-post. On the fourth day the young Prince fell into a profound sleep, from which he awaked in apparent possession of his faculties.

"Then you are not the Porphyry Rhinoceros?" he said, very slowly, as his eye fell upon the priest; "and this is my own dear little room at Sparkling Waters, though I do not understand all those candles. I thought it was the great hall in the Red Palace, and that all those animals of precious marbles, and my grandfather, the Duke, in his bronze and gold robes, were beating me and my tame snake to death with harlequins' laths.* It was terrible. But now I see it was all fancy and delirium."

The poor youth gave a sigh of relief, and feebly caressed the rugged old hand of the priest, which lay upon his counterpane. The Prince stayed for a long while motionless, but gradually a strange light came into his eyes, and a smile on to his lips. Presently he made a sign that the peasants should leave the room, and taking once more the good priest's hand, he looked solemnly in his eyes, and spoke in an earnest voice. "My father," he said, "I have seen and heard strange things in my sickness, and I cannot tell for certain now what belongs to the reality of my previous life, and what is merely the remembrance of delirium. On this I would fain be enlightened. Promise me, my father, to answer my questions truly, for this is a matter of the welfare of my soul, and therefore of your own."

The priest nearly jumped on his chair. So he had been right. The demons had been trying to tamper with the poor young Prince, and now he was going to have a fine account of it all.

"My son," he murmured, "as I hope for the spiritual welfare of both of us, I promise to answer all your interrogations to the best of my powers. Speak without reticence."

Alberic hesitated for a moment, and his eyes glanced from one long lit taper to the other.

"In that case," he said slowly, "let me conjure you, my father, to tell me whether or not there exists a certain tradition in my family, of the loves of my ancestor, Alberic the Blond, with a certain Snake Lady, and how he was unfaithful to her, and failed to disenchant her, and how a second Alberic, also my ancestor, loved this same Snake Lady, but failed before the ten years of fidelity were over, and became a monk. . . . Does such a story exist, or have I imagined it all during my sickness?"

"My son," replied the good priest testily, for he was most horribly disappointed by this speech, "it is scarce fitting that a young Prince but just escaped from the jaws of death—and, perhaps, even from the insidious onslaught of the Evil One—should give his mind to idle tales like these."

"Call them what you choose," answered the Prince gravely, "but remember your promise, father. Answer me truly, and presume not to question my reasons."

The priest started. What a hasty ass he had been! Why, these were probably the demons talking out of Alberic's mouth, causing him to ask silly irrelevant questions in order to prevent a good confession. Such were notoriously among their stock tricks! But he would outwit them. If only it were possible to summon up St. Paschal Baylon,* that new fashionable saint who had been doing such wonders with devils lately! But St. Paschal Baylon required not only that you should say several rosaries, but that you should light four candles on a table and lay a supper for two; after that there was nothing he would not do. So the priest hastily seized two candlesticks from the foot of the bed, and called to the peasant's wife to bring a clean napkin and plates and glasses; and meanwhile endeavoured to detain the demons by answering the poor Prince's foolish chatter, "Your ancestors, the two Alberics—a tradition in your Serene family—yes, my Lord—there is such—let me see, how does the story go?—ah yes—this demon, I mean this Snake Lady was a—what they call a fairy—or witch, malefica or stryx* is, I believe, the proper Latin expression—who had been turned into a snake for her sins—good woman, woman, is it possible you cannot be a little quicker in bringing those plates for His Highness's supper? The Snake Lady—let me see—was to cease altogether being a snake if a cavalier remained faithful to her for ten years, and at any rate turned into a woman every time a cavalier was found who had the courage to give her a kiss as if she were not a snake—a disagreeable thing, besides being mortal sin. As I said just now, this enabled her to resume temporarily her human shape, which is said to have been fair enough; but how can one tell? I believe she was allowed to change into a woman for an hour at sunset, in any case and without anybody kissing her, but only for an hour. A very unlikely story, my Lord, and not a very moral one, to my thinking!"

And the good priest spread the tablecloth over the table, wondering secretly when the plates and glasses for St. Paschal Baylon would make their appearance. If only the demon could be prevented from beating a retreat before all was ready! "To return to the story about which Your Highness is pleased to inquire," he continued, trying to gain time by pretending to humour the demon who was asking questions through the poor Prince's mouth, "I can remember hearing a poem before I took orders—a foolish poem too, in a very poor style, if my memory is correct—that related the manner in which Alberic the Blond met this Snake Lady, and disenchanted her by performing the ceremony I have alluded to. The poem was frequently sung at fairs and similar resorts of the uneducated, and, as remarked, was a very inferior composition indeed. Alberic the Blond afterwards came to his senses, it appears, and after abandoning the Snake Lady fulfilled his duty as a Prince, and married the Princess. . . . I cannot exactly remember what Princess, but it was a very suitable marriage, no doubt, from which Your Highness is of course descended.

"As regards the Marquis Alberic, second of the name, of whom it is accounted that he died in odour of sanctity (and indeed it is said that the facts concerning his beatification are being studied in the proper quarters), there is a mention in a life of Saint Fredevaldus, bishop and patron of Luna, printed at the beginning of the present century at Venice, with Approbation and Licence of the Authorities and Inquisition, a mention of the fact that this Marquis Alberic the second had contracted, having abandoned his lawful wife, a left-handed marriage* with this same Snake Lady (such evil creatures not being subject to natural death), she having induced him thereunto in hope of his proving faithful ten years, and by this means restoring her altogether to human shape. But a certain holy hermit, having got wind of this scandal, prayed to St. Fredevaldus as patron of Luna, whereupon St. Fredevaldus took pity on the Marquis Alberic's sins, and appeared to him in a vision at the end of the ninth year of his irregular connection with the Snake Lady, and touched his heart so thoroughly that he instantly forswore her company, and handing the Marquisate over to his mother, abandoned the world and entered the order of St. Romwald,* in which he died, as remarked, in odour of sanctity, in consequence of which the present Duke, Your Highness's magnificent grandfather, is at this moment, as befits so pious a Prince, employing his influence with the Holy Father for the beatification of so glorious an ancestor. And now, my son," added the good priest, suddenly changing his tone, for he had got the table ready, and lighted the candles, and only required to go through the preliminary invocation of St. Paschal Baylon—"and now, my son, let your curiosity trouble you no more, but endeavour to obtain some rest, and if possible——"

But the Prince interrupted him.

"One word more, good father," he begged, fixing him with earnest eyes; "is it known what has been the fate of the Snake Lady?"

The impudence of the demons made the priest quite angry, but he must not scare them before the arrival of St. Paschal, so he controlled himself, and answered slowly by gulps, between the lines of the invocation he was mumbling under his breath:

"My Lord—it results from the same life of St. Fredevaldus, that . . . (in case of property lost, fire, flood, earthquake, plague) . . . that the Snake Lady (thee we invoke, most holy Paschal Baylon!). The Snake Lady being of the nature of fairies, cannot die unless her head be severed from her trunk, and is still haunting the world, together with other evil spirits, in hopes that another member of the house of Luna (Thee we invoke, most holy Paschal Baylon!)—may succumb to her arts and be faithful to her for the ten years needful to her disenchantments—(most holy Paschal Baylon!—and most of all—on thee we call—for aid against the . . .)——"

But before the priest could finish his invocation, a terrible shout came from the bed where the sick Prince was lying—

"O Oriana, Oriana!" cried Prince Alberic, sitting up in his bed with a look which terrified the priest as much as his voice. "O Oriana, Oriana!" he repeated, and then fell back exhausted and broken.

"Bless my soul!" cried the priest, almost upsetting the table; "why, the demon has already issued out of him! Who would have guessed that St. Paschal Baylon performed his miracles as quick as that?"

VIII

Prince Alberic was awakened by the loud trill of a nightingale. The room was bathed in moonlight, in which the tapers, left burning round the bed to ward off evil spirits, flickered yellow and ineffectual. Through the open casement came, with the scent of freshly-cut grass, a faint concert of nocturnal sounds: the silvery vibration of the cricket, the reedlike quavering notes of the leaf frogs, and, every now and then, the soft note of an owlet, seeming to stroke the silence as the downy wings growing out of the temples of the Sleep God* might stroke the air. The nightingale had paused; and Alberic listened breathless for its next burst of song. At last, and when he expected it least, it came, liquid, loud, and triumphant; so near that it filled the room and thrilled through his marrow like an unison of Cremona viols.* It was singing on the pomegranate close outside, whose first buds must be opening into flame-coloured petals. For it was May. Alberic listened; and collected his thoughts, and understood. He arose and dressed, and his limbs seemed suddenly strong, and his mind strangely clear, as if his sickness had been but a dream. Again the nightingale trilled out, and again stopped. Alberic crept noiselessly out of his chamber, down the stairs and into the open. Opposite, the moon had just risen, immense and golden, and the pines and the cypresses of the hill, the furthest battlements of the castle walls, were printed upon it like delicate lace. It was so light that the roses were pink, and the pomegranate flower scarlet, and the lemons pale yellow, and the vines bright green, only differently coloured from how they looked by day, and as if washed over with silver. The orchard spread uphill, its twigs and separate leaves all glittering as if made of diamonds, and its tree-trunks and spalliers weaving strange black patterns of shadow. A little breeze shuddered up from the sea, bringing the scent of the irises grown for their root among the cornfields below. The nightingale was silent. But Prince Alberic did not stand waiting for its song. A spiral dance of fire-flies, rising and falling like a thin gold fountain, beckoned him upwards through the dewy grass. The circuit of castle walls, jagged and battlemented, and with tufts of trees profiled here and there against the resplendent blue pallor of the moonlight, seemed twined and knotted like huge snakes around the world.

Suddenly, again, the nightingale sang—a throbbing, silver song. It was the same bird, Alberic felt sure; but it was in front of him now, and was calling him onwards. The fire-flies wove their golden dance a few steps in front, always a few steps in front, and drew him up-hill through the orchard.

As the ground became steeper, the long trellises, black and crooked, seemed to twist and glide through the blue moonlit grass like black gliding snakes, and, at the top, its marble pillarets clear in the light, slumbered the little Gothic palace of white marble. From the solitary sentinel pine broke the song of the nightingale. This was the place. A breeze had risen, and from the shining moonlit sea, broken into causeways and flotillas of smooth and fretted silver, came a faint briny smell, mingling with that of the irises and blossoming lemons, with the scent of vague ripeness and freshness. The moon hung like a silver lantern over the orchard; the wood of the trellises patterned the blue luminous heaven; the vine-leaves seemed to swim, transparent, in the shining air. Over the circular well, in the high grass, the fire-flies rose and fell like a thin fountain of gold. And, from the sentinel pine, the nightingale sang.

Prince Alberic leant against the brink of the well, by the trough carved with antique designs of serpent-bearing mænads.* He was wonderfully calm, and his heart sang within him. It was, he knew, the hour and place of his fate.

The nightingale ceased: and the shrill song of the crickets was suspended. The silvery luminous world was silent.

A quiver came through the grass by the well, a rustle through the roses. And, on the well's brink, encircling its central blackness, glided the Snake.

"Oriana!" whispered Alberic. "Oriana!" She paused, and stood almost erect. The Prince put out his hand, and she twisted round his arm, extending slowly her chilly coil to his wrist and fingers.

"Oriana!" whispered Prince Alberic again. And raising his hand to his face, he leaned down and pressed his lips on the little flat head of the serpent. And the nightingale sang. But a coldness seized his heart, the moon seemed suddenly extinguished, and he slipped away in unconsciousness.

When he awoke the moon was still high. The nightingale was singing its loudest. He lay in the grass by the well, and his head rested on the knees of the most beautiful of ladies. She was dressed in cloth of silver which seemed woven of moon mists, and shimmering moonlit green grass. It was his own dear Godmother.

IX

When Duke Balthasar Maria had got through the rehearsals of the ballet called Daphne Transformed,* and finally danced his part of Phœbus Apollo to the infinite delight and glory of his subjects, he was greatly concerned, being benignly humoured, on learning that he had very nearly lost his grandson and heir. The Dwarf, the Jesuit, and the Jester, whom he delighted in pitting against one another, had severally accused each other of disrespectful remarks about the dancing of that ballet; so Duke Balthasar determined to disgrace all three together and inflict upon them the hated presence of Prince Alberic. It was, after all, very pleasant to possess a young grandson, whom one could take to one's bosom and employ in being insolent to one's own favourites. It was time, said Duke Balthasar, that Alberic should learn the habits of a court and take unto himself a suitable princess.

The young Prince accordingly was sent for from Sparkling Waters, and installed at Luna in a wing of the Red Palace, overlooking the Court of Honour, and commanding an excellent view of the great rockery, with the Verde Antique Apes and the Porphyry Rhinoceros. He found awaiting him on the great staircase a magnificent staff of servants, a master of the horse, a grand cook, a barber, a hairdresser and assistant, a fencing-master, and four fiddlers. Several lovely ladies of the Court, the principal ministers of the Crown, and the Jesuit, the Dwarf, and the Jester, were also ready to pay their respects. Prince Alberic threw himself out of the glass coach before they had time to open the door, and bowing coldly, ascended the staircase, carrying under his cloak what appeared to be a small wicker cage. The Jesuit, who was the soul of politeness, sprang forward and signed to an officer of the household to relieve His Highness of this burden. But Alberic waved the man off; and the rumour went abroad that a hissing noise had issued from under the Prince's cloak, and, like lightning, the head and forked tongue of a serpent.

Half an hour later the official spies had informed Duke Balthasar that his grandson and heir had brought from Sparkling Waters no apparent luggage save two swords, a fowling-piece, a volume of Virgil, a branch of pomegranate blossom, and a tame grass snake.

Duke Balthasar did not like the idea of the grass snake; but wishing to annoy the Jester, the Dwarf, and the Jesuit, he merely smiled when they told him of it, and said: "The dear boy! What a child he is! He probably, also, has a pet lamb, white as snow, and gentle as spring, mourning for him in his old home! How touching is the innocence of childhood! Heigho! I was just like that myself not so very long ago." Whereupon the three favourites and the whole Court of Luna smiled and bowed and sighed: "How lovely is the innocence of youth!" while the Duke fell to humming the well-known air, "Thyrsis was a shepherd-boy," of which the ducal fiddlers instantly struck up the ritornel.*

"But," added Balthasar Maria, with that subtle blending of majesty and archness in which he excelled all living Princes, "but it is now time that the Prince, my grandson, should learn"—here he put his hand on his sword and threw back slightly one curl of his jet-black peruke—"the stern exercises of Mars; and also, let us hope, the freaks and frolics of Venus."*

Saying which, the old sinner pinched the cheek of a lady of the very highest quality, whose husband and father were instantly congratulated by the whole Court.

Prince Alberic was displayed next day to the people of Luna, standing on the balcony among a tremendous banging of mortars; while Duke Balthasar explained that he felt towards this youth all the fondness and responsibility of an elder brother. There was a grand ball, a gala opera, a review, a very high mass in the cathedral; the Dwarf, the Jesuit, and the Jester each separately offered his services to Alberic in case he wanted a loan of money, a love-letter carried, or in case even (expressed in more delicate terms) he might wish to poison his grandfather. Duke Balthasar Maria, on his side, summoned his ministers, and sent couriers, booted and liveried, to three great dukes of Italy, carrying each of them, in a morocco wallet emblazoned with the arms of Luna, an account of Prince Alberic's lineage and person, and a request for particulars of any marriageable princesses and dowries to be disposed of.

X

Prince Alberic did not give his grandfather that warm satisfaction which the old Duke had expected. Balthasar Maria, entirely bent upon annoying the three favourites, had said, and had finally believed, that he intended to introduce his grandson to the delights and duties of life, and in the company of this beloved stripling, to dream that he, too, was a youth once more: a statement which the Court took with due deprecatory reverence, as the Duke was well known never to have ceased to be young.

But Alberic did not lend himself to so touching an idyll. He behaved, indeed, with the greatest decorum, and manifested the utmost respect for his grandfather. He was marvellously assiduous in the council chamber, and still more so in following the military exercises and learning the trade of a soldier. He surprised every one by his interest and intelligence in all affairs of state; he more than surprised the Court by his readiness to seek knowledge about the administration of the country and the condition of the people. He was a youth of excellent morals, courage, and diligence; but, there was no denying it, he had positively no conception of *sacrificing to the Graces*. He sat out, as if he had been watching a review, the delicious operas and superb ballets which absorbed half the revenue of the duchy. He listened, without a smile of comprehension, to the witty innuendoes of the ducal table. But worst of all, he had absolutely no eyes, let alone a heart, for the fair sex. Now Balthasar Maria had assembled at Luna a perfect bevy of lovely nymphs, both ladies of the greatest birth, whose husbands received most honourable posts, military and civil, and young females of humbler extraction, though not less expensive habits, ranging from singers and dancers to slave-girls of various colours, all dressed in their appropriate costume: a galaxy of beauty which was duly represented by the skill of celebrated painters on all the walls of the Red Palace, where you may still see their faded charms, habited as Diana, or Pallas, or in the spangles of Columbine, or the turban of Sibyls.* These ladies were the object of Duke Balthasar's most munificently divided attentions; and in the delight of his new-born family affection, he had promised himself much tender interest in guiding the taste of his heir among such of these nymphs as had already received his own exquisite appreciation. Great, therefore, was the disappointment of the affectionate grandfather when his dream of companionship was dispelled, and it became hopeless to interest young Alberic in anything at Luna save despatches and cannons.

The Court, indeed, found the means of consoling Duke Balthasar for this bitterness by extracting therefrom a brilliant comparison between the unfading grace, the vivacious, though majestic, character of the grandfather, and the gloomy and pedantic personality of the grandson. But, although Balthasar Maria would only smile at every new proof of Alberic's bearish obtuseness, and ejaculate in French, "Poor child! he was born old, and I shall die young!" the reigning Prince of Luna grew vaguely to resent the peculiarities of his heir.

In this fashion things proceeded in the Red Palace at Luna, until Prince Alberic had attained his twenty-first year.

He was sent, in the interval, to visit the principal courts of Italy, and to inspect its chief curiosities, natural and historical, as befitted the heir to an illustrious state. He received the golden rose from the Pope in Rome; he witnessed the festivities of Ascension Day from the Doge's barge at Venice; he accompanied the Marquis of Montferrat to the camp under Turin; he witnessed the launching of a galley against the Barbary corsairs by the Knights of St. Stephen in the port of Leghorn, and a grand bullfight and burning of heretics given by the Spanish Viceroy at Palermo; and he was allowed to be present when the celebrated Dr. Borri* turned two brass buckles into pure gold before the Archduke at Milan. On all of which occasions the heir-apparent of Luna bore himself with a dignity and discretion most singular in one so young. In the course of these journeys he was presented to several of the most promising heiresses in Italy, some of whom were of so tender age as to be displayed in jewelled swaddling clothes on brocade cushions; and a great many possible marriages were discussed behind his back. But Prince Alberic declared for his part that he had decided to lead a single life until the age of twenty-eight or thirty, and that he would then require the assistance of no ambassadors or chancellors, but find for himself the future Duchess of Luna.

All this did not please Balthasar Maria, as indeed nothing else about his grandson did please him much. But, as the old Duke did not really relish the idea of a daughter-in-law at Luna, and as young Alberic's whimsicalities entailed no expense, and left him entirely free in his business and pleasure, he turned a deaf ear to the criticisms of his counsellors, and letting his grandson inspect fortifications, drill soldiers, pore over parchments, and mope in his wing of the palace, with no amusement save his repulsive tame snake, Balthasar Maria composed and practised various ballets, and began to turn his attention very seriously to the completion of the rockery grotto and of the sepulchral chapel, which, besides the Red Palace itself, were the chief monuments of his glorious reign.

It was the growing desire to witness the fulfilment of these magnanimous projects which led the Duke of Luna into unexpected conflict with his grandson. The wonderful enterprises above-mentioned involved immense expenses, and had periodically been suspended for lack of funds. The collection of animals in the rockery was very far from complete. A camelopard of spotted alabaster, an elephant of Sardinian jasper,* and the entire families of a cow and sheep, all of correspondingly rich marbles, were urgently required to fill up the corners. Moreover, the supply of water was at present so small that the fountains were dry save for a couple of hours on the very greatest holidays; and it was necessary for the perfect naturalness of this ingenious work that an aqueduct twenty miles long should pour perennial streams from a high mountain lake into the grotto of the Red Palace.

The question of the sepulchral chapel was, if possible, even more urgent, for, after every new ballet, Duke Balthasar went through a fit of contrition, during which he fixed his thoughts on death; and the possibilities of untimely release, and of burial in an unfinished mausoleum, filled him with terrors. It is true that Duke Balthasar had, immediately after building the vast domed chapel, secured an effigy of his own person before taking thought for the monuments of his already buried ancestors, and the statue, twelve feet high, representing himself in coronation robes of green bronze brocaded with gold, holding a sceptre, and bearing on his head, of purest silver, a spiky coronet set with diamonds, was one of the curiosities which travellers admired most in Italy. But this statue was unsymmetrical, and moreover, had a dismal suggestiveness, so long as surrounded by empty niches; and the fact that only one-half of the pavement was inlaid with discs of sardonyx, jasper, and carnelian, and that the larger part of the walls were rough brick without a vestige of the mosaic pattern of lapislazuli, malachite, pearl, and coral, which had been begun round the one finished tomb, rendered the chapel as poverty-stricken in one aspect as it was magnificent in another. The finishing of the chapel was therefore urgent, and two more bronze statues were actually cast, those, to wit, of the Duke's father and grandfather, and mosaic workmen called from the Medicean works in Florence.* But, all of a sudden, the ducal treasury was discovered to be empty, and the ducal credit to be exploded.

State lotteries, taxes on salt, even a sham crusade against the Dey of Algiers,* all failed to produce any money. The alliance, the right to pass troops through the duchy, the letting out of the ducal army to the highest bidder, had long since ceased to be a source of revenue either from the Emperor, the King of Spain, or the Most Christian One. The Serene Republics of Venice and Genoa publicly warned their subjects against lending a single sequin to the Duke of Luna; the Dukes of Mantua and Modena began to worry about bad debts; the Pope himself had the atrocious taste to make complaints about suppression of church dues and interception of Peter's pence.* There remained to the bankrupt Duke Balthasar Maria only one hope in the world—the marriage of his grandson.

There happened to exist at that moment a sovereign of incalculable wealth, with an only daughter of marriageable age. But this potentate, although the nephew of a recent Pope, by whose confiscations his fortunes were founded, had originally been a dealer in such goods as are comprehensively known as drysalting;* and, rapacious as were the Princes of the Empire, each was too much ashamed of his neighbours to venture upon alliance with a family of so obtrusive an origin. Here was Balthasar Maria's opportunity: the Drysalter Prince's ducats should complete the rockery, the aqueduct, and the chapel; the drysalter's daughter should be wedded to Alberic of Luna, that was to be third of the name.

XI

Prince Alberic sternly declined. He expressed his dutiful wish that the grotto and the chapel, like all other enterprises undertaken by his grandparent, might be brought to an end worthy of him. He declared that the aversion to drysalters was a prejudice unshared by himself. He even went so far as to suggest that the eligible princess should marry, not the heir-apparent, but the reigning Duke of Luna. But, as regarded himself, he intended, as stated, to remain for many years single. Duke Balthasar had never in his life before seen a man who was determined to oppose him. He felt terrified and became speechless in the presence of young Alberic.

Direct influence having proved useless, the Duke and his counsellors, among whom the Jesuit, the Dwarf, and the Jester had been duly reinstated, looked round for means of indirect persuasion or coercion.

A celebrated Venetian beauty was sent for to Luna—a lady frequently employed in diplomatic missions, which she carried through by her unparalleled grace in dancing. But Prince Alberic, having watched her for half an hour, merely remarked to his equerry that his own tame grass snake made the same movements as the lady infinitely better and more modestly. Whereupon this means was abandoned. The Dwarf then suggested a new method of acting on the young Prince's feelings. This, which he remembered to have been employed very successfully in the case of a certain Duchess of Malfi,* who had given her family much trouble some generations back, consisted in dressing a number of domestics up as ghosts and devils, hiring some genuine lunatics from a neighbouring establishment, and introducing them at dead of night into Prince Alberic's chamber. But the Prince, who was busy at his orisons, merely threw a heavy stool and two candlesticks at the apparitions; and, as he did so, the tame snake suddenly rose up from the floor, growing colossal in the act, and hissed so terrifically that the whole party fled down the corridor. The most likely advice was given by the Jesuit. This truly subtle diplomatist averred that it was useless trying to act upon the Prince by means which did not already affect him; instead of clumsily constructing a lever for which there was no fulcrum in the youth's soul, it was necessary to find out whatever leverage there might already exist.

Now, on careful inquiry, there was discovered a fact which the official spies, who always acted by precedent and pursued their inquiries according to the rules of the human heart as taught by the Secret Inquisition of the Republic of Venice,* had naturally failed to perceive. This fact consisted in a rumour, very vague but very persistent, that Prince Alberic did not inhabit his wing of the palace in absolute solitude. Some of the pages attending on his person affirmed to have heard whispered conversations in the Prince's study, on entering which they had invariably found him alone; others maintained that, during the absence of the Prince from the palace, they had heard the sound of his private harpsichord, the one with the story of Orpheus and the view of Soracte* on the cover, although he always kept its key on his person. A footman declared that he had found in the Prince's study, and among his books and maps, a piece of embroidery certainly not belonging to the Prince's furniture and apparel, moreover, half finished, and with a needle sticking in the canvas; which piece of embroidery the Prince had thrust into his pocket. But, as none of the attendants had ever seen any visitor entering or issuing from the Prince's apartments, and the professional spies had ransacked all possible hiding-places and modes of exit in vain, these curious indications had been neglected, and the opinion had been formed that Alberic being, as every one could judge, somewhat insane, had a gift of ventriloquism, a taste for musical boxes, and a proficiency in unmanly handicrafts which he carefully secreted.

These rumours had at one time caused great delight to Duke Balthasar; but he had got tired of sitting in a dark cupboard in his grandson's chamber, and had caught a bad chill looking through his keyhole; so he had stopped all further inquiries as officious fooling on the part of impudent lacqueys.

But the Jesuit foolishly adhered to the rumour. "Discover *her*," he said, "and work through her on Prince Alberic." But Duke Balthasar, after listening twenty times to this remark with the most delighted interest, turned round on the twenty-first time and gave the Jesuit a look of Jove-like thunder. "My father," he said, "I am surprised—I may say more than surprised—at a person of your cloth descending so low as to make aspersions upon the virtue of a young Prince reared in my palace and born of my blood. Never let me hear another word about ladies of light manners being secreted within these walls." Whereupon the Jesuit retired, and was in disgrace for a fortnight, till Duke Balthasar woke up one morning with a strong apprehension of dying.

But no more was said of the mysterious female friend of Prince Alberic, still less was any attempt made to gain her intervention in the matter of the Drysalter Princess's marriage.

XII

More desperate measures were soon resorted to. It was given out that Prince Alberic was engrossed in study; and he was forbidden to leave his wing of the Red Palace, with no other view than the famous grotto with the Verde Antique Apes and the Porphyry Rhinoceros. It was published that Prince Alberic was sick; and he was confined very rigorously to a less agreeable apartment in the rear of the Palace, where he could catch sight of the plaster laurels and draperies, and the rolling plaster eyeball of one of the Twelve Cæsars under the cornice. It was judiciously hinted that the Prince had entered into religious retreat; and he was locked and bolted into the State prison, alongside of the unfinished sepulchral chapel, whence a lugubrious hammering came as the only sound of life. In each of these places the recalcitrant youth was duly argued with by some of his grandfather's familiars, and even received a visit from the old Duke in person. But threats and blandishments were all in vain, and Alberic persisted in his refusal to marry.

It was now six months since he had seen the outer world, and six weeks since he had inhabited the State prison, every stage in his confinement, almost every day thereof, having systematically deprived him of some luxury, some comfort, or some mode of passing his time. His harpsichord and foils had remained in the gala wing overlooking the grotto. His maps and books had not followed him beyond the higher story with the view of the Twelfth Cæsar. And now they had taken away from him his Virgil, his inkstand and paper, and left him only a book of hours.*

Balthasar Maria and his counsellors felt intolerably baffled. There remained nothing further to do; for if Prince Alberic were publicly beheaded, or privately poisoned, or merely left to die of want and sadness, it was obvious that Prince Alberic could no longer conclude the marriage with the Drysalter Princess, and that no money to finish the grotto and the chapel, or to carry on Court expenses, would be forthcoming.

It was a burning day of August, a Friday, thirteenth of that month, and after a long prevalence of enervating sirocco, when the old Duke determined to make one last appeal to the obedience of his grandson. The sun, setting among ominous clouds, sent a lurid orange gleam into Prince Alberic's prison chamber, at the moment that his ducal grandfather, accompanied by the Jester, the Dwarf, and the Jesuit, appeared on its threshold after prodigious clanking of keys and clattering of bolts. The unhappy youth rose as they entered, and making a profound bow, motioned his grandparent to the only chair in the place.

Balthasar Maria had never visited him before in this his worst place of confinement; and the bareness of the room, the dust and cobwebs, the excessive hardness of the chair, affected his sensitive heart; and, joined with irritation at his grandson's obstinacy and utter depression about the marriage, the grotto, and the chapel, actually caused this magnanimous sovereign to burst into tears and bitter lamentations.

"It would indeed melt the heart of a stone," remarked the Jester sternly, while his two companions attempted to soothe the weeping Duke—"to see one of the greatest, wisest, and most valorous Princes in Europe reduced to tears by the undutifulness of his child."

"Princes, nay kings and emperors' sons," exclaimed the Dwarf, who was administering Melissa water* to the Duke, "have perished miserably for much less."

"Some of the most remarkable personages of sacred history are stated to have incurred eternal perdition for far slighter offences," added the Jesuit.

Alberic had sat down on the bed. The tawny sunshine fell upon his figure. He had grown very thin, and his garments were inexpressibly threadbare. But he was spotlessly neat, his lace band was perfectly folded, his beautiful blond hair flowed in exquisite curls about his pale face, and his whole aspect was serene and even cheerful. He might be twenty-two years old, and was of consummate beauty and stature.

"My Lord," he answered slowly, "I entreat Your Serene Highness to believe that no one could regret more deeply than I do such a spectacle as is offered me by the tears of a Duke of Luna. At the same time, I can only reiterate that I accept no responsibility . . ."

A distant growling of thunder caused the old Duke to start, and interrupted Alberic's speech.

"Your obstinacy, my Lord," exclaimed the Dwarf, who was an excessively choleric person, "betrays the existence of a hidden conspiracy most dangerous to the state."

"It is an indication," added the Jester, "of a highly deranged mind."

"It seems to me," whispered the Jesuit, "to savour most undoubtedly of devilry."

Alberic shrugged his shoulders. He had risen from the bed to close the grated window, into which a shower of hail was suddenly blowing with unparalleled violence, when the old Duke jumped on his seat, and, with eyeballs starting with terror, exclaimed, as he tottered convulsively, "The serpent! the serpent!"

For there, in a corner, the tame grass snake was placidly coiled up, sleeping.

"The snake! the devil! Prince Alberic's pet companion!" exclaimed the three favourites, and rushed towards that corner.

Alberic threw himself forward. But he was too late. The Jester, with a blow of his harlequin's lath, had crushed the head of the startled creature; and, even while he was struggling with him and the Jesuit, the Dwarf had given it two cuts with his Turkish scimitar.

"The snake! the snake!" shrieked Duke Balthasar, heedless of the desperate struggle.

The warders and equerries waiting outside thought that Prince Alberic must be murdering his grandfather, and burst into prison and separated the combatants.

"Chain the rebel! the wizard! the madman!" cried the three favourites.

Alberic had thrown himself on the dead snake, which lay crushed and bleeding on the floor; and he moaned piteously.

But the Prince was unarmed and over-powered in a moment. Three times he broke loose, but three times he was recaptured, and finally bound and gagged, and dragged away. The old Duke recovered from his fright, and was helped up from the bed on to which he had sunk. As he prepared to leave, he approached the dead snake, and looked at it for some time. He kicked its mangled head with his ribboned shoe, and turned away laughing.

"Who knows," he said, "whether you were not the Snake Lady? That foolish boy made a great fuss, I remember, when he was scarcely out of long clothes, about a tattered old tapestry representing that repulsive story."

And he departed to supper.

XIII

Prince Alberic of Luna, who should have been third of his name, died a fortnight later, it was stated, insane. But those who approached him maintained that he had been in perfect possession of his faculties; and that if he refused all nourishment during his second imprisonment, it was from set purpose. He was removed at night from his apartments facing the grotto with the Verde Antique Monkeys and the Porphyry Rhinoceros, and hastily buried under a slab, which remained without any name or date, in the famous mosaic sepulchral chapel.

Duke Balthasar Maria survived him only a few months. The old Duke had plunged into excesses of debauchery with a view, apparently, to dismissing certain terrible thoughts and images which seemed to haunt him day and night, and against which no religious practices or medical prescription were of any avail. The origin of these painful delusions was probably connected with a very strange rumour, which grew to a tradition at Luna, to the effect that when the prison room occupied by Prince Alberic was cleaned, after that terrible storm of the 13th August of the year 1700, the persons employed found in a corner, not the dead grass snake, which they had been ordered to cast into the palace drains, but the body of a woman, naked, and miserably disfigured with blows and sabre cuts.

Be this as it may, history records as certain that the house of Luna became extinct in 1701, the duchy lapsing to the Empire. Moreover, that the mosaic chapel remained for ever unfinished, with no statue save the green bronze and gold one of Balthasar Maria above the nameless slab covering Prince Alberic. The rockery also was never completed; only a few marble animals adorning it besides the Porphyry Rhinoceros and the Verde Antique Apes, and the water-supply being sufficient only for the greatest holidays. These things the traveller can report. Also that certain chairs and curtains in the porter's lodge of the now long-deserted Red Palace are made of the various pieces of an extremely damaged arras, having represented the story of Alberic the Blond and the Snake Lady.

THE DOLL

I BELIEVE that's the last bit of *bric-à-brac* I shall ever buy in my life (she said, closing the Renaissance casket)—that and the Chinese dessert set we have just been using. The passion seems to have left me utterly. And I think I can guess why. At the same time as the plates and the little coffer I bought a thing—I scarcely know whether I ought to call it a thing—which put me out of conceit with ferreting about among dead people's properties. I have often wanted to tell you all about it, and stopped for fear of seeming an idiot. But it weighs upon me sometimes like a secret; so, silly or not silly, I think I should like to tell you the story. There, ring for some more logs, and put that screen before the lamp.

It was two years ago, in the autumn, at Foligno, in Umbria.* I was alone at the inn, for you know my husband is too busy for my *bric-à-brac* journeys, and the friend who was to have met me fell ill and came on only later. Foligno isn't what people call an interesting place, but I liked it. There are a lot of picturesque little towns all round; and great savage mountains of pink stone, covered with ilex, where they roll faggots down into the torrent beds, within a drive. There's a full, rushing little river round one side of the walls, which are covered with ivy; and there are fifteenth-century frescoes, which I dare say you know all about. But, what of course I care for most, there are a number of fine old palaces, with gateways carved in that pink stone, and courts with pillars, and beautiful window gratings, mostly in good enough repair, for Foligno is a market town and a junction, and altogether a kind of metropolis down in the valley.

Also, and principally, I liked Foligno because I discovered a delightful curiosity-dealer. I don't mean a delightful curiosity shop, for he had nothing worth twenty francs to sell; but a delightful, enchanting old man. His Christian name was Orestes,* and that was enough for me. He had a long white beard and such kind brown eyes, and beautiful hands; and he always carried an earthenware brazier under his cloak. He had taken to the curiosity business from a passion for beautiful things, and for the past of his native place, after having been a master mason. He knew all the old chronicles, lent me that of Matarazzo,* and knew exactly where everything had happened for the last six hundred years. He spoke of the Trincis, who had been local despots, and of St. Angela, who is the local saint, and of the Baglionis and Cæsar Borgia and Julius II, as if he had known them; he showed me the place where St. Francis preached to the birds, and the place where Propertius—was it Propertius or Tibullus?*—had had his farm; and when he accompanied me on my rambles in search of *bric-à-brac* he would stop at corners and under arches and say, "This, you see, is where they carried off those Nuns I told you about; that's where the Cardinal was stabbed. That's the place where they razed the palace after the massacre, and passed the ploughshare through the ground and sowed salt." And all with a vague, far-off, melancholy look, as if he lived in those days and not these. Also he helped me to get that little velvet coffer with the iron clasps, which is really one of the best things we have in the house. So I was very happy at Foligno, driving and prowling about all day, reading the chronicles Orestes lent me in the evening; and I didn't mind waiting so long for my friend who never turned up. That is to say, I was perfectly happy until within three days of my departure. And now comes the story of my strange purchase.

Orestes, with considerable shrugging of shoulders, came one morning with the information that a certain noble person of Foligno wanted to sell me a set of Chinese plates. "Some of them are cracked," he said; "but at all events you will see the inside of one of our finest palaces, with all its rooms as they used to be—nothing valuable; but I know that the signora appreciates the past wherever it has been let alone."

The palace, by way of exception, was of the late seventeenth century, and looked like a barracks among the neat little carved Renaissance houses. It had immense lions' heads over all the windows, a gateway in which two coaches could have met, a yard where a hundred might have waited, and a colossal staircase with stucco virtues* on the vaultings. There was a cobbler in the lodge* and a soap factory on the ground floor, and at the end of the colonnaded court a garden with ragged yellow vines and dead sunflowers. "Grandiose, but very coarse—almost eighteenth-century," said Orestes as we went up the sounding, low-stepped stairs. Some of the dessert set had been placed, ready for my inspection, on a great gold console in the immense escutcheoned anteroom. I looked at it, and told them to prepare the rest for me to see the next day. The owner, a very noble person, but half ruined—I should have thought entirely ruined, judging by the state of the house—was residing in the country, and the only occupant of the palace was an old woman, just like those who raise the curtains for you at church doors.

The palace was very grand. There was a ballroom as big as a church, and a number of reception rooms, with dirty floors and eighteenth-century furniture, all tarnished and tattered, and a gala room, all yellow satin and gold, where some emperor had slept; and there were horrible racks of faded photographs on the walls, and twopenny screens, and Berlin wool cushions,* attesting the existence of more modern occupants.

I let the old woman unbar one painted and gilded shutter after another, and open window after window, each filled with little greenish panes of glass, and followed her about passively, quite happy, because I was wandering among the ghosts of dead people. "There is the library at the end here," said the old woman, "if the signora does not mind passing through my room and the ironing-room; it's quicker than going back by the big hall." I nodded, and prepared to pass as quickly as possible through an untidy-looking servants' room, when I suddenly stepped back. There was a woman in 1820 costume seated opposite, quite motionless. It was a huge doll. She had a sort of Canova classic face, like the pictures of Mme. Pasta and Lady Blessington.* She sat with her hands folded on her lap and stared fixedly.

"It is the first wife of the Count's grandfather," said the old woman. "We took her out of her closet this morning to give her a little dusting."

The Doll was dressed to the utmost detail. She had on open-work silk stockings, with sandal shoes, and long silk embroidered mittens. The hair was merely painted, in flat bands narrowing the forehead to a triangle. There was a big hole in the back of her head, showing it was cardboard.

"Ah," said Orestes, musingly, "the image of the beautiful countess! I had forgotten all about it. I haven't seen it since I was a lad," and he wiped some cobweb off the folded hands with his red handkerchief, infinitely gently. "She used still to be kept in her own boudoir."

"That was before my time," answered the housekeeper. "I've always seen her in the wardrobe, and I've been here thirty years. Will the signora care to see the old Count's collection of medals?"

Orestes was very pensive as he accompanied me home.

"That was a very beautiful lady," he said shyly, as we came within sight of my inn; "I mean the first wife of the grandfather of the present Count. She died after they had been married a couple of years. The old Count, they say, went half crazy. He had the Doll made from a picture, and kept it in the poor lady's room, and spent several hours in it every day with her. But he ended by marrying a woman he had in the house, a laundress, by whom he had had a daughter."

"What a curious story!" I said, and thought no more about it.

But the Doll returned to my thoughts, she and her folded hands, and wide open eyes, and the fact of her husband's having ended by marrying the laundress. And next day, when we returned to the palace to see the complete set of old Chinese plates, I suddenly experienced an odd wish to see the Doll once more. I took advantage of Orestes, and the old woman, and the Count's lawyer being busy deciding whether a certain dish cover which my maid had dropped, had or had not been previously chipped, to slip off and make my way to the ironing-room.

The Doll was still there, sure enough, and they hadn't found time to dust her yet. Her white satin frock, with little *ruches** at the hem, and her short bodice, had turned grey with engrained dirt; and her black fringed kerchief was almost red. The poor white silk mittens and white silk stockings were, on the other hand, almost black. A newspaper had fallen from an adjacent table on to her knees, or been thrown there by some one, and she looked as if she were holding it. It came home to me then that the clothes which she wore were the real clothes of her poor dead original. And when I found on the table a dusty, unkempt wig, with straight bands in front and an elaborate jug handle of curls behind, I knew at once that it was made of the poor lady's real hair.

"It is very well made," I said shyly, when the old woman, of course, came creaking after me.

She had no thought except that of humouring whatever caprice might bring her a tip. So she smirked horribly, and, to show me that the image was really worthy of my attention, she proceeded in a ghastly way to bend the articulated arms, and to cross one leg over the other beneath the white satin skirt.

"Please, please, don't do that!" I cried to the old witch. But one of the poor feet, in its sandalled shoe, continued dangling and wagging dreadfully.

I was afraid lest my maid should find me staring at the Doll. I felt I couldn't stand my maid's remarks about her. So, though fascinated by the fixed dark stare in her Canova goddess or Ingres Madonna* face, I tore myself away and returned to the inspection of the dessert set.

I don't know what that Doll had done to me; but I found that I was thinking of her all day long. It was as if I had just made a new acquaintance of a painfully interesting kind, rushed into a sudden friendship with a woman whose secret I had surprised, as sometimes happens, by some mere accident. For I somehow knew everything about her, and the first items of information which I gained from Orestes—I ought to say that I was irresistibly impelled to talk about her with him—did not enlighten me in the least, but merely confirmed what I was aware of.

The Doll—for I made no distinction between the portrait and the original—had been married straight out of the convent, and, during her brief wedded life, been kept secluded from the world by her husband's mad love for her, so that she had remained a mere shy, proud, inexperienced child.

Had she loved him? She did not tell me that at once. But gradually I became aware that in a deep, inarticulate way she had really cared for him more than he cared for her. She did not know what answer to make to his easy, overflowing, garrulous, demonstrative affection; he could not be silent about his love for two minutes, and she could never find a word to express hers, painfully though she longed to do so. Not that he wanted it; he was a brilliant, will-less, lyrical sort of person, who knew nothing of the feelings of others and cared only to welter and dissolve in his own. In those two years of ecstatic, talkative, all-absorbing love for her he not only forswore all society and utterly neglected his affairs, but he never made an attempt to train this raw young creature into a companion, or showed any curiosity as to whether his idol might have a mind or a character of her own. This indifference she explained by her own stupid, inconceivable incapacity for expressing her feelings; how should he guess at her longing to know, to understand, when she could not even tell him how much she loved him? At last the spell seemed broken: the words and the power of saying them came; but it was on her death-bed. The poor young creature died in child-birth, scarcely more than a child herself.

There now! I knew even you would think it all silliness. I know what people are—what we all are—how impossible it is ever *really* to make others feel in the same way as ourselves about anything. Do you suppose I could have ever told all this about the Doll to my husband?

Yet I tell him everything about myself; and I know he would have been quite kind and respectful. It was silly of me ever to embark on the story of the Doll with any one; it ought to have remained a secret between me and Orestes. *He*, I really think, would have understood all about the poor lady's feelings, or known it already as well as I. Well, having begun, I must go on, I suppose.

I knew all about the Doll when she was alive—I mean about the lady—and I got to know, in the same way, all about her after she was dead. Only I don't think I'll tell you. *Basta:** the husband had the Doll made, and dressed it in her clothes, and placed it in her boudoir, where not a thing was moved from how it had been at the moment of her death. He allowed no one to go in, and cleaned and dusted it all himself, and spent hours every day weeping and moaning before the Doll. Then, gradually, he began to look at his collection of medals, and to resume his rides; but he never went into society, and never neglected spending an hour in the boudoir with the Doll. Then came the business with the laundress. And then he sent the Doll into a wardrobe? Oh no; he wasn't that sort of man. He was an idealizing, sentimental, feeble sort of person, and the amour with the laundress grew up quite gradually in the shadow of the inconsolable passion for the wife. He would never have married another woman of his own rank, given *her* son a stepmother (the son was sent to a distant school and went to the bad); and when he *did* marry the laundress it was almost in his dotage, and because she and the priests bullied him so fearfully about legitimating that other child. He went on paying visits to the Doll for a long time, while the laundress idyl went on quite peaceably. Then, as he grew old and lazy, he went less often; other people were sent to dust the Doll, and finally she was not dusted at all. Then he died, having quarrelled with his son and got to live like a feeble old boor, mostly in the kitchen. The son—the Doll's son—having gone to the bad, married a rich widow. It was she who refurnished the boudoir and sent the Doll away. But the daughter of the laundress, the illegitimate child, who had become a kind of housekeeper in her half-brother's palace, nourished a lingering regard for the Doll, partly because the old Count had made such a fuss about it, partly because it must have cost a lot of money, and partly because the lady had been a *real* lady. So when the boudoir was refurnished she emptied out a closet and put the Doll to live there; and she occasionally had it brought out to be dusted.

Well, while all these things were being borne in upon me there came a telegram saying my friend was not coming on to Foligno, and asking me to meet her at Perugia.* The little Renaissance coffer had been sent to London; Orestes and my maid and myself had carefully packed every one of the Chinese plates and fruit dishes in baskets of hay. I had ordered a set of the "Archivio Storico"* as a parting gift for dear old Orestes—I could never have dreamed of offering him money, or cravat pins, or things like that—and there was no excuse for staying one hour more at Foligno. Also I had got into low spirits of late—I suppose we poor women cannot stay alone six days in an inn, even with *bric-à-brac* and chronicles and devoted maids—and I knew I should not get better till I was out of the place. Still I found it difficult, nay, impossible, to go. I will confess it outright: I couldn't abandon the Doll. I couldn't leave her, with the hole in her poor cardboard head, with the Ingres Madonna features gathering dust in that filthy old woman's ironing-room. It was just impossible. Still go I must. So I sent for Orestes. I knew exactly what I wanted; but it seemed impossible, and I was afraid, somehow, of asking him. I gathered up my courage, and, as if it were the most natural thing in the world, I said—

"Dear Signor Oreste, I want you to help me to make one last purchase. I want the Count to sell me the—the portrait of his grandmother; I mean the Doll."

I had prepared a speech to the effect that Orestes would easily understand that a life-size figure so completely dressed in the original costume of a past epoch would soon possess the highest historical interest, etc. But I felt that I neither needed nor ventured to say any of it. Orestes, who was seated opposite me at table—he would only accept a glass of wine and a morsel of bread, although I had asked him to share my hotel dinner—Orestes nodded slowly, then opened his eyes out wide, and seemed to frame the whole of me in them. It wasn't surprise. He was weighing me and my offer.

"Would it be very difficult?" I asked. "I should have thought that the Count——"

"The Count," answered Orestes drily, "would sell his soul, if he had one, let alone his grandmother, for the price of a new trotting pony."

Then I understood.

"Signor Oreste," I replied, feeling like a child under the dear old man's glance, "we have not known one another long, so I cannot expect you to trust me yet in many things. Perhaps also buying furniture out of dead people's houses to stick it in one's own is not a great recommendation of one's character. But I want to tell you that I am an honest woman according to my lights, and I want you to trust me in this matter."

Orestes bowed. "I will try and induce the Count to sell you the Doll," he said.

I had her sent in a closed carriage to the house of Orestes. He had, behind his shop, a garden which extended into a little vineyard, whence you could see the circle of great Umbrian mountains; and on this I had had my eye.

"Signor Oreste," I said, "will you be very kind, and have some faggots—I have seen some beautiful faggots of myrtle and bay in your kitchen—brought out into the vineyard; and may I pluck some of your chrysanthemums?" I added.

We stacked the faggots at the end of the vineyard, and placed the Doll in the midst of them, and the chrysanthemums on her knees. She sat there in her white satin Empire frock,* which, in the bright November sunshine, seemed white once more, and sparkling. Her black fixed eyes stared as in wonder on the yellow vines and reddening peach trees, the sparkling dewy grass of the vineyard, upon the blue morning sunshine, the misty blue amphitheatre of mountains all round.

Orestes struck a match and slowly lit a pine cone with it; when the cone was blazing he handed it silently to me. The dry bay and myrtle blazed up crackling, with a fresh resinous odour; the Doll was veiled in flame and smoke. In a few seconds the flame sank, the smouldering faggots crumbled. The Doll was gone. Only, where she had been, there remained in the embers something small and shiny. Orestes raked it out and handed it to me. It was a wedding ring of old-fashioned shape, which had been hidden under the silk mitten. "Keep it, signora," said Orestes; "you have put an end to her sorrows."

MARSYAS IN FLANDERS*

I

"YOU are right. This is not the original crucifix at all. Another one has been put instead. *Il y a eu substitution*," and the little old Antiquary of Dunes* nodded mysteriously, fixing his ghostseer's eyes upon mine.

He said it in a scarce audible whisper. For it happened to be the vigil of the Feast of the Crucifix, and the once famous church was full of semi-clerical persons decorating it for the morrow, and of old ladies in strange caps, clattering about with pails and brooms. The Antiquary had brought me there the very moment of my arrival, lest the crowd of faithful should prevent his showing me everything next morning.

The famous crucifix was exhibited behind rows and rows of unlit candles, and surrounded by strings of paper flowers and coloured muslin, and garlands of sweet resinous maritime pine; and two lighted chandeliers illumined it.

"There has been an exchange," he repeated, looking round that no one might hear him. "Il y a eu substitution."

For I had remarked, as anyone would have done, at the first glance, that the crucifix had every appearance of French work of the thirteenth century, boldly realistic, whereas the crucifix of the legend, which was a work of St. Luke, which had hung for centuries in the Holy Sepulchre at Jerusalem and been miraculously cast ashore at Dunes in 1195, would surely have been a more or less Byzantine image, like its miraculous companion of Lucca.*

"But why should there have been a substitution?" I inquired innocently.

"Hush, hush," answered the Antiquary, frowning, "not here—later, later——"

He took me all over the church, once so famous for pilgrimages; but from which, even like the sea which has left it in a salt marsh beneath the cliffs, the tide of devotion has receded for centuries. It is a very dignified little church, of charmingly restrained and shapely Gothic, built of a delicate pale stone, which the sea damp has picked out, in bases and capitals and carved foliation, with stains of a lovely bright green. The Antiquary showed me where the transept and belfry had been left unfinished when the miracles had diminished in the fourteenth century. And he took me up to the curious warder's chamber, a large room up some steps in the triforium;* with a fireplace and stone seats for the men who guarded the precious crucifix day and night. There had even been beehives in the window, he told me, and he remembered seeing them still as a child.

"Was it usual, here in Flanders, to have a guardroom in churches containing important relics?" I asked, for I could not remember having seen anything similar before.

"By no means," he answered, looking round to make sure we were alone, "but it was necessary here. You have never heard in what the chief miracles of this church consisted?"

"No," I whispered back, gradually infected by his mysteriousness, "unless you allude to the legend that the figure of the Saviour broke all the crosses until the right one was cast up by the sea?"

He shook his head but did not answer, and descended the steep stairs into the nave, while I lingered a moment looking down into it from the warder's chamber. I have never had so curious an impression of a church. The chandeliers on either side of the crucifix swirled slowly round, making great pools of light which were broken by the shadows of the clustered columns; and among the pews of the nave moved the flicker of the sacristan's lamp. The place was full of the scent of resinous pine branches, evoking dunes and mountain-sides; and from the busy groups below rose a subdued chatter of women's voices, and a splash of water and clatter of pattens. It vaguely suggested preparations for a witches' sabbath.

"What sort of miracles did they have in this church?" I asked, when we had passed into the dusky square, "and what did you mean about their having exchanged the crucifix—about a *substitution?*"

It seemed quite dark outside. The church rose black, a vague lopsided mass of buttresses and high-pitched roofs, against the watery, moon-lit sky; the big trees of the churchyard behind waving about in the seawind; and the windows shone yellow, like flaming portals, in the darkness.

"Please remark the bold effect of the gargoyles," said the Antiquary pointing upwards.

They jutted out, vague wild beasts, from the roof-line; and, what was positively frightening, you saw the moonlight, yellow and blue through the open jaws of some of them. A gust swept through the trees, making the weathercock clatter and groan.

"Why, those gargoyle wolves seem positively to howl," I exclaimed.

The old Antiquary chuckled. "Aha," he answered, "did I not tell you that this church has witnessed things like no other church in Christendom? And it still remembers them! There—have you ever known such a wild, savage church before?"

And as he spoke there suddenly mingled with the sough of the wind and the groans of the weather-vane, a shrill quavering sound as of pipers inside.

"The organist trying his vox humana* for to-morrow," remarked the Antiquary.

II

Next day I bought one of the printed histories of the miraculous crucifix which they were hawking all round the church; and next day also, my friend the Antiquary was good enough to tell me all that he knew of the matter. Between my two informants, the following may be said to be the true story.

In the autumn of 1195, after a night of frightful storm, a boat was found cast upon the shore of Dunes, which was at that time a fishing village at the mouth of the Nys,* and exactly opposite a terrible sunken reef.

The boat was broken and upset; and close to it, on the sand and bent grass, lay a stone figure of the crucified Saviour, without its cross and, as seems probable, also without its arms, which had been made of separate blocks. A variety of persons immediately came forward to claim it; the little church of Dunes, on whose glebe it was found; the Barons of Croÿ, who had the right of jetsam on that coast, and also the great Abbey of St. Loup of Arras,* as possessing the spiritual overlordship of the place. But a holy man who lived close by in the cliffs, had a vision which settled the dispute. St. Luke in person appeared and told him that he was the original maker of the figure; that it had been one of three which had hung round the Holy Sepulchre of Jerusalem; that three knights, a Norman, a Tuscan, and a man of Arras, had with the permission of Heaven stolen them from the Infidels and placed them on unmanned boats; that one of the images had been cast upon the Norman coast near Salenelles;* that the second had run aground not far from the city of Lucca, in Italy; and that this third was the one which had been embarked by the knight from Artois. As regarded its final resting place, the hermit, on the authority of St. Luke, recommended that the statue should be left to decide the matter itself. Accordingly, the crucified figure was solemnly cast back into the sea. The very next day it was found once more in the same spot, among the sand and bent grass at the mouth of the Nys. It was therefore deposited in the little church of Dunes; and very soon indeed the flocks of pious persons who brought it offerings from all parts made it necessary and possible to rebuild the church thus sanctified by its presence.

The Holy Effigy of Dunes—Sacra Dunarum Effigies as it was called—did not work the ordinary sort of miracles. But its fame spread far and wide by the unexampled wonders which became the constant accompaniment of its existence. The Effigy, as above mentioned, had been discovered without the cross to which it had evidently been fastened, nor had any researches or any subsequent storms brought the missing blocks to light, despite the many prayers which were offered for the purpose. After some time, therefore, and a deal of discussion, it was decided that a new cross should be provided for the effigy to hang upon. And certain skilful stone-masons of Arras were called to Dunes for this purpose. But behold! the very day after the cross had been solemnly erected in the church, an unheard of and terrifying fact was discovered. The Effigy, which had been hanging perfectly straight the previous evening, had shifted its position, and was bent violently to the right, as if in an effort to break loose.

This was attested not merely by hundreds of laymen, but by the priests of the place, who notified the fact in a document, existing in the episcopal archives of Arras until 1790,* to the Abbot of St. Loup their spiritual overlord.

This was the beginning of a series of mysterious occurrences which spread the fame of the marvellous crucifix all over Christendom. The Effigy did not remain in the position into which it had miraculously worked itself: it was found, at intervals of time, shifted in some other manner upon its cross, and always as if it had gone through violent contortions. And one day, about ten years after it had been cast up by the sea, the priests of the church and the burghers of Dunes discovered the Effigy hanging in its original out-stretched, symmetrical attitude, but, O wonder! with the cross, broken in three pieces, lying on the steps of its chapel.

Certain persons, who lived in the end of the town nearest the church, reported to have been roused in the middle of the night by what they had taken for a violent clap of thunder, but which was doubtless the crash of the cross falling down; or perhaps, who knows? the noise with which the terrible Effigy had broken loose and spurned the alien cross from it. For that was the secret: the Effigy, made by a saint and come to Dunes by miracle, had evidently found some trace of unholiness in the stone to which it had been fastened. Such was the ready explanation afforded by the Prior of the church, in answer to an angry summons of the Abbot of St. Loup, who expressed his disapproval of such unusual miracles. Indeed, it was discovered that the piece of marble had not been cleaned from sinful human touch with the necessary rites before the figure was fastened on; a most grave, though excusable oversight. So a new cross was ordered, although it was noticed that much time was lost about it; and the consecration took place only some years later.

Meanwhile the Prior had built the warder's chamber, with the fireplace and recess, and obtained permission from the Pope himself that a clerk in orders should watch day and night, on the score that so wonderful a relic might be stolen. For the relic had by this time entirely cut out all similar crucifixes, and the village of Dunes, through the concourse of pilgrims, had rapidly grown into a town, the property of the now fabulously wealthy Priory of the Holy Cross.

The Abbots of St. Loup, however, looked upon the matter with an unfavourable eye. Although nominally remaining their vassals, the Priors of Dunes had contrived to obtain gradually from the Pope privileges which rendered them virtually independent, and in particular, immunities which sent to the treasury of St. Loup only a small proportion of the tribute money brought by the pilgrims. Abbot Walterius in particular, showed himself actively hostile. He accused the Prior of Dunes of having employed his warders to trump up stories of strange movements and sounds on the part of the still crossless Effigy, and of suggesting, to the ignorant, changes in its attitude which were more credulously believed in now that there was no longer the straight line of the cross by which to verify. So finally the new cross was made, and consecrated, and on Holy Cross Day of the year, the Effigy was fastened to it in the presence of an immense concourse of clergy and laity. The Effigy, it was now supposed, would be satisfied, and no unusual occurrences would increase or perhaps fatally compromise its reputation for sanctity.

These expectations were violently dispelled. In November, 1293, after a year of strange rumours concerning the Effigy, the figure was again discovered to have moved, and continued moving, or rather (Judging from the position on the cross) writhing; and on Christmas Eve of the same year, the cross was a second time thrown down and dashed in pieces. The priest on duty was, at the same time, found, it was thought, dead, in his warder's chamber. Another cross was made and this time privately consecrated and put in place, and a hole in the roof made a pretext to close the church for a while, and to perform the rites of purification necessary after its pollution by workmen. Indeed, it was remarked that on this occasion the Prior of Dunes took as much trouble to diminish and if possible to hide away the miracles, as his predecessor had done his best to blazon the preceding ones abroad. The priest who had been on duty on the eventful Christmas Eve disappeared mysteriously, and it was thought by many persons that he had gone mad and was confined in the Prior's prison, for fear of the revelations he might make. For by this time, and not without some encouragement from the Abbots at Arras, extraordinary stories had begun to circulate about the goings-on in the church of Dunes. This church, be it remembered, stood a little above the town, isolated and surrounded by big trees. It was surrounded by the precincts of the Priory and, save on the water side, by high walls. Nevertheless, persons there were who affirmed that, the wind having been in that direction, they had heard strange noises come from the church of nights. During storms, particularly, sounds had been heard which were variously described as howls, groans, and the music of rustic dancing. A master mariner affirmed that one Hallow Even, as his boat approached the mouth of the Nys, he had seen the church of Dunes brilliantly lit up, its immense windows flaming. But he was suspected of being drunk and of having exaggerated the effect of the small light shining from the warder's chamber. The interest of the townfolk of Dunes coincided with that of the Priory, since they prospered greatly by the pilgrimages, so these tales were promptly hushed up. Yet they undoubtedly reached the ear of the Abbot of St. Loup. And at last there came an event which brought them all back to the surface.

For, on the Vigil of All Saints,* 1299, the church was struck by lightning. The new warder was found dead in the middle of the nave, the cross broken in two; and oh, horror! the Effigy was missing. The indescribable fear which overcame every one was merely increased by the discovery of the Effigy lying behind the high altar, in an attitude of frightful convulsion, and, it was whispered, blackened by lightning.

This was the end of the strange doings at Dunes.

An ecclesiastical council was held at Arras, and the church shut once more for nearly a year. It was opened this time and re-consecrated by the Abbot of St. Loup, whom the Prior of Holy Cross served humbly at mass. A new chapel had been built, and in it the miraculous crucifix was displayed, dressed in more splendid brocade and gems than usual, and its head nearly hidden by one of the most gorgeous crowns ever seen before; a gift, it was said, of the Duke of Burgundy.

All this new splendour, and the presence of the great Abbot himself, was presently explained to the faithful, when the Prior came forward to announce that a last and greatest miracle had now taken place. The original cross, on which the figure had hung in the Church of the Holy Sepulchre, and for which the Effigy had spurned all others made by less holy hands, had been cast on the shore of Dunes, on the very spot where, a hundred years before, the figure of the Saviour had been discovered in the sands. "This," said the Prior, "was the explanation of the terrible occurrences which had filled all hearts with anguish. The Holy Effigy was now satisfied, it would rest in peace and its miraculous powers would be engaged only in granting the prayers of the faithful.

One-half of the forecast came true: from that day forward the Effigy never shifted its position; but from that day forward also, no considerable miracle was ever registered; the devotion of Dunes diminished, other relics threw the Sacred Effigy into the shade; and the pilgrimages dwindling to mere local gatherings, the church was never brought to completion.

What had happened? No one ever knew, guessed, or perhaps even asked. But, when in 1790 the Archiepiscopal palace of Arras was sacked, a certain notary of the neighbourhood bought a large portion of the archives at the price of waste paper, either from historical curiosity, or expecting to obtain thereby facts which might gratify his aversion to the clergy. These documents lay unexamined for many years, till my friend the Antiquary bought them. Among them, taken helter skelter from the Archbishop's palace, were sundry papers referring to the suppressed Abbey of St. Loup of Arras, and among these latter, a series of notes concerning the affairs of the church of Dunes; they were, so far as their fragmentary nature explained, the minutes of an inquest made in 1309, and contained the deposition of sundry witnesses. To understand their meaning it is necessary to remember that this was the time when witch trials had begun, and when the proceedings against the Templars* had set the fashion of inquests which could help the finances of the country while furthering the interests of religion.

What appears to have happened is that after the catastrophe of the Vigil of All Saints, October, 1299, the Prior, Urbain de Luc, found himself suddenly threatened with a charge of sacrilege and witchcraft, of obtaining the miracles of the Effigy by devilish means, and of converting his church into a chapel of the Evil One.

Instead of appealing to high ecclesiastical tribunals, as the privileges obtained from the Holy See would have warranted, Prior Urbain guessed that this charge came originally from the wrathful Abbey of St. Loup, and, dropping all his pretensions in order to save himself, he threw himself upon the mercy of the Abbot whom he had hitherto flouted. The Abbot appears to have been satisfied by his submission, and the matter to have dropped after a few legal preliminaries, of which the notes found among the archiepiscopal archives of Arras represented a portion. Some of these notes my friend the Antiquary kindly allowed me to translate from the Latin, and I give them here, leaving the reader to make what he can of them.

"Item. The Abbot expresses himself satisfied that His Reverence the Prior has had no personal knowledge of or dealings with the Evil One (Diabolus). Nevertheless, the gravity of the charge requires . . ." —here the page is torn.

"Hugues Jacquot, Simon le Couvreur, Pierre Denis, burghers of Dunes, being interrogated, witness:

"That the noises from the Church of the Holy Cross always happened on nights of bad storms, and foreboded shipwrecks on the coast; and were very various, such as terrible rattling, groans, howls as of wolves, and occasional flute playing. A certain Jehan, who has twice been branded and flogged for lighting fires on the coast and otherwise causing ships to wreck* at the mouth of the Nys, being promised immunity, after two or three slight pulls on the rack, witnesses as follows: That the band of wreckers to which he belongs always knew when a dangerous storm was brewing, on account of the noises which issued from the church of Dunes. Witness has often climbed the walls and prowled round in the churchyard, waiting to hear such noises. He was not unfamiliar with the howlings and roarings mentioned by the previous witnesses. He has heard tell by a countryman who passed in the night that the howling was such that the countryman thought himself pursued by a pack of wolves, although it is well known that no wolf has been seen in these parts for thirty years. But the witness himself is of opinion that the most singular of all the noises, and the one which always accompanied or foretold the worst storms, was a noise of flutes and pipes (quod vulgo dicuntur flustes et musettes*) so sweet that the King of France could not have sweeter at his Court. Being interrogated whether he had ever seen anything? the witness answers: 'That he has seen the church brightly lit up from the sands; but on approaching found all dark, save the light from the warder's chamber. That once, by moonlight, the piping and fluting and howling being uncommonly loud, he thought he had seen wolves, and a human figure on the roof, but that he ran away from fear, and cannot be sure.'

"Item. His Lordship the Abbot desires the Right Reverend Prior to answer truly, placing his hand on the Gospels, whether or not he had himself heard such noises.

"The Right Reverend Prior denies ever having heard anything similar. But, being threatened with further proceedings (the rack?) acknowledges that he had frequently been told of these noises by the Warder on duty.

"*Query:* Whether the Right Reverend Prior was ever told anything else by the Warder?

"*Answer:* Yes; but under the seal of confession. The last Warder, moreover, the one killed by lightning, had been a reprobate priest, having committed the greatest crimes and obliged to take asylum, whom the Prior had kept there on account of the difficulty of finding a man sufficiently courageous for the office.

"*Query:* Whether the Prior has ever questioned previous Warders?

"*Answer:* That the Warders were bound to reveal only in confession whatever they had heard; that the Prior's predecessors had kept the seal of confession inviolate, and that though unworthy, the Prior himself desired to do alike.

"*Query:* What had become of the Warder who had been found in a swoon after the occurrences of Hallow Even?

"*Answer:* That the Prior does not know. The Warder was crazy. The Prior believes he was secluded for that reason."

A disagreeable surprise had been, apparently, arranged for Prior Urbain de Luc. For the next entry states that:

"Item. By order of His Magnificence the Lord Abbot, certain servants of the Lord Abbot aforesaid introduce Robert Baudouin, priest, once Warder in the Church of the Holy Cross, who has been kept ten years in prison by His Reverence the Prior, as being of unsound mind. Witness manifests great terror on finding himself in the presence of their Lordships, and particularly of His Reverence the Prior. And refuses to speak, hiding his face in his hands and uttering shrieks. Being comforted with kind words by those present, nay even most graciously by My Lord the Abbot himself, *etiam** threatened with the rack if he continue obdurate, this witness deposes as follows, not without much lamentation, shrieking and senseless jabber after the manner of mad men.

"*Query:* Can he remember what happened on the Vigil of All Saints, in the church of Dunes, before he swooned on the floor of the church?

"*Answer:* He cannot. It would be sin to speak of such things before great spiritual Lords. Moreover he is but an ignorant man, and also mad. Moreover his hunger is great.

"Being given white bread* from the Lord Abbot's own table, witness is again cross-questioned.

"*Query:* What can he remember of the events of the Vigil of All Saints?

"*Answer:* Thinks he was not always mad. Thinks he has not always been in prison. Thinks he once went in a boat on sea, etc.

"*Query:* Does witness think he has ever been in the church of Dunes?

"*Answer:* Cannot remember. But is sure that he was not always in prison.

"*Query:* Has witness ever heard anything like that? (My Lord the Abbot having secretly ordered that a certain fool in his service, an excellent musician, should suddenly play the pipes behind the Arras.)

"At which sound witness began to tremble and sob and fall on his knees, and catch hold of the robe even of My Lord the Abbot, hiding his head therein.

"*Query:* Wherefore does he feel such terror, being in the fatherly presence of so clement a prince as the Lord Abbot?

"*Answer:* That witness cannot stand that piping any longer. That it freezes his blood. That he has told the Prior many times that he will not remain any longer in the warder's chamber. That he is afraid for his life. That he dare not make the sign of the Cross nor say his prayers for fear of the Great Wild Man.* That the Great Wild Man took the Cross and broke it in two and played at quoits* with it in the nave. That all the wolves trooped down from the roof howling, and danced on their hind legs while the Great Wild Man played the pipes on the high altar. That witness had surrounded himself with a hedge of little crosses, made of broken rye straw, to keep off the Great Wild Man from the warder's chamber. Ah—ah—ah! He is piping again! The wolves are howling! He is raising the tempest.

"*Item.* That no further information can be extracted from witness, who falls on the floor like one possessed and has to be removed from the presence of His Lordship the Abbot and His Reverence the Prior."

III

Here the minutes of the inquest break off. Did those great spiritual dignitaries ever get to learn more about the terrible doings in the church of Dunes? Did they ever guess at their cause?

"For there was a cause," said the Antiquary, folding his spectacles after reading me these notes, "or more strictly the cause still exists. And you will understand, though those learned priests of six centuries ago could not."

And rising, he fetched a key from a shelf and preceded me into the yard of his house, situated on the Nys, a mile below Dunes.

Between the low steadings one saw the salt marsh, lilac with sea lavender, the Island of Birds, a great sandbank at the mouth of the Nys, where every kind of sea fowl gathers; and beyond, the angry white-crested sea under an angry orange afterglow. On the other side, inland, and appearing above the farm roofs, stood the church of Dunes, its pointed belfry and jagged outlines of gables and buttresses and gargoyles and wind-warped pines black against the easterly sky of ominous livid red.

"I told you," said the Antiquary, stopping with the key in the lock of a big outhouse, "that there had been a *substitution*; that the crucifix at present at Dunes is not the one miraculously cast up by the storm of 1195. I believe the present one may be identified as a life-size statue, for which a receipt exists in the archives of Arras, furnished to the Abbot of St. Loup by Estienne Le Mas and Guillaume Pernel, stone masons, in the year 1299, that is to say the year of the inquest and of the cessation of all supernatural occurrences at Dunes. As to the original effigy, you shall see it and understand everything."

The Antiquary opened the door of a sloping, vaulted passage, lit a lantern and led the way. It was evidently the cellar of some mediæval building; and a scent of wine, of damp wood, and of fir branches from innumerable stacked up faggots, filled the darkness among thickset columns.

"Here," said the Antiquary, raising his lantern, "he was buried beneath this vault, and they had run an iron stake through his middle, like a vampire,* to prevent his rising."

The Effigy was erect against the dark wall, surrounded by brushwood. It was more than life-size, nude, the arms broken off at the shoulders, the head, with stubbly beard and clotted hair, drawn up with an effort, the face contracted with agony; the muscles dragged as of one hanging crucified, the feet bound together with a rope. The figure was familiar to me in various galleries. I came forward to examine the ear: it was leaf-shaped.

"Ah, you have understood the whole mystery," said the Antiquary.

"I have understood," I answered, not knowing how far his thought really went, "that this supposed statue of Christ is an antique satyr, a Marsyas* awaiting his punishment."

The Antiquary nodded. "Exactly," he said drily, "that is the whole explanation. Only I think the Abbot and the Prior were not so wrong to drive the iron stake through him when they removed him from the church."

APPENDIX A

FAUSTUS AND HELENA

NOTES ON THE SUPERNATURAL IN ART

THERE is a story, well-known throughout the sixteenth century, which tells how Doctor Faustus of Wittemberg, having made over his soul to the fiend, employed him to raise the ghost of Helen of Sparta,* in order that she might become his paramour. The story has no historic value, no scientific meaning; it lacks the hoary dignity of the tales of heroes and demi-gods, wrought, vague, and colossal forms, out of cloud and sunbeam, of those tales narrated and heard by generations of men deep hidden in the stratified ruins of lost civilisation, carried in the races from India to Hellas, and to Scandinavia. Compared with them, this tale of Faustus and Helena is paltry and brand-new; it is not a myth, nay, scarcely a legend; it is a mere trifling incident added by humanistic pedantry to the ever-changing mediæval story of the man who barters his soul for knowledge, the wizard, alchemist, philosopher, printer, Albertus, Bacon, or Faustus.* It is a part, an unessential, subordinate fragment, valued in its day neither more nor less than any other part of the history of Doctor Faustus, narrated cursorily by the biographer of the wizard, overlooked by some of the ballad rhymers, alternately used and rejected by the playwrights of puppet-shows; given by Marlowe himself no greater importance than the other marvellous deeds, the juggling tricks and magic journeys of his hero.

But for us, the incident of Faustus and Helena has a meaning, a fascination wholly different from any other portion of the story; the other incidents owe everything to artistic treatment: this one owes nothing. The wizard Faustus, awaiting the hour which will give him over to Hell, is the creation of Marlowe; Gretchen is even more completely the creation of Goethe; the fiend of the Englishman is occasionally grand, the fiend of the German is throughout masterly; in all these cases we are in the presence of true artistic work, of stuff rendered valuable solely by the hand of the artist, of figures well defined and finite, and limited also in their power over the imagination. But the group of Faustus and Helena is different; it belongs neither to Marlowe nor to Goethe,* it belongs to the legend. It does not give the complete and limited satisfaction of a work of art; it has the charm of the fantastic and fitful shapes formed by the flickering firelight or the wreathing mists; it haunts like some vague strain of music, drowsily heard in half-sleep. It fills the fancy, it oscillates and transforms itself; the artist may see it, attempt to seize and embody it for evermore in a definite and enduring shape, but it vanishes out of his grasp, and the forms which should have inclosed it are mere empty sepulchres, haunted and charmed merely by the evoking power of our own imagination. If we are fascinated by the Lady Helen of Marlowe, walking, like some Florentine goddess, with embroidered kirtle and madonna face, across the study of the old wizard of Wittemberg; if we are pleased by the stately pseudo-antique Helena of Goethe, draped in the drapery of Thorwaldsen's statues,* and speaking the language of Goethe's own Iphigenia,* as she meets the very modern Faust, gracefully masqued in mediæval costume; if we find in these attempts, the one unthinking and imperfect, the other laboured and abortive, something which delights our fancy, it is because our thoughts wander off from them and evoke a Faustus and Helena of our own, different from the creations of Marlowe and of Goethe; it is because in these definite and imperfect artistic forms, there yet remains the suggestion of the subject with all its power over the imagination. We forget Marlowe, and we forget Goethe, to follow up the infinite suggestion of the legend. We cease to see the Elizabethan and the pseudo-antique Helen; we lift our imagination from the book and see the mediæval street at Wittemberg, the gabled house of Faustus, all sculptured with quaint devices and grotesque forms of apes and cherubs and flowers; we penetrate through the low brown rooms, filled with musty books and mysterious ovens and retorts, redolent with strange scents of alchemy, to that innermost secret chamber, where the old wizard hides, in the depths of his mediæval house, the immortal woman, the god-born, the fatal, the beloved of Theseus and Paris and Achilles; we are blinded by this sunshine of Antiquity pent up in the oaken-panelled chamber, such as Dürer* might have etched; and all around we hear circulating the mysterious rumours of the neighbours, of the burghers and students, whispering shyly of Dr. Faustus and his strange guest, in the beer-cellars and in the cloisters of the old university town. And gazing thus into the fantastic intellectual mist which has risen up between us and the book we were reading, be it Marlowe or Goethe, we cease, after a while, to see Faustus or Helena, we perceive only a chaotic fluctuation of incongruous shapes; scholars in furred robes and caps pulled over their ears, burghers wives with high sugar-loaf coif and slashed boddices, with hands demurely folded over their prayer-books, and knights in armour and immense plumes, and haggling Jews, and tonsured monks, descended out of panels of Wohlgemüth* and the engravings of Dürer, mingling with, changing into processions of naked athletes on foaming short-maned horses, of draped Athenian maidens carrying baskets and sickles, and priests bearing oil-jars and torches, all melting into each other, indistinct, confused, like the images in a dream; vague crowds, phantoms following in the wake of the spectre woman of Antiquity, beautiful, unimpassioned, ever young, luring to Hell the wizard of the Middle Ages.

Why does all this vanish as soon as we once more fix our eyes upon the book? Why can our fancy show us more than can the artistic genius of Marlowe and of Goethe? Why does Marlowe, believing in Helen as a satanic reality, and Goethe, striving after her as an artistic vision, equally fail to satisfy us? The question is intricate: it requires a threefold answer, dependent on the fact that this tale of Faustus and Helena is in fact a tale of the supernatural—a weird and colossal ghost-story, in which the actors are the spectre of Antiquity, ever young, beautiful, radiant, though risen from the putrescence of two thousand years; and the Middle Ages, alive, but toothless, palsied, and tottering. Why neither Marlowe nor Goethe have succeeded in giving a satisfactory artistic shape to this tale is explained by the necessary relations between art and the supernatural, between our creative power and our imaginative faculty; why Marlowe has failed in one manner and Goethe in another is explained by the fact that, as we said, for the first the tale was a supernatural reality, for the second a supernatural fiction.

What are the relations between art and the supernatural? At first sight the two appear closely allied: like the supernatural, art is born of imagination; the supernatural, like art, conjures up unreal visions. The two have been intimately connected during the great ages of the supernatural, when instead of existing merely in a few disputed traditional dogmas, and in a little discredited traditional folklore, it constituted the whole of religion and a great part of philosophy. Gods and demons, saints and spectres, have afforded at least one-half of the subjects for art. The supernatural, in the shape of religious mythology, had art bound in its service in Antiquity and the Middle Ages; the supernatural, in the shape of spectral fancies, regained its dominion over art with the advent of romanticism. From the gods of the *Iliad* down to the Commander in *Don Giovanni*, from the sylvan divinities of Praxiteles to the fairies of Shakespeare, from the Furies of Æschylus to the Archangels of Perugino,* the supernatural and the artistic have constantly appeared linked together. Yet, in reality, the hostility between the supernatural and the artistic is well-nigh as great as the hostility between the supernatural and the logical. Critical reason is a solvent, it reduces the phantoms of the imagination to their most prosaic elements; artistic power, on the other hand, moulds and solidifies them into distinct and palpable forms: the synthetical definiteness of art is as sceptical as the analytical definiteness of logic. For the supernatural is necessarily essentially vague, and art is necessarily essentially distinct: give shape to the vague and it ceases to exist. The task set to the artist by the dreamer, the prophet, the priest, the ghost-seer of all times, is as difficult, though in the opposite sense, as that by which the little girl in the Venetian fairy tale sought to test the omnipotence of the emperor. She asked him for a very humble dish, quite simple and not costly, a pat of butter broiled on a gridiron. The emperor desired his cook to place the butter on the gridiron and light the fire; all was going well, when, behold! the butter began to melt, trickled off, and vanished. The artists were asked to paint, or model, or narrate the supernatural; they set about the work in good conscience, but see, the supernatural became the natural, the gods turned into men, the madonnas into mere mothers, the angels into armed striplings, the phantoms into mere creatures of flesh and blood.

There are in reality two sorts of supernatural, although only one really deserves the name. A great number of beliefs in all mythologies are in reality mere scientific errors—abortive attempts to explain phenomena by causes with which they have no connection—the imagination plays not more part in them than in any other sort of theorising, and the notions that unlucky accidents are due to a certain man's glance, that certain formulæ will bring rain or sunshine, that miraculous images will dispel pestilence, and kings of England cure epilepsy, must be classed under the head of mistaken generalizations, not very different in point of fact from exploded scientific theories, such as Descartes' vortices,* or the innate ideas of scholasticism. That there was a time when animals spoke with human voice may seem to us a piece of fairy-lore, but it was in its day a scientific hypothesis as brilliant and satisfying as Darwin's theory of evolution. We must, therefore, in examining the relations between art and the supernatural, eliminate as far as possible this species of scientific speculation, and consider only that supernatural which really deserves the name, which is beyond and outside the limits of the possible, the rational, the explicable—that supernatural which is due not to the logical faculties, arguing from wrong premises, but to the imagination wrought upon by certain kinds of physical surroundings. The divinity of the earlier races is in some measure a mistaken scientific hypothesis of the sort we have described, an attempt to explain phenomena otherwise inexplicable. But it is much more: it is the effect on the imagination of certain external impressions, it is those impressions brought to a focus, personified, but personified vaguely, in a fluctuating ever-changing manner; the personification being continually altered, reinforced, blurred out, enlarged, restricted by new series of impressions from without, even as the shape which we puzzle out of congregated cloud-masses fluctuates with their every movement—a shifting vapour now obliterates the form, now compresses it into greater distinctness: the wings of the fantastic monster seem now flapping leisurely, now extending bristling like a griffon's; at one moment it has a beak and talons, at others a mane and hoofs; the breeze, the sunlight, the moonbeam, form, alter, and obliterate it. Thus is it with the supernatural: the gods, moulded out of cloud and sunlight and darkness, are for ever changing, fluctuating between a human or animal shape, god or goddess, cow, ape, or horse, and the mere natural phenomenon which impresses the fancy. Pan* is the weird, shaggy, cloven-footed shape which the goat-herd or the huntsman has seen gliding among the bushes in the grey twilight; his is the piping heard in the tangle of reeds, marsh lily, and knotted nightshade by the river side: but Pan is also the wood, with all its sights and noises, the solitude, the gloom, the infinity of rustling leaves, and cracking branches; he is the greenish-yellow light stealing in amid the boughs; he is the breeze in the foliage, the murmur of unseen waters, the mist hanging over the damp sward, the ferns and grasses which entangle the feet, and the briars which catch in the hair and garments are his grasp; and the wanderer dashes through the thickets with a sickening fear in his heart, and sinks down on the outskirts of the forest, gasping, with sweat-clotted hair, overcome by this glimpse of the great god.

In this constant renewal of the impressions on the fancy, in this unceasing shaping and reshaping of its creations, consisted the vitality of the myths of paganism, from the scorching and pestilence-bearing gods of India to the divinities shaped out of tempest and snowdrift of Scandinavia; they were constantly issuing out of the elements, renewed, changed, ever young, under the exorcism not only of the priest and of the poet, but of the village boor; and on this unceasing renovation depended the sway which they maintained, without ethical importance to help them, despite philosophy and Christianity. Christianity, born in an age of speculation and eclecticism, removed its divinities, its mystic figures, out of the cosmic surroundings of paganism; it forbade the imagination to touch or alter them, it regularised, defined, explained, placed the Saviour, the Virgin, the saints and angels, into a kind of supersensuous world of logic, logic adapted to Heaven, and different therefore from the logic of earth, but logic none the less. Christianity endowed them with certain definite attributes, not to be found among mortals, but analogous in a manner to mortal attributes; the Christian supernatural system belongs mainly to the category of mistaken scientific systems; its peculiarities are due, not to overwrought fancy, but to overtaxed reason. Thus the genuine supernatural was well-nigh banished by official Christianity, regulated as it was by a sort of congress of men of science, who eliminated, to the best of their powers, any vagaries of the imagination which might show themselves in their mystico-logic system. But the imagination did work nevertheless, and the supernatural did reappear, both within and without the Christian system of mythology. The Heaven of theology was too ethical, too logical, too positive, too scientific, in accordance with the science of the Middle Ages, for the minds of humanity at large; the scholars and learned clergy might study and expound it, but it was insufficient for the ignorant. The imagination reappeared once more. To the monk arose out of the silence and gloom of the damp, lichen-grown crypt, out of the fœtid emanations of the charnal-house, strange forms of horror which lurked in his steps and haunted his sleep after fasting and scourging and vigils; devils and imps horrible and obscene, which the chisel of the stonecutter vainly attempted to reproduce, in their fluctuating abomination, on the capitals and gargoyles of cloister and cathedral. To the artisan, the weaver pent up in some dark cellar into which the daylight stole grey and faint from the narrow strip of blue sky between the over-hanging eaves, for him, the hungry and toil-worn and weary of soul, there arose out of the hum of the street above, out of the half-lit dust, the winter damp and summer suffocation of the underground workshop, visions and sounds of sweetness and glory, misty clusters of white-robed angels shedding radiance around them, swaying in mystic linked dances, mingling with the sordid noises of toil seraphic harmonies, now near, now dying away into distance, voices singing of the sunshine and flowers of Paradise. And for others, for the lean and tattered peasant, with the dull, apathetic resignation of the starved and goaded ox or horse, sleeping on the damp clay of his hut and eating strange flourless bread, and stranger carrion flesh, there came a world of the supernatural, different from that of the monk or the artisan, at once terrifying and consoling; the divinities cast out by Christianity, the divinities for ever newly begotten by nature, but begotten of a nature miserably changed, born in exile and obloquy and persecution, fostered by the wretched and the brutified; differing from the gods of antiquity as the desolate heath, barren of all save stones and prickly furze and thistle, differs from the fertile pasture-land; as the forests planted over the cornfield, whence issue wolves, and the Baron's harvest-trampling horses, differ from the forests which gave their oaks and pines to Tyrian ships; divinities warped, and crippled, grown hideous and malignant and unhappy in the likeness of their miserable votaries.

This is the real supernatural, born of the imagination and its surroundings, the vital, the fluctuating, the potent; and it is this which the artist of every age, from Phidias to Giotto, from Giotto to Blake,* has been called upon to make known to the multitude. And there had been artistic work going on unnoticed long before the time of any painter or sculptor or poet of whom we have any record; mankind longed from the first to embody, to fix its visions of wonder, it set to work with rough unskilful fingers moulding into shape its divinities. Rude work, ugly, barbarous, blundering scratchings on walls, kneaded clay vessels, notched sticks, nonsense rhymes; but work nevertheless which already showed that art and the supernatural were at variance, the beaked and clawed figures outlined on the wall were compromises between the man and the beast, but definite compromises, so much and no more of the man, so much and no more of the beast; the goddess on the clay vessels became a mere little owl; the divinities even in the nonsense verses were presented now as very distinct cows, now as very distinct clouds, or very distinct men and women; the vague, fluctuating impressions oscillating before the imagination like the colours of a dove's wing, or the pattern of a shot silk, interwoven, unsteady, never completely united into one, never completely separated into several, were rudely seized, disentangled by art; part was taken, part thrown aside; what remained was homogeneous, definite, unchanging; it was what it was and could never be aught else.

Goethe has remarked,* with a subjective simplicity of irreverence which is almost comical, that as God created man in his image, it was only fair that man, in his turn, should create God in *his* image. But the decay of pagan belief was not, as Hegel imagines,* due to the fact that Hellenic art was anthropomorphic. The gods ceased to be gods not merely because they became too like men, but because they became too like anything definite. If the ibis on the amulet, or the owl on the terra-cotta, represents a more vital belief in the gods than does the Venus of Milo or the Giustiniani Minerva,* it is not because the idea of divinity is more compatible with an ugly bird than with a beautiful woman, but because whereas the beautiful woman, exquisitely wrought by a consummate sculptor, occupied the mind of the artist and of the beholder with the idea of her beauty, to the exclusion of all else, the rudely-engraven ibis, or the badly-modelled owlet, on the other hand, served merely as a symbol, as the recaller of an idea; the mind did not pause in contemplation of the bird, but wandered off in search of the god: the goggle eyes of the owl and the beak of the ibis were soon forgotten in the contemplation of the vague, ever transmuted visions of phenomena of sky and light, of semi-human and semi-bestial shapes, of confused half-embodied forces; in short, of the supernatural. But the human shape did most mischief to the supernatural, merely because the human shape was the most absolute, the most distinct of all shapes: a god might be symbolised as a beast, but he could only be pourtrayed as a man; and if the portrait was correct, then the god was a man, and nothing more. Even the most fantastic among pagan supernatural creatures, those strange monsters who longest kept their original dual nature—the centaurs, satyrs, and tritons—became, beneath the chisel of the artist, mere aberrations from the normal, rare, and curious types like certain fair-booth phenomena, but perfectly intelligible and rational; the very Chimæra, she who was to give her name to every sort of unintelligible fancy, became, in the bas-reliefs of the story of Bellerophon* a mere singular mixture between a lion, a dog, and a bird—a cross-breed which happens not to be possible, but which an ancient might well have conceived as adorning some distant zoological collection. How much more rationalised were not the divinities in whom only a peculiar shape of the eye, a certain structure of the leg, or a definite fashion of wearing the hair remained of their former nature. Learned men, indeed, tell us that we need only glance at Hera to see that she is at bottom a cow; at Apollo, to recognise that he is but a stag in human shape: or at Zeus, to recognise that he is, in point of fact, a lion. Yet it remains true that we need only walk down the nearest street to meet ten ordinary men and women who look more like various animals than do any antique divinities, and who can yet never be said to be in reality cows, stags, or lions. The same applies to the violent efforts which are constantly being made to show in the Greek and Latin poets a distinct recollection of the cosmic nature of the gods, construing the very human movements, looks, and dress of divinities into meteorological phenomena, as has been done even by Mr. Ruskin,* in his *Queen of the Air*, despite his artist's sense, which should have warned him that no artistic figure, like Homer's divinities, can possibly be at the same time a woman and a whirlwind. The gods did originally partake of the character of cosmic phenomena, as they partook of the characters of beasts and birds, and of every other species of transformation, such as we may watch in dreams; but as soon as they were artistically embodied, this transformation ceased, the nature had to be specified in proportion as the form became distinct; and the drapery of Pallas, although it had inherited its purple tint from the storm-cloud, was none the less, when it clad the shoulders of the goddess, not a storm-cloud, but a piece of purple linen. "What do you want of me?" asks the artist. "A god," answers the believer. "What is your god to be like?" asks the artist. "My god is to be a very handsome warrior, a serene heaven, which is occasionally overcast with clouds, which clouds are sometimes very beneficial, and become (and so does the god at those moments) heavy-uddered cows; at others, they are dark, and cause annoyance, and then they capture the god, who is the light (but he is also the clouds, remember), and lock him up in a tower, and then he frees himself, and he is a neighing horse, and he is sitting on the prancing horse (which is himself, you know, and is the sky too), in the shape of two warriors, and also——" "May Cerberus* devour you!" cries the artist. "How can I represent all this? Do you want a warrior, or a cow, or the heavens, or a horse, or do you want a warrior with the hoofs of a horse and the horns of a cow? Explain, for, by Juno, I can give you only one of these at a time."

Thus, in proportion as the gods were subjected to artistic manipulation, whether by sculptor or poet, they lost their supernatural powers. A period there doubtless was when the gods stood out quite distinct from nature, and yet remained connected with it, as the figures of a high relief stand out from the background; but gradually they were freed from the chaos of impressions which had given them birth, and then, little by little, they ceased to be gods; they were isolated from the world of the wonderful, they were respectfully shelved off into the region of the ideal, where they were contemplated, admired, discussed, but not worshipped, even like their statues by Praxiteles and their pictures by Parrhasius.* The divinities who continued to be reverenced were the rustic divinities and the foreign gods and goddesses; the divinities which had been safe from the artistic desecration of the cities, and the divinities which were imported from hieratic, unartistic countries like Egypt and Syria; on the one hand, the gods shaped with the pruning-knife out of figwood, and stained with ochre or wine-lees, grotesque mannikins, standing like scarecrows, in orchard or corn-field, to which the peasants crowded in devout procession, leading their cleanly-dressed little ones, and carrying gifts of fruit and milk, while the listless Tibullus,* fresh from sceptical Rome, looked on from his doorstep, a vague, childish veneration stealing over his mind; on the other hand, the monstrous goddesses, hundred-breasted or ibis-headed, half hidden in the Syrian and Egyptian temples, surrounded by mysterious priests, swarthy or effeminate, in mitres and tawny robes, jangling their sistra and clashing their cymbals, moving in mystic or frenzied dances, weird, obscene, and unearthly, to the melancholy drone of Phrygian or Egyptian music, sending a shudder through the atheist Catullus,* and filling his mind with ghastly visions of victims of the great goddess, bleeding, fainting, lashed on to madness by the wrath of the terrible divinity. These were the last survivors of paganism, and to their protection clung the old gods of Greece and Rome, reduced to human level by art, stripped naked by sculptor and poet and muffling themselves in the homely or barbaric garments of low-born or outlandish usurpers; art had been a worse enemy than scepticism: Apelles and Scopas had done more mischief than Epicurus.*

Christian art was, perhaps, more reverent in intention, but not less desecrating in practice; even the Giottesques turned Christ, the Virgin, and the Saints, into mere Florentine men and women; even Angelico* himself, although a saint, was unable to show Paradise except as a flowery meadow, under a highly gilded sky, through which moved ladies and youths in most artistic but most earthly embroidered garments; and Hell except as a very hot place where men and women were being boiled and broiled and baked and fried and roasted by very comic little weasel-snouted fiends, which on a carnival car would have made Florentines roar with laughter. The real supernatural was in the cells of fever-stricken, starved visionaries; it was in the contagious awe of the crowd sinking down at the sight of the stained napkin of Bolsena;* in that soiled piece of linen was Christ, and God, and Paradise; in that and not in the panels of Angelico and Perugino, or in the frescoes of Signorelli and Filippino.*

Why? Because the supernatural is nothing but ever-renewed impressions, ever-shifting fancies; and that art is the definer, the embodier, the analytic and synthetic force of form. Every artistic embodiment of impressions or fancies implies isolation of those impressions or fancies, selection, combination and balancing of them; that is to say, diminution—nay, destruction of their inherent power. As, in order to be moulded, the clay must be separated from the mound; as, in order to be carved, the wood must be cut off from the tree; as, in order to be re-shaped by art, the mass of atoms must be rudely severed; so also the mental elements of art, the mood, the fancy must be severed from the preceding and succeeding moods or fancies; artistic manipulation requires that its intellectual, like its tangible materials, cease to be vital, but the materials, mental or physical, are not only deprived of vitality and power of self-alteration; they are combined in given proportions, the action of the one on the other destroys in great part the special power of each; art is proportion, and proportion is restriction. Last of all, but most important, these isolated, no longer vital materials, neutralised by each other, are further reduced to insignificance by becoming parts of a whole conception; their separate meaning is effaced by the general meaning of the work of art; art bottles lightning to use it as white colour, and measures out thunder by the beat of the chapel-master's roll of notes. But art does not merely restrict impressions and fancies within the limits of form; in its days of maturity and independence it restricts yet closer within the limits of beauty. Partially developed art, still unconscious of its powers and aims, still in childish submission to religion, sets to work conscientiously, with no other object than to embody the supernatural; if the supernatural suffers in the act of embodiment, if the fluctuating fancies which are Zeus or Pallas are limited and curtailed, rendered logical and prosaic even in the wooden pre-historic idol or the roughly kneaded clay owlet, it is by no choice of the artist—his attempt is abortive, because it is thwarted by the very nature of his art. But when art is mature, things are different; the artist, conscious of his powers, instinctively recognising the futility of aiming at the embodiment of the supernatural, dragged by an irresistible longing to the display of his skill, to the imitation of the existing and to the creation of beauty, ceases to strain after the impossible and refuses to attempt anything beyond the possible. The art, which was before a mere insufficient means, is now an all-engrossing aim; unconsciously, perhaps, to himself, the artist regards the subject merely as a pretext for the treatment; and where the subject is opposed to such treatment as he desires, he sacrifices it. He may be quite as conscientious as his earliest predecessor, but his conscience has become an artistic conscience, he sees only as much as is within art's limits; the gods, or the saints, which were cloudy and supernatural to the artist of immature art, are definite and artistic to the artist of mature art; he can think, imagine, feel only in a given manner; his religious conceptions have taken the shape of his artistic creations; art has destroyed the supernatural, and the artist has swallowed up the believer. The attempts at supernatural effects are almost always limited to a sort of symbolical abbreviation, which satisfies the artist and his public respecting the subject of the work, and lends it a traditional association of the supernatural; a few spikes round the head of a young man are all that remains of the solar nature of Apollo; the little budding horns and pointed ears of the satyr must suffice to recall that he was once a mystic fusion of man and beast and forest; a gilded disc behind the head is all that shows that Giotto's figures are immortals in glory; and a pair of wings is all that explains that Perugino's St. Michael is not a mere dainty mortal warrior; the highest mysteries of Christianity are despatched with a triangle and an open book, to draw which Raphael might employ his colour-grinder, while he himself drew the finely-draped baker's daughter from Trastevere.*

In all these cases the artist refused to grapple with the supernatural, and dismissed it with a mere stereotyped symbol, not more artistic than the names which he might have engraved beneath each figure. Religious associations were thus awakened without the artist, whether of the time of Pericles or of the time of Leo X.,* giving himself further trouble; the diffusion of religious ideas and feeling spared art from being religious. Let us, therefore, in order to judge fairly of what art can or cannot do for the supernatural, seek for one of the very rare instances in which the artist has had no symbolical abbreviations at his disposal, and has been obliged, if he would awaken any idea in the mind of the spectator, to do so by means of his artistic creations. The number of such exceptional instances is extremely limited in the great art of antiquity and the Renaissance, when artistic subjects were almost always traditionally religious or plainly realistic, and consequently intelligible at first sight. There is, however, an example, and that example is a masterpiece. It is the engraving by Agostino Veneziano, after a lost drawing by Raphael, generally called "Lo Stregozzo,"* and representing a witch going to the Sabbath. Through a swampy country, amidst rank and barren vegetation, sweeps the triumphal procession—strange, beautiful, and ghastly; a naked boy dashes headlong in front, bestriding a long-haired he-goat, and blowing a horn, little stolen children packed behind on his saddle; on he dashes, across the tufts of marsh-lily and bulrush, across the stagnant pools of water, clearing the way and announcing his mistress the witch. She thrones, old, parched, lank, high on the top of an unearthly car, made of the spine and ribs of some antediluvian creature, with springs and traces of ghastly jaw and collar and thigh bones, supported on either side by galloping skeletons, skeletons made up of skeletons, of all that is strangest in the bones and beaks of beasts and birds, on which ride young fauns and satyrs. To her chariot, by a yoke of human bones, are harnessed two stalwart naked youths, and two others sustain its plough-like end; grand, magnificently moving figures, bounding forward like wild horses, the unearthly carriage swinging and creaking as they go. And, as they go, brushing through the high, dry, maremma-grass, the witch cowers on her chariot, clutching in one hand a heap of babies, in the other a vessel filled with fire, whose smoke, mingling with her long, dishevelled hair, floats behind, sweeping through the rank vegetation, curling and eddying into vague, strange semblances of lions, apes, chimæras. Forward dashes the outrunner on his goat, onward bound the naked litter-bearers; up gallop the fauns and satyrs on the fleshless, monstrous carcases; up and down sways the creaking, cracking chariot of bones; one moment more, and the wild, splendid, hideous triumph will have swept out of sight, leaving behind only trampled marsh-plants and a trail of fantastic, lurid smoke among the ruffled, moaning reeds and grasses.

Such is Raphael's *Stregozzo*. It is a master-piece of drawing and of pictorial fancy, it is perhaps the highest achievement of great art in the direction of the supernatural: for Dürer is often hideous, Rembrandt* always obscure, and the moderns, like Blake and Doré,* distinctly run counter to the essential nature of art in their attempts after vagueness. When once told the subject of the print, by Agostino Veneziano, our imagination easily flies off on to the track of the supernatural; but, in so doing, it leaves the work behind, and on return to it we experience a return to the natural. If, on the other hand, we are not told the subject of the print, we very possibly see nothing supernatural in it: there are splendid figures worthy of Michael Angelo, and grotesque fancies, in the shape of the skeletons and coach of bones, worthy of Leonardo; as a whole, the print is striking, beautiful, and problematic, but it falls short of the effect which would be produced by the mere words "a witch riding through a marsh on a chariot of bones," if left to insinuate themselves into the imagination. Of the really supernatural, there is in it but one touch: and that in the only part of the drawing which is left vague; it is the confused shapes assumed by the eddying smoke among the rushes. All the rest is outside the region of the supernatural: it is problematic in subject, but clear, harmonious, and beautiful in treatment; the imagination may wander off from it, but in its presence it must remain passive. With this masterpiece we would fain compare a picture which seems to deal with a cognate subject; a picture as suggestive as it is absolutely artistically worthless. We saw it once, many years ago, among a heap of rubbishy smudges at a picture-dealer's in Rome, and we have never forgotten it—a picture painted by some German smearer of the early sixteenth century; very ugly, stupid, and unattractive; ill drawn, ill composed, of a uniform hard, vulgar brown. It represented, with no attempt at perspective, a level country spread out like a map, dotted here and there with little spired and turretted towns, also a castle or two, a few trees and some rivers, disposed with a child's satisfaction with their mere indication, as much as to say—"here is a town, there is a castle." Some peasants were represented working in the fields, a little train of horsemen coming out of a castle, and near one of the chess-board castles a grass plot with half-a-dozen lit stakes, to which tiny figures were carrying faggots, while men-at-arms and burghers, no bigger than flies, looked on. In the foreground of the great flat expanse lay a boor, a fellow dressed like a field-labourer, in heavy sleep on the ground. Round him on the grass were marked curious circles, and in them was moving a strange figure, in cloak and helmet, with clawed wings and horns, leering horridly, moving round on tiptoe, his arms outstretched, as if gradually encircling the sleeper in order to pounce upon him; despite the complete absence of artistic skill, the gradual inevitable approach of the demon, the irresistible network of circles with which he was surrounding his prey, was perfectly indicated. Above, in the sky, two figures, half demon, half dragon, floated leisurely, like a moored boat, as if a guard of the devil below. What is the exact subject of this picture? No one can tell; but its meaning is intense for the imagination, it has the frightful suggestiveness of some old book on witchcraft, prosaic and curt; of a page opened at random of Sprenger's *Malleus Malificarum.** Yes; over the plain, the towns, and castles, monotonous and dull, the fiends are hovering; even over the stakes where their votaries are being burnt; and see, the peasant asleep in the field, with his spade and hoe beside him, is being surrounded by magic circles, by the invisible nets of the demon, who prowls round him like a kite ready to pounce on to its quarry.

Why is there no need to write the word *witchcraft* beneath this picture? Why can this nameless smearer succeed where Raphael has failed? Because he is content to suggest to the imagination, and lets it create for itself its world of the supernatural; because he is not an artist, and because Raphael is; because he suggests everything and shows nothing, while Raphael creates, defines, perfects, gives form to that which is by its nature formless.

If we would bring home to ourselves this action of art on the supernatural, we must examine the only species of supernatural which still retains vitality, and can still be deprived of it by art. That which remains to us of the imaginative workings of the past is traditional and well-nigh effete: we have poems and pictures, Vedic hymns, Hebrew psalms, and Egyptian symbols; we have folklore and dogma; remnants of the supernatural, some labelled in our historic museums, where they are scrutinised, catalogue and eye-glass in hand; others dusty on altars and in chapels, before which we uncover our heads and cast down our eyes: relics of dead and dying faiths, of which some are daily being transferred from the church to the museum;

art cannot deprive any of these of that imaginative life and power which they have long ceased to possess. We have forms of the supernatural in which we believe from acquiescence of habit, but they are not vital; we have a form of the supernatural in which, from logic and habit, we disbelieve, but which is vital; and this form of the supernatural is the ghostly. We none of us believe in ghosts as logical possibilities, but we most of us conceive them as imaginative probabilities; we can still feel the ghostly, and thence it is that a ghost is the only thing which can in any respect replace for us the divinities of old, and enable us to understand, if only for a minute, the imaginative power which they possessed, and of which they were despoiled not only by logic, but by art. By *ghost* we do not mean the vulgar apparition which is seen or heard in told or written tales; we mean the ghost which slowly rises up in our mind, the haunter not of corridors and staircases, but of our fancies. Just as the gods of primitive religions were the undulating, bright heat which made mid-day solitary and solemn as midnight; the warm damp, the sap-riser and expander of life; the sad dying away of the summer, and the leaden, suicidal sterility of winter; so the ghost, their only modern equivalent, is the damp, the darkness, the silence, the solitude; a ghost is the sound of our steps through a ruined cloister, where the ivy-berries and convolvulus growing in the fissures sway up and down among the sculptured foliage of the windows, it is the scent of mouldering plaster and mouldering bones from beneath the broken pavement; a ghost is the bright moonlight against which the cypresses stand out like black hearse-plumes, in which the blasted grey olives and the gnarled fig-trees stretch their branches over the broken walls like fantastic, knotted, beckoning fingers, and the abandoned villas on the outskirts of Italian towns, with the birds flying in and out of the unglazed windows, loom forth white and ghastly; a ghost is the long-closed room of one long dead, the faint smell of withered flowers, the rustle of long-unmoved curtains, the yellow paper and faded ribbons of long-unread letters... each and all of these things, and a hundred others besides, according to our nature, is a ghost, a vague feeling we can scarcely describe, a something pleasing and terrible which invades our whole consciousness, and which, confusedly embodied, we half dread to see behind us, we know not in what shape, if we look round.

Call we in our artist, or let us be our own artist; embody, let us see or hear this ghost, let it become visible or audible to others besides ourselves; paint us that vagueness, mould into shape that darkness, modulate into chords that silence—tell us the character and history of those vague beings.... set to work boldly or cunningly. What do we obtain? A picture, a piece of music, a story; but the ghost is gone. In its stead we get oftenest the mere image of a human being; call it a ghost if you will, it is none. And the more complete the artistic work, the less remains of the ghost. Why do those stories affect us most in which the ghost is heard but not seen? Why do those places affect us most of which we merely vaguely know that they are haunted? Why most of all those which look as if they might be haunted? Why, as soon as a figure is seen, is the charm half-lost? And why, even when there is a figure, is it kept so vague and mist-like? Would you know Hamlet's father for a ghost unless he told you he was one? and can you remember it long while he speaks in mortal words? and what would be Hamlet's father without the terrace of Elsinore, the hour, and the moonlight? Do not these embodied ghosts owe what little effect they still possess to their surroundings, and are not the surroundings the real ghost?

Throw sunshine on to them, and what remains? Thus we have wandered through the realm of the supernatural in a manner neither logical nor business-like, for logic and business-likeness are rude qualities, and scare away the ghostly; very far away do we seem to have rambled from Dr. Faustus and Helen of Sparta; but in this labyrinth of the fantastic there are sudden unexpected turns—and see, one of these has suddenly brought us back into their presence. For we have seen why the supernatural is always injured by artistic treatment, why therefore the confused images evoked in our mind by the mere threadbare tale of Faustus and Helena are superior in imaginative power to the picture carefully elaborated and shown us by Goethe. We can now understand why under his hand the infinite charm of the weird meeting of antiquity and the Middle Ages has evaporated. We can explain why the strange fancy of the classic Walpürgis-night, in the second part of *Faust*, at once stimulates the imagination and gives it nothing. If we let our mind dwell on that mysterious Pharsalian plain, with its glimmering fires and flamelets alone breaking the darkness, where Faust and Mephistopheles wandering about meet the spectres of antiquity, shadowy in the gloom—the sphinxes crouching, the sirens, the dryads and oreads, the griffons and cranes flapping their unseen wings overhead; where Faust springs on the back of Chiron,* and as he is borne along sickens for sudden joy when the centaur tells him that Helen has been carried on that back, has clasped that neck; when we let our mind work on all this, we are charmed by the weird meetings, the mysterious shapes which elbow us; but let us take up the volume and we return to barren prose, without colour or perfume. Yet Goethe felt the supernatural as we feel it, as it can be felt only in days of disbelief, when the more logical we become in our ideas, the more we view nature as a prosaic machine constructed by no one in particular, the more poignantly, on the other hand, do we feel the delight of the transient belief in the vague and the impossible; the greater the distinctness with which we see and understand all around us, the greater the longing for a momentary half-light in which forms may appear stranger, grander, vaguer than they are. We moderns seek in the world of the supernatural a renewal of the delightful semi-obscurity of vision and keenness of fancy of our childhood; when a glimpse into fairyland was still possible, when things appeared in false lights, brighter, more important, more magnificent than now. Art indeed can afford us calm and clear enjoyment of the beautiful—enjoyment serious, self-possessed, wide-awake, such as befits mature intellects; but no picture, no symphony, no poem, can give us that delight, that delusory, imaginative pleasure which we received as children from a tawdry engraving or a hideous doll; for around that doll there was an atmosphere of glory. In certain words, in certain sights, in certain snatches of melody, words, sights, and sounds which we now recognise as trivial, commonplace, and vulgar, there was an ineffable meaning; they were spells which opened doors into realms of wonder; they were precious in proportion as they were misappreciated. We now appreciate and despise; we see, we no longer imagine. And it is to replace this uncertainty of vision, this liberty of seeing in things much more than there is, which belongs to man and to mankind in this childhood, which compensated the Middle Ages for starvation and pestilence, and compensates the child for blows and lessons, it is to replace this that we crave after the supernatural, the ghostly—no longer believed, but still felt. It was from this sickness of the prosaic, this turning away from logical certainty, that the men of the end of the eighteenth and the beginning of this century, the men who had finally destroyed belief in the religious supernatural, who were bringing light with new sciences of economy, philology, and history—Schiller, Goethe, Herder, Coleridge*—left the lecture-room and the laboratory, and set gravely to work on ghostly tales and ballads. It was from this rebellion against the tyranny of the possible that Goethe was charmed with that culmination of all impossibilities, that most daring of ghost stories, the story of Faustus and Helena. He felt the seduction of the supernatural, he tried to embody it—and he failed.

The case was different with Marlowe. The bringing together of Faustus and Helena had no special meaning for the man of the sixteenth century, too far from antiquity and too near the Middle Ages to perceive as we do the strange difference between them; and the supernatural had no fascination in a time when it was all permeating and everywhere mixed with prose. The whole play of *Dr. Faustus* is conceived in a thoroughly realistic fashion; it is tragic, but not ghostly. To Marlowe's audience, and probably to Marlowe himself, despite his atheistic reputation, the story of Faustus's wonders and final damnation was quite within the realm of the possible; the intensity of the belief in the tale is shown by the total absence of any attempt to give it dignity or weirdness. Faustus evokes Lucifer with a pedantic semi-biblical Latin speech; he goes about playing the most trumpery conjuror's tricks—snatching with invisible hands the food from people's lips, clapping horns and tails on to courtiers for the Emperor's amusement, letting his legs be pulled off like boots, selling wisps of straw as horses, doing and saying things which could appear tragic and important, nay, even serious, only to people who took every second cat for a witch, who burned their neighbours for vomiting pins, who suspected devils at every turn, as the great witch-expert Sprenger shows them in his horribly matter-of-fact manual. We moderns, disbelieving in devilries, would require the most elaborately romantic and poetic accessories—a splendid lurid background, a magnificent Byronian invocation of the fiend. The Mephistophilis of Marlowe, in those days when devils still dwelt in people, required none of Goethe's wit or poetry; the mere fact of his being a devil, with the very real association of flame and brimstone in this world and the next, was sufficient to inspire interest in him; whereas in 1800, with Voltaire's novels and Hume's treatises* on the table, a dull devil was no more endurable than any other sort of bore. The very superiority of Marlowe is due to this absence of weirdness, to this complete realism; the last scene of the English play is infinitely above the end of the second part of *Faust* in tragic grandeur, just because Goethe made abortive attempts, after a conscious and artificial supernatural, while Marlowe was satisfied with perfect reality of situation. The position of Faustus, when the years of his pact have expired, and he awaits midnight, which will give him over to Lucifer, is as thoroughly natural in the eyes of Marlowe as is in the eyes of Shelley the position of Beatrice Cenci* awaiting the moment of execution. The conversation between Faustus and the scholars, after he has made his will, is terribly life-like: they disbelieve at first, pooh-pooh his danger; then, half-convinced, beg that a priest may be fetched; but Faustus cannot deal with priests. He bids them, in agony, go pray in the next room. "Aye, pray for me, pray for me, and what noise soever you hear, come not unto me, for nothing can save me.... Gentlemen, farewell; if I live till morning, I'll visit you; if not, Faustus is gone to hell."* Faustus remains alone for the one hour which separates him from his doom; he clutches at the passing time, he cries to the hours to stop with no rhetorical figure of speech, but with a terrible reality of agony:

> Let this hour be but
> A year, a month, a week, a natural day,
> That Faustus may repent and save his soul.

Time to repent, time to recoil from the horrible gulf into which he is being sucked; Christ, will Christ's blood not save him? He would leap up to heaven and cling fast, but Lucifer drags him down. He would seek annihilation in nature, be sucked into its senseless, feelingless mass...and, meanwhile, the time is passing, the interval of respite is shrinking and dwindling. Would that he were a soulless brute and might perish, or that at least eternal hell were finite—a thousand, a hundred thousand years let him suffer, but not for ever and without end! Mid-night begins striking. With convulsive agony he exclaims as the rain patters against the window:

> O soul, be changed into small water-drops,
> And fall into the ocean, ne'er be found.

But the twelfth stroke sounds; Lucifer and his crew enter; and when next morning the students, frightened by the horrible tempest and ghastly noises of the night, enter his study, they find Faustus lying dead, torn and mangled by the demon. All this is not supernatural in our sense; such scenes as this were real for Marlowe and his audience. Such cases were surely not unfrequent; more than one man certainly watched through such a night in hopeless agony, conscious, like Faustus, of pact with the fiend—awaiting, with earth and heaven shut and bolted against him, eternal hell.

In this story of Doctor Faustus, which, to Marlowe and his contemporaries, was not a romance but a reality, the episode of the evoking of Helen is extremely secondary in interest. To raise a dead woman was not more wonderful than to turn wisps of straw into horses, and it was perhaps considered the easier of the two miracles; the sense of the ordinary ghostly is absent, and the sense that Helen is the ghost of a whole long-dead civilisation, that sense which is for us the whole charm of the tale, could not exist in the sixteenth century. Goethe's Faust feels for Helen as Goethe himself might have felt, as Winckelmann* felt for a lost antique statue, as Schiller felt for the dead Olympus: a passion intensely imaginative and poetic, born of deep appreciation of antiquity, the essentially modern, passionate, nostalgic craving for the past. In Marlowe's play, on the contrary, Faustus and the students evoke Helen from a confused pedantic impression that an ancient lady must be as much superior to a modern lady as an ancient poem, be it even by Statius or Claudian,* must be superior to a modern poem—it is a humanistic fancy of the days of the revival of letters. But, by a strange phenomenon, Marlowe, once realising what Helen means, that she is the fairest of women, forgets the scholarly interest in her. Faustus, once in presence of the wonderful woman, forgets that he had summoned her up to gratify his and his friends' pedantry; he sees her, loves her, and bursts out into the splendid tirade full of passionate fancy:

> Was this the face that launched a thousand ships,
> And burnt the topless towers of Ilium?
> Sweet Helen, make me immortal with a kiss!
> Her lips suck forth my soul! See, where it flies!
> Come, Helen, come, give me my soul again.

Here will I dwell, for Heaven is in these lips,
And all is dross that is not Helena.
I will be Paris, and for love of thee,
Instead of Troy shall Wittenberg be sacked;
And I will combat with weak Menelaus,
And wear thy colours on my plumed crest;
Yea, I will wound Achilles in the heel,
And then return to Helen for a kiss.
Oh! thou art fairer than the evening air
Clad in the beauty of a thousand stars;
Brighter art thou than flaming Jupiter
When he appeared to hapless Semele;
More lovely than the monarch of the sky
In wanton Arethusa's azure arms;
And none but thou shalt be my paramour.

This is real passion for a real woman, a woman very different from the splendid semi-vivified statue of Goethe, the Helen with only the cold, bloodless, intellectual life which could be infused by enthusiastic studies of ancient literature and art, gleaming bright like marble or a spectre. This Helena of Marlowe is no antique; the Elizabethan dramatist, like the painter of the fifteenth century, could not conceive the purely antique, despite all the translating of ancient writers, and all the drawing from ancient marbles. One of the prose versions of the story of Faustus,* contains a quaint account of Helen, which sheds much light on Marlowe's conception:

This lady appeared before them in a most rich gowne of purple velvet, costly imbrodered; her haire hanged downe loose, as faire as the beaten gold, and of such length that it reached downe to her hammes; having most amorous cole-black eyes, a sweet and pleasant round face, with lips as red as a cherry; her cheeks of a rose colour, her mouth small, her neck white like a swan; tall and slender of personage; in summe, there was no imperfect place in her; she looked around about with a rolling hawk's eye, a smiling and wanton countenance, which neerehand inflamed the hearts of all the students, but that they persuaded themselves she was a spirit, which make them lightly passe away such fancies.

This fair dame in the velvet embroidered gown, with the long, hanging hair, this Helen of the original Faustus legend, is antique only in name; she belongs to the race of mediæval and modern women—the Lauras, Fiammettas, and Simonettas of Petrarch, Boccaccio, and Lorenzo dei Medici; she is the sister of that slily sentimental coquette, the Monna Lisa of Leonardo.* The strong and simple women of Homer, and even of Euripides, majestic and matronly even in shame, would repudiate this slender, smiling, ogling beauty; Briseis, though the captive of Achilles' spear,* would turn with scorn from her. The antique woman has a dignity due to her very inferiority and restrictedness of position; she has the simplicity, the completeness, the absence of everything suggestive of degradation, like that of some stately animal, pure in its animal nature. The modern woman, with more freedom and more ideal, rarely approaches to this character; she is too complex to be perfect, she is frail because she has an ideal, she is dubious because she is free, she may fall because she may rise. Helen deserted Menelaus and brought ruin upon Troy, therefore, in the eyes of Antiquity, she was the victim of fate, she might be unruffled, spotless, majestic; but to the man of the sixteenth century she was merely frail and false. The rolling hawk's eye and the wanton smile of the old legend-monger would have perplexed Homer, but they were necessary for Marlowe; his Helen was essentially modern, he had probably no inkling that an antique Helen as distinguished from a modern could exist. In the paramour of Faustus he saw merely the most beautiful woman, some fair and wanton creature, dressed not in chaste and majestic antique drapery, but in fantastic garments of lawn, like those of Hero in his own poem:*

> The lining purple silk, with gilt stars drawn;
> Her wide sleeves green, and bordered with a grove
> Where Venus, in her naked glory strove
> To please the careless and disdainful eyes
> Of proud Adonis, that before her lies;
> Her kirtle blue....
> Upon her head she wore a myrtle wreath
> From whence her veil reached to the ground beneath;
> Her veil was artificial flowers and leaves
> Whose workmanship both man and beast deceives.

Some slim and dainty goddess of Botticelli,* very mortal withal, long and sinuous, tightly clad in brocaded garments and clinging cobweb veils, beautiful with the delicate, diaphanous beauty, rather emaciated and hectic, of high rank, and the conscious, elaborate fascination of a woman of fashion—a creature whom, like the Gioconda, Leonardo might have spent years in decking and painting, ever changing the ornaments and ever altering the portrait; to whom courtly poets like Bembo and Castiglione* might have written scores of sonnets and canzoni to her hands, her eyes, her hair, her lips, a fanciful inventory to which she listened languidly under the cypresses of Florentine gardens. Some such being, even rarer and more dubious for being an exotic in the England of Elizabeth, was Marlowe's Helen; such, and not a ghostly figure, descended from a pedestal, white and marble-like in her unruffled drapery, walking with solid step and unswerving, placid glance through the study, crammed with books, and vials, and strange instruments, of the mediæval wizard of Wittenberg. Marlowe deluded himself as well as Faustus, and palmed off on to him a mere modern lady. To raise a real spectre of the antique is a craving of our own century; Goethe attempted to do it and failed, for what reasons we have seen; but we have all of us the charm wherewith to evoke for ourselves a real Helena, on condition that, unlike Faustus and unlike Goethe, we seek not to show her to others, and remain satisfied if the weird and glorious figure haunt only our own imagination.

APPENDIX B

TO

FLORA PRIESTLEY AND *ARTHUR LEMON**

Are Dedicated

DIONEA, AMOUR DURE,

AND THESE PAGES OF INTRODUCTION AND APOLOGY

PREFACE

We were talking last evening—as the blue moon-mist poured in through the old-fashioned grated window, and mingled with our yellow lamplight at table—we were talking of a certain castle whose heir is initiated (as folk tell) on his twenty-first birthday to the knowledge of a secret so terrible as to overshadow his subsequent life.* It struck us, discussing idly the various mysteries and terrors that may lie behind this fact or this fable, that no doom or horror conceivable and to be defined in words could ever adequately solve this riddle; that no reality of dreadfulness could seem aught but paltry, bearable, and easy to face in comparison with this vague we know not what.

And this leads me to say, that it seems to me that the supernatural, in order to call forth those sensations, terrible to our ancestors and terrible but delicious to ourselves, sceptical posterity, must necessarily, and with but a few exceptions, remain enwrapped in mystery. Indeed, 'tis the mystery that touches us, the vague shroud of moonbeams that hangs about the haunting lady, the glint on the warrior's breastplate, the click of his unseen spurs, while the figure itself wanders forth, scarcely outlined, scarcely separated from the surrounding trees; or walks, and sucked back, ever and anon, into the flickering shadows.

A number of ingenious persons of our day, desirous of a pocket-superstition, as men of yore were greedy of a pocket-saint to carry about in gold and enamel, a number of highly reasoning men of semi-science have returned to the notion of our fathers, that ghosts have an existence outside our own fancy and emotion; and have culled from the experience of some Jemima Jackson, who fifty years ago, being nine years of age, saw her maiden aunt appear six months after decease, abundant proof of this fact. One feels glad to think the maiden aunt should have walked about after death, if it afforded her any satisfaction, poor soul! but one is struck by the extreme uninterestingness of this lady's appearance in the spirit, corresponding perhaps to her want of charm while in the flesh. Altogether one quite agrees, having duly perused the collection of evidence on the subject, with the wisdom of these modern ghost-experts, when they affirm that you can always tell a genuine ghost-story by the circumstance of its being about a nobody, its having no point or picturesqueness, and being, generally speaking, flat, stale, and unprofitable.

A genuine ghost-story! But then they are not genuine ghost-stories, those tales that tingle through our additional sense, the sense of the supernatural, and fill places, nay whole epochs, with their strange perfume of witchgarden flowers.

No, alas! neither the story of the murdered King of Denmark (murdered people, I am told, usually stay quiet, as a scientific fact), nor of that weird woman who saw King James the Poet three times with his shroud wrapped ever higher; nor the tale of the finger of the bronze Venus closing over the wedding-ring, whether told by Morris in verse patterned like some tapestry, or by Mérimée* in terror of cynical reality, or droned by the original mediæval professional storyteller, none of these are genuine ghost-stories. They exist, these ghosts, only in our minds, in the minds of those dead folk; they have never stumbled and fumbled about, with Jemima Jackson's maiden aunt, among the arm-chairs and rep* sofas of reality.

They are things of the imagination, born there, bred there, sprung from the strange confused heaps, half-rubbish, half-treasure, which lie in our fancy, heaps of half-faded recollections, of fragmentary vivid impressions, litter of multi-coloured tatters, and faded herbs and flowers, whence arises that odour (we all know it), musty and damp, but penetratingly sweet and intoxicatingly heady, which hangs in the air when the ghost has swept through the unopened door, and the flickering flames of candle and fire start up once more after waning.

The genuine ghost? And is not this he, or she, this one born of ourselves, of the weird places we have seen, the strange stories we have heard—this one, and not the aunt of Miss Jemima Jackson? For what use, I entreat you to tell me, is that respectable spinster's vision? Was she worth seeing, that aunt of hers, or would she, if followed, have led the way to any interesting brimstone or any endurable beatitude?

The supernatural can open the caves of Jamschid and scale the ladder of Jacob:* what use has it got if it land us in Islington or Shepherd's Bush?* It is well known that Dr. Faustus,* having been offered any ghost he chose, boldly selected, for Mephistopheles to convey, no less a person than Helena of Troy. Imagine if the familiar fiend had summoned up some Miss Jemima Jackson's Aunt of Antiquity!

That is the thing—the Past, the more or less remote Past, of which the prose is clean obliterated by distance—that is the place to get our ghosts from. Indeed we live ourselves, we educated folk of modern times, on the borderland of the Past, in houses looking down on its troubadours' orchards and Greek folks' pillared courtyards; and a legion of ghosts, very vague and changeful, are perpetually to and fro, fetching and carrying for us between it and the Present.

Hence, my four little tales are of no genuine ghosts in the scientific sense; they tell of no hauntings such as could be contributed by the Society for Psychical Research,* of no spectres that can be caught in definite places and made to dictate judicial evidence. My ghosts are what you call spurious ghosts (according to me the only genuine ones), of whom I can affirm only one thing, that they haunted certain brains, and have haunted, among others, my own and my friends'—yours, dear Arthur Lemon, along the dim twilit tracks, among the high growing bracken and the spectral pines, of the south country; and yours, amidst the mist of moonbeams and olive-branches, dear Flora Priestley, while the moonlit sea moaned and rattled against the mouldering walls of the house whence Shelley* set sail for eternity.

VERNON LEE

Maiano, *near* Florence,
June 1889

EXPLANATORY NOTES

ABBREVIATIONS

H	Vernon Lee, *Hauntings* (1890)
FM	Vernon Lee, *For Maurice: Five Unlikely Stories* (1927)
OED	*Oxford English Dictionary*
SL I	*Selected Letters of Vernon Lee, 1856–1935*, vol. I, ed. Amanda Gagel (London and New York, 2016)
SL II	*Selected Letters of Vernon Lee, 1856–1935*, vol. II, ed. Sophie Geoffroy (London and New York, 2021)
Symonds	John Addington Symonds, *The Renaissance in Italy* (New York, 1881)

WINTHROP'S ADVENTURE

First published in the January 1881 number of *Fraser's Magazine*, as well as in the April 1881 number of the American *Appletons' Journal*, as 'A Culture-Ghost: or, Winthrop's Adventure'. Nearly half a century later, Lee included it, with the shortened title 'Winthrop's Adventure', in *For Maurice* (1927), along with a lengthy account of how it came to be written. The origins of both this story and its later reimagining as 'A Wicked Voice' lay in her visits, with John Singer Sargent, to Bologna's Accademia Filarmonica in 1873, where they found themselves 'spell-bound' by painter Corrado Giaquinto's (1703–66) portrait of the celebrated castrato singer Carlo Broschi, known as Farinelli (1705–82). On a 'thunder-stormy night in a derelict villa', Lee wrought herself into a state of near-panic, writing

> into the small hours, sitting quite alone in an Italian country house with all the servants long gone to bed, the lamp guttering and owls hooting. So that night over the first version of *Winthrop's Adventure* was a *bonâ fide*, indeed my only, ghostly experience, complete with cold hands, dank hair, a thumping heart and eyes one didn't dare to raise from the writing table for fear of dark corners; and, as regards the final wrench, the opening of doors, the (at last!) refuge in bed, all *that* was so terrible as to have left no more memory behind than if I had fainted before my manuscript till the next morning. (*FM*, xxxv)

3 *Julian Winthrop*: based on John Singer Sargent; Lee would later describe the story as 'about how "I", who was also of course John, spent a thunder-stormy night in a derelict villa and there encountered . . . a vocal ghost who was Farinelli's' (*FM*, xxxiv).

Bellosguardo: hill outside Florence (the name means 'beautiful view'); at the time a neighbourhood particularly favoured by British and American residents.

4 *Gubbio majolica*: fine, tin-glazed Renaissance Italian earthenware; particularly renowned is the work of master potter Giorgio Andreoli (*c.*1465/70–1553), who worked in the Umbrian town of Gubbio.

5 *Barbella*: perhaps Lee has borrowed the name from Charles Burney's friend, the Neapolitan violinist and composer Emanuele Barbella (1718–77).

some now disused clef: one of the C clefs, five of which were utilized by composers until the end of the eighteenth century; today only the tenor is in regular use (the alto is occasionally used). Lee recalled how in Bologna she and Sargent 'would spend hours over the portfolios of prints and the unreadable (for they were bristling with various clefs of *Ut* [C]) scores of the music school'.

"Sei Regina, io son pastore": 'You are queen, I am a shepherd'. Invented aria, perhaps suggestive of an alternative version of *Il re pastore* ('The Shepherd King'), a libretto by Pietro Metastasio (the subject of one of the essays in *Studies of the Eighteenth Century in Italy*) which was set by around 25 composers in the eighteenth century, most famously Mozart in 1775 (in 1751 Metastasio recommended the first version, by composer Giuseppe Bonno, to Farinelli, then in Spain). One hears echoes here of the line 'io sono Aminta, e son pastore' ('I am Aminta, and I am a shepherd'), blended with the aria 'Bella Regina' ('Beautiful Queen').

9 *Lombardy*: region of Northern Italy; Lee's 'quaint Lombard city' of M—— is difficult to place exactly (Milan, the Lombard capital, is a very poor fit). The best candidates would seem to be Modena and Mantua, both of which are close to 'the neighbouring Bologna'. Modena is nearer to Bologna, but is actually in the Emilia-Romagna region. The reference to the Montagues and Capulets (see note to p. 19 [*Montagus and Capulets*]) suggests Mantua. Some details fit either city (the presence of a cathedral) or neither (i.e. the equestrian statue described in the story), while others suggest Bologna itself, where Lee and Singer encountered the portrait that inspired the story (see Headnote). Probably it is best to regard M— as, to some extent at least, a composite invention.

snuffy: here, most likely, 'bearing the marks of a snuff user' (as the same adjective is later applied to his coat).

10 *friskiness*: liveliness.

Cremonese fiddle: the Lombard city of Cremona was home to the Amati, Guarneri, Stradivari, and Rugeri families and the centre of violin production in the seventeenth and eighteenth centuries (see note to p. 15 [*Amati's fiddles*]).

soldino: i.e. penny.

11 *chlamys-robed auletes, and citharoedi*: in ancient Greece, the chlamys was a short cloak, the aulos a reed instrument, and the cithara a stringed instrument; 'auletes' and 'citharoedi' are aulos- and cithara-players, respectively.

tamtams: Chinese gongs.

Palestrina: Giovanni Pierluigi da Palestrina (*c.*1525–94), great Renaissance composer of sacred music and madrigals.

12 *Raphael*: painter and architect (1483–1520); with Leonardo da Vinci and Michelangelo, one of the 'big three' of the Italian High Renaissance in art.

Cenci fashion: refers to the pose of the figure traditionally identified as Beatrice Cenci (1577–99) in the famous 1599 portrait formerly attributed to Bolognese painter Guido Reni (1575–1642).

Greuze: French painter Jean-Baptiste Greuze (1725–1805); even admirers and friends such as philosopher Denis Diderot and writer and salonnière Manon Roland commented on the excessive 'greyness' of his canvases.

Rinaldi: fictitious; as discussed in the headnote, inspired partly by the celebrated castrato singer Farinelli (1705–82).

13 *Madame Banti*: Brigida Banti (1757–1806), renowned Italian soprano of humble origins; in his *Memoirs*, Mozart's librettist, Lorenzo Da Ponte, wrote: 'Accustomed from early girlhood to singing in cafés and about the streets, she brought to the Opera, whither her voice only had elevated her, all the habits, manners, and customs of a brazen-faced Corisca [wanton nymph]' (trans. Elisabeth Abbott (New York, 2000), 234). Lee is more sympathetic, writing of 'the poor untaught girl who was later to be called Banti, the most pathetic female singer of the latter part of the eighteenth century' (*S18*, 139–40). A Victorian history of opera gives the following account of Banti's posthumous laryngeal bequest (a legacy Lee is presumably extending to include the lungs as well): 'Banti died at Bologna . . . bequeathing her larynx (of extraordinary size) to the town, the municipality of which caused it to be duly preserved in a glass bottle' (Henry Sutherland Edwards, *History of Opera, from its Origin in Italy to the Present Time*, vol. 2 (London, 1862), 12).

the green bronze condottiere . . . bronze charger: there are a number of equestrian statues of Renaissance *condottieri* (mercenary or military leaders), famous examples being Donatello's statue of Erasmo da Narni ('Gattamelata') in Padua (1453) and Andrea del Verrocchio's of Bartolomeo Colleoni in Venice (1480s). If Lee has Mantua in mind, this statue might be imagined to be of Ludovico Gonzago (1412–78).

14 *Guido of Arezzo's "Micrologus"*: Guido of Arezzo (*c.*990–1050?), Benedictine monk and music theorist whose treatise *Micrologus* (*c.*1026) originated Western solmization: the association of notes with particular syllables, initially ut–re–mi–fa–so–la (whence, ultimately, the nickname 'Fa Diesis'). Burney wrote: 'Guido . . . is one of those favoured names to which the liberality of posterity knows no bounds. He has long been regarded in the empire of music as Lord of the Manor' (*History of Music*, vol. 1 (London, 1782), 458).

15 *Amati's fiddles*: the Amati were a family of Cremonese violin makers; Andrea Amati (*c.*1505–77) had made a group of stringed instruments for the Court of French king Charles IX (1550–74).

15 *marenghi*: 'A Lombard coin struck by Napoleon after the battle of Marengo, and by which people still occasionally count' (Lee's note). Gold coin worth 20 lire.

Basta!: enough!

16 *Convent of the Clarisse*: the Poor Clares are a Franciscan order of nuns; there was a Poor Clares convent in Mantua (the *Convento di Santa Lucia*), suppressed in 1786, a few years after the Marchese Negri was supposed to have entered it (if, again, M— is to be identified, or identified primarily, with Mantua). Elizabeth Gaskell, a likely early influence on Lee as a Gothic writer, had published her story, 'The Poor Clare', in 1856.

the Dance of Death: also called the *Danse Macabre*, a medieval genre which found representation in art, literature, and music.

Guastalla: town in Emilia-Romagna.

18 *Per Bacco!*: By Bacchus! (the Roman god of wine).

"*Libertas*": Latin for 'liberty'.

Crevalcuore: Crevalcore, town near Bologna.

19 *Montagus and Capulets*: the Montecchi (usually spelled 'Montague' in English) and Capuleti, feuding medieval families immortalized in Shakespeare's *Romeo and Juliet* (set in Verona and Mantua).

20 *the imperial eagle of Austria... German Caesars*: the double-headed eagle of the Holy Roman Empire and the Austrian Empire (*Kaiserthum*, with 'Kaiser' being linguistically a 'German Caesar') which succeeded it in 1804, and of which Lombardy had been a part, until being incorporated into the new Kingdom of Italy in 1866.

21 *Rondò di Cajo Gracco... that old opera of Cimarosa's*: Domenico Cimarosa (1749–1801), major opera composer of the late eighteenth century whose music Lee admired (and about whom she wrote in *Studies of the Eighteenth Century in Italy* and elsewhere). Cimarosa never composed a *Cajo Gracco* (i.e. Gaius Gracchus, a Roman Tribune), though Leonardo Leo and Giovanni Buononcini both did; he did compose a *Caio Mario* (*Gaius Marius*). 'Mille pene mio tesoro' is an (invented) aria for Lee's (invented) opera. It is a particularly late-eighteenth-century showpiece type of aria called a *rondò* (not to be confused with a 'rondo', without accented 'o'). Aria 'titles' are simply the first few words of the lyric; this one translates to 'A thousand pains, my darling [treasure]', and recalls the arias 'Mille pene' from the second act of Christoph Willibald Gluck's *Orfeo ed Euridice* (1762) and 'il mio tesoro' from the second act of Mozart's *Don Giovanni* (1787).

22 *albo lapillo*: Latin, 'white stone'; i.e. to have his name remembered as significant, as the Romans marked memorable days on the calendar with a white stone or piece of chalk.

the Ducal family of Sforza: the House of Sforza was one of the most powerful and important in Renaissance Italy.

It was St. John's Eve: the night before the Feast Day of St John the Baptist (24 June), on which 'Saint John's Fires' are traditionally lit throughout Europe; as with other solstice celebrations, it has supernatural associations as well.

23 *Carthusian monastery*: the Carthusians are a Catholic religious order founded in the eleventh century.

illustrissimo: most illustrious.

24 *classic distaff*: old-fashioned spindle.

Charlemagne... "Reali di Francia": *I Reali di Francia* ('The Royalty of France') is a compilation of legends by Tuscan writer and ballad singer Andrea da Barberino (*c.*1370–1431) concerning Charlemagne (748–814), the first Holy Roman Emperor ('Emperor of the Romans').

Milord Vellingtone: clearly a reference to the Duke of Wellington, but the meaning is obscure, as the first (and famous) Duke had then been dead for a quarter-century; perhaps that is the joke?

Bologna... St Petronius's Day... the Caracci: Saint Petronius was a fifth-century bishop, and subsequently a patron saint, of the city of Bologna; the Carracci were a family of Bolognese artists.

26 *Avvocato*: title for a lawyer; indicates the acquisition of an aristocratic property by a wealthy member of the middle classes.

28 *corpo di Bacco!*: by the body of Bacchus!

Via!: Go! Come on!

Abate: priest, abbot.

29 *saint of ours... tongs*: tenth-century English (and therefore 'ours') bishop St Dunstan, supposed to have held the devil's nose with a pair of tongs.

Forestiere: 'a stranger—a foreigner', as the priest called him earlier.

30 *silkworms*: silk cultivation in Italy dates from the eleventh century CE, and flourished in Bologna and elsewhere, including Veneto where 'A Wicked Voice' (which also depicts implements of sericulture) is set.

31 *pressed the repeater*: 'repeating watches' chimed on demand.

32 *"oeil de boeuf"*: literally ox-eye or bull's-eye; particularly prominent in Baroque architecture.

a black silk bag: 'bag-wigs' were fashionable in the eighteenth century.

OKE OF OKEHURST; OR, THE PHANTOM LOVER

Initially published as a 'shilling shocker' by William Blackwood, titled 'A Phantom Lover: A Fantastic Story' (Edinburgh and London, 1886). Lee had offered the story to Blackwood as 'Oke of Okehurst', in a letter showing that she had not forgotten his rejection of 'Medea' on the basis of its supposed historical accuracy ('On the slight chance of its fitting into Maga [*Blackwood's Magazine*] I send you herewith another eerie story called *Oke of Okehurst*. No one with the best wile in the world could take *this* for a historical treatise')

(*SL* II, 169). On Blackwood's offering to publish the story as a book rather than in the pages of 'Maga', Lee declared herself thrilled ('I have always dearly wished to produce a shilling dreadful, little guessing that I had produced one unconsciously'). Upon its publication, a reviewer for the *St. James's Gazette* wrote, '"A Phantom Lover" is probably the best shilling story since "Dr. Jekyll." It is short, it is startling.' In *Hauntings* (1890) the story, third in order, was titled 'Oke of Okehurst; or, The Phantom Lover'. As is so often the case in Lee's fiction, the novella blends and crystallizes a range of her contemporaneous experiences: places visited, personal encounters and infatuations, intellectual discoveries. The old Kentish manor where 'Oke' takes place is based on Godington House near Ashford, where Lee and Mary visited the poet and editor Alfred Austin and his wife, who lived in the old dower house of the estate. (This is almost alone among Lee's fantastic tales in having an English setting; there is also 'The Hidden Door', in Lee's words 'a North country ghost story', written at around the same time as 'Oke'. 'The Hidden Door', which verges on genre parody, was published alongside tales by F. Marion Crawford, Anne Crawford, and Mary Robinson in *Unwin's Annual* of 1887.) There is no doubt something of Austin—of both Austins—in William Oke, Lee's 'regular Kentish Tory' squire, conventional to a fault and full of talk of 'the Primrose League, and the iniquities of Mr. Gladstone'. (After visiting the Austins Lee wrote to her mother, 'Of course they are blue Tories, Mrs Austin being Secretary of a Primrose League', apparently the first time Lee had heard of the Conservative organization, newly formed in honour of Gladstone's parliamentary nemesis, the late Benjamin Disraeli; her first impression of Alfred Austin had been of 'rather a self conceited little man, who spouts a sort of utilitarian toryism' (*SL* II, 87–9).) Meanwhile, Oke's wife, cousin, and tormentor—the 'graceful', 'exquisite', 'exotic', and above all 'wayward' Alice Oke—is modelled after Lady Archibald Campbell, with whom Lee had become fascinated after seeing her perform in John Fletcher's pastoral play *The Faithful Shepherdess* a few weeks before her trip to Kent: 'I am enclined [*sic*] to think Lady A. must be a very clever, delightful, fantastic wayward creature . . . a very tall . . . strong, but extremely supple & graceful creature, with mobile nervous face . . . perhaps a little touched by the craziness in her family. I am dying to know her' (*SL* II, 62). Lee invests both of her Okes with a little—more than a little—'craziness', adds a catalyst in the form of a painter-narrator modelled (like Winthrop) on Sargent, and invites the reader to witness the slow unfolding of the tragedy which follows. As discussed in the Introduction, Lee's reading in psychological theory influenced the novella: Lee admired immensely her friend Paul Bourget's *Essais de la Psychologie Contemporaine* (1881–5), a series of psychological studies of eminent writers (his portrait of Baudelaire's 'malsain' ('unhealthy') mind contains one of the earliest discussions of late-nineteenth-century 'decadence'), agreeing to review Bourget's second series the same week she announced to Mary Robinson, 'I am writing Oke of Okehurst'. While at work on her story, Lee also devoured Hippolyte Taine's pioneering work of empirical psychology, *On Intelligence* (1870), reading it alongside Tolstoy's *War and Peace* ('I am quite happy over La Guerre et la Paix, still more so over

Taine's *De l'Intelligence*'). Here Taine deconstructs the comforting, common-sense distinction between hallucination and the apprehension of reality, which he calls 'a true hallucination': 'external perception, even when accurate, is an hallucination'. 'Phantom' is his term for all such mental events: everything we perceive is 'a phantom or hallucinatory semblance' ('Un fantôme ou simulacre hallucinatoire'). The floating apparition of a dead man's head and real people seen in the street (Taine's examples) are both and equally 'internal phantoms' ('fantômes intérieurs'), and determining which phantoms correspond to external realities can be a tricky business: 'Hence we see that the objects we touch, see, or perceive by any one of our senses, are nothing more than semblances or phantoms precisely similar to those which arise in the mind of a hypnotized person, a dreamer, a person laboring under hallucinations, or afflicted by subjective sensations . . . the phantom is produced . . . whether the sensation be normal or abnormal' (Hippolyte Taine, *On Intelligence*, vol. 2, trans. T. D. Haye (New York, 1875), 1–2). The French quotations (Lee read the French edition) are taken from Hippolyte Taine, *De l'Intelligence, Tome Second* (Paris, 1870).

Note that the story is presented here as it appeared in *Hauntings*; a chapter numbering error which crept into the tale upon its book publication has been corrected, however.

37 *To COUNT PETER BOUTOURLINE*: Russian poet; Lee would include him as one of the interlocutors in her book *Althea: A Second Book of Dialogues on Aspirations and Duties* (1894), as 'Boris'.

39 *the Park*: Hyde Park, London.

the Blues: the Royal Horse Guards, a cavalry regiment of the British Army; merged with the Royal Dragoons in 1969 to form the Blues and Royals.

a velvet coat: a sartorial feature associated with Bohemianism and aestheticism.

40 *Academy*: the Royal Academy of Arts, founded in the eighteenth century, which had moved in the 1860s to Burlington House on Piccadilly. John Singer Sargent, on whom the narrator of 'A Phantom Lover' is likely based, had exhibited at the Royal Academy since 1882, though he did not make a real splash there until 1887, with his *Carnation, Lily, Lily, Rose*. Like Lee's narrator, Sargent was a much sought-after portraitist.

41 *Morris furniture, Liberty rugs, and Mudie novels*: the poet, novelist, and designer William Morris (1834–96), enormously influential in the Arts and Crafts Movement, co-founded the decorative arts firm Morris, Marshall, Faulkner, & Co. in 1861 (it became Morris & Co. in 1875); Arthur Lasenby Liberty (1843–1917) opened his high-end department store in Regent Street in 1875 (Liberty & Co. would become famous for its own fabric designs, but imported Oriental carpets are likely what the narrator has in mind here). Mudie's, founded in 1842, was the preeminent commercial circulating library of the Victorian era.

a large red-brick house . . . of the time of James I: based on Godington House near Ashford in Kent, which this description well matches (its Jacobean exterior was constructed around a medieval hall). Lee and Mary Robinson had visited the poet Alfred Austin, who lived in a house on the estate, in 1885. A 1900 guidebook describes the manor house as a 'fine square Elizabethan [*sic*] structure with its red brick front, its clear outlines and its white stone windows... The park itself is richly timbered with stately oaks and beeches; indeed, one old oak standing close to the northern part of the house is said to be as old as any in East Kent' (Charles Igglesden, *A Saunter through Kent with Pen and Pencil* (Ashford, Kent, 1900), 51).

41 *My host received me in the hall... ship's hull*: cf. the description of Godington in *A Saunter through Kent*: 'It would be difficult in any country house to find such a grand old entrance hall as at Godington, with its loftiness, its great span, its dome-like ceiling, its rich oak carving... Rich oak carving we find everywhere, not only in the hall, but alongside the staircase, on the balustrades' (53). Visitors to Godington today may see the 'heraldic monsters' of the staircase's 'parapet' and the Toke family 'coats-of-arms' in the hall, among other details recorded by Lee. (Did the historical Toke family who lived there, as well as the great oak tree on the estate, suggest the name 'Oke'? As always with Lee, it is difficult to pin her ideas down to a single source.)

42 *damascened*: ornamented with a watered pattern.

43 *majolica*: fine, tin-glazed Renaissance Italian earthenware.

the Sleeping Beauty: Lee includes a variant of the Sleeping Beauty folk tale in *Tuscan Fairy Tales*, titled 'The Glass Coffin' (a different version of the story, bearing the same title, appears in the Grimm brothers' collection).

Vandyck: Sir Anthony Van Dyck (1599–1641), Flemish portrait painter, after 1632 court painter to Charles I, who granted him a knighthood.

44 *Baudelaire*: French poet Charles Baudelaire (1821–67), who explored the effects of hashish, wine, and opium in his book *Paradis Artificiels* (1860).

46 *Titian's and Tintoretto's women*: Titian (Tiziano Vecellio) (*c.*1485–1576) and Tintoretto (Jacopo Robusti) (1518–94), outstanding representatives of the Venetian school of Renaissance painting.

47 *Narcissus*: mythical youth of great beauty, condemned by Apollo to gaze unceasingly at his own reflected image.

48 *the Christian soldier kind of thing*: a potent strain of Victorian Christian militarism was captured in the hymn 'Onward, Christian Soldiers' (lyrics written in 1865 by Sabine Baring-Gould—discussed in the Introduction for his writing on myth and folklore—the music in 1871 by Arthur Sullivan of Gilbert and Sullivan fame).

50 *flat, stale, and unprofitable*: Hamlet, in his first meditation on suicide, laments: 'How weary, stale, flat and unprofitable | Seem to me all the uses of the world' (*Hamlet* 1.2); Lee also uses the phrase, or part of it, in the novella's dedication and in the Preface to *Hauntings*.

52 *Scotch wars...Agincourt*: the two Wars of Scottish Independence (1296–1328 and 1332–57) and the Battle of Agincourt (1415), a victory by the outnumbered English forces (Henry V's 'happy few') against the French.

57 *by some Bolognese master*: suggests representatives of the Baroque 'Bolognese School' such as Ludovico (1555–1619), Agostino (1557–1602) and Annibale (1560–1609) Carracci, Guido Reni (1575–1642), and Guercino (Giovanni Francesco Barbieri) (1591–1666). Reflecting on her youthful tastes in art, Lee would write, 'I spurned the Renaissance masters (Raphael, Titian, Michelangelo, et cetera), insisting that there was nothing to be found in their work but "technical" qualities. I much preferred the Bolognese painters (Guido Reni, Guercino, the Carracci brothers), on account of the "soul" they put into their canvases.' Vernon Lee, *Psychology of an Art Writer*, ed. Lucas Zwirner (New York, 2018), 25–6.

58 *Herrick, Waller, and Drayton...Dryope*: the fictitious Christopher Lovelock is modelled after real 'Cavalier Poets' (associated with, and loyal to, Charles I) such as Robert Herrick (bap. 1591–1674), Edmund Waller (1606–87), and (according to some classifications) Michael Drayton (1563–1631); most conspicuously, his name recalls that of the archetypal Cavalier poet Richard Lovelace (1618–57) (he also leaves a 'love lock' at the story's end). In Greek mythology, Dryope is a nymph who is transformed into a tree. This is usually, as in Ovid, a poplar, but as Lee and her narrator are careful to point out, the real clue here is not in the myth but in the name, which derives from 'oak'.

61 *genre painter*: painter of scenes from everyday life; in the words of an exactly contemporaneous text: 'Just as we call those genre canvases, whereon are painted idyls of the fireside, the roadside, and the farm, pictures of "real life"' (*OED*).

63 *spalliered*: i.e. 'espaliered', trained on a wooden lattice.

64 *ling*: heather.

65 *Appledore*: Kentish village.

68 *the Black Prince or Sidney*: knight and military commander Edward the Black Prince (1330–76) and poet, courtier, and soldier Sir Philip Sidney (1554–86), both associated with the chivalric ideal.

70 *the Primrose League,...Mr. Gladstone*: the two are related, as the former was a Conservative mass organization formed initially to frustrate the legislative agenda of the latter, Liberal Prime Minister William Ewart Gladstone (1809–98), during his second premiership. The League was founded in 1883 by Lord Randolph Churchill, and named after what was supposedly the late Tory statesman Benjamin Disraeli's favourite flower. Chief among the 'iniquities' discussed here would surely have been Gladstone's unhurried efforts to raise the Siege of Khartoum (1884–5) in which the popular General Charles George Gordon was killed. (Also see headnote to the story.)

74 *oast-houses*: kilns for hop-drying; Kent is, and has long been, a major English hop-growing region.

76 *a blue-ribbon man*: i.e. a teetotaller.

80 *like Jacob with the angel*: in Genesis 32.22–32, the Patriarch Jacob, while journeying back to Canaan, wrestles all night long with a figure variously called 'a man', 'God', and an 'angel'—a favourite subject for artists.

seedy: unwell.

81 *the "Vita Nuova"*: Dante Alighieri's exploration of the theme of courtly love (1294, first published in English translation in 1846).

82 *too much Buddhist literature... esoteric*: likely a reference to the brand of occult Buddhism promulgated by Theosophists such as Helena Blavatsky, Henry Steel Olcott, and Alfred Sinnett; Sinnett's recently published book *Esoteric Buddhism* (1883) shares Alice Oke's (and the novella's) interest in the topic of reincarnation.

Morris's 'Love is Enough': *Love is Enough, or The Freeing of Pharamond: A Morality* (1873), a long, masque-like poem by William Morris.

AMOUR DURE

First published in *Murray's Magazine* as 'Amour Dure: Passages from the Diary of Spiridion Trepka', and subsequently as the first story in *Hauntings*. Lee had been unable to sell the story, as 'Medea da Carpi', to William Blackwood, who viewed it as too 'historical', to Lee's amusement, or bemusement (see headnote to 'Oke of Okehurst').

84 SPIRIDION: Spiridon or Spyridon is a Greek name; there is a Saint Spyridon (*c*.270–348 CE) from Cyprus; Lee may have taken the name from George Sand's Gothic novel *Spiridion* (1839).

Urbania: Lee's 'Urbania' is at best a blend of history and imagination; in the sixteenth century, the real town of Urbania (which is in the Metauro Valley by the Apennines, rather than 'on the high Apennine ridge') would still have been called Castel Durante, as it was not renamed until 1636 (after Pope Urban VIII); as many of the references in the story demonstrate, Lee often has in mind the city of Urbino as well (for whose rulers, prominent among them Duke Federico da Montefeltro, Castel Durante served as a summer residence).

Vandals: Germanic tribe originally from present-day Poland; by extension any barbarian invader. Ironically, at the end of the story Spiridion will himself commit a fateful 'act of vandalism'.

Grimm or Mommsen: Herman Friedrich Grimm (1828–1901), art historian and critic and son of folklorist Wilhelm Grimm, and Theodor Mommsen (1817–1903) ('boring Mommsen', as Lee once called him in a letter), classical scholar and historian, especially famous for his multivolume *History of Rome* (1854–6).

Apennine... Montemurlo: the Apennine mountain range stretches along the length of Italy; the specific setting here is the Umbria–Marche Apennines. Penna San Giovanni, Fossombrone, and Mercatello are all in the Marche region; Sigillo is in Umbria, and Montemurlo is in Tuscany.

85 *Æneas Sylvius' Commentaries*: Enea Silvio Bartolomeo Piccolomini, Pope Pius II (1405–64), author of the autobiographical *Commentaries* (posthumously published in 1584).

86 *Signorelli's frescoes... La Fille de Mme. Angot*: Italian painter Luca Signorelli (*c*.1445–1523) is best known for his fresco cycle in Orvieto Cathedral's San Brizio Chapel (1499–1504), which had inspired two poems in Eugene Lee-Hamilton's 1884 collection *Apollo and Marsyas, and Other Poems*: 'On Signorelli's Fresco of the Resurrection' and 'On Signorelli's Fresco of the Binding of the Lost'; Lee may be thinking here, however, of one of the frescoes from his *Life of St Benedict* in the convent of Monte Oliveto, 'Benedict Discovers Totila's Deceit' (1499–1502), which foregrounds a particularly striking set of swaggering, *condottieri* like soldiers in 'parti-coloured' hose. The (Urbino-born) painter Raphael's good looks (and large eyes) were captured in several portraits. The Virgin Mary (Madonna) and her older cousin Elizabeth; their meeting while both were pregnant (with Jesus and John the Baptist, respectively), called the Visitation, was the subject of paintings by Raphael and Giotto, among many others (the meaning of the reference here is thus simply 'both young and old women'). The Sienese architect, engineer, and painter Francesco di Giorgio Martini (1439–1502) worked on the Ducal Palaces of both Urbino and Urbania. The American Elias Howe (1819–67) invented his lockstitch machine in 1845. The overheard discussions revolve around the politicians Marco Minghetti (1818–86) and Benedetto Cairoli (1825–89), the latter's failure to predict the French occupation of Tunisia in Northern Africa, and (most probably) the building of the new *Re Umberto* line of ironclad battleships. *La Fille de Madame Angot* ('The Daughter of Madame Angot') was an enormously popular 1872 operetta by French composer Charles Lecocq (1832–1918).

Mercury: Roman counterpart to Hermes, wing-footed god of travellers and trade.

Raphaels and Francias and Peruginos: three Renaissance painters. Raphael (1483–1520) was a pupil in Pietro Perugino's (*c*.1445/50–1523) shop; Francesco Francia (1447–1517) was influenced by both artists (a dubious story, related by Vasari, has him dying of depression at his inferiority to Raphael).

the Empire: i.e. in the early nineteenth-century Empire style, under Napoleonic rule.

the three Fates: in Greek and Roman mythology, three goddesses (as the Greek *Moirai*, Clotho, Lachesis, and Atropos; as the Roman *Parcæ*, Nona, Decima, and Morta) who spun out, measured, and cut the thread of man's destinies. There is a story in which the Greek *Moirai* change a mortal (Galanthis, servant to Alcmene, mother of Heracles) into a cat (or a weasel), but the connection here may be to witchcraft more generally.

86 *Sor Asdrubale*: a seeming connection to the historical Castel Durante/Urbania, near which local tradition places the Battle of Metaurus (207 BCE), in which the Carthaginian general Hasdrubal (i.e. *Asdrubale*) Barca (245–207 BCE) was defeated by the legions commanded by rival Roman politicians Gaius Claudius Nero and Marcus Livius Salinator.

the Pontifical Government: since 1625 the Duchy of Urbino had been a possession of the Papal States, which ceased to exist in 1870; presumably the meaning here is that Sor Asdrubale regrets the *end* of papal rule over the region.

San Pasquale Baylon: Paschal Baylón (1540–92), Franciscan lay brother; See also note to p. 235 [*St. Paschal Baylon*, 'Prince Alberic and the Snake Lady'].

87 *Dryasdusts*: dull, unimaginative scholars; after novelist Walter Scott's meta-character Jonas Dryasdust (and especially, perhaps, after that character's appropriation by Thomas Carlyle).

Gualterio's and Padre de Sanctis' histories: fictitious, though there is a 'Messer Raffaello Gualterio' of Orvieto mentioned in Vasari's 'Vita di Simone Mosca' (there was also a contemporary historian and politician named Filippo Antonio Gualterio).

Medea... Carpi: in Greek mythology, Medea of Colchis, on the coast of the Black Sea, married Jason after helping him win the Golden Fleece; when he later abandoned her for King Creon's daughter Glauce, she murdered Creon, Glauce, and her own children by Jason. Long associated with witchcraft and the use of poisons, and often mentioned in connection with Lucrezia Borgia. Carpi is a town in the Emilia-Romagna region of Italy.

Bianca Cappello... Lucrezia Borgia: Bianca Cappello (1548–87), Venetian noblewoman and mistress (subsequently wife) of Francesco I de' Medici, who in Symonds's words 'brought disgrace upon his line by marrying the infamous Bianca Capello [*sic*], after authorizing the murder of her previous husband. Bianca, though incapable of bearing children... pretend[ed] to have borne a son... Of the three mothers who served in this nefarious transaction, Bianca contrived to assassinate two, but not before one of the victims to her dread of exposure made full confession at the point of death' (Symonds, vol. 2, 695). Lucrezia Borgia (1480–1519), daughter of Rodrigo Borgia (1431–1503; afterwards Pope Alexander VI) and sister of Cesare Borgia (1475–1507), was long painted by historians (and novelists, poets, and librettists) as a serial poisoner and *femme fatale*, a judgment that began to be revised in the nineteenth century; Symonds wrote: 'History has at last done justice to the memory of this woman, whose long yellow hair was so beautiful, and whose character was so colourless. The legend which made her a poison-brewing Mænad has been proved a lie... Instead of viewing her with dread as a potent and malignant witch, we have to regard her with contempt as a feeble woman, soiled with sensual foulness from the cradle' (Symonds, vol. 1, 420–1).

a Malatesta of the Rimini family: the Malatesta were the ruling family of Rimini, a city on the Adriatic coast, approximately twenty miles north of Urbino; of the most infamous representative of the family, the fifteenth-century *condottiero* Sigismondo Pandolfo Malatesta (1417–68), Burckhardt wrote: 'Unscrupulousness, impiety, military skill and high culture have been seldom combined in one individual as in Sigismondo Malatesta' (Jacob Burckhardt, *The Civilisation of the Renaissance in Italy* (London, 1892), 33).

the Pico family: rulers of the city of Mirandola in the Emilia-Romagna region; the family's most famous representative was the philosopher and scholar Giovanni Pico della Mirandola (1463–94), the subject of one of the essays in Walter Pater's *The Renaissance*. His nephew was (like his father) named Giovanni Francesco Pico della Mirandola (1470–1533), whose name, however, was truncated as 'Gianfrancesco' rather than 'Giovanfrancesco'. This Pico was, interestingly, the author of a 1523 treatise in dialogue form titled *Strix* ('The Witch') in which Medea, among other mythological figures, is discussed.

Stimigliano: a village in the Lazio region; as nineteenth-century guidebooks point out, there is an Orsini castle in nearby Monte Rotondo.

the Orsini family: another old and powerful princely family which played a major role in shaping the course of medieval and Renaissance Italian history.

Orvieto: city in Umbria.

88 *Cupids*: the Roman equivalent to the Greek Eros is Amor or Cupid, son of Mars and Venus and god of love.

Varano of Camerino: Camerino is a town in the Apennines, in the Marche region bordering Umbria, long ruled by the noble da Varano family.

the barefooted sisters at Pesaro: presumably the Poor Clares convent in the city of Pesaro (the capital of the Province of Pesaro and Urbino); one member of this family, Camilla Battista da Varano (1458–1524), did in fact become a Poor Clare nun, in the abbey at Urbino.

89 *Narni*: Umbrian town, today perhaps best known for having given its name, in the Latin form (Narnia), to C. S. Lewis's fantasy world.

90 *Ulysses and the Sirens*: in the Odyssey, Circe warns Odysseus (Ulysses in Latin) not to let his crew hear the song of the bird-like Sirens, which lures men to their destruction.

Marcantonio Frangipani: Lee's fictitious representative of the historical Frangipani clan (an old Roman family) is well named, as Mark Antony (as depicted by Plutarch and others) was Cleopatra's besotted lover (see note to p. 91 [*Baroccio . . . Cleopatra at the feet of Augustus*]).

the convent of the Clarisse: the Poor Clares, or Order of Saint Clare, had monasteries in many Italian cities, including Urbino.

Ordelaffi . . . Romagnole family: the Ordelaffi were yet another noble Italian family, who ruled in the historical region of Romagna.

90 *Don Arcangelo Zappi*: fictitious; perhaps Lee has borrowed the name from poet, and member of the Arcadian Academy, Giambattista Felice Zappi (1667–1719), whom she discusses in her *Studies of the Eighteenth Century in Italy*.

91 *the taking of Rome fifteen years ago... Italianissimi*: the process of Italian unification (in which Piedmont played a central role throughout, prompting Sor Asdrubale's references to the 'Piedmontese') culminated in the capture of Rome on 20 September 1870; *Italianissimi* means 'most Italian' or truly Italian (and here, pro-unification).

Baroccio... Cleopatra at the feet of Augustus: Federico Barocci (*c.*1535–1612), known as Il Baroccio, painter whose native city was Urbino. The subject of this imagined painting is taken from the account by the first-century CE biographer Plutarch, later used by Shakespeare, among others; after the defeat of Mark Antony by Octavian (afterwards Caesar Augustus), Antony's paramour Cleopatra pleads with the victor.

Jean Goujon: French sculptor (*c.*1510–*c.*1565).

92 *Arethusa*: wood-nymph from Greek mythology; there are many artistic depictions of Arethusa, but the context suggests that Lee has in mind the numerous and famous Greek coins on which the head appears in profile, like Medea da Carpi's miniature.

posy: emblematic device, from 'poesy', poem or poetic composition.

Antonio Tassi, Gianbologna's pupil: perhaps an imaginary relation of the painter Agostino Tassi (1578–1644); the Flemish sculptor Giambologna (1529–1608) is a historical figure, however, whose equestrian statues include that of Cosimo I in Florence's *Piazza dell Signoria*.

familiaris ejus... ritibus sacrato: Lee has Spiridion translate most of this Latin: 'of his familiar angel or genius, vulgarly called "idolino" ["little idol", but in Italian, not Latin, hence "vulgarly" or "vernacularly" so-called]... being consecrated by the astrologers with certain rites'. There is a famous 'Idolino of Pesaro', a bronze Roman statue which later belonged to the Duke of Urbino—another connection, perhaps, with the city.

93 *Siena and Lucca*: Tuscan cities.

as Ovid might... of Pontus: the Roman poet Ovid (43 BCE–17/18 CE) was banished by Augustus to Tomis in the Black Sea region of Pontus; his sense of desolation and depression is expressed in works including the *Epistulae ex Ponto* ('Letters from Pontus').

amori: love affairs, amours; presumably fleeting and thus the opposite of an 'amour dure'.

bright washball-blue and gamboge walls: i.e. the colour of blue soap balls or bars; gamboge is orange-yellow.

94 *beau monde*: fashionable society.

like Goethe in Rome... welch mich versengend erquickt... Fraus: the German writer Johann Wolfgang von Goethe (1749–1832) made a pilgrimage to

Italy in 1786, which was the basis for his travel book *Italienische Reise* ('Italian Journey'), as well as the cycle of poems originally titled *Erotica Romana* (later *Roman Elegies*), one of which Spiridion (slightly mis)quotes here: Goethe waits to glimpse a 'creature' at a window who will 'scorch [him] with love'. *Frau* is German for 'woman'.

'cute: shrewd, sharp: from 'acute'.

Vittoria Accoramboni: (1557–85) Umbrian noblewoman whose life—and murder—formed the basis of Jacobean dramatist John Webster's tragedy *The White Devil* (1612).

Don Quixote: the mad knight of Miguel de Cervantes's great novel, honouring the old ideals of courtly love, idealizes a neighbouring farm-girl.

the race of... Bianca Cappellos: there are two Annia Galeria Faustinas, mother and daughter: the first was married to the Emperor Antoninus Pius, the second to the Emperor Marcus Aurelius. Of Faustina the Younger, historian Edward Gibbon wrote in his *History of the Decline and Fall of the Roman Empire*: 'Faustina, the daughter of Pius and the wife of Marcus, has been as much celebrated for her gallantries as for her beauty. The grave simplicity of the philosopher [Marcus Aurelius] was ill-calculated to engage her wanton levity, or to fix that unbounded passion for variety, which often discovered personal merit in the meanest of mankind. The Cupid of the ancients was, in general, a very sensual deity; and the amours of an empress, as they exact on her side the plainest advances, are seldom susceptible of much sentimental delicacy. Marcus was the only man in the empire who seemed ignorant or insensible of the irregularities of Faustina; which, according to the prejudices of every age, reflected some disgrace on the injured husband. He promoted several of her lovers to posts of honour and profit, and during a connexion of thirty years, invariably gave her proofs of the most tender confidence, and of a respect which ended not with her life' ((Cincinnati, 1859), 41). Marozia (*c*.890–937 CE) was a Roman noblewoman, characterized by Gibbon as one 'of two sister prostitutes' whose enormous 'influence' over the papacy 'was founded on their wealth and beauty, their political and amorous intrigues: the most strenuous of their lovers were rewarded with the Roman mitre, and their reign may have suggested to darker ages the fable of a female pope' (189). For Bianca Cappello, see note to p. 87 [*Bianca Cappello... Lucrezia Borgia*].

the Caffè Greco... Via Palombella: the Antico Caffè Greco is the oldest café in Rome, frequented, over the years, by Goethe, Lord Byron, and Richard Wagner, among others. Baedeker's 1881 *Handbook for Travellers* recommends the *Palombella* wine-house on the Via della Palombella ('at the back of the Pantheon to the right (with a better room on the first floor)').

Hamlet and... Doleful Countenance: Shakespeare's Prince Hamlet and Cervantes's Don Quixote (see note to p. 94 [*Don Quixote*]), dubbed 'El Caballero de la Triste Figura' (Knight of the Doleful or Sorrowful Countenance); i.e. archetypal figures of melancholy.

95 *Tacitus and Sallust... the great Malatestas... Cæsare Borgia*: Roman historians Publius Cornelius Tacitus (*c*.56–*c*.120 CE), whose *Annals* and *Histories* chronicle the rise and growth of the Roman Empire (with unforgettable portraits of such emperors as Caligula and Nero), and Sallust (86–*c*.35 BCE), author of *Catiline's War* and *The Jugurthine War*. For the Malatestas, see note to p. 87 [*a Malatesta of the Rimini family*]. Cesare Borgia, brother to Lucrezia (see note to p. 87 [*Bianca Cappello... Lucrezia Borgia*]) (in the course of his military campaigns, Borgia captured Urbino in 1502).

oubliette: dungeon.

96 *Trattoria La Stella d'Italia*: la Stella d'Italia (Star of Italy) has long been a symbolic representation of Italy; it took on special significance as an emblem of national unity after the political unification of Italy.

Plato as well as Petrarch: i.e. she could read Ancient Greek as easily as Italian.

"la pessima Medea"... her namesake of Colchis: 'the wicked Medea'; Bianca Cappello was known as 'la pessima Bianca'. Colchis was the homeland of the mythological Medea, on the East coast of the Black Sea (see note to p. 87 [*Medea... Carpi*]).

97 *Capuchin*: a religious order of Franciscan friars.

"chained up in hell... immortal bard": from the *Inferno* of Dante Alighieri (*c*.1265–1321) (the region of 'Caina' is named after the biblical fratricide Cain).

98 *Tramontana*: northern wind.

Vallombrosa: literally 'shaded valley', resort area outside of Florence; in a letter to Mary Robinson, Lee wrote: 'suddenly you turn a corner, and enter what from a distance had seemed a cold blue shadow on the mountain side, a dense forest of dark fir... After coming out of that Tuscan valley of olives & vines, you can't think how startling & lovely it is. Then, always climbing through the fir woods, you get to big meadows full of orchids and forget me nots—closed in by firs, with a great expanse of pale yellow beech wood on all the rocks above. That is Vallombrosa' (*SL* I, 412).

mewed up: caged, confined.

100 *Bronzino*: Mannerist Italian painter Agnolo di Cosimo (1503–72), known as Bronzino, renowned for his portraits, especially of the Medici family, which Symonds called 'Hard and cold, yet obviously true to life' (Symonds, vol. 1, 815). Of his portraits of academician Bartolomeo and his wife Lucrezia Panciatichi, Vasari wrote, 'so natural that they seem truly alive, and nothing is wanting in them save breath'. Lee probably had the portrait of Lucrezia Panciatichi in the Uffizi in mind here; Lucrezia wears a gold necklace bearing the words, 'Amour Dure Sans Fin' (love lasts without end). (The same painting figures in Henry James's novel *The Wings of the Dove*, in which one character muses, 'Splendid as she is, one doubts if she was good.')

stomacher: 'An ornamental covering for the chest (often covered with jewels) worn by women under the lacing of the bodice' (*OED*).

101 *it looks... of the Inquisition*: i.e. like a dungeon where suspected heretics are tortured by agents of the Catholic Inquisition.

rusks: wine biscuits.

"*Evivva, Medea!*": Long live Medea!

102 *Parcæ or Norns*: essentially, the Roman and Norse equivalents, respectively, of the three Fates of Greek mythology (see note to p. 86 [*the three Fates*]).

"*Nino*"... "*Viscere mie*": in Italian, 'Nino' is a diminutive of several names, but this sounds closer in meaning to the Spanish *niño* ('child'); 'mie viscere' literally means 'my insides' and is, indeed, a 'term of affection' (it can be found, for instance, in Goldoni's plays).

103 *San Giovanni Decollato*: 'the beheaded St John'. In the New Testament (Mark 6:21–9 and Matthew 14:3–11), Salome, the 'daughter of Herodias', dances for King Herod and demands John the Baptist's head on a platter ('charger'). Countless artists and writers would take inspiration from the story, famously Oscar Wilde in his play *Salome*, one year after the appearance of *Hauntings*.

104 *oratory*: in the context of Catholicism, a place of prayer (often private) technically distinguished from a parish church.

106 *the pedlar in "Winter's Tale"*: the rogue Autolycus, whose 'unbraided wares' are enumerated in Act IV, scene iv of Shakespeare's play.

107 *the daughter of Herodias*: see note to p. 103 [*San Giovanni Decollato*].

112 *Posen and Breslau*: Poznań and Wrocław, cities in Western Poland; in 1885, both were in the German Empire. The same year (1887) that 'Amour Dure' appeared in *Murray's Magazine*, Lee's essay collection *Juvenilia* was published, containing the essay 'Christkindchen', with similar recollections of Lee's own childhood Christmases in Germany.

DIONEA

The second story in *Hauntings*, for which collection it was long believed to have been written; like 'Voix Maudite' ('A Wicked Voice') and 'A Wedding Chest', however, it was first published in the jointly published bilingual monthly *Les Lettres et les Arts | Art and Letters: An Illustrated Review* (Dec. 1888; titled 'Dionéa' in the French-language edition), where it is strikingly illustrated by French painter and illustrator Paul Édouard Rosset-Granger (1853–1942). In June 1883, Lee wrote to her mother from Paris:

> I saw at the Louvre a very beautiful & singular thing, which I recommend to Eugene as a possible sonnet. It is a torso, half draped, of a Venus, found on the seashore at a place in Africa called *Tripoli Vecchio*—somewhere near Carthage, I presume—It has evidently been rolled for years & years in the surf, for it is all worn away, every line & curve softened, so that it looks ~~like~~ exquisitely soft and strange & creamy, hands, breasts & drapery all indicated clearly but washed by the sea into something soft, vague & lovely. (*SL* I, 423)

Eugene took the recommendation, and 'On a Surf-Rolled Torso of Venus' appeared the following year in *Apollo and Marsysas, and Other Poems*; meanwhile Lee's own response to the statue evolved into 'Dionea'. Another crucial influence on the story was the German poet Heinrich Heine's conceit, elaborated in the 1854 essay *Die Götter im Exil* ('The Gods in Exile'), of the survival of the classical deities as malevolent, or at least baleful, refugees in a Christian world. Imagining a recapitulation of the old myths in which 'the poor gods were compelled to flee ignominiously and conceal themselves under various disguises on earth', Heinrich writes of a

> metamorphosis into demons which the Greek and Roman gods underwent when Christianity achieved supreme control of the world. The superstition of the people ascribed to those gods a real but cursed existence . . . the Church . . . by no means declared the ancient gods to be myths, inventions of falsehood and error, as did the philosophers, but held them to be evil spirits, who, through the victory of Christ, had been hurled from the summit of their power, and now dragged along their miserable existences in the obscurity of dismantled temples or in enchanted groves, and by their diabolic arts, through lust and beauty, particularly through dancing and singing, lured to apostasy unsteadfast Christians who had lost their way in the forest. (*The Prose Writings of Heinrich Heine*, ed. Havelock Ellis (London, 1887), 268–9)

This idea influenced Walter Pater as well (see headnote to 'Marsyas in Flanders'). In her introduction to *Tuscan Fairy Tales*, Lee seems also to put Heine's conception into the 'mouths of the people'; identifying fairy tales with 'inanimate relics of much earlier beliefs . . . fragment[s] of broken-down mythology', she reports (or invents) an exchange with 'a woman from Barga' who declares to her, 'All the fairies, *folletti* [goblins or elves], and such like, were locked up by the council of Trent' (7–8).

115 *Sabina*: region in central Italy originally inhabited by the ancient Italian people called the *Sabini* (Sabines); the town of Palombara Sabina is associated historically with the Savelli family (see note to p. 118 [*the Savelli popes and . . . miracles*]).

Montemirto Ligure: 'Montemirto' (Lee's invention) literally means 'Mount myrtle' (a plant sacred to Aphrodite/Venus); Liguria is a region of northwestern Italy on the Ligurian Sea, where 'Ligure' is a component of many place names.

Republican: like his fellow revolutionaries Giuseppe Garibaldi and Giuseppe Mazzini (see note to p. 119 [*Mazzinian times*]), De Rosis wanted, and presumably fought, to see Italy united as a republican state (in the event, it was unified under a monarchy).

Lerici and Porto Venere: towns on the Ligurian coast of Italy (the classical Portus Veneris may derive its name from a now-lost temple to Venus).

Venus Verticordia: epithet for Venus (and the subject of an 1869 painting by Pre-Raphaelite painter Dante Gabriel Rossetti); 'Verticordia' means literally 'changer' or 'turner of hearts'. The goddess was supposed to convert (women's) hearts from lasciviousness to chastity, attributes which De Rosis subsequently inverts.

scapulars: article of devotion hung from strings over the shoulders (from Latin 'scapulae', shoulders), usually fashioned from squares or rectangles of cloth, wood or paper.

116 *the Superior of the College De Propagandâ Fidē*: missionary training college ('de propaganda fide' means 'for the propagation of the faith') whose students came from countries all over the world; it would thus be a strange 'jabber' indeed which was not at all spoken, or recognized, there.

117 *Διονεα—Dionea*: as De Rosis goes on to explain, in Greek mythology Dione is 'one of the loves of Father Zeus, and mother of no less a lady than the goddess Venus' (the Roman counterpart to the Greek Aphrodite, goddess of love and beauty); sometimes Aphrodite herself was called 'Dione'. (*Dionaea* is also the Latin name for the carnivorous Venus flytrap.)

Norma, Odoacer, Archimedes... Themis: names with pagan associations—(spuriously) Gaulish (from Bellini's 1831 opera *Norma*), Roman-barbarian, and Greek, respectively.

Calendar: the Catholic Calendar of Saints.

"Flos Sanctorum... Extravagant Saints": the *Flos Sanctorum*, i.e. 'The Blossom of the Saints' (1599–1610), is the work of Spanish hagiographer and Jesuit priest Pedro de Ribadeneira (1527–1611). As a notoriously credulous and fanciful work—here in an imagined posthumous edition with further additions—it is a fitting place to find (or place) a fictitious saint.

Saint Dionea,... Emperor Decius: refers to the Decian persecution of 250 CE; cf. martyrologist John Foxe (1516–87) in his *Acts and Monuments*: 'Vincentius speaketh of forty virgins, martyrs, in the forenamed city of Antioch, who suffered in the persecution of Decius' (*Acts and Monuments*, Vol. 1 (London, 1841), 177). (Also, Decius' demand that everyone resident in the Roman Empire sacrifice to the Roman gods grimly foreshadows the story's climax.)

118 *the Savelli Popes and... miracles*: the Savelli were an aristocratic Roman family; Popes Honorius III (1160–1227) and Honorius IV (1210–87) were Savellis. In the chapel of the Savelli family in the Basilica of Santa Maria in Ara Coeli in Rome there is a tomb of Andrew Savelli (d. 1306), but no record of his being canonized as a saint.

119 *the sea... myrtle-bushes... the rose-hedge... pigeons*: all associated with Aphrodite/Venus.

Burne Jones or Tadema: English Pre-Raphaelite painter and illustrator Sir Edward Coley Burne-Jones (1833–98) and Dutch-born English painter Sir Lawrence Alma-Tadema (1836–1912), who '[i]ncreasingly... concentrated on scenes of domestic tranquility, languid beauty and statuesque female figures, utilising the wet white ground of the Pre-Raphaelites to achieve a vivid Mediterranean light' (*The Bulfinch Guide to Art History*, ed. Shearer West (Boston, 1996), 210).

Carrara: Tuscan city known for its marble quarries.

119 *Theresienstadt and Spielberg*: Bohemian town (now Terezín, in Czechia) and Austrian city.

Mazzinian times: reference to Italian revolutionary Giuseppe Mazzini (1805–72), founder of the group *Giovane Italia* (Young Italy), of which De Rosis seems to have been a member; Mazzini spent many years in exile from his homeland, as has De Rosis (as the reader has just learned; he indeed resembles Mazzini—a doctor's son from Genoa—in several respects).

120 *the big ironclads at Spezia*: reference to ship-building arms race with Austria-Hungary (see note to p. 86 [*Signorelli's frescoes... La Fille de Mme. Angot*, 'Amour Dure']); La Spezia is a Ligurian port city and site of an important naval base.

Theocritus... Longus... Zola... Amyot: the Hellenistic Greek poet Theocritus (early 3rd cent. BCE) is the founder of pastoral poetry. Longus is the author of the pastoral romance *Daphnis and Chloe* (mid-3rd cent. CE), which the French writer Jacques Amyot (1513–93), best known for his rendition of Plutarch's *Lives*, translated in 1559. The French novelist Émile Zola (1840–1902) was a pioneer of literary naturalism, controversial for his frank depictions of sexuality.

Heine's little book: the 1854 essay *Die Götter im Exil* ('The Gods in Exile') by German poet and writer Heinrich Heine (1797–1856), which likely influenced Walter Pater's 'Denys L'Auxerrois' (see note to p. 271 [*Marsyas*, 'Marsyas in Flanders']) as well as 'Dionea'. (Perhaps De Rosis calls Heine 'my friend'—and this likely more in the sense of fellow-traveller than of acquaintance—owing to the poet's participation in the 'Young Germany' movement, connected to 'Young Italy' and other republican groups throughout Europe.)

pizzo di Cantù: distinctively serpentine bobbin lace made in the Northern Lombard city of Cantù.

121 *Easter of the Roses*: Pentecost; 'In Italy it was called "the Easter of the Roses", because it was customary to scatter red roses from the roof of the church... to represent the fiery tongues of Pentecost' (Robert Owen, *Sanctorale Catholicum, Or, Book of Saints* (London, 1880), 269).

Leonardo da Vinci's women: with particular reference, no doubt, to the Tuscan polymath's most famous painting, the *Mona Lisa* or 'La Gioconda' (*c.*1503–6), though Walter Pater wrote in his essay on Leonardo in *The Renaissance* of 'the unfathomable smile, always with a touch of something sinister in it, which plays over all Leonardo's work' ((Oxford, 1986), 79).

creatures of Satan: i.e. through his association or identification with Beelzebub, the 'Lord of the Flies'.

122 *"Decameron"*: classic collection of tales by Italian writer and humanist Giovanni Boccaccio (1313–75).

123 *Diderot and Schubert*: French philosopher and writer Denis Diderot (1713–84), author of the anti-clerical novel *La Religieuse* ('The Nun'), and

Franz Schubert (1797–1828), composer of hundreds of *lieder* (art-songs) including 'Die junge Nonne', published in 1825.

amore and morte and mio bene: 'love', 'death', 'my love' (Italian).

the monk playing the virginal in Giorgione's "Concert": the painting (also known as *The Interrupted Concert*) is today known to be the work of Titian (1488/90–1576) rather than fellow Venetian School master Giorgone (1477/78–1510).

124 *any of the Anchorites recorded by St Jerome*: most famous for his Latin translation of the Bible, Jerome (*c*.347–410) wrote biographies of Christian hermits Paul of Thebes (*c*.226/7–*c*.341) and Hilarion the Great (291–371).

125 *charcoal*: suicide by carbon monoxide poisoning, by burning charcoal in a closed room; Lee's friend, the poet Amy Levy, would commit suicide by this method the following year, in 1889.

worked like Jacob: the Old Testament Patriarch Jacob serves the deceptive Laban for multiple seven-year spans in order to marry his daughter Rachel (Genesis 25:18–21).

126 *Don Juan*: legendary seducer.

127 *You remember what... cigarettes enchantées*: the French critic Charles Augustin Sainte-Beuve (1804–69) quoted the novelist Honoré de Balzac (1799–1850) as saying, 'Concevoir... c'est jouir, c'est fumer des cigarettes enchantées; mais sans l'exécution, tout s'en va en rêve et en fumée' ('to conceive'—i.e. to dream about or, as De Rosis puts it here, 'project' a creative work—'is a pleasure, like smoking enchanted cigarettes; but without execution, the whole thing goes up in smoke and dreams' (a quotation also applied by John Addington Symonds to Leonardo da Vinci in the third volume of Symonds's *Renaissance in Italy*).

the persecutions of Apollo... from Wagner: in *Gods in Exile* (see note to p. 120 [*Heine's little book*]), Heine imagines Apollo's fate: '[he] stooped so low as to accept service with cattle-breeders, and as once before he had tended the cows of Admetus, so now he lived as a shepherd in Lower Austria [i.e. Styria]. Here, however, he aroused suspicion through the marvellous sweetness of his singing and, being recognised by a learned monk as one of the ancient magic-working heathen gods, he was delivered over to the ecclesiastical courts' for torture (*The Prose Writings of Heinrich Heine*, ed. Havelock Ellis (London, 1887), 268). The king and queen of the Roman underworld, Pluto and Proserpina, appear, rather reduced in dignity, in 'The Merchant's Tale' in Geoffrey Chaucer's *Canterbury Tales* (*c*.1400). The historical, though highly mythologized, thirteenth-century poet and Minnesinger (German poet-singers akin to troubadours) Tannhäuser was the subject of an 1845 opera by Richard Wagner, drawing upon the legend of Tannhäuser's dalliance with Venus in the fairy otherworld of Venusberg. The four-volume work to which De Rosis refers is the *Minnesinger* (1838–56) compiled by German philologist Friedrich Heinrich von der Hagen (1780–1856).

127 *Pan*: goat-legged Greek nature god much in evidence in late-Victorian literature (e.g. Arthur Machen's 1894 novella 'The Great God Pan').

Fata Morgana: Italian version of King Arthur's sister, the enchantress Morgan le Fay (both mean 'Morgana the fairy'); also and by extension, a mirage.

"Procul a mea... alios age rabidos": the concluding lines from Latin poet Catullus' (84–54 BCE) 'Attis' poem; the quotation should read 'era' (mistress, ruler, sweetheart, or as here, 'queen') rather than 'Hera' (the Greek queen of the gods), as the 'more terrible goddess' being addressed here is the fertility goddess Cybele, whose devotees, like Attis in this version of the myth, castrated themselves: 'from my house be all thy fury, O my queen; others drive thou in frenzy, others drive thou to madness'.

128 *Gibson's and Dupré's studio*: Welsh Neoclassical sculptor John Gibson (1790–1866) and Italian sculptor Giovanni Dupré (1817–82).

wide-shouldered Amazon: in Greek mythology, legendary race of warrior women.

129 *the Veglia*: ancient custom within the farming communities of Tuscany during the winter months, involving courting, singing, fairy tales, and other activities.

Mme. Angot: see note to p. 86 [*Signorelli's frescoes... La Fille de Mme. Angot*, 'Amour Dure'].

Cervantes' Licentiate: from the short story 'El licenciado Vidriera' ('The Lawyer of Glass') in Cervantes's *Novelas ejemplares* ('Exemplary Novels') (1613).

130 *Hermann and Dorothea*: narrative poem by Goethe, published in 1782–4; the reference here may be to the charitable distribution of linen to a camp of refugees fleeing French revolutionary troops in the poem.

a Memling Madonna: i.e. a portrait of the Virgin Mary by Early Netherlandish painter Hans Memling (*c.*1430–94) (see also note to p. 137 [*a Madonna of Van Eyck's*]).

131 *like the lion of Una*: reference to Edmund Spenser's epic poem *The Faerie Queene* (1590–6), in which the beauty and goodness of the princess Una transform a menacing lion into a protector and companion, a scene depicted in paintings by William Bell Scott (1811–90) and Briton Rivière (1840–1920), as well as on a coin minted in 1839, with Queen Victoria as Una and Britain as the lion.

the Fates of the Parthenon... Endymion, Adonis, Anchises: sculptures of three goddesses (two of which are in fact likely to be Aphrodite and Dione) on the East Pediment of the Parthenon on the Acropolis in Athens, formerly identified as the Three Fates (the *Moirae*: Clotho, Lachesis, and Atropos) (see note to p. 86 [*the Three Fates*, 'Amour Dure']); in Greek mythology Endymion was a shepherd loved by the moon goddess Selene, Adonis a youth loved by the goddesses Aphrodite and Persephone, and the Trojan hero Anchises a lover of Aphrodite.

La Rochefoucauld: French moralist François de La Rochefoucauld (1613–80), of whose *Maxims* Voltaire remarked, 'there is scarcely more than one truth running through the book—that "self-love is the motive of everything" '.

the unæsthetic sex, as Schopenhauer calls it: German philosopher Arthur Schopenhauer (1788–1860), who wrote in his 1851 essay 'On Women', 'One would be more justified in calling them the unaesthetic sex than the beautiful. Neither for music, nor for poetry, nor for fine art have they any real or true sense and susceptibility, and it is mere mockery on their part, in their desire to please, if they affect any such thing.'

132 *"Flower of the myrtle... is the sea"*: an example of a stornello, a popular Italian verse form, Tuscan in origin; in his essay 'Popular Songs of Tuscany', John Addington Symonds describes it in this way: 'The stornello, or ritournelle, never exceeds three lines, and owes its name to the return which it makes at the end of the last line to the rhyme given by the emphatic word of the first. [Robert] Browning, in his poem of "Fra Lippo Lippi", has accustomed English ears to one common species of the stornello, which sets out with the name of a flower, and rhymes with it' (*Sketches in Italy and Greece* (London, 1879), 109–10). Some examples from 'Fra Lippo Lippi' (the 'and so on' is the speaker's):

> Flower o' the broom,
>
> Take away love, and our earth is a tomb!
>
> Flower o' the quince,
>
> I let Lisa go, and what good in life since?
>
> Flower o' the thyme—and so on.

133 *Chineseries*: i.e. *chinoiseries*, Chinese porcelain, art-objects, etc.

134 *"And the three fairies said... the third of the three fairies"*: version of the Greek myth in which Paris of Troy chooses Aphrodite's gift (the beautiful Helen) over those offered by Hera and Athena, with Christian-era trappings (Holy Roman Emperor, Pope, etc.).

the Eternal Feminine: in German, *das Ewig-Weibliche*, a conception of essential 'Womanliness' associated particularly with Goethe.

Zeuxis and the ladies... Juno: refers to an anecdote in which the 5th century BCE Greek painter Zeuxis used five models to fashion a composite portrait—of Helen of Troy, not Juno (Roman equivalent to the Greek Hera, queen of the Olympian gods), though the painting was, according to Latin writer Cicero, within the Temple of Juno in the city of Croton (today Crotone in Calabria, Southern Italy).

136 *Suabian mountain sprite*: Swabia is a region, historically a Duchy, in south-western Germany; Sabine Baring-Gould names it as the site of one possible Venusberg (see note to p. 127 [*the persecutions of Apollo... from Wagner*]). ('[Les] Dieux in Exil' is the French for Heine's title.)

136 *St Augustine, Tertullian... Lady Isis*: Christian polemicist Tertullian (*c*.155–*c*.240 CE) and theologian Augustine of Hippo (354–430 CE) both battled heresy in their writings, including pagan cults centring upon the worship of Greco-Roman and (like Isis) Egyptian deities.

137 *like a Madonna of Van Eyck's*: this could describe more than one of early Netherlandish painter Jan van Eyck's (*c*.1390–1441) paintings of the Virgin Mary.

A WICKED VOICE

Once thought to have first appeared in *Hauntings* as the fourth and final story, this thoroughgoing reimagination of 'A Culture-Ghost' was written originally in French and published three years earlier, as 'Voix maudite', in the French 'revue illustrée' (illustrated review) *Les Lettres et les arts* (Aug. 1887) (see headnote to 'Dionea'). Lee then translated (and slightly modified) her French tale for her 1890 collection. In 1970, the story would be translated 'back' into French from this English version, and titled 'Une voix maléfique' (Lee's 'The Virgin of the Seven Daggers' would follow a similarly tortuous path from its original appearance as 'La Madone aux sept glaives' to its later translation as 'La Vierge aux sept poignards'). Regarding 'The Transformations of the Culture-Ghost', as she characterized the passage from the earlier tale to the later one, Lee wrote:

> I recast it some fifteen years afterwards with a full-fledged technique and self-criticism. The Singer whom I had prepared for ghostly functions by a violent death, had now to be assassinated for something better than a vague intrigue with somebody's great-grand-aunt. Or rather: had he not better do the murdering himself? haunt not in pointless solitude merely to sing a posthumous song; but haunt in company with an appropriate victim, be doomed to ghostly repetition of that murderous song of his? (For he had obviously to do the murdering with a song.) He had to become a vocal villain, deliberately revenging himself for virtuous disdain by inspiring a shameful passion in the proud lady whom his singing stabbed to death. His voice... I mean the voice of my new version, was a wicked voice, and the story was called after it. As wicked (in the original French it was even wickeder, a Voix Maudite) as ever you could make it: a voice seeking fresh victims even in its posthumous existence. (*FM*, xxix–xl.)

139 *Chi ha inteso, intenda*: 'Whoever has understood, let him understand' (Italian). The dedication is to singer Mary Wakefield; the Palazzo Barbaro in Venice was owned by the parents of John Singer Sargent's cousin, the painter Ralph Wormeley Curtis (1854–1922).

Wagner... the divine Mozart: Richard Wagner (1813–83), one of the titans of nineteenth-century music, composed operas or 'music-dramas' including *Tannhäuser* (1845), *Tristan und Isolde* (1865), *Die Meistersinger von Nürnberg* (1868), and the operatic tetralogy *Der Ring des Nibelungen*

(1869–76). In Lee's time the forty-plus operas of German-born English composer George Frideric Handel (1685–1759), among them *Giulio Cesare* (1724), *Tamerlano* (1724), *Rodelinda* (1725), and *Serse* (1738), were almost entirely neglected; today they are widely performed. The works of operatic composer and reformer Christoph Willibald Gluck (1714–87) include *Orfeo ed Euridice* (1862) and *Iphigénie en Tauride* (1779); Wolfgang Amadeus Mozart (1756–91) wrote over twenty operas including *Le Nozze di Figaro* (1786), *Don Giovanni* (1787), and *Die Zauberflöte* (1791).

O cursed human voice... of Satan!: in the original (French) story, the corresponding paragraph (there, the fourth) begins, 'O Maudite, Maudite voix humaine, violon de chair et d'os fabriqué par un luthier auprès duquel pâlissent les Stradivarius et les Amati' (*Les Lettres et les Arts* 126) ('O wicked, wicked human voice, violin of flesh and bone, fashioned by a luthier beside whom the Stradivarius and Amati pale') (see note to p. 10 [*Cremonese fiddle*, 'Winthrop's Adventure']).

Sophocles and Euripides: two of the three great Athenian tragedians (the other being Aeschylus). Three of Gluck's greatest operas—*Alceste* (1767), *Iphigénie en Aulide* (1774), and *Iphigénie en Tauride* (1779)—are based directly or indirectly on dramas by Euripides.

Ogier the Dane: legendary knight who appeared first in the medieval French *chansons de geste*, and subsequently in Norse adaptations and Danish folklore (there is, in fact, a 1789 Danish opera based on the legend, *Holger Danske*, by German composer Friedrich Ludwig Æmilius Kunzen (1761–1817), but this was little known in the nineteenth century). Perhaps Lee got the idea for a Wagnerian music-drama based on the Ogier legend from Sabine Baring-Gould's discussion of the sleeping hero motif, where it is linked with the story of Siegfried, used by Wagner in his *Ring* cycle: 'In Scandinavian mythology we have Siegfrid or Sigurd thus resting, and awaiting his call to come forth and fight... Ogier the Dane, or Olger Dansk, will in like manner shake off his slumber and come forth from the dream-land of Avallon to avenge the right' (*Curious Myths of the Middle Ages* (London, 1884), 105). Lee's letters indicate that she was reading Baring-Gould's book a few months before beginning work on 'Voix Maudite'.

140 *were-wolves*: perhaps a nod to Sabine Baring-Gould's 1865 study of lycanthropy in folklore, *The Book of Were-Wolves*; in July of 1886 Lee wrote to her mother, 'I am sending off a copy of the book on Mediaeval Myth [Baring-Gould's *Curious Myths of the Middle Ages*]; I hope E. [Eugene] may find something in it. I will look out about the Were-Wolf book by the same author' (*SL* II, 197).

the square of San Polo: the Campo San Polo in Venice, once the site of large weekly markets.

141 *ailes de pigeon*: hair worn in rows of curls (French, literally 'pigeon wings').

the Arcadian Academy: Lee had written at length about the *Accademia dell'Arcadia*, the famed Italian literary society founded in 1690, noting that the Italian academies of the time 'were all local—very limited in numbers and fame—all except one, whose name resounded with equal glory from Trent to Messina, from Savona to Treviso, which comprised among its members all the great writers, philosophers, or artists, all the noble lords, all the rich bankers, all the astute lawyers, all the well-known doctors, all the sainted priests, all the beautiful ladies, that lived or travelled in Italy' (*S18*, 15–16). In keeping with the Academy's practice or affectation, Lee's imagined Arcadian has taken a 'pastoral' *nom de plume* (Goethe's, for example, was 'Megalio Melpomeneo').

141 *Zaffirino*: 'little sapphire'; a connection with the poet Sappho of Lesbos (*c*.610–*c*.570 BCE) has also been suggested (see Catherine Maxwell, 'Sappho, Mary Wakefield, and Vernon Lee's "A Wicked Voice"', *MHRA* 102.4 (2007), 960–74).

142 *Rossini and Donizetti*: Gioachino Rossini (1792–1868) and Gaetano Donizetti (1797–1848), leading composers of the bel canto era of Italian opera; among their many works still in the operatic repertory are Rossini's *The Barber of Seville* (1816) and *William Tell* (1829) and Donizetti's *The Elixir of Love* (1832), *Lucia di Lammermoor* (1835), and *Don Pasquale* (1843).

the Procuratessa Vendramin...the Brenta: the Vendramin were a wealthy Venetian family; the theatre and opera house they built in 1622 is still in existence (now the Teatro Goldoni). A Procuratessa was the wife of a Procurator of St Mark, a powerful Venetian office (one member of the family, Andrea Vendramin, was Procurator before becoming Doge in 1476). The Brenta River runs to the Adriatic from the region of Trento.

143 *gentildonna*: noblewoman (Italian).

parcere subjectis et debellare superbos... Virgil: 'to spare the vanquished and subdue the proud', from book 6 of the Latin poet Virgil's (70–19 BCE) epic poem, the *Aeneid*.

Cosmas and Damian: third-century Christian martyrs, by tradition twin brothers and physicians; Venice's San Giorgio Maggiore is one of many churches claiming to possess relics of the saints.

Patriarch of Aquileia: Aquileia was a Roman city at the head of the Adriatic Sea; the Patriarchate of Aquileia was for centuries an episcopal see.

Saint Justina: Paduan saint and patroness (not to be confused with St Justina of Antioch or St Justina of Mainz).

145 *Swinburne and Baudelaire*: English poet Algernon Charles Swinburne (1837–1909) and French poet Charles Baudelaire (1821–67) both wrote on scandalous topics including lesbianism (and specifically the poet Sappho, whom the name 'Zaffirino' is possibly meant to recall) (see note to p. 141 [*Zaffirino*]).

146 *Biondina in Gondoleta*: famous song ('The Blonde in the Gondola'), of the type called *canzone veneziana*, with lyrics attributed to the Venetian poet Antonio Lamberti (1757–1832) and music by German composer Johann Simon Mayr (1763–1845); there is a later setting by Giovanni Battista

Perucchini (1784–1870), but this seems less likely to be the version referred to here. (See also note to p. 152 [*Gritti*].)

147 *Iphigenia, with Agamemnon and Achilles... peacock*: in Greek mythology, the princess Iphigenia is sacrificed by her father, Agamemnon (king of Mycenae) en route to the Trojan War, to appease the goddess Artemis (Iphigenia is told, by way of deception, that she is to wed the warrior Achilles); Euripides' two plays—and Gluck's two operas—*Iphigenia in Aulis* and *Iphigenia at Tauris* are both based on the story (see notes to p. 139 [*Sophocles and Euripides*] and [*Wagner... the divine Mozart*]). The peacock suggests that the goddess depicted on the panel is the Greek queen of the Olympians, Hera (Juno to the Romans).

149 *the theme of the "prowess of Ogier"*: Magnus, as a good Wagnerian, conceives his opera in terms of *leitmotive* ('leading-motives'), constantly recurring musical themes, subject to modification and combination, which are associated with particular characters, concepts, situations, and so on.

150 *the Giudecca*: island in the Venetian lagoon.

St. Mark's: Venice's iconic, Italo-Byzantine cathedral.

Florian's: famous café in Venice, founded in 1720.

La Camesella or Funiculì, funiculà: the Neapolitan song (*canzone napolitana*) 'Levate 'a cammesella', and the popular 1880 tune written in honour of the new funicular (inclined cable) railway on Mount Vesuvius (its Neapolitan refrain, quoted later in the story, means 'let's go!').

151 *Bordogni or Crescentini*: Marco Bordogni (1789–1856) and Girolamo Crescentini (1762–1846), both operatic singers and (more relevant here) singing teachers and writers of singing exercises.

"Bis, Bis!": encore!

152 *Santa Lucia*: yet another traditional *canzone napolitana*.

Gritti: Francesco Gritti (1740–1811), but the lyrics are more probably by Antonio Lamberti (see note to p. 146 [*Biondina in Gondoleta*]). The confusion may have arisen from their appearance in a collection of work by both men: *Favole del Gritti / Canzonette ed Apologhi del Lamberti* (Padova, 1819).

153 *the spies of the old Republic*: the *Inquisitori* (inquisitors) of the Council of Ten (*il Consiglio dei Dieci*), Venice's powerful ruling body, employed a network of *confidenti*, spies and informants including gondoliers, at least in the popular imagination: '[The Inquisition's] universal and fiendish vigilance was maintained by a multitude of spies in all the public places of the city... Their informers infested all ranks of society, from the highest to the lowest. Nobles, monks, prostitutes, gondoliers, and domestic servants enabled them to watch the secret springs of action in fashion, religion, passion, pleasure, and privacy' (William H. Stiles, *Austria*, Vol. 1 (London, 1852), 276).

154 *Padua... St. Anthony's*: the Basilica of St Anthony in the coastal city of Padua (Padova), part of the Venetian Republic until 1797 (one of its 'Terra Firma' or mainland territories). Writing on the subject of Venice's patronage

of music, Lee noted, in *Studies of the Eighteenth Century in Italy*: 'It spent large sums on the musical establishment of [Padua's] great, half-Gothic, half-Byzantine basilica of St. Anthony', a phrase her narrator will echo in the next paragraph (149).

154 *Gregorian modulation*: Gregorian chant or plainsong is particularly marked by modal, rather than tonal, modulation.

Feast of Fools: European feast day celebrated in the later Middle Ages, called in Latin, e.g., *festum fatuorum*, *festum stultorum*, *festum hypodiaconorum*; associated with carnivalesque mockery and licence.

Hoffmannlike: suggestive of the fantastic world of E. T. A. Hoffmann's (1776–1822) fiction.

Lalande and Burney: Joseph Jérôme Lefrançois de Lalande (1732–1807), French astronomer and author of the book of travel *Voyage d'un François en Italie* (1769), which contains an interview with violinist Giovanni Tartini in which he discusses the composition of his 'Devil's Sonata' (see note to p. 154 [*Guadagni, the soprano for... Tartini*]); and Charles Burney (1726–1814), historian of music.

Terra Firma: see note to p. 154 [*Padua... St. Anthony's*].

Guadagni, the soprano for... Tartini: castrato singer Gaetano Guadagni (16 February 1728–11 November 1792) and composer and violinist Giovanni Tartini (1692–1770) were both associated with the Basilica of St Anthony. Guadagni, famous for creating the role of Orpheus in Gluck's *Orfeo ed Euridice* (of which 'Che faro senza Euridice' is the most famous aria), was a member of the *capella*, while Tartini, one of the first possessors of a Stradivarius violin, was *maestro di capello*. Tartini's legendary encounter with the evil one was recorded by, among others, Charles Burney, the occultist Helena Blavatsky (in her 1880 story 'The Ensouled Violin'), and Lee, in *Studies of the Eighteenth Century in Italy*: 'Early in the century Tartini had received a visit from the Devil, and had heard the Fiend play the violin more beautifully than even he himself had ever played... the demon's performance left a deep impression... of weirdness which can be seen not only in his fantastically-beautiful works but in his haggard face, with intense, wildly-staring eyes, as it is portrayed in the gallery of the Philharmonic Academicians of Bologna' (150).

156 *Ave Maria*: 'Hail Mary', Roman Catholic prayer of praise.

peronospora: downy mildew.

Euganean hills: volcanic in origin, these hills on the Padovan-Venetian plain inspired a poem by Percy Bysshe Shelley (1792–1822), the 'Lines Written among the Euganean Hills'.

157 *a great golden Danaë cloud*: in Greek mythology, Zeus visited, and impregnated, the mortal woman Danaë while in the form of a golden shower of rain (in paintings like the famous series by Titian (1488/90–1576), the divine manifestation is more cloud-like in appearance); the child would be the hero Perseus.

159 *the divine Schumann*: German composer Robert Schumann (1810–56).

160 *Tritons*: mermen of Greek myth.

Murano-glass: the island of Murano, in the Venetian lagoon, was renowned for glassmaking.

rifiorituras: vocal decoration or 'flowering' by the singer ('rifioritura' is literally a 'reflowering'), particularly common in eighteenth-century operatic performance.

161 *cadenza*: improvised passage or flourish near the end of the aria.

THE LEGEND OF MADAME KRASINSKA

Published in *The Fortnightly Review* (March 1890) and subsequently in Lee's second collection of shorter fiction, *Vanitas: Polite Stories* (1892).

163 *Little Sisters of the Poor*: Catholic organization of nuns, founded in France in 1839, devoted to the elderly poor (as the erstwhile Madame Krasinska exclaims, 'Ah, the old! The old!... Have you ever tried to imagine what it is to be poor and forsaken and old?'). The order had only come to Florence in 1882, moving in 1888 to a new house in the via Andrea del Sarto, where presumably this scene takes place.

Cecchino: diminutive of 'Cecco'; interestingly, the name resembles that of two men, both named Eugenio Cecconi, either or both of whom might be relevant here: the archbishop who had supported the establishment of the *Piccole Sorelle dei Poveri* in Florence, and a Tuscan painter whose work Lee possessed.

164 *the Maremma*: coastal region of Western central Italy, even today little industrialized. In her essay 'In the Tuscan Maremma' Lee wrote: 'Time does not seem to exist for the Maremma; all periods have left their handiwork, but it has been effaced and harmonized by a nature untamed by man, and inimical towards him' (*Harper's Monthly Magazine*, vol. 106, no. 632 (Jan. 1903), 237).

165 *fastest*: 'fast' (as in 'fast-living') can suggest dissipation, but a milder sense, reserved for ladies, seems applicable to the Baroness Fosca and her 'ferociously frank conversation': 'Studiedly unrefined in habits and manners, disregardful of propriety or decorum' (*OED*).

Lucretia Borgia: see note to p. 87 [*Bianca Cappello... Lucrezia Borgia*, 'Amour Dure'].

smart: stylish, elegant.

crâne: swaggering, bold, audacious.

Deadly Nightshade: highly toxic plant whose Linnaean designation connects 'beautiful lady' (*belladonna*) with the third of the Greek fates (*Atropos*), associated with the end of life. The idea may have sprung into Cecco's mind by association with Lucrezia Borgia, infamous as a poisoner.

167 *Giotto's tower*: the *Campanile del Giotto*, part of the complex of Florence's celebrated Cathedral, was begun in 1334 by the great painter turned architect Giotto di Bondone (*c.*1267–1337) in his old age, and not completed until 1359.

Solferino: the Battle of Solferino, fought 24 June 1859 between the French and Sardinian armies against Austria, as part of the Second War of Italian Independence. Jean-Henri Dunant's 1862 book *Un Souvenir de Solferino*, describing the death and suffering he witnessed in the aftermath of the battle, led to the founding of the Red Cross.

the station: the *stazione Maria Antonia*, built in 1848; its design has been attributed to the British engineer Isambard Kingdom Brunel (1806–59).

168 *an invisible cloak*: 'Leonbruno', the last of the stories collected by Lee in *Tuscan Fairy Tales*, features such a magic cloak, a staple of European, particularly Welsh, folklore (Lee's mother was Welsh).

169 *obligato*: 'obbligato', obligatory (Italian), particularly in the context of musical accompaniment.

170 *prunella*: sturdy material of wool and silk.

171 *Viccolo del Beccamorto*: there is a Vicolo del Beccamorto in Palermo, Sicily.

Chanoinesse: canoness (French).

Netta: we do not learn until the last sentence of the story that this is short for 'Antoinette' (perhaps Lee is thinking of Princess Antonietta Strozzi, the chief benefactor of Florence's Little Sisters of the Poor).

172 *Gyp*: pseudonym of aristocratic, prolific, and bestselling novelist (and self-declared 'anti-Semite') Sibylle-Gabrielle Marie-Antoinette de Riquetti de Mirabeau, Comtesse de Martel de Janville (1849–1932), a contemporary of Lee whose fiction often satirized fashionable society. Two of her most popular novels of the 1880s ('Madame Krasinska' is presumably set in the early 1890s or perhaps shortly before), *Autour du Mariage* and *Autour du Divorce*, feature a 'May–December' marriage like Netta's.

brougham: one-horse carriage.

173 *Lung' Arno*: the riverside embankment.

The foundry: the Pignone foundry on the Arno, set up in 1842 and one of Florence's most thriving industrial enterprises by the late nineteenth century.

the check-string: used to signal the driver to stop the carriage.

chest protectors: felt, bib-like defences against the cold.

frictioning gloves: by rubbing the extremities, these were supposed 'to promote circulation, thereby freeing obstructions by opening the pores and assisting nature to throw off morbid matter', according to an 1875 advertising circular.

variosities: varieties.

174 *Tornabuoni's*: an old Florentine patrician family; perhaps also a nod to the via Tornabuoni, a possible location for 'the big chemist's' of the

story, which Netta, channelling the Sora Lena's memories, will later call 'the English chemist's' (both Roberts & Co. and the American & British Pharmacy were there, as was Doney's café (see note to p. 176 [*Doney's*])).

antipyrine: a benzene derivative.

175 *Father Agostino*: Padre Agostino da Montefeltro, popular preaching friar who had come to Florence in 1888.

176 *Addio, mia bella, addio*: popular song of the Risorgimento attributed to the poet Carlo Alberto Bosi (1813–86).

Sacré Coeur: perhaps the Istituto del Sacro Cuore, a Catholic girls' school opened in 1881. There is also a church, the Chiesa del Sacro Cuoro, which had been built in the 1870s.

Doney's: popular and elegant café-restaurant on the via Tornabuoni.

Cascine: according to the 1874 *Cook's Handbook to Florence*, 'the Hyde Park, the Champs Elysées, of Florence'.

178 *chaffing*: engaging in banter.

179 *the red, green, and white lanterns*: colours of the Italian tricolor flag.

Garibaldi's hymn: patriotic song associated with Italian general Giuseppe Garibaldi (1807–82); music writer Hugh Reginald Haweis (1838–1901) (whom Lee called 'odious'), in Italy in the eventful year of 1860, wrote: 'The part which music played in the Italian Revolution was remarkable. A certain gay and intrepid march tune, characteristically called "Garibaldi's Hymn", was shouted, blown, scraped and rattled on drums in and out of season. The whole spirit of the volunteer movement seemed to be in it' (*My Musical Life* (London, 1886), 104).

"*Faites votre jeu, messieurs... manque*": roulette lingo. Netta is running the game.

180 *tresette*: popular Italian card game.

moreen: strong fabric with a watered finish.

magenta: shortly before the Battle of Solferino (see note to p. 167 [*Solferino*]), the French–Sardinian forces had scored another victory against the Austrians (4 June 1859) in the Lombardy town of Magenta. A newly synthesized dye was named after the battle in 1860.

Montepulciano: vintage from Tuscan town of that name, renowned for its wine.

181 *San Bonifazio*: the Ospedale di Bonifacio, founded in the fourteenth century; an asylum in the nineteenth century (see Introduction).

the Aeneid, translated by Caro: Virgil's epic poem, a legendary account of the foundation of Rome in Italy, was translated into Italian by the poet Annibale Caro (1507–66) (published in 1581).

Berlin-wool cushion: see note to p. 254 [*Berlin wool cushions*, 'The Doll'].

Etna... Mongibello: two names for the same active Sicilian volcano.

181 *"Casta Diva!"*: most famous aria in Vincenzo Bellini's bel canto opera *Norma* (1831); the title means, ironically in context, 'chaste goddess'.

182 *the old Jews' quarter*: the Florentine ghetto, which we are soon to learn is 'condemned to destruction', was near the old Mercato Vecchio; the 1889 Baedeker's *Handbook* notes: 'In the vicinity is the Ghetto, or former Jewish quarter, which is now closed. It is intended to rebuild the entire quarter as far as the via Tornabuoni.' Anglo-Jewish poet Amy Levy (1861–89), who met, and became infatuated with, Lee in Florence in 1886, published an essay, 'The Ghetto at Florence', the same year.

escutcheoned and stanchioned: escutcheoned means decorated with coats of arms; stanchions are supports, usually with reference to windows.

Ghibelline nobles: rival party to the Guelphs in late medieval Italy; Ghibellines, more likely to be noble, supported the Holy Roman Emperor against the Pope.

184 *Dante's grandfather*: i.e. around the early thirteenth century.

pipkins: pots, or perhaps pails.

185 *niello*: decorative black-coloured alloy used in metalwork.

"Pater noster qui es in caelis": beginning of the Lord's Prayer (or 'paternoster'): 'Our Father, who art in Heaven.'

THE VIRGIN OF THE SEVEN DAGGERS

This story has its origins in an 1888–9 journey to Spain: 'I found myself, for reasons of health, banished to the South of Spain in mid-winter. No doubt the nervous depression this journey was meant to cure intensified my dislike for things Spanish' (*FM*, xix). Here Lee had the idea of bringing together two seemingly diametrically opposed archetypes: 'the typical Spanish hero' Don Juan ('the conquering super-rake and super-ruffian, decoying women, murdering fathers, insulting even dead men and glorying in wickedness') and the Virgin Mary, in the incarnation of a 'knife-riddled Spanish Madonna'. An old legend of the Alhambra provided the final spark for the tale: 'There was an Infanta, so my friend had told me, buried with all her treasure and court somewhere beneath the deserted Moorish palace . . . And with the vision in those jade green waters, there wavered into my mind the suspicion that there might well have been an almost successful rival of Don Juan's gloomy Madonna' (*FM*, xx–xxi). The idea of the buried infanta may also owe something to the 'Legend of the Three Beautiful Princesses' told by Washington Irving in his *Tales of the Alhambra* (1832) in connection with the Torre de las Infantas; Irving tells of a trio of beautiful infantas whose father keeps them virtual prisoners in the Alhambra, in the keeping of a duenna and a 'broad-shouldered renegado', with luxurious surroundings (fountain, caged birds) similar to those in Lee's story; two of the infantas flee with their suitors (Spanish cavaliers like Don Juan); the third remains behind, dies, and is buried 'in a vault beneath the tower', where her spirit is supposed to linger. Initially published in French, as 'La Madone aux sept glaives', in *Feuilleton du journal des débats du Samedi* (Feb. 1896), the story subsequently appeared in English as 'The Virgin of the Seven Daggers: A Moorish Ghost Story of the Seventeenth Century' (*English Review*, Jan.–Feb. 1909) and (with a few minor changes) in *For Maurice: Five Unlikely Tales* (1927).

186 *DEDICATED... JOSE FERNANDEZ GIMENEZ*: the Spanish diplomat José Fernandez Gimenez, the source of the legend quoted in the headnote.

Grenada... the Sierra: Granada, situated at the foot of the Sierra Nevada mountains, is the capital of the province of Granada in Southern Spain. Though likely not the origin of the city's name, 'granada' is Spanish for 'pomegranate', which is depicted in the city's coat of arms (and referenced later in the story).

the well-nigh Africa sun: 'the sunshine', in the *English Review*.

Our Lady of the Seven Daggers: most likely Lee has in mind the Basilica Nuestra Señora de las Angustias (Our Lady of Sorrows), or La Virgen de las Angustias, in Granada.

the pompous... of the later Philips: another of the few slight discrepancies between the *English Review* and *For Maurice* versions of the story; the former reads, 'of the reign of Philip IV'. Philip IV reigned 1621–65, while 'the later Philips' opens the door for the reign of Philip V (1700–46, with a seven-month interruption in 1724), which saw the appearance of more elaborately ornate Baroque works (on the other hand, the construction of the church of La Virgen de las Angustias dates from late in the reign of Philip III—perhaps it is he who is meant to be included in the amended timeframe).

Morisco rebels: the Moriscos (Spanish, 'little Moors') were ostensibly Christianized Spanish Muslims (and their descendants), who remained in many respects an alien community; the Moriscos of Granada were expelled after revolting in 1568–71.

like a tirade... by Gongora: playwright Pedro Calderón de la Barca (1600–81) and lyric poet Luis de Góngora (1561–1627), two outstanding writers of the Spanish Golden Age.

retablo: in the Renaissance Spanish context, this suggests a large, elaborately carved, gilded, painted, and/or sculpted altarpiece of wood.

187 *farthingale*: hooped petticoat or similar structure for expanding and giving shape to the skirt of a woman's dress, originating in Spain in the sixteenth century.

heartsease: wild pansy.

Charles the Melancholy: Charles II of Spain (1661–1700), known as *El Hechizado* ('the Bewitched').

188 *the King's Alguazils and the Holy Officer's delators*: 'alguacil' ('alguazil' is the Portuguese rather than the Spanish spelling) can refer to several governmental positions; here is likely meant the bailiffs involved in the Spanish Inquisition's tribunals; delators are 'denouncers' or informers.

188 *the voice of Syphax*: this imagined castrato singer seems to draw upon or blend two historical figures, Farinelli (see note to p. 299 [headnote to 'Winthrop's Adventure']), who was a royal favourite in the court of Charles II's successor, Philip V (1683–1746), and Giovanni Francesco Grossi (1653–97), who was called 'Siface' (Syphax) after winning fame for singing that role in the 1671 revival of Francesco Cavalli's opera *Scipione Affricano* (Syphax was a king of Numidia who allied with Carthage against Rome).

189 *Albaycin*: the Albaicín, where the Alhambra is located, once contained the city's Jewish quarter (the *Realejo*).

Domingo Zurbaran of Seville: surely Francisco de Zurbarán (1598–1664), apprenticed in Seville and known as the 'Spanish Caravaggio'; the slip in naming, if it is a slip, may be related to Zurbarán's commission to execute a series of paintings for the Dominican monastery San Pablo el Real in Seville, fourteen of which focus on the life of St Dominic (Domingo de Guzmán).

the tower of the Sail: i.e. the Alhambra's Torre de la Vela, properly 'watch tower' ('vela' can mean 'sail' as well as 'vigil/watch'). Its bell is rung on 2 January (the date marking the end of Muslim rule in Iberia, in 1492); tradition holds that 'damsels' who join in the ringing will be married before year's end. Lee was in Granada on 2 January 1889: 'This is the anniversary of the Conquest: worse luck to them! The bell of the Alhambra is ringing all day' (*SL* II, 506).

the arms of Castile and Aragon: the two most important kingdoms of Spain, which had been united by the union of Ferdinand and Isabella in 1469.

the anniversary of... the Infidels: see note to p. 189 [*the tower of the sail*].

190 *the Alhambra*: Islamic palace and fortress, converted into the Royal Court of Ferdinand and Isabella after the 1492 *Reconquista*, and a major tourist attraction since the nineteenth century; on her first visit, Lee wrote in her Commonplace Book that its 'architecture of cobweb and soapbubble' was more 'monotonous and wearisome... than any other medieval building' (quoted in *SL* II, 511).

Tower of the Cypresses: the Alhambra boasts several towers with colourful names—the Tower of Heads, the Tower of the Witch, etc.—as well as a Walk of the Cypresses (Paseo de los Cipreses), but Lee has invented this tower.

the Morisco village of Andarax: Laujar de Andarax, whose residents were active in the 1500 rebellion of Granada Muslims in response to forced conversions to Catholicism, and scene of one of its bloodiest reprisals.

191 *Titian*: Venetian painter of the Renaissance, Tiziano Vecellio (*c.*1488–1576).

192 *the Cid... the Mosque*: Lee is giving the fictitious Don Juan historical (if quasi-legendary) ancestors: 'el Cid', Rodrigo Díaz de Vivar (*c.*1043–99), was a Castilian knight later transformed into a chivalric hero in the twelfth-century *Song of the Cid*; Hernán Pérez del Pulgar (1451–1531) was a knight whose exploits in the 1482–91 Granada War, as related by

Washington Irving, include entering secretly into the city, still under Moorish control, and making his way to the chief mosque: 'Here the cavalier, pious as brave, threw himself on his knees, and drawing forth a parchment scroll on which was inscribed in large letters AVE MARIA, nailed it to the door of the mosque, thus converting the heathen edifice into a Christian chapel and dedicating it to the blessed Virgin' (*Chronicle of the Conquest of Granada* (New York, 1863), 490). (This is the Cathedral of Granada, dedicated to the Virgin of the Incarnation.)

Venus...Juno...Minerva: Venus (Greek Aphrodite) is the Roman goddess of beauty, Juno (Hera) is the queen of the gods, and Minerva (Athena) is the goddess of wisdom.

the snows of Mulhacen: part of the Sierra Nevadas, Mulhacén is the highest mountain in Iberia.

"The Jew...Bonaventura": in other words he is a *converso*, a recent (and in this case, apparently, purely nominal) convert to Catholicism; the popular association of Jews with sorcery and necromancy is particularly relevant here.

powder magazine: Lee's fictitious Tower of the Cypresses here joins the (real) Torre de Siete Suelos (Tower of the Seven Floors) and Torre de Agua (Water Tower) in suffering damage during Napoleon's use of the Alhambra as a barracks. (Napoleon's forces also planned to blow up the complex altogether; perhaps Lee is thinking of this averted explosion.)

King Yahya: presumably refers to the Caliph of Cordoba Yahya ibn Ali (d. 1035); awareness of political uncertainty (he was later ousted) might conceivably have prompted such an action.

193 *Tetuan*: Tétouan, city in northern Morocco; this would be the Tétouan rebuilt by Muslim refugees from Spain in the wake of the Reconquista, the fall of Granada specifically (see note to p. 189 [*the anniversary of...the Infidels*]).

194 *"Jab...trum"*: Lee's necromantic ritual, a mixture of heterogeneous elements drawn from different cultural traditions and sheer nonsense, structured as an inversion of Christian ritual (e.g. 'credo', 'esto nobis'), is a parody; one of the many depictions of such ceremonies that Lee might have had in mind is Renaissance artist Benvenuto Cellini's dramatic account of his attempt to make contact through sorcery with his beloved Angela: 'The necromancer having begun to make his tremendous invocations, called by their names a multitude of demons, who were the leaders of the several legions...in the Hebrew language as likewise in Latin and Greek; insomuch, that the amphitheatre was almost in an instant filled with demons a hundred times more numerous than at the former conjuration' (*The Life of Cellini* (Philadelphia, 1812), 173). In *The Art of Iugling or Legerdemaine* Samuel Rid facetiously describes the macaronic patter of the magician: 'Credo, passe passe...as Ailif, Casil, zaze, Hit, metmeltat, Saturnus, Iupiter, Mars, Sol, Venus, Mercurie, Luna? Or thus: Drocti, Micocti, et Senarocti, Velu barocti, Asmarocti, Ronnsee, Faronnsee, hey

passe passe: many such obseruations to this arte, are necessary, without which all the rest, are little to the purpose' (London, 1614, n.p.).

Esto Nobis: recalls liturgical texts in which God or Christ is called upon to 'be for us'...something: a tower of strength, a foretaste of heaven, etc. Here the biblical monster Leviathan is apparently addressed, but without a direct object. In his *Transcendental Magic* (1854–6), esotericist Éliphas Lévi assured the would-be necromancer that 'The Latin words, est, sit, esto, fiat, have the same force [as Kabbalistic 'keys of magical transformation' spoken in Hebrew] when pronounced with full understanding'.

194 *"Osiris... Belshazar"*: Osiris, the reborn Egyptian god of fertility and the dead, with whose cult necromancy was associated; Apollo was among other things the god of oracles, some of whom were also associated with communication with the dead. The biblical story of Belshazzar's Feast, in which a mysterious hand writes a message of doom on the wall, also suggests supernatural revelation.

197 *into the outer world*: here ends the first half of the story, as it appeared in the *English Review* (January 1909).

198 *Damascus work*: steel ornamented with a watered pattern.

200 *a Mecca rosary*: i.e. Islamic prayer beads.

the histories of... Sheba: the Quranic version of the Old Testament story of Joseph (Jusuf) and Potiphar's wife (Zulaykha, variously transliterated) was put into verse by the fifteenth-century Persian poet and scholar Jāmī, in a work translated into English by Victorian orientalist Ralph Thomas Hotchkin Griffith (1826–1906), who called it 'the Ovid of the East' (in the Hebrew Bible and Quran, theirs is an entirely one-sided love story, as Potiphar's wife/Zulaikha tries unsuccessfully to seduce Joseph, before accusing him of rape). In the Books of I Kings and II Chronicles, the Queen of Sheba (thought to be in East Africa or possibly southern Arabia) comes to visit King Solomon in Jerusalem bearing gifts and 'hard questions'; a subsequent cycle of legends elaborates this narrative into a love story.

201 *Oriana, for whom Amadis... Proteus*: Oriana, Amadis, and Galaor are characters in the Spanish prose romance *Amadís of Gaul*, which also inspired the sixteenth-century *Felixmarte de Hircania*. The following references are all from Greek/Roman mythology: the abduction of Helen (married to King Menelaus of Sparta) by the Trojan prince Paris (who had won her by choosing Aphrodite/Venus as the fairest of the goddesses) sparked the Trojan War; after Zeus/Jupiter/Jove seduced the nymph Callisto, his wife Hera/Juno had her turned into a bear; the dawn-goddess Aurora (Eos in Greek) made her human lover Tithonus immortal, though he continued to age (the subject of a poem by Tennyson); Proteus was the shapeshifting sea-god and god of change, chosen by Lee as the emblematic figure for her book by that name (see Introduction).

202 *the Castilian... of the sainted King Ferdinand*: Ferdinand III of Castile (*c.*1200–52), canonized in 1671; i.e. the Chief Eunuch is speaking Old Castilian (Medieval Spanish).

204 *stomacher*: ornamented, triangular piece of cloth worn beneath the bodice; puce is a dark purple-brown colour.

205 *Berber of the Rif*: North African ethnic group; the Rif is a region in Morocco (which Lee had visited en route to Spain).

207 *the great hospital, founded by... God*: San Juan de Dios Hospital, founded in 1544 by the Augustinian Monks of San Jerónimo.

208 *the monogram I.H.S.*: a Christogram (abbreviation of the name of Christ).

210 *Archpriest Morales*: perhaps suggested by the historian Ambrosio de Morales (1513–91), who was in holy orders, though he died a decade before Calderón was born.

Purgatory of St Patrick... my Ludovic Enio: Calderon's play *El Purgatorio de San Patricio* draws upon the ancient legend of a cavern on an island in Lough Derg in County Donegal, Ireland, supposed to have been visited by St Patrick, where he witnessed the suffering of the damned. One of the 'Curious Myths of the Middle Ages' related by Sabine Baring-Gould (see Introduction), the story would appear in many works of popular as well as 'high' literature; in *Orlando Furioso*, Ariosto writes: '[Rogero] next for Ireland shaped his course; | And saw fabulous Hibernia, where | The goodly, sainted elder made the cave, | In which men cleansed from all offences are; | Such mercy there, it seems, is found to save'. Ludovico Enio, or Luis Ennius, is the Don Juan-like protagonist of Calderón's play. This paragraph differs significantly from its counterpart in the English periodical version of the story; there, the relevant portion reads: 'Were it presented in the shape of a play, adorned with graces of style and with flowers of rhetoric, it would be indeed (with the blessing of heaven) well calculated to spread the glory of our holy church. But alas, my dear friend... [etc.]'.

PRINCE ALBERIC AND THE SNAKE LADY

First published in the July 1896 number of *The Yellow Book*, the iconic periodical of the decadent 1890s. The story was then included in *Pope Jacynth and Other Fantastic Tales* (1904). The tale, which blends mythic archetype with exacting particularity of historical detail, may have drawn upon any number of possible sources available to Lee. In one of the versions of the Venusberg legend recorded in Sabine Baring-Gould's *Curious Myths of the Middle Ages* (see Introduction), the Venus figure appears as a snake-woman, encountered by the hero in the 'bowels of the earth': 'He came to an enchanted land, where was a beautiful woman wearing a golden crown, but from her waist downward she was a serpent. She gave him gold and silver, and entreated him to kiss her three times. He complied twice, but the writhing of her tail so horrified him, that he fled without giving her the third kiss. Afterwards he prowled about the mountains... filled with a craving for the society of the lady, but he never could find it again' (*Curious Myths* (London, 1873), 223). The essence of this tale might have transferred, *mutatis mutandis*, to 'Prince Alberic and the Snake Lady', in the story of Alberic's ancestor told to him by the itinerant singer of 'fairy tales': 'And Alberic runs forward, and seizes the serpent in both arms, and lifts it up, and three times presses his warm lips against its cold and slippery skin, shutting his eyes in horror. And when the knight of Luna opens them again, behold! O wonder! In his arms no longer a dreadful snake, but a damsel, richly dressed and beautiful beyond compare' (p. 233). In fact, the figure of the serpent- or dragon-woman who requires a kiss, often from a knight, to be restored to a lady is a common topos in medieval and folk tales across Europe (*Lybeaus Desconus*, ed. Eve Salisbury and James Weldon (Kalamazoo, Michigan, 2013), 26–7). Another of Baring-Gould's 'Curious Myths', concerning the fairy Melusina, a mermaid or serpent-woman figure ('half her body being that of a very beautiful lady, the other half ending in a snake'), likely made its own contribution to the conception of the story as well. One notes too that, while yet an adolescent, Lee wrote a sketch, 'Capo Serpente: A Legend of the Roman Campagna', about an artist's fatal encounter with a snake-man:

> In the scorched Campagna, by the ruined tomb, dwells the Serpent King, the terrible Capo Serpente. The peasant dreads him, and avoids the tall, dry grass by the pool of stagnant water.
>
> But the artist, the stranger from the land where there are neither green trees nor gay flowers [both the structure and this observation are put into the contemporaneous Winthrop], sits down by the ruined tomb, and paints, unconscious of the danger.
>
> When the sun sheds upon the broken arches of the aqueduct a rosy tint, when the Alban hills are purple, when the dome of St Peter's rises black upon a golden sky, a huge green serpent glides from beneath the tall grass.
>
> His body is covered with scales, his head is that of a beautiful youth, and on it he wears a golden crown. He steals along and rises up before the eyes of the painter.
>
> The artist wishes to fly, he is rooted to the ground; he cannot take his eyes off the beautiful but terrible face; again he makes an effort to escape, in vain, the serpent exerts a fascination over his mind.
>
> His friends seek him. They find him lying in the high grass by the stagnant pool near the ruined tomb. 'He has had a fit', say his artist friends.
>
> The old peasant in the goatskin dress and leather thongs, knows better. He shakes his head, and mutters, crossing himself: 'He has seen the Capo Serpente'.

Meanwhile in *Tuscan Fairy Tales*, Lee writes, 'People have heard of the fairies (*fate*), who were lovely women six days of the week, and turned into snakes on the seventh' (6). 'Alberic' is moreover set in 'Luna', a fictionalized or counterfactual Massa-Carrara, where Lee apparently focused her story-gathering efforts for that early collection, and where legends involving shape-shifting snake-women can indeed be traced (see e.g. Michele Armanini, *Ligures apuani: Lunigiana storica, Garfagnana e Versilia prima dei Romani* (Padova, 2015) and Carlo Gabrielli Rosi, *Leggende e luoghi della paura tra Liguria e Toscana, Massa Carrara e Provincia* (Pisa, 1991)); perhaps Lee heard such tales and stored them away for future use rather than including them in her collection. This is not even to touch the question of literary influence: Lee's conception of the snake-woman has been plausibly claimed as a response to John Keats's poem 'Lamia' and E. T. A. Hoffmann's fairy tale *Der goldene Topf* ('The Golden Flower-Pot'), among other sources (see e.g. Andrew Smith, *The Ghost Story, 1840–1920: A Cultural History* (Manchester, 2010), 81–5, and Vineta Colby, *Vernon Lee: A Literary Biography* (Charlottesville and London, 2003), 230), while in 1875, Lee wrote the Biblioteca Nazionale in Florence in search of a 3 copy of Philostratus' *Life of Apollonius*, with its classical version of the lamia myth (a vampiric snake-woman).

211 *TO HER HIGHNESS*... *SARÀWAK*: differs slightly from that used in *The Yellow Book*: '[To H.H. the Ranee Brooke of Saràwak]'. Margaret, Lady Brooke (1849–1936) was at the centre of a group of literary figures in the 1890s including Joseph Conrad and W. H. Hudson; in his 1891 collection *A House of Pomegranates*, Oscar Wilde had dedicated the fairytale 'The Young King' to her.

the Duchy of Luna: Lee's invention; in 1906, when her friend Maurice Baring contemplated a work of historical fiction, she advised him to 'boldly invent a state to suit [his] purpose', adding 'as I did in *Alberic*, if you remember, though I had Massa Carrara [a Tuscan province] in my mind' (quoted in Colby, *Vernon Lee*, 354).

Monsieur le Brun... *Alexander and Roxana*: Charles Le Brun (1619–90) was court painter to 'The Sun King', Louis XIV of France (1638–1715), as well as Inspector-General of the Gobelins tapestry manufactory in Paris. Macedonian king and conqueror Alexander the Great (356–323 BCE), who married the Bactrian princess Roxana in 327 BCE, was depicted in a series of Gobelins tapestries designed by Le Brun, who also featured him in historical paintings.

Marius of the Flowers: perhaps an obscure Neapolitan painter named Marius Mazzi (1603–73?) and known as 'Marius des Fiori' and 'Marius des Fleurs'; an eighteenth-century 'Lexicon of Painters' by Ludwig von Winckelmann (from which the birth and death dates are taken) notes laconically that he was 'a very famous flower-painter'.

the Red Palace at Luna: probably based on the Palazzo Cybo-Malaspina at Massa, commonly called the Palazzo Rosso (Red Palace), the Renaissance portion of which was begun in 1563 by Duke Alberico I (a possible source for Lee's Alberic).

Apollo and the Graces: in Greek and Roman mythology, the Graces were minor goddesses of beauty, grace, and charm; when in the company of Apollo (the god of music, among other things), they were usually imagined to be dancing to his playing of the lyre. Many artists depicted the Graces in their work, perhaps most famously Sandro Botticelli (1445–1510) in his painting *Primavera*.

212 *Oriana*: in the famous chivalric romance *Amadis of Gaul*, Oriana is the daughter of the king of Britain and beloved of the knight Amadis; in the epic poem *L'Amadigi* by Bernardo Tasso (father of Torquato), she has become more of a benevolent *fata* or 'fairy lady'; possibly Lee derived the name from this story.

the Chronicles of Archbishop Turpin... Boiardo: first of several references to the body of medieval legends about Charlemagne and his paladins known as the Matter of France; the so-called Chronicle of Turpin, also called the *Historia Caroli Magni* (History of Charlemagne), is a twelfth-century work which influenced Matteo Maria Boiardo's epic poem *Orlando Innammorato* ('Orlando in Love') (1483–95). Boiardo's work in turn was followed by Ludovico Ariosto's *Orlando Furioso* ('Orlando Mad') (1516) and Torquato Tasso's *Gerusalemme Liberata* ('Jerusalem Delivered') (1581): all elaborations on the same body of material centring upon the mythologized Charlemagne and his companions (especially the heroic knight Roland, or Orlando). In none of these texts can the tale of Alberic the Blond and the Snake Lady Oriana be found.

Susanna and the Elders: an episode from the apocryphal portion of the Book of Daniel, in which a pair of lecherous old men spy upon the beautiful (and married) Susanna, then try to blackmail her into sexual intercourse, a subject frequently treated by painters, including Guido Reni and Artemisia Gentileschi.

215 *a gala coral with bells by Benvenuto Cellini*: a 'coral' in this sense is a teeth-cutting toy, sometimes made of coral; Samuel Johnson, defining it in his *Dictionary* as 'The piece of coral which children have about their necks, imagined to assist them in breeding teeth', curiously misquotes Pope's *The Rape of the Lock* in order to provide an example with bells attached: 'Her infant grandame's coral [actually "whistle"] next it grew; | The bells she gingled [jingled], and the whistle blew'. It is clearly not a suitable gift for an eight-year-old boy. Cellini (1500–71) was a goldsmith and artist best known today for his racy *Autobiography*, translated into English by John Addington Symonds, among others.

216 *the Twelve Cæsars*: presumably the same 'twelve Caesars'—i.e. the first twelve rulers of the Roman Empire (technically, Julius Caesar was not Emperor)—whose lives are told in the lively *De vita Caesarum* by Suetonius (*c.*69–122 CE): Julius Caesar, Augustus, Tiberius, Caligula, Claudius, Nero, Galba, Otho, Vitellius, Vespasian, Titus, and Domitian.

satyrs: in Greek mythology, half-goat nature deities.

the Giraffe of Cipollino... Monkeys: i.e. Cipollino marble, also known as onion-stone, and verd antique (from *verde antico*, 'ancient green'), a variety of decorative stone.

the feast of St Balthasar... wellknown: Balthazar or Balthasar is one of the Three Magi in the story of Jesus' birth (Balthasar, Caspar, and Melchior); Balthasar is the one supposed to have brought the gift of myrrh. All three figures are saints in Roman Catholicism; Balthasar's feast day is 6 January.

217 *Neptune... Bernini*: Neptune is the Roman counterpart to the Greek sea god Poseidon; Gian Lorenzo Bernini (1598–1680) was the preeminent sculptor of the Baroque period.

225 *Virgil*: major Roman poet (70–19 BCE), author of the *Eclogues*, the *Georgics*, and the *Aeneid*.

caracole: a half-turn to left or right on horseback, or a succession of such movements.

229 *the Holy Sepulchre... Tasso*: now Alberic's fictitious ancestor has been written into Tasso's *Gerusalemme Liberata* (1581) as well as the *Historia Caroli Magni* and *Orlando Innammorata* (see note to p. 212 [*the Chronicles of Archbishop Turpin... Boiardo*]); Godfrey de Bouillon and Tancred, historical figures who helped take Jerusalem in the First Crusade (1096–9), feature in Tasso's epic poem.

230 *pipkins*: earthenware cooking pots.

the stories of... Jerusalem Delivered: 'The King of Portugal's Cowherd' is one of the stories in Lee's book *Tuscan Fairy Tales* (in it, the cowherd receives a magic gun from a witch/fairy, kills two ogres with it, unhorses all comers at the joust, and so marries the King's daughter). The second tale, if not invented, is unknown, though an Italian folktale centring upon a magic griffin feather is told in Thomas Frederick Crane's *Italian Popular Tales* (1885) (the Brothers Grimm tell a different tale demonstrating the curative powers of griffin feathers). *Orlando Innammorata*, *Orlando Furioso*, and *Gerusalemme Liberata* are all elaborations of the same Carolingian cycle of legends (see note to p. 212 [*the Chronicles of Archbishop Turpin... Boiardo*]).

231 *the worshippers of Macomet... the rest*: 'Macomet' is a rare variant of Muhammed (momentarily Lee will refer to 'the Wizard Macomet'); we are still, presumably, in the fictional world of Tasso, where the historical (if mythologized) figures of Tancred and Bohemond (*c.*1054–1111) can be found alongside the wholly fictional Reynold or Rinaldo.

232 *Brillamorte*: of course, Lee's counterfactual knight needs a unique, specially named sword like those wielded by Roland (Durandal), Charlemagne (Joyeuse), Ogier (Cortana), Rinaldo (Froberge), and so on; the name of Alberic's blade denotes 'Shining Death', perhaps an oblique nod to Olivier's Hautclere ('High Brightness')

the hero Hercules... the great dragon: the eleventh of the twelve labours of the Greek mythological hero Hercules (Herakles); he had to retrieve 'the apples which Hera had received at her wedding from Ge (the Earth), and which she had entrusted to the keeping of the Hesperides and the dragon Ladon, on Mt Atlas, in the country of the Hyperboreans' (*Smaller Classical Dictionary*, 255).

the vain Narcissus... the Meek Damsel: in Greek mythology, Narcissus was a beautiful youth, condemned by Apollo to gaze always at his own reflected image; he is transformed into a daffodil. When Venus' lover Adonis is killed by a wild boar, she changes his blood into anemone flowers. The angel Gabriel is the 'Messenger' who brings Mary ('the Meek Damsel') news that she will bear the son of God, along with—in legend and many paintings—one or a 'sheaf' of lilies, symbolic of purity.

234 *Phœbus Apollo*: Phoebus or 'bright' is the epithet most often applied to Apollo, indicating his role as sun god (clearly another reference to Louis XIV, who cultivated an association or identification with the god, dancing in the role of Apollo at the age of fourteen in the *Ballet Royal de la Nuit* (1653); see also note to p. 240 (*Daphne Transformed*).

harlequins' laths: Harlequin (Italian Arlecchino), one of the main stock characters of the commedia dell'arte, carries a *batte* (slapstick).

235 *St. Paschal Baylon*: Paschal Baylón (1540–92), Franciscan lay brother, also mentioned in 'Amour Dure'. The encyclopedic *Acta Sanctorum* ('Acts of the Saints'), quoted here by Ebenezer Cobham Brewer (of *Brewer's Dictionary of Phrase and Fable* fame), records some instances of the saint's devil-fighting prowess: '*The Devil assails St. Pascal Baylon under divers forms* (A.D. 1540–1592). The celestial favours shown to St Pascal made the devils mad with rage, and they beset him in divers ways. Sometimes they rushed upon him in the form of lions and tigers, seeking to devour him; sometimes they tried to scare him by assuming horrible shapes; sometimes they beat him till all his body was black and blue... but the saint, well accustomed to these attacks, was never alarmed... the devils [then] tried another tack, and offered to impress upon his body the marks of the divine wounds... but Pascal, discovering this ruse also, said to the foul fiend, "You ravening wolf, how dare you take on yourself the clothing of a lamb? Off with you!" And the fiend, terrified at these words, fled' (*A Dictionary of Miracles: Imitative, Realistic, and Dogmatic* (Philadelphia, 1894), 99).

malefica or strix: two Latin words with variable, evolving meanings, though both had come to mean 'witch' in early modern Europe.

236 *left-handed marriage*: usually refers to a union between a man and woman of unequal social status, which in this context would raise issues regarding the passing on of a title and/or property.

237 *St Romwald*: this is 'St Romuald' in the story's original *Yellow Book* appearance, i.e. Romuald (*c*.951–*c*.1025/7), a Ravenna-born monk who founded the eremitic *Ordo Camaldulensium* (presumably the order mentioned in the story) in Tuscany. Interestingly however, 'Romuald' is also the name of the priestly victim-lover of the female vampire in Théophile Gautier's 'La Morte Amoreuse', considered a possible influence on Lee's story.

238 *the downy wings... of the Sleep God*: the Greek god of sleep Hypnos (the Roman counterpart is Somnus, who appears in book 11 of Ovid's *Metamorphoses*), often depicted with wings sprouting from his brow.

Cremona viols: see note to p. 10 [*Cremonese fiddle*, 'Winthrop's Adventure'].

239 *serpent-bearing mænads*: frenzied woman followers of the Greek wine god Dionysus; in Euripides' tragedy the *Bacchae*, as elsewhere in art and literature, they appear as snake-handlers.

240 *Daphne Transformed*: an imagined ballet based on the Greek myth, most famously told in Ovid's *Metamorphoses*, of a nymph pursued by a love-smitten Apollo. Fleeing to her father (the river God Peneus) for protection, Daphne was transformed into a laurel tree (Apollo—and, later, Roman Emperors—wore a wreath of laurel leaves). It is a scene depicted in many works of art and music: Jacopo Peri's *Dafne* (*c.*1597) is considered the first opera.

241 *"Thyrsis was a shepherd-boy...ritornel"*: an imagined aria (àir) about the mythological Arcadian herdsman Thyrsis, Tirsi in Italian, who made an appearance in numerous musical works including the first opera, Peri's *Dafne*. The ritornello ('little return') of an aria is a repeated orchestral passage.

"the stern exercises of Mars...the freaks and frolics of Venus": i.e. the business of war and love, respectively.

242 *habited as Diana...turban of Sibyls*: dressed as the Roman hunting goddess Diana (equivalent to the Greek Artemis), the Greek goddess of wisdom Athena, the Commedia dell'Arte stock character Columbine, or the female oracles of antiquity, turbaned, or quasi-turbaned, particularly perhaps as in several paintings of turban-wearing Sibyls with cherubs by Guercino (1591–1666)), or the Delphic Sibyl depicted in one of Michelangelo's frescoes in the Sistine Chapel.

243 *the golden rose...Dr. Borri*: the golden rose, an ornament upon which a papal blessing is bestowed, is sometimes given to sovereigns (and thus, perhaps, a possible threat to Balthasar Maria's authority, in his eyes). The Fèsta de ła Sènsa (Feast of the Ascension) is a major traditional celebration in Venice; the Doge's role was to sail into the Adriatic to ritualize the city's 'marriage' to the sea. The Spanish Inquisition held its tribunal ('the burning of heretics') at the Palazzo Chiaramonte in Palermo, Sicily, from 1600 to 1782. 'Dr Borri' is the Milanese alchemist Giuseppe Francesco Borri (1627–95).

244 *Sardinian jasper*: 'Red and white veined marble, from Sardinia, called by the Italians Sardinian Jasper' (*A Companion to the Museum, Late Sir Ashton Lever's* (London, 1790), 108).

the Medicean works in Florence: the Opificio delle Pietre Dure or Manufactory of Florentine Mosaic, founded by grand ducal decree by Ferdinando I de' Medici in 1588.

245 *the Dey of Algiers*: Ottoman honorific title applied to the ruler of Algiers, Tripoli, and/or Tunis in North Africa, first used in the later seventeenth century.

Peter's pence: direct donations (in some contexts a de facto tax) paid to the papal treasury.

245 *drysalting*: writing in 1725, Daniel Defoe lists 'cocheneal, indigo, gauls, shumach, logwood, fustick, madder' as among the substances in which a drysalter trades. (Given the Italian context, perhaps the drysalting of fish or cheeses specifically is implied here.)

246 *Duchess of Malfi*: the historical Giovanna d'Aragoṇa, Duchess of Amalfi (1478–1510), whose travails and murder at the hands of her brothers formed the basis for Jacobean playwright John Webster's harrowing revenge tragedy *The Duchess of Malfi* (1613), among other Italian and English literary works.

the Secret Inquisition of the Republic of Venice: see note to p. 153 [*the spies of the old Republic*, 'A Wicked Voice'].

the story of Orpheus... of Soracte: in Greek legend, the quintessential poet-singer Orpheus must descend into the underworld to bring back his lover Eurydice (killed by snakebite); Monte Soratte (Soracte in antiquity), outside of Rome, was associated with the Roman god Soranus, who in turn had associations with both the underworld god Dis Pater and Apollo. Perhaps Lee had seen a painting by Poussin's brother-in-law and pupil Gaspard Dughet (1615–75), described here by Gustav Friedrich Waagen, in which Soratte was used as backdrop for the myth: 'On the right is a rising ground with cattle descending from it, and stately trees. On the left a hill of very gradual elevation; more on the left trees ahead. Between these trees and the hill lies the Campagna of Rome, the horizontal lines of which are broken by the fine forms of Mount Soracte. In the middle of the foreground is Eurydice bitten by the asp, with female companions, and Orpheus reposing' (*Galleries and Cabinets of Art in Great Britain* (London, 1857), 153–4).

248 *a book of hours*: devotional book for laymen, popular in the Middle Ages.

249 *Melissa water*: medicinal infusion of lemon balm (Latin *melissa*) in water, originally developed by Carmelite nuns. Perhaps, too, Lee is thinking of Melissa or Melusina, the legendary fairy who is half-woman and half-snake or -fish, as described in Sabine Baring-Gould's *Curious Myths of the Middle Ages*.

THE DOLL

First appeared in 1896 in *The Cornhill Magazine* as 'The Image', with a dedication ('À MME LOUIS ORMOND') to her goddaughter Violet Sargent (younger sister to John Singer Sargent), who had married Louis Francis Ormond in 1891. This might seem an inauspicious tale to dedicate to a young woman in the early years of marriage, though Lee appears to have approved of Ormond, describing him to her mother as 'Good looking, quite French... The young man is really a delightful creature' (quoted in Karen Corsaro and Daniel Williman, *John Singer Sargent and His Muse* (Lanham, 2014), 44). Republished in *For Maurice*, with very minor changes and without the dedication, as 'The Doll' (the version reproduced here).

252 *Foligno, in Umbria*: Foligno is a town in the central Italian region of Umbria (today divided into the provinces of Perugia and Terni).

Orestes: in Greek mythology, the son of Agamemnon and Clytemnestra. As the avenger of his father's death at the hands of his mother and her lover Aegisthus, he featured in the tragedies of Aeschylus, Sophocles, and Euripides. Perhaps, however, Lee has chosen the name primarily, if subtly, to link the character with the Baglioni family who are the principal subjects of Francesco Matarazzo's *Chronicle* (see note to p. 252 [*Matarazzo*]): 'In the heart of pious Umbria they scorned the Church, and gave themselves pagan names—Ercole, Troilo, Ascanio, Annibale, Atalanta, Penelope, Lavinia, Zenobia' (Will Durant, *The Renaissance* (New York, 1953), 241). See also note to p. 141 [*Norma, Odoacer, Archimedes... Themis*, 'Dionea'].

Matarazzo: Francesco Matarazzo (*c.*1443–1518), author of the vividly told *Cronaca della Città di Perugia* ('Chronicle of the City of Perugia') of which John Addington Symonds, who called the book 'more fascinating than a novel', wrote: 'His chronicle is a masterpiece of naïve, unstudied narrative. Few documents are so important for the student of the sixteenth century in Italy' (*Sketches in Italy and Greece* (London, 1879), 72). Matarazzo, who enjoyed the patronage of the powerful Baglioni family (see note to p. 253 [*the Trincis... St Angela... Tibullus*]), invests them with a larger-than-life glamour even as he is chronicling their crimes; as Symonds drily observed: 'He seems unable to write about them without using the language of an adoring lover' (74).

253 *the Trincis... St. Angela... Tibullus*: the Trinci family were lords of Foligno throughout the fourteenth and early fifteenth centuries, a reign, like that of the Baglione in nearby Perugia, accompanied by much violence and terror: 'Some of the bloodiest pages in mediaeval Italian history are those which relate the vicissitudes of the Trinci family [and] the exhaustion of Foligno by internal discord' (John Addington Symonds, *Italian Byways* (New York, 1883), 98). Angela of Foligno (1248–1309) was a penitent and mystical writer who later gained the epithet 'Mistress of Theologians'; Jacob Burckhardt singled out the Baglioni family, de facto rulers of Perugia, as peculiarly bloodthirsty even by the standards of the time. The legendary *condottiero* Cesare Borgia (1475–1507) invaded Perugia in 1503 in the name of the pope (his father Rodrigo Borgia, Alexander VI), chasing off one Baglioni and installing another in his place. In 1506, after having compelled the submission of Gianpaolo Baglioni, Alexander's successor Julius II entered Perugia virtually unguarded; Niccolò Machiavelli would later marvel at the humiliated ruler's failure to murder the pontiff in cold blood: 'All prudent men who were with the Pope remarked on his temerity, and on the pusillanimity of Giovanpagolo [Gianpaolo]; nor could they conjecture why the latter had not, to his eternal glory, availed himself of this opportunity for crushing his enemy, and at the same time enriching

himself with plunder' (*Discourses* (London, 1883), 92–3). According to legend as recorded in the fourteenth-century *Little Flowers of St Francis*, Francis of Assisi (*c.*1181–1226) preached to the birds 'betwixt Carmano and Bevagna', a town about five miles from Foligno. Also born in Assisi (then Asisium), between 54 and 47 BC, was the Roman elegiac poet Sextus Propertius; the birthplace of his contemporary Albius Tibullus, with whom he is often compared, is not known.

253 *stucco virtues*: i.e. plaster angels.

lodge: outbuilding near the entrance, usually occupied by a caretaker. The fact that a cobbler has set up shop here suggests the 'ruined' state of the palace's owner, as does the presence of a 'soap factory' within.

254 *Berlin wool cushions*: Berlin wool work embroidery patterns were very popular in the nineteenth century; the presence of 'Berlin work' here is perhaps another sign of reduced circumstances; Isabella Beeton, in her *Book of Needlework*, offers the middle-class reader 'all the stitches which are used in Berlin Work', promising that they are 'neither too great in number nor too simple or too elaborate in execution for those who aspire to become Berlin workers' (*Book of Needlework* (London, 1870), 559).

Canova... Mme. Pasta... Lady Blessington: Antonio Canova (1757–1822), celebrated Neoclassical sculptor who created busts and portrait statues for several members of the Bonaparte family; in 1811 he produced a series of ideal heads in marble. There are many portraits of superstar opera soprano Giuditta Pasta (1797–1852) and Irish writer Marguerite Gardiner Countess of Blessington (1789–1849), some in short-bodiced dresses of white satin (see note to p. 259 [*Empire frock*]).

255 *ruches*: ruffles or pleats.

256 *Ingres Madonna*: French Neoclassical painter Jean-Auguste-Dominique Ingres (1780–1867); of his 'Madonnas', the most appropriate reference here would probably be to the one featured in his 1824 painting *The Vow of Louis XIII*, inasmuch as it borrows directly from Raphael's 1511 *Madonna of Foligno*.

257 *Basta*: enough (Italian).

258 *Perugia*: chief city, and today capital, of Umbria, and subject of Matarazzo's *Chronicles* (see note to p. 252 [*Matarazzo*]).

"Archivio Storicho": *Archivio Storico Italiano*, journal founded in 1842 by Jean-Baptiste Vieusseux which included reprints of historical documents, such as the fifteenth-century chronicles which Lee had consulted while researching her essay 'The Italy of the Elizabethan Dramatists' (included in *Euphorion*, 1884). In its pages had appeared such primary sources as the *Cronaca della Città di Perugia dal 1309 al 1491* attributed to 'Graziani of Perugia', a work Burckhardt pairs with Matarazzo's as representing the two most 'admirable historical narratives' of the period.

259 *Empire frock*: dress in the Neoclassical style of the Napoleonic empire, featuring a 'short bodice' as described earlier in the story.

MARSYAS IN FLANDERS

Noted in some anthologies as having been written and/or published in an unnamed magazine in 1900, but no such appearance has been definitely established as yet; the story was ultimately included in *For Maurice: Five Unlikely Stories* (1929). Perhaps the continued exhumation of Lee's letters and commonplace-books will yield more information about the story's writing and early publication (if any) in the near future. Several aspects of the story might point to its possible conception, if not composition, in the late 1890s (in light, for instance, of Lee's travels in France, and perhaps of Pater's recent death, soon after publishing 'Apollo in Picardy'). (A more speculative connection might link this story, with its church antiquary, with the early stories of M. R. James, though such influence, if any, might have gone either way.)

260 MARSYAS IN FLANDERS: Lee's title invokes that of an 1831 short story by Honoré de Balzac, 'Jésus-Christ en Flandre' ('Christ in Flanders'); indeed, the story itself clearly represents, at least in part, a conscious attempt to produce a kind of infernal inversion or sequel to the earlier tale, which purports to relate a medieval legend of Christ coming ashore at a beach near Ostend. The last paragraph of Balzac's story contains *en germe* much of Lee's, from the sea-bourne 'relic' of Christ (or a supposed Christ) connected to a little church by the sea, to the invocation of revolutionary France: 'The Convent of Mercy was built for sailors on this spot, where for long afterwards (so it was said) the footprints of Jesus Christ could be seen in the sand; but in 1793, at the time of the French invasion, the monks carried away this precious relic, that bore witness to the Saviour's last visit to earth' (*The Unknown Masterpiece* (New York, 1900), 63). As for Marsyas: it used to be said that Lee's title was too much of a 'spoiler', but the number of readers for whom this is true today is surely vanishingly small. Accordingly, the modern reader may wish to wait until the gloss at the end of the story for explication of this name (see note to p. 271 [*Marsyas*]).

Antiquary of Dunes: the antiquary is the church's archivist or record-keeper; 'Dunes' may be a fictionalized Dunkirk, where a nearby Abbey of Our Lady of the Dunes was founded in 1107 ('Dunkirk' literally means 'Church in the Dunes').

the Holy Sepulchre... of Lucca: the Church of the Holy Sepulchre is a fourth-century church in the Old City of Jerusalem, supposed to contain the sites of Jesus' crucifixion, burial, and resurrection; in the *duomo* (cathedral) of the Tuscan city of Lucca is a relic known as the Volto Santo di Lucca (Holy Face of Lucca), a wooden Christ crucified, 'a more or less Byzantine image' in Lee's words, supposed to have arrived on Tuscan shores in the eighth century; in September a 'Festa di Santo Croce' is held in Lucca, like 'the Feast of the Crucifix' celebrated in Dunes. In her later introduction to the story Lee notes that it 'evidently embod[ies] the legend of the Holy Face of Lucca', though attributing 'its true origin' in a 'ghostly adventure' half-remembered from a French textbook.

261 *triforium*: 'A gallery or arcade in the wall over the arches at the sides of the nave and choir, and sometimes of the transepts, in some large churches' (*OED*).

262 *vox humana*: pipe organ stop supposed to sound like human voices.

the mouth of the Nys: perhaps suggested by the Flemish river of Lys.

Abbey of St. Loup of Arras: Arras is a city in the Artois region of northern France, particularly prominent in the Middle Ages in the cloth and wool industry; a tapestry came to be known simply as an 'arras' (later in Lee's story a fool is hiding, like Hamlet, behind one). The Benedictine Abbey of St Vaast (not St Loup) in Arras was suppressed during the French Revolution.

the Norman coast near Salenelles: Sallenelles is in the Calvados department of Normandy; in the introduction to *For Maurice*, Lee says that the story was inspired in part by the sight of 'a blackened Gothic church in a silted up Norman estuary'.

263 *until 1790*: i.e. at the time of the Revolution, when the abbey was (as we presently read) 'sacked'.

266 *the Vigil of All Saints*: Halloween.

267 *the proceedings against the Templars*: the Knights Templar, a military order (and financial powerhouse), was dissolved in 1312, soon after King Philip IV of France had begun persecuting its French members.

causing ships to wreck: in order to plunder them; a family of wreckers features in Lee's short novel *Penelope Brandling: A Tale of the Welsh Coast in the Eighteenth Century* (1903).

268 *quod vulgo dicuntur flustes et musettes*: 'As they are called in the vernacular' (Latin); a 'musette' is a bagpipe (more usually so-called in the Baroque period; 'muse' is more likely to have been the term used in the earlier period.

269 *etiam*: and furthermore (Latin).

white bread: then a delicacy, made from fine flour.

270 *the Great Wild Man*: the motif of the hairy 'wild man' or 'l'homme sauvage' was common in medieval art and folklore.

quoits: game where hoops, discs, or loops of rope are thrown at a spike.

271 *like a vampire*: it is possible, though by no means necessary, for Lee to have been influenced here by Bram Stoker's recently published (1897) novel *Dracula*.

Marsyas: in Greek mythology, a satyr or silenus (woodland deities comparable to the 'wild men' of folklore; see note to p. 270 [*the Great Wild Man*]), flayed alive as punishment for challenging Apollo to a musical competition—his *aulos* (double pipes or flutes) against the Olympian's lyre—and losing. The flaying of Marsyas was a popular subject in art (Titian's painting of that name is perhaps the most famous example), and there are many statues, classical and later, of Marsyas' torment, including a pair in Florence's Uffizi Gallery, discussed by Giorgio Vasari in his *Life* of Andrea del Verrocchio. Lee makes a point of having her narrator say, 'The figure was familiar to me in various galleries' (his ear is pointed, i.e. 'leaf-shaped', like a satyr's). Eugene Lee-Hamilton had dramatized the myth in a poem, reviewed by Symonds in 1885:

> Apollo and Marsyas takes its name from the Greek legend of the rivalry between the satyr and the Olympian deity. Marsyas, for Mr. Lee-Hamilton, symbolises all that is remote, wild, pain-compelling, and orgiastic in the music of the world. Apollo represents its pure, defined, and chastened melodies... Of his personal susceptibility to the influence of Marsyas Mr. Lee-Hamilton makes no secret; and, in the lyrical contention which he has written for these rival powers, he puts far better poetry into the mouth of the satyr than that which he has invented for the god. (*The Academy* 27 (January 1885), 71)

Two earlier fictions, or quasi-fictions, by Walter Pater, both centring upon uncanny pagan returns in medieval Europe, are also crucial influences here: 'Denys l'Auxerrois' (1887) and 'Apollo in Picardy' (1893). In her essay 'Dionysus in the Euganean Hills: W. H. Pater: In Memoriam', Lee discusses both pieces in articulating the broader conceit, which animates such tales as 'Dionea' as well, of the classical deities 'in exile' in the modern world as a source of disquiet and even terror:

> Of course more than one divinity of the Pagans went into exile... [Venus, Zeus, and] Apollo, of whom, in a much finer companion-piece to *Denys l'Auxerrois*, Pater himself fabled a reappearance in mediæval Picardy; let alone no end of gods and goddesses who lurked in peasant legend, sometimes disguised as local saints, or... carrying off mortal brides in the shape of wild men of the woods even to this day. Exile like this, implying an in-and-out existence of alternate mysterious appearance and disappearance is, therefore, a kind of *haunting*; the gods who had it partaking of the nature of ghosts even more than all gods do, *revenants* as they are from other ages, and with the wistful eeriness of all ghosts, merely to think on whom makes our hair, like Job's, rise up; tragic beings and, as likely as not, malevolent towards living men,... of all gods Dionysus is the one fittest for such sinister exile. (*The Contemporary Review* 120 (September 1921), 347–8)

(For a discussion of the association of Marsyas with Dionysus in Lee's 'Marsyas' and Pater's 'Denys l'Auxerrois' see Patricia Pulham's *Art and the Transitional Object in Vernon Lee's Supernatural Tales*.) Once again, too, Lee draws (like Pater) upon Heinrich Heine's 'The Gods in Exile', particularly its discussion of Marsyas' antagonist Apollo.

APPENDICES

FAUSTUS AND HELENA: NOTES ON THE SUPERNATURAL IN ART

This typically erudite essay probing the relationship between art and the supernatural was first published in 1880 in *Cornhill Magazine*; it was reprinted the following year in Lee's essay collection, *Belcaro: Being Essays on Sundry Aesthetical Questions*.

273 *Doctor Faustus of Wittemberg... Helen of Sparta*: the German folk legend of Faust, a scholar who sells his soul to the devil for worldly knowledge, emerged in the sixteenth century and formed the basis of countless literary and other works; the figure's association with the university town of Wittenberg is playwright Christopher Marlowe's invention. In raising Helen of Troy—in classical literature the most beautiful woman in the world—Faustus commits the abominable crime of necromancy (before being spirited off to Troy by Paris, sparking the Trojan War, she was married to King Menelaus of Sparta).

Albertus, Bacon, or Faustus: German theologian and philosopher Albertus Magnus or Albert the Great (*c*.1200–1280) and English philosopher and proto-scientist Robert Bacon (*c*.1220–1292), both earned posthumous reputations as wizards; the German alchemist Johann Georg Faust or John Faustus (*c*.1480–1540) was the historical figure on whom the legend of Faust is primarily based.

Marlowe... Goethe: refers to the two great literary treatments of the legend: *The Tragical History of the Life and Death of Doctor Faustus* by Elizabethan playwright Christopher Marlowe (1564–93) and the two-part verse drama *Faust* by German poet Johann Wolfgang von Goethe (1749–1832), in which Gretchen or Margarete is Faust's lover.

274 *Thorwaldsen's statues*: refers to the work of Danish sculptor Bertel Thorvaldsen (1770–1844), whose strict Neoclassicism parallels the 'pseudo-antique' quality Lee sees in Goethe's Helen.

Goethe's own Iphigenia: *Iphigenie auf Tauris*, Goethe's version of Euripides' tragedy *Iphigenia in Tauris*, was first performed in 1779, and subsequently revised.

Dürer: Albrecht Dürer (1471–1528), German painter and printmaker.

Wohlgemüth: Nuremberg artist Michael Wolgemut (1434–1519), who served as master to Durer, known for his painted wooden retables.

275 *the gods of the Iliad... Perugino*: the *Iliad* is, with the *Odyssey*, one of two foundational Greek epic poems attributed to Homer; in the story of Don Giovanni (most famously in Mozart's operatic treatment) Il Commendatore (The Commander) returns from the dead in the form of a statue to drag Don Giovanni (Don Juan) to Hell; Praxiteles was a Greek sculptor (fourth century BCE) whose statues include satyrs ('sylvan divinities'); fairies add a supernatural dimension to Shakespeare's play *A Midsummer Night's Dream* (*c*.1595); the Furies or Erinyes are female tormentors and figures of vengeance who appear in Greek tragedian Aeschylus' trilogy the *Oresteia*; Pietro Perugino, Renaissance painter and teacher of Raphael. All of these are offered as examples of supernatural elements in great works of Western art (pictorial, sculptural, literary, and musical).

276 *Descartes' vortices*: French mathematician and philosopher René Decartes (1596–1650) developed a 'vortex theory' of planetary motion which vied

with, and eventually was discarded in favour of, Newton's theory of universal gravitation.

277 *Pan*: see note to p. 127 [*Pan*, 'Dionea'].

278 *Phidias... Blake*: Greek sculptor Phidias (*c.*480–430 BCE), Florentine painter Giotto di Bondone (*c.*1267–1337), and English poet and artist William Blake (1757–1827).

279 *Goethe has remarked*: the quotation is more usually attributed to Voltaire.

as Hegel imagines: see German philosopher Georg Friedrich Wilhelm Hegel's *Lectures on Aesthetics* (1818–29), an influence on Lee.

the Venus of Milo or the Giustiniani Minerva: the Venus de Milo is an ancient Greek statue of the goddess of love, Aphrodite, now at the Louvre Museum, Paris; the Giustiniani Minerva, also known as the Athena Giustiniani, is a Roman copy of a Greek statue of the goddess of wisdom, once in the possession of banker and art collector Vincenzo Giustiniani (1564–1637) and currently in the Vatican Museums.

Chimaera... Bellerophon: in Greek mythology, the hero Bellerophon slew the hybrid monster Chimera.

280 *Mr. Ruskin*: influential Victorian art critic John Ruskin (1819–1900); Lee refers to *The Queen of the Air: Being a Study of the Greek Myths of Cloud and Storm* (1869).

Cerberus: in Greek mythology, three-headed guard dog of the underworld.

281 *Parrhasius*: ancient Greek painter from Ephesus.

Tibullus: Albius Tibullus (*c.*55–19 BCE), Latin elegiac poet.

Catullus: Roman poet(*c.*84–*c.*54); the reference is to his treatment of the myth of Cybele, the Phrygian mother goddess, and her ecstatic follower Attis, who castrates himself.

Apelles and Scopas... Epicurus: Apelles of Kos and Skopas of Paros, Greek painter and sculptor, respectively, of the fourth century BCE. The Greek philosopher Epicurus (341–270 BC) is associated with materialism and a form of hedonism.

the Giottesques... Angelico: the 'Giottesques' were fourteenth-century followers of Giotto; Fra Angelico (*c.*1395–1455) was a Dominican friar and painter.

the stained napkin of Bolsena: in 1263, during Mass in Bolsena, Italy, the communion bread was seen to bleed onto the linen cloth beneath it.

Signorelli and Filippino: Italian Renaissance painters Luca Signorelli (*c.*1441–1523) and Filippino Lippi (1457–1504).

283 *Raphael... Trastevere*: the major Renaissance artist Raphael (1483–1520) used his mistress Margarita Luti (known as La Fornarina, 'the baker's daughter') as a model.

the time of Pericles... the time of Leo X: i.e., Golden Age Athens, in which forms of secular enlightenment prompted a religious reaction, and the reign of the Medici pope whose papacy (1513–21) saw, and perhaps contributed to, the Protestant schism.

283 *Agostino Veneziano... "Lo Stregozzo"*: the Renaissance engraver Agostino de' Musi (*c.*1490–*c.*1540) from Venice ('Veneziano'); 'Lo Stregozzo' is also known as 'The Carcass', 'The Witches' Procession', and 'The Magician' (the source drawing is no longer attributed to Raphael).

284 *Rembrandt*: Rembrandt van Rijn (1606–69), Dutch painter.

Doré: Gustave Doré (1832–83), French engraver and artist.

285 *Sprengler's Malleus Malificarum*: properly *Malleus Maleficarum* or 'The Hammer of Witches', 1486 treatise on witchcraft dubiously attributed to theologian Jacob Sprenger.

287 *Walpürgis-night... Chiron*: Walpürgisnacht is the night of 30 April, an event associated with witchcraft; Faust is conducted on that night to a Satanic revel on the plain of Pharsalia, historically important as the site of Julius Caesar's decisive military victory over Pompey the Great in 48 BCE. Dryads are tree-nymphs, oreads mountain-nymphs. Chiron was the wisest and best of the centaurs (half-horses, half-men) in Greek mythology; Goethe has Faust ride on his back.

288 *Schiller... Coleridge*: German philosopher and playwright Friedrich Schiller (1759–1805), German philosopher and poet Johann Gottfried von Herder (1744–1803), and English poet and critic Samuel Taylor Coleridge (1772–1834).

289 *Voltaire's novels and Hume's treatises*: philosophers Voltaire (1698–1778) and David Hume (1711–76); the point is that devils are not frightening in a post-Enlightenment age.

Shelley... Cenci: reference to Percy Bysshe Shelley's verse play *The Cenci* (1819); the historical Beatrice Cenci (1577–99) was executed for the murder of her father, who had raped her.

"Aye... hell": this and the following three quotations are from Marlowe's *Doctor Faustus*.

290 *Winckelmann*: German art historian Johann Joachim Winckelmann (1717–68).

Statius or Claudian: Publius Papinius Statius (*c.*45–*c.*96 CE) and Claudius Claudianus (*c.*370–*c.*404 CE), used by Lee as examples of second-rate Latin poets.

291 *One of the prose versions of the story of Faustus*: from the 1592 English *Faustbuch* (*The Historie of the Damnable Life and Deserved Death of Doctor John Faustus*), though the text in the edition at the British Library differs somewhat.

the Lauras... Leonardo: i.e. women addressed or portrayed in works by Renaissance poets and artists.

292 *Homer... Achilles' spear*: i.e. fictitious women in classical literature, as depicted by epic poet Homer and playwright Euripides (Briseis is captured by the warrior Achilles in Homer's *Iliad*).

Hero in his own poem: from Marlowe's *Hero and Leander* (1598), based on the Greek myth of two young lovers living on opposite sides of the Hellespont; Hero is a priestess of Aphrodite, the goddess of love.

Botticelli: Sandro Botticelli (1445–1510), Italian Renaissance painter best known for *The Birth of Venus*.

Bembo and Castiglione: Italian Renaissance writers Pietro Bembo (1470–1547) and Baldassare Castiglione (1478–1529); Castiglione's most famous work is *The Book of the Courtier*, though both men wrote love sonnets in the style of Petrarch (1304–74).

PREFACE TO *HAUNTINGS*

295 *TO FLORA PRIESTLEY AND ARTHUR LEMON*: Flora Priestley (1859–1944) was a friend of Vernon Lee and John Singer Sargent, who painted her several times; Arthur Lemon (1850–1912) was an English painter resident, like Lee, in Italy.

a certain castle... his subsequent life: a Gothic premise used by a number of writers, including Lee herself, quasi-facetiously, in 'A Hidden Door', published in 1886.

296 *the murdered King of Denmark... by Mérimée*: references to (1) Shakespeare's *Hamlet*, (2) a legend about James I of Scotland being warned of his death by 'a woman of Yreland, that clepid herselfe as a suthesayer' (an episode much expanded by Dante Gabriel Rossetti in his 1881 ballad 'The King's Tragedy'), and (3) a medieval legend related in Sabine Baring-Gould's *Curious Myths of the Middle Ages* and developed by, among others, William Morris (1834–96), Prosper Mérimée (1803–70), and Lee herself (see Introduction):

There is a curious story told by Fordun in his 'Scotichronicon'... He relates that in the year 1050, a youth of noble birth had been married in Rome, and during the nuptial feast, being engaged in a game of ball, he took off his wedding-ring, and placed it on the finger of a statue of Venus. When he wished to resume it, he found that the stony hand had become clinched, so that it was impossible to remove the ring. Thenceforth he was haunted by the Goddess Venus, who constantly whispered in his ear, 'Embrace me; I am Venus, whom you have wedded; I will never restore your ring.' However, by the assistance of a priest, she was at length forced to give it up to its rightful owner.

rep: ribbed fabric used in upholstering.

the caves of Jamschid... the ladder of Jacob: Jamshid, king in Persian mythology, who developed from the Avestan hero Yima (as related in the *Vendidad*, translated by Mary Robinson's future husband, James Darmesteter, in 1880); the magical 'cup of Jamshid' appears in legend and literature including the *Rubaiyat* of Omar Khayyam (called 'Jamshyd's Sev'n-ring'd Cup' in Edward FitzGerald's famous English version of 1859).

296 *Islington or Shepherd's Bush*: London districts, here apparently suggesting the prosaic, unromantic, modern, and/or dull.

Dr. Faustus: see note to p. 273 [*Doctor Faustus of Wittemberg... Helen of Sparta*, 'Faustus and Helena'].

297 *Society for Psychical Research*: British society founded in 1882 for the scientific investigation of the paranormal.

Shelley: the English Romantic poet Percy Bysshe Shelley (1792–1822) last lived at Villa Magni, near Lerici; he drowned after a boating accident while returning there from Livorno.

The Oxford World's Classics Website

www.worldsclassics.co.uk

- Browse the full range of Oxford World's Classics online
- Sign up for our monthly e-alert to receive information on new titles
- Read extracts from the Introductions
- Listen to our editors and translators talk about the world's greatest literature with our Oxford World's Classics audio guides
- Join the conversation, follow us on Twitter at OWC_Oxford
- Teachers and lecturers can order inspection copies quickly and simply via our website

www.worldsclassics.co.uk

MORE ABOUT **OXFORD WORLD'S CLASSICS**

American Literature

British and Irish Literature

Children's Literature

Classics and Ancient Literature

Colonial Literature

Eastern Literature

European Literature

Gothic Literature

History

Medieval Literature

Oxford English Drama

Philosophy

Poetry

Politics

Religion

The Oxford Shakespeare